1.25

Dear Reader:

Ten years ago, I began to write the book that would change my life. That book was *The Bronze Horseman*. I had written three previous novels—none of them set in Russia, the country of my birth. I came to the United States when I was ten and spent the rest of my adolescence and youth wanting to be an American. So when I became a writer, I was intent on writing about American characters and conflicts, not about the country my parents and I fled in 1973.

But in 1996, soon after the birth of my third child and deep in the middle of writing another book, an image came to me in the middle of a sleepless night, a vision of a Red Army soldier and a young factory girl walking alone during war in Leningrad. He was tall and she was small. They were desperately in love, and they were starving.

From that image, as if from a renewable well-spring, came forth *The Bronze Horseman*, its follow-up *Tatiana and Alexander*, and the soon-to-be-published-by-Madison Park Press *The Summer Garden*.

The Bronze Horseman has been published in twenty one countries and translated into fourteen languages.

I'm very pleased that Madison Park Press is giving readers another opportunity to discover the book that has turned the life of its author into the before and after.

I hope that reading it will give you an entrance into another world, into an experience of a life most of us here in the United States have never known, a life in which a war was fought in our villages and cities, and all the people we knew found themselves in terrible danger, always a breath away from betrayal or death. Despite this, first love wound its way into the hearts of my two heroes with the strength of a wildflower pushing through cement.

This fall, more awaits you in the story of my heroine Tatiana and her Alexander. But it all began with *The Bronze Horseman*. I hope you enjoy the journey.

THE
BRONZE
HORSEMAN

A Novel

Paullina Simons

William Morrow
75 Years of Publishing
An Imprint of HarperCollins*Publishers*

Maps by David Lindroth

Designed by Bernard Klein

ISBN 978-0-06-019926-5

Printed in the U.S.A.

For my beloved grandparents, Maria and Lev Handler, who have lived through World War I, the Russian Revolution and the Russian Civil War, who have lived through World War II, the siege of Leningrad and evacuation, through famine and purges, through Lenin and Stalin, and in the golden twilight of their lives, through twenty non-air-conditioned summers in New York. God bless you.

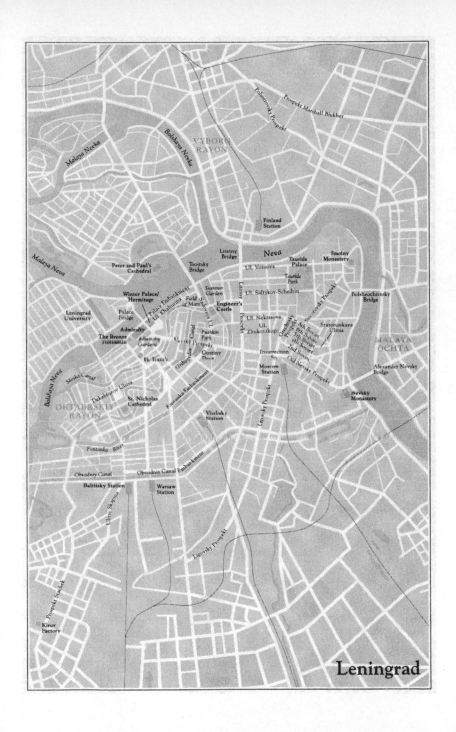

Leningrad

Hence in a season of calm weather
Though inland far we be,
Our Souls have sight of that immortal sea
Which brought us hither,
Can in a moment travel thither,
And see the Children sport upon the shore,
And hear the mighty waters rolling evermore.

                    William Wordsworth

FINLAND

Lake Ladoga

Lodeynoye
Pole

PRESENT-DAY BORDER

Vyborg

R. Svir

Gulf of Finland

Karelian Isthmus

Kokkorevo

Syastroy

Kronstadt

Leningrad

Morozovo
Shlisselburg

Lisiy Nos

Kobona

Volkhov

Lomonosov

Dubrovka

Sinyavino

R. Neva

Peterhof

Mga

Pulkovo

Tsarskoye Selo

R. Izhora

Tikhvin

Gatchina

SOVIET UNION

Narva

Kingisepp

R. Luga

R. Volkhov

Tolmachevo

Luga

Novgorod

Lake Ilmen

0   50 Miles

Book One

LENINGRAD

Part One

THE LUCENT DUSK

THE FIELD OF MARS

1

Lіgнт came through the window, trickling morning all over the room. Tatiana Metanova slept the sleep of the innocent, the sleep of restless joy, of warm, white Leningrad nights, of jasmine June. But most of all, intoxicated with life, she slept the exuberant sleep of undaunted youth.

She did not sleep for much longer.

When the sun's rays moved across the room to rest at the foot of Tatiana's bed, she pulled the sheet over her head, trying to keep the daylight out. The bedroom door opened, and she heard the floor creak once. It was her sister, Dasha.

Daria, Dasha, Dashenka, Dashka.

She represented everything that was dear to Tatiana.

Right now, however, Tatiana wanted to smother her. Dasha was trying to wake her up and, unfortunately, succeeding. Dasha's strong hands were vigorously shaking Tatiana, while her usually harmonious voice was dissonantly hissing, "Psst! Tania! Wake up. Wake up!"

Tatiana groaned. Dasha pulled back the sheet.

Never was their seven-year age difference more apparent than now, when Tatiana wanted to sleep and Dasha was . . .

"Stop it," Tatiana muttered, fishing helplessly behind her for the sheet and pulling it back over her. "Can't you see I'm sleeping? What are you? My mother?"

The door to the room opened. Two creaks on the floor. It *was* her mother. "Tania? You awake? Get up right now."

Tatiana could never say that her mother's voice was harmonious. There was nothing soft about Irina Metanova. She was small, boisterous, and full of indignant, overflowing energy. She wore a kerchief to keep her hair back from her face, for she had probably already been down on her knees washing the communal bathroom in her blue summer frock. She looked bedraggled and done with her Sunday.

"What, Mama?" Tatiana said, not lifting her head from the pillow. Dasha's hair touched Tatiana's back. Her hand was on Tatiana's leg, and Dasha bent over as if to kiss her. Tatiana felt a momentary tenderness, but before Dasha could say anything, Mama's grating voice intruded. "Get up quick. There's going to be an important announcement on the radio in a few minutes."

Tatiana whispered to Dasha, "Where were *you* last night? You didn't come in till well past dawn."

"Can I help it," Dasha whispered with pleasure, "that last night dawn was at midnight? I came in at the perfectly respectable hour of midnight." She was grinning. "You were all asleep."

"Dawn was at three, and you weren't home."

Dasha paused. "I'll tell Papa I got caught on the other side of the river when the bridges went up at three."

"Yes, you do that. Explain to him what you were doing on the other side of the river at three in the morning." Tatiana turned over. Dasha looked particularly striking this morning. She had unruly dark brown hair and an animated, round, dark-eyed face that had a reaction for everything. Right now that reaction was cheerful exasperation. Tatiana was exasperated herself—less cheerfully. She wanted to continue sleeping.

She caught a glimpse of her mother's tense expression. "What announcement?"

Her mother was taking the bedclothes off the sofa.

"Mama! What announcement?" Tatiana repeated.

"There is going to be a government announcement in a few minutes. That's all I know," Mama said doggedly, shaking her head, as if to say, *what's not to understand?*

Tatiana was reluctantly awake. Announcement. It was a rare event when music would be interrupted for a word from the government. "Maybe we invaded Finland again." She rubbed her eyes.

"Quiet," Mama said.

"Or maybe they invaded us. They've been wanting their borders back ever since losing them last year."

"We didn't invade them," said Dasha. "Last year we went to get *our* borders back. The ones we lost in the Great War. And you should stop listening to adult conversations."

"We didn't lose our borders," Tatiana said. "Comrade Lenin gave them away freely and willingly. That doesn't count."

"Tania, we are not at war with Finland. Get out of bed."

6

Tatiana did not get out of bed. "Latvia, then? Lithuania? Byelorussia? Didn't we just help ourselves to them, too, after the Hitler-Stalin pact?"

"Tatiana Georgievna! Stop it!" Her mother always called her by her first and patronymic names whenever she wanted to show Tatiana she was not in the mood to be fooled with.

Tatiana pretended to be serious. "What else is left? We already have half of Poland."

"I said stop!" Mama exclaimed. "Enough of your games. Get out of bed. Daria Georgievna, get that sister of yours out of bed."

Dasha did not move.

Growling, Mama left the room.

Turning quickly to Tatiana, Dasha whispered conspiratorially, "I've got something to tell you!"

"Something good?" Tatiana was instantly curious. Dasha usually revealed little about her grown-up life. Tatiana sat up.

"Something great!" said Dasha. "I'm in love!"

Tatiana rolled her eyes and fell back on the bed.

"Stop it!" Dasha said, jumping on top of her. "This is serious, Tania."

"Yes, all right. Did you just meet him yesterday when the bridges were up?" She smiled.

"Yesterday was the third time."

Tatiana shook her head, gazing at Dasha, whose joy was infectious. "Can you get off me?"

"No, I can't get off you," Dasha said, tickling her. "Not until you say, 'I'm happy, Dasha.' "

"Why would I say that?" exclaimed Tatiana, laughing. "I'm not happy. Stop it! Why should I be happy? *I'm* not in love. Cut it out!"

Mama came back into the room, carrying six cups on a round tray and a silver *samovar*—an urn with a spigot used for boiling water for tea. "You two will stop at once! Did you hear me?"

"Yes, Mama," said Dasha, giving Tatiana one last hard tickle.

"Ouch!" said Tatiana as loudly as possible. "Mama, I think she cracked my ribs."

"I'm going to crack something else in a minute. You're both too old for these games."

Dasha stuck out her tongue at Tatiana. "Very grown-up," Tatiana said. "Our Mamochka doesn't know you're only two."

Dasha's tongue remained out. Tatiana reached up and grabbed the slippery thing between her fingers. Dasha squealed. Tatiana let go.

"What did I say!" Mama bellowed.

Dasha leaned over and whispered to Tatiana, "Wait until you meet him. You've never met anybody so handsome."

"You mean better-looking than that Sergei you tortured me with? Didn't you tell me *he* was so handsome?"

"Stop it," hissed Dasha, smacking Tatiana's leg.

"Of course." Tatiana grinned. "And wasn't that just last week?"

"You'll never understand because you are still an incorrigible child." There was another smack. Mama yelled. The girls stopped.

Tatiana's father, Georgi Vasilievich Metanov, came in. A short man in his forties, he sported a full head of untidy black hair that was just beginning to turn to salt and pepper. Dasha got her curly hair from Papa. He walked past the bed, glanced vacantly at Tatiana, her legs still under the sheets, and said, "Tania, it's noon. Get up. Or there's going to be trouble. I need you dressed in two minutes."

"That's easy," Tatiana replied, jumping up on the bed and showing her family that she was still wearing her shirt and skirt from yesterday. Dasha and Mama shook their heads; Mama nearly smiled.

Papa looked away toward the window. "What are we going to do with her, Irina?"

Nothing, Tatiana thought, nothing as long as Papa looks the other way.

"I need to get married," Dasha said, still sitting on the bed. "So I can finally have a room of my own to get dressed in."

"You're joking," said Tatiana, jumping up and down on the bed. "You'll just be in here with your husband. Me, you, him, all sleeping in one bed, with Pasha at our feet. Romantic, isn't it?"

"Don't get married, Dashenka," her mother said absentmindedly. "Tania is right for once. We have no room for him."

Her father said nothing, turning on the radio.

Their long, narrow room had one full bed on which Tatiana and Dasha slept, one sofa on which Mama and Papa slept, and one low metal cot on which Tatiana's twin brother, Pasha, slept. His cot was at the foot of the girls' bed, so Pasha called himself their little footdog.

Tatiana's grandparents, Babushka and Deda, lived in the adjacent room, joined to theirs by a short hallway. Occasionally Dasha would sleep on the small sofa in the hallway if she came in late and didn't want to disturb her parents and thereby get into trouble the next day. The hall sofa was only about one and a half meters long, more suitable for Tatiana to sleep on, since she was just over one and a half meters long herself. But Tatiana didn't need to sleep in the hall because she rarely came in late, whereas Dasha was a different story.

"Where's Pasha?" Tatiana asked.

"Finishing breakfast," Mama replied. She couldn't stop moving. While Papa sat on the old sofa, still as a building, Mama bustled all around him, picking up empty packs of cigarettes, straightening books on the shelf, wiping down the little table with her hand. Tatiana continued to stand on the bed. Dasha continued to sit.

The Metanovs were lucky—they had two rooms *and* a sectioned-off part of the communal hallway. Six years earlier they had built a door to partition the very end of the corridor. It was almost like having an apartment of their own. The Iglenkos down the hall had to sleep six to a large room—off the corridor. Now *that* was unlucky.

The sunshine filtered in through the billowing white curtains.

Tatiana knew there would be only an instant, a brief flicker of time that bathed her with the possibilities of the day. In a moment it would all be gone. And in a moment it all was. Still . . . that sun streaking through the room, the distant rumble of buses through the open window, the slight wind.

This was the part of Sunday that Tatiana loved most: the beginning.

Pasha walked in with Deda and Babushka. Despite being Tatiana's twin, he looked nothing like her. A compact, dark-haired boy, a smaller version of their father, he acknowledged Tatiana by casually nodding in her direction and mouthing, "Nice hair."

Tatiana stuck out her tongue. She just hadn't brushed and tied it up yet.

Pasha sat on his low cot, and Babushka snuggled up next to him. Because she was the tallest of the Metanovs, the whole family deferred to her in all matters except matters of morality, in which everyone deferred to Deda. Babushka was imposing, no-nonsense, and silver-haired. Deda was humble and dark and kind. He sat next to Papa on the sofa and murmured, "It's something big, son."

Papa nodded anxiously.

Mama continued to clean anxiously.

Tatiana watched Babushka stroke Pasha's back. "Pasha," Tatiana whispered, crawling to the edge of the bed and pulling on her brother. "Want to go to Tauride Park later? I'll beat you in war."

"Dream on," said Pasha, "You will never beat me."

The radio began to make a series of clicking sounds. It was 12:30 P.M. on June 22, 1941.

"Tania, be quiet and sit down," Papa ordered his daughter. "It's about to begin. Irina, you, too. Sit."

Comrade Vyacheslav Molotov, Joseph Stalin's Foreign Minister, began:

Men and women, citizens of the Soviet Union—the Soviet government and its head, Comrade Stalin, have instructed me to make the following announcement. At 4 A.M., without declaration of war and without any claims being made on the Soviet Union, German troops attacked our country, attacked our frontier in many places, and bombed from the air Shitomir, Kiev, Sevastopol, Kaunas, and other cities. This attack has been made despite the fact that there was a nonaggression pact between the Soviet Union and Germany, a pact the terms of which were scrupulously observed by the Soviet Union. We have been attacked, although during the period of the pact the German Government had not made the slightest complaint about the USSR's not carrying out its obligations . . .

The government calls upon you, men and women citizens of the Soviet

9

Union, to rally even more closely around the glorious Bolshevik Party, around the Soviet government and our great leader, Comrade Stalin. Our cause is just. The enemy will be crushed. Victory will be ours.

The radio went dead, and the family sat in stunned and heavy silence. Finally Papa said, "Oh, my God." And from the sofa he stared at Pasha. Mama said, "We have to immediately go and get our money out of the bank."

Babushka Anna said, "Not evacuation again. Can we survive another one? Almost better to stay in the city."

Deda said, "Can I even get another evacuation teaching post? I'm nearly sixty-four. It's time to die, not move."

Dasha said, "The Leningrad garrison doesn't go to war, right? The war comes to the Leningrad garrison?"

Pasha said, "War! Tania, did you hear? I'm going to enlist. I'm going to go and fight for Mother Russia."

Before Tatiana could say what she was thinking—which was an immeasurably excited "Wow!"—her father jumped up off the sofa and, responding only to Pasha, exclaimed, "What are you thinking? Who do you think will take you?"

"Come on, Papochka," said Pasha with a smile. "The war always needs good men."

"Good men, yes. Not children," barked Papa as he kneeled on the floor, looking under Tatiana and Dasha's bed.

"War, why, that's not possible," Tatiana said slowly. "Didn't Comrade Stalin sign a peace treaty?"

Mama poured tea and said, "Tania, it's for real. It's for real."

Tatiana tried to keep the thrill out of her voice when she said, "Will we have to . . . *evacuate*?"

Papa pulled an old, ratty suitcase from under the bed.

"So soon?" said Tatiana.

She knew of evacuation from the stories Deda and Babushka had told her of the unrest around the time of the Revolution of 1917, when they went just west of the Ural Mountains to live in a village whose name Tatiana could never remember. Waiting for the train with all their belongings, crowding in, crossing the Volga on barges . . .

It was the change that excited Tatiana. It was the unknown. She herself had been to Moscow once for a minute when she was eight—did that even count? Moscow wasn't exotic. It wasn't Africa or America. It wasn't even the Urals. It was just Moscow. Beyond the Red Square there was nothing, not even a little beauty.

As a family the Metanovs had taken a couple of day trips to Tsarskoye Selo and Peterhof. The summer palaces of the tsars had been turned by the Bolsheviks into lavish museums with landscaped grounds. When Tatiana wandered the halls of Peterhof, treading carefully on the cold, veined marble, she could not believe there had been a time when people had *all this* to live in.

But then the family would return to Leningrad, to their two rooms on Fifth Soviet, and before Tatiana got to her room, she would have to walk past the six Iglenkos who lived off the corridor with their door open.

When Tatiana was three, the family vacationed in the very Crimea that this morning had been attacked by the Germans. What Tatiana remembered from that trip was that it was the first time she ate a raw potato. Also the last. She saw tadpoles in a little pond and slept covered with a blanket in a tent. She vaguely remembered the smell of salt water. It was in the frigid April Black Sea that Tatiana felt her first and last jellyfish, floating past her tiny naked body and making her shriek with delighted terror.

The thought of evacuation filled Tatiana with stomach-churning excitement. Born in 1924, the year of Lenin's death, *after* the revolution, *after* the hunger, *after* the civil war, Tatiana had been born *after* the worst but *before* anything good either. She had been born *during*.

Lifting his black eyes to her, as if measuring her emotions, Deda spoke. "Tanechka, what are you even thinking?"

She tried to make her face calm. "Nothing."

"What's going on in that head of yours? It's war. Do you understand?"

"I understand."

"Somehow I don't think you do." Deda paused. "Tania, the life you know is over. Mark my words. From this day forward, nothing will be as you have imagined."

Pasha exclaimed, "Yes! We're going to boot the Germans back to hell, where they belong." He smiled at Tatiana, who smiled back.

Mama and Papa were quiet.

Papa said, "Yes. And then what?"

Babushka went to sit on the sofa next to Deda. Placing her large hand on his, she pursed her lips and nodded, in a way that showed Tatiana that Babushka knew things and was keeping them to herself. Deda knew, too, but whatever it was they knew did not measure up to Tatiana's tumult. That's all right, she thought. They don't understand. They are not young.

Mama broke the silence of seven people. "What are you doing, Georgi Vasilievich?"

"Too many children, Irina Fedorovna. Too many children to worry about," he said dolefully to her, struggling with Pasha's suitcase.

"Really, Papa?" said Tatiana. "Which of your children would you like not to worry about?"

Without replying, Papa went to Pasha's drawers in the armoire they all shared and started haphazardly throwing the boy's clothes into the suitcase.

"I'm sending him away, Irina. I'm sending him away to camp in Tolmachevo. He was going to go anyway next week with Volodya Iglenko. He'll just go a little sooner. Volodya will go with him. Nina will be glad to have them go a week early. You'll see. Everything will be all right."

Mama opened her mouth and shook her head. "Tolmachevo? He will be safe there? Are you sure?"

"Absolutely," said Papa.

"Absolutely not," said Pasha. "Papa, war has started! I'm not going to camp. I'm going to enlist."

Good for you, Pasha, thought Tatiana, but Papa whipped around to glare at her brother, and, sucking in her breath, Tatiana suddenly understood everything.

Grabbing Pasha by the shoulders, Papa started to shake him. "What are you saying? Are you crazy? *Enlist?*"

Pasha fought to break free. Papa would not let go.

"Papa, let go of me."

"Pavel, you're my son, and you will listen to me. The first thing you're going to do is get out of Leningrad. Then we'll discuss enlisting. Right now we have a train to catch."

There was something embarrassing and awkward about a physical scene in a small room with so many people watching. Tatiana wanted to turn away, but there was nowhere to turn. Across from her were her grandmother and grandfather, behind her was Dasha, to the left of her were her mother and father and brother. She looked down at her hands and closed her eyes. She imagined lying on her back in the middle of a summer field eating sweet clover. No one was around her.

How did things change in a matter of seconds?

She opened her eyes and blinked. One second. She blinked again. Another second.

Seconds ago she was sleeping.

Seconds ago Molotov spoke.

Seconds ago she was exhilarated.

Seconds ago Papa spoke.

And now Pasha was leaving. Blink, blink, blink.

Deda and Babushka were diplomatically silent, as always. Deda, God love him, never missed an opportunity to keep quiet. Babushka was quite the opposite of him in that respect, but in this particular instance she had obviously decided to follow his lead. Perhaps it was his hand tightly squeezing her leg each time she opened her mouth, but for whatever reason, she did not speak.

Dasha, unafraid of their father and not discouraged by the distant prospect of war, got up and said, "Papa, this is crazy. Why are you sending him away? The Germans are nowhere near Leningrad. You heard Comrade Molotov. They're at the Crimea. That's thousands of kilometers from here."

"Be quiet, Dashenka," said Papa. "You have no idea about the Germans."

"They're not here, Papa," Dasha repeated in her strong voice that allowed for no argument. Tatiana wished she could speak as persuasively as Dasha. Her own voice was echo soft, as if some female hormone hadn't come her way yet. In many ways it barely had. She'd got her monthlies only last year, and even then . . . she *barely* got her monthlies. They were more like quarterlies. They came in the winter, decided they didn't like it, and left till fall. In the fall they came and stayed as if they were never leaving. Since then Tatiana had seen them twice. Maybe if they came more often, Tatiana would have a meaningful voice like Dasha's. You could set the clock by Dasha's monthlies.

"Daria! I'm not going to argue with *you* on this point!" exclaimed Papa. "Your brother is not staying in Leningrad. Pasha, get dressed. Put on some trousers and a nice shirt."

"Papa, please."

"Pasha! I said get dressed. We cannot waste time. I guarantee those children's camps are going to completely fill up in one hour, and then I won't be able to get you in."

Perhaps it was a mistake to tell that to Pasha, because Tatiana had never seen her brother move more slowly. He must have spent a good ten minutes looking for the one dress shirt he owned. They all averted their eyes while Pasha changed. Tatiana closed her eyes again, searching for her meadow, for the pleasant summer smell of white cherry and nettles. She wanted some blueberries. She realized she was a little hungry. Opening her eyes, she glanced around the room. "I don't want to go," complained Pasha.

"It's just for a little while, son," said Papa. "It's a precaution. You'll be safe in camp, out of harm's way. You'll stay maybe a month, until we see how the war is going. Then you'll come back, and if there's evacuation, we'll get you and your sisters out."

Yes! Tatiana wanted to hear that.

"Georg." Deda spoke softly. "Georg."

"Yes, Papochka?" Tatiana's father said respectfully. No one loved Deda more than Papa, not even Tatiana.

"Georg. You cannot keep the boy out of conscription. You can't."

"Of course I can. He is only seventeen."

Deda shook his neat gray head. "Exactly—seventeen. They'll take him."

The look of trapped fear slid across Papa's face and was gone. "They won't take him, Papochka," said Papa hoarsely. "I don't even know what you're talking about." He was clearly unable to say what he felt: *everyone stop talking and let me save my son the only way I know how.* Deda sat back against the sofa cushions.

Feeling bad for her father and wanting to be helpful, Tatiana began to say, "We're not yet—" but Mama cut in with, "Pashechka, take a sweater, darling."

"I'm not taking a sweater, Mama," he exclaimed. "It's the middle of summer!"

"We had frost two weeks ago."

13

"And now it's hot. I'm not taking it."

"Listen to your mother, Pavel," said Papa. "The nights will be cold in Tolmachevo. Take the sweater." Pasha sighed deeply, rebelliously, but took the sweater and threw it inside the suitcase. Papa closed it and locked it. "Everyone, listen. Here's my plan . . ."

"What plan?" Tatiana said with mild frustration. "I hope this plan includes some food. Because—"

"I know why," Papa snapped. "Now, be quiet and listen. This concerns you, too." He started telling them what he needed them to do.

Tatiana fell back on the bed. If they weren't evacuating this *instant*, she didn't want to hear any more.

Pasha went to boys' camp every summer, in Tolmachevo, Luga, or Gatchina. Pasha preferred Luga because it had the best river for swimming. Tatiana preferred Pasha in Luga because he was close to their *dacha*, their summer house, and she could go and visit him. The Luga camp was only five kilometers from their *dacha* straight through the woods. Tolmachevo, on the other hand, was twenty kilometers from Luga, and there the counselors were strict and expected you up by sunrise. Pasha said it was a bit like being in the army. Well, now it would be almost like enlisting, she thought, not listening to her father speak.

She felt Dasha pinch her hard on the leg. "Ouch!" she said, deliberately loudly, hoping her sister would get into trouble for hurting her. No one cared. No one said anything. They didn't even look her way. All eyes were on Pasha as he stood—reedy and awkward in his brown trousers and frayed beige shirt—in the middle of the room, in the half bloom of late adolescence, so beloved. And he knew it.

He was everyone's favorite child, favorite grandchild, favorite brother.

Because he was the only son.

Tatiana lifted herself off the bed and came to stand by Pasha. Putting her arm around him, she said, "Cheer up. You're so lucky. You're going to camp. I'm not going anywhere."

He stepped slightly away from her, but only slightly; stepped away not because he was uncomfortable with her, Tatiana knew, but because he did not feel himself to be lucky. She knew that her brother wanted to become a soldier more than anything. He didn't want to be in some silly camp. "Pasha," she said cheerfully, "first you have to beat *me* in war. *Then* you can enlist and fight the Germans."

"Shut up, Tania," said Pasha.

"Shut up, Tania," said Papa.

"Papa," said Tatiana, "can I pack *my* suitcase? I want to go to camp, too."

"Pasha, are you ready? Let's go," said Papa, not even replying to Tatiana. There *were* no girls' camps.

"I have a joke for you, dear Pasha," said Tatiana, not wanting to give up and not put off by her brother's reluctance.

14

"Don't want to hear your stupid jokes, dear Tania."

"You'll like this one."

"Why do I doubt it?"

Papa said, "Tatiana! This is no time for jokes."

Deda intervened on Tatiana's behalf. "Georg, let the girl speak."

Nodding at Deda, Tatiana said, "A soldier is being led to his execution. 'Some bad weather we're having,' he says to his convoy. 'Look who's complaining,' they say. '*We* have to go back.' "

Nobody moved. No one even smiled.

Pasha raised his eyebrows, pinched her, and whispered, "Nice going, Tania."

She sighed. Someday her spirit would soar, she thought, but not this day.

2

"Tatiana, no long good-byes. You'll see your brother in a month. Come downstairs and hold the front door open for us. Your mother's back is bothering her," Papa told her as they got ready to carry Pasha's things along with bags of extra food for camp.

"All right, Papa."

The apartment was laid out like a train—a long corridor with nine rooms attached. There were two kitchens, one at the front of the apartment, one at the back. The bathrooms and the toilets were attached to the kitchens. In the nine rooms lived twenty-five people. Five years ago there were thirty-three people in the apartment, but eight people had moved or died or—

Tatiana's family lived in the back. It was better to live in the back. The rear kitchen was the bigger of the two, and it had stairs leading up to the roof and down to the courtyard; Tatiana liked taking the rear stairs because she could sneak out without passing crazy Slavin's room.

The rear kitchen had a bigger stove than the front kitchen and a bigger bath. And only three other families shared the rear kitchen and bathroom with the Metanovs—the Petrovs, the Sarkovs, and crazy Slavin, who never cooked and never bathed.

Slavin was not in the hall at the moment. Good.

As Tatiana walked down the corridor to the front door, she passed the shared telephone. Petr Petrov was using it, and Tatiana had time to think how lucky they were that their telephone worked. Tatiana's cousin Marina lived in an apartment where the telephone was broken all the time—faulty wiring. It was difficult to get in touch with her, unless Tatiana wrote or went to see her personally, which she did not do often, since Marina lived on the other side of town, across the river Neva.

As Tatiana neared Petr, she saw that he was very agitated. He was obviously waiting for a connection, and though the cord was too short to allow him to pace, he was pacing with his whole body while standing in one place. Petr got his connection just as Tatiana was passing him in the narrow corridor; Tatiana knew this because he screamed into the phone. "Luba! Is that you? Is that you, Luba?"

So unexpected and sharp was his cry that Tatiana jumped away from him, knocking into the wall. Getting her bearings, she passed him quickly and then slowed down to listen.

"Luba, can you hear me? We have a bad connection. Everyone is trying to get through. Luba, come back to Leningrad! Did you hear? War has started. Take whatever you can, leave the rest, and get the next train. Luba! No, not in an hour, not tomorrow—*now*, do you understand? Come back immediately!" Short pause. "Forget our things, I tell you! Are you listening to me, woman?"

Turning around, Tatiana caught a glimpse of Petr's stiff back.

"Tatiana!" Papa was glaring at her with an expression that said, *if you don't come here right now* . . .

But Tatiana dawdled to hear more. Her father yelled across the corridor, "Tatiana Georgievna! Come here and help." Like her mother, her father said her full name only when he wanted Tatiana to know how serious he was. Tatiana hurried, wondering about Petr Petrov and about why her brother couldn't open the front door himself.

Volodya Iglenko, who was Pasha's age and was going to the Tolmachevo camp with him, walked downstairs with the Metanovs, holding his own suitcase and opening his own door. He was one of four brothers. He *had* to do things for himself. "Pasha, let me show you," Tatiana said quietly. "It's like this. You put your hand on the handle, and you pull. The door opens. You walk outside. It shuts behind you. Let's see if you can do it."

"Just open the door, Tania," said Pasha. "Can't you see I'm carrying my suitcase?"

Out on the street they stood still for a moment.

"Tania," said Papa. "Take the hundred and fifty rubles I gave you and go and buy us some food. But don't dawdle, like always. Go immediately. Do you hear?"

"I hear, Papa. I'll go immediately."

Pasha snorted. "You're going back to bed," he whispered to her.

Mama said, "Come on, we better go."

"Yes," Papa said. "Come on, Pasha."

"So long," Tatiana said, knocking Pasha on the arm.

He grunted unhappily in reply and pulled her hair. "Tie your hair up before you go out, will you?" he said. "You'll scare off the passersby."

"Shut up," Tatiana said lightly. "Or I'll cut it off completely."

"All right, let's go now," said Papa, tugging at Pasha.

Tatiana said good-bye to Volodya, waved to her mother, took one last look at Pasha's reluctant back, and returned upstairs.

Deda and Babushka were on their way out with Dasha. They were going to the bank to get their savings out.

Tatiana was left alone.

She breathed a sigh of relief and fell onto her bed.

Tatiana knew she had been born too late into the family. She and Pasha. She should have been born in 1917, like Dasha. After her there were other children, but not for long: two brothers, one born in 1919 and one in 1921, died of typhus. A girl, born in 1922, died of scarlet fever in 1923. Then in 1924, as Lenin was dying and the New Economic Plan—that short-lived return to free enterprise—was coming to an end, while Stalin was scheming to enlarge his power base in the presidium through the firing squad, Pasha and Tatiana were born seven minutes apart to a very tired twenty-five-year-old Irina Fedorovna. The family *wanted* Pasha, their boy, but Tatiana was a stunning surprise. No one had twins. Who had twins? Twins were almost unheard of. *And* there was no room for her. She and Pasha had to share a crib for the first three years of their life. Since then Tatiana slept with Dasha.

But the fact remained—she was taking up valuable bed space. Dasha couldn't get married because Tania took up the space where Dasha's prospective husband would lie. Dasha often expressed this to Tatiana. She would say, "Because of you I'm going to die an old maid." To which Tatiana would immediately reply, "Soon, I hope. So I can marry and have my husband sleep next to me."

After graduating from school last month, Tatiana had gotten a job so she wouldn't have to spend another idle summer in Luga reading and rowing boats and playing silly games with the kids down the dusty road. Tatiana had spent all of her childhood summers at their dacha in Luga and on nearby Lake Ilmen in Novgorod, where her cousin Marina had a *dacha* with her parents.

In the past Tatiana had looked forward to cucumbers in June, tomatoes in July, and maybe some raspberries in August, looked forward to mushroom picking and blueberry picking, to fishing on the river—all such small pleasures. But this summer was going to be different.

Tatiana realized she was tired of being a child. At the same time she didn't know how to be anything else, so she got a job at the Kirov factory, in the south of Leningrad. That was *nearly* adult. She now worked and constantly read the newspaper, shaking her head at France, at Marshal Pétain, at Dunkirk, at Neville Chamberlain. She tried to be very serious, nodding purposefully at the crises in the Low Countries and the Far East. Those were Tatiana's concessions to adulthood—Kirov and *Pravda*.

She liked her job at Kirov, the biggest industrial plant in Leningrad and probably in all of the Soviet Union. Tatiana had heard that somewhere in that factory workers built tanks. But she was skeptical. She had not seen one.

She made silverware. Her job was to put the knives, forks, and spoons into boxes. She was the second-to-last person in the assembly line. The girl after

17

her taped the boxes shut. Tatiana felt bad for that girl; taping was just so boring. At least Tatiana got to handle three different types of utensils.

Working at Kirov was going to be fun this summer, Tatiana thought, lying on her bed, but not as much fun as evacuation would have been.

Tatiana would have liked to get in a few hours of reading. She had just started Mikhail Zoshchenko's sadistically funny short stories on the ironic realities of Soviet life, but her instructions from her father had been very clear. She looked at her book longingly. What was the hurry anyway? The adults were behaving as if there were a fire. The Germans were two thousand kilometers away. Comrade Stalin would not let that traitor Hitler get deep into the country. And Tatiana never got to be home alone.

As soon as Tatiana had realized there was going to be no immediate evacuation, she became less excited about the war. Was it *interesting*? Yes. But Zoshchenko's story *"Banya"*—"The Bathhouse"—about a man going to the Soviet bathhouse and washing his clothes there, too, and losing his coat checks, was hilarious. *Where is a naked man to put those coat checks? The checks were washed away during the bath. Only the string remained. I offer the string to the coat attendant. He won't take it. Any citizen can cut up string, he says. There won't be enough coats to go around. Wait until the other customers have gone. I'll give you whatever coat is left.*

Since no one was evacuating, Tatiana read the story twice, lying on the bed, her legs up on the wall, weak from laughter by the second time.

Still, orders were orders. She had to go out and get food.

But today was Sunday, and Tatiana did not like to go out on Sundays unless she got dressed up. Without asking, she borrowed Dasha's high-heeled red sandals, in which Tatiana walked like a newborn calf with two broken legs. Dasha walked better in them; she was much more used to them.

Tatiana brushed out her very blonde long hair, wistfully wishing for thick dark curls like the rest of the family's. Hers was so straight and *blah* blonde. She always wore it tied back in a ponytail or in braids. Today she tied it up in a ponytail. The straightness and the blondeness of her hair were inexplicable. In her daughter's defense, Mama would say that she herself had had straight blonde hair as a child. Yes, and Babushka said that when *she* got married she had weighed only forty-seven kilos.

Tatiana put on the only Sunday dress she owned, made sure her face and teeth and hands were sparkling clean, and left the apartment.

A hundred and fifty rubles was a colossal amount of money. Tatiana didn't know where her father got that kind of money, but it appeared magically in his hands, and it was not her place to ask. She was supposed to come back with—what did her father say? Rice? Vodka? She had already forgotten.

Mama did tell him, "Georg, don't send her out. She won't get anything."

Tatiana had nodded in agreement. "Mama is right. Send Dasha, Papa."

"No!" Papa exclaimed. "I know you can do it. Just go to the store, take a bag with you, and come back with—"

What did he tell her to come back with? Potatoes? Flour?

Tatiana walked past the Sarkovs' room and saw Zhanna and Zhenya Sarkov sitting in armchairs, sipping tea, reading, looking very relaxed, as if it were just another Sunday. How lucky they are to have such a big room all to themselves, thought Tatiana. Crazy Slavin was not in the hall. Good.

It was as if Molotov's announcement two hours ago had been an aberration in an otherwise normal day. Tatiana almost doubted that she had heard Comrade Molotov correctly until she got outside and turned the corner on Grechesky Prospekt, where teeming clusters of people were rushing toward Nevsky Prospekt, the main shopping street in Leningrad.

Tatiana could not remember when she had last seen such crowds on Leningrad streets. Quickly she turned around and went the other way to Suvorovsky Prospekt. She wanted to beat the crowds. If they were all going to the Nevsky Prospekt stores, she was going the opposite way down to Tauride Park, where the grocery stores, though understocked, were also underpatronized.

A man and a woman walked by, stared at Tatiana in her dress, and smiled. She lowered her gaze but smiled, too.

Tatiana was wearing her splendid white dress with red roses. She had the dress since 1938, when she had turned fourteen. Her father bought it from a market vendor in a town called Swietokryst in Poland, where he had gone on a business trip for the Leningrad waterworks plant. He went to Swietokryst, Warsaw, and Lublin. Tatiana thought her father was a world traveler when he came back. Dasha and Mama received chocolates from Warsaw, but the chocolates went a long time ago—two years and three hundred and sixty three days ago. But here Tatiana was, still wearing her dress with crimson roses embroidered on the thick, smooth, snow-white cotton. The roses weren't buds; they were blooms. It was a perfect summer dress, with thin shoulder straps and no sleeves. It was fitted through the waist and then billowed out in a flowing skirt to just above her knees, and if Tatiana spun around fast enough, the skirt whirled up in a parachute.

There was only one problem with this dress in June 1941: it was too small for Tatiana. The crisscross satin straps at the back of the dress that Tatiana could once tie completely closed had to be constantly loosened.

It vexed Tatiana that the body she was increasingly uneasy with could outgrow her favorite dress. It wasn't as if her body were blossoming to look like Dasha's, full of hips and breasts and thighs and arms. No, not at all. Tatiana's hips, though round, remained small, and her legs and arms remained slender, but the breasts got larger, and *there* was the problem. Had the breasts remained the same size, Tatiana wouldn't have had to leave the straps loose, exposing her bare spine under the crisscrosses from her shoulder blades to the small of her back for all the world to see.

Tatiana liked the notion of the dress, she liked the feeling of the cotton against her skin and the stitched roses under her fingers, but she did not like the feeling of her exploding body trapped inside the lung-squeezing material. What she enjoyed was the memory of her skinny-as-a-stick fourteen-year-old self putting on that dress for the first time and going out for a Sunday walk on Nevsky. It was for that feeling that she had put on the dress again this Sunday, the day Germany invaded the Soviet Union.

On another level, on a conscious, loudly-audible-to-the-soul level, what Tatiana also loved about the dress was a small tag that said FABRIQUÉ EN FRANCE.

Fabriqué en France! It was gratifying to own a piece of anything not made badly by the Soviets, but instead made well and romantically by the French; for who was more romantic than the French? The French were masters of love. All nations were different. The Russians were unparalleled in their suffering, the English in their reserve, the Americans in their love of life, the Italians in their love of Christ, and the French in their hope of love. So when *they* made the dress for Tatiana, they made it full of promise. They made it as if to tell her, put it on, *chérie*, and in this dress you, too, shall be loved as we have loved; put it on and love shall be yours. And so Tatiana never despaired in her white dress with red roses. Had the Americans made it, she would have been happy. Had the Italians made it, she would have started praying, had the British made it, she would have squared her shoulders, but because the French had made it, she never lost hope.

Though at the moment, Tatiana walked down Suvorovsky with her dress uncomfortably tight against her swelling adolescent chest.

Outside was fresh and warm, and it was a jolt to the consciousness to remember that on this sunny lovely day full of promise, Hitler was in the Soviet Union. Tatiana shook her head as she walked. Deda had never trusted that Hitler and said so from the start. When Comrade Stalin signed the nonaggression pact with Hitler in 1939, Deda said that Stalin had gone to bed with the devil. And now the devil had betrayed Stalin. Why was that such a surprise? Why had we expected more from him? Had we expected the devil to behave honorably?

Tatiana thought Deda was the smartest man on earth. Ever since Poland was trampled over in 1939, Deda had been saying that Hitler was coming to the Soviet Union. A few months ago in the spring, he suddenly started bringing home canned goods. Too many canned goods for Babushka's liking. Babushka had no interest in spending part of Deda's monthly pay on an intangible such as *just in case.* She would scoff at him. What are you talking about, war? she would say, glaring at the canned ham. Who is going to eat this, ever? I will never eat this garbage, why do you spend good money on garbage? Why can't you get marinated mushrooms, or tomatoes? And Deda, who loved Babushka more than a woman deserved to be loved by a man, would bow his head, let her vent her feelings, say nothing, but the following month be back carrying more cans of ham. He also bought sugar and he bought coffee and he bought tobacco, and he bought some vodka, too. He had less luck with keeping these items stocked because for every birthday, anniversary, May Day, the vodka was broken open and the tobacco smoked and the coffee drunk and the sugar put into bread and pie dough and tea. Deda was a man unable to deny his family anything, but he denied himself. So on his own birthday he refused to open the vodka. But Babushka still opened the bag of sugar to make him blueberry pie. The one thing that remained constant and grew by a can or two each month was the ham, which everyone hated and no one ate.

Tatiana's task of buying up all the rice and vodka she could get her hands on was proving much harder than she had anticipated.

The stores on Suvorovsky were empty of vodka. They carried cheese. But cheese would not keep well. They had bread, but bread would not keep well. The salami was gone, the canned goods, too. And the flour.

With a quickening pace Tatiana walked down Suvorovsky, eleven blocks in all, over a kilometer, and every store was empty of canned or long-term provisions. It was only three o'clock.

Tatiana passed two savings banks. Both were closed. Signs, hastily hand-written, said CLOSED EARLY. This surprised her. Why would the banks close early? It's not as if they could run out of money. They were banks. She chuckled to herself.

The Metanovs had waited too long, Tatiana realized, sitting around as they did, packing Pasha, bickering, looking dejectedly at one another. They should have been out the door in an instant, but instead Pasha was sent to camp. And Tatiana had read Zoshchenko. She should have been out an hour earlier. If only she had gone to Nevsky Prospekt, she could be standing in line right now with the rest of the crowds.

But even though she strolled down Suvorovsky disheartened at not being able to find even a box of matches to buy, Tatiana felt the warm summer air carrying with it an anomalous scent of provenance, a scent of an order of things to come that she neither knew nor understood. Will I always remember this day? Tatiana thought, inhaling deeply. I've said that in the past: oh, this day I'll remember, but I have forgotten the days I thought I would never forget. I remember seeing my first tadpole. Who would have thought? I remember tasting the salt water of the Black Sea for the first time. I remember getting lost in the woods by myself the first time. Maybe it's the firsts you remember. I've never been in a real war before, Tatiana thought. Maybe I'll remember this.

Tatiana headed toward the stores near Tauride Park. She liked this area of the city, away from the hustle of Nevsky Prospekt. The trees were lush and tall, and there were fewer people. She liked the feeling of a bit of solitude.

After looking inside three or four grocers, Tatiana wanted to just give up. She was seriously considering going back home and telling her father she

21

wasn't able to find anything, but the thought of telling him she had failed in the one small task he had assigned her filled her with anxiety. She walked on. Near the corner where Suvorovsky met Ulitsa Saltykov-Schedrin, there was a store with a long line of people stretching out into an otherwise empty street.

Dutifully she went and stood behind the last person in line.

Shifting from foot to foot, Tatiana stood and stood, asked for the time, stood and stood. The line moved a meter. Sighing, she asked the lady in front of her what they were standing in line for. The lady shrugged aggressively, turning away from Tatiana. "What, what?" the lady grumbled, holding her bag closer to her chest, as if Tatiana were about to rob her. "Stand in line like everybody else, and don't ask stupid questions."

Tatiana waited. The line moved another meter. She asked for the time again.

"Ten minutes after the last time you asked me!" barked the woman.

When she heard the young woman in front of the grumpy lady say the word "banks" Tatiana perked up.

"No more money," the young woman was saying to an older woman standing next to her. "Did you know that? The savings banks have run out. I don't know what they're going to do now. Hope you have some in your mattress."

The older woman shook her head worriedly. "I had 200 rubles, my life savings. That's what I have with me now."

"Well, buy, buy. Buy everything. Canned goods are especially—"

The older woman shook her head. "Don't like canned goods."

"Well, then buy caviar. I heard one woman bought ten kilos of caviar at Elisey on Nevsky. What's she going to do with this caviar? But it's none of my business. I'm buying oil. And matches."

"Buy some salt," the older woman said wisely. "You can drink tea without sugar, but you can't eat porridge without salt."

"Don't like porridge," the younger woman said. "Never liked it. Won't eat it. It's gruel, that's what it is."

"Well, buy caviar then. You like caviar, don't you?"

"No. Maybe some sausage," the younger woman said thoughtfully. "Some nice smoked *kolbasa*. Listen, it's been over twenty years that the proletariat has been the tsar. I know by now what to expect."

The woman in front of Tatiana snorted loudly. The two women ahead of her turned around.

"You *don't* know what to expect!" the woman said in a loud tone. "It's war." She gave a mirthless grunt that sounded like a train engine sputtering.

"Who asked you?"

"War, comrades! Welcome to reality, brought to you by Hitler. Buy your caviar and butter, and eat them tonight. Because mark my words, your two hundred rubles will not buy you a loaf of bread next January."

"Shut up!"

Tatiana lowered her head. She did not like fighting. Not at home, not on the street with strangers.

Two people were leaving the store with big paper bags under their arms. "What's in them?" she inquired politely.

"Smoked *kolbasa*," a man told her gruffly, hurrying on. He looked as if he were afraid Tatiana would run after him and beat him to the ground to get his cursed smoked *kolbasa*. Tatiana continued to stand in line. She didn't even like sausage.

After thirty more minutes she left.

Not wanting to disappoint her father, she hurried to the bus stop. She was going to catch bus Number 22 to Elisey on Nevsky Prospekt, since she knew for sure they sold at least caviar there.

But then she thought, caviar? We will have to eat it next week. Surely caviar won't last until winter? But is that the goal? Food for the winter? That just couldn't be, she decided; winter was too far away. The Red Army was invincible; Comrade Stalin said so himself. The German pigs would be out by September.

As she rounded the corner of Ulitsa Saltykov-Schedrin, the rubber band holding her hair snapped and broke.

The bus stop was across the street on the Tauride Park side. Usually she got bus 136 from here to go across town to visit cousin Marina. Today bus 22 would take her to Elisey, but she knew she needed to hurry. From the way those women were talking, soon even the caviar would be gone.

Just ahead of her, Tatiana spotted a kiosk that sold ice cream.

Ice cream!

Suddenly the day was filled with possibilities. A man sat on a little stool under a small umbrella to shield himself from the sun as he read the paper.

Tatiana quickened her pace.

From behind her she heard the sound of the bus. She turned around and saw her bus in the middle distance. She knew if she ran, she could catch it easily. She stepped off the curb to cross the street, then looked at the ice cream stand, looked at the bus again, looked at the ice cream stand, and stopped.

Tatiana *really* wanted an ice cream.

Biting her lip, she let the bus pass. It's all right, she thought. The next one will come soon, and in the meantime I'll sit at the bus stop and have an ice cream.

Walking up to the kiosk man, she said eagerly, "Ice cream, yes?"

"It says ice cream, doesn't it? I'm sitting here, aren't I? What do you want?" He lifted his eyes from the newspaper to her, and his hard expression softened. "What can I get you, dearie?"

"Have you got . . ." She trembled a little. "Have you got crème brûlée?"

"Yes." He opened the freezer door. "A cone or a cup?"

"A cone, please," Tatiana replied, jumping up and down once.

23

She paid him gladly; she would have paid him double. In anticipation of the pleasure she was about to receive, Tatiana ran across the road in her heels, hurrying to the bench under the trees so she could eat her ice cream in peace, while she waited for the bus to take her to buy caviar because war had started.

There was no one else waiting for the bus, and she was glad for the fine moment to feast on her delight in seclusion. She took off the white paper wrapping, threw it in the trash can next to the bench, smelled the ice cream, and took a lick of the sweet, creamy, cold caramel. Closing her eyes in happiness, Tatiana smiled and rolled the ice cream in her mouth, waiting for it to melt on her tongue.

Too good, Tatiana thought. Just too good.

The wind blew her hair, and she held it back with one hand as she licked the ice cream in circles around the smooth ball. She crossed and uncrossed her legs, swung her head back, lolled the ice cream in her throat, and hummed the song everyone was singing these days: "Someday we'll meet in Lvov, my love and I."

It was a perfect day. For five minutes there was no war, and it was just a glorious Sunday in a Leningrad June.

When Tatiana looked up from her ice cream, she saw a soldier staring at her from across the street.

It was unremarkable in a garrison city like Leningrad to see a soldier. Leningrad was full of soldiers. Seeing soldiers on the street was like seeing old ladies with shopping bags, or lines, or beer bars. Tatiana normally would have glanced past him down the street and moved on, except that this soldier was standing across the street and staring at her with an expression Tatiana had never seen before. She stopped eating her ice cream.

Her side of the street was already in the shade, but the side where he stood swam in the northern afternoon light. Tatiana stared back at him for just a moment, and in the moment of looking into his face, something moved inside her; *moved* she would have liked to say *imperceptibly*, but that wasn't quite the case. It was as if her heart started pumping blood through all four chambers at once, pouring it into her lungs and flooding it through her body. She blinked and felt her breath become shorter. The soldier was melting into the pavement under the pale yellow sun.

The bus came, obstructing Tatiana's view of him. She almost cried out and got up, not to get on the bus, no, but to run forward, across the street, so she would not lose sight of him. The bus doors opened, and the driver looked at her expectantly. Tatiana, mild-mannered and quiet, nearly shouted at him to get out of her way.

"Are you getting on, young lady? I can't be waiting forever."

Getting on? "No, no, I'm not going."

"Then what the hell are you doing waiting for the bus!" the driver hollered and slammed the doors shut.

Tatiana backed away toward the bench and saw the soldier running around the bus.

He stopped.

She stopped.

The bus doors opened again. "Need the bus?" asked the driver.

The soldier looked at Tatiana, then at the bus driver.

"Oh, for the sake of Lenin and Stalin!" the driver bellowed, slamming the doors shut for the second time.

Tatiana was left standing in front of the bench. She backed away, tripped, and sat quickly down.

In a casual tone, with a shrug and a roll of his eyes, the soldier said, "I thought it was my bus."

"Yes, me, too," she uttered, her voice croaky.

"Your ice cream is melting," he said helpfully.

And it was, melting right through the bottom point of the waffle cone, onto her dress. "Oh, no," she said. Tatiana brushed the ice cream, only to spread it in a smear. "Great," she muttered, and noticed that her hand wiping the dress was trembling.

"Have you been waiting long?" the soldier asked. His voice was strong and deep and had a trace of . . . she didn't know. Not from around here, she thought, keeping her gaze lowered.

"Not too long," she replied quietly, and, holding her breath, raised her eyes to get a better look at him. And raised them and raised them. He was tall.

He was wearing a dress uniform. The beige fatigues looked like his Sunday best, and his cap was ornate, with an enameled red star on the front. He wore wide parade shoulder boards in gray metallic lace. They looked impressive, but Tatiana had no idea what they meant. Was he a private? He was carrying his rifle. Did privates carry rifles? On the left side of his chest he wore a single silver medal trimmed in gold.

Underneath his umber cap he was dark-haired. The youth and dark hair were to his advantage, Tatiana thought, as her shy eyes met his eyes, which were the color of caramel—one shade darker than her crème brûlée ice cream. Were they a soldier's eyes? Were they a man's eyes? They were peaceful and smiling.

Tatiana and the soldier stared at each other for a moment or two, but it was a moment or two too long. Strangers looked at each other for half a nothing before averting their eyes. Tatiana felt as if she could open her mouth and say his name. She glanced away, feeling unsteady and warm.

"Your ice cream is still melting," the soldier repeated helpfully.

Blushing, Tatiana said with haste, "Oh, this ice cream. I'm finished with it." She got up and threw it emphatically in the trash, wishing she had a handkerchief to wipe her stained dress.

Tatiana couldn't tell if he was young like her; no, he seemed older. Like a young man, looking at her with a man's eyes. She blushed again, continuing to stare at the pavement between her red sandals and his black army boots.

A bus came. The soldier turned away from her and walked toward it. Tatiana watched him. Even his walk was from another world; the step was too sure, the stride too long, yet somehow it all seemed right, looked right, felt right. It was like stumbling on a book you thought you had lost. Ah, yes, there it is.

In a minute the bus doors were going to open and he was going to hop on the bus and wave a little good-bye to her and she was never going to see him again. *Don't go!* Tatiana shouted to him in her mind.

As the soldier got closer to the bus, he slowed down and stopped. At the last minute he backed away, shaking his head at the bus driver, who made a frustrated motion with his hands, slammed the door shut, and peeled away from the curb.

The soldier came back and sat on the bench.

The rest of her day flew out of her head without even a farewell.

Tatiana and the soldier were having a silence. How can we be having a silence? Tatiana thought. We just met. Wait. We haven't met at all. We don't know each other. How could we be having *anything*?

Nervously she looked up and down the street. Suddenly it occurred to her that he might be hearing the thumping in her chest, for how could he *not*? The noise had scared away the crows from the trees behind them. The birds had flown off in a panic, their wings flapping fervently. She knew—it was her. *Now* she needed her bus to come. Now.

He was a soldier, yes, but she had seen soldiers before. And he was good-looking, yes, but she had seen good-looking before. Once or twice last summer she had even met good-looking soldiers. One, she forgot his name now—as she forgot most things now—had bought her an ice cream.

It wasn't this soldier's uniform that affected her, and it wasn't his looks. It was the way he had stared at her from across the street, separated from her by ten meters of concrete, a bus, and the electric wires of the tram line.

He took a pack of cigarettes from the pocket of his uniform. "Would you like one?"

"Oh, no, no," Tatiana replied. "I don't smoke."

The soldier put the cigarettes back in his pocket. "I don't know anyone who doesn't smoke," he said lightly.

She and her grandfather were the only ones Tatiana knew who didn't smoke. She couldn't continue to be silent; it was too pathetic. But when Tatiana opened her mouth to speak, all the words she thought of saying sounded so stupid that she just closed her mouth and begged silently for the bus to come.

It didn't.

Finally the soldier spoke again. "Are you waiting for bus 22?"

"Yes," Tatiana replied in a tinny voice. "Wait, no." She saw a bus with three digits coming up. It was Number 136.

"This is the one I'm going to take," she said without thinking and quickly got up.

"One thirty-six?" she heard him mutter behind her.

Tatiana walked toward it, took out five kopecks, and climbed aboard. After paying, she made her way to the back of the bus and sat down just in time to see the soldier getting on and making his way to the back.

He sat one seat behind her on the opposite side.

Tatiana scooted over to the window and tried not to think of him. Where did she intend to go on bus 136? Oh, yes, that's the bus she took to Marina's on Polustrovsky Prospekt. She would go there. She'd get off at Polustrovsky and go ring Marina's doorbell.

Tatiana could see the soldier out of the corner of her eye.

Where was *he* going on bus Number 136?

The bus passed Tauride Park and turned at Liteiny Prospekt.

Tatiana straightened out the folds of her dress and traced the embroidered shapes of the roses with her fingers. Bending over between the seats, she adjusted her sandals. But mainly what she did was hope at every stop that the soldier would not get off. Not here, she thought, not here. And not here either. Where she wanted him to get off, Tatiana didn't know; all she knew was that she didn't want him to get off *here*.

The soldier didn't. Tatiana could tell he sat very calmly, looking out his window. Occasionally he would turn toward the front of the bus, and then Tatiana could swear he was looking at her.

After crossing Liteiny Bridge over the river Neva, the bus continued across town. The few stores Tatiana saw out the window either had long lines or were closed.

The streets became progressively emptier—bright, deserted Leningrad streets.

Stop after stop after stop went by. She was getting farther into north Leningrad.

Her head clearing briefly, Tatiana realized she had long since passed Marina's stop near Polustrovsky. Now she couldn't even tell where she was anymore. Unsettled, she moved tensely around on the seat.

Where was she going? She didn't know, but she couldn't get off the bus. First of all, the soldier was making no move to ring the bell, and second, she didn't know where she was. If Tatiana got off here, she would have to cross the street and take the bus back.

What was she hoping for anyway? To watch where he got off and then come back here another day with Marina? The thought made Tatiana twitch with disquiet.

Come back to find her soldier.

It was ridiculous. Right now she was hoping merely for a graceful retreat and a way back home.

Little by little, other people trickled off the bus. Finally there was no one left except Tatiana and the soldier.

The bus sped on. Tatiana didn't know what to do anymore. The soldier was not getting off the bus. What have I gotten myself into? she thought. She decided to get off, but when she rang the bell, the bus driver turned around and said, "You want to get off here, girl? Nothing here but industrial buildings. You meeting somebody?"

"Uh, no," she stammered.

"Well, then wait. Next will be the last stop."

Mortified, Tatiana sat back down with a thump.

The bus pulled into a dusty terminal.

The driver said, "Last stop."

Tatiana got off the bus into a hot, earth-covered bus station, which was a square lot at the end of an empty street. She was afraid to turn around. She put her hand on her chest to still her relentless heart. What was she supposed to do now? Nothing to do but take the bus back. Slowly she walked out of the station.

After—and only after—taking the deepest breath, Tatiana finally looked to her right, and there he was, smiling cheerfully at her. He had perfect white teeth—unusual for a Russian. She couldn't help but smile back. Relief must have shown in her face. Relief and apprehension and anxiety; all that, and something else, too.

Grinning, the soldier said, "All right, I give up. Where *are* you going?"

What could Tatiana say?

His Russian was slightly accented. It was correct Russian, just slightly accented. She tried to figure out if the accent and the white teeth came from the same place and, if so, where that place was. Georgia, maybe? Armenia? Somewhere near the Black Sea. He sounded as if he came from around salt water.

"Excuse me?" Tatiana said at last.

The soldier smiled again. "Where are you *going?*"

Looking up at him, Tatiana got a crick in her neck. She was a waif of a girl, and the soldier towered over her. Even in her high heels she barely came up to the base of his throat. Another thing she must ask him, if she could get her tongue back from him—the height. The teeth, the accent, and the height, all from the same place, comrade?

They had stopped stupidly in the middle of the deserted street. There wasn't much activity around the bus terminal on a Sunday when war had started. Instead of hanging around near buses, people were standing in lines buying food. Not Tatiana, no, she was stopped stupidly in the middle of the street.

"I think I missed my stop," Tatiana muttered. "I have to go back."

"Where *were* you going?" he repeated politely, still standing across from her, not moving, not making a move to move. Standing completely still, eclipsing the sun.

"Where?" she asked rhetorically. Her hair was a big mess, wasn't it? Tatiana never wore makeup, but she wished she had a little lipstick. Something, anything, so she wouldn't feel so plain and silly.

"Let's get out of the street," the soldier said. They crossed. "You want to sit?" He pointed to a bench by the bus stop sign. "We can wait for the next bus here." They sat. He sat too close to her.

"You know, it's the oddest thing," Tatiana began after a prolonged throat clearing. "My cousin Marina lives on Polustrovsky Prospekt—I was going there—"

"That was several kilometers ago. A dozen bus stops."

"No," Tatiana said, flustered. "I must have just missed it."

He made a serious face. "Don't worry. We'll get you right back. The bus will come in a few minutes."

Glancing at him, she asked, "Where were . . . *you* going?"

"Me? I'm with the garrison. I'm on city patrol today." His eyes were twinkling.

Oh, perfect, Tatiana thought, looking away. He was merely on city patrol, and I was headed practically to Murmansk. What an idiot. Embarrassed, her face all red, she suddenly felt light-headed. She looked down at her shoes. "Except for the ice cream, I haven't eaten all day," she said feebly, her consciousness yielding to unconsciousness in a matter of suspended seconds. The soldier's arm went around her back, and his calm, firm voice said, "No. No, don't faint. Stay up."

And she did.

Woozy and disoriented, she didn't want to see his tilted head looking at her solicitously. She smelled him, something pleasant and masculine, not alcohol or sweat like most Russians. What was it? Soap? Cologne for men? Men in the Soviet Union did not wear cologne. No, it was just him.

"I'm sorry," Tatiana said weakly, attempting to stand up. He helped her. "Thank you."

"Not at all. Are you all right?"

"Absolutely. Just hungry, I think."

He was still holding her. The perimeter of her upper arm was inside his hand, which was the size of a small country, perhaps Poland. Trembling slightly, Tatiana straightened herself, and he let her go, leaving a warm empty space where his hand had been.

"Sitting on the bus, now out in the sun . . ." the soldier said with some concern in his voice. "You'll be all right. Come on." He pointed. "There's our bus."

The bus came, driven by the same driver, who looked at them with raised eyebrows and said nothing.

This time they sat together, Tatiana near the window, the soldier with his uniformed arm draped over the wooden back of the seat behind her.

Looking at him in this proximity was truly impossible. There was just no hiding from his eyes. But it was his eyes that Tatiana wanted most to see.

"I don't normally faint," she said, looking out the window. That was a lie. She fainted all the time. All someone had to do was bump a chair against her knee and she was on the floor unconscious. The teachers at school used to send home two or three notes a month about her fainting.

She glanced at him.

Smiling irrepressibly, the soldier said, "What's your name anyway?"

"Tatiana," she said, noticing the slight stubble on his face, the sharp line of his nose, his black brows, and the small gray scar on his forehead. He was tanned under the stubble. His white teeth were outstanding.

"Tatiana," he repeated in his deep voice. "Tatiana," he said, slower, gentler. "Tania? Tanechka?"

"Tania," she replied and gave him her hand. Before he told her his name, he took it. Her small, slender, white hand disappeared in his enormous, warm, dark one. She thought he must have heard her heart through her fingers, through her wrist, through all the veins under her skin.

"I am Alexander," he said.

Her hand remained outstretched in his.

"Tatiana. Such a good *Russian* name."

"Alexander, too," she said and lowered her eyes.

Finally, reluctantly, she pulled her hand away. His large hands were clean, his fingers long and thick, and his nails trimmed. Neat nails on a man were another anomaly in Tatiana's Soviet life.

She looked away onto the street. The window of the bus was dirty. She wondered who washed it and when and how frequently. Anything not to think. What she *felt* though, was almost as if he were asking her not to turn away from him, almost as if his hand were about to come up and turn her face to him. She turned to him, lifted her eyes, and smiled. "Want to hear a joke?"

"Dying to."

"A soldier is being led to his execution," Tatiana began. " 'Some bad weather we're having,' he says to his convoy. 'Look who's complaining,' they say. 'We have to go back.' "

Alexander laughed so instantly and loudly, his merry eyes never leaving her face, that Tatiana felt herself—just a little bit—melting within.

"That's funny, Tania," he said.

"Thank you." She smiled and said quickly, "I have another joke: 'General, what do you think about the upcoming battle?' "

Alexander said, "I know this one. The general says, 'God knows it will be lost.' "

Tatiana continued, " 'Then why should we try?' "

And Alexander finished, " 'To find out who is the loser.' "

They both smiled and looked away from each other.

"Your straps are untied," she heard him say.

"My what?"

"Your straps. At the back of the dress. They've come undone. Here, turn your back to me a little more. I'll tie them for you."

She turned her back to him and felt his fingers pulling on the satin ribbons. "How tight do you want them?"

"That's good," she said hoarsely, not breathing. It occurred to her that he must be seeing down to the small of her bare back underneath the straps, and she became suddenly and keenly self-conscious.

When she turned to him, Alexander cleared his throat and asked, "Are you going to get off at Polustrovsky? To see your cousin Marina? Because it's coming up. Or do you want me to take you home?"

"Polustrovsky?" Tatiana repeated, as if hearing the word for the first time. It took her a moment. "Oh, my." Placing her hand on her forehead, she said, "Oh, no, you won't believe—I can't go home. I'm going to get in so much trouble."

"Why?" Alexander said. "What can I do to help?"

Why did she think he meant it? And moreover, why did she suddenly find herself relieved and strengthened and not afraid of going home?

After she told him about the rubles in her pocket and the failed quest for food, Tatiana finished with, "I don't know why my father would delegate this task to me. I'm the least capable of anyone in my family of actually succeeding."

"Don't sell yourself short, Tatiana," said Alexander. "Besides, I can help you."

"You can?"

He told her he would take her to one of the officers-only army stores called *Voentorgs*, where she could buy many of the things she needed.

"But I'm not an officer," she pointed out.

"Yes, but I am."

"You are?"

"Yes," he said. "Alexander Belov, first lieutenant. Impressed?"

"Skeptical," she said. Alexander laughed. Tatiana didn't want him to be old enough to be a first lieutenant. "What's the medal for?" she asked, looking at his chest.

"Military valor," he said with an indifferent shrug.

"Oh?" Her mouth lifted in a timid, admiring smile. "What did you do that was so military and valiant?"

"Nothing much. Where do you live, Tania?"

"Near Tauride Park—on the corner of Grechesky and Fifth Soviet," she instantly replied. "Do you know where that is?"

Alexander nodded. "I patrol everywhere. You live with your parents?"

31

"Of course. With my parents, my grandparents, my sister, and my twin brother."

"All in one room?" Alexander asked, without inflection.

"No, we have two!" Tatiana exclaimed happily. "And my grandparents are on a housing list to get another room when one becomes available."

"How long," asked Alexander, "have they been on this housing list?"

"Since 1924," replied Tatiana, and they both laughed.

They were on the bus forever and a second.

"I've never known anyone who was a twin," said Alexander as they got off. "Are you close?"

"Yes, but Pasha can be very irritating. He thinks because he is a boy he always has to win."

"You mean he doesn't?"

"Not if I can help it," said Tatiana, glancing away from his teasing eyes. "Do you have any brothers or sisters?"

"No," said Alexander. "I was my mother and father's only child." He blinked and then quickly continued, "We've come full circle, haven't we? Fortunately, we're not far from the store. Do you feel like walking, or do you want to wait for bus 22?"

Tatiana watched him.

Did he just say, *was*?

Did he just say, I *was* my mother and father's only child? "We can walk," Tatiana let out slowly, staring thoughtfully into his face and not moving. From his high forehead to his square jaw, his facial bones were prominent and clearly visible to her curious eyes. And all were set in what seemed like cement at the moment. As if he were grinding his teeth together. Carefully, she asked, "So where are you from, Alexander? You have a slight . . . accent."

"I don't, do I?" he asked, looking down at her feet. "Are you going to be all right walking in those shoes?"

"Yes, I'll be fine," she replied. Was he trying to change the subject? Her dress strap had fallen off her shoulder. Suddenly Alexander reached out and with his index finger pulled the strap back up, his fingertip tracing her skin. Tatiana turned red. She hated that about herself. She turned red all the time for no reason.

Alexander stared at her. His face relaxed into—what *was* that in his eyes? It looked almost like bedazzlement. "Tania—"

"Come on, let's walk," Tatiana said, mindful of the protracted daylight and the burning embers and his voice. There was something nauseating about these sudden feelings clinging to her like wet clothes.

The sandals were hurting her feet, but she didn't want to let him know it. "Is the store far from here?"

"Not far," he said. "We will have to stop at the barracks for a minute. I've got to sign out. I'll have to blindfold you the rest of the way. I can't have you knowing where the soldiers' barracks are, can I?"

Tatiana was not about to look at Alexander to see if he was joking.

"So," she said, trying to sound casual, "here we are, and we haven't talked about the war." She put on her purposeful serious face. "Alexander, what do *you* think of Hitler's actions?"

Why did he look infinitely amused by her? What had she said that was so amusing? "Do you really want to talk about the war?"

"Of course," she maintained. "It's a grave matter."

The look of wonder did not leave his eyes. "It's just war," he said. "It was so inevitable. We've been waiting for it. Let's go this way."

They walked past Mikhailovsky Palace or Engineer's Castle, as it was sometimes called, over the short Fontanka Canal bridge at the aqueous intersection of the Fontanka and Moika canals. Tatiana loved the slightly arched granite bridge, and sometimes she would climb on top of the low parapets and walk the ledge. Not today, of course. She wasn't going to be a child today.

They walked past the western end of *Letniy Sad*, the Summer Garden, and came out onto the grassy parade grounds of *Marsovo Póle*, the Field of Mars. "We need to leave this country to Hitler," said Alexander, "or we need to stay and fight for Mother Russia. But if we stay, it's a fight to the death." He pointed. "The barracks are just across the field."

"To the death? Really?" Tatiana looked up excitedly and slowed down on the grass. She wanted to take off her shoes. "Are *you* going to go to the front?"

"I go where they send me." Alexander slowed down, too, then stopped. "Tania, why don't you take off your shoes? You'll be more comfortable."

"I'm fine," she said. How did he know her feet were killing her? Was it that obvious?

"Go on," he prodded gently. "It will be easier for you to walk on the grass."

He was right. Breathing a sigh of relief, she bent, unstrapped the sandals, and slipped them off. Straightening up and raising her eyes to him, she said, "That is a little better."

Alexander was silent. "Now you're really tiny," he said at last.

"I'm not tiny," she returned. "You're just outsized." Blushing, she lowered her gaze.

"How old are you, Tania?"

"Older than you think," Tatiana said, wanting to sound old and mature. The warm Leningrad breeze blew her blonde hair over her face. Holding her shoes with one hand, she attempted to sort out her hair with the other. She wished she had a rubber band for her ponytail. Standing in front of her, Alexander reached out and brushed the hair away. His eyes traveled from her hair to her eyes to her mouth where they stopped.

Did she have ice cream all around her lips? Yes, that must be it. How awkward. She licked her lips, trying to clean the corners. "What?" she said. "Do I have ice cream—"

"How do you know how old I think you are?" he asked. "Tell me, how old are you?"

"I'm going to be seventeen soon," she said.

"When?"

"Tomorrow."

"You're not even *seventeen*," Alexander echoed.

"Seventeen *tomorrow*!" she repeated indignantly.

"Seventeen, right. Very grown up." His eyes were dancing.

"How old are *you*?"

"Twenty-two," he said. "Twenty-two, *just*."

"Oh," she said, and couldn't hide the disappointment in her voice.

"What? Is that very old?" Alexander asked, failing to keep the smile off his face.

"Ancient," Tatiana replied, failing to keep the smile off her face.

Slowly they walked across the Field of Mars, Tatiana barefoot and carrying the red sandals in her slightly swinging hands.

Once they got to the pavement, she put her sandals back on and they crossed the street, stopping at a nondescript brown stucco four-story building, distinguished by its lack of a front door. A deep, darkened passageway ran inside. "These are the Pavlov Barracks," Alexander said, "where I'm stationed."

"These are the famous Pavlov Barracks?" Tatiana looked up at the grubby building. "Surely this can't be it."

"What were you expecting? Maybe a snowcapped palace?"

"Do I come in?"

"Just to the gate. I'm going to turn in my weapon and sign out. You'll wait, all right?"

"I'll wait." After walking through the long archway, they came to a manned iron gate, deep inside the entranceway. A young sentry lifted his hand in salute to Alexander. "Proceed, Lieutenant. Who is this with you?"

"Tatiana. She'll wait for me here, Sergeant Petrenko."

"Of course she will," the guard said, eyeing Tatiana surreptitiously, but not so surreptitiously that she didn't notice. Tatiana watched Alexander walk beyond the iron gate across a courtyard, salute a tall officer, then stop and chat briefly to a cluster of smoking soldiers, breaking into a laugh and striding off. Nothing distinguished Alexander from the others, except that he was taller than anyone else and had darker hair and whiter teeth, broader shoulders and a wider stride. Nothing but that he was vivid and they were muted.

Petrenko asked if she wanted to sit down.

She shook her head. Alexander had told her to wait right here, and she wasn't going to move. Certainly she wasn't going to be sitting in some other soldier's chair, though she would have liked to sit.

As she stood looking through the garrison gate, waiting for Alexander, Tatiana felt herself floating on the cloud of fate that laced her afternoon with improbability and desire.

Desire for life.

One of her Deda's favorite sayings was, "Life is so unpredictable. That's what I like least about it. If only life were more like *math.*"

This one day Tatiana had to disagree with him.

She would take a day like this over any day in school or in the factory. She decided she would take a day like this over any other day in her life.

Taking a short step toward the guard, Tatiana asked, "Tell me, are civilians allowed inside?"

Smiling, Petrenko said with a wink, "Well, it depends what the sentry gets for it."

"That will be quite enough, Sergeant," Alexander said, walking briskly past him. "Let's go, Tania." He didn't have his rifle anymore.

Just as they were about to walk through the passageway onto the street, a soldier jumped out at them from a secret door Tatiana had not seen. He startled her so much that she actually yelped as if stung. Placing his hand on Tatiana's back, Alexander shook his head. "Dimitri, why?"

The soldier laughed noisily. "Your faces! That's why."

Tatiana composed herself. Was she wrong, or did Alexander move not just closer to her but closer and to the front, as if to stand not next to her but to shield her? How absurd.

Smiling, the soldier said, "So, Alex, who is your new friend?"

"Dimitri, this is Tatiana."

Dimitri shook Tatiana's hand vigorously, not letting go. Graciously, she pulled away.

Dimitri was average height by Russian standards, short compared to Alexander. He had a Russian face: broad, slightly washed-out features, as if the colors had all run dry. His nose was wide and turned up, his lips extremely thin. They were two rubber bands loosely strung together. His throat was nicked in several places by his razor. Underneath his left eye he had a small black birthmark. Dimitri's sidecap did not have an enameled red star like Alexander's, nor were his shoulder boards metallic. Dimitri's were red, with one thin blue stripe. His uniform tunic bore no medals.

"Very nice to meet you," said Dimitri. "So where are you two headed?"

Alexander told him.

"If you like," said Dimitri, "I'll be glad to help carry the purchases back to your house."

"We can manage, Dima, thanks," said Alexander.

"No, no, it's nothing." Dimitri smiled. "It'll be my pleasure." He was looking at Tatiana.

"So, Tatiana, how did you happen to run into our lieutenant?" asked Dimitri, walking alongside her while Alexander trailed behind. Tatiana turned

35

around and found him staring at her with anxiety. Their glances touched and moved apart. Alexander caught up and led them down the street. The *Voentorg* store was just around the corner.

"I ran into him on the bus," Tatiana replied to Dimitri. "He took pity on me and offered his help."

"Well, it was certainly lucky for you," Dimitri said. "No one likes to help out a damsel in distress as much as our Alexander."

"I'm hardly a damsel in distress," Tatiana muttered, while Alexander prodded her with his hand, directing her inside the store and ending the conversation.

Tatiana was amazed at what she found behind a simple glass door with a sign on it that said OFFICERS ONLY. First, there was no line. Second, the store was stocked full of sacks and bags and smelled of smoked ham and fish, enveloped in the aroma of cigarettes and coffee.

Alexander asked her how much money she had, and she told him, thinking the sum would stun him. He merely shrugged and said, "We could spend it all on sugar, but let's be provident, shall we?"

"I don't know what I'm buying for. So how can I be provident?"

"Buy," he said, "as if you're never going to see these goods again."

She gave him her money without a second thought.

He bought for her four kilos of sugar, four kilos of white flour, three kilos of oats, five kilos of barley, three kilos of coffee, ten cans of marinated mushrooms, and five cans of tomatoes. Also she bought a kilo of black caviar, and with the few rubles that were left she bought two cans of ham to please her Deda. To please herself she bought a small bar of chocolate.

Smiling, Alexander told her he would pay for the chocolate out of his own money and bought her five bars.

He suggested she buy matches. Tatiana mildly scoffed at this, because, she pointed out—she thought cleverly—you couldn't eat matches. He suggested she buy some motor oil. She told him she didn't have a car. He said to buy it anyway. She didn't want to. She didn't want to be spending her father's money on something as silly as oil and matches.

"But, Tania," Alexander pointed out, "how are you going to put the flour you're buying to good use if you don't have a match to light the fire? It'll be hard to bake that bread."

She relented only after she found out the matches were a few kopecks, and even then she bought only one box of 200.

"Don't forget the motor oil, Tania."

"When I get a car, I'll buy the motor oil."

"What if there is no kerosene this winter?" said Alexander.

"So what?" she said. "We have electricity."

He folded his arms. "Buy it," he said.

"Did you say this winter?" Tatiana waved him off. "What are you talking about, winter? It's June. We're not going to be fighting the Germans this winter."

"Tell that to the Londoners," said Alexander. "Tell that to the French, to the Belgians, to the Dutch. They've been fighting . . ."

"If you can call what the French did fighting."

Laughing, Alexander said, "Tatiana, buy the motor oil. You won't regret it."

She would have listened to him, but the voice of her father in her head was stronger, admonishing her for wasting his money. She refused.

She asked the shop assistant for a rubber band and tied up her hair nice and neat while Alexander was paying. Tatiana asked how they were going to get all the provisions home.

Dimitri said, "Don't worry. That's why I came along."

"Dima," said Alexander. "I really think we'll be all right."

"Alexander," said Tatiana. "We do have a lot of . . ."

"Dimitri the packhorse," said Dimitri. "Glad to be of service to you, Alexander." He smirked.

Tatiana noted the smirk, remembering her feeling that when Dimitri walked into the store, past the glass door with the sign OFFICERS ONLY, he had been as surprised as Tatiana to find himself inside the *Voentorg*.

"Are you and Alexander in the same unit?" Tatiana asked Dimitri as they piled her provisions into wooden apple crates and left the store.

"Oh, no, no," said Dimitri. "Alexander is an officer, and I'm just a lowly private. No, he is a number of ranks above me. Which," Dimitri said with his smirk, "allows him to send *me* to the front in Finland."

"Not Finland," corrected Alexander mildly. "And not to the front, but to check out reinforcements at Lisiy Nos. What are you complaining about?"

"I am not complaining. I'm lauding your farsightedness."

Tatiana stole a glance at Alexander, uncertain how to respond to the ironic stretching of Dimitri's rubber lips.

"Where is this Lisiy Nos?" she asked.

"The Karelian Isthmus," Alexander replied. "Are you going to be all right walking?"

"Of course." Tatiana couldn't wait to get home. Her sister would die when Tatiana showed up with two soldiers. She carried the lightest crate, the one with the caviar and coffee.

"Is that too heavy for you?" Alexander asked.

"No," she said. Actually, it was quite heavy, and she didn't know how she was going to get to the bus. They were going to the bus, weren't they? They weren't planning to walk to Fifth Soviet from the Field of Mars?

The pavement was narrow, so they walked in single file, Alexander leading, Tatiana second, and Dimitri bringing up the rear.

"Alexander," Tatiana panted, "are we planning to . . . walk home?" She was out of breath.

Alexander stopped walking. "Give me that," he said.

"I'm really fine."

He put down his crate, took hers, and placed it on top, lifting both crates easily. "Your feet must be killing you in those shoes. Come on. Let's go."

The pavement expanded, and now she could walk next to Alexander. Dimitri flanked her on the left. "Tania, do you think we'll get some vodka for our trouble?"

"I think my father might find some vodka for you, yes."

"So, Tania, tell us," Dimitri asked, "do you go out much?"

Go out? What a strange question. "Not much," she said shyly.

"Ever go to a place named Sadko?"

"No," she said. "But my sister often does. She says it's nice."

Dimitri leaned over a little. "Next weekend, do you want to come to Sadko with us?"

"Umm, no, thank you," she said, lowering her eyes.

"Come on," Dimitri said. "It'll be fun. Right, Alexander?"

Alexander did not respond.

They walked three in a row along the wide pavement. Tatiana was in the middle. When other pedestrians headed toward them, it was Dimitri who stepped behind Tatiana to let them pass.

Tatiana noticed that Dimitri moved behind her with a reluctant sigh, as if it were a last resort, a battle, as if he were ceding territory to the enemy. At first Tatiana thought the passersby were the enemy, but soon she realized that, no, she and Alexander were the enemy because they never moved over, continuing to walk side by side, shoulder to shoulder.

Quietly Alexander asked, "Are you tired?"

Tatiana nodded.

"You want to rest a minute?" He put down his crates.

Dimitri did, too, eyeing Tatiana. "So, Tania, where do *you* go for fun?"

"Fun?" she said. "I don't know. I go to the park. We go to our *dacha* in Luga." Turning to Alexander, she asked, "So will you tell me where you're from, or am I going to have to guess?"

"I think you're going to have to guess, Tania."

"Somewhere around salt water, Alexander."

"You mean he didn't tell you yet?" said Dimitri, standing very close to them.

"I can't get a straight answer out of him."

"Now, *that's* surprising."

"Very good, Tania," Alexander said. "I'm from Krasnodar, by the Black Sea."

"Yes, Krasnodar," said Dimitri. "Have you ever been there?"

"No," she replied. "I've never been anywhere."

Dimitri glanced at Alexander, who picked up his crates and said curtly, "Let's go."

They passed a church and crossed Grechesky Prospekt. Tatiana was so lost in thinking of a way to see Alexander again that she walked right past her apartment building. She was a few hundred meters down the block, almost near the corner of Suvorovsky, when she stopped.

"You want another rest?" Alexander asked.

"No," she said, trying to hide the feelings from her voice. "We missed my apartment building."

"Missed it?" exclaimed Dimitri. "How can that be?"

"We just did, that's all," said Tatiana. "It's at the other corner."

Smiling, Alexander lowered his head. Slowly they walked back.

After entering the front door, Tatiana said, "I'm on the third floor. Will you two be all right?"

"Do we have a choice?" Dimitri asked. "Is there an elevator? Of course not," he added. "This isn't America. Is it, Alexander?"

"I shouldn't think so," Alexander replied.

They climbed the stairs in front of Tatiana. "Thank you," she whispered behind Alexander, mostly to herself; in fact, she was just thinking out loud. The thoughts were too loud, that was all.

"You're welcome," he said, without turning around.

Stumbling, she continued upward.

When she opened the door to her communal apartment, Tatiana hoped that crazy Slavin would not be lying on the floor in the middle of the corridor. This time her hopes went unanswered. He was there, his torso in the corridor, his legs inside his room, a snake of a man, thin, unkempt, malodorous, his ragged mop of greasy gray hair covering most of his face.

"Slavin has been pulling his hair out again," she whispered to Alexander, who was right behind her.

"I think that's the least of his problems," Alexander whispered back.

With a growl, Slavin let Tatiana walk by but grabbed hold of Alexander's leg and laughed hysterically.

"Comrade," said Dimitri, coming up behind Alexander and sticking his boot on top of Slavin's wrist, "let go of the lieutenant."

"It's all right, Dimitri," said Alexander, moving Dimitri away with his elbow. "I can handle him."

Slavin squealed with delight and squeezed Alexander's boot harder. "Our Tanechka is bringing home a handsome soldier," Slavin shrieked. "Excuse me . . . *two* handsome soldiers! What's your father going to say, Tanechka? Is he going to approve? I don't think so! I don't think so at all. He doesn't like you to bring home boys. He'll say two is too much for you. Give one to your sister, give her one, my sweet." With glee, Slavin laughed wildly. Alexander yanked his leg away.

Slavin reached out to grab hold of Dimitri, then looked up into Dimitri's face and let his hand drop without touching him.

Calling after all three of them, Slavin screeched, "Yes, Tanechka, bring

39

them home. Bring more! Bring them all—because they'll all be dead in three days. Dead! Shot by Comrade Hitler, such a *good* friend of Comrade Stalin!"

"He was in a war," Tatiana said by way of explanation, relieved to be past him. "He ignores me when I'm alone."

"Why do I doubt that?" said Alexander.

Flushing, Tatiana said, "He really does. He is bored with us because we ignore him."

Leaning into her, Alexander said, "Isn't communal living grand?"

That surprised her. "What else is there?"

"Nothing," he replied. "This is what it's going to take to reconstruct our selfish, bourgeois souls."

"That's what Comrade Stalin says!" Tatiana exclaimed.

"I know," said Alexander, keeping a serious face. "I'm quoting him."

Trying not to laugh, Tatiana led him to her front door. Before opening it, she glanced back at Alexander and Dimitri and said with an excited sigh, "All right. Home." Opening the door, she said, smiling, "Come in, Alexander."

"Can I come in, too?" Dimitri asked.

"Come in, Dimitri."

Tatiana's family were in Babushka and Deda's room around the big dining table. Tatiana stuck her head in from the hallway. "I'm home!"

No one even looked up. Mama said blankly, "Where've you been?" She could have been saying, *more bread?*

"Mama, Papa! Look at the food I've bought."

Papa looked up briefly from his glass of vodka. "Good, daughter," he said. She could have returned empty-handed. With a small sigh, she glanced at Alexander standing in the hallway. What *was* that on his face? Sympathy? No, not quite. *Warmer.* She whispered to him, "Put the crates down and come in with me."

"Mama, Papa, Babushka, Deda," said Tatiana, walking into the room and trying to keep the thrill out of her voice for the imminent introduction, "I want you to meet Alexander—"

"And Dimitri," said Dimitri quickly, as if Tatiana had forgotten him.

"And Dimitri," Tatiana finished.

Everyone shook hands and stared incredulously at Alexander and then at Tatiana. Mama and Papa remained seated at the table with a bottle of vodka between them and two shot glasses. Deda and Babushka went to sit on the couch to give the soldiers more room at the table. Tatiana thought her parents looked sad. Were they drinking to Pasha and chasing him down with pickles?

Papa stood up. "You did very well, Tania. I'm proud of you." He motioned to Alexander and Dimitri. "Come. Have some vodka."

Alexander politely shook his head. "No, thank you. I have duty later."

"Shake your head for yourself," said Dimitri, stepping forward.

40

Papa poured, frowning at Alexander. What kind of man refused a drink of vodka? Alexander may have had his reasons for refusing her father's hospitality, but Tatiana knew that because of that, her father was going to like Dimitri better. Such a small act, yet the feelings that would follow would be so permanent. And yet because he refused, Tatiana liked Alexander better.

"Tania, I don't suppose you bought any milk?" Mama asked her.

"Papa told me dry goods only."

"Where are you from?" Tatiana's father asked Alexander.

"Krasnodar region," he said.

Papa shook his head. "I lived in Krasnodar in my youth. You don't sound like you're from there."

"Well, I am," said Alexander mildly.

To change the subject, Tatiana asked, "Alexander, would you prefer some tea instead? I can make you some tea."

He moved closer to her, and she had to summon her breath. "No, thank you," he said warmly. "I can't stay long, Tania. I've got to get back."

Tatiana took off her sandals. "Excuse me," she said. "My feet are . . ." She smiled. She had tried hard to pretend they did not bother her, but the blisters on her big toe and little toe were bleeding.

Alexander glanced at her feet, shaking his head. Then he looked into her face. That expression seeped into his almond eyes again. "Barefoot is better," he said very quietly.

Dasha came into the room. She stopped and stared at the two soldiers.

She looked healthy, radiant with the day, and Tatiana suddenly thought her sister looked *too* healthy and *too* radiant, but before she could utter a sound, Dasha exclaimed, her voice thick with pleasure, "Alexander! What are *you* doing here?" Dasha didn't even glance at Tatiana, who, perplexed, looked at Alexander and said, "You know Dasha . . . ?" but then broke off in the middle of the question, seeing realization and conscience and unhappiness strike his mute, comprehending face.

Tatiana looked at Dasha, then back to Alexander. She felt herself paling from the inside out. *Oh, no,* she wanted to say. *Oh, no, how can this be?*

Alexander's face became impassive. He smiled easily at Dasha and said, not looking at Tatiana, "Yes. Dasha and I have met."

"You can say *that* again!" Dasha said with a laugh and a pinch of his arm. "Alexander, what are you *doing* here?"

Tatiana glanced around the room to see if anyone else had noticed what she had noticed. Dimitri was eating a pickle. Deda was reading the newspaper, his glasses on. Papa was having another drink. Mama was opening up some cookies, and Babushka had her eyes closed. No one else saw.

Mama said, "The soldiers just came back with Tatiana. Brought food."

"Really?" Dasha said, her face turning up to Alexander, full of mild curiosity. "How do you know my sister?"

"I don't," said Alexander. "I ran into her on the bus."

41

"You ran into my little sister?" said Dasha. "Incredible! It's like destiny!" She tweaked him lightly on the arm again.

"Let's go sit down," said Alexander. "I think I will have that drink after all." He moved to the table in the middle of the room by the wall, while Dasha and Tatiana remained by the door. Dasha leaned over and whispered, "He is the one I told you about!" Dasha must have thought she was whispering.

"One what?"

"This morning," hissed Dasha.

"This morning?"

"Why are you being so dumb? He's the one!"

Tatiana got it. She hadn't been dumb. There was no morning. There was only waiting for the bus and meeting Alexander. "Oh," she said, refusing to allow herself to feel anything. She was too stunned.

Dasha went to sit in the chair next to him. Glancing sadly at Alexander's uniformed back, Tatiana went to put the food away.

"Tanechka," Mama called after her, "put it away in the right place, not like usual."

Tatiana heard Alexander say, "Don't bother with shots. Pour mine straight into a glass."

"Good man," said Papa, pouring him a glass. "A toast. To new friends."

"To new friends," everyone chimed in.

Dimitri said, "Tania, come and have a toast with us," and Tatiana came in, but Papa said, no, Tania was too young to drink, and Dimitri apologized, and Dasha said she would drink for herself *and* her sister, and Papa said like she didn't already, and everyone laughed except Babushka, who was trying to nap, and Tatiana, who wanted the day to be instantly over.

From the hallway, as she picked up the crates and carried them one after the other into the kitchen, she heard tidbits of conversation.

"Work on the fortifications must be speeded up."

"Troops must be moved to the frontiers."

"Airports must be put in working order. Guns must be installed in forward positions. All of this must go ahead at fever pace."

A little later she heard Papa say, "Oh, our Tania works at Kirov. She's just graduated from school—a year early! She plans to go to Leningrad University next year when she turns eighteen. You'd never know it by looking at her—but she graduated a year early. Did I already say that?"

Tatiana smiled at her father.

"I don't know why she wanted to work at Kirov," said Mama. "It's so far, it's practically outside Leningrad. She can't take care of herself," she added.

"Why *should* she, when you've been doing everything for her all her life," Papa snapped.

"Tania!" yelled Mama. "Wash our dishes from dinner while you're out there, won't you?"

In the kitchen Tatiana put away all she had bought. As she carried the crates, she would glance into the room to see Alexander's back. Karelia and the Finns and their borders, and the tanks, and weapons superiority and the treacherous marshy woods where it was so hard to gain ground and the war with Finland of 1940 and . . .

She was in the kitchen when Alexander and Dasha and Dimitri came out. Alexander did not look at her. It was as if he were a pipeline full of water, and Dasha had turned the faucet off.

"Tania, say good-bye," Dasha said. "They're going."

Tatiana wished she were invisible. "Good-bye," she said from a distance, wiping her floured hands on her white dress. "Thanks again for your help."

Dasha said, holding on to Alexander's arm, "I'll walk you out."

Dimitri came up to Tatiana and asked if he could call on her again. She may have said yes, she may have nodded. She barely heard him.

Leveling his eyes on her, Alexander said, "It was nice to meet you, Tatiana."

Tatiana may have said, "You, too." She didn't think so.

The three of them went, and Tatiana was left standing in the kitchen. Mama came out and said, "The officer forgot his cap."

Tatiana took it from Mama's hands, but before she could take one step to the corridor, Alexander had returned—by himself. "Forgot my cap," he said.

Tatiana gave it to him without speaking and without looking at him.

As he took the cap from her, his fingers rested against hers for a moment. That made her look up. Tatiana stared at him with sadness. What did grown-ups do? *She* wanted to cry. She could do nothing but gulp down the aching in her throat and act grown-up.

"I'm sorry," Alexander said so quietly that Tatiana thought she might have misheard him. He turned and walked out.

Tatiana found her mother frowning at her. "What do you think *you're* doing?"

"Be grateful we got some food, Mama," said Tatiana, and started to make herself something to eat. She buttered a piece of bread, ate part of it with absentminded abandon, then jumped up and threw the rest out.

There was nowhere for her to go. Not in the kitchen, not in the hallway, not in the bedroom. What she wanted was a little room of her own where she could go and jot down small things in her diary.

Tatiana had no little room of her own. As a result she had no diary. Diaries, as she understood them from books, were supposed to be full of personal writings and filled with private words. Well, in Tatiana's world there were no private words. All private thoughts you kept in your head as you lay down next to another person, even if that other person happened to be your sister. Leo Tolstoy, one of her favorite writers, wrote a diary of his life as a young boy, an adolescent, a young man. That diary was *meant* to be read by thousands of people. That wasn't the kind of diary Tatiana wanted to keep. She wanted to keep one in which she could write down Alexander's name and no one would read it. She wanted to have a room where she could say his name out loud and no one would hear it.

Alexander.

Instead, she went back into the bedroom, sat next to her mother, and had a sweet biscuit.

Her parents talked about the money Dasha was not able to get out of the bank, which had closed early, and a little about evacuation, but said nothing about Pasha—for how could they?—and Tatiana said nothing about Alexander—for how could she? Her father talked about Dimitri and what a fine young man he seemed to be. Tatiana sat quietly at the table, summoning her teenage strength. When Dasha returned, she motioned for Tatiana to come into their bedroom. Tatiana dutifully went. Whirling around, Dasha said, "So what did you think?"

"Of what?" said Tatiana in a tired voice.

"Tania, of him! What did you think of *him?*"

"He's nice."

"Nice? Oh, come on! What did I tell you? You've never met anyone so handsome."

Tatiana managed a small smile.

"Wasn't I right? Wasn't I?" Dasha laughed.

"You were right, Dasha," said Tatiana.

"Isn't it incredible that you met him?"

"Isn't it?" said Tatiana without feeling, standing up and wanting to get out of the room, but Dasha blocked the door with her twitching body, unwittingly challenging Tatiana, who was not up to a fight, not a big one, not a small one. Challengeless, she said and did nothing. That's the way it had always been. Dasha was seven years older. She was stronger, smarter, funnier, more attractive. She always won. Tatiana sat back down on the bed.

Dasha sat next to Tatiana. "What about Dimitri? Did you like him?"

"I guess. Listen, don't worry about *me*, Dash."

"Who's worried?" Dasha said, ruffling Tatiana's hair. "Give Dima a chance. I think he actually liked you." Dasha said that almost as if she were surprised. "Must be your dress."

"Must be. Listen, I'm tired. It's been a long day."

Dasha put her arm on Tatiana's back. "I really like Alexander, Tania," she said. "I like him so much, I can't even explain."

Tatiana felt a chill. Having met Alexander, having walked with Alexander, having smiled at Alexander, Tatiana grimly understood that Dasha's relationship with him was not some transient fling soon to be ended on the steps of Peterhof or in the gardens of the Admiralty. Tatiana had no doubt her sister meant it this time. "Don't explain anything, Dasha," said Tatiana.

"Tania, someday you'll understand."

Squinting sideways, Tatiana looked up at her sister sitting on the edge of the bed. She opened her mouth. A moment passed.

She wanted to say, but, Dasha, Alexander crossed the street for *me*.

He got on the bus for *me*, and went to the outskirts of town for *me*.

But Tatiana couldn't say any of that to her older sister.

What she wanted to say to Dasha was, you've had plenty. You can get yourself a new one any time you want. You're charming and bright and beautiful, and everybody likes you. But him I want for myself.

What she wanted to say was, *but what if he likes me best?*

Tatiana said nothing. She wasn't sure any of it was true. Especially the last part. How could he like Tatiana best? Look at Dasha with her hair and her flesh. And maybe Alexander crossed the street for Dasha, too. Maybe he went across town, across the river for Dasha at three o'clock in the bright morning when the Neva bridges were up. Tatiana had nothing to say. She closed her mouth. What a waste, what a joke it all had been.

Dasha studied her. "Tania, Dimitri is a soldier. . . . I don't know if you're quite ready for a soldier."

"What does that mean?"

"Nothing, nothing. But we might need to spruce you up a bit."

"Spruce me up, Dasha?" said Tatiana, her heart backing into her lungs.

"Yes, you know, maybe a little lipstick, maybe have a little talk . . ." Dasha pulled Tatiana's hair.

"Maybe we'll do that. Another day, though, all right?"

In her white dress with red roses, Tatiana curled up, facing the wall.

3

Alexander was walking fast down Ligovsky.

They were silent for a few minutes, and then Dimitri, still not catching his breath, said, "Nice family."

"Very nice," said Alexander calmly. He was not out of breath. And he did not want to talk to Dimitri about the Metanovs.

"I remember Dasha," Dimitri said, barely keeping up with Alexander. "I've seen her with you a few times at Sadko, haven't I?"

"Yes."

"Her sister is something, though, don't you think?"

Alexander didn't reply.

Dimitri continued. "Georgi Vasilievich said Tania was nearly seventeen." His head shuddered. "Seventeen! Remember us at seventeen, Alexander?"

Alexander kept on walking. "Too well." He wished he could remember himself at seventeen *less*. Dimitri was talking to him. "I didn't hear. What?"

"I said," Dimitri said patiently, "do you think she is a young seventeen or an old seventeen?"

"Too young for you, Dimitri, regardless," Alexander said coolly.

Dimitri was silent. "She is very pretty," he finally said.

"Yes. Still too young for you."

"What do you care? You're close to the older sister, I'm going to get to know the younger." Dimitri chuckled. "Why not? We could make a . . . foursome, don't you think? Two best friends, two sisters . . . there's a symmetry—"

"Dima," said Alexander, "what about Elena last night? She told me she liked you. I can introduce you next week."

Waving him off, Dimitri said, "You actually *talked* to Elena?" He laughed. "No. I can get dozens like Elena. Besides, why not Elena, too? No. Tatiana is not like the others." He rubbed his hands together and smiled.

Not a muscle moved on Alexander's face. Not a tic in his eye, not a tightening of his lips, not a furrowing of his brow. Nothing moved, except his legs, faster and faster down the street.

Dimitri broke into a trot. "Alexander, wait. About Tania . . . I just want to make sure . . . you don't mind, do you?"

"Of course, not, Dima," Alexander said evenly. "Why would I?"

"Absolutely!" He slapped Alexander on the back. "You're a good man. Quick question—do you want me to arrange entertainment for—"

"No!"

"But you'll be on duty all night. Come on, we'll have fun like always?"

"No. Not tonight." He paused. "Not again, all right?"

"But—"

"I'm late," said Alexander. "I'm going to run. I'll see you at the barracks."

UNCHARTED TIDES

1

THE next morning when Tatiana woke up, the first image in her mind was Alexander's face. Tatiana did not speak to Dasha, tried in fact not to look at her sister, who, as she was leaving said, "Happy birthday."

"Yes, Tanechka, happy birthday," said Mama, hurrying out. "Don't forget to lock up."

Papa kissed her on the head and said, "Your brother is seventeen today, too, you know."

"I know that, Papa."

Papa worked as a pipe engineer at the Leningrad waterworks plant. Mama was a seamstress at a Nevsky hospital uniform facility. Dasha was an assistant to a dentist. She had worked for him since leaving university two years ago. They had had a romance, but once it was over, Dasha continued there because she liked the job. It paid well and demanded little from her.

Tatiana went to Kirov, where the whole morning she sat in on meetings and patriotic speeches. The manager of her department, Sergei Krasenko, asked if anyone wanted to join the People's Volunteer Army to dig trenches down south to help defeat the hated Germans.

Today the German was hated. Yesterday he was beloved. What about tomorrow?

Yesterday Tatiana had met Alexander.

Krasenko continued to speak. The fortifications north of Leningrad, along the old frontier with Finland, were to be put into full defensive order. The Red Army suspected that the Finns were going to want Karelia back. Tatiana perked up. Karelia, Finland. Alexander spoke about that yesterday. Alexander . . . Tatiana perked down.

The women listened to Krasenko, but no one sprang up to volunteer for anything. No one, that is, except Tamara, the woman who followed Tatiana on the assembly line. "What have I got to lose?" she whispered with fervor as she scrambled to her feet. Tatiana had suspected that Tamara's job was just too boring.

Today before lunch she received goggles, a protective mask for her hair, and a brown factory coat. After lunch she was no longer packaging spoons and forks. Now small cylindrical metal bullets came to her down the assembly line. They fell by the dozen into small cardboard containers, and Tatiana's job was to put the containers into large wooden crates.

At five o'clock Tatiana took off her coat and her mask and goggles, splashed water on her face, retied her hair into a neat ponytail, and left the building. She walked on Prospekt Stachek, along the famous Kirov wall, a concrete structure seven meters tall that ran fifteen city blocks. She walked three of those blocks to her bus stop.

And waiting for her at the bus stop was Alexander.

When she saw him—Tatiana couldn't help herself—her face lit up. Putting her hand on her chest, she stopped walking for a moment, but he smiled at her and she blushed and, gulping down whatever was in her throat, walked toward him. She noticed that his officer's cap was in his hands. She wished she had scrubbed her face harder.

The presence of so many words inside her head made her incapable of small talk, just at the time when she needed small talk most. "What are you doing here?" she asked timidly.

"We're at war with Germany," Alexander said. "I have no time for pretenses."

Tatiana wanted to say something, anything, not to let his words linger in the air. So she said, "Oh."

"Happy birthday."

"Thank you."

"Are you doing something special tonight?"

"I don't know. Today is Monday, so everyone will be tired. We'll have dinner. A drink." She sighed. In a different world, perhaps, she might have invited him over for dinner on her birthday. Not in this world.

They waited. Somber people stood all around them. Tatiana did not feel somber. She thought, but is this what I'm going to look like when I'm here by myself, waiting for the bus like them?

Is this what I am going to look like for the rest of my life?

And then she thought, we're at war. What is the rest of my life even going to look like?

"How did you know I'd be here?"

"Your father told me yesterday you worked at Kirov. I took a chance you'd be waiting for the bus."

"Why?" she asked lightly. "Have we had so much luck with public transportation?"

Alexander smiled. "You mean *we* in the sense of the Soviet people? Or do you mean you and I?"

She blushed.

Bus Number 20 came with room for two dozen people. Three dozen piled on. Alexander and Tatiana waited.

"Come, let's walk," he said finally, leading her away.

"Walk where?"

"Walk back home. I want to talk to you about something."

She looked at him doubtfully. "Home is eight kilometers from here." She glanced at her feet.

"Are your shoes comfortable today?" He was smiling.

"Yes, thank you," she said, cursing herself for her little-girl awkwardness.

"I'll tell you what," he suggested. "Why don't we walk one long block over to Govorova Ulitsa, and take tram Number 1 from there? Can you walk one long block? Everybody here is waiting for the bus or the trolleybus. We'll catch tram Number 1 instead."

Tatiana thought about it. "I don't think that tram drops me off at my apartment," she said at last.

"No, it doesn't, but you can change at the Warsaw railroad station for tram Number 16 that will take you to the corner of Grechesky and Fifth Soviet, or you can change with me for tram Number 2, which will drop me off close to my barracks and you at the Russian Museum." He paused. "Or we can walk."

"I'm not walking eight kilometers," said Tatiana. "No matter how comfortable my shoes are. Let's go to the tram." She already knew she would not be getting off at some railroad station to catch another tram back home by herself.

When the tram didn't come for twenty minutes, Tatiana agreed to walk a few kilometers to tram Number 16. Govorova turned into Ulitsa Skapina and then meandered diagonally northward until it ended in the embankment of the Obvodnoy Canal—the Circular Canal

Tatiana didn't want to get to her tram. She didn't want him to get to his. She wanted to walk along the blue canal. How to tell him that? There were other things, too, to ask him. Always she tried to be less forward. Always she tried to find the right thing to say and didn't trust the etiquette pendulum swinging in her head, so she simply said nothing, which was perceived either as painful shyness or haughtiness. Dasha never had that problem. She just said the first thing that came into her head.

Tatiana knew she needed to trust her inner voice more. It was certainly loud enough.

Tatiana wanted to ask Alexander about Dasha.

But he began with, "I don't know how to tell you this. You might think I'm being presumptuous. But . . ." He trailed off.

"If I think you're being presumptuous," Tatiana remarked, "you probably are."

He stayed silent.

"Tell me anyway."

"You need to tell your father, Tatiana, that he has to get your brother back from Tolmachevo."

As she heard those words, she saw the imperially ornate Warsaw train station across the street, and she was thinking fleetingly about what it would be like to see Warsaw and Lublin and Swietokryst, and suddenly there was Pasha and Tolmachevo, and . . .

Tatiana wasn't expecting it. She had wanted something else. Instead, Alexander had mentioned Pasha, whom he did not know and had never met.

"Why?" Tatiana asked at last.

"Because there is some danger," Alexander said after a pause, "that Tolmachevo will fall to the Germans."

"What are you talking about?" She did not understand, and even if she did, she would not want to. She would *choose* not to understand. She didn't want to get upset. She had been too happy that Alexander had come to see her unbidden, of his own free will. Yet there was something in his voice—Pasha, Tolmachevo, Germans, these three words were flowing together in one sentence, said by a near-stranger with warm eyes in a cool tone. Had he come all the way to Kirov to alarm her? What for?

"What can *I* do?" she asked.

"Talk to your father about getting Pasha out of Tolmachevo. Why did he send him there?" he exclaimed. "To be safe?" Alexander shuddered, and something passed over his face. Unblinking, she watched him intently for more, for less, for an explanation. But there was nothing else. Not even words.

Tatiana cleared her throat. "There are boys' camps there. That's why he sent him."

He nodded. "I know. Many, many Leningraders sent their boys there yesterday." His face was blank.

"Alexander, the Germans are down in Crimea," said Tatiana. "Comrade Molotov said so himself. Didn't you hear his speech?"

"Yes, they are in Crimea. But we have a border with Europe that's two thousand kilometers long. Hitler's army is on every meter of that border, Tania, south from Bulgaria north to Poland." He paused. She didn't say anything. "For right now, Leningrad is the safest place for Pasha. Really."

Tatiana was skeptical. "Why are you so sure?" She became animated. "Why does the radio keep talking about the Red Army being the strongest army in the world? We have tanks, we have planes, we have artillery, we have guns. The radio is not saying what you're saying, Alexander." She spoke those words almost as a rebuke.

He shook his head. "Tania, Tania, Tania."

"What, what, what?" she said, and saw that Alexander, despite his serious face, nearly laughed. That made her nearly laugh herself, despite her own serious face.

"Tania, Leningrad has lived for so many years with a hostile border with Finland only twenty kilometers to the north that we forgot to arm the south. And that's where the danger is."

"If that's where the danger is, then how come you're sending Dimitri up to Finland where, as you suggest, all is quiet?"

Alexander was silent. "Reconnaissance," he said at last. Tatiana felt he left something unsaid. "My point is," he went on, "all of our precautionary defenses are focused in the north. But south and southwest, Leningrad does not have a single division, a single regiment, not one military unit deployed. Do you understand what I'm telling you?"

"No," she said, a little defiantly.

"Talk to your father about Pasha," he repeated.

They fell silent as they walked side by side through the quiet streets. Subdued was the sunlight, still the leaves, and only Alexander and Tatiana moved languidly through the summer, slowing down at the end of every block, looking at the pavement, looking up to the street signs. Tatiana was thinking, please don't let this end so soon. What was he thinking?

"Listen," Alexander said, "about yesterday . . . I'm sorry about the mishap. What could I do? Your sister and I . . . I didn't know she was your sister. We had met at Sadko—"

"I know. Of course. You don't have to explain," interjected Tatiana. He brought it up. That meant so much.

"Oh, but I do. I'm sorry if I've"—he paused—"upset you."

"No, not at all. Everything is fine. She had told me about you. She and you—" Tatiana stopped, wanting to add that she was all right with that, but got stuck on her words. "So what's Dimitri like? Is he nice? When is he coming back from Karelia?" Did she say that for effect? Tatiana wasn't sure. She just wanted to change the subject.

"I don't know. When his entrenching assignment is finished. In a few days."

"Listen, I'm getting tired. Can we catch a tram?"

"Sure," Alexander said slowly. "Let's wait for the Number 16."

They were seated on the tram when he spoke again. "Tatiana, your sister and I weren't serious. I will tell her—"

"No!" she exclaimed. The two stolid men in front of her turned around quizzically. "No," she repeated, more quietly, but no less adamantly. "Alexander, it's impossible." She put her hands over her face and then took them away. "She is my older sister. Do you understand?"

I was my mother and father's only child. His violin words echoed in her chest.

More gently, Tatiana said, "She is my *only* sister." She paused. "And she is serious about *you.*" Did she need to say more? She didn't think so, but judging by the displeased look on his face, yes, she did. "There will be other boys," she finally added with a gallant shrug, "but I will never have another sister."

All Alexander said was, "I'm not a boy."

"Men, then," Tatiana stammered. This was too difficult for her.

"What makes you think there will be other men?"

Dumbstruck, Tatiana nonetheless persisted. "Because you make up half the world. But I know for a fact I have only one sister."

When Alexander didn't comment, she ventured, "You do like Dasha, don't you?"

Quietly he replied, "Of course. But—"

"Well, then," Tatiana interrupted, "it's settled. No reason to speak any more about it." She sighed heavily.

"No," Alexander said, sighing briefly. "Guess not."

"All right, then." She stared out the window.

Whenever Tatiana thought of what she might like to be in life, she always thought of her grandfather and the dignity with which he conducted his simple existence. Her grandfather could have been anything, but he chose to become a math teacher. Tatiana didn't know if it was the teaching of irrefutable math that made Deda approach more intangible issues with the same black-and-white code or if it was the very essence of his character that drew him to math's absolutes, but whatever it was, Tatiana had always marveled at it. Whenever people asked her what she wanted to be when she grew up, she invariably said, "I want to be like my grandfather."

Tatiana knew what Deda would do. He would never step on his sister's heart.

The tram moved past Insurrection Square. Alexander asked her to get off a few stops before Fifth Soviet, near the redbrick Grechesky Hospital on Second Soviet and Grechesky. "I was born in this hospital," Tatiana offered, pointing.

"So, Tania, tell me, do you like Dimitri?"

It was a good minute before Tatiana could answer him.

What answer was he looking for? Was he asking as a spy for Dimitri or for himself? And what should she say? If it was for Dimitri and Tatiana said no, she did not like him, then she would hurt Dimitri's feelings, and she didn't want to do that.

If it was for Alexander and she said yes, she liked Dimitri, then she would hurt Alexander's feelings, and she didn't want to do that either. What were girls supposed to say? Weren't they supposed to play some kind of game? Lure, pull, pretend.

Alexander was Dasha's. Did Dasha's younger sister owe him an honest answer?

Did he want one?

He wanted one.

"No," she finally said. Tatiana didn't want to hurt Alexander's feelings most of all.

She saw by his face that she had given him the right answer.

"Dasha says I should give him a chance though. What do you think?"

"No," he replied at once.

They were stopped at the corner of Second Soviet and Grechesky Prospekt. The dome of the church across from her building glistened a few hundred meters in the distance. Tatiana couldn't take the thought of him leaving. Now that he had come, asked the impossible, and been refused, she was afraid she would not see him like this again. Alone like this again.

She couldn't let him leave just yet. Not just yet. "Alexander," she asked quietly, looking into his face, "are your . . . mother and father still in Krasnodar?"

"No," he said. "They're not in Krasnodar."

She didn't look away. His eyes poured into her. "Tania, so many things I can't explain but want to."

"So explain," Tatiana said softly, holding her breath.

"Just remember, what's happening right now in the Red Army—the confusion, the unpreparedness, the disorganization—none of it can be understood except through the events of the last four years. Do you see?"

Tatiana stood still. "I don't see. What does it have to do with your parents?"

Alexander stepped a shade closer, shielding her from the setting sun. "My parents are dead. My mother in 1936, my father in 1937." He lowered his voice even more. "Shot," he whispered. "By the NKVD—the not-so-secret police. Now I have to go, all right?"

Tatiana's shocked face must have slowed him, because he patted her on the arm and said, smiling grimly, "Don't worry. Sometimes things don't work out the way we hope, do they? No matter how much we plan, or how much we wish. True?"

"No, they don't," replied Tatiana, lowering her gaze. For some reason she didn't think he was talking just about his parents. "Alexander, do you want to—"

"I have to go," he cut in. "I'll see you."

All she wanted to ask was, when? but all she said was, "All right."

Tatiana didn't want to go back to her apartment, inside the kitchen, inside. She wanted to be on the tram again, or at the bus stop, even at the store, on the street—anywhere, as long as it wasn't in the apartment without him.

When Tatiana got to her building, she stood dumbly on the landing, mindlessly drawing the outline of the figure eight with her fingers, readying herself for the climb up and beyond.

With a heavy heart she ambled upstairs.

2

The family was discussing the war. There was no birthday dinner, but there was plenty of drink. And plenty of loud argument. What was going to happen to Leningrad? As Tatiana arrived, her father and grandfather were disagreeing on Hitler's intentions—as if they both knew him personally. All Mama wanted to know was why Comrade Stalin had not spoken to the people. Dasha wanted to know if she should continue working.

"As opposed to what?" snapped an irritated Papa. "Look at Tania. She is barely seventeen, and *she* doesn't ask if she should continue working."

Everybody looked at Tatiana, including Dasha—unhappily.

Tatiana put down her bag. "Seventeen today, Papa."

"Ah, yes!" Papa exclaimed. "Of course. The day has been so crazy. Let's drink a toast to Pasha's health." He paused. "And to Tania's."

The room was somehow smaller because Pasha wasn't with them.

Tatiana leaned against the wall, wondering when would be a good time to bring up her brother and Tolmachevo. Hardly anyone even noticed she was holding up the wall, except Dasha, who glanced at her from the couch and said, "Why don't you have some chicken soup? It's outside on the stove," and Tatiana thought that was a good idea. In the kitchen, she poured herself two ladlefuls of carrots and a bit of chicken and then sat on the window ledge and looked out into the yard as the soup got cold next to her. She couldn't eat anything hot. She was burning up inside.

When Tatiana walked back into their rooms, she heard her mother say consolingly to her father, "This war will *not* continue into winter. By then it will all be over."

Papa was quiet, rubbing the folds of his shirt. He said, "You know, Napoleon, too, came to the Soviet Union with his armies in June."

"Napoleon!" Mama screeched. "What does Napoleon have to do with this, Georgi Vasilievich? Please. I beg of you."

Tatiana opened her mouth to speak, to say something about Tolmachevo, but not only was she not sure of the message she was supposed to relay to her mature, all-knowing, insufferable family, it suddenly occurred to her that she might have to explain how she came by this information on the Germans' *future* advance into Russia.

Might? she thought. She closed her mouth.

Papa sat by Mama's side, looking into his empty glass. "Let's have another shot," he said. "And drink to Pasha."

"Let's go to Luga!" exclaimed Mama. "Let's go to our *dacha*, get away from the city."

How could Tatiana not say something now? "Maybe," she coughed up, with the confidence of a lamb, spluttering at her own audacity, "maybe we could bring Pasha back from camp in the meantime."

Papa, Mama, Dasha, Deda, and Babushka all stared at Tatiana with confusion and remorse, as if, one, they had been surprised she could speak and, two, they were sorry for saying grown-up things in the presence of a child.

Mama started to cry. "We *should* bring him back. Today is his birthday, and he is all by himself."

It's my birthday, too, Tatiana thought. She got up, deciding to go and have a bath.

"Where are you going?" Papa called to her.

"To wash."

"To wash what?" snapped Mama. "Take some plates into the kitchen, will you?"

"To wash myself," replied Tatiana, gathering the dirty plates from the table.

Dasha went out, Tatiana didn't ask where. She suspected it was to see Alexander. She was not one to feel sorry for herself, and she wasn't going to start now. If there was anything to feel sorry for, it was the turn of events that allowed feeling into her heart, only to have that feeling squashed by the ludicrous hands of fate. She wasn't going to allow pointless self-pity inside—that angry fiend.

Tatiana forced herself to reread some of Chekhov's stories, which never failed to ease her with their inertness. Reading seven of his short stories put her right to sleep, the last one about a girl sitting on a bench with an older man.

She kept hearing Deda and Papa argue about the war. Deda said that many people did not view it as sheer tragedy. The idea of war was terrible, but might not war bring freedom to them? Might not this new horror bring in its wake some good? Might it not lift from Russia's back the savage burden of the Bolsheviks and give the nation a chance for a new, normal, and humane life?

Tatiana heard Papa's voice, laden with vodka. "*Nothing* will lift from Russia the savage burden of the Bolsheviks. *Nothing* will bring us a normal life."

Tatiana thought Papa was a pessimist. Vodka tended to make him even more morose.

Something had to bring them all a chance for a new life. But what? As if she had any answers. She slept.

She was awakened at one forty-five in the morning by a sound she had never heard before coming from outside. It was a screeching siren piercing the dusky night. She cried out, and her father came over and told her not to worry, it was just an air-raid siren. She wanted to know if she had to get up; were the Germans bombing them already?

"Go to sleep, Tanechka, dear," said Papa, but how could she, with the siren shrieking and Dasha not home? The siren stopped after a few minutes, but Dasha was still not home.

3

At the morning meeting at Kirov the next day, Tatiana was told that the workday, in honor of the war effort, was extended until seven in the evening, until further notice. Until further notice, Tatiana guessed, was until the war ended. Krasenko informed the workers that he and the Party secretary from Moscow decided to step up production of the KV-1, heavy tank for the defense of Leningrad. Krasenko said that Leningrad would be defended with what tanks, ammunition, artillery they could make at Kirov. Stalin would not redeploy arms from the southern front to the Leningrad front to protect the city.

Whatever Leningrad could produce to defend itself—arms and food—would have to be sufficient.

After *that* meeting so many workers volunteered for the front that Tatiana thought the factory would be closed down. But no such luck. She and another worker—a worn, middle-aged woman named Zina—returned to their projectile assembly line.

Late in the day the nail gun broke, and Tatiana had to nail the crates shut with a hammer. By seven her back and her arm ached.

Tatiana and Zina walked along the Kirov wall, and before she got to the bus stop, Tatiana saw Alexander's black-haired head rising above the tide of others.

"I have to go," Tatiana said, losing a breath and speeding up. "See you tomorrow."

Zina mumbled something in return.

"Hello," she greeted him, her heart racing, her voice steady. "What are you doing here?" She was too tired to feign disinterest. She smiled.

"I'm coming to take you home. Did you have a nice birthday? Did you talk to your parents?"

"No," Tatiana replied.

"No to both?"

"I didn't talk to them, Alexander," Tatiana said, avoiding the birthday issue. "Maybe Dasha can talk to them? She is a lot braver than I am."

"Is she?"

"Oh, much," said Tatiana. "I'm a big chicken."

"I tried to talk to her about Pasha. She is even less concerned than you."

He shrugged. "Look, it's not my place. I'm just doing what I can." He glanced at the line of people. "We'll never get on this bus. Want to walk?"

"As long as it is up the tram steps," she said. "I can't move today. I'm so tired." She paused, adjusting her ponytail. "Have you been waiting long?"

"Two hours," he replied, and Tatiana suddenly felt less tired. She stared at Alexander with surprise.

"You've been waiting two hours?" What she didn't say was, you've been waiting two hours *for me*? "My day has been extended till seven. I'm sorry you waited so long," she said softly to him.

They fell away from the crowd, crossed the street, and headed toward Ulitsa Govorova.

"Why are you carrying that?" Tatiana asked, pointing to Alexander's rifle. "Are you on duty?"

"I'm off duty until ten," he said. "But I've been ordered to carry my weapon with me at all times."

"They're not here yet, are they?" Tatiana said, trying to be jovial.

"Not yet," came his short reply.

"Is the rifle heavy?"

"No." He paused and smiled. "Would you like to carry it?"

"Yes," she said. "Let's see. I've never held a rifle before." Taking it from him, she was surprised by how heavy it was and how hard it was to hold it with both hands. She carried it for a while and then gave it back to Alexander. "I don't know how you do it," she said. "Carry your weapon and all your other things, too."

"Not just carry it, Tania, but fire it. And run forward, and fall on the ground, and jump up with it in my hands, with all my other things on my back."

"I don't know how you do it." She wished she could be physically strong like that. Pasha would never beat her at war again.

The tram came, and they got on. It was crowded. Tatiana gave up her seat to an elderly lady, while Alexander looked as if he never intended to sit down. He held on to the brown overhead strap with one hand and his rifle strap with the other. Tatiana held on to the partially rusted metal handle. Every once in a while the tram would lurch and she would bump into him, and every time she would apologize. His body felt as hard as the Kirov wall.

Tatiana wanted to sit down with him alone somewhere and ask him about his parents. Certainly she couldn't ask him on the tram. And was knowing about his parents a good thing? Wouldn't knowledge about his life just make her feel closer to him, when what she needed was to feel as far away from him as possible?

Tatiana remained silent as the tram took them to Vosnesensky Prospekt, where they caught tram Number 2 to the Russian Museum.

"Well, I'll be going," Tatiana said—*extremely* reluctantly—after they got off.

"Do you want to sit for a minute?" Alexander suddenly asked. "We can rest on one of the benches in the Italian Gardens. Want to?"

"All right," Tatiana said, trying not to skip with joy as she walked in little steps next to him.

After they sat down, Tatiana could tell that something was weighing heavily on his mind, something he wanted to say and couldn't. She hoped it wasn't about Dasha. She thought, aren't we past that? She wasn't. But he was older. He should have been.

"Alexander, what's that building over there?" she asked, pointing across the street.

"Oh, that's the European Hotel," Alexander replied. "That and the Astoria are the best hotels in Leningrad."

"It looks like a palace. Who is allowed to stay there?"

"Foreigners."

Tatiana said, "My father went to Poland on business once a few years ago, and when he came back, he told us that in his Warsaw hotel *Polish* people from Krakow were staying! Can you imagine? We didn't believe him for a week. How could *Polish* people be staying in a hotel in *Warsaw?*" She chuckled. "That's like me staying at the European over there."

Alexander looked at her with an amused expression and said, "There *are* places where people can actually travel as they please in their own country."

Tatiana waved him off. "I guess," she said. "Like Poland." She swallowed hard and cleared her throat. "Alexander . . . I'm so sorry about your mother and father." She touched him gently on the shoulder. "Please tell me what happened."

With a suspended breath of relief escaping his mouth, Alexander said, "Your father is right, you know." He paused. "I'm not from Krasnodar."

"Really? Where are you from?"

"Have you ever heard of a town called Barrington?"

"No. Where is that?"

"Massachusetts."

She thought she had misheard. Her eyes became saucers. "Massachusetts?" she gasped. "As in, as in *America?*"

"Yes. As in America."

"You're from Massachusetts, *America?*" Tatiana said, astonished.

"Yes."

For a full minute, maybe two, Tatiana could not speak. Her heart drummed deafeningly and electrifyingly in her ears. She willed her jaw to stay shut.

"You're just teasing me," she said at last. "I am not that gullible."

Alexander shook his head. "I'm not teasing."

"You know why I don't believe you?"

"Yes," Alexander said. "You're thinking, who would want to come *here?*"

"That's exactly what I'm thinking."

"Communal living *was* a great disillusionment for us," Alexander told Tatiana. "We came here—my father anyway—so full of hope, and suddenly there were no showers."

"Showers?"

"Never mind. Where was the hot water? We couldn't even take a bath in the residential hotel we were staying at. Do you have hot water?"

"Of course we don't. We boil water on the stove and add it to the cold water in the bath. Every Saturday we go to the public bathhouse to wash. Like everybody in Leningrad."

Alexander nodded. "In Leningrad, in Moscow, in Kiev, in all of the Soviet Union."

"We're lucky. In the big cities we actually have running water. In provincial towns they don't even have that. Deda told me that about Molotov."

"He is right." Alexander nodded. "But even in Moscow the toilets flushed sporadically at best; the smell accumulated in the bathrooms. My parents and I, we adjusted somehow. We cooked on firewood and thought we were the Ingalls family."

"The who?"

"The Ingalls family lived in the American West in the late eighteen hundreds. Yet here *we* were, and this was socialist utopia. I said to my father once, with some irony, that he was right, this was much better than Massachusetts. He replied that you didn't build '*socialism in one country*' without a struggle. For a while I think he really believed it."

"When did you come?"

"In 1930, right after the 1929 stock market crash." Alexander looked at her blank expression and sighed. "Never mind. I was eleven. Never wanted to leave Barrington in the first place."

"Oh, no," Tatiana whispered.

"Cooking on a little Primus stove with kerosene got us down. Living in the dark. Living with unclean smells, it blackened our spirits in ways we never imagined. My mother took to drink. Well, why not? Everyone drank."

"Yes," said Tatiana. Her father drank.

"And after she drank, and the toilet was occupied by other foreigners living in our Moscow palace"—he paused—"*not* like the European—my mother would trot to the local park and relieve herself in the public toilets there—just a hole in the ground for my mother." He shivered at those words, and Tatiana shivered, too, in the balmy Leningrad evening. Gently she touched Alexander's shoulder again, and because he didn't move away, and because they sat canopied under the covering trees, and because there was not another soul around, Tatiana pressed her slender fingers against the fabric of his uniform and did not take them away.

"On Saturdays," Alexander continued, "my father and I—like you, your mother, and sister—would go to the public baths and wait two hours in line to get in. My mother went by herself on Fridays, wishing, I think, that she

59

had given birth to a daughter, so she wouldn't be all alone, so she wouldn't suffer over me so much."

"Did she suffer over you?"

"Tremendously. At first I was all right, but as the years went by, I started to blame them for my life. We were living in Moscow at the time. Seventy of us, idealists—and not just idealists, but idealists with children—lived as you do, sharing three toilets and three small kitchens on one long floor."

"Hmm," Tatiana said.

"How do *you* like it?"

She thought. "There are only twenty-five of us on our floor. But . . . what can I say? I like our *dacha* in Luga better." She glanced at him. "The tomatoes are fresh, and the morning air smells so clean."

"Yes!" Alexander exclaimed, as if she had said the magic word: *clean*.

"And," she added, "I like not being on top of other people all the time. Having a little bit of . . ." She trailed off. She couldn't think of the right word.

His legs outstretched, Alexander turned a little more to her, looking into her face.

"You know what I mean?" Tatiana said diffidently.

He nodded. "I do, Tania."

"So should we rejoice that the Germans attacked us?"

"That's just trading Satan for the devil."

Shaking her head, Tatiana said, "Don't let them catch you talking like that." But she was youthfully curious. "Which is Satan?"

"Stalin. He is marginally more sane."

"You and my grandfather," Tatiana murmured.

"What, your grandfather agrees with me?" Alexander smiled.

"No." She smiled back. "You agree with my grandfather."

"Tania, don't go kidding yourself for a minute. Hitler may be viewed by some people, especially down in the Ukraine, as their deliverer from Stalin, but you'll see how quickly he will destroy those illusions. The way he destroyed them in Austria and Czechoslovakia and Poland. In any case, after the war is over, whatever the outcome for the world, I have a feeling that here in the Soviet Union we will all go back to the same place." Alexander struggled with his words. "Have you been . . . protected by your family?" he asked with concern. "From the way it has been?"

Pressing her fingers into his shoulder, Tatiana said, "We really haven't had much personal experience with it." She didn't like to talk about it. It frightened her a little. "I once heard that someone at Papa's work was arrested. And a man and his daughter at the apartment vanished a few years ago, and the Sarkovs came to live in their place." She contemplated her words. Her father maintained that the mordant and heavyset Sarkovs were NKVD informers. "I have been somewhat protected, yes."

"Well, not me," said Alexander, taking out a cigarette and his lighter.

"Not at all. And so I cannot turn my mind away from my parents, who came here with such hope and were so crushed by the beliefs they supported almost from birth." He lit up. "You don't mind if I smoke?"

"Not at all," Tatiana said, watching him. She liked his face. "What was it?" she asked. "American living must not be that great if an American like your father could forsake his country."

Alexander didn't speak while he smoked the whole cigarette. "Let me tell you exactly what it was: Communism in America in the twenties—the Red Decade—was quite fashionable among the rich."

Alexander's father, Harold Barrington, wanted him to become a member of the Communist youth group, the Young Pioneers of America, in their town when Alexander turned ten. The group had a tiny membership, Harold had said, and they needed strength. Alexander refused. He was already in the Cub Scouts, he told his father. Barrington was a small town in eastern Massachusetts, named after the Barringtons, who had lived there since Benjamin Franklin. Alexander's progenitor had fought in the Revolutionary War. In the nineteenth century the Barringtons produced four mayors, and three of Alexander's forebears served and died in the Civil War.

Alexander's father wanted to make his own mark on the Barrington clan. He wanted to go his own way. Alexander's mother, Gina, came from Italy at the turn of the century when she was eighteen to embrace the American way of life, and when she changed her name to Jane and married Harold Barrington at nineteen, she embraced it with her heart. She had left her family in Italy to go her own way, too.

At first Jane and Harold were radicals, then they were socialist democrats, and then they were Communists. They lived in a country that let them, and they embraced Communism with all their hearts. A modern, progressive woman, Jane Barrington did not want to have children, and Margaret Sanger, the founder of Planned Parenthood, said she didn't have to.

After eleven years of being a radical with Harold, Jane decided she wanted to have children. It took her five years of miscarriages to have one child— Alexander—who was born to her in 1919 when she was thirty-five and Harold thirty-seven.

Alexander lived and breathed the Communist doctrine from the time he was old enough to understand English. In the comfort of his American home, surrounded by a blazing fire and woolen blankets, Alexander spoke words like "proletariat, equality, manifesto, Leninism," before he was old enough to know what they meant.

When he was eleven, his parents decided to live the words they had been speaking. Harold Barrington was constantly getting himself arrested for less-than-peaceful demonstrations on the streets of Boston, and finally he went to the American Civil Liberties Union and asked for their help in seeking voluntary asylum in the USSR. To do it he was willing and ready to renounce his American citizenship and move to the Soviet Union, where he could be one with the people. No social classes. No unemployment. No prejudice. No religion. The Barringtons did not admire the no-religion part, but they were progressive, intellectual people, who were willing and able to put God aside to help build the great Communist experiment.

Harold and Jane Barrington surrendered their passports, and when they first arrived in Moscow, they were feted and fed as royalty. Only Alexander seemed to notice the smell in the bathrooms, the lack of soap, and the brazenly destitute with rags on their feet who collected outside their restaurant windows, waiting for the dirty dishes to be brought into the kitchen so they could eat the scraps. The drunken squalor in the beer bars to which Harold Barrington took Alexander was so depressing that Alexander finally stopped going. He didn't care how much he wanted to be with his father.

At the residential hotel where they were staying, they received special treatment, along with other expatriates from England, Italy, and Belgium.

Harold and Jane got their new Soviet passports, thereby permanently severing their ties with the United States. As a minor, Alexander would not be getting his Soviet passport until he was sixteen and had to register for the compulsory military service.

Alexander went to school, learned Russian, made many friends. He was slowly adjusting to his new life when in 1935 the Barringtons were told that they would have to leave their rent-free accommodation and fend for themselves. The Soviet government could no longer keep them. The trouble was, the Barringtons could not find a room for themselves in Moscow. Not a single room in any communal apartment anywhere. They moved to Leningrad and, after weeks of going from one housing committee to another, finally found two rooms in a squalid building on the south side of the Neva. Harold found work at Izhorsk factory. Jane's drinking increased. Alexander kept his head down and concentrated on school.

It all ended in May 1936, the month Alexander turned seventeen years old.

Jane and Harold Barrington were arrested in the least expected way—but also the most ordinary. One day she did not come home from the market.

All Harold wanted was somehow to get a message to Alexander, but they had had bitter words and he had not seen the boy in two nights.

Four days after his wife's disappearance, there was a soft knock on Harold's door at three in the morning.

What Harold did not know was that representatives of the People's Commissariat of Internal Affairs had already come for Alexander.

* * *

A man named Leonid Slonko was Jane's interrogator at the Big House. "What funny things you say, Comrade Barrington," he said to her. "How did I know you were going to say them?"

"You've never met me before," she said.

"I've met thousands like you."

Really, thousands, she wanted to say. Are there really thousands of us coming from the United States?

"Yes, thousands," confirmed Slonko, as if she'd spoken. "They all come. To make us better, to live the capitalist-free life. Communism requires a sacrifice, you know that. You must put away your bourgeois aesthetic and look at us as a new reformed Soviet woman and not as an American."

"I have put away my bourgeois aesthetic," Jane said. "I've given away my home, my job, my friends, my entire life. I came here and started a new life because I believed. All you had to do was not betray me."

"And how did we do that? Did we do that by feeding you? By clothing you? By giving you a job? A place to live?"

"Then why am I here?" she asked.

"Because it is you who have betrayed us," said Slonko. "We cannot abide your disillusionment when we are trying to rebuild the human race for the benefit of all mankind. When we are trying to eradicate poverty and misery from this earth."

Slonko added, "And let me ask you, Comrade Barrington, when you expressed contempt for our country by calling on the U.S. embassy in Moscow a few weeks ago, did you perhaps forget that you have given up your allegiance to the United States by advocating the overthrow of democracy? By being connected with the Popular Front? By giving up your American citizenship? You are not an American citizen. They do not care whether you live or die." Slonko laughed. "How silly all of you are. You come here from your countries, decrying their governments, their customs, their ways of life that are repulsive to you. Yet at the first sign of trouble, who is it that you contact?" Slonko slapped the table. "Be assured, comrade, that the American government couldn't care less about you right now. They've forgotten who you are. The file on you and your husband and your son has been sealed by the U.S. Department of Justice and put into a vault. You are ours now."

It was true. Jane had gone to the U.S. embassy in Moscow two weeks before her arrest. She had taken the train with Alexander. She must have been followed. The reception she got at the embassy was chilly at best: the Americans had no interest in helping either her or her son.

"Was I followed?" she asked Slonko.

"What do you think?" he said. "You've shown that your fealty is a fickle thing. We were right to follow you. We were right not to trust you. Now you will be tried for treason under Article 58 of the Soviet Constitution. You know that, too. You know what's ahead of you."

"Yes," she said. "I just wish it would come quicker."

"What would be the point of that?" Slonko was a big, imposing man of advanc-

ing age, but he still looked strong and skilled. "You understand how you look to the Soviet government. You have broken with the country you were born in, then spat on the country that provided for you and your family. You were doing quite well in America, quite well—you, the Barringtons of Massachusetts—until you decided to change your life. You came here. Fine, we said. We were convinced you were all spies. We watched you because we were cautious, not vindictive. We watched you and then we wanted you to stand on your own two feet. We promised you we would take care of you, but for that we needed your undying loyalty. Comrade Stalin expects—no, requires—nothing less.

"You went to the embassy because you changed your mind about us the way you changed your mind about America. They said, sorry, but we don't know you. We said, sorry, but we don't want you. So what's there for you to do? Where do you go? They won't have you, we don't want you. You have shown us you cannot be trusted. Now what?"

"Now death," said Jane. "But I beg you, spare my only son." She lowered her head. "He was just a young boy. He never surrendered his U.S. citizenship."

"He surrendered it when he registered for the Red Army and became a Soviet citizen," said Slonko.

"But the U.S. State Department doesn't have a subversive file on him. He never joined the Communists there, he is not part of this. I beg you—"

"Why, comrade," Slonko said, "he is the most dangerous of you all."

Jane saw her husband once before appearing in front of a tribunal presided over by Slonko. After a speedy trial, she was put in front of the firing squad, turned blind to the wall.

Until his arrest Harold Barrington's concern for Alexander did not outweigh his despair at being caught with his dreams around his ankles.

He had been in prison before; incarceration did not bother him. Being in prison for his beliefs was a badge of honor, and he had worn that badge proudly in America. "I have sat in some of the best jails in Massachusetts," Harold used to say. "In New England no one compares to me in what I endure for my beliefs."

The Soviet Union had turned out to be a land of soup kitchens. Communism wasn't working as well in Russia as everyone hoped because it was Russia. It would work great in America, Harold thought. That was the place for Communism. Harold wanted to bring it back home.

Home.

He couldn't believe he was still calling it home.

The Soviet Union was well and good, but it wasn't his home, and the Soviet Communists knew it. They were done protecting him, no matter how much he had refused to believe it. Now he was the enemy of the people. He understood.

Harold derided America. He despised America with its shallowness and false morality, he hated the individualist ethic, and he thought the idea of democracy was embraced only by a special kind of idiot. But now that he was sitting in a Soviet concrete cell, Harold wanted to get his boy back *to this America, at any cost, at any price.*

The Soviet Union couldn't save Alexander. Only America could do that.

What have I done to my son? Harold thought. What have I left behind for him? Harold couldn't remember what Communism was anymore. All he saw was Alexander's admiring face as Harold stood on a pulpit in Greenwich, Connecticut, screaming invective on a Saturday afternoon in 1927.

Who is the boy I call Alexander? If I don't know, how will he? I found my way, but how will he find his in a country that does not want him?

All Harold wanted during his year of endless interrogations, denials, pleas, and confusion was to see Alexander once before he died. He called on Slonko's humanity.

"Don't call on my humanity," Slonko said. "I have none. Also, humanity has nothing to do with Communism, with creating a higher social order. That, comrade, takes discipline, perseverance, and a certain detached attitude."

"Not just detached," said Harold, "but severed."

"Your son will not be coming to visit you," Slonko said. "Your son is dead."

Speechless, Tatiana sat next to Alexander as both her hands caressed his arm up and down. "I'm so sorry," she whispered, wanting desperately to touch his face but unable to bring herself to do so. "Alexander, you hear me? I'm so sorry."

"I hear you. It's all right, Tania," he said, getting up. "My parents are gone, but I'm still here. That's something."

She could not move from the bench. "Alexander, wait, wait. How did you get from 'Barrington' to 'Belov?' And what happened to your father? Did you ever see your parents again?"

He looked at his watch. "What happens to time when I'm with you?" he muttered. "I have to run. We'll save that for another day." He gave her his hand to help her up. "A later day."

Her heart swelled. There would be another day, then? Slowly they walked out of the park. "Have you told Dasha any of this?" Tatiana asked.

"No, Tatiana," Alexander replied, not looking at her.

She was treading softly next to him. "I'm glad you told *me*," she said at last.

"Yes, me, too," said Alexander.

"Promise you'll tell me the rest someday?"

"Someday I'll make that promise." He smiled.

"I can't believe you're from *America*, Alexander. That's definitely a first for me." She blushed when she said it.

He bent and kissed her gently on the cheek. His lips were warm and his stubble prickly. "Be careful walking home," Alexander said after her. Her heart aching, Tatiana nodded, watching him walk away with a feeling that resembled despair.

What if he turned around and saw her? How silly she must look standing there staring at him. Before she could think another thought, Alexander turned around. Caught, she tried to move, her slow legs betraying her confusion. He saluted her. What must he think, seeing me gaping at him as he walks away. She wished she had more guile and made a vow to herself to get some. And then she raised her hand and saluted him back.

4

At home Dasha was on the roof. Each building had already designated their air-raid workers, first clearing debris from the attics, then taking shifts on the roofs, watching for German planes.

Dasha was sitting down on the tar roofing paper, smoking a cigarette and talking loudly with the two youngest Iglenko brothers, Anton and Kirill. Near them were buckets of water and heavy bags of sand. Tatiana wanted to sit next to her sister but couldn't.

Dasha got up and said, "Listen, I'm off. Will you be all right here?"

"Of course, Dasha. Anton will protect me." Anton was Tatiana's closest friend.

Dasha touched her sister's hair. "Don't stay up here too long. Are you tired? You're home so late. We knew Kirov would be too far for you. Why don't you get a job with Papa? You'll be home in fifteen minutes."

"Don't worry, Dash. I'm fine." She smiled as if to prove it.

After Dasha left, Anton Iglenko tried to jolly Tatiana out of her mood, but she didn't want to talk to anyone. She just wanted to think for a minute, for an hour, for a year. Tatiana needed to think herself *out* of what she was feeling.

Finally she relented and played the dizzy geography game. She put her hands over her eyes while Anton spun her around, stopping her suddenly, and she had to point in the direction of Finland. In the direction of Krasnodar. Which way the Urals? Which way *America*?

Then Tatiana spun Anton.

They named as many geographical locations as they could think of, and when they were done, they counted up their correct points. As the winner, Tatiana got to jump up and down.

Tonight Tatiana did not jump up and down. She sat down heavily on the roof. All she could think about was Alexander and America.

Anton, a scrawny blond boy, said, "Don't look so glum. It's all exciting."

"Is it?" she said.

"Why, yes. In two years, I'll be able to join. Petka left yesterday."

"Left yesterday for where?"

"For the front." He laughed. "In case you didn't notice, Tania, there's a war on."

"I noticed, all right," said Tatiana, shaking a little. "Have you heard from Volodya?" Volodya was with Pasha in Tolmachevo.

"No. Kirill and I wish we could have gone. Kirill can't wait to turn seventeen. He says the army will take him at seventeen."

"The army will take him at seventeen," said Tatiana, getting up.

"Tania, will somebody take you at seventeen?" Anton smiled.

"I don't think so, Anton," she replied. "I'll see you tomorrow. Tell your mother I have some chocolate for her if she wants. Tell her to come by tomorrow evening."

Tatiana went downstairs. Her grandparents were reading quietly on the couch. The small lamp was on. She squeezed in snugly between them, almost on both their laps.

"What's the matter, dear?" said her grandfather. "Don't be afraid."

"Deda, I'm not afraid," said Tatiana. "I'm just very, very confused." And I have no one to talk to, she thought.

"About the war?"

Tatiana considered. Telling them was out of the question. Instead, she asked, "Deda, you always said to me, 'Tania, there is so much still ahead of you. Be patient with life.' Do you still feel that way?"

Her grandfather didn't reply at first, and she felt she had her answer. "Oh, Deda," she mouthed plaintively.

"Oh, Tania," he said, putting his protective arm around her while her grandmother patted her knee. "Things have changed overnight in this world."

"It does seem that way," said Tatiana.

"Maybe you should be *less* patient."

"That's what I thought." She nodded. "I think patience is overrated as a virtue anyway."

"But be no less moral," said Deda. "No less righteous. Remember the three questions I told you to ask yourself to know who you are."

She wished Deda wouldn't remind her. She had no interest in asking herself those questions tonight. "Deda, in this family we leave the righteousness to you," Tatiana said, smiling weakly. "There is nothing left for the rest of us."

His head of thick gray hair shaking, her grandfather said, "Tania, that's *all* that's left."

In her bed Tatiana lay quietly and thought about Alexander. She thought about him not just telling her about his life but *drowning* her in it, the way he himself was drowned in it. As she listened to him, Tatiana had stopped breathing, her mouth remaining slightly open, so that Alexander could breathe his sorrow—from his words, from his own breath—into her lungs. He needed someone to bear the weight of his life.

Needed *her*.

Tatiana hoped she was ready.

She could not think about Dasha.

5

On the way to Kirov on Wednesday morning, Tatiana saw firemen building new water storage basins and installing what looked like fire hydrants. Was Leningrad expecting that many more fires? she wondered. Were the German bombs going to incinerate the city? She could not imagine it. It was as unimaginable as America.

In the distance the great Smolny Cathedral and Monastery was beginning to take on an unrecognizable shape and form. Camouflage nets were being draped over it by workers, who were dousing the nets in green, brown, and gray paint. What were the workers to do with the harder-to-cover—though also harder to spot from the air—spires of Peter and Paul's Cathedral and the Admiralty? For the time being they remained in full luminescent view.

Before she left work, Tatiana scrubbed her hands and face until they glistened, then stood in front of the mirror next to her locker and thoroughly brushed out her hair, leaving it long and down. This morning she had put on a wraparound floral print skirt and a blue blouse with short sleeves and white buttons. As she checked herself in the mirror, she couldn't decide—did she look twelve or thirteen? Whose kid sister was she? Oh, yes, Dasha's. Please be waiting for me, she thought before rushing out.

She hurried to the bus stop, and there was Alexander, his cap in his hands, waiting for her.

"I like your hair, Tania," he said, smiling.

"Thank you," she muttered. "I wish I didn't smell like I worked with petroleum all day. Petroleum and grease."

"Oh, no," he said, rolling his eyes. "You weren't making bombs again?"

She laughed.

They looked at the sulky, overworked crowd waiting for the bus and then at each other and together said, "Tram?" and nodded, crossing the street.

"At least we're still working," Tatiana said lightly. "Pravda says things are not so good with work in your America these days. Full employment here in the Soviet Union, Alexander."

"Yes," Alexander said, leaning into her as they walked. "There is no unemployment in the Soviet Union or in the Dartmoor jail—and for the same reason."

Smiling, Tatiana wanted to call him a subversive but didn't.

While they waited for the tram, Alexander said, "I brought you something." He handed her a package wrapped in brown paper. "I know Monday was your birthday. But I didn't have a chance before today . . ."

"What is it?" Sincerely surprised, she took the package from him. A small lump came up in her throat.

Lowering his voice, he said, "In America we have a custom. When you're given presents for your birthday, you're supposed to open them and say thank you."

Tatiana nervously looked down at the present. "Thank you." Gifts were not something she was used to. Wrapped gifts? Unheard of, even when they came wrapped only in plain brown paper.

"No. Open first. Then say thank you."

She smiled. "What do I do? Do I take the paper off?"

"Yes. You *tear* it off."

"And then what?"

"And then you throw it away."

"The whole present or just the paper?"

Slowly he said, "Just the paper."

"But you wrapped it so nicely. Why would I throw it away?"

"It's just paper."

"If it's just paper, why did you wrap it?"

"Will you please open my present?" said Alexander.

Eagerly Tatiana tore open the paper. Inside were three books—one hefty hardcover collection by Aleksandr Pushkin called *The Bronze Horseman and Other Poems,* and two smaller books, one by a man she'd never heard of, named John Stuart Mill; the book was called *On Liberty.* It was in English. The last one was an English-Russian dictionary.

"*English*-Russian?" Tatiana said, smiling. "It's less helpful than you might think. I speak no English. Was this yours from when you came here?"

"Yes," he said. "And without it you won't be able to read Mill."

"Thank you so much for all of them," she said.

"The *Bronze Horseman* book was my mother's," said Alexander. "She gave it to me a few weeks before they came for her."

Tatiana didn't know what to say. "I love Pushkin." Very quietly.

"I thought you might. All Russians do."

"Do you know what the poet Maikov wrote about Pushkin?"

"No," Alexander said.

Flustered by his eyes, Tatiana tried to remember the lines. "He said . . . let's see . . . *His sounds do not seem made in this world's fashion . . . as if pervaded with his deathless leaven . . . All earthly stuff—emotions, anguish, passion—had been transmuted to the stuff of heaven.*"

"All earthly stuff—emotions, anguish, passion—had been transmuted to the stuff of heaven," Alexander repeated.

Tatiana turned red and looked down the street. Where was that tram? "Have you ever read Pushkin yourself?" she asked in a tiny voice.

"Yes, I have read Pushkin myself," Alexander replied, taking the wrapping paper out of her hands and throwing it away. " 'The Bronze Horseman' is my favorite poem."

"Mine, too!" echoed Tatiana, looking up at him wondrously. *"There was a time, our memories keep its horrors fresh and near us, of this a tale now suffer me, to tell before you gentle readers, a grievous story it will be."*

"Tania, you quote from Pushkin like a true Russian."

"I *am* a true Russian."

Their tram arrived.

At the Russian Museum, Alexander asked, "Would you like to walk a bit?"

Tatiana couldn't say no even if she wanted to.

Even *if* she wanted to.

They walked toward the Field of Mars.

"Do you ever work?" she asked him. "Dimitri is off on missions in Karelia—don't *you* need to do something?"

"Yes, I stay behind," Alexander said with a grin, "and teach the rest of the soldiers how to play poker."

"Poker?"

"It's an American card game. Someday maybe I'll teach you how to play. Also, I've been deputized as the officer in charge of all recruitment and training of the People's Volunteer Army. I'm on duty from seven until six. I do sentry duty every other evening from ten to midnight." He paused.

Tatiana knew. That must be when Dasha went to see him.

Alexander quickly continued. "For all this I get my weekends off. I don't know how long that's going to last. I suspect not long. I'm here with the Leningrad garrison to protect the city. That's my post. When we run out of men at the front, that's when we'll send me."

But then we would run out of you, she thought. "Where are we going?"

"To *Letniy Sad*—the Summer Garden. But wait." Alexander stopped not far from his barracks. Across the street, lining the Field of Mars, were some benches. "Why don't you sit, and I'll go and get us some dinner."

"Dinner?"

"Yes, for your birthday. We'll have a birthday dinner." He offered to bring her some bread and meat. "Maybe I can even find some caviar." He smiled. "As a true Russian, Tania, you like caviar, don't you?"

"Mmm," she said. "What about matches?" she asked, trying not to sound too teasing, unsure how he would like it. "Aren't I going to perhaps need some matches?" Remembering the *Voentorg* store.

"If you need to light something, we will light it on the eternal flame in the Field of Mars. We walked past it last Sunday, remember?"

She remembered. "Can't touch that bold Bolshevik flame," she said, stepping away. "That's nearly sacrilegious."

Alexander laughed. "Sometimes we cook shish kebabs on it on our nights off. Is that sacrilegious? Besides, I thought there was no God."

Tatiana gazed up at him, but not for long. Was he teasing *her*? "That's right. There *is* no God."

"Of course not," he said. "We *are* in Communist Russia. We're all atheists."

Tatiana remembered a joke. "Comrade One says to Comrade Two, 'How is the potato crop this year?' Comrade Two replies, 'Very good, very good. With God's help the crop will reach all the way to His feet.' Comrade One says,

'Comrade! What are you saying? You know the Party says there is no God.' Comrade Two says, 'There's no potatoes either.' "

Alexander laughed. "You are so right about the potatoes. There aren't any. Now, go on," he said. "Wait on the bench for me. I'll be right back."

She walked across the street and sank down onto the bench. She smoothed out her hair, stuck her hand into her canvas bag, caressed the books he had given her, and was awash with—

What was she doing? She was so tired, she wasn't thinking. Alexander should not be here with her.

He should be here with Dasha. I know that for a fact, Tatiana thought, because if Dasha asks me where I've been, I won't be able to tell her. Standing up, Tatiana began to walk away when she heard Alexander calling her. "Tania!"

He came up, out of breath, carrying two paper bags. "Where are you going?"

She didn't have to say anything. He saw her face.

"Tania," Alexander said amiably, "I promise, I will just feed you and send you home. Let me feed you, all right?" Holding the bags in one hand, he placed the other hand on her hair. "It's for your birthday. Come on."

She couldn't go, and she knew it. Did Alexander know it, too? That was even worse. Did he know what a bind she found herself in, what unspeakable flux of feeling and confusion?

They crossed the Field of Mars on their way to the Summer Garden. Down the street the river Neva glowed in the sunlight, though it was nearly nine o'clock in the evening.

The Summer Garden was the wrong place for them.

Alexander and Tatiana couldn't find an empty bench amid the long paths, the Greek statues, the towering elms, and the intertwined lovers, like tangled rose branches all.

As they walked, her head was lowered.

They finally found a spot near the statue of Saturn. It was not the ideal place for them to sit, Tatiana thought, since Saturn's mouth was wide open and he was stuffing a child into it with derelict zeal.

Alexander had brought a little vodka and some bologna ham and some white bread. He had also brought a jar of black caviar and a bar of chocolate. Tatiana was quite hungry. Alexander told her to have all the caviar. She protested at first, but not vigorously. After she had eaten more than half, scooping the caviar out with the small spoon he had brought, she handed him the rest. "Please," she said, "finish it. I insist."

She had a gulp of vodka straight from the bottle and shuddered involuntarily; she hated vodka but didn't want him to know what a baby she was. Alexander laughed at her shuddering, taking the bottle from her and having a swig. "Listen, you don't have to drink it. I brought it to celebrate your birthday. Forgot the glasses, though."

He was spread out all over the bench and sitting conspicuously close. If she breathed, a part of her would touch a part of him. Tatiana was too overwhelmed to speak, as her intense feelings dropped into the brightly lit well inside her.

"Tania?" Alexander asked gently. "Tania, is the food all right?"

"Yes, fine." After a small throat clearing, she said, "I mean, it's very nice, thank you."

"Do you want some more vodka?"

"No."

She avoided his smiling eye as best she could when he asked her, "Have you ever had too much vodka?"

"Hmm." She nodded, still not looking up. "I was two. Gulped down half a liter or something. Had to be taken to the children's ward of Grechesky Hospital."

"Two? Not since?" His leg accidentally touched hers.

Tatiana blushed. "No, not since." She moved her leg and changed the subject to the Germans. She heard him sigh, then talk a little about what was happening at the garrison. But when Alexander was the only one talking, Tatiana was able to gaze at him, her eyes roaming around his face. She noticed his dark stubble, and she wanted to ask him if he was *ever* clean-shaven but decided it was too forward and didn't. The stubble was most pronounced around his mouth, where the black frame of the facial hair made his lips more vivid. She wanted to ask him about his slightly chipped side tooth but didn't do that either. She wanted to ask him to put away that soft, smiling look in his ice cream eyes.

She wanted to smile back.

"So, Alexander . . . do you still speak English?"

"Yes, I speak English. I don't get to practice. I haven't spoken it since my mother and father—" He broke off.

With a shake of her head, Tatiana said, "No, I'm sorry, I didn't mean to— I only wanted to know if you knew any words you could teach me in English."

Alexander's eyes gleamed so brightly that Tatiana felt as if all the blood in her body had rushed to her cheeks. "Tania, what words," he asked slowly, "would you like me to teach you in English?"

She couldn't answer him, afraid she would stammer. "I don't know," she finally managed. "How about *vodka?*"

"Oh, well, that's easy," he said. "It's *vodka.* " And laughed.

Alexander had a good laugh. A sincere, chortling, deep, male laugh, starting in his chest and infectiously ending in hers. Picking up the vodka bottle, he unscrewed the cap. "What should our toast be to?" he asked, raising the bottle. "It's your birthday—we will drink to you. Here's to next year's birthday. *Salut.* I hope it's a good one."

"Thank you. I'll drink a sip to that," she said, taking the bottle from him. "I like to celebrate my birthday with Pasha by my side."

Not responding to her comment, Alexander put the vodka away, looking at Saturn. "Another statue would have been better, don't you agree?" he asked. "My food is getting stuck in my throat, watching Saturn devour one of his own children whole."

"Where else would you have liked to sit?" asked Tatiana, sucking on a small piece of chocolate.

"I don't know. Maybe near Mark Antony over there." He looked around. "You think there is a statue of Aphro—"

"Can we go?" Tatiana said, suddenly rising. "I need to walk off all this food." What was she doing here?

But as they strolled out of the park and to the river, Tatiana wanted to ask if he was ever called something other than Alexander. It was an inappropriate question, and she didn't ask. A walk along the granite embankment on a vanishing evening would just have to be good enough. She could not also ask what endearing, affectionate name Alexander liked to be called by.

"Do you want to sit?" Alexander asked after a while.

"I'm fine," Tatiana replied. "Unless you want to."

"Yes, let's sit."

They sat on one of the benches overlooking the Neva. Across the river was the golden spire of Peter and Paul's Cathedral. Alexander took up nearly half the seat, his long legs spread apart, his arms draped on the back of the bench. Tatiana gingerly perched down, careful not to let her leg touch his.

Alexander had a casual, unconcerned ease about himself. He moved, sat, rested, and draped as if he were completely unaware of the effect he was having on a timorous girl of barely seventeen. All his confident limbs projected a sanguine belief in his own place in the universe. This was all given to me, he seemed to say. My body, my face, my height, my strength. I did not ask for it, I did not make it, I did not build it. I did not fight for it. This is a gift, for which I say my daily thanks as I wash and comb my hair, a gift I do not abuse or think of again as I go through my day. I am not proud of it, nor am I humbled by it. It does not make me arrogant or vain, but neither does it make me falsely modest or meek.

I know what I am, Alexander said with every movement of his body.

Tatiana had forgotten to breathe. Taking a breath now, she turned to the Neva.

"I love looking at this river," Alexander said quietly. "Especially during the white nights. We have nothing like this in America, you know."

"Maybe in Alaska?"

"Maybe," he said. "But this—the river gleaming, the city around its banks, the sun setting behind Leningrad University on the left, and rising in front of us on Peter and Paul's . . ." Shaking his head, he stopped talking. They sat silently.

"How did Pushkin put it in 'The Bronze Horseman'?" Alexander asked her. "*And rather than let darkness smother . . . the lustrous heaven's golden light . . .*" He broke off. "I can't remember the rest."

Tatiana knew "The Bronze Horseman" practically by heart. She continued for him, "*One twilight glow speeds on the other . . . to grant but half an hour to night.*"

Alexander turned his head to look at Tatiana, who continued to look at the river.

"Tania . . . where did you get all those freckles?" he asked softly.

"I know, they're so annoying. It's the sun," she replied, blushing and touching her face as if wanting to scrub off the freckles that covered the bridge of her nose and spread in sprinkles under her eyes. Please stop looking at me, she thought, afraid of his eyes and terrified of her own heart.

"What about your blonde hair?" he continued, just as softly. "Is that the sun, too?"

Tatiana became acutely aware of his arm behind her on the bench. If he wanted to, he could move his hand a few centimeters and touch the hair that fell down her back. He didn't.

"White nights are something, don't you think?" he said, not taking his gaze off her.

She muttered, "We make up for them with the Leningrad winter, though."

"Yes, winter is not much fun around here."

Tatiana said, "Sometimes in the winter, when the Neva freezes, we go sledding on the ice. Even in the dark. Under the fleeting northern lights."

"You and who?"

"Pasha, me, our friends. Sometimes me and Dasha. But she's much older. I don't tag along with her too much." Why did she say that about Dasha's being much older? Was she trying to be mean? Shut up already, Tatiana said to herself.

"You must love her very much," said Alexander.

What did he mean by that? She would rather not know.

"Are you as close to her as you are to Pasha?" he asked.

"Different. Pasha and I—" Tatiana broke off. She and Pasha ate out of the same bowl together. Dasha prepared and served them that bowl. "My sister and I share a bed. She tells me I can never get married because she doesn't want my husband sleeping in bed with us."

Their stares locked. Tatiana could not look away. She hoped he didn't notice her crimson color in the golden sunlight.

"You're too young to get married," Alexander said quietly.

"I know," Tatiana said, as always a little defensive about her age. "But I'm not *too* young."

Too young for what? Tatiana wondered, and no sooner had she wondered than in a measured voice Alexander said, "Too young for *what*?"

The expression in his eyes was just too much for her. Too much on the Neva, too much in the Summer Garden, too much.

She didn't know what to say. What would Dasha say? What would a grown-up say?

"Not too young to serve in the People's Volunteers," she finally said. "Maybe I can join? And you could train me?" She laughed and then lost herself in her embarrassment.

Unsmiling, Alexander flinched a little but said, "You are too young for even the People's Volunteers. They won't take you until—" He did not finish. And she felt his unfinished sentence but couldn't grasp the meaning of the hesitation in his voice, nor of the palpitations of his lips. There was an indentation in the middle of his bottom lip, almost like a soft nesting crevice—

Suddenly Tatiana could not look at Alexander's lips for a second longer while the two of them sat by the river in the sunlit night. She shot up from the bench. "I'd better be heading home. It's getting late."

"All right," Alexander said, also standing, much more slowly. "It's such a nice evening."

"Yes," she quietly agreed without looking at him. They started to walk along the river.

"Alexander, your *America*, do you miss it?"

"Yes."

"Would you ever go back if you could?"

"I suppose," he replied evenly.

"Could you?"

He looked at her. "How would I get there? Who would let me? What claim do I have on my American name?"

Tatiana had an urge to take his hand, to touch him, to ease him somehow. "Tell me something about *America*," she asked. "Did you ever see an ocean?"

"Yes, the Atlantic, and it's quite something."

"Is it salty?"

"Yes, and cold and immense, and it's got jellyfish and white sailboats."

"I saw a jellyfish once. What color is the Atlantic?"

"Green."

"Green like the trees?"

He looked around, at the Neva, at the trees, at her. "Green a little bit like the color of your eyes."

"So kind of muddy, murky green?" Emotion was pressing hard on her chest, making it difficult for her to breathe. I don't need to breathe now, she thought. I've breathed all my life.

Alexander suggested walking back through the Summer Garden.

Tatiana agreed but then remembered the sinuous lovers. "Maybe we shouldn't. Is there a quicker way?"

"No."

The tall elms cast long shadows as the sun fell behind them.

They walked through the gate and down the narrow path between the statues.

"The park looks different at night," she remarked.

"You've never been here at night?"

"No," she admitted, quickly adding, "but I've been out at night in other places. Once I—"

Alexander leaned in to her. "Tania, you want to know something?"

"What?" she said, leaning away.

"The less you've been out at night, the better I like it."

Speechless, she staggered ahead, looking at her feet.

He walked alongside, narrowing his soldier's stride to stay by her. It was a warm night; her bare arms twice touched the rough material of his army shirt.

"This is the best time, Tatiana," Alexander said. "Do you want to know why?"

"Please don't tell me."

"There will never be a time like this again. Never this simple, this uncomplicated."

"You call this uncomplicated?" Tatiana shook her head.

"Of course." Alexander paused. "We're just friends, walking through Leningrad in the *lucent dusk*."

They stopped at the Fontanka Bridge. "I've got duty at ten," he said. "Otherwise I'd walk you home—"

"No, no. I'm going to be fine. Don't worry. Thank you for dinner."

Looking into Alexander's face was not possible. Her saving grace was her height. Tatiana stared at his uniform buttons. She was not afraid of them.

He cleared his throat. "So tell me," he asked, "what do they call you when they want to call you something other than Tania or Tatiana?"

Her heart jumped. "Who's *they*?"

Alexander said nothing for what seemed like minutes.

Tatiana backed away from him, and when she was five meters away, she looked at his face. All she wanted to do was look into his wonderful face. "Sometimes," she said, "*they* call me Tatia."

He smiled.

The silences tormented her. What to do during them?

"You are very beautiful, Tatia," said Alexander.

"Stop," she said—inaudibly—as sensation left her legs.

He called after her, "If you wanted to, you could call me Shura."

Shura! That's a marvelous endearment. I would love to call you Shura, she wanted to tell him. "Who calls you Shura?"

"Nobody," Alexander replied with a salute.

Tatiana didn't just walk home. She flew. She grew brilliant red wings, and on them she sailed through the azure Leningrad sky. Closer to home, her heavy-with-guilt heart brought her down and the wings disappeared. She tied up her hair and made sure his books were at the very bottom of her bag. But she couldn't go upstairs for a number of minutes as she stood against the wall of the building, clenching both fists to her chest.

Dasha was sitting at the dining table with—surprisingly—Dimitri.

"We've been waiting for you for three hours," said Dasha petulantly. "Where have you been?"

Tatiana wondered if they could smell Alexander walking next to her through Leningrad. Did she smell of fragrant summer jasmine, of the warm sun on her bare forearms, of the vodka, of the caviar, of the chocolate? Could they see the extra freckles on the bridge of her nose? I've been walking under the lights of the North Pole. I've been walking and warming my face with the northern sun. Could they see it all in her exquisitely anguished eyes?

"I'm sorry you've been waiting. I work too late these days."

"Are you hungry?" Dasha asked. "Babushka made cutlets and mashed potatoes. You must be starved. Have some."

"I'm not hungry. I'm tired. Dima, will you excuse me?" said Tatiana, going to wash.

Dimitri stayed for another two hours. The grandparents wanted their room back at eleven, so Dimitri and Dasha and Tatiana went out onto the roof and sat until dusk fell after midnight, talking in the waning light. Tatiana couldn't talk much. Dimitri was friendly and light on the tongue. He showed the girls blisters on his hands from digging trenches for two straight days. Tatiana would feel him glancing at her, seeking eye contact and smiling when he got it.

Dasha, said, "So tell me, Dima, are you very close to Alexander?"

"Yes, Alexander and I go back a *very* long way," replied Dimitri. "We are like brothers."

Tatiana, through her haze, blinked twice as her brain tried to focus on Dimitri's words.

Dear God, Tatiana prayed in bed that night, turning to the wall and pulling the white sheet and the thin brown blanket over herself. *If You are there somewhere, please teach me how to hide what I never knew how to show.*

6

All Thursday long, as she worked on the flamethrowers, Tatiana thought about Alexander. And after work he was waiting for her. Tonight she didn't ask why he had come. And he didn't explain. He had no presents and no questions. He just came. They barely spoke; just their arms banged against each other, and once when the tram screeched to a stop, Tatiana fell into him, and he, his body unmoving, straightened her by placing his hand around her waist.

"Dasha talked me into coming by tonight," he said quietly to Tatiana.

"Oh," Tatiana said. "That's fine. Of course. My parents will be glad to see you again. They were in a great mood this morning," she continued. "Yesterday Mama got through to Pasha on the telephone, and apparently he is doing great—" She stopped talking. Suddenly she felt too sad to continue.

They walked as slowly as they could to tram Number 16 and stood silently, their arms pressed against each other, until it stopped at Grechesky Hospital.

"I'll see you, Lieutenant." She wanted to say *Shura* but could not.

"I'll see you, Tatia," said Alexander.

Later that night was the first time the four of them met at Fifth Soviet and all went out for a walk together. They bought ice cream, a milk shake, and a beer, and Dasha clung to Alexander's arm like a barnacle. Tatiana maintained a polite distance from Dimitri, using every faculty in her meager possession of faculties not to watch Dasha clinging to Alexander. Tatiana was surprised at how profoundly unpleasant she found it to look at her sister touching him. Dasha going to see him in some nebulous, unimagined, unexplored Leningrad, unseen by Tatiana's eyes, was infinitely preferable.

Alexander seemed as casual and content as any soldier would be with someone like Dasha on his arm. He barely glanced at Tatiana. How did Dasha and Alexander look together? Did they look right? Did they look more right than she and Alexander? She had no answers. She didn't know how she looked when she was close to Alexander. She knew only how she *was* when she was close to Alexander.

"Tania!" Dimitri was talking to her.

"Sorry, Dima, what?" Why did he raise his voice?

"Tania, I was saying don't you think Alexander should transfer me from the rifle guard division to somewhere else? Maybe with him to the motorized?"

"I guess. Is that possible? Don't you have to know how to drive a tank or something in the motorized?"

Alexander smiled. Dimitri said nothing.

"Tania!" exclaimed Dasha. "What do you know about what you have to do in the motorized? Be quiet. Alex, are you going to be storming rivers and charging at the enemy?" She giggled.

"No," said Dimitri. "First Alexander sends me. To make sure it's safe. Then he goes himself. And gets another promotion. Right, Alexander?"

"Something like that, Dima," Alexander said, walking beside him. "Though sometimes when I go myself, I also take you."

Tatiana could barely listen. Why was Dasha walking so close to him? And how could he go himself *and* take Dimitri with him? What did that mean?

"Tania!" Dimitri said. "Tania, are you listening to me?"

"Yes, of course," she said. Why does he keep raising his voice?

"You seem distracted."

"No, not at all. It's a nice evening, isn't it?"

"Do you want to take my arm? You look like you're ready to fall down."

Carelessly glancing at Tatiana, Dasha said, "Watch out, or any minute she is going to faint."

That night when Tatiana got into bed, she pulled the blanket over her head, pretending to be asleep even when Dasha lay down next to her and whispered, "Tania, Tania, are you sleeping? Tania?" and nudged her lightly. Tatiana didn't want to talk to Dasha in the dark, divulging confidences. She just wanted to say his name once out loud. *Shura.*

7

Friday at work Tatiana noticed that hardly anyone worthwhile was left at Kirov. Only the very young, like her, and the very old. The few men that remained were all over sixty or in management positions, or both.

In the first five days of war there had been suspiciously little news from the front. The radio announcers lauded wide-scale Soviet victories, while saying nothing at all of the German military power, nothing at all of the German position in the Soviet Union, nothing at all of danger to Leningrad or of evacuation. The radio was on all day as Tatiana filled her flamethrowers with thick petroleum and nitrocellulose, while through the open double doors the metal machine poured projectiles of different sizes onto the conveyor belt.

She heard *clink, clink, clink* from the metal rounds like the passing of seconds, and there were many seconds in her long day, and all she heard during them was *clink, clink, clink.*

And all Tatiana thought about was seven o'clock.

During lunch she heard on the radio that rationing might start next week. Also during lunch Krasenko told his waning staff that probably by Monday they were going to start military exercises, and that the working day was going to be extended until eight in the evening.

Before she left, Tatiana scrubbed her hands for ten minutes to get the petroleum smell out and failed. As she hurried out of the factory doors with Zina and made her way down the Kirov wall, she wanted to tell someone of her ambivalence and distress.

But then she saw Alexander's officer's cap tilted to the side, and she saw him take the cap off his head and hold it in his hands as he waited for her to walk up to him, and Tatiana forgot everything. She had to keep herself from breaking into a run. They crossed the street and made their way to Ulitsa Govorova.

"Let's walk a bit." Tatiana couldn't believe it was she who uttered those words after her day. But she didn't feel her day. She knew she wasn't going to have a minute with him on the weekend.

"What's a bit?"

She took a deep breath. "Let's walk all the way."

Slowly they strolled through the nearly deserted streets, anonymous to everyone. The railroad tracks and farm fields lay to their right, the industrial buildings of the Kirov borough rose to their left. There were no air-raid sirens, no planes flying overhead, just the pale sun shining. There were no other people.

"Alexander, why isn't Dima an officer like you?"

Alexander paused for a few moments. "He wanted to be an officer. We entered Officer Candidate School together."

Tatiana didn't know that. She told him Dimitri had not said a word about it.

"He wouldn't. We went in together, thinking we were going to stay together, but unfortunately Dima didn't make it."

"What happened?"

"Nothing happened. He couldn't stay underwater long enough without panicking, couldn't hold his breath, couldn't be quiet enough under false fire, didn't keep his cool, lost his nerve, his time in the five-mile wasn't good enough. Couldn't do fifty push-ups in a row. He just didn't make it. On many levels. He is a good soldier. A pretty good soldier," Alexander amended. "But he wasn't cut out to be an officer."

"Not like *you*," said Tatiana, taking an excited breath on the *you*.

With amusement Alexander glanced at her and shook his head. "I," he said, "am too angry a fighter."

The tram stopped right in front of them. Reluctantly they climbed aboard.

"How does Dimitri feel about it all?"

Tatiana had stopped trying to avoid Alexander as the tram bumped them together. She lived for that bumping now. Every time the tram moved, she moved with it in Alexander's direction, barely holding on to the handle. And he stood there like an inverted pyramid, catching her waist with his arm. Tonight, as he caught her, his hand remained around her. He motioned her to continue talking. But she couldn't until he took his hand away.

He took his hand away. "About what? Not becoming an officer?"

"No. About you."

"About how you'd think."

The tram stopped. To steady her, Alexander took hold of Tatiana's upper arm. Goose bumps broke out all over her body. Letting her go, he continued. "I think Dimitri often feels that things come too easily to me."

"What things?" Tatiana asked bravely.

"Don't know. Things in general. The army, the shooting range . . ." He stopped.

She looked at him, waiting. What was he going to say next? What else came too easily to Alexander?

"Nothing comes easily to you, Alexander," Tatiana said at last. "You've had the hardest life."

"And it has barely begun," he said. But when he spoke again, Tatiana detected a forced mildness. "Listen, Dimitri and I have a long history together. If I know Dima, in due course he will tell you things about me that you will not want to believe. I'm surprised he hasn't already."

"Things that are true or things that are complete lies?"

"I cannot answer that," Alexander replied. "Some will be true, some will be complete lies. Dimitri's got a gift, if you will, for mixing lies with just enough of the truth to drive you crazy."

"Some gift," she said. "So how will I know?"

"You won't. It will all sound true." Alexander glanced at her. "If you want to know the truth, ask me and I will tell you."

"If I ask, you'll tell me the truth about anything?" She looked up at him. "Yes."

Tatiana held her breath because for a moment her heart had stopped beating. It stopped as she bit her lip to keep the question off her tongue. *Do you love me?* she wanted to ask him. She wanted to slap herself into a terror that would paralyze her and make even thinking that impossible, but she could not. He wanted a question? That was the question yelling through her closed teeth and her silence and her breathless heart.

"You have a question for me, Tania?" he asked mildly.

"No," she replied, looking down at the metal handle and at the gray head of the woman in front of her.

"Here we are," Alexander said, as they got off at Obvodnoy Canal. They didn't take their second tram as usual. They ambled the five kilometers back home.

They passed an iron gate with a door behind it. The gate and the door did not look like an entryway to a building, but as if they had been built and now led to nowhere. Pointing, Alexander said, "Those gates, those doors, they can all be listening, now, yesterday, tomorrow, to you at Kirov, lying with a glass to the wall on the other side of your bed—"

"I know you're kidding. My grandparents are on the other side of my bed. You're not saying they're informers?"

"I'm not saying that." He paused. "What I'm saying is . . . no one at all can be trusted. And no one is safe."

"No one?" Tatiana asked teasingly, looking at him. "Not even you?"

"Especially not me."

"Can't be trusted or is not safe?" She smiled.

He smiled back. "Is not safe."

"But you're an officer in the Red Army!"

"Yes? Tell that to the officers in the Red Army in 1937 and 1938. They were all shot. Which is why now no one wants to take responsibility for this war."

Silently she sidled up to him and finally asked, "Am *I* safe?"

"Tatiana," he whispered, leaning close to her ear, "we are followed, always, everywhere. The day might come when someone will jump out at you from a secret door, and then you will be presented to a man behind a desk, and he will want to know what Alexander Belov spoke to you about on your walks home."

"You have told me way too much, Alexander Belov," Tatiana declared, leaning away from him. "Why did you do that if you thought I was going to be interrogated about you?"

"I needed to trust someone."

"Why didn't you tell Dasha and risk *her* life?"

Alexander paused before he replied. "Because I needed to trust *you*."

"You can trust me," Tatiana said cheerfully, shoving him lightly with her body. "But do me a favor, don't tell me anything else, all right?"

"It's too late," he said, shoving her lightly back.

"Are you saying we're doomed?" she asked, laughing.

"Eternally," replied Alexander. "Can I buy you an ice cream?"

"Yes, please." She beamed.

"Crème brûlée, right?"

"Always."

They sat on a bench while she ate it, but even after she was done, they continued to sit and talk and not move until Alexander glanced at his watch and got up.

It was nearing ten o'clock by the time they stopped at the corner of Grechesky and Second Soviet, three blocks away from her building.

Tatiana paused. "So are you coming a little later?" She sighed. "Dasha said you might be."

"Yes." He sighed also. "With Dimitri."

Tatiana was silent. They stood facing each other.

He was so near her she could smell him. Tatiana had never known anyone to smell as good and as clean as Alexander.

She thought he wanted to say something to her. He had opened his mouth, bent his head forward, frowned. She waited tensely, wanting it desperately, not wanting it, hating her ugly brown work boots, wishing she were wearing red sandals, remembering they were Dasha's, remembering she had no nice shoes of her own, wanting to be *barefoot* in front of him, and swelling with feeling and guilt previously unknown to her. Tatiana took a step back.

Alexander took a step back. "Go," he said. "I will see you tonight."

She walked away, feeling his eyes behind her. Turning around, she found him looking at her from a distance.

8

Alexander and Dimitri came by after eleven. It was still bright outside. Dasha was not home yet. Her boss had her working overtime, taking gold out of people's teeth. During times of crisis people liked to have gold instead of hard currency to barter with; gold kept its value. Dasha worked later and later, hating it, wanting everyone to behave as if life could still go on in the Leningrad summer as it had been—slow, warm, dusty, and full of young people in love.

Tatiana, Dimitri, and Alexander stood awkwardly in the kitchen as water dripped into the cast-iron sink. "So what's the matter with you two glum kids?" said Dimitri, looking from Tatiana to Alexander.

"Well, *I'm* tired," said Tatiana. It was only a partial lie.

"And I'm hungry," said Alexander, glancing at her.

"Tania, let's go for a walk."

"No, Dima."

"Yes. We'll leave Alexander here to wait for Dasha." Dimitri smiled. "They don't need us. Those two would love to be left by themselves. Am I right, Alexander?"

"They're not going to have much luck here," Tatiana muttered. Thank goodness.

Alexander walked over to the window and looked down into the courtyard.

"I really can't," Tatiana protested. "I'm . . ."

Dimitri took Tatiana by the arm. "Come on, Tanechka. You've eaten already, haven't you? Let's go. We'll be back soon, I promise."

Tatiana saw Alexander's squared shoulders.

She wanted to call him Shura. "Alexander," she said, "you want us to bring you something back?"

"No, Tania," he replied, glancing back at her. His unhappy eyes flashed for a moment and were subdued by his own will.

"Why don't you go inside? Babushka made meat *pirozhki*. Go have some. There is *borscht*, too."

Dimitri's hand was already yanking Tatiana down the hall. They stepped over Slavin in the corridor, who was resting quietly on the floor, and it looked as if they would pass him without incident, but just as Tatiana neared him, he stirred, lifted his head, and grabbed her ankle.

Roughly Dimitri stepped on his wrist, and Slavin yelped, letting go, looking up at Tatiana, and wailing, "Stay home, Tanechka dear, it's too late for you to go out at night! Stay home!" He did not look at Dimitri, who cursed at him and stepped on his wrist again.

On the street Dimitri asked if she wanted an ice cream. She didn't want him to buy her one but said, "All right. A vanilla cone." She ate the ice cream unhappily as they walked. The night was warm. She was thinking about only one thing.

"What are you thinking about?"

"War," she lied. "How about you?"

"You," he replied. "I've never met anyone like you, Tania. You're quite different from the kind of girl I usually meet."

Tatiana muttered a hapless thank-you, concentrating on her ice cream.

"I hope Alexander goes inside and eats," she said. "Dasha might not be home for another hour."

"Tania," Dimitri said, "is that what you want to talk about? Alexander?" Even Tatiana with her untrained ear heard a chill in Dimitri's voice.

"No, of course I don't," she said hurriedly. "I'm just making conversation." She changed the subject. "What did you do today?"

"Dug more trenches. The front line to the north is nearly complete. We'll be ready for those Finns next week." He smirked. "So Tania, I know you must be thinking it—why am I not an officer like Alexander?"

Tatiana said nothing.

"Why haven't you asked me about it?"

"I don't know." Her heart beat a little faster.

"It's almost as if you already know."

"Know? No." She wanted to throw out what was left of the ice cream and run home.

"Have you been speaking to Alexander about me?"

"No," she said, high-strung.

"How come you haven't asked why I'm just a *frontovik* and he's an officer?"

Tatiana had no answer for that. This was too stupid. She hated lying. Not saying anything, keeping a straight face, averting her eyes was difficult enough. But outright lying? Her tongue and throat weren't used to it.

"Alex and I had every intention of being officers together. That was our original plan."

"What plan?"

Dimitri didn't answer, and Tatiana's question hung in the air and then got lodged in her head.

Her hands began to shake slightly.

She did not want to be out at night alone with Dimitri.

She did not feel safe.

They got to the corner of Suvorovsky and Tauride Park. Though the sun was still thirty degrees in the sky, under the trees the park was in shade.

"You want to walk around the gardens for a bit?" Dimitri asked.

"What time is it?"

"I don't know."

"You know what?" Tatiana said. "I really have to get back."

"You don't have to."

"I do, Dimitri. My parents are not used to my being out late at night. They'll get upset."

"They won't get upset. They like me." He moved closer to her. "Your father likes me very much. Besides," he added, "your parents are too busy thinking about Pasha to notice what time *you* come and go."

Tatiana stopped and turned around. "I'm going back." And she started to walk up Suvorovsky away from him.

He grabbed her arm. "Tania, don't walk away from me." Without letting go, he said, "Come. Come and sit with me on the bench over by the trees."

"Dimitri," she said, not moving, "I'm not going by the trees with you. Can you let go?"

"Come with me by the trees."

"No, Dimitri, let me go *now*."

He stepped up to her, holding her very hard. His fingers dug into her skin. "Well, what if I don't *want* to let go, Tanechka? What are you going to do then?"

Tatiana did not move away from him. His free arm went around her waist, and he brought her close to him. "Dima," said Tatiana, composed and unafraid, looking him right in the face, "what are you doing? Have you lost your mind?"

"Yes," he said and bent his face to kiss her. With a small cry Tatiana turned her face down and sharply away.

"No! Let go of me, Dimitri," she said. She did not lift her head.

Suddenly he let go of her. "I'm sorry," he said with a tremor in his voice.

"I have to go home right now," she said, walking as fast as she could. "Dima, you're too old for me."

"No. No. Please. I'm only twenty-three."

"That's not what I mean. I'm too young for you. I need someone who"— she paused in thought—"expects less," she finished.

"How much less?"

"Who expects *nothing*."

"I'm really sorry, Tania," he said. "I didn't mean to scare you off like that."

"That's fine," she said, not looking at him. "I'm just not the kind of girl who goes by the trees." With *you*, she thought with a pang in her heart, remembering the Summer Garden.

"I know that now. I think that's why I really like you. I just don't know how to act around you sometimes."

"Be respectful and patient."

"Fine, I'll be as patient as Job." Dimitri leaned in to her. "Because, Tanechka," he said, "I have no intention of leaving you alone."

She hurried up Suvorovsky.

Suddenly Dimitri said, "I hope Dasha likes Alexander."

"Dasha does like Alexander."

"Because *he* really likes her."

"Oh, yes?" Tatiana said weakly. "How do you know?"

"He has almost stopped his previously uncontrolled extracurricular activities. Don't say that to Dasha, of course. It'll just hurt her feelings."

Tatiana wanted to say to Dimitri that she had no idea what he was talking about, but she was too afraid that he would tell her.

When they got home, Dasha and Alexander were sitting together on the small sofa in the hallway, reading from a volume of Zoshchenko's short stories and laughing. The only thing Tatiana could say was a sullen and grumpy, "That's *my* book."

For some reason Dasha found that very funny, and even Alexander smiled. As Tatiana walked past him, his legs were sticking so far out that she tripped over them and would have fallen face forward for sure, had he not instantly grabbed her. And just as instantly let go.

"Tania," Alexander said, "what's that on your arm?"

"What? Oh, it's nothing." Making hasty excuses about exhaustion, she said good night and disappeared into her grandparents' room, where she sat between her Deda and Babushka on the sofa and listened to the radio. They chatted quietly about Pasha, and soon she felt better.

Later that night she was facing the wall when she heard Dasha whispering to her. "Tania? Tania?"

Tatiana turned to her sister. "What is it? I'm tired."

Dasha kissed her shoulder. "Tania, we never talk anymore. Our Pasha left, and we never talk. You miss him, don't you? He'll be back soon."

"I miss him. You're busy. We'll talk tomorrow, Dashenka," said Tatiana.

"I'm in *love*, Tania!" Dasha whispered.

Tatiana whispered back, "I'm glad for you, Dasha." And she turned to the wall.

Dasha kissed the back of Tatiana's head. "I think this is really it, I do. Oh, Tanechka, I just don't know what to do with myself!"

"Have you tried sleep?"

"Tania, I can't think about anything else. He is driving me crazy. He is so . . . hot and cold. Tonight he was fine, relaxed and funny, but other days . . . I just can't figure him out."

Tatiana didn't say anything.

Dasha continued, "I know I can't expect too much at once. The fact that he is finally coming around at all is a miracle. I couldn't get him to come over until last Sunday, when he came with Dima and you."

Tatiana wanted to point out that it wasn't Dasha who got Alexander to come over, but of course said nothing.

"I'm not looking a gift horse in the mouth. I think he likes our family. Did you know he's from Krasnodar? He hasn't been back there since he joined the army. Doesn't have any brothers or sisters. Doesn't talk about his parents. He is . . . I can't explain. So closemouthed. Doesn't like to say too much about his own business." She paused. "Asks me about mine, though."

"Oh?" was all Tatiana could manage.

"He tells me he wishes it weren't war."

"Yes," said Tatiana. "We all wish it weren't war."

"But that sounds hopeful, doesn't it? As if a better life with him would be possible once the war was over. Tania," said Dasha into Tatiana's hair, "do you like Dimitri?"

Tatiana fought for her voice. "I like him fine," she whispered.

"He really likes you."

"No, he doesn't."

"Yes, he does. You have no idea about these things."

"I have some idea, and he doesn't."

"Is there anything you want to talk to me about, want to ask me?"

"No!"

Dismissively, Dasha said, "Tania, you mustn't be so shy. You're seventeen already. Why can't you just give in a little?"

"Give in to Dimitri?" whispered Tatiana. "Never, Dasha."

In the minutes before she fell asleep, Tatiana realized she was less afraid of the intangible of war than she was of the tangible of heartbreak.

9

On Saturday, Tatiana went to the Leningrad public library and borrowed a *Russian*-English phrase book. She was already somewhat familiar with the odd alphabet, having learned it in school. She spent most of the afternoon trying to speak some of the more ridiculous phrases out loud. The *Ths*, *Ws*, and the soft *Rs* were very difficult. *"The weather will be thunder and rain tomorrow"* was constructed to torment her. She could say *"be"* pretty well.

On Sunday, when Alexander came by, he single-handedly glued paper strips on their windows to keep the glass from shattering in the explosive waves that might come during shelling, if and when bombs fell on Leningrad. "Everyone must tape their windows," he said. "Soon the patrols are going to walk around the city to check that all the windows have been taped. We won't be able to find replacement glass anywhere if the Germans get to Leningrad."

The Metanovs watched him with great interest, with Mama commenting every few minutes on how tall he was, and on his good work and how steady his hands were, and how solidly he stood on the windowsill. Mama wanted to know where he'd learned how to do that. Dasha replied impatiently, "Well, he *is* in the Red Army, Mama!"

"Did they teach you to stand on the windowsill in the Red Army, Alexander?" Tatiana asked.

"Oh, shut up, Tania," Dasha said, laughing, but Alexander laughed, too, and he did not say *shut up, Tania.*

"What is that design you made on our windows?" Mama said as Alexander jumped down from the sill.

Tatiana, Dasha, Mama, and Babushka looked at the shape of the glued paper on the window. Instead of being the white crisscross that the women had seen on other windows in Leningrad, Alexander's design looked like a tree. A thick trunk, slightly bent to one side, with elongated leaves growing from it, longer at the bottom, tapering off at the top.

"What *is* that, young man?" Babushka demanded imperiously.

Alexander said, "That, Anna Lvovna, is a palm tree."

"A *what?*" said Dasha, standing close to him. Why always so close?

"A palm tree."

Tatiana, standing by the door, watched him without blinking.

"A palm tree?" Dasha said quizzically.

"It's a tropical tree. Grows in the Americas and the South Pacific."

"Hmm," said Mama. "Strange choice for our windows, don't you think?"

"Better than just an old crisscross," muttered Tatiana.

Alexander smiled at her. And lightly she smiled back.

Gruffly, Babushka said, "Well, young man, when you do *my* windows, don't do any fancy things. Just a simple crisscross for me. I don't need any palm trees."

Afterward Alexander and Dasha went out by themselves, leaving Tatiana with her moody and exhausted family. Tatiana went to the Leningrad library, where she spent hours mouthing alien English sounds to herself. It seemed extremely difficult: to read in this language, to speak it, to write it. Next time she saw Alexander, she would ask him to say a few things to her in English. Just to hear how they sounded. She was already thinking about the next time she saw Alexander, as if it were a certainty. She vowed to tell him that maybe, perhaps, he shouldn't come to Kirov anymore. She made the promise to herself that night as she lay in bed and faced the wall, she made the promise to the wall, touching the old wallpaper with her fingers, stroking it up and down and saying, I promise, I promise, I promise. Then she reached down to the floor between the bed and the wall and touched the *Bronze Horseman* book Alexander had given her. Maybe she would tell him that another day. After she heard some English from him, and after he talked to her about the war, and after—

There was another air-raid siren. Dasha returned home well after it, waking Tatiana, whose fingers remained on the listening wall.

10

On Monday at work, Krasenko called her to his office and told her that although she was doing a good job on the flamethrowers, he had to transfer her to one of the tank-production facilities immediately, because the order had come through from Moscow that Kirov had to make 180 tanks a month regardless of capability or manpower.

"Who's going to make the flamethrowers?"

"They'll make themselves," said Krasenko, lighting a cigarette. "You're a nice girl, Tania. Go. Have some soup at the canteen."

"Do you think the People's Volunteers would take me?" she asked him.

"No!"

"I heard that 15,000 people have already joined from Kirov to entrench the Luga line. Is that true?"

"What's true is that you can't go. Now, get out of here."

"Is Luga in danger?" Pasha was near Luga.

"No," Krasenko replied. "The Germans are far away. It's just a precaution. Now, go."

In tank production there were many more people and the assembly line was much more intricate, but because of that, Tatiana had less to do. She placed the pistons in the cylinders that went below the combustion chambers on the tank's V-12 diesel engine.

The facility was the size of an airplane hangar, gray and dark inside.

By the end of the day the diesel engine was in place, thanks to Tatiana, and the tread was on the tires, and the frame was tightly bolted, but there was no inside, no instruments, no panels, no weapons, no missile boxes, no ammunition launchers, and no hull roof—basically nothing that would make the machine anything other than a heavily armored car. But unlike the crating of the small-arms ammunition, or the making of flamethrowers, or the greasing of high-explosive GP bombs, making half a tank gave Tatiana a sense of accomplishment that she had not had in her entire first month of full-time work. She felt as if she had made the KV-1 herself. Another note of pride: in the afternoon Krasenko had told her the Germans could not even conceive of a tank this well built, well armed, this facile, this agile, this simple, yet armored with 45 mm of steel all around, supplied with an 85-mm gun. They thought their Panzer IV was the best tank there was. "Tania," he told her, "you did an excellent job on the diesel engine. Maybe you should be a mechanic when you grow up."

At eight in the evening Tatiana ran outside with her clean hands and her straightened-out collar and her brushed-out hair, not believing she could be running at the end of an eleven-hour day, yet running nonetheless, so afraid that Alexander wouldn't be waiting for her.

But he was.

He was waiting for her but not smiling.

Out of breath, Tatiana tried to regain her composure. She was alone with him for the first time since last Friday, alone in a sea of strangers. She wanted to say, *I'm so happy you came to see me.* What had happened to *don't come and see me anymore?*

Someone yelled out her name; Tatiana reluctantly turned around. It was

Ilya, a boy of sixteen, who worked alongside her on the tank tracks. "You catching the bus?" Ilya asked, glancing at Alexander, who said nothing.

"No, Ilya, but I'll see you tomorrow." Tatiana motioned for Alexander to cross the street.

"Who was *that*?" Alexander asked.

Puzzled, Tatiana glanced at him. "Who? Oh, just some boy I work with."

"Is he bothering you?"

"What? No, no." Ilya actually *was* bothering her a little bit. "I started in a new department. We're building tanks to send to the Luga line," she said proudly.

Nodding, he said, "How fast can you make them?"

"My department is making one every two days," she replied. "That's good, right?"

"To help at the Luga line," Alexander said, "you're going to need ten a day."

Detecting something . . . she looked up at him, tried to figure it out but couldn't. "Are you all right?"

"Yes."

She thought. "What's the matter?"

"Nothing."

The people near the tram stop were standing silently, smoking. No one was talking to anyone else. "You want to walk back home?" Tatiana asked shyly.

Alexander shook his head. "I've been in military training all day."

Nudging him with her fingers, Tatiana said teasingly, "I thought you already were in the military."

"Yes. Not for me, for them. Maneuvers, gun training, more air-raid shelters." He sounded depleted for some reason. Was she that close to the nuances of his voice? Of his face?

"What's the matter?" she asked again.

"Nothing," he repeated. But then he took her arm, pulling up her sleeve a little to reveal the dark bruises on the underside. "Tania, what's this?"

Ah. "Nothing." She tried to pull her arm away. He would not let go as he stood very close to her.

"Really nothing," she said, unable to look up at him. "Come on. I'm fine."

"I don't believe you," Alexander said. "I told you, don't take up with Dimitri."

"I'm not taking up with him," Tatiana said.

They glanced at each other, and then Tatiana stared at his uniform buttons.

"Alexander, it's nothing," she said. "He was just trying to get me to sit with him."

"I want you to tell me if he grabs you this hard again, do you hear?" Alexander said, letting go of her.

She didn't want his tender, firm fingers to let go of her. "Dima is a nice enough man. He is just used to a different kind of girl, I think." She coughed. "Who isn't? Well, listen, I took care of it. I'm sure it won't happen again."

"Oh?" Alexander said. "Like you took care of talking about Pasha to your family?"

Tatiana didn't speak at first but then said, "Alexander, I told you it was going to be hard for me. You can't even get my twenty-four-year-old sister to do it. Why don't *you* try? Come over for dinner one night, have some vodka with Papa, and bring it up. See how they take it. Show me how it's done. Because I can't do it."

"You can't talk to your own family about your brother, but you can stand up to Dimitri?"

"That's right," Tatiana replied, raising her voice a little, and thought unhappily, are we fighting? Why are we fighting?

There was a seat for them on the tram. Tatiana held on to the bench in front of her. Alexander's hands were folded in his lap. He was quiet and didn't look at her. Something continued to upset him. Was it Dimitri? Still they sat close, his arm pressed into her arm and his leg pressed into her leg. His leg felt made of marble. Tatiana didn't move her body away from him; as if she could, as if that were even an option. She was magnetized to him.

Trying to alleviate the tension between them, Tatiana brought up the war. "Where is the front now, Alexander?"

"Moving north."

"But it's far still. Right? Far from . . . ?"

He didn't look at her. "For all our military bravado, we are a civilian country." He snorted. "Our silly maneuvers, our exercises, our grounded planes, our pathetic tanks. We didn't know who we were dealing with."

She pressed lightly into his side, assimilating him through her skin. "Alexander, why does Dimitri seem so reluctant to go and fight? I mean, it *is* to get the Germans out of our country."

"He doesn't care about the Germans. He cares about only one thing—" He broke off.

Tatiana waited.

"You will learn something about Dimitri, Tania. He treats self-preservation as his inalienable right."

She gazed at him. "Alexander, what is . . . inalienable?"

He smiled. "A right that no one can assail."

Tatiana thought. "Who says that? Do we even have those kinds of rights? Aren't they usually reserved for the state?"

"We? Where?"

"Here." She lowered her voice. "In the Soviet Union."

"No, Tania. Here we do not. Here those rights *are* reserved for the state." Alexander paused. "And Dimitri. Especially self-preservation."

"Inalienable. I've never heard anyone say that word before," Tatiana said thoughtfully.

"No, you wouldn't," he said, his face softening. "How was the rest of your Sunday? What did you do? How is your mother? Every time I see her, she looks ready to fall down."

"Yes, too much worry for Mama these days." Tatiana turned to the window. She didn't want to speak about Pasha again. "You know what I did yesterday? I learned some English words. Want to hear?"

"Let's get off, and then yes, very much. Any *good* words?"

She didn't know quite what he meant, but she blushed anyway.

They got off the tram, and as they were walking past Warsaw Station, Tatiana saw a crowd of people huddled together: women with their children, old people with luggage, waiting in a focused disorder.

"What are they waiting for?" she asked.

"A train. They are the smart ones. They're leaving this city," said Alexander.

"Leaving?"

"Yes." He paused. "Tania . . . as you should be leaving."

"Leaving and going where?"

"Anywhere. Away from here."

Why was it that a week ago the thought of evacuation was so thrilling, yet today it felt like a death sentence? It wasn't evacuation. It was exile.

"What I hear," Alexander continued, "is that we're getting routed by the Germans. Trounced. We're unprepared, unequipped; we have no tanks and no weapons."

"Don't worry," Tatiana said with false levity. "We'll have a tank tomorrow."

"We have nothing except men, Tania. No matter what the cheerful radio reports say."

"They are quite cheerful," Tatiana said, trying to sound cheerful herself— and failing.

"Tania?"

"Yes?"

"Are you listening? The Germans are eventually headed for Leningrad. It's not safe. You really have to leave."

"But my family is staying put!"

"So? Leave without them."

"Alexander, what are you talking about?" Tatiana exclaimed and laughed. "I've never been anywhere by myself in my whole life! I barely go to the store by myself. I can't go by myself. Where? By myself to the Urals or to some place where they evacuate people? Is that where you want me to go? Or maybe to *America*, where you're from? Will I be safe there?" Tatiana chuckled. It was just preposterous.

"Certainly if you went where I'm from, you'd be safe there," Alexander said grimly.

* * *

After she came home that night, Tatiana struck up a conversation with her father about evacuation and about Pasha.

Papa listened to her long enough for him to take three puffs of his cigarette. Tatiana counted. Then he got up and, stubbing out the cigarette to punctuate his words, said, "Tanyusha, where in hell are you getting your ideas from? The Germans are not coming here. I'm not going away from here. And Pasha is safe. I know it. Listen, if it will make you feel better, Mama will call him tomorrow to make sure all is well. All right?"

Deda said, "Tania, I did ask to be evacuated east to the Molotov Oblast near the Urals. I have a cousin in Molotov."

"He's been dead for ten years, Vasili," said Babushka, shaking her large head. "Since the hunger of '31."

"His wife still lives there."

"She died of dysentery in '28."

"That was his second wife. His first wife, Naira Mikhailovna, still lives there."

"Not in Molotov. Remember? She lives where we used to live, in that village called—"

"Woman!" Deda interrupted. "Do you want to come with me or not?"

"*I'll* come with you, Deda," Tatiana said brightly. "Is Molotov nice?"

"I'll come with you, too, Vasili," said Babushka, "but don't pretend we have people in Molotov. We might as well go to Chukhotka."

Tatiana intervened. "Chukhotka . . . isn't that near the Arctic circle?"

"Yes," said Deda.

"Isn't that near the Bering Strait?"

"Yes," he said again.

"Well, maybe we *should* go to Chukhotka," Tatiana said. "If we have to go somewhere."

"Chukhotka? Who is going to let me go there?" Deda exclaimed. "Do you think I can teach math there?"

"Tania *is* a fool," agreed Mama.

Tatiana fell quiet. She wasn't thinking about Deda teaching math. She was thinking about something ridiculous. So outlandish that if she weren't in front of her judgmental family, she would have laughed.

"Why are you thinking about the Bering Strait, Tania?" asked Deda.

"She always thinks about preposterous things," Dasha piped in. "She's got a preposterous inner life."

"I have no inner life, Dasha," said Tatiana. "What's on the other side of the Bering Strait?"

"Why, Alaska," said Deda. "What does that have to do with anything?"

"Yes, Tania, shut up, will you?" said Mama.

The next night Tatiana's father came home with ration cards for the family. "Can you believe it?" he said. "Rations already. Well, we can manage.

93

They're not bad, actually." Workers got 800 grams of bread a day. Also, one kilo of meat a week and half a kilo of cereals. It seemed like plenty of food.

"Mama, did you try to call Pasha?" Tatiana wanted to know.

"I did," she replied. "I even went to the intercity telephone bureau on Ulitsa Zhelyabova. Couldn't get through. I'll try again tomorrow."

Information from the front was ominous. The war bulletins—posted all over Leningrad on wooden boards where the daily papers had once been posted—were haunting in their vagueness. The radio announcer said that the Red Army was winning but the German forces were gaining some ground.

How could the Red Army be winning if the Germans were gaining ground? Tatiana wondered.

A few days later Deda said the chances were very good that he was going to get the evacuation post in Molotov and suggested that the family start thinking about packing.

"I'm not leaving without Pasha," snapped Mama. "Besides," she said, in a calmer voice, "at the uniform factory I'm now making Red Army uniforms. I'm needed for the war effort." She nodded. "It's all right. The war will be over soon. You heard on the radio. The Red Army is winning. They're repelling the enemy."

Deda shook his head. "Oh, Irina Fedorovna," he said calmly, "the enemy is the best-armed, best-trained enemy in the world. Have you not heard? England has been fighting them for eighteen months. Alone. England, with their RAF, have not beaten the enemy."

"Yes, but, Papochka," interjected Papa coming to the defense of his wife, "now the Nazis are engaged in a *real* war, not just some air war. The Soviet front is massive. The Germans are going to have a hard time with us."

"I say we don't stay to find out how hard."

Mama repeated, "I'm not leaving."

Dasha said, "I'm with Mama on this."

I bet you are, thought Tatiana.

Pasha was no longer there, so he didn't speak.

They sat in their long, narrow room, Papa and Mama smoking, Baba and Deda shaking their quiet gray heads, Dasha sewing.

Tatiana kept to herself, thinking, well, *I* am not leaving either.

She was entrenched. She had dug a trench all around herself called *Alexander*, and she couldn't leave. Tatiana lived for that evening hour with him that propelled her into her future and into the barely formed, painful feelings that she could neither express nor understand. *Friends walking in the lucent dusk.* There was nothing more she could have from him, and there was nothing more she wanted from him but that one hour at the end of her long day when her heart beat and her breath was short and she was happy.

At home Tatiana surrounded herself with her family to protect herself, yet withdrew from them, wanting to be away from them. She watched them at night, as she did now, watched their mood, didn't trust it.

"Mama, did you call Pasha?"

"Yes. I got through. But there was no answer," Mama said. "No answer at the camp. I think I may have gotten the wrong number. I called the village Dohotino, where the camp was, but there was no answer from the Soviet council there either. I'll try again tomorrow. Everybody is trying to call. The lines must be overloaded."

Mama tried again and again, but there was no word from Pasha, and there was no good news from the front, and there was no evacuation.

Alexander stayed away from the apartment at night. Dasha worked late. Dimitri was up near Finland.

But every single day after work Tatiana brushed her hair and ran outside, thinking, *please be there*, and every single day after work Alexander was. Though he never asked her to go to the Summer Garden anymore or to sit on the bench under the trees with him, his hat was always in his hands.

Exhausted and slow, they meandered from tram to canal to tram, reluctantly parting at Grechesky Prospekt, three blocks away from her apartment building.

During their walks sometimes they talked about Alexander's America or his life in Moscow, and sometimes they talked about Tatiana's Lake Ilmen and her summers in Luga, and sometimes they chatted about the war, though less and less because of the anxiety over Pasha, and sometimes Alexander taught Tatiana a little English. Sometimes they told jokes, and sometimes they barely spoke at all. A few times Alexander let Tatiana carry his rifle as a balancing stick while she walked a high ledge on the side of Obvodnoy Canal. "Don't fall into the water, Tania," he once said, "because I can't swim."

"Is that true?" she asked incredulously, nearly toppling over.

Grabbing the end of his rifle to steady her, Alexander said with a grin, "Let's not find out, shall we? I don't want to lose my weapon."

"That's all right," Tatiana said, precariously teetering on the ledge and laughing. "I can swim perfectly well. I'll save your weapon for you. Want to see?"

"No, thank you."

And sometimes, when Alexander talked, Tatiana found her lower jaw drifting down and was suddenly and awkwardly aware that she had been staring at him so long that her mouth had dropped open. She didn't know what to look at when he talked—his caramel eyes that blinked and smiled and shined and were grim or his vibrant mouth that moved and opened and breathed and spoke. Her eyes darted from his eyes to his lips and circled from his hair to his jaw as if they were afraid she would miss something if she didn't stare at everything all at once.

There were some pieces of his fascinating life that Alexander did not wish to talk about—and didn't. Not about the last time he saw his father, not about how he became Alexander *Belov*, not about how he received his medal of valor. Tatiana didn't care and never did more than gently press him. She would take from him what he needed to give her and wait impatiently for the rest.

11

"My days are too long," Tatiana said to him one Friday evening, smiling the beaten smile of someone who had worked solidly for twelve hours. "I made you a whole tank today, Alexander! With a red star and a number thirty-six. Do you know how to operate a tank?"

"Better than that," he replied. "I know how to command it."

"What's the difference?"

"I do nothing except shout orders and get killed."

Tatiana didn't smile back. "How is that better?" she muttered. "I want to get transferred to the breadmaking facility. Instead of tanks, some lucky people are making bread."

"The more the better," said Alexander.

"Tanks?"

"Bread."

"They promised all of us a *bonus*—can you believe it?—if we made tanks over our quota. A bonus!" Tatiana chuckled. "The economics of profit during war: strange that we should want to work harder for a couple of extra rubles—goes against everything they've been teaching us from birth—but there it is."

"There it is, indeed, Tania," said Alexander. "But don't worry, they won't stop reconstructing you until you won't want to work harder even for a couple of extra rubles."

"Stop being subversive." She smiled. "No wonder you're not safe. In any case, it nearly killed Zina. She said she was ready to join the volunteers, that it couldn't be worse than this pressure."

Alexander was thoughtful. The pavement was wide, but they walked close together, their arms bumping. "Zina is right," he said finally. "Don't make any mistakes. You've heard the story of Karl Ots, haven't you?"

"Who?"

"He used to be the Kirov plant director when it was still called Putilov Works. Karl Martovich Ots. After Kirov's assassination in 1934, Ots tried to maintain order, to protect his workers from the threat of . . . retaliation, for lack of a better word."

Tatiana had heard something about Sergei Kirov from her father and grandfather. "Arrest? Death?" she said.

Alexander nodded. "Yes and yes. Anyway, one day when a T-28 tank was being inspected, a bolt was found to be missing. The tank had been about to be delivered to the army. There was of course a scandal and a frenzied search for the 'enemy saboteurs' to reveal themselves." Alexander took a breath. Tatiana waited.

"Now, Ots knew," he continued as they stopped at a junction, "that it had just been a stupid mistake, an oversight of the mechanic who had forgotten to screw in the bolt—no more, no less. Ots knew, so he refused to permit a witch hunt."

"Let me guess," Tatiana said. "He failed."

"It was like walking into a tornado and saying, but it's just wind."

"A tornado?" Tatiana asked quizzically.

Alexander went on. "Hundreds more people vanished from the factory."

Tatiana bowed her head. "Ots?"

"Hmm. With him vanished his able successor, the heads of the bookkeeping department, the tank-production units, the personnel department, the machine-tool shop, not to mention former Putilov plant workers—those who had moved on and were employed elsewhere in high positions in the government, such as the Novosibirsk Party Secretary, the Secretary of the Neva Party region—oh, and let's not forget the Mayor of Leningrad. He disappeared, too."

The light had turned green, then red, then green again. When it was red, the two of them crossed the street, not touching arms anymore. Tatiana was deep in thought. Finally she spoke. "So what you're saying is, be careful with the bolts?"

"That's what I'm saying."

"Zina is right. We don't need that kind of pressure. She is exhausted. All she wants is to go to Minsk and join her sister." Minsk was the capital of Byelorussia.

Alexander rubbed his eyes and adjusted his cap. "Tell her," he said tensely, "to forget Minsk. Concentrate on the tanks. How many are you supposed to make in a month?"

"One hundred and eighty. We're falling short."

"They're asking too much of you."

"Wait, wait." Tatiana put her hand on his arm and then, surprised at herself, took it away. "Why forget Minsk?"

"Minsk fell to the Germans thirteen days ago," Alexander said with grave finality.

"What?"

"Yes."

"*Thirteen* days ago? Oh, no, no." She shook her head. "No, Alexander, it can't be. Minsk is only a few kilometers south of . . ." Tatiana couldn't say it.

"Not a few, Tania, many," he said by way of comforting her. "Hundreds of kilometers."

"No, Alexander," said Tatiana, feeling her legs giving out. "Not that many. Why didn't you tell me?"

"Tania, it's classified army information! I tell you as much as I can, and then no more. I keep hoping you will hear something on the radio that sounds like the truth. When I know you haven't heard, I tell you some more. Minsk fell after only six days of war. Even Comrade Stalin was surprised."

"Why didn't he tell us when he spoke to us last week?"

"He called you his brothers and sisters, didn't he? He wanted you to rise up with anger and fight. What good would it do to tell you how deep in the Soviet Union the Germans are?"

"How deep are they?"

When Alexander didn't answer, she asked in a despondent voice, barely able to get the words out, "What about our Pasha?"

"Tania!" he said loudly. "I don't understand what you want me to do. I have been coming here and telling you from day *one* to get him out of Tolmachevo!"

Tatiana turned her face away from him and struggled not to cry. She didn't want him to see that.

"They're not in Luga yet," said Alexander, quieter. "They haven't reached Tolmachevo. Try not to worry. But I'll just tell you that on the first day of war, we lost 1,200 planes."

"I didn't know we had 1,200 planes."

"About that many."

"So what are we going to do?"

"*We?*" said Alexander, glancing at her and pausing. "I told you, Tania. Leave Leningrad."

"And I told *you* my family isn't going without Pasha."

Alexander said nothing. They continued to walk.

"Are you tired?" he asked quietly. "You want to go home?"

I am tired. I don't want to go home.

When Tatiana didn't reply, Alexander said, "Want to walk to Palace Bridge? I think they still sell ice cream in a shop near the river."

After having ice cream, Alexander and Tatiana were walking along the Neva embankment heading west into the sunset and across from the green-and-white splendor of the Winter Palace when on the opposite side of the street Tatiana spotted a man who made her stop suddenly.

A tall, thin, middle-aged man with a long, gray Jovian beard stood outside the Hermitage Museum with an expression of absolute shattered regret.

Tatiana instantly reacted to his face. What could make a man look this way? He was standing next to the back of a military truck, watching young men carry wooden crates down the ramp from the Winter Palace. It was these crates the man looked at with such profound heartbreak, as if they were his vanishing first love.

"Who *is* that man?" she asked, tremendously affected by his expression.

"The curator of the Hermitage."

"Why is he looking at the crates that way?"

Alexander said, "They are his life's sole passion. He doesn't know if he is ever going to see them again."

Tatiana stared at the man. She almost wanted to go and comfort him. "He's got to have more faith, don't you think?"

"I agree, Tania." Alexander smiled. "He's got to have a little more faith. After the war is over, he will see his crates again."

"The way he is looking at them, after the war is over he is going to bring them back single-handedly," declared Tatiana. Four gray armored trucks were parked outside the museum. "What do you think is going on?"

Alexander said nothing but he stopped her from walking further, motioning her to watch. In a moment four more men appeared out of the wide green doors carrying wooden crates down the ramp. The crates had holes drilled in them.

"Paintings?"

He nodded.

"Four truckloads of paintings?"

"That's nothing, I'm sure it's a small percentage of their load."

"Alexander, why are they getting the paintings out of the Hermitage?"

"Because there's a war on."

"So they're getting the artwork out?" Tatiana said indignantly.

"Yes."

"If they're so worried Hitler is going to come to Leningrad, why don't they get the people out?"

Alexander smiled at her, and she nearly forgot her question. "Tania, who will be left to fight the Nazis if the people leave? Paintings can't fight for Leningrad."

"Wait, we are not trained in fighting."

"No, but *we* are. That's why I'm here. Our garrison is thousands of soldiers strong. We will barricade the city and fight. First we will send the *frontovik*—"

"You mean Dimitri?"

"Yes, him. Into the streets with a gun. When he is dead, we will send me, with a tank, like the one you've been making for me. When I'm dead, all the barricades down, all the weapons and tanks gone, they will send you with a rock."

"And when *I'm* dead?" Tatiana asked.

"You're the last line of defense. When you're dead, Hitler will march through Leningrad the way he marched through Paris. Do you remember that?"

"That's not fair. The French didn't fight," Tatiana said, wanting to be anywhere right now but standing in front of men loading artwork from the Hermitage onto armored trucks.

"They didn't fight, Tania, but *you* will fight. For every street and for every building. And when you lose—"

"The art will be saved."

"Yes! The art will be saved," Alexander said emotionally. "And another artist will paint a glorious picture, immortalizing you, with a club in your raised hand, swinging to hit the German tank as it's about to crush you, all against the backdrop of the statue of Peter the Great atop his bronze horse. And that picture will hang in the Hermitage, and at the start of the next war the curator will once again stand on the street, crying over his vanishing crates."

Tatiana watched the men disappear behind the green doors and descend the ramp a few minutes later with more crates. "You make it sound so romantic," she said to him. "You make dying for Leningrad sound almost worthwhile."

"*Isn't* it worthwhile?"

"Maybe it's not so bad to be a Nazi." Tatiana raised her right arm outward and upward. "We can salute the Führer. We salute Comrade Stalin now anyway." She bent her arm in a salute. "We won't be free, we'll all be slaves. But so what? We'll have food. We'll have our life. A free life is better, but any life is better than no life, right?"

When Alexander, staring at her, did not reply, Tatiana continued, "We won't be able to go to other countries. But we can't now. Who wants to go to the dissolute Western free world slums anyway, where strangers kill each other for fifty—what is it?—*cents*? Isn't that what they teach us in Soviet schools?" Tatiana peered into Alexander's eyes. "You know," she said, "maybe I *would* rather die in front of the Bronze Horseman with a rock in my hand and have someone else live the free life that I can't even fathom."

"Yes," Alexander said hoarsely, "*you* would," and in a gesture both desperate and tender, he placed his palm on Tatiana's bare skin, right below her throat. His palm was so large it covered her from her clavicle to the top of her breast. Her heart nearly flew out of her chest into his hand.

Tatiana looked up at him helplessly and watched him bend to her, but a uniformed guard stepped up to the curb and shouted across the street, "Move it, you two! Move it! What are you standing gawking for? What's there to gawk at? That's enough! You've seen it all. Move on!"

Alexander took his hand away from Tatiana, turned around, and glared at the guard, who backed off, muttering that Red Army officers were as bound by the law as anyone else.

When they said good-bye to each other a few minutes later, they did not speak about what had happened, but neither could Tatiana look up at Alexander, which was just as well, because Alexander didn't look at Tatiana.

At home was a dinner of cold potatoes and cold fried onions. Tatiana ate quickly and then went up to the roof to sit and look at the sky for enemy planes, but the planes could have come and razed the whole city, because all Tatiana could see was Alexander's impassioned eyes, all Tatiana could feel was Alexander's impassioned hand on her rapidly beating heart.

Somewhere in those weeks Tatiana's innocence was lost. The innocence of honesty was gone forever, for she knew she would have to live in deceit; every day in verse and prose, in close quarters, in the same bed, every night when her foot touched Dasha's, she would live in deceit. Because she felt for him.

But what Tatiana felt for Alexander was true.

What Tatiana felt for Alexander was impervious to the drumbeat of conscience.

Oh, to be walking through Leningrad white night after white night, the dawn and the dusk all smelting together like platinum ore, Tatiana thought, turning away to the wall, again to the wall, to the wall, as ever. Alexander, my nights, my days, my every thought. You will fall away from me in just a while, won't you, and I'll be whole again, and I will go on and feel for someone else, the way everyone does.

But my innocence is forever gone.

12

Two days later, on the second Sunday in July, Alexander and Dimitri, dressed in their civilian clothes, called on Tatiana and Dasha. Alexander wore black linen trousers and a white cotton button-down short-sleeved shirt. Tatiana had never seen him in a short-sleeved shirt before, seen skin beyond his face and hands. His forearms were muscular and tanned. His face was clean-shaven. She had never seen him clean-shaven. By the time the evening hour fell, Alexander always had stubble. Tatiana thought, her heart catching on him, that he looked almost impossibly handsome.

"Where do you girls want to go? Let's go somewhere special," said Dimitri. "Let's go to Peterhof."

They packed some food and went to catch the train from Warsaw Station. Peterhof was an hour's train ride away. All four of them walked a block along Obvodnoy Canal, where Alexander and Tatiana ambled every day. Tatiana walked in silence. Once when Alexander jumped off the narrow pavement and strolled ahead of her with Dasha, his *bare* arm brushed against her *bare* arm.

On the train Dasha said, "Tania, tell Dima and Alex what you call Peterhof. Tell them."

Tatiana came out of her thoughts. "What? Oh. I call it the Versailles of the Soviet Union."

Dasha said, "When Tania was younger, she wanted to be a queen and live in the Great Palace, didn't you, Tanechka?"

"Hmm."

"What did the kids in Luga used to call you?"

"Can't remember, Dasha."

"No, they called you something so funny. The queen of . . . the queen of . . ."

Tatiana glanced at Alexander, who glanced at Tatiana.

"Tania," asked Dimitri, "what would have been your first act as queen?"

"To restore peace to the monarchy," she said. "And then to behead all transgressors."

Everybody laughed. Dimitri said, "I really missed you, Tania." Alexander stopped laughing and stared out the window. Tatiana, too, stared out the window. They were sitting diagonally across from each other on facing seats.

Touching her neat ponytail, Dimitri said, "Tania, why don't you ever wear your hair down? I saw it down once. It looked so pretty."

Dismissively Dasha said, "Dima, forget it, she's so stubborn. We tell her and tell her. Why do you keep it so long if you don't do something with it? But no. She never wears it down, do you, Tania?"

"No, Dasha," said Tatiana, wishing for her wall, for anything, just so her flushed face would not be in view of Alexander's quietly full eyes.

"Take it out of your ponytail now, Tanechka," said Dimitri. "Go on."

"Go on, Tania," said Dasha.

Slowly Tatiana pulled the rubber band out of her hair and turned to the window, not speaking again until their stop.

In Peterhof they did not take an organized tour but meandered around the palace and the Elysian manicured grounds instead, finally finding a secluded spot on the lawn under the trees near the Great Cascade Fountain to have their picnic.

With gusto they ate their lunch of hard-boiled eggs and bread and cheese. Dasha had even brought vodka, and she and Alexander and Dimitri drank from the bottle, while Tatiana refused. Then everybody had a smoke except Tatiana.

"Tania," Dimitri said, "you don't smoke, you don't drink. What do you do?"

"Cartwheels!" exclaimed Dasha. "Right, Tania? In Luga, Tania taught all the boys how to do cartwheels."

"*All* the boys?" said Alexander.

"Yes, yes," echoed Dimitri. "There were boys in Luga?"

"Like flies around Tania."

"What are you talking about, Dasha?" Tatiana said, suddenly embarrassed. With an effort, she did not meet Alexander's eyes.

Dasha pinched Tatiana on the thigh. "Tania, tell Dima and Alex how those wild beasts never left you alone." She laughed. "You were like honey to bears."

"Yes, tell us, Tania!" said Dimitri.

Alexander said nothing.

Tatiana was beet red. "Dasha, I was maybe seven. There was a group of us. Boys *and* girls."

"Yes, and they all buzzed around you," Dasha drew out, looking fondly at Tatiana. "Our Tania was the *cutest* child. She had round button eyes and those little freckles and not just blonde but white-blonde hair! She was like a ball of white sunshine rolling around Luga. None of the old ladies could keep their hands off her."

"Just the old ladies?" Alexander asked evenly.

"Do a cartwheel, Tania," said Dimitri with his hand on her back. "Show us what you can do."

"Yes, Tania!" Dasha said. "Come on. This is the perfect place for it, don't you think? Here in front of a majestic palace, fountains, lawn, gardenias blooming—"

"Germans in Minsk," said Tatiana, trying not to look at Alexander, lying on the blanket on his side, propped up by his elbow. He looked so casual, so familiar, so . . .

And yet, at the same time, utterly untouchable and unattainable.

"Forget the Germans," Dimitri said. "This is the place for love."

That's what Tatiana was afraid of.

"Come on, Tania," Alexander said softly, sitting up and crossing his legs. "Let's see these famous cartwheels." He lit a cigarette.

Dasha prodded her. "You never say no to a cartwheel."

Tatiana wanted to say no today.

Sighing, she got up from their old blanket. "Fine. Though, frankly, I don't know what kind of a queen I'd make, doing cartwheels for my subjects."

Tatiana was wearing a dress, not *the* dress but a casual pink sundress. Walking a few meters away from them, she said, "Are you ready?" And from a distance she saw Alexander's eyes swallowing her. "Watch," she said, putting her right foot forward. She flung herself upside down on her right arm, swinging her body in a perfect arc around onto her left arm and then her left foot, and then, without taking a breath and with her hair flying, Tatiana whirled around again, and again and again in an empyrean circle, down a straight trajectory on the grass toward the Great Palace, toward childhood and innocence, away from Dimitri and Dasha and Alexander.

As she walked back, her face flushed and her hair everywhere, she allowed herself a glance at Alexander's face. Everything she had wanted to see was there.

Laughing, Dasha fell on top of Alexander and said, "What did I tell you? She's got hidden talents."

Tatiana lowered her gaze and sat down on the blanket.

Rubbing Tatiana's back, Dimitri said, "Hmm, Tania, what else do you have in your bag of tricks?"

"That's it," she replied tersely.

A little later, Dimitri asked, "Dasha, Tania, how would you girls define love?"

"What?"

"How would you define love? What does love mean to you?"

"Dima! Who wants to know?" Dasha smiled at Alexander.

"It's just a question, Dasha." Dimitri drank some more vodka. "This is a good place, a fine Sunday, for that question." He smiled at Tatiana.

"I don't know. Alexander, should I answer it?" Dasha asked.

Shrugging and smoking, Alexander said, "Answer if you want."

The blanket was too small for the four of them, Tatiana thought. She was sitting in a lotus position, Dima was lying on his stomach to her left, and Alexander and Dasha were in front of her, Dasha leaning into Alexander.

"All right. Love . . . let's see," said Dasha. "Help me out, Tania, will you?"

"Dash, you can do this. I know you can." Tatiana didn't want to say that Dasha had had lots of field experience.

"Hmm . . . love. Love is . . . when he comes by when he says he's going to," she said, nudging Alexander. "Love is when he is late but says he is sorry." She smiled. "Love is when he doesn't look at any other girls but me." Nudging him again, twice. "How's that?"

"Very good, Dasha," said Alexander.

Tatiana coughed.

"Tania! What? *You're* not satisfied with that?" Dasha asked.

"No, no. It's very good." But the teasing hesitation was clearly in her voice.

"What, clever clogs? What didn't I say?"

"Oh, no, Dash. Everything. But it sounds to me what you described is what it's like to *be* loved." She paused. No one else spoke. "Isn't love what you give *him*, not what he gives *you*? Is there a difference? Am I completely wrong?"

"Completely," said Dasha, smiling at Tatiana. "What do you know?"

"Nothing," Tatiana said, not looking at anyone.

"Tanechka?" said Dimitri. "What do *you* think love is?"

Tatiana felt she was being set up.

"Tania? Tell us. What does love mean to you?" Dimitri repeated.

"Yes, go ahead, Tania," said Dasha. "Tell Dimitri what love means to you." And then in a teasing, affectionate voice, she said, "To Tania, let's see, love is being left alone for a whole summer to read in peace. Love is—sleeping late, that's the number one love. Love is—crème brûlée ice cream; no, *that* is the number one love. Tania, tell the truth, if you could sleep late all summer, and read while you ate ice cream all day, tell me you would not be in bliss!" Dasha laughed. "Love is, oh, I know—Deda! *He* is number one. Love is this Great Palace. Love is telling us those silly jokes, trying to make us laugh. Love is, Pasha—he is *definitely* number one. Love is—oh! Naked cartwheels!" Dasha exclaimed with joy.

"Naked cartwheels?" asked Alexander, who had not taken his eyes off Tatiana.

Dimitri said, "Can we see *those?*"

"Oh, Tania! They should see how you do those cartwheels! At Lake Ilmen she would catapult herself naked five times right into the water." Delight was all over Dasha's face. "Wait! That's it! That's what you were called. The kids used to call you the cartwheel queen of Lake Ilmen!"

"Yes," said Tatiana calmly. "Not the naked cartwheel queen of Lake Ilmen."

Alexander was trying not to laugh.

Dasha and Dimitri were rolling on the blanket.

Throwing a piece of bread at her sister, all red in the face, Tatiana said, "I was seven then, Dashka."

"You're seven now."

"Shut up."

Dasha knocked Tatiana back, throwing herself on top of her, "Tania, Tania, Tania," she squealed, tickling Tatiana. "You're the funniest girl." And when she was very close to Tatiana's face, she said, "Look at all your freckles." Dasha bent her head and kissed them. "They've really popped out. You must be walking outside a lot. You don't walk home from Kirov, do you?"

"No, and get off me. You are way too heavy," said Tatiana, tickling her sister back and pushing her off.

Dimitri said, "Tania, you didn't answer the question."

"Yes," said Alexander. "Let Tatiana answer the question."

It took Tatiana a few moments to get her breath back. Finally she said, "Love is . . ." And with a pulsing heart she thought about what she *could* say and what would be a big lie. What would be the truth? Partial truth, whole truth? How much could she give right now? Knowing who was listening. "Love is," she repeated slowly, looking only at Dasha, "when he is hungry and you feed him. Love is knowing when he is hungry."

Dasha said, "But, Tania, you don't know how to cook! He'd pretty much starve, wouldn't he?"

Dimitri cackled. "What about when he is horny? What do you do then?" He laughed so hard he started hiccuping. "Is love knowing when he is horny? And feeding him?"

"Shut the hell up, Dimitri," said Alexander.

"Dima, you are just so crass," said Dasha. "You have no class." Turning to Alexander and smiling, she pushed him lightly and said in an eager voice, "All right, now your turn."

Tatiana, sitting motionless in her lotus position, looked beyond Alexander to the Great Palace, thinking of the gilded throne room and all her dreams blossoming here in Peterhof when she was a child.

"Love is, to be loved," said Alexander, "in return."

Her lower lip trembling, Tatiana would not take her eyes off Peter the Great's Summer Palace.

Dasha leaned into him with a smile. "That's nice, Alexander."

Only when they all got up and folded their blanket to catch the train back did it occur to Tatiana that no one had asked Dimitri what love meant to him.

That night, as she was turned to the wall, remorse over Alexander ate Tatiana up from the whites of her bones. To turn away from Dasha like this was to admit the unadmittable, to accept the unacceptable, to forgive the unforgivable. Turning away meant that deception was going to become her way of life, as long as she had a dark wall to turn her face to.

How could Tatiana live a life, *breathe* in a life where she could sleep next to her sister with her back turned every night? Her sister, who took her mushroom picking in Luga a dozen years ago with only a basket, no knife and no paper bag, "so that the mushrooms wouldn't be afraid," Dasha had said. Her sister, who taught Tatiana how to tie her shoelaces at five and to ride her bike at six, and to eat clover. Her sister, who looked after her summer after summer, who covered for all her pranks, who cooked for her and braided her hair and bathed her when she was small. Her sister, who had once taken her out at night with her and her wild beaus, letting Tatiana see how young men behaved with young women. Tatiana had stood awkwardly against the wall of Nevsky Prospekt, eating her ice cream, while the older boys kissed the older girls. Dasha never took Tatiana with her again and after that night became more protective of Tatiana than ever.

Tatiana could not continue like this one more day.

She had to ask Alexander to stop coming to Kirov.

Tatiana felt one way. That was indisputable. But she had to behave another way. That was indisputable, too.

Turning away from the wall and to Dasha, Tatiana reached out and gently stroked the length of her sister's thick curls.

"That feels nice, Tanechka," murmured Dasha.

"I love you, Dasha," said Tatiana, as her tears trickled down on the pillow.

"Mmm, love you, too. Go to sleep."

All the while her mind was laying down the unassailable law of right and wrong, Tatiana's breath was whispering his name in the rhythmic beat of her heart. SHU-rah, SHU-rah, SHU-rah.

On the Monday after Peterhof, when a smiling Alexander met an unsmiling Tatiana at Kirov, she said to him before even a hello, "Alexander, you can't come anymore."

He stopped smiling and stood silently in front of her, at last prodding her with his hand. "Come on," he said. "Let's walk."

They walked the long block to Govorova.

"What's the matter?" He was looking at the ground.

"Alexander, I can't do this anymore. I just can't."

He stayed quiet.

"I can't make it," said Tatiana, strengthened by the concrete pavement under her feet. She was glad they were walking and she didn't have to look at his face. "It's too hard for me."

"Why?" he asked.

"Why?" Flummoxed by that question, she fell silent. Not one of her answers could she speak aloud.

"We're just friends, Tania, right?" Alexander said quietly. "*Good* friends. I come because I know you're tired. You've had a long day, you have a long way home, and a long evening ahead of you still. I come because sometimes you smile when you're with me, and I think you are happy. Am I wrong? That's why I come. It's not a big thing."

"Alexander!" she exclaimed. "Yes, we have the pretense of not really being up to much. But *please.*" She took a breath. "Why don't we tell Dasha then that you take me home from Kirov? Why do we get off every single day *three blocks* before my building?"

Slowly he said, "Dasha wouldn't understand. It would hurt her feelings."

"Of course it would. It *should!*"

"But, Tania, this has nothing to do with Dasha."

Tatiana's efforts to remain calm were costing her white fingers blood. "Alexander, this has *everything* to do with Dasha. I can't lie in bed with her night after night, afraid. Please," she said.

They came to the tram stop. Alexander stood in front of her. "Tania, look at me."

She turned her head away. "No."

"Look at me," he said, taking both her hands in his.

She raised her eyes to Alexander. His big hands felt so comforting.

"Tatia, look at me and say, Alexander, I don't want you to come anymore."

"Alexander," she said in a whisper, "I don't want you to come anymore."

He did not let go of her hands, nor did she pull away.

"After yesterday you don't want me to come anymore?" he asked, his voice faltering.

Tatiana could not look at him when she spoke. "After yesterday most of all."

"Tania!" he exclaimed suddenly. "Let's tell her!"

"What?" She thought she had misheard.

"Yes! Let's tell her."

"Tell her what?" Tatiana said, her tongue suddenly full of frozen fear. She shivered in her sleeveless top. "There is nothing *to* tell her."

"Tatiana, please!" Alexander's eyes flashed at her. "Let's tell the truth and live with the consequences. Let's do the honest thing. She deserves that. I'm going to end it with her and then—"

"No!" She tried to pull her hands away. "Please, no. Please. She'll be devastated." She paused. "We *have* to think about other people."

"What about *us*?" He squeezed her hands. "Tania . . ." he whispered, "what about you and me?"

"Alexander!" Her nerves were raw. "Please . . ."

"*You* please!" he said loudly. "I'm sick to death of this—all because you don't want to do the honorable thing."

"When is it honorable to hurt other people?"

"Dasha will get over it."

"Will Dimitri?"

When Alexander did not reply, Tatiana repeated, "Will Dimitri?"

"Let *me* worry about Dimitri, all right?"

"And you're wrong. Dasha will not get over you. She thinks you're the love of her life."

"She thinks wrong. She doesn't even know me."

Tatiana couldn't listen anymore. She yanked her hands away. "No, no. Stop talking."

Alexander stood in front of her on the pavement. "I'm a soldier in the Red Army. I'm not a doctor in America. I'm not a scientist in Britain. I'm a soldier in the *Soviet Union*. I could die any minute a thousand different ways to Sunday. This might be the last minute we will have together. Don't you want to spend that minute with me?"

Mesmerized by him, Tatiana muttered, "Right now, I just want to crawl into bed—"

"Yes," he exclaimed fervently, "crawl into bed *with me!*"

Weakening, Tatiana shook her head. "We have nowhere to go . . ." she whispered.

Alexander came up close and cupped her face as he said in a trembling, encouraged voice, "We'll work it out, Tatiasha, I promise, somehow we'll—"

"No!" she cried.

His hands lowered.

"You . . . misunderstood," she stammered. "I meant that there is nothing for us to do."

And then his eyes lowered.

And hers, too. "She is my sister," Tatiana said. "Why can't you just understand? I will not break my sister's heart."

Alexander took a step back and said coldly, "Oh, that's right, you already told me. There will be other boys. But never another sister." Without another word he turned around and began walking away.

Tatiana ran after him. "Alexander, wait!"

He kept walking.

Tatiana could not keep up. "Please, wait!" she called into Ulitsa Govorova. She held on to the wall of a yellow stucco building, whispering, *please come back.*"

Alexander came back. "Let's go," he said flatly. "I have to get back to the barracks."

Tatiana persisted. "Listen to me. If we stop now, at least there will be nothing to tell the people who are close to us, who love us, who depend on us not to betray them. Dasha—"

"Tatiana!" Alexander came at her so suddenly that she staggered back, letting go of the wall and nearly falling to the pavement. He grabbed her by the arms. "What are you talking about?" he said. "The betrayal—it's an objective thing. What, you think just because we haven't *told* them yet it's not betrayal?"

"Stop."

He didn't. "You think when you can't look at me because you're afraid that everybody will see what I see, it's not betrayal? When your face lights up a block away as you fly out of your stupid job? When you leave your hair down, when those lips of yours quiver? Are they not betraying you?" He was breathing hard.

"Stop it," she said, red, upset, trying unsuccessfully to wrest herself away from him.

"Tatiana, every single minute that you have spent with me, you have lied to your sister, lied to Dimitri, to your parents, to God, and to yourself. When will you stop?"

"Alexander," Tatiana said in a whisper, "*you* stop."

He let go.

She was panting. "You're right," Tatiana said, unable to get a breath out. "But I haven't lied to myself. That's why I can't do this anymore." She paused. "Please . . . I don't want to fight with you. And I don't have the strength to hurt Dasha. I don't have the strength for any of this."

"The strength or the desire, Tania?"

Opening her hands pleadingly, she said, "The strength. I've never lied like this in my life." Realizing what she was admitting, Tatiana flushed with embarrassment, but what could she do? She had to bravely continue. "You have no idea what it costs me every day, every minute, every night to hide from Dasha. My blank stare, my gritted teeth, my casual disregard—do you have any idea what it costs me?"

"Oh, I do," he said, the grimmest of soldiers. "I'm the one who knows the truth. That's why I want to end this charade."

"End it and then what?" Tatiana exclaimed, flaring up. "Have you thought this all the way through?" She raised her voice. "End it and then what? I've still got to live with Dasha!" She laughed with exasperation. "What do you think, you think you can *call* on me after you are through with her? You think after you tell him, after I tell her, you'll be able to come over, have dinner? Chat with my family? And, Alexander, what about *me*? Where am *I* supposed to go? To the barracks with you? Don't you understand that I sleep in the same bed with her? And that I have nowhere else to go!" Tatiana yelled. "Understand," she said, "you can do what you like, you can end it with Dasha, but if you do, you will never be able to see me again."

"Don't threaten me, Tatiana," Alexander said loudly, his eyes blazing. "And I thought *that* was the whole point of *this*."

Tatiana groaned, ready to cry.

Lowering his voice, he said, "All right, don't be upset." He rubbed her arm.

"Then stop upsetting me!"

He took his hand away.

"Go on with your life," Tatiana said. "You're a man." She lowered her eyes. "Go on with Dasha. *She* is right for you. She is a woman and I'm—"

"Blind!" Alexander exclaimed.

Tatiana stood on Ulitsa Govorova, desolately failing in the battle of her heart. "Oh, Alexander," she said, "what do you *want* from me . . ."

"Everything!" he whispered fiercely.

Tatiana shook her head, clenching her fists to her chest.

Running his hand down the length of her hair, Alexander said, "Tatia, I'm asking you for the last time."

"And I'm telling you for the last time," she said, barely able to get the words out.

Standing tall, Alexander stopped touching her.

She took a step forward, putting her gentle hand on him. "Shura . . . I don't own Dasha's life," Tatiana said. "I cannot sacrifice my sister's life. I can't give it away to please you and me—"

"That's fine," he interrupted, pulling his arm away. "You've made it very clear. I can see I was wrong about you. You can stop now. But I'm telling you, I'm going to do it my way, not your way. I *will* end it with Dasha, and you will not see me again."

"No, please . . ."

"Will you just go?" Alexander said, pointing down the street. "Walk away from me to the canal. Go home. Go to your Dasha."

"Shura . . ." she said with anguish.

"Don't call me that." His voice was cold. He folded his arms. "Go, I said! Walk away."

Tatiana blinked. Every night when they parted, an aching breath left her lungs where Alexander had been. She felt physically emptier in his absence.

And up in her room she surrounded herself with other people to feel him less, to want him less. But invariably every night Tatiana had to climb into bed with her sister, and every night Tatiana would turn to the wall begging for strength.

I can do this, she thought. I've spent seventeen years with Dasha and only three weeks with Alexander. I can do this. Feel one way. Behave one way, too.

Tatiana turned and walked away.

14

True to his word, the next time Dasha came to see him, Alexander took her for a short walk down Nevsky and told her that he needed some time to himself to think things through. Dasha cried, which he hated, because he hated to see women cry, and she pleaded, which he also did not like much. But he did not relent. Alexander could not tell Dasha he was furious with her younger sister. Furious with a shy, tiny thing who could fit into the palm of his hand if she crouched, yet who would not surrender one stride, not even for him.

A few days later Alexander almost felt glad he wasn't seeing Tatiana's face anymore. He found out that the Germans were just eighteen kilometers south of the barely fortified Luga line, which in turn was just eighteen kilometers south of *Tolmachevo*. Information came into the garrison that the Germans had combed through the entire town of Novgorod in a matter of a few hours. Novgorod, the town southeast of Luga, was where Tatiana cartwheeled into Lake Ilmen.

The People's Volunteer Army, though tens of thousands strong, had just begun digging the trenches in Luga.

Anticipating the threat of the Finns, most of the resources for field mining, antitank trenching, and concrete reinforcements had gone to the north of Leningrad. The Finnish-Soviet front line in southern Karelia was the best-defended line in the Soviet Union—and the quietest. Dimitri must be happy, Alexander thought. Hitler's precipitous advance south of Leningrad, however, had caught the Red Army by surprise. They scrambled to build a line of defense along 125 kilometers of the Luga River from Lake Ilmen to Narva. There were some entrenchments, some gun emplacements, some tank traps dug, but not nearly enough. The Leningrad command, realizing that something had to be done and done immediately, loaded the concrete tank barriers from Karelia and trucked them down to Luga.

And all the while the Red Army had been retreating after days of constant fighting.

It wasn't just retreating. It was relinquishing ground to the Germans at the rate of 500 kilometers in the first three weeks of war. There was no more air support, and the few tanks the Red Army had were insufficient, despite Tatiana's best efforts. In the middle of July the army comprised mostly rifle squads against the German Panzer units of tanks, mobile artillery, planes, and foot soldiers. The Soviets were running out of arms and out of men.

The hope for defending the Luga line now fell to the hordes of People's Volunteers, who had no training and, worse, no rifles. They were just a wall of old men and young women standing up against Hitler. What weapons they could pick up, they picked up from the dead Red Army soldiers. Some volunteers had shovels, axes, and picks, but many did not have even that.

Alexander didn't want to think about how sticks held up to German tanks. He knew.

Smoke and Thunder

1

TATIANA'S world changed after Alexander stopped coming to see her. She was now one of the last people to leave work. As she slowly walked out the double doors of the factory, she still turned her head expectantly, hoping that maybe she would see his head, his uniform, his rifle, his cap in his hands.

Down the length of the Kirov wall Tatiana walked, waiting for the buses to pick up passengers. She sat on the bench and waited for him. And then she walked the eight kilometers back to Fifth Soviet, looking for him, seeing him, in fact, everywhere. By the time she would get home at eleven or later, the dinner her family had prepared at seven was old and cold. At home everyone listened tensely to the radio, not speaking about the only thing that was on their minds—Pasha.

Dasha came home one evening in tears and told Tatiana that Alexander wanted to take a break. She cried for five straight minutes while Tatiana gently patted her back. "Well, I'm not going to give up, Tania," said Dasha. "I'm not. He means too much to me. He is going through something. I think he is afraid of commitment, like most soldiers. But I'm not going to give up. He said he needed a little time to think. That doesn't mean forever; that's just until he sorts himself out, right?"

"I don't know, Dashenka." What kind of person said he was going to do something and then did? No person Tatiana knew.

Dimitri came to see her once, and they spent an hour together surrounded by her family. She was mildly surprised that he hadn't been by more often, but he made some—Tatiana thought lame—excuse. He seemed distracted.

He had no information on the position of the Germans in the Soviet Union. His mouth on her cheek at the end of the night was as distant as Finland.

Up on the roof the kids from the building looked for excitement, for incendiary bombs to put out. There weren't any bombs. It was quiet at night, except for the laughing of Anton and his friends next to her, except for the beating of her heart.

Up on the roof Tatiana thought about the *evening minute*, the minute she used to walk out the factory doors, turn her head to the left even before her body turned, and look for his face. The *evening minute* as she hurried down the street, her happiness curling her mouth upward to the white sky, the red wings speeding her to him, to look up at him and smile.

At night she was still turned to the wall, her back to the absent Dasha, who was never home.

Tatiana would have continued this wretched way, but one morning the Metanovs heard on the radio that the Germans were trouncing their way through the countryside and, despite all measures taken by the heroic Soviet soldiers, were nearly at Luga. It wasn't the Luga part that stunned the family and made them unable to eat or talk to each other. It was that they all knew that Luga was mere kilometers from Tolmachevo, where Pasha was safely, they thought—no, were *sure*—ensconced at camp.

If the Germans were about to steamroll through Luga, what was to happen to Tolmachevo? Where was their son, their grandson, their brother?

Tatiana tried to console her family with hollow words. "He is fine, he'll be all right." When that didn't work, she tried, "We'll get in touch with him. Come on, Mama, don't cry." When that didn't work, she tried, "Mama, I can feel him still out there. He is my twin brother. He is all right, I'm telling you." Nothing worked.

There remained no word on Pasha, and Tatiana, despite her brave talk, became increasingly afraid for her brother.

The local *Soviet* had no answers. The borough *Soviet* also had no answers. Tatiana and her mother went there together.

"What can I tell you?" the stern, mustachioed woman told Mama. "My information says only that the Germans are near Luga. It doesn't say anything about Tolmachevo."

"Then why isn't there any answer when we try to call the camps?" Mama demanded. "Why are the phones not working?"

"Who do I look like, Comrade Stalin? Do I have all the answers?"

"Can we get to Tolmachevo?" Mama asked.

"What are you talking about? Can you get to the front? Can you take a bus, comrade, to the front? Yes, sure. Good luck to you." The woman's gray mustache moved as she laughed. "Natalia, come here, you have to hear this."

Tatiana wanted to say something rude back, but she couldn't muster the courage. Wishing she had tried harder to convince her family about Pasha, she led her mother out of the borough council office.

* * *

That night when Tatiana was pretending to sleep, her face to the wall, her hand on the floor below on Alexander's copy of The Bronze Horseman, she overheard her parents whispering tearfully to each other. It started with her mother's quiet sobbing, followed by her father's comforting "Shh, shh." Then he was sobbing, too, and Tatiana wanted to be anywhere but where she was.

Little whispers came to her, fragmented sentences, mournful longings.

"Maybe he is all right," she heard her mother say.

"Maybe," echoed her father.

"Oh, Georg. We can't lose our Pasha. We can't." She moaned. "Our boy."

"Our favorite boy," added Papa. "Our only son."

Mama sobbed.

Tatiana heard the sheets rustling. Her mother sniffed.

"What kind of God would take him away?"

"There is no God. Come now, Irina," Papa said in a comforting voice. "Not so loud. You'll wake the girls."

Mama cried out. "I don't care," she said, nonetheless lowering her voice to a whisper once more. "Why couldn't God take one of them?"

"Irina, don't say that. You don't mean it."

"Why, Georg, why? I know you feel the same way. Wouldn't you give up Tania for our son? Or even Dasha? But Tania is so timid and weak, she's never going to amount to anything."

"What kind of a life can she have here anyway, timid or not?" said Tatiana's father.

"Not like our son," said Mama. "Not like our Pasha."

Tatiana put the sheet over her ears so she wouldn't hear any more. Dasha continued to sleep. Mama and Papa soon fell asleep themselves. But Tatiana remained awake, the words crashing their agonizing tune on her ears. *Why couldn't God take Tania instead of Pasha?*

2

The next day after work, filled with apprehension, not believing her own nerve, Tatiana went to Pavlov Barracks. To a smiling Sergeant Petrenko she gave Alexander's name and waited, standing against the wall, hoping for some strength in her legs.

Minutes later Alexander walked through the gate. The sharply tense expression on his face dissolved momentarily into . . . but only momentarily. He had circles under his eyes. "Hello, Tatiana," he said coolly, and stood a polite distance from her in the dank passageway. "Is everything all right?"

"Sort of," Tatiana replied. "What about you? You look—"

Blinking, Alexander replied, "Everything is fine. How have you been?"

"Not so good," Tatiana admitted and became immediately afraid he would think it was because of him. "One thing . . ." She wanted to keep her voice from breaking. There was fear for Pasha, but there was something else, too. She didn't want Alexander to know it. She would try to hide it from him.

"Alexander, is there a way you could find out for us about Pasha . . . ?"

He looked at her with pity. "Oh, Tania," he said. "What for?"

"Please. Could you?" She added, "My parents, they're in despair."

"Better not to know."

"Please. Mama and Papa need to know. They just can't function." I need to know. I just can't function.

"You think it would be easier if they knew?"

"Absolutely. It's always better to know. Because then they could deal with the truth." She looked away even as she was speaking. "This is breaking them apart, the uncertainty over him." When Alexander didn't reply, Tatiana, chewing her lip, said, "If they knew, then Dasha and I and maybe Mama, too, would go to Molotov with Deda and Babushka."

Alexander lit a cigarette.

"Will you try—Alexander?" She was glad to say his name out loud. She wanted to touch his arm. So happy and so miserable to see his face again, she wanted to come closer to him. He wasn't wearing his full uniform. He must have come from his quarters, because he wore a barely buttoned shirt that was not even tucked into his army trousers. Couldn't she come closer to him? No, she couldn't.

He smoked silently. Tilting his head, he didn't stop looking at her. Tatiana tried not to show him the expression in her eyes. She mustered a pale smile.

"You will go to Molotov?" Alexander asked.

"Yes."

"Good," Alexander said without inflection or hesitation. "Tania, whether or not I will find out about Pasha, know this—*you* have to go. Your grandfather is lucky to get a post. Most people are not getting evacuated."

"My parents say the city is still the safest place right now. That's why so many thousands are coming to Leningrad from the countryside," Tatiana said with quiet authority.

"No place in the Soviet Union is safe," said Alexander.

"Careful," she said, lowering her voice.

Alexander leaned toward her, and Tatiana raised her eyes to him, not just eagerly but avidly. "What? What?" she whispered, but before he could say anything, Dimitri sprinted out of the gate.

"Hi!" he said to Tatiana, frowning. "What are you doing here?"

"I was coming up to see you," said Tatiana quickly.

"And I'm having a smoke," said Alexander.

"He needs to stop smoking just as you're coming up to see me," Dimitri said to Tatiana. He smiled. "Very nice of you to come, though. I'm

116

touched." He put his arm around her. "Let me walk you home, Tanechka," he said, leading her away. "Do you want to go somewhere? It's a nice evening."

"See you, Tania," she heard Alexander call after her. Tatiana was ready to break down.

Alexander went to see Colonel Mikhail Stepanov.

Alexander had served under Colonel Stepanov in the Winter War of 1940 with Finland, when the colonel was a captain and Alexander was a second lieutenant. The colonel had had many chances for promotion, not just to brigadier but to major general, but he refused, preferring to keep his rank and run the Leningrad garrison.

Colonel Stepanov was a tall man, nearly as tall as Alexander. He was slender and carried himself stiffly, but the movements of his body were gentle, and in his blue eyes hung a sad haze that remained even when he smiled at Alexander.

"Good morning, sir," Alexander said, saluting him.

"Good morning, Lieutenant," said the colonel, coming out from behind his desk. "At ease, soldier." They shook hands. Then Stepanov stepped away and went back behind his desk. "How are you?"

"Very well, sir."

"What's going on? How is Major Orlov treating you?"

"Everything is fine, sir. Thank you."

"What can I do for you?"

Alexander cleared his throat. "I just came for some information."

"I said at ease."

Alexander moved his feet apart and placed his hands behind his back. "The volunteers, sir, what's been happening to them?"

"The volunteers? You know what's been happening, Lieutenant Belov. You've been training them."

"I mean near Luga, near Novgorod."

"Novgorod?" Stepanov shook his head. "The volunteers were involved in some battles there. The situation in Novgorod is not good."

"Oh?"

"Untrained Soviet women throwing grenades at Panzer tanks. Some didn't even have grenades. They threw rocks." Colonel Stepanov peered into Alexander's face. "What's your interest in this?"

"Colonel," said Alexander, clicking his heels together, "I'm trying to find a seventeen-year-old boy who went to a boys' camp near Tolmachevo. There is no answer from the camps, and his family is panicked." Alexander paused, staring at the colonel. "A young boy, sir. His name is Pavel Metanov. He went to a camp in Dohotino."

The colonel stood quietly for a few moments, studying Alexander, and finally said, "Go attend to your duties. I'll see what I can find out. I'm not promising anything."

Alexander saluted him. "Thank you, sir."

Later that evening Dimitri came to the quarters Alexander shared with three other officers. They were all playing cards. A cigarette hung languidly in Alexander's mouth as he was shuffling. He barely turned his head to look at Dimitri.

Crouching beside Alexander's chair, Dimitri cleared his throat.

"Salute your commanding officer, Chernenko," said Second Lieutenant Anatoly Marazov, not looking up from his cards. Dimitri stood and saluted Marazov. "Sir," he said.

"At ease, Private."

"What's going on, Dima?" Alexander asked.

"Not much," said Dimitri quietly, crouching again. "Nowhere to go and talk?"

"Talk right here. Everything all right?"

"Fine, fine. Rumors are we're staying put."

"We're not staying put, Chernenko," said Marazov. "We're staying to defend Leningrad."

"The Finns are calling themselves co-belligerents." Dimitri snorted derisively. "If they ally with the Germans, we're as good as dead. We might as well hang up our arms."

"That's the spirit," said Marazov. "Belov, did you give me this soldier?"

Alexander turned to Dimitri. "Lieutenant Marazov is right. Dima, I'm surprised by your attitude. Frankly, it's not like you." Alexander stopped his voice from inflection.

Dimitri smiled slyly. "Alexander," he said, "not quite what we hoped for when we joined the army?"

When Alexander didn't reply, Dimitri said, "I mean, *war*."

"No, war was not what I hoped for. Is it what anyone hopes for?" Alexander paused. "Is it what you hoped for?"

"Not at all, as you know. But I had far fewer choices than you."

"You had choices, Belov?" asked Marazov.

Putting down his cards, Alexander stubbed out his cigarette and stood up. "I'll be right back," he said to the other officers and strode out. With smaller footsteps Dimitri followed behind. There were too many officers in the corridor; they walked downstairs and through the side door, out onto the cobbled courtyard. It was past one in the morning. The sky was three shades darker than gray.

A few feet away from them three soldiers stood smoking. But this was as alone as they were going to get. Alexander said, "Dima, you need to stop this nonsense. I *had* no choices. Don't go believing that. What choices did I have?"

"The choice to be somewhere else."

Alexander made no reply. He wished he were anywhere else, other than standing in front of Dimitri, who said, "Finland is too dangerous for us right now."

"I know." Alexander did not want to talk about Finland.

"Too many men on both sides, NKVD border troops everywhere. The Lisiy Nos area is full of troops—theirs and ours—and barbed wire and mines. It's not safe at all. I don't know what we're going to do. Are you sure the Finns will come down to Lisiy Nos from Vyborg?"

Alexander smoked and said nothing. Finally he spoke. "Yes. Eventually. They will want their old borders back. They'll come to Lisiy Nos."

"What else can we do? We'll bide our time then," Dimitri said. When Alexander didn't comment, Dimitri continued. "Will the right time ever come again, Alex?"

"I don't know, Dima. We'll have to wait and see."

Dimitri sighed. "Well, in the meantime, can you move me out of the First Rifle Regiment?"

"Dima, I already got you out of the Second Infantry Battalion."

"I know, but I'm still too close to possible attack. Marazov's men are the second line. I'd rather be recon, or clean-up. Or running supplies, something like that." He paused. "Best chance for success in running, don't you think?"

"You want to be running supplies? Ammunition to front-line troops?" Alexander asked with surprise.

"I was thinking more of mail and cigarettes to rear units."

Alexander smiled. "I'll see what I can do, all right?"

"Come on," Dimitri said, stubbing out his cigarette on the pavement. "Try to be more cheerful. What's the matter with you these days? Everything is all right still. The Germans aren't here; we're having a great summer."

Alexander said nothing.

"Alex," said Dimitri, "I wanted to talk to you about something. . . . Tania is such a nice girl."

"What?"

"Tania. She is such a nice girl."

"Yes."

Dimitri said nothing for a while. "And I want her to stay that way. She really shouldn't be coming here. And talking to *you*, of all people."

"I agree."

"I know we're all good friends, and she is the kid sister of your fancy-woman, but frankly, I don't want *your* reputation rubbing off on *my* nice girl. After all," Dimitri said, "she is not like one of your garrison hacks—"

Taking a step toward Dimitri, Alexander said, "That's enough."

Dimitri laughed. "I'm just joking. Is Dasha still coming to see you? I haven't been over there much. Tania works crazy hours. Dasha still comes, though, right?"

"Yes." Every night without fail Dasha would show up, trying everything she knew to get him back. But he wasn't about to tell Dimitri his business with Dasha.

"Well, all the more reason Tania shouldn't come here. It would upset Dasha needlessly, wouldn't it, if she were to find out?"

"I'm sure you're right." Alexander stared at Dimitri, who did not blanch. "Have you got another cigarette?"

Dimitri immediately reached into the pocket of his khaki trousers. "Love it. A first lieutenant asking a lowly private for a fag. I always like it when you ask me to do something for you."

Alexander took the cigarette and said nothing.

Dimitri cleared his throat. "If I didn't know any better, I'd say you had some feelings for the diminutive Tanechka."

"But you know better, don't you?"

Dimitri shrugged. "I guess. Just the way you were looking at her—"

"Forget it," said Alexander, cutting him off and taking a deep drag of the cigarette. "It's in your head."

Dimitri gave a sigh. "I know, I know," he said. "What can I say? I've fallen bad for that girl."

The cigarette slowly burned to ash between Alexander's fingers. "You *have?*" he asked at last.

"Yes. Why is that such a surprise?" Dimitri laughed wholeheartedly. "You think a cad like me is too low for a girl like Tania?"

"No, not at all," Alexander said. "But from what I've heard, you haven't stopped your Sadko activities."

Dimitri shrugged. "What does that have to do with anything?" Before Alexander could reply, Dimitri came a little closer to him, lowered his voice, and said, "Tania is young and has asked me to go slow. I am very respectful of her wishes and patient with her." He arched his eyebrows. "She is really coming around, though—"

Alexander threw down the cigarette butt and stamped it out with his boot. "All right, then," he said. "We're finished here." He started walking back to his building.

Dimitri caught up with him and grabbed him by the arm.

Alexander whirled around, yanking his arm easily from Dimitri's grip. "Don't grab me, Dimitri." His eyes flashed. The sky turned another shade of gray. "I'm not Tatiana."

Taking a few quick steps back from Alexander, Dimitri said, "All right, all right. Stop it." He took another step back. "You've really got to do something about that temper of yours, Alexander *Barrington*." He enunciated every syllable. And then he backed farther away and smiled. He seemed smaller, his little teeth sharper and more yellow, his hair more greasy, his eyes narrower in the coming of night.

3

Tatiana ran to work the next morning, carrying hope with her. She had learned to ignore the ignoble, ever-present, blue-uniformed NKVD militia troops standing by the front doors of Kirov with their obscene rifles, walking through the factory floors, almost marching, carrying their weapons close to their hips. A few of them would look at her as she passed by, and it was the only time in her life when she wished she were smaller than she already was and less noticeable. With their grave, unyielding faces, they stared at Tatiana, hardly blinking, while she blinked frequently as she hurried past them, pushing through the doors, to the relative anonymity of the assembly line.

So that the workers didn't get bored and therefore negligent on any one production facet of the KV-1, they were moved around every two hours. Tatiana went from working the pulley that lifted the treadless tank and placed it on tread, to painting the red star on a finished tank ready to be flatbedded and put into production. She spray-painted not only the red star but the white words FOR STALIN! on the hull that stood out markedly against the glossy green paint.

Ilya, the skinny boy with the crew cut, had not left Tatiana alone after Alexander stopped coming at night. He would ask her all sorts of questions that she was too polite not to answer, but in the end even Tatiana gave way to slight rudeness. I have to concentrate on my work, she would tell him, wondering how in the world he always managed to get a position next to her, no matter how many times she got transferred during the day to different tank-building responsibilities. In the canteen Ilya would get his plate and sit next to her and Zina, who could not stand him and frequently told him so.

But today Tatiana felt sorrier for him. "He is just lonely," she said, biting into her meat cutlet, lapping up the gravy, her mouth full. "He doesn't seem to have anybody. Stay, Ilya." So Ilya stayed.

Tatiana could afford to be generous. She couldn't wait for her day to end. After going to see Alexander yesterday, she was certain he would come after work to see her at Kirov. She wore her lightest skirt and her lightest, softest blouse, and even had a bath in the morning, having just taken one the night before.

That evening she ran out of the Kirov doors, her golden hair shining and down, her face scrubbed and pink, and turned her smiling head, breathless for Alexander.

He wasn't there.

It was after eight, and she sat on the bench until after nine with her hands on her lap. Then she got up and walked home.

There was no news of Pasha, and Mama and Papa were miserable. They kept crying intermittently. Dasha was not home. Deda and Babushka were slowly packing their things. Tatiana went out onto the roof and sat watching the airships float like white whales across the northern sky, listening to Anton and Kirill reading Tolstoy's *War and Peace*, evoking their brother Volodya, lost in Tolmachevo. Tatiana listened with half an ear, thinking of her brother Pasha, lost in Tolmachevo.

Alexander didn't come to see her. He had no news. Or the news he had was bad and he couldn't face her. But Tatiana knew the truth: he didn't come to see her because he was done. Done with her, with her childish ways, done with that part of his life. They had been friends walking in the Summer Garden, but he was a man, and now he was done.

He was right, of course, not to come. And she would not cry.

But to face Kirov day after day without him and without Pasha, too, to face evening after evening without him and without Pasha, to face war, to face herself without Alexander and without Pasha filled Tatiana with such a pervasive emptiness that she nearly groaned out loud, right in front of the laughing Anton and Kirill.

She needed just one thing now—to lay her eyes on the boy who had breathed the same air as her for seventeen years, in the same school, in the same class, in the same room, in the same womb. She wanted her friend and her twin back.

Tatiana thought she could feel Pasha while sitting out on the roof under the darkening sky; the white nights had ended on July 16. Her brother was not harmed. He was waiting for Tatiana to come for him, and she would not fail him. She wasn't going to be like the rest of her family, sitting around, smoking, fretting. Doing nothing. Tatiana knew: five minutes with Pasha's light heart and she would forget much of the last month.

She would forget Alexander. And she needed to do something to forget Alexander.

After everyone had gone to bed, Tatiana went downstairs, got a pair of kitchen scissors, and began to mercilessly lop off her blonde hair, watching it fall in long strands into the communal sink. Afterward the small, grimy mirror showed only a vague reflection. All she saw was her sulky lips and her sad, hollow eyes that glowed greener without the hair to frame her face. The freckles on her nose and under her eyes stood out even more prominently. Did she look like a boy? All the better. Did she look younger? More frail? What would Alexander think of all her hair gone? Who cared? She knew what he would think. Shura, Shura, Shura.

Just as dawn was breaking, Tatiana put on the only pair of beige trousers she could find, packed some baking soda and peroxide for her teeth, her toothbrush—she never took trips without her toothbrush—retrieved Pasha's sleeping bag from his old days at camp, left a one-sentence note for her family, and set out for Kirov on foot.

During her last morning at work Tatiana was assigned to the diesel engines. She screwed the glow plugs into the combustion chambers. The plugs warmed up the compressed air in the cylinders before ignition could take place. She was very good at that part of the assembly, having performed it many times before, so she did her job mindlessly, while all morning struggling with her nerve.

At lunchtime she went to see Krasenko, bringing a willing Zina along, and told him they both wanted to join the People's Volunteer Army. Zina had talked about joining the volunteers for over a week.

Krasenko told her she was too young.

She persisted.

"Why are you doing this, Tania?" Krasenko asked with sympathy in his voice. "Luga is not for a girl like you."

She told him she knew how hopeless things were there. The bulletin boards at work shouted, "At Luga—to the trenches!" She said she knew that boys and girls of fourteen and fifteen were working in the fields digging trenches. She and Zina wanted to do all they could to help the Red Army soldiers. Zina nodded mutely. Tatiana knew she needed special dispensation from Krasenko. "Please, Sergei Andreevich," she said.

"No," he said.

Tatiana persisted. She told Krasenko she would take leave that was due to her, starting tomorrow, and get down to Luga one way or another if she had to. She was leaving, with or without his help. Tatiana was not afraid of Krasenko. She knew he liked her. "Sergei Andreevich, you can't keep me here. How would it look if you were keeping eager volunteers from helping their motherland, helping the Red Army?"

Zina stood nodding by Tatiana's side.

Krasenko sighed heavily and wrote them both passes and permissions to leave Kirov and stamped their domestic passports. As they were about to leave, he got up and wished her luck. Tatiana wanted to tell him she was going to go and find her brother, but she didn't want him to talk her out of it, so she said nothing except thank you.

The girls went to a dark, gymnasium-size room, where after a physical exam they were outfitted with pickaxes and shovels that Tatiana found much too heavy for her, and were then sent to Warsaw Station on the bus to catch the special military truck transportation destined for Luga.

Tatiana wondered if they were going to be armored trucks like the ones that transported paintings from the Hermitage or like the ones that Alexander said he sometimes drove to the south of Leningrad.

They weren't. They were just regular trucks covered with khaki tarpaulin, the kind Tatiana saw constantly around Leningrad.

Tatiana and Zina climbed aboard. Forty more people piled in. Tatiana observed the soldiers loading crates onto the truck. They would have to sit on them. "What's in them?" she asked one of the soldiers.

"Grenades," he replied, grinning.

Tatiana stood.

The trucks left Warsaw Station in a convoy of seven and started down the highway, bound south for Luga.

In Gatchina everyone was told to get off and take a military train the rest of the way.

"Zina," Tatiana said to her friend, "it's good we're taking the train. That way we can get off in Tolmachevo, all right?"

"What are you, crazy?" said Zina. "We're all going to Luga."

"I know. You and I will get off, and then we'll get back on another train and go to Luga."

"No."

"Zina, yes. Please. I have to get off in Tolmachevo. I have to find my brother."

Zina stared at Tatiana with incredulity. "Tania! When you told me Minsk had fallen, did I say to you, come with me because I have to find my sister?" she said, her small, dark eyes blinking, her mouth tight.

"No, Zina, but I don't think Tolmachevo has fallen to the Germans yet. I still have hope."

"I'm not getting off," Zina said. "I'm going like everybody else to Luga, and I'm going to help our soldiers, like everybody else. I don't want to get shot by the NKVD as a deserter."

"Zina!" Tatiana exclaimed. "How can you be a deserter? You're a volunteer. Please come with me."

"I'm not getting off, and that's it," Zina said, turning her head away from Tatiana.

"Fine," said Tatiana. "But *I'm* getting off."

4

A corporal stuck his head into Alexander's quarters and shouted that Colonel Stepanov wanted to see him.

Colonel Stepanov was writing in his journal. He looked more tired than he had three days ago. Alexander patiently waited. The colonel looked up, and Alexander saw black bags under his blue eyes and taut lines in his face effected by the exertion of his will upon unwilling subjects.

"Lieutenant, sorry it took me a while. I'm afraid I don't have much good news for you."

"I understand."

The colonel looked down into his journal.

"The situation in Novgorod was desperate. When the Red Army realized the Germans were surrounding the nearby villages only kilometers away, they recruited the young men from several camps around Luga and Tolmachevo to help entrench the town. One of those camps was Dohotino. I don't know specifically about a Pavel Metanov . . ." The colonel cleared his throat. "As you know the German advance was much faster than we anticipated."

It was Soviet-speak. It was like listening to the radio. They said *this*, but they meant *that*.

"Colonel? What?"

"The Germans got past Novgorod."

"What happened to the young boys from the camps?"

"Lieutenant, beyond what I already told you, I don't know." He paused. "How well did you know this boy?"

"I know his family well, sir."

"A personal stake in this?"

Alexander blinked. "Yes, sir."

Colonel Stepanov was very quiet, playing with his pen, looking at the pages in his journal, not looking at Alexander, even when he spoke at last. "I wish I had something better to tell you, Alexander. The Germans ran over Novgorod with their tanks. Remember Colonel Yanov? He perished. The Germans shot soldiers and civilians indiscriminately, they pillaged what they could, and then they burned the town."

Not backing away from the table, not looking away from Colonel Stepanov's face, Alexander said steadily, "Let me understand. The Red Army sent underage boys into battle?"

Stepanov stood up behind his desk. "Surely you're not telling us how to run our war, Lieutenant?"

"I don't mean to be disrespectful." Alexander struck his heels together, saluted the colonel, but didn't move. "But to use untrained boys along with battle-trained, command-experienced officers as fodder for the Nazis is sheer military madness."

Colonel Stepanov did not come out from behind the desk. The two men were quiet, one young, the other already old at forty-four. Then the colonel spoke. "Tell the family their son died to save Mother Russia," he said, his voice cracking. "He died in the service of our great leader, Comrade Stalin."

Later that morning Alexander was called to the entry gate. He made his way downstairs, fearing it was Tatiana. He couldn't face her just yet. He was going to meet her at Kirov in the evening. He saw Dasha standing with Petrenko. She looked shaken and tense.

"What's the matter?" he asked her, leading her aside, hoping she, too, wouldn't ask him about Tolmachevo and Pasha, but she stuck a piece of paper into his hand and said, "Look at this, just look what my crazy sister has done!"

He opened the note. It was the first time he was seeing Tatiana's handwriting. It was round, small, and neat. *Dear Mama and Papa,* the note read. *I've gone to join the People's Volunteers to find Pasha and bring him back for you. Tania.*

Making every effort to control his facial expression, Alexander gave the note back to Dasha with careful fingers and said, "She left when?"

"Yesterday morning. We got up and she was gone."

"Dasha, why didn't you come to me right away? She's been gone since *yesterday?*"

"We thought she was just kidding. That she would come back."

"Did you hope," Alexander enunciated slowly, "that she would come back with Pasha?"

"We don't know! She gets these ideas into her head. I honestly don't know what she is thinking. She can't go to the store by herself, much less to the front. Mama and Papa are beside themselves. They were so worried about Pasha, and now this."

"Are they worried, or are they angry?" asked Alexander.

"They're frantic. They're deathly afraid for her. She—" Dasha broke off. Tears were in her eyes. "Dearest," Dasha said, coming close to him. She put her arms around him, but Alexander's face remained as closed as a bank on a holiday. "Alexander," she said, "I didn't know who to turn to. Help us, please. Help us find my sister. We can't lose my Tania . . ."

"I know," he said.

"Please?" Dasha said. "Will you do this . . . for me?"

Patting her on the back, Alexander stepped away. "Let me see what I can do."

Alexander bypassed his immediate commander, Major Orlov, and went straight to Colonel Stepanov. He got authorization to take twenty volunteers and two sergeants to drive an armored truck loaded with munitions south to the Luga line. Alexander knew that the line badly needed to be strengthened. He told Stepanov he would be back in a few days.

Before dismissing Alexander, Stepanov said, "Bring yourself back. Bring the men back, Lieutenant." He paused. "As always."

"I will do my best, sir," said Alexander. He had not seen many volunteers come back to the garrison.

Before he left, he went to see Dimitri and offered him a spot on the squad. Dimitri refused. "Dima," said Alexander, "you should come."

"I'll go where they send me," said Dimitri, shaking his head, "but I'm not swimming voluntarily into the jaws of the shark. Have you heard about what's happened to Novgorod?"

Alexander drove the armored truck himself. It was filled with men, thirty-five Nagant rifles, thirty-five brand-new Tokarev rifles, two boxes of hand grenades, three crates of field mines, seven boxes of ammunition, a stack of oval artillery shells, and a keg of gunpowder for the mortars. Alexander thought it was good that the truck was armored.

He wished he had one of the tanks Tatiana had made.

The three towns followed in order from Leningrad: Gatchina was first, then Tolmachevo, then Luga. By the time Alexander reached Gatchina, he could already hear the distant thunder of artillery. His fleet of men trembled behind him as he made his way down the unpaved road. He heard bombs exploding like fireworks, and as if in a dream his father's face flashed before him, wanting to know what Alexander was doing near death's door before it was his time. He said, "Dad, I'm going for her," and Sergeant Oleg Kashnikov, a brawny young soldier, said, "What did you say, Lieutenant?"

"Nothing. Sometimes I do that. Talk to my father."

"But, Lieutenant, that wasn't Russian," Kashnikov said. "It sounded like English, but what do I know?"

"Not English, just gibberish," said Alexander.

When Alexander and his men got out at Luga, the noise of artillery fire was no longer distant. The land was flat, and in the horizon there was smoke and sound. It wasn't a sound signifying nothing, thought Alexander. It was the thunder of anger and of death.

During the evening of one Fourth of July barbecue, the family had gone out sailing on the sea in Nantucket Sound and watched the fireworks from their boat. Seven-year-old Alexander lifted his head up to the sky, enchanted by the rainbow lights exploding loudly overhead. He couldn't imagine anything more spectacular than these vibrant colors showering the sky with life.

Straight ahead was the approach to Luga River. To the left were fields, and to the right was a forest. Alexander spotted children who were maybe ten years old picking what remained of this year's crops. On the perimeter of the fields, soldiers and older men and women were digging trenches. He knew that after the crops were picked, the fields would be mined.

Calmly, holding his rifle tightly, Alexander told his men to stay put while he went to find Colonel Pyadyshev, who was organizing the defense line for a twelve-kilometer stretch along the river. Pyadyshev was pleased about the extra arms and immediately had his soldiers unload them and prepare to divide them up. "Only seventy rifles, Lieutenant?" he said to Alexander.

"All we have, sir," Alexander replied. "More are coming."

Then Alexander took his twenty charges closer to the river bank, where they received shovels and dug for a few hours. With a pair of binoculars Alexander searched the forest on the other side of the river and determined that the Germans had already advanced to contact, though they had not yet brought themselves into full offensive position.

The men had a bite to eat out of the canned goods they had brought with them. They drank water from the river. Alexander then left his two sergeants, Kashnikov and Shapkov, in charge, and went to find the group of volunteers who had come with the Kirov Works over four days ago.

He didn't find anyone that day. But the next day he found Zina. She was in the field, bent over with her shovel. She was digging out the potatoes and

127

throwing them into the basket, dirt and all. Alexander suggested she clean the dirt off first, to make more room for actual potatoes. Zina glared at him, prepared to say something rude, but then looked at his red star and his rifle and said nothing. Alexander saw that she did not recognize him. Not everyone can have my memory for faces, he thought. "I'm looking for your friend," he said to Zina. "Is she here with you? Young girl, Tatiana."

Zina looked up at him, and fear flashed through her eyes.

"Haven't seen her," Zina said. "I think she must be over there." She waved her arm.

What's she afraid of? wondered Alexander, breathing a relieved sigh. "So she is here. Over where?"

"I don't know. We got separated after we got off the train."

"Separated where?"

"Don't know." She was plainly nervous. She missed her basket completely, and the potatoes fell on the ground. Not picking them up, she continued to dig.

Alexander banged the ground twice with his rifle. "Comrade Atapova! Stop. Straighten up. Stand up, stop moving." Zina quickly did. "Do you remember me?"

She shook her head.

"Aren't you wondering how I know your name?"

"You have a way of finding these things out," mumbled Zina.

"I'm Alexander Belov," he said. "I used to come to Kirov to meet Tatiana. That's how I know your name. Now do you remember?"

Relief showed on Zina's dirt-covered, unfriendly face.

"Tatiana's family is very worried about her. Do you know where she is?"

Relief mixed with defensiveness. "Listen," Zina barked, "she wanted me to get off with her, but I said I couldn't. I'm not a deserter."

"Get off with her where? And you can't be a deserter," said Alexander. "You're in the volunteer army."

Zina didn't seem to or want to understand. "Well, in any case I haven't seen her for days. She didn't come to Luga with us. She jumped off the train at Tolmachevo."

Alexander paled. "When you say jumped off the train . . ."

"I mean, the train slowed down a bit at an intersection, and she stepped down the rung and jumped. I saw her rolling down the hill."

Steeling his face, he said, "Why did you let her jump off the train?"

Raising her voice, Zina said, "*Let* her? Who *let* her? I said, don't do it. She wanted me to come with her." She laughed. "She wanted *me* to jump off a train! Why should *I* go with her? I'm not looking for my brother. I came to join the People's Volunteer Army. For Mother Russia."

As he stepped away from her, Alexander said, "So for Mother Russia you would jump off the train, comrade?"

Zina had no answer. She turned away from him and continued to dig the potatoes, mumbling, "I wasn't jumping off any train. I wasn't going to be a deserter."

Alexander quickly went to find some of his men. He took Kashnikov and five volunteers and drove the truck, now emptied of munitions, north to Tolmachevo. The town itself was nearly deserted. They drove through the streets, finally finding a woman carrying a child and a satchel. The woman told them Dohotino was three kilometers west. "But you won't find nobody there," she said. "Nobody there at all."

They drove there anyway. The woman was right. All the huts had been long abandoned and the village bombed. There had been a fire, which had burned a swath through half a dozen homes. Still Alexander called out for her. "Tania!" he called. "Tatiana!"

He looked inside every single hut, even the burned-down ones. His men called for her also. It sounded foreign to him, her name coming off strangers' tongues. But Kashnikov was a good sergeant. He didn't question Alexander. The men were glad to help, if only to get away from the monotony of trench digging.

"Tania! Tania!" Their voices echoed through the small farming village in the middle of fields and woods. They did not find a soul. They found bits and pieces on the ground, blankets, singed backpacks, toothbrushes.

On the outskirts of Dohotino there was a small sign with an arrow: DOHOTINO BOYS CAMP. The seven men walked two kilometers through a wooded path and came out at a small meadow where ten abandoned tents stood in a row near a large pond.

Alexander looked through the tents and discovered that there should have been eleven, not ten. One of the tents had been taken down and its stakes removed. The ground was still fresh where the stakes had been pulled out. Alexander thought that was a good idea and had the soldiers remove the other ten tents. The tents were big and made of thick canvas.

The fire that had been set up by the campers felt cold to his touch, as if it hadn't been lit in weeks. There was not a trace of old food around, of trash left by young boys or by a young Tatiana.

It was late in the evening when they returned to Luga. He and his men pitched their newly found tents by the forest in the rear of the army camp. Covered in his trench coat, Alexander lay on the ground. He couldn't sleep for a long time.

Back in America, in the Cub Scouts, they used to pitch tents and sleep in the woods and eat berries and fish they caught in the lake, and have fires at night. They opened up their cans of ham, they toasted marshmallows, they sang Cub Scout songs, and stayed up late, and during the day learned how to survive in the woods and how to make knots. It was an idyllic existence when Alexander was just a boy of eight, nine, ten. The summer months he spent at Cub Scout camp were by far the best months of his childhood.

He knew that if Tatiana hadn't broken her neck jumping off the train, she must have found the empty camp. Maybe, if she were smart, she took the missing tent. But what would she do next? Would she come back to Leningrad?

Alexander couldn't see that. If she had set out to find Pasha, he didn't see how she could return without some answer as to his whereabouts. After Tolmachevo where would she go?

Luga. There was nowhere else. She would go to Luga, because that's where she would think Pasha had gone—to help build the Luga line.

Invigorated and hopeful, he slept.

The next morning at sunup Alexander heard the distant roar of planes. He hoped they were Soviet planes.

No such luck. The black swastika was clearly apparent even from 300 meters below. Sixteen planes in two formations swooped, and he saw something drop from them. He heard screams of panic, but there were no bombs. In a few moments white and brown pieces of paper floated down like tiny parachutes. One landed in front of his tent. He picked it up. *Soviet Man!* the paper proclaimed. *The end is here! Join the winning side—and live! Surrender—and live! Nazism is superior to Communism. You will have food, you will have jobs, you will have freedom! Now!*

Another piece of paper was an actual pass to cross the front line. Shaking his head, Alexander dropped both to the ground and went to wash in the Luga tributary that ran through the woods.

By nine in the morning Alexander saw more planes, all of them with the Nazi insignia. They flew just a hundred meters above ground. The heavy machine guns inside the planes made popping sounds as they shot at workers in the fields.

Everyone ran for the trees, for cover. One of the tents caught fire. The Nazis weren't throwing bombs, Alexander thought as he put on his helmet and jumped down into a trench. No, they were *saving* their precious bombs.

Then Alexander saw they might have been saving *some* bombs, but not the fragmentation bombs, which ultimately fell from the planes and burst overhead. Alexander heard screams muffled by the continued shelling.

He looked in the trenches for his men but couldn't find anyone he knew. The bombing continued for another thirty minutes, after which the planes flew away, but not before they threw out new leaflets. *Surrender or die!* was all these said.

Surrender or die.

The black smoke floating overhead, the scattered fires, the groaning human beings looked apocalyptic to Alexander. Bodies floated in the Luga. On the banks of the river, right along the ditches and the concrete reinforced holes, injured people writhed on the ground. Alexander found Kashnikov, who was alive but missing part of his ear. The wound was bleeding freely onto his uniform. Shapkov was in working order. Alexander spent the rest of the morning helping to move the wounded into field tents and the rest of the day digging not trenches but mass graves. He and sixteen of his men dug a large hole by the forest, into which they put the bodies of twenty-three people who had died that morning. Eleven women, nine men, one old man, and two children under ten. None of them soldiers.

Alexander looked into the face of every one of the women, his heart stopping each time.

Then he walked among the dozens of wounded, but again he did not find Tatiana. He even looked for Pasha, just in case, having seen a picture of him when he was a thirteen-year-old boy, standing in swimming trunks by Tatiana, pulling at her blonde braids.

He looked for Pasha reflexively. He knew that Pasha was not in Luga.

Alexander could not find Zina again.

He finally went to talk to Colonel Pyadyshev. After standing at attention for a few moments, Alexander said, "Hard to work in these conditions, isn't it, sir?"

"No, Lieutenant," said Pyadyshev, a brooding, balding man. "What conditions would these be? The conditions of war?"

"No, sir. The conditions of being ill prepared to face a relentless enemy. I am merely expressing a measure of sympathy for the struggle ahead. Tomorrow we will resume fortifying the line."

"Lieutenant, you will resume tonight, until there is no more light. What do you think, is tomorrow a holiday for the Nazis? You think they won't bomb us again?"

Alexander was sure they would bomb again.

"Lieutenant Belov," continued Colonel Pyadyshev, "you just got here, and today you worked very hard . . ."

"Got here three days ago, sir," said Alexander.

"Three days ago, good. Well, the Germans have been bombing the line for the last ten days. There was bombing yesterday—I don't know where you were—and the day before. Every morning like clockwork, from nine to eleven. First they throw the leaflets telling us all to join their side, then they bomb us. We spend the rest of the day burying the bodies and digging trenches. Their main units are advancing on us at a rate of fifteen kilometers a day. They've mowed us down in Minsk, they've mowed us down in Brest Litovsk, and they're finishing mowing us down in Novgorod. We're next. You're right, we have no chance. But when you tell me that we're ill prepared, I tell you no, we do everything we can, and then we die. That's the whole point." Pyadyshev lit a cigarette with trembling hands and leaned on his small table.

Alexander saluted him. "We will continue to do all we can."

While there was still light, Alexander walked with three of his men around the front-line camp. As he passed the hundreds of soldiers on the Luga shores, waiting for the Germans, playing cards, smoking cigarettes, he was surprised by how many wore ranking colors on their shoulders. It seemed to Alexander that one out of every ten men was an officer. Many were lieutenants, some first, some second, but there were captains, and quite a number of majors, all on the front line, ready to face the enemy. *Front line.* Who was left to command the troops if the majors were down on the ground? Alexander didn't want to think about it.

He combed the fields diligently, using the grid method and going up and down, looking into the face of every person either shoveling out potatoes or shoveling out trenches. He did not find her.

Alexander went back to talk to Pyadyshev. "One more question, sir. Some volunteers came from Kirov Works about five days ago. Is there any place besides here they might have been diverted to, to help in the war effort? Could any of them have been sent farther east?"

"I command these twelve kilometers, and the rest I don't know about. These twelve are the last line of defense between here and Leningrad. After this there is nothing left. There is only retreat. Or surrender."

"There is no surrender, Colonel," Alexander said firmly. "Death before surrender."

Now it was the colonel's turn to blink. "Go back to Leningrad, Lieutenant Belov. Go back to Leningrad while you still can. And take the volunteers you brought with you. Save *them.*"

The next morning when Alexander went to speak to Pyadyshev, he saw that the colonel's tent had been dismantled overnight, the stakes had been removed, and the holes where the stakes had been filled in. More and more soldiers arrived at the river, and the front was split into three sectors, each with its own commander, since it became increasingly clear that it was difficult to organize such a large regiment of troops with just one command post. The new commander's tent was pitched fifty meters from Pyadyshev's old tent. The new commander not only did not know where Pyadyshev was, he did not even know *who* Pyadyshev was. The date was July 23.

Alexander did not have time to marvel at the speedy work of the NKVD, because at nine the shelling started again and lasted this time until noon. The Germans were trying to kill the front-line soldiers before they attacked with ground troops. They were biding their time, but not for long. Alexander suspected that it was only a matter of days before part two of the *blitzkrieg.* Either he was going to find Tatiana or he was going to remain at Luga and stand in front of the German tanks.

With a heavy heart Alexander walked up and down the river, looking for her. The rest of Alexander's men were taken into the entrenching service. Those who had been trained by him had been given rifles. They were told it was a crime punishable by death to get separated from their weapons. "To lose your gun is a crime against the Motherland!" But during the next air raid he watched three of his men drop their rifles as they ran for cover. When the air raid was over, they smiled sheepishly at Alexander, who smiled wearily back, shaking his head.

Another day went by. As soldiers took their positions along the banks, as they set up artillery cannons and mined the potato fields, as they loaded what vegetables they could onto trucks that carried them back to Leningrad, the tight feeling inside Alexander's chest did not let up from morning until night.

Pasha was lost, that much was obvious. But where was Tatiana? Why couldn't he find her?

5

Tatiana jumped off the train and rolled down the hill without much ado. It was a breeze compared to what they used to do in Luga, taking a running jump and heaving themselves down a hard, pebbled, steep embankment to the river. The grassy hill was positively soft by comparison. The shoulder on which she fell hurt a little.

Finding the boys' camp in Dohotino abandoned traumatized Tatiana, and for one day she stayed in one of the tents at the camp, not knowing what to do. She swam in the pond and ate blueberries. She had brought a few dried and toasted bread pieces in her knapsack, but she was saving them.

When she and her brother were younger, they used to race across the Luga River to see who could swim the fastest. Pasha was slightly bigger and stronger than Tatiana, but what she had that he did not was endurance. The first time they raced, he won. The second time they raced, he won. The third time he did not win. Tatiana smiled as she thought back to that, smiled at the memory of Pasha screaming in his frustration, at the memory of herself squealing in her delight.

She wasn't going to give up on her brother yet. Tatiana figured that Pasha and his campmates had been taken into volunteer work somewhere near Luga. She decided to go ahead to Luga to look for Pasha and maybe find Zina, too, and convince her to return to Leningrad. She didn't want Zina on her conscience, the way Pasha lay on her conscience.

But the following morning as she set out, the German planes shelled the village of Dohotino, where Tatiana was walking completely alone. She ran and hid in one of the huts, but suddenly a small incendiary bomb fell through the roof and set ablaze the wooden wall in front of her. She saw the old kerosene lamp just in time. Forgetting everything, she ran like mad, and the house exploded seconds later, incinerating the hut she had been in, three surrounding huts, and a stable nearby. She was left without her tent, or her sleeping bag, or her knapsack, or her toast.

Tatiana dropped into the bushes behind the huts, crawled on her stomach through the nettles, and hid herself under a fallen oak. The bombing continued over the village and nearby Tolmachevo for another hour. She could see the nettles burning—nettles *she had just crawled through* burning. The bombs fell into the forest, igniting the top branches, which fell in flames to the ground on which Tatiana lay.

I'm going to die, she thought. Alone, in this village, under an oak. No one will ever find me. Who in my family will come to look for me? I'm going to die here alone in the woods and turn to moss, and on Fifth Soviet they will open up another bottle of vodka and chase me down with pickles, and say, this is for our Tania.

After the bombing ended, she stayed under her oak for another hour or so, just in case. Her face and arms felt swollen and stung—nettles. Better that than the bombs. She was grateful for the forethought that had kept her domestic passport with a stamp from Krasenko in her shirt pocket. Without it she wouldn't get far; she'd be detained in one of many army checkpoints, or perhaps in a local *Soviet* office.

Tatiana walked back to Tolmachevo and knocked at a house, where she asked for something to eat. The family let her stay with them until morning, when she left and spotted a military truck near the town *Soviet*. Showing her passport, she asked for a lift to Luga. The truck dropped her off at the easternmost end of the Luga defense line, closest to Novgorod.

The first day Tatiana dug for potatoes and then dug trenches across the field. Not seeing any groups of boys dressed in camp uniforms, she asked an army sergeant about camp volunteers, and he mumbled something about Novgorod. "The camp volunteers were sent there," he said, and walked away.

Novgorod? Lake Ilmen? Is that where her Pasha was? Is that where she was meant to go? Tatiana washed in the stream and slept near a tree on the grass.

The following morning the German planes shelled the potatoes, and the trenches, and Tatiana.

The fragmentation bombs were too terrifying to watch, exploding as if they meant to kill just her. She realized she had to get out of Luga at all costs. Wondering how in the world she was going to make her way to Novgorod, Tatiana wandered through the smoke. No sooner had she thought about Lake Ilmen than three soldiers came up to her, asking her if she was injured and then ordering her to follow them to the hospital field tent. Reluctantly she followed. She was even more reluctant when she found out what they wanted her to do—which was to tend to the dying. And there were many dying. Soldiers, civilian women, village children, old people. All in the hastily put-up army tent, all dying.

Having never seen death up close before, Tatiana shut her eyes and wanted to go back home, but there was no turning around and no going back. The NKVD militia stood by the entrance flaps, ready to maintain order and make sure that a volunteer like Tatiana stayed where she was supposed to.

Her heart and teeth clenched, Tatiana learned how to clot wounds by pressing on them with sterile bandages. The wounds clotted, and then the wounded died. What Tatiana could not do was give blood transfusions, because there wasn't any blood. What she could not do was stop the limbs from infection; what she could not do was stop the limbs from pain. The doctors refused to give morphine to the dying, under orders instead to give it to the less severely wounded, who could go back to the front line.

Tatiana saw that many people could have been saved had there been some blood, or any of that new medicine, penicillin; at the very least they could have been spared the agony of death with morphine. The pervasive helplessness she felt the first night in the field hospital nearly drowned the helplessness she felt at not finding her brother.

The next morning one of the soldiers, mortally wounded in the chest, asked her if she was a boy or a girl.

"I'm a girl," she said sadly.

"Prove it," he said, but before she had a chance to prove it, the soldier died.

On the radio near the officers' tents, Tatiana heard heavily accented German voices inviting her in Russian to go to Germany with them. They threw passes for her to cross the front line, and when she didn't go, they tried to kill her with bombs and machine-gun fire. Then the Germans were quiet until evening, when the shelling resumed. In between the attacks Tatiana washed the dying and bandaged their wounds.

The following afternoon she went a kilometer into the fields to get a potato to eat. She heard the planes before she saw them and thought, but it isn't evening yet, instantly dropping down between the low bushes. For fifteen minutes she lay there. When the planes left, Tatiana got up and ran back to the field tent, only to discover a bonfire in its place, with charred and groaning bodies crawling out of it.

Hundreds of surviving volunteers got helmets and buckets and cups and whatever else they could find and ran down to the river and back to help put out the fire. It took three hours, well into evening, when there was more shelling, and then night. There was no tent for the wounded anymore. They lay on the ground on blankets or on the grass, moaning their last breaths into the summer air. Tatiana couldn't help anyone. Wearing a green helmet with a red star that she had used to bring water up from the river, all Tatiana could do was sit by one woman who had lost her child in the attack and who herself was gravely wounded in the stomach. She now lay in front of Tatiana, crying for her small girl. Pulling the helmet tighter over her head, Tatiana took the woman's hand and held it until the woman stopped crying for her small girl.

Then she got up and went near the tree line and lay down on the ground. I'm next, she thought. I can feel it. I'm next.

How was she supposed to get to Novgorod, one hundred kilometers east of here?

She washed and slept in the field with the helmet on her head, and as soon as morning broke, she looked across the river and saw the turrets and the guns of the German tanks on the other side. A corporal, who had been sleeping nearby, gathered together Tatiana and a few other volunteers and ordered them to leave immediately and return to the city of Luga.

She pulled the corporal aside and quietly asked him if there was a way she could get to Novgorod instead. The corporal pushed her hard away with his rifle and yelled, "Are you out of your mind? Novgorod is in German hands!"

The look on Tatiana's face stopped him. "Comrade—what's your name?" he said more reasonably.

"Tatiana Metanova."

"Comrade Metanova. Listen to me, you are too young to be here. How old are you, fifteen?"

"Seventeen."

"Please. Return to Luga immediately. I think there are still military trains running from Luga Station back to Leningrad. Are you from Leningrad?"

"Yes." She did not want to cry in front of a stranger. "All of Novgorod is in German hands?" she said faintly. "What about our volunteers there?"

"Will you just shut the hell up about Novgorod!" the corporal yelled. "Did you not hear me? There are no Soviets left in Novgorod. And soon there will be no Soviets left in Luga, you included. So do yourself a favor, get out of here. Let me see your passport."

She showed him.

Handing it back to her, he said, "You have dispensation from Kirov. Go back to Kirov. Go home."

How did she go home without Pasha? But Tatiana couldn't tell the corporal that.

There were nine in Tatiana's group. She was the smallest and the youngest. It took them the rest of the day to walk through the fields and the forests, twelve kilometers back to Luga. Tatiana said that they were getting to Luga just in time for the evening bombing. Her weary companions dismissed her. She felt as if she were back with her family.

The group got to Luga Station at six-thirty and waited for the train.

The train did not come, but at seven o'clock Tatiana heard the German planes. The volunteers were huddled inside the small station that had at first seemed so safe, the building made of brick and looking as if it could withstand a little shelling and gunfire.

But during the raid one of the women became so afraid that she screamed and ran outside, where she was instantly cut down. The other eight people watched in horror, but it soon became obvious that what the Germans wanted was to take out the very station that hid them. The Nazis were intent on knocking out the railroad. The planes weren't leaving until the station was no longer standing. Tatiana sat on the floor with her knees to her chest and pulled the green helmet over her closed eyes. She thought that the helmet would muffle the sound of death.

The train station crumbled like wet paper. Tatiana crawled from the beams and the fire, but there was nowhere for her to go. Through the smoke she could feel bodies around her. Hot and faint, she felt for them with her hands. The gunfire came from right outside the door, but when the lattice beam fell from the ceiling, all sounds faded away, all faded away, and there was no more fear. Only regret was left. Regret for Alexander.

6

Alexander started to lose hope. In the distance across the river, the natural front boundary, he could see the Germans amassing their troops and tanks and battalions of gun-ready, aggressive, and impeccably trained soldiers who would stop at nothing, certainly not at the hundreds of shovel-bearing volunteers.

As far as his eye could see, there were only two Soviet tanks. On the other side of the river there were at least thirty Panzers. Alexander's platoon of twenty men had been reduced to twelve, and fields of mines now lay between him and Leningrad. Three of his men died when a mine they were planting went off. They didn't have experience with mines, only with rifles, but all of their rifles had been taken by the army, all but Alexander's and his two sergeants'.

Turning away from the river, he didn't know which way to look.

In the late evening the new colonel called Alexander into his command quarters. Alexander didn't like him nearly as much as he had liked Pyadyshev.

"Lieutenant, how many men do you have left in your charge?"

"Just twelve, sir."

"Plenty."

"Plenty for what?"

"The Germans have just bombed the Luga train station," the colonel said. "Now the trains from Leningrad carrying more men and ammunition can't reach the front. We need you and your men to clear the debris scattered on the railroad tracks so the engineers can repair the railroad and we can resume service by tomorrow morning."

"It's getting dark, sir."

"I know, Lieutenant. I wish I could give you daylight, but I can't. The white nights are behind us, and this has to be done immediately."

As Alexander was about to leave, the colonel said, almost as an aside, "Oh, and I heard there were volunteers hiding out in the station when the bombs destroyed it. You might want to remove them."

At Luga Station, Alexander and his men used kerosene lamps to survey the damage. The once brick building lay broken on the ground, and the rail tracks were knocked out for fifty meters.

Alexander called out, "Is anybody under there? Speak up!"

No one answered.

Coming closer to the wreckage, he repeated, "Anybody in there?"

He thought he heard a moan.

"They're all dead, Lieutenant," said Kashnikov. "Look at it."

"Yes, but listen—Anyone there?" He started moving the large pieces of stone himself. "Help me, will you?"

"We should get to the tracks first," suggested Kashnikov. "So the engineers can restore electricity to the railroad."

Straightening out and leveling his cool gaze on him, Alexander said, "Railroad tracks before people, Sergeant?"

"On orders from the colonel, Lieutenant," Kashnikov mumbled.

"No, Sergeant! On orders from *me*. Now, move." Alexander pushed away boulders and bits of window and doorframes. There was little light, and it was hard to see. Dust and debris settled on his hands, and he cut himself on the broken glass without even feeling it. He realized it when the blood dripped from one hand to the other.

Alexander definitely heard something besides crickets. "Did you hear that?" he said. It was a soft moan.

"No, sir," said Kashnikov, looking at him with concern.

"Kashnikov, have your hands fallen off? Quicker, I tell you."

They worked quicker.

Finally, underneath the brick and burned beams, they found one body. Then two. Then three. Then a pile of bodies lying one on top of another in a pyramid underneath the rubble. Alexander thought they were *too* neat. Random force could not have stacked them. They had been placed this way. They could not have stacked themselves. He strained to listen. There was that moan again. He moved one dead man, another dead woman, anxiously shoving the kerosene lamp into their faces. Another moan.

At the bottom, underneath the third body, Alexander found Tatiana.

Her back was to him, and on her head was an army helmet. He recognized neither the clothes on her body nor the helmet on her head, but even before he removed the helmet, he knew it was her by the shape of the soft, small frame he had watched so intently for many days.

"Tatia . . ." he said in a disbelieving voice.

Alexander threw off the rest of the bodies, cleared off the last of the beams, and pushed the hair back from her face. She was barely conscious, and in the bleak yellow light from the lamps she looked barely alive, but it was from her that the soft moans had come and were continuing every few seconds.

Her clothing, her hair, her shoes, her face were covered with dust and blood. "Tania, come on," he said, rubbing her cheek, kneeling by her. "Come on." Her cheek was warm. That was a good sign.

"Is this *the* Tania?" asked Kashnikov.

Alexander didn't reply. He was thinking of how best to pick her up. He could not tell, covered in blood as she was, where she was injured.

"I think she's dying," said Kashnikov.

"Oh, you're a fucking doctor now?" Alexander snapped. "She's not dying. Now, stop talking. Stay here with the men to clear the area. They need your help. I'm putting you in charge, Sergeant. Afterward quickly make your way back to Leningrad. Do you hear me? Can you do that? We've given them our arms, and eight of our men, and we found her. We are finished here in Luga. So hurry." Carefully he turned Tatiana over and lifted her into his arms. She was limp and still moaning.

"What about the wounded, Lieutenant?"

"Do you hear any more noise? You didn't even hear this one. Now suddenly you're concerned. The rest are dead. Check them out yourself if you wish. I will get her to the medic."

"Do you need me to come with you? She'll need a stretcher," Kashnikov said.

"No she won't," said Alexander. "I'll carry her myself."

It was eleven o'clock at night by the time Alexander had walked three kilometers back to the encampment with Tatiana in his arms and searched for the medic.

He did not find him, but he found the medic's assistant, Mark, asleep in a tent.

"The medic is dead," Mark said. "Fragment cut him in two."

"Do we have another medic?"

"No," said Mark. "I'll have to do."

"You'll do."

He took one look at Tatiana's soaked body and said, "She's bled out. Leave her outside." He lay back down on his cot.

"She's not bled out," said Alexander. "I don't think it's her blood." The assistant obviously wanted to be asleep again. Alexander wasn't having any of it.

"It's hard to tell with so little light," Mark said. "If she lives till morning, I'll look at her then."

Alexander didn't budge, holding Tatiana in his arms. "Corporal," he said, "you will look at her now."

Sitting up on his cot, Mark sighed. "Lieutenant, it's very late."

"Late for what? Do you have a sheet or another bed for her?"

"A bed? What is this, a resort? Let me get you a sheet."

Mark laid the white sheet on the ground. Alexander first kneeled with Tatiana in his arms, then set her down. Examining her, Mark peered at her head, at her scalp, at her face and teeth. He looked at her neck and lifted her arms. When he lifted her leg, Tatiana moaned louder than before.

"Ah," said Mark. "Do you have your knife?"

Alexander gave him his knife.

She was wearing long trousers. Mark cut open one trouser leg, then the other. Alexander saw that her right ankle and the shin above it were swollen and black. "Broken shinbone," Mark said. "So much blood on her and just this so far. It's badly broken, though, fractured in several places. Let's see the rest." Unbuttoning her shirt, he cut open her once white vest and examined her chest, ribs, and stomach.

Blood stained her fragile body.

Alexander wanted to look away.

Mark sighed. "I can't tell what's hers, what isn't," he said. "Nothing on the legs is oozing fresh blood." He touched her stomach. "You were right. She doesn't feel clammy or cold."

Staying back, Alexander said nothing. His heart was heavy and relieved.

"See here? She's got three broken ribs on the right side. Where did you find her?"

"Under the train station. Under brick and dead bodies."

"Well, that explains it. She's lucky to be alive. Charmed, I'd say." Mark stood up. "I have no bed for her in our hospital tent. Get her there and leave her on the ground. In the morning someone will take care of her."

"I'm not leaving her on the ground until morning."

"What are you worried about? She is not as injured as some of the others." Mark shook his head. "You should see them."

"I'm an officer in the Red Army, Corporal," said Alexander. "I've seen wounded men. You're sure you don't have a cot for her somewhere?"

Mark shrugged. "There's no shrapnel in her eyes, no life-threatening wounds. I'm not kicking out someone with a stomach wound to make room for her."

"Of course not," said Alexander.

"I don't know what we're going to do with her tomorrow," Mark said. "She needs a proper hospital. Her leg needs to be set and put in a cast immediately. We certainly can't do it here."

Alexander shook his head. The railroad was bombed out, and the army had taken his truck. "Don't worry about her tomorrow," he said. "Have you got some more towels and some bandages for tonight?" Bending down, Alexander covered Tatiana with the sheet she lay on and picked her up. "And another sheet."

Mark reluctantly went to his medic's bag.

"What about some morphine?"

"No, Lieutenant." He laughed. "I have no morphine for her. No morphine for a girl with some broken bones. She'll have to live through the pain."

Mark placed three towels and some bandages on top of Tatiana, and Alexander carried her to his tent.

After laying her down on the sheet, he pulled closed her shirt and went to the stream to get some water in a pail. When he returned, he cut a towel into small pieces, dipped one of them in the cool water, and began washing her face and hair. He cleaned her forehead and her cheeks and her eyes and her mouth. "Tatia," he whispered, "what kind of a crazy girl are you?" Alexander saw her open her eyes. Mutely they watched each other. "Tatia," he whispered again.

Her hand reached up to his face. "Alexander?" she said weakly, with no surprise. "Am I dreaming?"

"No," he said.

"I must be . . ." She trailed off. "I was just dreaming . . . of your face. What's happened?"

"You're in my tent. What were you doing at Luga Station? It's been destroyed by the Germans."

Tatiana took a moment to answer. "Going back to Leningrad, I think," she replied. "What are *you* doing here?"

He could have lied; he thought once he would have wanted to, feeling so angry and betrayed at the way she had discarded him. But the truth was so plain. "Looking for you."

Her eyes filled again. "What's happened? Why am I so cold?"

"Nothing," he said hastily. "The medic's assistant, Mark, had to cut open your trousers and your—"

Tatiana lifted her hands and felt through her open clothes. Alexander looked away. He had managed to pretend so well with her at Kirov, to keep his distance, but he couldn't pretend that finding her alive and covered with blood meant nothing, that saving her meant nothing, that she meant nothing

She brought her hand to her face and stared at the blood. "Is it my blood?"

"I don't think so."

"Then what's wrong with me? Why can't I move?"

"Your ribs are broken—"

She groaned.

"And your leg."

"My back," she whispered. "Something is wrong with my back."

Anxious and concerned, Alexander said, "What's the matter?"

"I don't know. It's burning."

"It's probably the ribs," he said. "I broke a rib in the Winter War last year. It feels like your back is on fire."

"Oozing."

Leaving the wet rag in the bucket of water, Alexander looked into her face. "Tania, can you hear me all right?"

"Hmm."

"Can you sit up?"

Tatiana tried to sit up. "I can't," she whispered. Her hands were holding her ripped tunic and undershirt together.

Alexander's whole heart was giving out. He lifted her to a sitting position. "Let me take the clothes off you. They're no good to you anyway; they're all blood-soaked. You can't wear them."

She shook her head.

"I have to take them off you," he said. "I will look at your back, and then I'll clean you. You don't want to get an infection. You will if you have open wounds. I'll clean you, I'll wash the blood off your hair, and then I'll bandage your ribs and leg. You'll feel better right away once they're bandaged."

She shook her head, sitting against him.

"Don't be scared, Tania," Alexander said. He held her to him, and after a few moments, when she didn't say anything, he carefully took off her tunic and then her vest. Small and hurt and weak, she pressed her naked body against him; her blood-covered back was underneath his hands, and her skin felt warm. She needs me so much to take care of her, Alexander thought, gently feeling for any gashes. And I desperately need to take care of her. "Where does it hurt?"

"Where you're touching me," she whispered. "Right under your fingers."

He leaned over her shoulder to take a look. Her back was grimy, but the blood was already thick. "I think you've probably been cut. I'll wash your back in a minute, but I think you're all right." Alexander pressed her head against his chest. His lips pressed against her damp hair.

He lowered her onto the white sheet. Her hands covered her breasts, and she closed her eyes. "Tatiasha," Alexander said, "I need to clean you."

Her eyes remained closed. "Let me do it myself," she whispered.

"All right," he said, "but you can't even sit up by yourself."

She didn't reply at first. "Give me a wet towel, and I'll do it myself."

"Tatia, let me take care of you." He stopped and took a breath. "Please. Don't be afraid. I will never hurt you."

"I know that," she muttered, unable or unwilling to open her eyes.

"I tell you what," Alexander said. "Don't worry. Stay like that. I'll—wash around you."

He washed her hair, her arms, her stomach, and the top of her chest, all under the glimmering light of a kerosene lamp in the corner of the tent. Tatiana groaned loudly when he touched her blackened rib cage.

As he cleaned her, Alexander soothingly whispered, "One of these days, just one, I'm not saying now, but soon, maybe you can explain to me what you were doing in a train station during bombing. All right? I want you to think about what you're going to tell me. Look how lucky you are. Move your arms a bit. After I dry you, I'll bandage your ribs. They'll heal on their own in a few weeks. You'll be as good as new."

Her eyes remaining closed, Tatiana turned her face away, her hands on her breasts. Alexander removed her torn trousers, leaving her in her underwear, and washed her legs. She flinched and fainted when he touched her broken shin. He waited for her to come to.

"It hurts very much?"

"Like it's about to be cut off," muttered Tatiana. "Do you have anything for the pain?"

"Just vodka."

"I'm not much for vodka."

As he was drying her stomach with a towel, Tatiana, her eyes still closed, her hands still covering herself, whispered, "Please . . . don't look at me." Her voice broke.

His own voice breaking, Alexander said, "It's all right, Tatiasha." He bent down and kissed the top of her soft breast above her hand. "It's all right." He left his lips on her skin for a moment and then straightened up. "I have to turn you over, I have to clean the rest of you."

"I can't turn over by myself," she said.

"I will turn you over." And he did, cleaning her back with the same careful, tender meticulousness he had washed the rest of her. "Your back is all right. Many glass cuts. It's the ribs that are burning you."

Her face in the sheet, Tatiana muttered, "What am I going to wear? This was all I had."

"Don't worry. We'll find you something tomorrow." Turning her around, Alexander sat her up and patted her dry. He bandaged her from behind so his face wouldn't be just centimeters from her breasts, which she continued to keep covered. He wrapped the bandage around her ribs, tying it carefully under her arms, wanting to kiss the top of her shoulder. He didn't.

After laying Tatiana down, he covered her upper body with a blanket and then tightly bandaged her leg, using a wood splint for extra support. "How is that?" he asked, managing a smile. "Told you, good as new. Now, come here, hold on to me." She could barely lift her arms to his neck.

Alexander moved her to his trench-coat bed on the ground, and when he set her down, Tatiana held on to him for a moment before she let go. He covered her with a woolen blanket.

Pulling the blanket to her neck, she said, "Why am I so cold? I'm not going to die, am I?"

"No," Alexander said as he cleaned up the sheets and the towels. "You're going to be fine." He smiled. "We just have to get you back to the city."

"I can't walk. How are we going to do that?"

Patting her good leg lightly, Alexander said, "Tania, when you're with me, don't worry. I will take care of everything."

"I'm not worried," Tatiana replied, staring at him intensely in the dim light.

"Maybe the railroad will be repaired tomorrow. That's only three kilometers from here. I wish I still had my truck, but the army took it. They need it more." He paused. "We need to leave early tomorrow morning." He moved a little closer to her. "Where were you before you decided to go under the German fire?"

"Downriver. Under the German fire." Tatiana swallowed. "They're on the other side."

"I know. Tomorrow or the next day they'll be on this side. We will need to leave at dawn. Now, stay here, and don't go anywhere." He smiled. "My Primus stove is right outside. I'm going to go and get some clean water from the stream, wash, and then I'll make you some tea." Out of his rucksack he took a bottle of vodka and brought it to her lips, lifting her head slightly.

"I don't—"

"Please drink it. You're going to be extremely sore. This will make it a bit better. Have you ever had anything broken before?"

"My arm, years ago," Tatiana replied, and drank with a shudder.

"Why did you cut your hair?" Alexander asked, holding her head, looking down at her. He needed to shut his eyes for a moment not to continue to look at her so close to him.

"I didn't want it to be in the way," she said. "You hate it?" She looked up at him with her sweet, defenseless eyes.

"I don't hate it," Alexander said hoarsely. It took all his strength not to lean down and kiss her. He laid her on his coat and left the tent, needing to gather himself emotionally. Her helplessness and vulnerability had made his barely hidden feelings for her float to the surface, where they bobbed now, tantalizingly *in* reach, achingly *out*. He went to the stream and then made her some tea and went back inside. She was half awake and half conscious. He wished he had some morphine.

"I have some chocolate for you. Do you want a piece?"

Tatiana moved onto her good side and sucked on a small piece of chocolate as Alexander sat by her on the grass, his knees drawn up.

"Do you want the rest?"

He shook his head. "Why did you do this crazy thing, Tania?"

"To find my brother." She glanced at him and looked away.

"Why didn't you just come back to the barracks and ask me?"

"I had already gone once. I thought if you knew something, you'd come and see me." She looked at him. "Did you—"

"I'm sorry," said Alexander. He watched her round face pale. She was trying to be so brave. "Tania, I'm really sorry," he said, "but Pasha was sent to Novgorod."

With a choking whimper, Tatiana said, "Oh . . . no. Please, don't say any more. Please." She started to shiver and couldn't stop. "I'm so cold," she said, her hand coming up to rest on his boot. "Can you give me my tea before I fall asleep?"

He held her head up and the cup to her mouth as she drank.

"I'm tired," she whispered, leaning back. Her eyes never left his face. Just like at Kirov.

Alexander started to move away before her voice sounded. "Where are you going?"

"Nowhere. Right here," he replied. "I'll sleep here, and early tomorrow we'll set out for home."

"You'll be cold on the grass," she whispered. "Come here."

Alexander shook his head.

"Please, Shura," said Tatiana in her dulcet voice, her hand stretching out to him. "Please come near me."

He couldn't say no even if he wanted to. Turning off the lamp, he removed his boots and his bloodied and soiled uniform, fumbled around his rucksack for a clean undershirt, and lay down on his trench coat next to Tatiana, covering them both with the woolen blanket.

It was pitch black in the tent. He lay on his back, and she lay on her left side, in the crook of his arm. Alexander heard the noise of the crickets. He heard her soft breath. He *felt* her warm breath on his shoulder and chest. He *felt* her naked body under his arm, pressing against his side. He couldn't breathe.

"Tania?"

"Yes?" Her expectant voice quivering.

"Are you tired? Too tired to talk?"

"Not too tired to talk." Less expectantly.

"Start at the beginning, and don't stop until you get to Luga Station. What happened to you?"

After she told him everything, he waited a moment and then asked incredulously, "Did you cover yourself by crawling under a pile of bodies before the station collapsed?"

"Yes," she replied.

Alexander was silent for a few moments. "Nice military maneuver, Tatia."

"Thank you."

They were quiet, and then he heard her crying. He held her closer. "I'm sorry about your brother."

"Shura," Tatiana said, speaking so softly he had to strain to hear, "remember I told you about how Pasha and I used to go to Lake Ilmen in Novgorod?"

"I remember, Tania." He stroked her hair.

"My Aunt Rita and Uncle Boris and my cousin Marina —"

"*The* cousin Marina?"

"What do you mean?"

"The cousin Marina you were going to visit on the bus?" He smiled in the dark and felt her hand lightly pinch his stomach.

"Yes. They had a *dacha* and a rowboat on that lake, and Pasha and I used to take turns rowing. I'd row halfway across the lake and he'd row halfway. Well, one day we got into a stupid argument about where halfway actually was. He just didn't want to let me row, so he kept arguing and arguing, and then yelling, and then screaming, and finally he said, 'You want this oar? Well, here, you can have it,' and he swung it at me and knocked me right out

145

of the boat into the lake." Tatiana shivered. Alexander heard her laugh a little. "I went into the water, and I was fine, but I didn't want him to think I was fine, so I held my breath and went under the boat, and I heard him from above yelling for me, more and more panicked, more and more frantic, and suddenly he jumped into the water to rescue me, and I swam to the other side of the boat, climbed in, picked up one of the oars and whistled for him. As soon as he turned around, I whacked him on the head." Tatiana wiped her face with the hand that had just been touching Alexander. "Well, with my luck, he of course lost consciousness. He had put on a life jacket—"

"Unlike you?"

"Unlike me. I saw him floating in the water facedown, and I thought he was just playing a trick on me, too. I wanted to see how long he could hold his breath. I was convinced he couldn't hold it as long as me. So I let him float for a minute, then another minute. Finally I jumped in and pulled him to the boat. Don't know how I got him in. And rowed all the way back to shore by myself while he lay there and moaned that I had hit him too hard. Oh, did I get it from my parents when they saw the bruise on Pasha's head. And after I'd been thoroughly punished, then he told everybody that he was just faking and was conscious the whole time." She started to cry again. "Do you know how I feel now? Like I'm waiting any minute for Pasha to come out of the water and tell me this was all just a big joke."

His voice cracking, Alexander said, "Tatiasha, the fucking Germans just hit him too hard with that oar."

"I know," she whispered. "I'm so sad he was alone without all of us." She fell silent, and Alexander, too, as he lay and listened to her breath recover its rhythm. That he was alone without *you*, Tatiana, thought Alexander. He would have felt better had he been with *you*.

He listened to her paused breath, as if she were trying to ask him something. He continued to stroke her hair to give her strength. "What, Tatia?"

"Shura, are you asleep?"

"No."

"I've missed you . . . coming to Kirov. Is that all right to say?"

"And I've missed *you*," Alexander said, rubbing his lips against her gold-silk, down-feather hair. "And it's all right to say."

There was nothing else from her, except her hand, moving on his chest, gently, tenderly, up and down. He held her close. A groan of pain escaped her, and another, and another.

Minutes passed.

Minutes.

And then hours.

"Shura, are you asleep?"

"No."

"I just wanted to say . . . thank you, soldier."

Alexander's eyes stared into the blackness, as he tried to envisage moments of his own life, of his childhood, of his mother and father, of Barrington. He saw nothing. Felt nothing but Tatiana lying on his fallen-asleep arm, caressing his chest. She stopped and placed her hand on his rapid heart. He felt her lips lightly press against his shirt, and then she slept. And finally he slept, too.

When Alexander first saw a tinge of blue-gray light from outside the tent, he said, "Tania?"

"I'm awake," she said, her hand still on his chest.

He disentangled himself and went to wash by the stream in the woods, where it was still dark. There was no doing it on the banks of the Luga River. The Germans were only seventy-five meters across the water, their cannons and artillery pointed at the Soviet men who slept hugging their machine guns. Not Alexander—he had slept hugging Tatiana.

Coming back to the tent with clean water, he sat Tatiana up covered in the blanket, helped her wash, and then gave her some bread and some more tea.

"How are you feeling this morning?" he asked. "Spry?" He smiled.

"Yes," she said weakly. "I think I can hop on my good leg." He saw by her constricted face she was in terrible pain.

Alexander told her he would be right back and went to wake up the medic and ask for some clothes for her and some medication. Mark had no medication, but he found her a dress that belonged to one of the nurses who had died a few days ago. "Corporal, I need one lousy gram of morphine."

"I don't have it," Mark snapped. "They shoot you for stealing morphine. I don't have it for a broken leg. Bring her to me with intestinal damage and I won't have it. You want her to have our precious morphine or a captain in the Red Army?"

Alexander did not answer that question.

After returning, he sat Tatiana up and slipped the dress over her head, taking care not to hurt her or to look at her bare and bandaged body.

"You're a good man, Alexander," she said, reaching up and laying her small palm onto his face.

"But a man first," he said quietly, leaning into her hand. He paused briefly before continuing. "Your leg must hurt so much. Have some vodka again. It'll dull the pain."

"All right," she said. "Anything you say."

He let her have a few swigs. "Ready to go?"

"Leave me," Tatiana said. "Go yourself, leave me. They'll have room for me in the field tent eventually. People die, beds become free."

"You think I came all the way to Luga to leave you waiting for a hospital bed?" He dismantled his tent and packed up his trench coat and blanket. She sat on the ground. "Let me help you up. Can you stand on one leg?"

"Yes," she said, groaning. Tatiana stood in front of Alexander, barely coming up to the top of his chest. All he wanted to do was kiss her head. Please don't look up at me, Alexander thought. She was very unsteady, holding on to his arms and swaying. "Put your rucksack on me," she said. "It'll be easier for you."

He did. "Tania, I'm going to crouch in front of you, and you're going to grab my neck. Just hold on tight, hear me?"

"I will. What about your rifle?"

"You on my back, rifle in my hands," Alexander said. "Come on, we've got to go."

She grabbed on to him, and he stood up with her on his back, taking hold of his weapon. "Ready?"

"Yes."

Alexander heard her groaning. "It hurts?"

Her arms around his neck squeezed him. "It's not bad."

Alexander carried Tatiana on his back for three kilometers to Luga Station, which despite his hope was not repaired yet. "What now?" she asked anxiously when he stopped to rest.

He offered her a drink of water. "Now we walk through the woods to the next station."

"How many kilometers is that?"

"Six," he replied.

She shook her head. "Alexander, no. You can't carry me for six more kilometers."

"Do you have any other ideas?" he asked, crouching in front of her. "Let's go."

They were on a forest road making their way to the next train station north when they heard the planes just over the trees. Alexander himself would have continued walking, but he did not want to be walking with Tatiana on his back. If a bomb fell, she would be the first one to get hit.

He walked off the path, bringing her into the woods and setting her down by a fallen tree. "Lie down," he told her, helping her lean back. He lay by her side, holding on to his rifle. "Turn onto your stomach," he said. "And cover your head." She didn't move. "Don't be afraid, Tania."

"How can I be afraid now?" she said haltingly, lying on her back looking up at him. She wasn't moving. She placed her hands on his chest.

"Go on," he said, staring at her. "What? Do you need me to help? I should have taken your green helmet from the station."

"Alexander—"

"Now that it's morning, I'm suddenly Alexander again?"

Gazing up at him, Tatiana whispered, "Oh, Shura . . ." And Alexander could no longer bear it. He bent to her face and kissed her.

Her lips were as soft and young and full as he had imagined them to be. Tatiana's whole body started to tremble as she kissed him back with such tenderness, such passion, such need that Alexander involuntarily emitted a

148

small groan. He was bewildered by her hands pressing his head into hers and not letting go. "Oh, God . . ." he whispered into her parted mouth.

The crashing noise of the bombs overhead stopped them. Alexander felt that *something* had to stop *him*. The tip of the pine tree nearby caught fire, and bits of burning branches fell down into the damp forest very close to them. He turned her onto her stomach and lay next to her in the moss with his arm and half his body covering her. "Are you all right?" he whispered. "Bombs frighten you?"

"Bombs are the least of it," she whispered back.

As soon as the shelling stopped, Alexander said, "Let's go. We've got to get to the train. Let's hurry."

As she got up, she wouldn't raise her eyes at him. Turning his back to her, he crouched, and she climbed on. He carried her, his arms under her knees, his hands holding his rifle.

"I'm heavy," she said into his back.

"You're no heavier than my ruck," he said, panting. "Just hang on. We'll be there soon."

Every once in a while his rifle bumped her broken leg, and Alexander would feel her constrict in pain, but she didn't moan, didn't cry out. At one point he felt her put her head down on his back. He hoped she was all right.

Under a black smoky sky, amid burning woods, Alexander carried Tatiana on his back six kilometers to the next station. The nearby shelling had stopped, but the sound of explosions and artillery guns carried on all around.

At the station Alexander set her down on the ground and sank down next to her. She sidled closer to him and closer still.

"Tired?" she asked him gently.

He nodded.

They waited. The station was full of other people—women with little babies, with their elderly parents, with all their belongings. Grimy and shell-shocked, they waited for the train. Alexander took out a piece of his remaining bread and split it with Tatiana.

"No, you have it," she said. "You need it more than I do."

"Did you eat anything yesterday?" Alexander asked her. "No, of course you didn't."

"I had a raw potato, some blueberries in the forest. And the chocolate you gave me." The length of her body and leg pressed against his side. She leaned her head on his arm and closed her eyes.

Alexander put his arm around her. "You're going to be all right," he said, kissing her forehead. "You'll see. Just a little longer, and you're going to be fine. I promise."

The train came. It was a cattle train, with no room to sit. "Do you want to wait, maybe?" he asked. "For a passenger train?"

"No," she replied weakly. "I'm not feeling well. Best get to Leningrad soon. Let's get on. I'll stand on one leg."

Alexander lifted her onto the platform first and then jumped up himself. The carriage was crowded with dozens of other people. They stood near the edge, where they could see the countryside through the open doors. For several hours they stood compressed against each other, Tatiana leaning on him, her head on his chest, and Alexander supporting her as best he could by her arms. He couldn't hold her tightly around her ribs or on her back. At one point he felt her body start to drift down. "No, stay up, stay up," he said to her, keeping her upright.

And she stayed up, her arms going around him.

The doors to the carriage were left open in case people wanted to jump off. The train moved past fields and dirt roads that were filled with Soviet farmers dragging their cows and pigs and goats behind them and refugees pulling carts filled with their earthly possessions. Ambulances tried to get through the same roads past the crowds of people; motorcyclists, too. Alexander watched Tatiana's somber face.

"What are you thinking, Tatia?"

"Why are those silly people carrying their whole lives on their backs? If *I* were leaving, I wouldn't take anything. Just myself."

He smiled. "What about all your things? You have things, don't you?"

"Yes. But I wouldn't take any of them."

"Not even my *Bronze Horseman* book? You should take *that*."

She looked up, attempting a smile. "Maybe that. But either I'm leaving to save myself or I'm saddling myself, slowing myself down, making it easier for the enemy. Don't you think we should ask ourselves what our purpose is? Are we leaving our home? Are we starting a new life? Or are we planning to continue the old one elsewhere?"

"Those are all good questions."

"Yes." Pensively, she stared out at the fields.

Alexander bent and rubbed his cheek against Tatiana's shorn head, his hand pressing her to him a little tighter. He had only one thing left over from his former life; otherwise America did not exist, except in his memory.

"I wish I could have found my brother," he heard her whisper.

"I know," said Alexander with emotion. "I wish I could have found him for you."

After a pained breath, Tatiana remained silent.

The train arrived at Warsaw Station in the early evening. They sat quietly on the bench overlooking the Obvodnoy Canal and waited for the Number 16 tram to take them to Grechesky Hospital near Tatiana's house. The tram came. Alexander said, "You want to get on?"

"No," she replied.

They sat.

The second tram came.

"This one?"

"No," she replied.

The third came.

"No," Tatiana said before he even asked, and put her head on his arm.

Four trams came and went—and still they sat, close to each other, not speaking, looking out on the canal.

"In just one more breath," Tatiana said finally, "on the next tram, you are going to take me back to my old life."

Alexander said nothing.

Uttering a small cry, Tatiana whispered, "What are we going to do?"

He didn't reply.

"At Kirov that day," she asked, "when we fought, did you . . . have a plan?"

He did want to get her out of Leningrad. She wasn't safe in the city. "Not really."

"I didn't think so," she said, her head against his arm.

Another tram came and went.

"Shura, what do I tell my family about Pasha?"

Tightening his lips, he touched her face. "Tell them you're sorry. Tell them you did your absolute best."

"Maybe, like me, he's alive somewhere?"

"You're not somewhere," said Alexander. "You're with me."

Tatiana swallowed before she continued. "Yes, but until yesterday, I wasn't. I was somewhere, too." She looked at him hopefully. "Maybe?"

Alexander shook his head. "Oh, Tania."

Tatiana looked away. "Did you have trouble finding me?"

"Not much." He didn't want to tell her how he had searched every meter of Luga for her.

"But how did you know to look for me in Luga?"

"I looked for you in Tolmachevo, too."

"But how did you know to look for me at all?" Tatiana asked.

Alexander saw her looking at him with an expression of want and hope he couldn't endure. "Listen . . ." he said. "It was Dasha who asked me to find you."

"Oh?" Tatiana's face fell. "Oh." She moved away from him until no part of her body was touching his.

"Tatia . . ."

"Look, our tram is here," she said, trying to get herself up. "Let's go."

Alexander took her arm. "Let me help."

"I'm fine," she said, and hopped once while still holding on to him, groaning in pain.

The tram doors opened. "Stop," Alexander urged. "Let me help you, I said."

"And I said I'm fine."

"Stop," he said more firmly. "Or I'm going to let go of you."

"Then let go."

With exasperation he sighed and went around to stand in front of her. "Stop hopping. Do your ribs like that? Hold on to me," he said, "and I'll carry you inside."

When they were sitting down and on their way, Alexander asked, "Why are you upset?"

"I'm not upset."

After a moment he put his arm around her. Tatiana sat stolidly looking out the window.

In fifteen minutes of not talking they were at the hospital on Grechesky. Alexander carried her inside, where the nurses immediately found a bed for her, put her in a clean hospital gown, and instantly gave her something for the pain.

"Much better with the morphine?" He smiled. "The doctor will be here in just a minute. He'll set your leg and put it in a cast; you'll sleep. Meantime I'm going to go. I'll tell your family you're here, and then I'm going to go and retrieve my men." He sighed. "I'm sure they're still stuck in Luga."

Tatiana leaned back against the pillows and said coolly, "Thank you for helping me."

Alexander sat on the edge of the bed. Tatiana turned her head away. He placed two fingers under her chin and turned her face back to him. There were tears in her eyes. "Tatia?" he said. "Why are you upset? Had Dasha not come to me, I never would have gone and found you." He shrugged. "I don't know why, but this is how it's supposed to be. You're home, you're all right." He caressed her cheek. "You're just going through too much right now, too much is broken . . ."

She sniffed, trying to turn her head away again, but he wouldn't let her, feeling overwhelming, crushing tenderness. "Shh . . . come here," he said, and hugged her gently. "Tania, whatever questions you have, the answer is *yes* to all of them," he whispered, kissing her hair. He felt her attempting to move away.

"I have no questions," she said evenly. "They've all been answered. You did this for Dasha. She will be so grateful."

Shaking his head, Alexander laughed once with disbelief. Allowing Tatiana to slip down on the pillow, he said, "Did I kiss you for Dasha, too?"

She turned red.

"Tania," he said quietly, "we cannot be having this conversation. Not after what we've just been through."

"You're right. We should not be talking at all." She wouldn't look at him.

"We should. Just not about this."

"Go, Alexander. Go and tell my sister how you saved me for her."

"I didn't save you for her," he said, standing up. "I saved you for me. And you're not being very fair, Tania."

"I know." She nodded sadly, staring at the blanket. "There is nothing fair about any of this."

Alexander took Tatiana's hand, struggling with himself not to kiss her again, not to cause her further pain and himself further pain. In the end, with a hurting heart, he pressed his lips into the trembling palm of her hand and left.

IMPALED IN SPACE

1

AFTER Alexander left, Tatiana wanted to cry, but her ribs hurt too much. She put her arm over her face when the nurse, Vera, came in and said, "Now, now, there, there, you'll be all right. Your family will be here soon. Don't cry, you'll hurt yourself. You've got broken ribs. Why don't you sleep? I'll give you something to sleep."

"Do you have some more morphine?"

"I already gave you two grams. How much more do you want?" Vera chuckled.

"Another kilo?"

Tatiana slept.

When she opened her eyes, her family was sitting on chairs around her bed, looking alternately endeared and horrified by her. Dasha was holding her hand. Mama was wiping her face. Babushka was anxiously tapping on Deda's hand. Papa was looking at her with reproachful eyes.

"Tania, you've been out for two days," said Dasha, who would not stop kissing Tatiana's cut hair.

Mama stroked her hands. "What were you thinking?" she kept repeating in a wailing voice.

"I wanted to get our Pasha," Tatiana said, squeezing her mother's hand. "I'm sorry I didn't."

"Tania, what nonsense you talk," said Papa, walking to the window. "Didn't you go to school? Didn't you graduate a year early? What did they teach you there? Obviously not sense."

Mama said, "Tanechka, you are our baby girl, our angel baby girl. What would we have done if we had lost you, too?" She sobbed. "How could we go on?"

Papa told Mama not to talk nonsense. "We have not lost Pasha! Volunteers come back from the line all the time. There is hope."

"Tell that to Nina Iglenko," said Dasha. "You can't step into the corridor without hearing her cries for Volodya."

"Nina has four sons," Papa said grimly, "who are all going to the front if this war is not over soon. She better get used to losing them." He lowered his head. "But we have only one, and I have to have hope."

If Tatiana had had the strength, she would have turned away from all of them, unable to face them with the truth of what she had seen on the Luga River. If she told them that she had wrapped dead bodies, that she had watched people die in front of her, that she had seen burning and mangled limbs and small children struck down, her family would not have believed her. Tatiana hardly believed it herself.

"You really are completely insane, Tania," said Dasha. "Putting us all through such hell, and risking my poor Alexander's life. He went to find you, you know. I begged him to do it. He didn't want to; he had to go over his commanding officer's head."

"Tatiana," said Deda, "he saved your life."

"Did he?" she said feebly.

"Oh, you poor thing," said Mama, rubbing Tatiana's hand. "You don't remember anything. Georg, she doesn't remember. What you must have gone through."

"Mama, didn't you hear?" said Dasha. "The station fell on her. Alexander dug her out from fallen bricks!"

"That man, Dashenka!" exclaimed Papa. "Where did you find him? He's gold, pure gold. Hold on to him."

"I intend to, Papa."

At that moment the man who was pure gold walked in with Dimitri. The family flocked to him. Papa and Deda shook his hands vigorously. Mama and Babushka hugged him. Dasha bent him to her and kissed him on the mouth.

And kissed him and kissed him.

And kissed him.

"Enough, Daria Georgievna," said Papa. "Let the soldier breathe."

Dimitri came over to Tatiana and put his arm around her. His eyes were concerned and amused. "Well, Tanechka," he said, kissing her head, "you seem to be quite fortunate to have your life."

"Tatiana, I think you have something to say to Lieutenant Belov," said Papa solemnly.

"They are going to give our lieutenant *another* medal for military valor," Dimitri snorted. "After dropping off Tatiana, he returned for his men, bringing eleven out of twenty of them back to Leningrad. And most of these men were untrained. Better even than Finland, right, Alex?"

155

Stepping up to the bed, Alexander said, "Tania, how are you feeling?"

"Wait, what happened in Finland?" asked Dasha, glued to Alexander's arm.

"How are you feeling, Tania?" Alexander repeated.

"Great," Tatiana replied, unable to look at him. She smiled at her mother. "I'm all right, Mama. I'll be home soon."

Dasha said, "What happened in Finland?" Still glued to Alexander.

"I don't want to talk about it," Alexander said.

"I'll tell them," Dimitri said brightly. "In Finland, Alexander brought back only four out of thirty men, yet somehow he managed to turn even that defeat into a victory. A medal and a promotion. Didn't you, Alexander?"

Not replying to Dimitri, Alexander asked Tania, "How is your leg?"

"Fine," she replied. "It will be as good as new soon."

"Not soon!" exclaimed Mama. "September! You're in a cast until September, Tania. What are you going to do?"

"I guess," said Tatiana, "I will be in a cast until September."

Mama, shaking her head and sniffling, said, "No, Alexander *carried* her on his back, Georg, on his *back*." She grabbed Alexander's hands and said, "How can we ever thank you?"

"No thanks necessary," Alexander replied, smiling at Tatiana's mother. "Just take care of Tania."

"Alex, it's a good thing our Tania only weighs about three kilos," Dasha said with a giggle.

"Thank him, Tania," persisted Papa, practically storming Tatiana's bed in his anxiety and gratitude. "Thank the man for saving your life, for goodness' sake!"

Forming a thin smile, with Dimitri still holding her hand, Tatiana somehow managed to look straight at Alexander as she said, "Thank you, Lieutenant."

Before he had a chance to respond, Dasha hugged him again. "Alexander, you see what you've done for our family? How can I *ever* thank you?" She smiled, rubbing up to him.

Blessedly, the nurse came in and told everyone they had to leave.

Dimitri leaned down and pressed his rubbery mouth to the corner of Tatiana's mouth. "Good night, dear," he said. "I'll come and see you tomorrow."

She wanted to scream.

Dasha remained behind to straighten Tatiana's blankets and move a pillow under her leg. She seemed agitated in a way Tatiana had not seen in weeks. "Tania," she whispered, "if there is a God, thank God for you. After he brought you back, we had a long talk. I was so grateful to him for finding you, and I convinced him to give us another chance. With the war so close, I said, what did we have to lose? I said, Alexander, look at what you did for me; you wouldn't have done it if you didn't have feelings for me. And he said, Dasha,

I never said I didn't have feelings for you." Dasha kissed Tatiana's head. "Thank you, my lovely baby, thank you for staying alive long enough for him to find you."

"You're welcome," said Tatiana in a dull voice. If he was in Dasha's life again, he would be in her life again.

Why did that feel so hollow?

"Tania . . . do you think Pasha is alive somewhere?"

Tatiana thought of the leaflets floating down from the sky like confetti, of the shells exploding in midair like metal rain, of the bleakness of the artillery guns pointed at her and at Alexander. And at Pasha.

"I don't think so," said Tatiana, closing her eyes. Whatever had happened to him, Pasha felt permanently lost.

Tatiana's eyes were still closed an hour later when she thought she heard the door creak. As she opened her eyes, Alexander was sitting on her bed. How did he do that, carry his body and his rifle with such quiet?

"What are you doing here?" she asked.

"Came to see how you were."

"You just leave Dasha?"

He nodded. "I'm on my way to St. Isaac's. I do air-raid duty above the dome, in the rotunda arcade. Until one Petrenko is on duty before me. He is a good soldier. He covers me if I'm a little late." St. Isaac's Cathedral was the tallest structure in Leningrad.

"What are you doing *here*?" Tatiana repeated.

"Wanted to make sure you were all right. And I wanted to talk to you about Dasha—"

"I'm great. Really. And you shouldn't do this. Come around like this. Dasha is right. I've made enough of a mess already. You shouldn't be late for your patrol."

"Don't worry about *me*. How are you feeling?"

"Fine," she said, glaring at him. "You're quite the hero, aren't you, Alexander?" she said. "My family thinks Dasha could not have done better." Tatiana lowered her eyes.

"Tatia . . ."

"She told me that you two are back together," Tatiana said with false brightness. "Why not? With the war so close, what have you got to lose, right? The whole Luga fiasco really worked out all the way around."

"Tatia . . ."

"Don't Tatia me," she snapped.

Alexander sighed. "What would you like me to do?"

"Just leave me alone, Alexander."

"How can I, Tatiana?"

"I don't know. But you better find a way. And you see how solicitous Dimitri is being? This has brought out all his best qualities, too," Tatiana said. "I never knew he could be so kind."

"Yes, he's kissing you kindly," said Alexander, his eyes darkening.

"He *is* being very kind."

"And you're letting him."

"Oh?" Tatiana said, "Well, at least I'm not *knocking* him."

Alexander sucked in his breath. So did Tatiana. She couldn't believe herself.

"What?" he said scathingly. "Is that *next* for you two?"

Shaken, she did not reply.

A nurse came in and left the door open, "for some fresh air."

When they were alone again, he said, "Tania, I don't know what you want me to do. I told you from the beginning, let's not play this game." He paused. "But now it's too late. Now Dimitri—" Alexander broke off, shaking his head. "Now it's become doubly difficult."

All she wanted was for him to kiss her again. "Which leads me for the *third* time to my *next* question," she said angrily. "What are you doing here?"

"Don't be upset."

"I'm not upset!"

Alexander lifted his hand to touch her. She whirled her face away.

"Oh," he said, getting up. "From *me* you turn away." He was at the door when he spun around. "And for your information," he barked, "it's impossible for *you* to be knocking *him*."

Tatiana was told by vivacious Vera that she would have to remain in the hospital until the middle of August, until her ribs healed enough for her to walk around on crutches. Her shinbone was fractured in three places and had been set in a cast from her knee to her toes.

Tatiana's family brought her food, which she ate with relish. *Pirozhki* with cabbage, chicken cutlets, some hamburger patties, and blueberry pie, which she didn't enjoy as much as she used to, having practically lived on blueberries during her stint in the volunteer army.

First Mama and Papa visited her every day. Soon it became every other day. Dasha would breeze in, radiant, healthy, cheerful, arm in arm with the uniformed Lieutenant Alexander Belov, kiss Tatiana on the head, and say she really couldn't stay. Dimitri would come over and, with his arm around her, sit by her side and then leave with them.

One night when to pass the time the four of them were playing cards, Dasha told Tatiana that her dentist had evacuated. He had asked Dasha to come with him to Sverdlovsk on the other side of the Urals, but Dasha had refused, finding work instead with Mama at the uniform factory. "Now I can't evacuate. I'm indispensable to the war effort, too," said Dasha, smiling at Alexander and showing Tatiana a handful of gold teeth.

"Where did you get those?" Tatiana asked.

Dasha replied that she got them as payment from the patients who came to the dentist in the last month, asking that the gold be taken out of their mouths.

"You took their gold teeth?" Tatiana asked with surprise.

"The gold teeth were my payment," Dasha said unapologetically. "We can't all be so pure as you."

Tatiana didn't pursue it. Who was *she* to pontificate to Dasha?

Tatiana changed the subject to war. War was like weather—always something to talk about. Alexander said the Luga line was about to fall any day, and she again felt the stamp of failure. All that effort on the part of thousands, only to have it crumble in a few days. She stopped asking. Being in the hospital imbued her with a sense of the unreal, even more than being in the deserted Dohotino village. She was stuck between four gray walls with a window, and she saw no one except the people who sporadically came to see her. She knew nothing except what she chose to ask about. Maybe if she didn't ask about war, by the time she left the hospital, the war would somehow be over.

And then what? Tatiana would ask herself.

Nothing, she would answer in the dark of night. Nothing except the life I had. I'll go back to work. Maybe next year I'll go to university, as I planned. Yes, I'll go to university, I'll study English, and I'll meet someone. I'll meet some nice Russian university student who is studying to be an engineer. We'll get married and go to live with his mother and grandmother in their communal apartment. And then we'll have a child.

Tatiana could not imagine that life. She could not imagine any life except this hospital bed, except this hospital window facing the buildings on Grechesky Prospekt, except eating oatmeal for breakfast and soup for lunch and boiled chicken for dinner. All she wanted was for Alexander to come and see her on his own. She wanted to say she was wrong, to say she had no right to behave badly. She wanted to feel him close to her again.

She read Zoshchenko's funny short stories about the ironic realities of Soviet life but couldn't find any humor in them all of a sudden.

Tatiana lay in her room day in and day out, and the days were long, and at night she couldn't sleep. The tears she saw in her mother's eyes ate at her heart, and the silence of her father ate at her even more. The feeling of failure over Pasha sickened her. But the absence of Alexander ate at Tatiana most of all.

At first she was sorry, then she was angry, then she was angry at herself for being angry. Then she felt hurt. Finally she felt resigned.

And it was on the day she felt resigned that Alexander came in the middle of the afternoon when she wasn't expecting him at all—right after lunch— and brought her an ice cream.

"Thank you," she said quietly.

"You're welcome," he replied just as quietly, and then sat in the chair by her bed and watched her eat it. "I'm on city patrol," he said. "I'm walking around the streets, making sure the windows are all taped, checking to see if there are any strange disturbances."

"By yourself?"

"No," he said, rolling his eyes. "With a group of seven forty-year-old men who have never carried a rifle."

"Teach them how, Alexander. You must be a good teacher."

Glancing at her, he said, "We've just spent the whole morning putting up tank barricades on Moscow Prospekt leading south. No trams are running there now." He paused. "But Kirov is still open and pushing out those tanks. They're just now deciding to move the production east. Little by little, other industries are leaving in trucks and the last of the trains." He paused again. "Tania? Are you listening to me?"

"What?" She broke free of the deafening noise in her head.

"How is the ice cream?"

"Very good. An unexpected treat."

"I think that's a good way to think about many things in life," Alexander said, getting up. "I have to be going."

"No!" Tatiana said quickly, and then more quietly, "Wait."

Alexander sat back down.

"About the other night . . ." she said. "I'm sorry. I—"

Alexander shook his head. "Forget it."

Tatiana couldn't think of anything to say besides low-spirited words. "Why did you take so long to come by?"

"What do you mean? I come by and see you every day."

Tatiana didn't say anything, and neither did he.

They looked at each other.

"I would have come alone," he said. "I just thought there was little point. It wasn't going to make you or me feel better."

An image sprang up, an image of *him bending over her, washing blood from her naked body.* She breathed with difficulty. Another image . . . *sleeping next to him, in his arms, her lips pressed to his chest, her hands touching him. Feeling closer to him than to anyone on earth. Standing with her arms around him on the train.* And worse—*the visceral sensation of his lips parting her lips.* She turned her face from him. "You're right, I know," she whispered.

Alexander got up, and this time Tatiana didn't stop him. "I'll see you," he said, bending over her and pressing his lips to her head.

Well, my *head*, that's something, thought Tatiana. When he was by the door, she asked, "Will you come again? If you can. For just a few minutes."

With his cap in his hands, he said, "Tania . . ."

"I know. You're right. Don't."

"Tania, all the nurses here . . . someone will mention my visit in front of your family. It'll just end badly."

But it will end. "You're right," she said. "Don't."

After he left, Tatiana thought in loathing self-flagellation, I'm a very bad sister. I've always thought of myself as a good sister, but I realize that I have never been tested before. The first time I *have* been—look how I'm behaving.

2

One night a week later, Tatiana woke up feeling her face being stroked. She wanted to open her eyes, but it felt so much like a dream, and she felt so drugged and tired that she let her eyes stay closed. A man with big hands and vodka on his breath was stroking her face. She knew only one man with big hands. She kept her eyes shut, but she knew that her breathing pattern had changed from sleepy breaths to shallow rasps. He stopped touching her. "Tatia?"

She so wanted the illusion to continue. The illusion of being touched by Alexander in the middle of an August night. Tatiana opened her eyes.

It *was* Alexander. He wasn't wearing his hat. There was that look in his molasses eyes again; even in the dark she could make it out.

"Did I wake you?" He smiled.

She sat up. "Yes, I think." She reached out and touched his arm. "It seems like the middle of the night."

"It is," he said. He stared at her blanket, and she looked at the top of his black head. "It's around three."

They were speaking in just above a whisper.

"What's the matter?" she asked. "Are you all right?"

"I'm fine. I just wanted to see if you were all right. I keep . . . thinking of you here by yourself. Are you sad? Lonely?"

"Yes and yes," Tatiana said. She smelled vodka on him. "Have you been drinking?"

"Hmm." His wandering eyes were slightly unfocused. "For the first time in a while. I had a night off tonight. Marazov and I went out, had a few drinks." He stopped. "Tatia . . ."

Her heart pounding, she waited breathlessly. His hands were on her blanket. Her legs were underneath the blanket. "Shura," she said, and suddenly, for an instant, felt happy. The way she felt coming out of Kirov and turning her head and seeing his smile. *Happier.*

Alexander said, "I can't find the right words. I thought maybe after I'd had enough to drink . . ."

"Every word you're saying is the right word," Tatiana told him. "What?"

Alexander took her hands and pressed them to his chest. His head remained bent. He said nothing.

What to do? Tatiana was a child. Any other girl would know what to do. She didn't even know what the right thing might be. I'm like a newborn. How I wish I knew what to do now in this moment with him. In my hospital bed, with my ribs taped up, with my leg in a cast, yes, but *alone* with him.

Dasha's face appeared between them, as if Tatiana's conscience could not let her heart have even a moment of stolen joy. That is how it should be, she said to herself, wanting desperately to lift his head and kiss him. Suddenly Dasha's face evaporated. Tatiana leaned toward him and kissed his hair. It smelled of soap and smoke. Alexander looked up. They were centimeters away from each other; she smelled his delicious, vodka-laden, Alexander-laden breath. "I'm *so* happy you came to see me, Shura," she whispered, feeling an aching pull in her lower body.

Alexander tilted his head and kissed her deeply on the lips. He let go of her hands, and she wrapped her arms around his neck, pressing herself against him. They kissed as if in a fever . . . they kissed as if the breath were leaving their bodies.

The aching in her stomach got to be too much to bear; Tatiana opened her mouth and moaned. Alexander took her face into his hands. "You sweet thing," he murmured. "You're the *sweetest* thing. I don't know what to do, what to do, Tania." He kissed her lips and licked them with his tongue and kissed her eyes and her cheeks and her neck. Tatiana moaned again, still holding on to him; she felt herself incinerating from within. His lips were so insistent and hungry that Tatiana, suddenly unable to breathe or sit, started to float down onto the bed.

Alexander held her up. Tatiana felt his hands gently moving up and down on her partially exposed back where her nightgown opened. Slowly he untied the strings of her gown. Alexander was completely clothed, sitting on her bed and kissing her as he pulled the nightgown down. Tatiana breathed out, shuddering.

He pulled back from her face, still holding her, still whispering. His eyes were blazing. "Tania, you are too much for me . . . I can't take you, not in small doses, not in large ones, not here, not on the street, nowhere." His hands moved around to hold her just above her bandaged ribs.

"Shura," she whispered, her whole aching weakness in her voice. "What's happening to me? What *is* this?"

Alexander cupped her breasts and fondled them. Flattening out his palms, he rubbed her nipples in circles. Tatiana moaned. He rubbed them harder. Pulling away and staring at her breasts, he muttered, "Oh, God . . . look at you . . ." Tatiana watched him as he bent down to her breast, put her nipple in his mouth, and sucked it, while rubbing her other nipple with his fingers. Then he sucked the other nipple. Watching and feeling Alexander's lips on her nipples utterly overwhelmed Tatiana. Her hands clutching his head, she moaned so loudly that he pulled away and lightly put his hand over her mouth. "Shh," he whispered. "They'll hear you outside." His right hand never stopped. Spanning her, his thumb and his little finger kneaded her nipples. Tatiana moaned just as loudly. His left hand went around her mouth a little firmer. "Shh," he said, smiling, short of breath.

"Shura, I'm going to die."

"No, Tatia."

"Breathe on me . . ."

He breathed on her. She kissed him hotly, her hands not leaving his hair. The friction and pressure on her breasts from his fingers was making her delirious; she moaned with such abandon that Alexander moved away. Tatiana sat in the blue light, topless, naked to the hips, gazing at him and panting. Her hands were gripping the hospital sheet.

"Tania," Alexander said, looking at her with wonder and lust. "How can you be so innocent in this day and age? How can you be so *innocent?*"

"I'm sorry," she said. "I wish I knew more."

Moving flush with her, he held her to him. "Knew more?"

"Had more experience. I just—"

"You're joking, right?" Alexander whispered fiercely. "Don't you understand me at all? It's your innocence that's driving me *mad*. Can't you see that?"

His hands caressed her. "Don't moan," he said. "They'll have me arrested."

Tatiana wanted him to—but she wasn't brave enough to say it. Gently she pushed his head downward. The only thing she could manage in a stilted whisper was, "Please . . ."

Smiling, he went to lock the door. The door wouldn't lock. He took his rifle and stuck it against the door handle.

Alexander came back to Tatiana, laid her flat on the bed, covered her mouth, bent to her breasts, and sucked her nipples until she nearly fainted, quivering the whole time and groaning into the palm of his hand.

"God, is there more?" she whispered, panting.

"Have you ever had more?" Alexander asked, panting himself.

Tatiana stared into his face. To tell him the truth? He was a *man*—how could she tell him? She didn't want to lie to him. She said nothing.

He sat up, pulling her up, too. "Have you? Tell me the truth. Please. I must know. Have you ever had more?"

She didn't want to lie to him. "No," she said. "I haven't had more."

His eyes glazed with amazement, heartache, and desire, Alexander lowered his head and said, "Oh, Tania, what are we going to do?"

"Shura . . ." Tatiana whispered, having forgotten *everything else* in the universe. She took his hands and put them on her breasts. "Please, Shura, please."

Alexander quietly moved his hands away to rest on her legs. "We can't here."

"Then where?"

He couldn't even look up at her.

Tatiana saw he didn't have an answer. "What about you?" she said, nearly crying. "Don't you want more? Don't you need something for yourself?"

"God, yes." His voice was hoarse.

"What is it? What can I do?"

Smiling lightly, he whispered, "What are you offering?"

"I have no idea." Tatiana timidly touched his thigh. "But I'll do anything." She kissed his neck. "*Anything*," she whispered. "You tell me what to do and I'll do it." She moved her hand a little higher. Her fingers were trembling.

Now it was Alexander's turn to groan. He gripped her hand, and said, "Tania, wait—is this how you want it to be for you?"

"I don't know," she moaned back, licking his lips. "I want it any—"

Suddenly the door moved and light streaked into the room. A nurse's voice sounded from the outside. "Tatiana? Are you all right? What's wrong with the door?"

Quickly Tatiana pulled up her nightgown, and Alexander went to his rifle, picked it up, turned on the light in the room, and opened the door.

"Everything is fine," he said, an air of formality enveloping him. "Just came to say good night to Tatiana."

"Good night?" the nurse shrieked. "Are you an idiot or something? It's four in the morning. There are no visiting hours at four in the morning."

"Nurse! You're forgetting yourself," said Alexander, raising his voice. "I'm a lieutenant in the Red Army."

Substantially more quietly, the nurse said, "I heard screams, I thought she was hurt."

"I'm fine," said Tatiana, and her voice was all croaky. "We were just laughing."

"And I was just leaving," Alexander said.

"You're going to wake up my other patients," the nurse said.

"Good night, Tatiana," Alexander said, his eyes boring into her. "I hope your leg feels better."

"Thank you, Lieutenant," Tatiana said. "Come again soon."

"Just not at four in the morning," the nurse mumbled, coming inside to check on Tatiana. Behind the nurse's back, Alexander pressed his fingers to his lips and blew Tatiana a kiss. Then he was gone.

There was no more sleep to be had that night, or the following morning. Tatiana had Vera bathe her twice, and kept obsessively brushing her teeth and tongue all day to make sure her breath was clean. She had no food, only water to drink, though by the afternoon, she nibbled on some bread left over from lunch.

Tatiana had thought that guilt would overtake her, that the force of conscience would make her unable to face herself and her thoughts. But that wasn't the case. The only thing she kept reliving was the evening minute on fiery wings with Alexander on her breasts and lips.

Nothing in Tatiana's former life had prepared her for Alexander.

There was school and there was Fifth Soviet, and there was Luga. In Luga, Tatiana had had many friends and many endless summers of mindless adventures. In Luga there had been nothing but the abandon of childhood, and in every step of that childhood there was Pasha, in her games and in her days.

It wasn't that Tatiana had not been occasionally and peripherally aware that every once in a while one of Pasha's friends looked at her for a little too long or stood too close to her. It was that she herself had never looked too long at anyone.

Until Alexander.

He was new. Transcendentally new. Immemorially new. She had thought all the while that their instant familiarity was based on the things she understood—compassion, empathy, fondness, friendship. Two people resoundingly coming together. Needing to sit close together on the tram, to bump into each other, to make each other laugh. Needing each other. Needing *happiness*. Needing *youth*.

But now Tatiana could not believe her preternatural *desire* for him. Her suffocating *need* for him. Simply could not fathom it. The throbbing in her lower stomach continued unabated all day as she bathed and brushed her teeth and brushed her hair.

That evening before Vera left, Tatiana asked her for some lipstick.

When Dasha, Alexander, and Dimitri came to see her, Dasha took one look at Tatiana and said, "Tania, I've never seen you wear lipstick before. Look at your lips." Dasha said it as if realizing for the first time that Tatiana actually *had* lips.

Dimitri came over, sat on her bed, and said, smiling, "Yes, just look at them."

Only Alexander kept quiet. Tatiana couldn't read his expression because she could not bring herself to raise her eyes. She realized that the consequence of last night was going to be her complete inability to ever look at him in public again.

They stayed for a short time. Alexander got up and said he had to be getting back.

Tatiana sat catatonically until she heard a knock on the door, and Alexander came in, closing the door behind him. She pulled herself up straight. He came over in long purposeful strides, sat at the edge of her bed, and in a tender, possessive gesture wiped the lipstick off her lips. "What *is* that?" he asked.

"All the other girls wear it," Tatiana said, quickly wiping her mouth, breathless at the sight of him. "Including Dasha."

"Well, I don't want you to have anything on your lovely face," he said, stroking her cheeks. "God knows, you don't need it."

"All right," she said, wiping her mouth, and waited. Her head fell back on the pillow as she raised her expectant, earnest eyes to him, her expectant, earnest lips to him.

Alexander was quiet. "Tania," he finally said with a great sigh, "about last night . . ."

She groaned.

"See," he said, the resolve in his eyes fading, "that's exactly what you can't do."

"All right," she said hoarsely, holding on to his sleeve. Reaching up, she traced his lips with her fingers. "Shura . . ."

Alexander moved his face away and stood up. The sheen had gone from his eyes. Tatiana stared at him in bewilderment. "I'm sorry about last night," he said coolly. "I had too much to drink. I took advantage of you—"

"No," she said, shaking her head.

He nodded. "I did. It was a terrible mistake. I shouldn't have come here; you know it even better than I do."

Speechlessly Tatiana shook her head.

"God, I know, Tania," said Alexander, his face constricted. "But we live an impossible life. Where can we—"

"Right here," she whispered, turning bright red, not looking at him.

The nurse walked in to check on Tatiana, looking askance at Alexander. They remained mute until she walked out.

"Right here?" Alexander said. "What, with the nurses outside the door? For fifteen minutes right here, that's what you want for yourself?"

Tatiana didn't reply. She felt as if she would have taken five minutes with the nurses *inside* the door. Her eyes remained lowered.

"All right, and *then* what?" Alexander said, letting out a heavy breath. "What then for us?" He paused. "What then for you?"

"I don't know," she said, biting her lip to keep herself from crying. "What then for everyone?"

"Everyone has it off in the alleys against the wall!" Alexander exclaimed. "And on garden benches, and in their barracks, and in communal apartments with their parents on the sofa! Everyone else does not have Dasha in her bed. Does not have Dimitri." He glanced away. "Everyone else is not you, Tatiana."

She turned onto her side, away from him.

"You deserve better than that."

She didn't want him to see her tears.

"I came here to apologize to you and to say I won't let it happen again."

She closed her eyes, trying not to shake, blinded for a moment. "All right."

Alexander walked around the bed to stand in her line of sight. He wasn't letting go of his rifle. Tatiana wiped her face. "Tania, please don't cry," he said emotionally. "Last night I came here ready to sacrifice everything, you included, to satisfy the burning inside me I've had since the day we met. But God was looking out for you, and He stopped us, and more important He stopped *me*, and I, in the gray of the morning, am less confused . . ." Alexander paused. "Though only more desperate for you." He took a long breath, staring at his rifle.

Tatiana could not find her voice to speak.

Alexander said, "You and I—" then broke off, shaking his head. "But the time is all wrong for us."

She turned onto her back, putting her arm over her face. The time, the place, the life. "Couldn't you have thought this through before you came here?" she said. "Couldn't you have had this talk with yourself before last night?"

"I cannot stay away from you," he said. "Last night I was drunk. But tonight I'm sober. And I'm sorry."

Tears choking her throat, Tatiana said nothing.

Alexander left without touching her.

3

Luga had burned, Tolmachevo had fallen, the German general von Leeb's men cut the Kingisepp-Gatchina rail line, and despite the efforts of hundreds of thousands of volunteers digging trenches under mortar fire, none of the front lines would hold. Despite all orders not to surrender the railroad, the railroad was surrendered.

And Tatiana was still in the hospital unable to walk, unable to hold the crutches, unable to stand on her broken shinbone, unable to close her eyes and see anything else besides Alexander.

Tatiana couldn't wring the hurt out of herself. Couldn't drench the flame out of herself.

In the middle of August, a few days before Tatiana was to come home, Deda and Babushka came to tell Tatiana they were leaving Leningrad.

Babushka said, "Tanechka, we're too old to stay in the city during war. We'll never make it through the bombing, or the fighting, or a siege. Your father wants us to leave, and he is right, we need to go. We'll be better off in Molotov. Your grandfather was assigned a good teaching post and during the summer we will stay in—"

"What about Dasha?" Tatiana interrupted with hope. "She is going to come with you, right?"

Deda said that Dasha would not leave Tatiana behind.

It's not me she cannot leave behind, thought Tatiana.

Deda said that when the cast came off Tatiana's leg, she, Dasha, and maybe their cousin Marina, too, would evacuate to Molotov. "Evacuating you right now is too difficult with a broken leg," concluded Deda.

Yes, Tatiana thought, without Alexander to carry me, it is difficult indeed. "So Marina is staying in Leningrad, too?"

167

"Yes," Deda replied. "Your Aunt Rita is very sick, and Uncle Boris is up at Izhorsk. We asked her if she wanted to come with us, but she said she could not leave her mother in the hospital and her father as he prepares to fight the Germans."

Marina's father, Boris Razin, was an engineer at Izhorsk, a factory much like Kirov, and as the Germans neared it, the workers, in between making tanks and artillery shells and rocket launchers, were preparing for battle.

"Marina should definitely go with you," said Tatiana. "She—" Tatiana tried to think of a mild description. "—She does not do well under pressure."

Deda said, "Yes, we know. But as always, it is the ties and bonds of love and family that keep people from saving themselves. Lucky for us, your grand-mother and I are our own bonds. I would say not just bonds, but chains." He smiled at Babushka.

"Now, remember, Tanechka," said Babushka, patting her blanket, "Deda and I love you very much. You know that, don't you?"

"Of course, Babushka," said Tatiana.

"When you come to Molotov, I'm going to introduce you to my good friend, Dusia. She is old, very religious, and is going to eat you right up."

"Great," muttered Tatiana, smiling wearily.

Deda kissed her on the forehead. "There are difficult days ahead for all of us. Ahead of *you* particularly, Tania. You and Dasha. Now that Pasha is not here, your parents need you more than ever. Your mettle will be tested, along with everyone else's. There will be only one standard, the standard of sur-vival at all cost, and it will be up to you to say at what price survival. Hold your head high, and if you're going to go down, go down knowing you have not in any way compromised your soul."

Pulling him by the arm, Babushka said, "That's enough. Tania, you do whatever you have to do to survive, and damn your soul. We expect to see you in Molotov next month."

"Never compromise on what your heart tells you to be right, my grand-daughter," Deda said, getting up and hugging her. "You hear me?"

"Loud and clear, Deda," Tatiana said, hugging him back.

Later that evening, when Dasha came with Alexander and Dimitri, Tatiana mentioned that Deda had asked the girls to join them when Tatiana's cast was off in September, and Alexander said, "That won't be possible. There will be no trains in September."

He usually avoided speaking to Tatiana, keeping his careful, silent dis-tance.

Tatiana would have liked to speak back to him, but her feelings remained in unquelled turmoil, and she didn't trust her outer face to hide the tremor in her voice or the softness in her eyes when she looked at him. So she said nothing, as usual, and didn't look at him. Dimitri sat by her side.

Dasha spoke. "What does *that* mean?"

"It means there will be no trains," Alexander repeated. "There were trains in June when you girls could have left, and there were trains in July, but Tatiana here broke her leg. In September, when her leg will be healed, there will not be a single train leaving Leningrad unless a miracle happens between now and when the Germans get to Mga."

"What kind of miracle?" asked Dasha hopefully.

"German unconditional surrender," replied Alexander dryly. "Once we lost Luga, our fate was sealed. We are certainly going to try to stop the Germans at Mga, the central point for rail travel to the rest of the Soviet Union. In fact, we are told that under no circumstances are we allowed to surrender Mga to the Germans. It is now against the law to give up railroads to the Nazis." Alexander smiled. "But I have an uncanny ability to see the future. The law *will* be broken, and there will be no trains in September."

Tatiana heard the subtext in his even voice. *Tania, I told you and told you to leave this damned city, you didn't listen to me, and now with a broken leg you can't go anywhere.*

4

Tatiana's life was positively joyous in the hospital compared to what she encountered when she came back home in the middle of August.

When she returned, finally able to walk—badly—on crutches, Tatiana found Dasha cooking dinner for Alexander, and Alexander sitting behind the table happily eating, joking with Mama, talking politics with Papa, smoking, relaxing, and not leaving. And not leaving.

And not leaving.

Tatiana sat morosely and nibbled at her food like an overstuffed mouse. When was he going to leave? It was getting so late. Didn't he have taps?

"Dimitri, what time is taps for you?"

"Eleven," Dimitri replied. "But Alexander has the night off tonight."

Oh.

"Tania, did you hear? Mama and Papa are now sleeping in Deda and Babushka's room," Dasha said, smiling. "You and I have a room to ourselves, can you believe it?"

There was something in Dasha's voice that Tatiana did not like. "No," said Tatiana. When was Alexander leaving?

Dimitri went back to the barracks. Before eleven o'clock Mama and Papa got ready to go to bed. Mama leaned to Dasha and whispered, "He can't stay overnight, do you hear me? Your father will go through the roof. He'll kill us both."

"I hear you, Mama," Dasha whispered back. "He'll leave soon, I promise."

Not soon enough, Tatiana thought.

Their parents went to bed, and Dasha took Tatiana aside and whispered, "Tania, can you go up on the roof and play with Anton? Please? I just want to have an hour alone with Alexander—in a *room*, Tania!"

Tatiana left Dasha *alone* with Alexander. In her room.

She went to the kitchen and threw up in the sink. The nauseating din inside her head continued even after she went up onto the roof and sat with Anton, who was supposed to be on night duty. Anton was not a very good sky-watcher. He was sleeping. Fortunately the sky was quiet. Even from far away there was no sound of war. Tatiana sifted the sand in the bucket and cried in the moonless night.

I've done this, she thought. This is all because of me. Shuddering at herself, she laughed out loud. Anton twitched. I've done this to myself, and I have no one else to blame.

Had she not decided to single-handedly bring Pasha back, had she not joined the volunteers and walked off God knows where and got blown up and had her leg broken, she and Dasha would have left with Deda and Babushka for Molotov. And the unthinkable would not be happening in her room right now.

She sat on the roof until Dasha came upstairs sometime later and motioned for her to come to bed.

The following evening Mama told Tatiana that now that she was home by herself all day with a broken leg and nothing to do, she would have to start cooking dinner for the family.

All Tatiana's life Babushka Anna, who did not work, had cooked. On the weekends Tatiana's mother cooked. Sometimes Dasha cooked. During holidays like New Year everybody cooked; everybody, that is, except Tatiana, who cleared up.

"I'd be glad to, Mama," said Tatiana. "If I only knew how."

Dismissively Dasha said, "There is nothing to it."

"Yes, Tania," said Alexander, smiling. "There's nothing to it. Make something delicious. A cabbage pie or something."

Why not? Tatiana thought; while her leg was healing, she needed to busy her idle hands. She would try. She could not continue sitting in the room and reading all day, even if the reading was a Russian-English phrase book. Even if it was rereading Tolstoy's *War and Peace*. She could not continue sitting in her room, thinking about Alexander.

The crutches had been killing her ribs, so Tatiana stopped using them. She hobbled to the store on her cast leg. The first thing she would cook in her life would be a cabbage pie. She would have also liked to make a mushroom pie but couldn't find any mushrooms in the store.

The yeast dough took Tatiana three attempts and five hours in all. She made some chicken soup to go with the pie.

Alexander came for dinner, along with Dimitri. Extremely nervous about

Alexander trying her food, Tatiana suggested that perhaps the two soldiers wanted to go back and eat at the barracks. "What, and miss your first pie?" Alexander said teasingly. Dimitri smiled.

They ate and drank and talked about the day and about war, and about evacuation, and about hopes for finding Pasha, and then Papa said, "Tania, this is a little salty."

Mama said, "No, she just didn't let the dough rise enough. And there are too many onions. Why didn't you try to get something else besides cabbage?"

Dasha said, "Tania, next time cook the carrots a little longer in the soup. And put a bay leaf in. You forgot the bay leaf."

Smiling, Dimitri said, "It's not too bad for your first effort, Tania."

Alexander passed Tatiana his plate, and said, "It's great. Can I please have some more pie? And here's my bowl for the soup."

After dinner Dasha took Tatiana away and whispered in her pleading voice, "Can you and Dimitri go on the roof for a little while? It's not going to be too late tonight. He's got to get back. Please?"

Kids from the apartment building were constantly on the roof. Dimitri and Tatiana were not alone.

But Dasha and Alexander were alone.

What Tatiana needed was not to see her sister and him. Him for a lifetime. Her for two weeks. In two weeks, when the summer would end, Dasha's infatuation would surely end, too. Nothing could survive the Leningrad winter.

But how could Tatiana not see Alexander? Maybe she could lie to everyone else, but she could not lie to herself. She held her breath the whole day until the evening hour when she would finally hear him walking down the corridor. The last two nights he stopped at her door, smiled, and said, "Hello, Tania."

"Hello, Alexander," she replied, blushing and looking down at his boots. She couldn't meet his eyes without trembling somewhere on her body.

Then she fed him.

Then Dasha took Tatiana aside and whispered.

Tatiana had been ready, gritted teeth and all, to put Alexander away. She had known all along what the right thing was, and she was prepared to do it.

But why did her face have to be rubbed in the right thing night after night?

As the days went on, Tatiana realized she was too young to hide well what was in her heart but old enough to know that her heart was in her eyes.

She was afraid she would glance at Alexander and something in her look would catch Dimitri's attention, something would make him think, wait a minute, why is she looking at *him?* Or worse, what is *that* in her eyes? Or worse still, why is she looking *away?* Why can't she look at him like everyone else? Like I look at Dasha, like Dasha looks at me?

Looking at Alexander condemned Tatiana, but not looking at him equally betrayed her, maybe even more so.

And Dimitri seemed to catch it all. Every glance away, every glance toward, Dimitri's quietly studying eyes were on Alexander, on Tatiana.

Alexander was older. He could hide better.

Most of the time he treated her as if he had never met her before last night or tonight, before an hour ago, maybe a witching hour, maybe a drunken hour, certainly a smoking hour, but he managed somehow to behave toward her as if she were nothing to him. As if he were nothing to her.

But how?

How did he hide their Kirov walks and their arms against each other, how did he hide his life that he poured into her, how did he hide his unstoppable hands on her breasts, and his lips on her, and all the things he had said to her? How did he hide Luga from them all? Luga, when he washed her bloodied body? When she lay naked against him as he kissed her hair and held her with his tender arms, while his heart beat wildly in his chest. How did he hide his eyes? When they were alone, Alexander looked at Tatiana as if there were no one else in the world but her.

Was *that* the lie?

Was *this* the lie?

Maybe that's what grown-ups did. They kissed your breasts and then pretended it meant nothing. And if they could pretend really well, it meant they were really grown-up.

Or maybe they kissed your breasts and it really *was* nothing.

How was that possible? To touch another human being that way and have it mean nothing?

But maybe if you could do that, it meant you were really grown-up.

Tatiana didn't know, but she was baffled and humiliated by it—imagining herself in Alexander's hands when he could barely be bothered to call her by name.

Tatiana would lower her head and wish for them all to disappear. But every once in a while when Alexander would be sitting down at the table, and she was in the room, and everyone was talking while she was moving or picking up teacups, she would see him glance at her, and for a flicker she would see his true eyes.

All Tatiana had with Alexander were meaningless gestures. He would open the door for her, and as she walked by him, a bit of her brushed a bit of him, and that kept her going for a day. Or when she made him tea and handed him the cup, the very tips of his fingers would—accidentally?—touch the very tips of hers, and that kept her going for another day. Until the next time she saw him. Until the next time a part of him would brush against a part of her. Until the next time he said, "Hello, Tania." But one time, when Dimitri had already walked inside and Dasha was elsewhere, with a big smile on his face Alexander said, "Hello, Tania! I'm home." And it made her laugh, though she didn't want to. And when she looked up at him, he was soundlessly laughing, too.

One night when Alexander tasted her cheese *blinchiki*, he said, "Tania, I think that's the best yet." And that lifted her spirits, until Dasha kissed him and said, "Tanechka, you really have been a godsend for us all."

Tatiana didn't smile, and then she saw Dimitri watching her not smiling, and then she smiled but knew it was not enough. Later, when Dasha and Alexander were sitting together on the couch, Dimitri said, "Dasha, I must say that I have never seen Alexander as happy with anyone as he is with you," and everybody smiled, including Alexander, who did not look at an unsmiling Tatiana. Yes, and we have me to thank for it, she thought grimly, catching Dimitri's eyes.

She continued to learn to cook new things, how to make sweet pies because she saw that Alexander liked them, finishing them off in one sitting, followed by his tea and cigarettes.

"Do you know what else I like?" he said once.

Tatiana's heart stopped for a moment.

"Potato pancakes."

"I don't know how to make those."

Where was everyone else? Mama and Papa were in the other room. Dasha had gone to the bathroom. Dimitri was not there. Alexander smiled into her face, and his smile was contagious, and it was for her. "Potatoes, flour, some onions. Salt."

"Is that from—"

Dasha came back.

The next day Tatiana made potato pancakes ladled with sour cream, and the whole family devoured them, saying they had never tasted anything so delicious. "Where did you learn to make *that*?" asked Dasha.

The only small pleasure Tatiana had during her long days was feeding Alexander. The pleasure was most intense and most untinged by hurt in the hours before the family returned home, when she was making the food and looking forward to seeing his face. During dinner emotions were already gathering clouds, and soon after dinner two things happened: either Alexander left to go back to barracks, which was bad enough, or Dasha asked to be left alone with him, which was worse.

Where had they gone before they had a room of their own to go to? Tatiana could not conceive of the things Alexander had said to her in the hospital about alleys and benches. Dasha, always the protective older sister, certainly never talked to Tatiana about those things. Didn't talk to Tatiana about anything.

No one talked to Tatiana about anything.

Tatiana never saw Alexander alone.

He hid everything.

But one evening after dinner, when they all went out onto the roof, Anton asked Tatiana if she wanted to play their dizzy geography game. Tatiana said she was going to have trouble twirling on one leg.

"Come on, try," said Anton. "I'll hold you up."

"All right," Tatiana said, wanting a bit of giddiness. She hopped around and around on her one good leg, while keeping her eyes closed. Anton's friendly hands were on her arms, and he laughed hysterically as she got all the countries in the world completely out of whack, and when she opened her eyes, she saw Alexander looking at her with such a black expression that it hurt her even to breathe, as if her ribs were rebroken. She straightened herself out and went to sit next to Dimitri, thinking that perhaps even grownups couldn't hide *everything*.

"That's a fun game, Tania," said Dimitri, putting his arm around her.

"Yes, Tania," said Dasha, "when are you ever going to grow up?"

Alexander said nothing.

Of all the small mercies Tatiana was grateful for, the one she was most grateful for was her broken leg's preventing her from going on solitary walks with Dimitri. She was also grateful for the constant buzz of people in the apartment that stopped her from being alone with Dimitri. But that night when they got back downstairs from the roof, Tatiana discovered to her panic that her parents had themselves gone for a walk in the balmy August night, leaving the two couples alone together.

Tatiana saw Dimitri's insinuating smile and felt his insinuating closeness. Dasha smiled at Alexander and said, "Are you tired?"

Tatiana could barely continue to stand on one leg.

It was Alexander who came to her rescue. "No, Dasha," he said, "I have to be going tonight. Come on, Dimitri."

Dimitri said he didn't have to be going, not taking his eyes off Tatiana.

Alexander said, "Yes, you do, Dima. Lieutenant Marazov needs to see you tonight before taps. Let's go."

Tatiana was grateful for Alexander. Though it was a bit like the Germans cutting off your legs and then wanting you to be grateful to them for not killing you.

When Mama and Papa came back from their walk, Tatiana quietly asked them never to leave the apartment in the evening again, not even for a cold glass of beer on a warm August night.

During the days Tatiana went out for slow walks around the block to check the local stores for any food. She had begun to notice an absence of beef and pork. She could not find even the 250 grams of meat a week per person that was allotted them. Only occasionally did she find chicken.

Tatiana still found the ever-present cabbage, apples, potatoes, onions, carrots. But butter was more scarce. She had to put less in her yeast dough. The pies started tasting worse, though Alexander still ate them cheerfully. She found flour, eggs, milk. She couldn't buy a lot; she couldn't carry a lot. She would buy enough to make one pie for dinner, and then in the afternoons she would take a nap and study her English words before turning on the radio.

Tatiana listened to the radio every afternoon, because the second thing her father said when he came home was, "Any news from the front?" The first thing he said was, "Any news?" leaving out the unspoken. *Any news about Pasha?*

So Tatiana felt obliged to listen to the radio to find out the minimum about the Red Army's position, or about von Leeb's army's advance. She didn't want to hear it. On occasion, yes—listening to bleak reports from the front lifted her spirits. Even defeat at the hands of Hitler's men was better than what she had to endure inside herself every day. She turned on the radio in the hope that hopeless news elsewhere would cheer her up.

She knew if the announcer started listing open radio frequencies, then nothing extraordinary had happened that day. Usually there was some news. But even before the announcer came on, there was a series of dismal little rings and pauses, like a rat-ta-tat-tat of a typewriter. The radio information bulletin itself lasted a few seconds. Maybe three short sentences about the Finnish-Russian front.

"The Finnish armies are quickly regaining all the territory they lost in the war of 1940."

"The Finns are coming closer to Leningrad."

"The Finns are at Lisiy Nos, only twenty kilometers from the city limits."

Then followed a few sentences about the German advance. The newsreader read slowly, stretching out the no-news bulletin to impart meaning that wasn't there. After he listed the cities south of Leningrad that were under German control, Tatiana had to go and open a map.

When she found out that Tsarskoye Selo was in German hands, she was shocked and even forgot about Alexander for the moment it took her to get her bearings. Tsarskoye Selo, like Peterhof, was a summer palace of the old tsars, it was the summer writing place of Alexander Pushkin, but the worst thing was that Tsarskoye Selo was just ten kilometers southeast of the Kirov factory, which was located on the city limits of Leningrad.

Were the Germans ten *kilometers* from Leningrad?

"Yes," Alexander said that night. "The Germans are very close."

The city had changed in the month Tatiana spent in Luga and in the hospital. The golden spires of the Admiralty and Peter and Paul's Cathedral had been spray-painted gray. Soldiers were on every street, and the NKVD militia in their dark blue uniforms were even more conspicuous than the soldiers. Every window in the city was taped against explosion; the people on the streets walked quickly and with a purpose. Tatiana sometimes sat on a bench near the church across the street and watched them. In the sky floated the ubiquitous airships, some round, some oval. The rations became slightly more restrictive, but Tatiana was still able to get enough flour to make potato pies, mushroom pies, and cabbage pies. Alexander often brought some of his rations with him when he came for dinner. There was chicken enough to make chicken soup with well-cooked carrots. Bay leaf was gone.

Dimitri got Tatiana out onto the roof while Dasha and Alexander were downstairs alone in Tatiana's room. Putting his arm around her, Dimitri said, "Tania, please. I'm feeling so sad. How long am I going to wait? Just a little more tonight?"

Placing her hand on his arm, Tatiana asked, "What's the matter?"

"I just need a little comfort from you," he said, hugging her, kissing her cheeks, trying to bring his mouth to hers. There was something that felt almost unnatural in Dimitri's touching her. She couldn't put her finger on it. "Dima, please," she whispered, moving slightly away from him and motioning for Anton, who skipped over and chatted with them until Dimitri got fed up and left.

"Thanks, Anton," said Tatiana.

"Anytime," he replied. "Why don't you just tell him to leave you alone?"

"Anton, you wouldn't believe it, but the more I do, the more he comes around," said Tatiana.

"Older men are all like that, Tania," said Anton with authority, as if he knew about such things. "Don't you understand anything? You have to give in. *Then* he'll leave you alone!" He laughed.

Tatiana laughed, too. "I think you may be right, Anton. I think that's how older men work."

She continued to busy Dimitri with cards or books, with jokes or vodka. Vodka, in particular, was good. Dimitri tended to have a little too much and then fall asleep on the small sofa in the hallway, and Tatiana would take her grandmother's cardigan and go up onto the roof without him and sit with Anton and think of Pasha, and think of Alexander.

She passed the time with Anton, told jokes, read Zoshchenko and *War and Peace*, and looked at the Leningrad sky, wondering how much longer for the Germans to get to Leningrad.

Wondering how much longer for everything.

And after the other kids left to go to sleep, Tatiana continued to sit by the kerosene lamp on the roof and mouth little English words to herself from the dictionary and the phrase book. She learned to say *"Pen." "Table." "Love." "The United States of America." "Potato pancakes."* She wished she had two minutes alone with Alexander to tell him some of the amusing phrases she was learning.

One night at the very end of August, with Anton asleep next to her, Tatiana tried to think of a way to make her life right again.

Once it had been right. As right as it *could* be. Suddenly after June 22 there was such havoc, constant, cheerless, and unending. But not all of it cheerless.

Tatiana missed the evening hour with Alexander at Kirov more than she could admit even to herself. The evening hour when they had sat apart and together and ambled through the empty streets; when they talked and were silent, and the silence flowed into their words as Lake Ladoga flowed into the Neva that flowed into the Gulf of Finland that flowed into the Baltic Sea. The evening hour when they smiled and the white of his teeth blinded her eyes, when he laughed and his laughter flew into her lungs, when she never took her eyes off him and no one saw but him, and he was all right with it.

The evening hour at Kirov when they were alone.

What to do? How to fix this? Somehow she had to make herself right again inside. For her own sake, for her sister's, and for Alexander's.

It was two in the morning. Tatiana was cold, wearing only an old sundress with a cardigan over it. She was thinking that she would rather spend the rest of her life on the roof than downstairs with Mama and Papa's forlorn hope for Pasha, or with Dasha's supplicating whisper . . . *Tania, go away so I can be alone with him.*

Tatiana thought about the war. Maybe if the German planes came whizzing by and dropped a bomb on our building, I could save everyone else but die in the process. Would they mourn me? Would they cry? Would Alexander wish things were different?

Different how?

Different when?

She knew that Alexander already wished things were different. He wished they had been different from the start.

But even at the start, on the bus still, together, untouched by anything but each other, was there a place where Tania and Shura could have gone when they wanted to be alone for two minutes to speak English phrases to one another? Other than the walk home from Kirov?

Tatiana didn't know of such a place.

Did Alexander?

This was a pointless exercise, designed only to pummel herself further. As if she needed it.

All I want is some relief, Tatiana thought. Why is that too much to ask?

Nothing brought her relief. Not Alexander's aloofness, not his occasional short temper with Dasha, not his moodiness, not his winning at cards all the time—nothing eased either Tatiana's feeling for him or her need for him. He didn't have many nights off. He usually had to be back for taps, while other nights he had sky duty at St. Isaac's. He had only one or two evenings off each week, but it was one or two evenings too many.

And tonight was one of those evenings. *Please, Tania, please go away so I can be alone with him.*

She heard a distant rumble. Overhead the airships floated by.

The hours at night and at morning and at day before night break, again the hours. Something had to be done. But what?

Tatiana came downstairs. She made herself a cup of tea to warm her cold hands and was sitting exhausted on the kitchen windowsill, looking out onto the dark courtyard, when out of the corner of her eye she saw Alexander walk past the door. She heard his footsteps slow down and then trail back. He stood in the doorway. For a moment they did not speak.

"What are you doing?" he asked quietly.

She said coolly and bravely, "Waiting for you to leave, so I can go to bed."

Alexander walked tentatively into the kitchen.

She glared at him.

He came closer. The thought of being able to smell him made Tatiana's heart weak. He stopped short of that.

"I hardly ever stay late," he said.

"Good for you."

Now that no one was watching her, Tatiana stared unblinking at him.

Looking at her with remorse and understanding, Alexander said, "Tatiasha, it's been *very* hard for you, I know. I'm sorry. It's my fault. I blame myself. What did I tell you? I never should have come into your hospital room that night."

"Oh, because before it was bearable."

"It was better than this."

"You're right, it was." Tatiana wanted to jump down from the sill and go to him. She wanted to ride the tram, to sit on the bench, to sleep in a tent with him. She wanted to feel him next to her again. On her again. But what she said was, "Tell me, did you *arrange* for Dima to be in Leningrad every night? Because every night that he is here, he tries to take liberties with me."

Alexander's eyes flared. "He told me he had taken some."

"Really?" Is that why Alexander had been so cold? "What did Dima say?" Tatiana was too tired to be angry at Dimitri. Alexander came closer. Just a little more, she thought, and I'll be able to smell you.

"Never mind that," said Alexander, sounding pained.

"And you thought he was telling the truth?"

"You tell *me*."

"Alexander, you know what?" She swung her legs off the sill and put down her cup.

Alexander came closer. "No, what, Tatia?" he said softly.

Tatiana smelled his maleness, his shampoo, his soap. Wanly she smiled. Then her smile vanished. "Please," she said, "do me a favor and stay away from me. All right?"

"I'm doing my level best," he said, taking a step back.

"No," Tatiana said, and broke off. "Why are you coming over?" she whispered. "Don't continue with Dasha." She sighed deeply. "Like after Kirov. Go ahead. Go fight your war. And take Dimitri. He won't take no for an answer, and I'm getting sick and tired of all this." Of all of you, she wanted to say but didn't. "Soon I'm going to get tired of saying no to him," Tatiana added for effect.

"Stop it," Alexander said. "I can't leave now. The Germans are too close. Your family is going to need me." He paused. "*You* are going to need me."

"I'm not. I'm going to be fine. Please, Alexander . . . this is just too hard for me. Can't you see that? Say good-bye to Dasha, say good-bye to me, and take your Dimitri with you." She paused. "Please, please, go away."

"Tania," Alexander said, nearly inaudibly, "how can I not come and see you?"

She blinked.

"Who is going to feed me, Tania?"

Tatiana blinked again. "Well, that's fine," she said, very upset. "I'll be making dinner for you and having it off with your best friend while you're knocking my sister. Did I get the terms right this time? That *is* perfect, isn't it?"

Alexander turned on his heels and walked out.

The first thing Tatiana did when she woke up the next morning was go and see Vera at Grechesky Hospital. While Vera was looking at her ribs, Tatiana asked, "Vera, is there anything for me to do around here? Is there any job for me at the hospital maybe?"

Vera's kind face studied her. "What's the matter? You look so sad. Is it because of the leg?"

"No, I'm . . ." The kindness got to Tatiana, who nearly opened her mouth and poured her heartache on Vera's bleached and unsuspecting head. Nearly. She got hold of herself. "I'm all right. Just can't go anywhere. Bored to tears. I stay on the roof all night, looking for bombs. Tell me, is there anything for me to do?"

Vera remained thoughtful. "We could use a hand around here."

Tatiana instantly perked up. "Doing what?"

"There is so much to do. You can sit behind the desk and do paperwork, or you can serve food in the cafeteria, or you can bandage wounds or take temperatures or, when you get better, maybe even learn nursing."

Tatiana smiled broadly. "Vera, that's fantastic!" Then she frowned. "But what will I do about Kirov? I'm supposed to go back and make tanks there as soon as my cast comes off. When is it coming off, by the way?"

"Tatiana! The front is at Kirov," exclaimed Vera. "You're not going to Kirov. You're not that brave. They give you a rifle there now and train you in combat before you can continue to work. You got out just in time, you know. But here we're always shorthanded. Too many people volunteer, and not enough of them come back." She smiled. "Not everyone can be lucky like you, having an officer dig you out of the rubble."

If Tatiana could have skipped home, she would have.

That night at dinner, barely able to contain her enthusiasm, Tatiana told her family she had found a job close to home.

"That's right! Go to work," said Papa. "Finally! You can eat lunch there instead of eating here."

"Tania can't go yet," said Alexander. "Her leg will never heal, and she'll limp for life."

"Well, she can't continue doing nothing and getting a dependent ration!" Papa exclaimed loudly. "We can't feed her. At work I heard they're about to lower rations again. It's only going to get harder."

"I'll go to work, Papa," said Tatiana, still cheerfully. "And I'll eat less, all right?"

Alexander glared at her from across the table, stabbing the mashed potatoes with his fork.

Papa threw down his fork. "Tania, this is all your fault! You should have left with your grandparents! It would be easier on our food situation, and you wouldn't be placing yourself in danger by remaining in Leningrad." He shook his head. "You should have left with them."

"Papa, what are you talking about?" asked Tatiana, *not* cheerfully and a notch louder than she ever spoke to her father. "You know I couldn't have left with Deda because of my leg." She frowned.

"All right, Tania," said Dasha, putting her hand on Tatiana's arm. "Stop it."

Mama threw down *her* fork. "Tania! If you hadn't gone and done something idiotic, you wouldn't have a broken leg in the first place!"

Tatiana ripped her arm from under Dasha's and turned to her mother. "Mama! Maybe if you hadn't said you would rather *I* had died instead of Pasha, I wouldn't have gone and tried to find him for you!"

Mama and Papa stared speechlessly at Tatiana, while everyone else in the room was mute as well. "I never said that!" Mama cried, standing up from the table. "Never."

"Mama! I heard you."

"Never!"

"I heard you! 'Why couldn't God have taken our Tania instead?' You remember, Mama? Remember, Papa?"

"Tania, come on," said Dasha in a trembling voice. "They didn't mean it."

"Come on, Tanechka," said Dimitri, placing his hand on Tatiana. "Calm down."

"Tatiana!" shouted Papa. "Don't you dare talk that way to us when this whole thing has been your fault!"

Tatiana tried to take a deep breath, but she could not, and she could not calm down. "My fault?" she yelled to her father. "It's *your* fault! You're the one who sent Pasha to his death and then sat and did nothing at all to get him back—"

Papa shot up and hit her across the face so hard that she fell sideways from her chair.

Alexander shot up and shoved Tatiana's father away. "No," he said. "No."

"Get out!" yelled Papa. "This is family business. Get the hell out!"

Alexander helped Tatiana to her feet. They stood between the couch and the dining table, close to Dasha, who was holding her shaking head in her hands. She wouldn't get up. She and Dimitri continued to sit. Papa and Mama both stood next to each other and panted.

Tatiana's nose was bleeding. But now Alexander was between her and her father. Pressing herself against Alexander and holding on to his sleeve, Tatiana shouted, "Papa, you can hit me all you want. You can kill me, too, if you like! It still won't bring Pasha back. And nobody is leaving, because there is *nowhere* for us to go!"

Screaming, Papa went for her again but couldn't get past Alexander. "No," Alexander said, shaking his head, one of his arms extended behind him holding Tatiana, one of his arms in front of Papa.

A wailing Dasha finally stood up and rushed to her father, grabbing his arms. "Papochka, Papochka, don't, please." Whirling to Tatiana, Dasha cried, "Look what you've done!" And tried to get around Alexander, who stopped her.

"What are you doing?" he asked quietly.

Uncomprehending, Dasha stared at him. "What, you're defending her still? Look what she's done!"

Mama was crying. Papa was still screaming, red in the face. Dimitri continued to stare into his plate. Tatiana was behind Alexander as he and Dasha squared off. "Stop it," he said. "She hasn't done anything. All of you, stop it. Maybe if you had listened to her back in June when you could have gotten Pasha out, you wouldn't all be standing here fighting each other, and your son and brother might still be alive. Now it's too late. But now you keep your hands off her."

Turning to Tatiana, Alexander asked, "Are you all right?" Taking a napkin off the table, he handed it to her and said, "Hold the bridge of your nose to stop the bleeding. Go on. Quick."

Then he faced Tatiana's father. "Georgi Vasilievich," said Alexander, "I understand you were trying to save your son." He paused. "Believe me, I know what you were doing. But don't take it out on Tania."

Papa threw down his vodka glass, cursed, and stumbled into the next room. Mama followed him, slamming the door behind her. Tatiana heard Mama's sobs. "It's always like this," she said unsteadily. "She cries, and someone goes in to apologize. Usually it's me."

Dasha was still standing glaring at Alexander. "I cannot believe," she said, "that you just sided with her against me."

"Don't give me that shit, Dasha," Alexander said loudly. "You think I sided against you because I wouldn't let you hit your little sister who has a broken leg? Why don't you pick on someone your own size? Or why don't you hit me? I know why," Alexander went on angrily. "Because you'd only be able to do it *once*."

"You're right," Dasha said, and tried to slap him.

He grabbed her hand, pushing it hard away. "You're out of control, Dasha," he said. "And I'm leaving."

Dimitri, who hadn't said a word, sighed, stood and left with Alexander.

As soon as they were out the door, Dasha went for Tatiana, who couldn't stand and fell onto the dining table, right against the mashed potatoes she had made an hour ago.

"Now look what you've done!" Dasha yelled. "Look what you've done!"

The door swung open, and Alexander came through. Grabbing Dasha by the arm and yanking her away from Tatiana, he said, "Tania, can you give us a minute, please?"

Tatiana went out, shutting the door behind herself, still holding the napkin to her nose.

She heard Alexander shouting and then Dasha shouting.

She and Dimitri stood in the hallway and looked at each other dumbly. Shrugging, Dimitri said, "He's like that. He's got that foundling temper."

Tatiana wanted to say that she had never seen him lose it before tonight but remained silent, trying to listen. Dimitri said, "He needs to stay out of it and let the family take care of its own business. Don't you think? Tomorrow it will all be better."

Tatiana said, "Reminds me of that old joke: 'Vasili, why do you beat me all the time? I haven't done anything wrong.' And Vasili replies, 'You should be thankful. If I knew what you were doing, I'd kill you.' "

Dimitri laughed as if that were the funniest thing he had heard all day.

She heard Alexander's voice from inside the room. "Can't you see?" he was yelling at Dasha. "She isn't driving me away, *you* are—by your behavior. How do you think I can ever take your side when you hit your sister?"

Dasha said something.

"Dasha, don't give me your stupid apologies. I don't need them." Pause. "I can't continue, no."

From inside the door Tatiana heard hysterical sobbing. "Please, Alex, please don't go, please, I'm sorry, you're right, my love, you're right. Please don't go. What can I do? Do you want me to apologize to her?"

"Dasha, if you touch your sister again, I will finish with you instantly," Tatiana heard Alexander say. "Do you understand?"

"I will never hit her again," Dasha promised.

Silence from the room.

Tatiana was dumbstruck.

Not knowing where to look, she wiped her bleeding nose and looked at Dimitri, shrugging her shoulders. "Can't have a moment alone even to fight," she said. "Well, at least that worked out." Her body began to slide down.

Dimitri picked her up, sat her on the sofa in the hallway, and wiped her face, patting her back. "Are you all right?" he kept saying.

The Sarkovs knocked on their hall door, also wanting to know if everything was all right. One fight in the communal apartment and everyone knew. Everyone heard. Everything.

"It's great," said Tatiana. "Just a little argument. Everything is fine."

Summarily, Dasha walked out of the room and apologized sullenly to Tatiana. She went back inside to be with Alexander and closed the door. Tatiana asked Dimitri to go and then limped upstairs to the roof, where she sat and prayed for a bomb.

She saw Alexander walk out of the stairwell doors and come toward her. Tatiana was sitting talking to Anton, and though her heart had skipped a beat, she didn't acknowledge him. Her hands were in Anton's hands. Anton nudged her and stopped talking. Sighing, Tatiana turned to Alexander. "What?" she said unhappily.

"Give me your hand," he whispered.

"No."

"Give me your hand."

Loudly she said, "Anton, you remember Dasha's Alexander? Shake hands, why don't you?"

Anton let go of Tatiana and shook hands with Alexander, who said, "Anton, will you excuse us for a moment?"

Reluctantly Anton scooted away on his haunches, still staying close enough to overhear.

"Let's move away from him," Alexander said to Tatiana.

"It's hard for me to move around so much. I'm fine right here."

Without arguing further, Alexander picked Tatiana up and walked a few steps away to set her down in the corner of the roof where there was no Anton and no Mariska—the seven-year-old girl who practically lived on the roof because her parents were drunk down on the second floor.

"Give me your hands, Tania."

Unwillingly Tatiana complied. Her hands were shaking. "Are you all right?" he asked quietly. "Does this happen often?"

"I'm fine. It happens every once in a while." She shook her head, *"Why?"*

"I will never let anyone hurt you," he said.

"But what good is it? Now they're all angry at me. You've just had a bit of Dasha, you're going to leave, but I'm still here, in that bed, in that room, in that hallway. I'm still the trash."

His face was full of pity and feeling. "I haven't had a bit of Dasha. I will not let them hurt you. I don't give a shit if Dasha finds out about us, or if Dimitri—" He broke off. Tatiana strained to listen. "I don't give a shit if I expose us to all the world. I will not let anyone hurt you." He paused, peering into her face. "And you know it. So if you don't want to see me hang, or ruin your plans to spare Dasha from the truth, I suggest you be more careful around people who might hit you."

"Where do you come from?" she asked. "Do they not do this in your *America*? Here in Russia, parents hit their children, and the children take it.

183

Big sisters hit their little sisters, and the little sisters take it. That's just how it is."

"I understand," Alexander said. "But you're too small to let anyone hit you. Plus, he is drinking too much. It makes him more volatile. You must be more careful around him."

His hands were soothing and warm. Tatiana half-closed her eyes, imagining only one thing. Her mouth parted in a silent moan.

"Babe, don't do that," Alexander said, his hands holding hers tighter.

"Shura, I'm lost," said Tatiana. "I don't know what to do. I'm completely lost."

Suddenly she pulled her hands away and with her eyes motioned behind him. Dasha was coming toward them from the stairwell.

She stopped near them and said, "I came to see my sister." She looked from Alexander to Tatiana. "I didn't know you were still here. You said you had to go."

"I did have to go," Alexander said, standing up. He gave Dasha a quick peck. "I'll see you in a few days, and you, Tania, go and get your nose looked at. Make sure it's not broken."

Tatiana was barely able to nod.

After he left, Dasha sat next to her. "What did he want?"

"Nothing. He wanted to see if I was all right." In that instant something overcame Tatiana, and before she opened her mouth and told Dasha *everything,* she said, "You know what, Dasha? You're my older sister and I love you, and I'm going to be all right tomorrow, but right now you're the last person I want to talk to. I realize I do it too often—bow to you when you want me to talk, or to go away, or whatever. Well, tomorrow I will bow to you again, but right now I don't want to talk to you. I just want to sit here and think." Tatiana paused and said pointedly, "So *please, Dasha, go away.*"

Dasha didn't move. "Look, I'm sorry, Tania, I really am. But you shouldn't have said what you said to Papa and Mama. You know how broken up they are about Pasha. You know they already blame themselves."

"Dasha, I don't want to hear your backhanded apology!"

"What's gotten into you?" asked Dasha. "You never talked that way before. To anyone."

"Please, Dasha, please. Go away."

Tatiana sat on the roof until morning, wrapped in the old cardigan, her legs cold, her face cold.

She was stunned by her unwavering intimacy with Alexander. Though they hadn't spoken much, though he had been cool to her, though the last words they had exchanged were bitter, she had no doubt as she laid into her mother and father that if she needed defending, the man who went to find her at Luga would stand up for her. That conviction had given her the strength to yell at Papa, to say the insulting thing to him, no matter how true it was. No matter how much she had wanted to say it, she never would have dared had she not felt Alexander's strength.

And when Tatiana stood behind him, she felt even braver, not caring for her bleeding nose, for her throbbing ribs. She knew he would not let even Dasha hurt her; she knew this as she knew her own heart, and that knowledge in the dark of night suddenly made her at peace with herself, at peace with her life, and at peace even with Dasha.

Dimitri, for all his purported feelings for Tatiana, had done nothing, as she knew he wouldn't. Her opinion of Dimitri hadn't changed a whit. Dimitri was a Soviet man. She did not blame Dimitri for this—for being true to his nature.

Yet she was using all her strength to deny her own: Tatiana knew that she belonged irrevocably to Alexander.

She thought she could extricate herself from him, that she could go on with her life somehow, that he could go on with his.

It was all a sham.

This wasn't a way of getting over a passing crush on your older sister's swain. This was the moon of Jupiter and the sun of Venus aligning in the sky over her head.

5

When Alexander walked into his quarters, Dimitri was lying down in his top bunk.

"What's going on?" said Alexander tiredly.

"You tell me," said Dimitri.

"Let's see. Didn't I just see you? I'm going to sleep. I have to wake up at five tomorrow."

"I'll get to the point, then," Dimitri said, hopping off the bunk. "I want you to end the charade you're playing with my girl."

"What are you talking about?"

"Can't I just have this one thing for myself? You already have a good life, don't you? Think about all the things you have that you want. You're a lieutenant in the Red Army. You have a company of men obeying your every order. I'm not in your company—"

"No, but you're in mine, Private," said Anatoly Marazov, jumping off the bunk next to Alexander's. "It's late, and we all have long days ahead of us. You shouldn't be here raising your voice. You're here by privilege."

Dimitri saluted him. Alexander stood by quietly.

"At attention, Private," Marazov said, coming up to Dimitri. "I thought when you came here you were just relaxing, waiting for your friend."

"It's just a small matter between me and the lieutenant, sir," said Dimitri.

"It's only a *small* matter, Private, when I'm *not* woken up out of a much-needed sleep. As soon as I'm awake, it ceases to be a *small* matter and becomes something else entirely. Now, at ease." Marazov, who was in his long johns, walked around Dimitri, who was fully uniformed, and said, "Can this small matter wait till morning?"

Alexander stepped in. "Lieutenant, can you give us a few minutes?"

Trying not to smile, Marazov bowed his head. "As you wish, Lieutenant."

"We will take it out in the hall."

They stepped out into the corridor; Alexander closed the door behind him. "Dima, what's the problem? Don't get yourself into trouble with your commanding officer."

"Cut the shit. Tell me, when is it enough for you?" Remaining at a distance from Alexander, Dimitri hissed, "You can have any girl in the world. Why do you want mine?"

It took all of Alexander's strength not to ask Dimitri the same question. "I have no idea what you're talking about. She was getting hurt. I helped her."

Dimitri continued, "I'm just a grunt. I have to follow everybody's orders and eat everybody's shit. She is the only one who treats me like a human being."

She can't help it. She treats everybody like that. "But, Dima," Alexander said, "you also have *your* life. Think of all the things you don't have that you don't want. You have not been sent down south, where men are falling into Hitler's meat grinder. Marazov's unit is staying here until the front comes to Leningrad. I've taken care of that. To help you." He paused. "Because I'm your friend." He took a step toward Dimitri. "I have been very good to you over the years. What has happened to our friendship?"

"Love happened," snapped Dimitri. "She is more important to me now. I want to survive this fucking war—for her."

"Oh, Dimitri," said Alexander and fell silent. "So survive—for her. Who's stopping you?"

Dimitri whispered, "Whatever silly crush she might have, it's not real. How could it be? She doesn't know who you are." Dimitri paused. "Or *does* she?"

Alexander's heart skipped erratically before he answered. The lightbulb next to them was broken. The one down the hall flickered on and off. Sounds of men laughing came from some of the rooms. Water was running. And still they stood silently across from one another. Alexander wondered what Dimitri was referring to. His indiscreet past? America? He glared at Dimitri. "Of course she doesn't," he said at last. "She knows absolutely nothing."

"Because if she did, Alexander, it would make things very dangerous, don't you think? For *us*."

Alexander took a step toward Dimitri, who put out his palms and backed into the wall. "Dimitri," said Alexander, "don't fuck with me. I told you, she knows nothing."

"I don't want to hurt anyone," Dimitri said in a small voice, his hands up. "I just want my chance with Tania."

His teeth clenched, Alexander turned away and went back to his quarters.

Lying on his bed with his arms behind his head, Marazov said casually, "Alexander, you want me to take care of Chernenko for you? Is he giving you trouble?"

Alexander shook his head. "Don't worry. I can handle him."

"We could reassign him."

"He's already been reassigned. Four times."

"Oh, nobody wants him, so you give him to me?"

"Not to you, to Kashnikov."

"Yes, and Kashnikov is mine."

Getting out a flask and taking a swig of vodka, then passing it to Alexander, Marazov said, "We don't have enough men to throw in front of Hitler's tanks to hold Leningrad. We are going to have to surrender, aren't we?"

"Not if I can help it," said Alexander. "We're going to fight on the streets with rocks, if we have to." He smiled.

Marazov saluted him from across the bunks and fell down onto his pillow. "Lieutenant Belov, I haven't seen much of you off duty. You can't believe some of the girls that are coming to the club lately." He grinned.

Alexander grinned back and shook his head. "No more for me."

Marazov lifted his head in surprise. "I don't understand the words that are coming out of your mouth, Lieutenant. I hear you. I *think* you're speaking Russian, but I just can't believe what I'm hearing. What in fuck's name is going on?"

When Alexander didn't answer, Marazov said, "Wait, wait. You're not . . . oh, no!" He laughed infectiously. "Now I *know* you're full of shit. What happened to you? You're not dying, are you?"

"I'm not sleeping, that's for fucking sure," said Alexander.

"Who can I wake up? I can't keep this to myself."

He leaned over his bunk and hit the sleeping soldier beneath him with a pillow. "Grinkov, wake up. You won't believe it when I tell you—"

"Fuck off," Grinkov said, throwing the pillow to the floor and turning away.

Alexander laughed. "Stop it, you crazy bastard," he said to Marazov. "Stop it before I have *you* reassigned."

"Who is it?"

"Don't know what you're talking about," said Alexander, putting a pillow over his face.

"Wait, is it the girl you keep muttering about in your sleep?"

Taking the pillow off his face, Alexander said with surprise, "I don't mutter in my sleep."

"Oh, yes you do," said Marazov. "And how. Grinkov, what does Belov mutter when he is sleeping?"

"Fuck off," Grinkov said again, turning to the wall.

"No, that's not it. It's some girl's name. It's . . . it's . . . Alexander, you're a fiend for keeping it from your fellow officers."

"Yes, because you can be trusted," said Alexander, turning on his side.

Marazov clapped his hands. "I want to meet this one," he said. "I need to meet the girl who has taken our wandering Alexander's horse and cart."

Later, as he lay with a heavy chest, unable to sleep, Alexander knew that it was not as easy as a walk in the fields to reconstruct your heart. If his life in the Soviet Union had taught him anything, it had taught him that. But he was going to try—after he had spoken to her. Everything would be easier to carry after he had spoken to her.

Alexander knew that before he *had* light instead of darkness, he had to *deserve* light instead of darkness. The time for him had obviously not come. He still had to earn his stars.

6

In the morning Mama asked Tatiana if she was pleased with herself. No, Tatiana replied. Not particularly.

After they had all left, she started to get ready to go to the hospital. There was a knock on the door, and when she opened it, she found Alexander standing outside.

"I can't let you in," Tatiana said, pointing to Zhanna Sarkova, who walked out of her room and stood in the corridor looking suspiciously at them. Anxiety and excitement mixed in equal measure inside Tatiana. She couldn't let him inside, couldn't close the door, not with Sarkova standing watching them, yet—

"Don't worry," Alexander said, striding in. "I've got a whole platoon waiting for me downstairs. We're going to barricade the southeastern streets." He paused. "Terrible news. Mga fell to the Germans yesterday."

"Oh, no, not Mga." Tatiana remembered Alexander's words about the trains. "What does it mean for us?"

Alexander shook his head. "It's the end. I just wanted to make sure you were all right after yesterday. And," he said pointedly, "that you weren't going to work."

"I am."

"Tatia, no."

"Shura, I am."

"No." He raised his voice.

Glancing behind him, Tatiana said, "I want you to know that that woman is definitely going to say something to my family about you coming by. I guarantee it."

"That's why you're going to give me my cap that I left here yesterday. During inspection this morning, I got fined. I need it."

Tatiana left the door open while Alexander went into the bedroom to retrieve his cap.

"Please don't go to the hospital," he said, coming out and standing in the hallway.

"Alexander, I'm going crazy. All day, every day. In the hospital at least I'll see some real suffering. It'll cheer me up."

"Your leg is never going to heal if you stand all day on it. You have a couple more weeks until the cast comes off. Go to work then."

"I am not staying here for another two weeks—the only hospital they'll put me in in two weeks will be a mental hospital!"

"I wish Kirov weren't on the front line," Alexander said softly. "You could go back to work there. I would meet you every day." He paused. "Like I used to, remember?"

Did she *remember*?

Tatiana's heart was pounding. But there was Sarkova standing in the corridor watching them through their open door.

Alexander muttered, "That's it. I'm fed up," and shut the door.

Tatiana opened her mouth and then closed it again. "Oh, no," she said. "We're in more and more trouble."

He came closer to her.

She backed away from him.

Alexander took another step toward her. "How is your nose?"

"It's fine. It's not broken."

"And how would you know?" He came closer.

She put her palms out. "Shura, *please*."

There was a loud knock on the door. "Tanechka, are you all right?"

"Fine, thank you," Tatiana called out.

The door knob turned, and Sarkova opened the door. "I just wanted to know if you'd like me to make you anything to eat."

"No, thank you, Zhanna," said Tatiana, keeping a straight face.

Sarkova glared at Alexander, who turned to Tatiana and rolled his eyes. Tatiana nearly burst out laughing.

"We were just leaving," she said.

"Oh, where are you going?"

"Well, I'm going to work—"

Alexander whispered, "No you're not."

"And Lieutenant Belov is going to build barricades."

Alexander turned to Zhanna. "Barricades, Comrade Sarkova," he said, striding toward her. "Do you know what those are? Structures nearly three meters high by four meters thick, stretching for twenty kilometers."

Sarkova backed away into the hall.

189

"And each barricade is supplied with eight machine-gun rests, ten anti-tank positions, thirteen mortar positions, and forty-six machine-gun points."

"Oh."

"That's how we protect the city we love," Alexander said, slamming the door.

Tatiana stood behind him shaking her head, a smile of delight on her face. "You've done it now." She grabbed her bag. "Let's go, barricade-builder."

They went out, locking the door behind them and leaving Sarkova in the communal kitchen, grumbling into her tea.

As he was helping her down the stairs, Alexander took hold of her hand. Tatiana tried to pull away. "Alexander—"

"No." He brought her to him on the stairwell landing.

Tatiana felt the rumbling inside her, the rumbling of wood crackling on the rack of fire. "Look," she said, "I will ask Vera to put me to work in the hospital canteen. Maybe you can come for lunch?" She smiled. "I'll serve you."

Alexander shook his head. "Though few things give me more pleasure than to have you feed me"—he smiled—"we'll be too far south. I won't be able to get back in time for lunch."

"Shura, let go of me. We're on a landing in my building . . ."

He held onto her hand. Sensing something, she said, "What's wrong?"

Alexander hesitated, and his chocolate eyes melted sadness onto her. "Oh, Tania. I have to talk to you." He sighed. "I have to talk to you about Dimitri."

"What about him?"

"I can't now. I need to talk to you at length and *alone*. Come and see me tonight at St. Isaac's."

Tatiana's turbulent heart hammered in her chest. St. Isaac's! "Alexander, I can barely walk to the hospital three blocks away. How am I going to get to St. Isaac's?" But Tatiana knew: if she had to crawl dragging one leg behind her, she would get herself to the cathedral.

"I know. I don't want you to walk all that way without help. The streets are safe, but you . . ." He stroked her face. "Do you have a friend who can take you up there?" he asked. "Not Anton. A female friend. A single female friend you can trust, who can help you and drop you off nearby? Then you can just walk a block or two by yourself."

Tatiana was quiet. "How am I going to get back home?" she said.

Alexander smiled, bringing her closer to him. "As always," he said, "I will take you home myself."

She stared at his tunic buttons.

"Tania, we desperately need to have a minute," he said. "And you know it."

She knew it. "This isn't right."

"It's the only thing that's right."

"All right. Go."

"Will you come?"

"I will try. Now, go."

"Lift your—"

Before he stopped speaking, Tatiana raised her face to him. They kissed deeply. "Do you have *any* idea what I feel?" Alexander whispered, his hands in her hair.

"No," Tatiana replied, holding on to him, her legs numb. "I only have an idea what I feel."

That night a miracle happened. Tatiana's cousin Marina's phone was working. Tatiana begged Marina to visit her, and Marina came, around eight. Tatiana couldn't stop hugging her. "Marinka, you are living proof that there is indeed a God in the heavens. I needed you so much," she said. "Where have you been?"

"There is no God, you know that. Where have I been?" Marina said, laughing. "Let go of me. Where have *you* been? I heard all about your escapades in Luga." She blinked. "I'm sorry about our Pasha." Brightening a bit, she said, "Why do you look like a boy?"

"I have so much to tell you."

"Obviously." Marina sat down at the table in the room where just yesterday Tatiana had stood behind Alexander. "Is there anything to eat? I'm so hungry."

Marina was a big-hipped, small-breasted, dark-eyed girl with short black hair and clusters of birthmarks on her face. She was nineteen and in her second year at Leningrad University. Marina was the closest thing Tatiana had to a best friend and a confidante. Marina, Tatiana, and Pasha had spent many summer days romping around Luga and nearby Novgorod. The difference in their ages had become apparent only a year or so ago. Tatiana simply no longer belonged with Marina's crowd.

Tatiana hastily gave Marina some bread, some cheese, some tea and said, "Marina, eat quick, because I need to go for a walk, all right? You look pretty in that dress. How was your summer?"

"We can't go for a walk. You can't walk. Look at you. Talk to me here." Mama and Papa were in the next room with Dasha, listening to the radio. Tatiana and Marina were alone in the room; Tatiana's family was not speaking to her after yesterday. Chewing, Marina looked Tatiana over. "Start with the hair. What happened to your hair? And why is your skirt so long?"

"I cut my hair. And the skirt hides the cast. Get up. We need to go." Tatiana pulled on Marina's arm. She was in a hurry. Alexander told her to come after ten, and here it was nearly nine, and she was still at Fifth Soviet. Was she prepared to tell Marina everything to get her to help? She pulled again at Marina's plump arm. "Let's go. Enough eating."

"How are you going to walk? You can barely hobble. And why do we need to go anywhere? When is the cast coming off?"

"Then let's go for a hobble. The cast feels as if it's never coming off. How do I look?"

Marina stopped eating and eyed Tatiana. "What did you just say?"

"I said let's go."

"All right," Marina said, wiping her mouth and standing up. "What is going on?"

"Nothing. Why?"

"Tatiana Metanova! I know that something is seriously wrong."

"What are you talking about?"

"Tania! I've known you for seventeen years, and you have never asked me how you looked."

"Maybe if your phone were working more often, I would. Are you going to answer me, or can we just go?"

"Your hair is too short, your skirt is too long, your blouse is white and tight—what the hell is going on?"

Finally Tatiana got Marina out the door. They walked slowly down Grechesky, to Insurrection Square, where they took a tram down Nevsky Prospekt to the Admiralty. Tatiana walked supported by Marina's arm. She had a little trouble walking and talking at the same time. The walking took most of her energy.

"Tania, tell me, why did you jump off a moving train? Is that how you broke your leg?"

"It's not how I broke my leg," said Tatiana, "and I jumped off a moving train because that was what I had to do."

"Did a ton of bricks fall on you because they had to, too?" Marina asked with a chortle. "Is that how you broke your leg?"

"Yes, and are you going to stop?"

Marina laughed. "I'm sorry about Pasha, Tanechka," she said, much more quietly. "He was the best boy."

"Yes," said Tatiana. "I wish I had found him."

"I know." Marina paused. "This has not been a great summer. I haven't seen you since before the war started."

Tatiana nodded. "You almost saw me. I was very close to coming and visiting you the day the war started."

"Why didn't you?"

Tatiana wished she could have told Marina everything—about her emotion and her conscience, about her fear and confusion. What Tatiana did instead was tell Marina about Dasha and Alexander, and herself and Dimitri, and herself and Luga, and Alexander's search for her. What Tatiana didn't tell Marina was the truth.

Tatiana could barely trust *herself* not to slip in front of Dasha amid the ice of constant lies on which she skated. How could she trust Marina, who had nothing at stake? Tatiana didn't tell her, sensing that truth forged a chasm between her and all the people she loved. How can that be? Tatiana thought, as they came to the Admiralty Gardens and sat on a bench. How can it be that deceit and treachery and secrecy bonded her to other human beings instead of truth and trust and openness? How could it be that she could not trust a member of her own family with a personal matter? This life just seems to breed contempt for other human beings.

The Admiralty Gardens were laid out on the banks of the Neva, between the Palace Bridge and St. Isaac's. Tatiana was not far from Alexander. If she strained, she might be able to hear him breathe. She smiled. Tall leafy elms branched out over the footpaths and the benches much the same as they did in the Summer Garden. The difference was, in the Summer Garden Tatiana had walked and sat with *him*.

"Tania," Marina said, "is there a reason we're here?"

"No, Marina," said Tatiana. "We're just sitting and talking." She wished she had a watch. How late was it already?

"I used to come to this park," Marina said. "Once I even brought you. Remember?"

Tatiana, suddenly blushing, said, "Yes . . . I do."

Marina said, "I've had some good times in my life. They don't seem so far away. You think we'll have them again?"

"Sure, Marinka," said Tatiana. "I'm counting on it. I *haven't* had any good times yet." She smiled at her cousin.

Marina laughed. "Not even with Dima?"

"Of course, not!" Tatiana said, and didn't say anything else.

Marina put her arm around Tatiana. "Don't be sad, Tania. You'll get out of this city somehow."

Tatiana shook her head. "No. There are no more trains, Marinka. Mga fell."

Marina was quiet. "We haven't heard from Papa for three days," she said. "He's been fighting at Izhorsk. That's near Mga, isn't it?"

"Yes," Tatiana said faintly. "It is."

Marina held Tatiana closer. "I don't think anyone is getting out of this city," she said. "My mama is so sick. My papa is . . ."

"I know," said Tatiana, patting her cousin's leg. "We'll make it, Marina. We just have to be strong."

"Yes, especially you," Marina said, with a shake of her head, shuddering away her unhappy thoughts. "Will you tell me why you brought me here?"

"No."

"Tania . . ."

"No. I have nothing to tell."

Marina tickled Tatiana's arm. "Tania, tell me about Dimitri."

"There is nothing to tell."

Marina giggled. "I can't believe you of all people are seeing a soldier!" She looked askance at Tatiana. "Oh, no—you're not meeting him here later, are you?"

"No!" Tatiana cried. "Dima and I are just friendly."

"Yes, sure. Soldiers have only one way of being friendly, Tania."

Now it was Tatiana's turn to look askance at her cousin. "What are you talking about?"

"Remember I went out with a soldier last year?" Marina made a derisive clicking sound with her tongue. "I glimpsed the life he lived and said forget it, I want no part of it. But this summer I was seeing someone nice, another student. He enlisted and went down to Fornosovo." She stopped. "Haven't heard from him since."

"What do you mean?" said Tatiana. "What did you want no part of with soldiers? War, you mean?"

"Tania, not war. Women."

"Women?" she said weakly.

"Women—good-time girls, pick-me-up girls, garrison hacks, harlots—all kinds of women come to the bars and the clubs and the barracks offering themselves to garrison soldiers, and the soldiers accept. All of them. It's just what they do. Like having a smoke. Every time they're off duty, every time they have time off at the weekend, every time they get furlough." Marina shook her head. "I don't know how you're keeping Dimitri away. Easy women, difficult women, young girls like you, it's all the same to soldiers— just one big conquest party to them."

In a small, horrified voice, Tatiana said, "Marinka, what are you talking about? Not in Leningrad. That's only in the West. In *America*."

Marina burst out laughing. "Tania, I love you," she said, putting an arm around her. "I really do. You are just—"

"That's not Alexander," muttered a shaken Tatiana.

"Who? Oh, Dasha's guy. No? Ask Dasha." Marina laughed. "How do you think he met her?"

Dasha did meet Alexander in Sadko. "You're not saying . . ."

"Ask Dasha, Tania."

"You don't know what you're talking about!" Tatiana was sorry she'd ever called her.

When Tatiana remained silent, Marina continued. "Look, the point I'm making is that you have to be careful with a soldier like Dimitri, especially you of all people. They expect certain things. And when they don't get the things they expect, they take them anyway. Do you understand?"

Tatiana kept quiet. How in the world had they started talking about this?

"Are you still friendly with Anton Iglenko? He is a nice boy, and he really likes you."

"Marina!" Tatiana shook her head. "Anton is my friend." She sat breathing heavily, keeping her hands steady on her lap. "He doesn't like me."

Marina smiled, ruffling Tatiana's hair. "You're adorable, Tania. And blind as always. Remember Misha? Remember how stuck on you he was?"

"Who?" Tatiana strained to remember. "Misha from Luga?"

Marina nodded. "For three summers in a row. Pasha couldn't keep him away from you."

"You're crazy." Tatiana and Misha used to hang upside down from trees together. She taught him how to do cartwheels. And Pasha, too.

Marina asked, "Tania, have you ever talked to Dasha about these things?"

"God, no!" Tatiana exclaimed, trying to get up. She felt as if she were being stabbed repeatedly with a blunt kitchen utensil.

Marina helped her stand. "Well, I suggest you do. She's your older sister. She should help you. But be careful with Dimitri, Tania. You don't want to be just another notch in some soldier's belt."

Tatiana tried to think of Alexander as she knew him. She knew nothing about that part of him. A vision of his head appeared, softly kissing the top of her breast when she lay wounded in his tent. She shook her head. What Marina was describing, *that was not her Alexander.*

Then Tatiana remembered Dimitri's comment about Alexander's extracurricular activities. She felt ill. "Let's go home," she said dejectedly, and slowly they walked back to the tram stop on Nevsky. Tatiana told Marina that she didn't have to go all the way back home with her. "I'm going to be fine. I can walk home from Insurrection Square. Honestly. Look, your bus home will come any minute. Don't worry for a second about me."

Marina said she could not leave Tatiana alone at night in the middle of the city. It hadn't occurred to Tatiana that she should be afraid of anything. "Alexander told us that violent crime has fallen off dramatically since war began. It's almost nonexistent."

"Oh, well, if Alexander told you . . ." Marina said, peering at Tatiana's face. "Are you all right?"

"I'm great. Ou," Tatiana said, and then she saw a sad reluctance in Marina that she had not seen at first, so wrapped up was she in her own upset haze. Focusing, she studied Marina for a moment. She couldn't see. Reaching out, she touched Marina's face. Marina blinked. Tatiana saw. "Who is home, Marina?" Tatiana asked quietly. "Who are you going home to?"

"No one," Marina replied, just as quietly. "Mama's in the hospital. Papa's gone. Down the hall, the Lublins—"

"Marinka," Tatiana said softly, "don't stay by yourself. Come and live with us. We have room now. Deda and Babushka have left. You don't want to be alone. Come on. You'll sleep with Dasha and me."

"Really?" Marina said.

Tatiana nodded. "Really."

"Tania, have you asked your parents about this?"

"I don't need to. Just pack your things and come. Your mother is my father's sister. He will not say no. Come, all right?"

Marina gave Tatiana a hug. "Thank you," she whispered. "I've been feeling so alone in those rooms without Mama and Papa."

Tatiana patted Marina, and said, "I know— Look! Your bus!"

Waving to Tatiana, Marina ran across Nevsky to catch her bus, and Tatiana sat on the bench and waited for her tram to go back home.

She felt sick to her stomach.

Her tram came; the doors opened. The conductor looked at her. Tatiana shook her head. The tram left.

How could she not go to see him? *She could not stay away from him.*

Getting up, Tatiana limped past the Admiralty Gardens to St. Isaac's.

Two soldiers were walking toward her. Stopping in front of Tatiana, they banged their rifles on the pavement and asked where she was headed. She told them.

One soldier said St. Isaac's was closed this time of night. She said yes, but she was looking for a Lieutenant Belov. They knew him, and their serious faces relaxed. One soldier said, "I told you, Viktor, that we should have enrolled in officers' school, and you didn't believe me."

"I thought it'd be more work, not more—" He glanced at Tatiana and broke off. "And who are you?"

"His cousin from Krasnodar."

"Oh. Cousin," said Viktor. "Well, come with us. We'll take you to him. I don't know how you're going to get up to the observation arcade with that cast. It's about two hundred steps up a spiral staircase."

"I'll make it," Tatiana said.

St. Isaac's had never seemed so far away from Nevsky, even though it was less than a kilometer. By the time they got to the cathedral, she was panting and her leg was throbbing. In front of the cathedral on the banks of the Neva, Tatiana saw the shape of the statue of Peter the Great on his steed—the Bronze Horseman—a faint silhouette covered with a wooden form filled with canvas and sand. The Bronze Horseman was built by Catherine the Great as a tribute to Peter the Great for building Leningrad. Tonight nothing could be seen of the black horse or the majestic rider or his outstretched hand; just sandbags to protect the statue from the Germans.

Viktor said, "Tomorrow they're going to impose a curfew on the whole city. No more evening excursions. So make this meeting with Lieutenant Belov count, *cousin.*"

They brought her inside the cavernous granite hall. She heard the light beating of the pendulum the Communists had placed inside the cathedral to turn the place of worship into a science museum.

The guard at the narrow opening to the staircase asked if Tatiana was clean.

"Well, I think so. She's not carrying any bombs."

"Did you search her?"

"Let me," said Viktor. He ran his hands over her ribs, making Tatiana grimace. She felt an increasing anxiety. Being alone with three soldiers in a dark, ominous building, with Alexander high up and unable to hear her, made her fear things she could not imagine. It was an irrational fear, she told herself, as Viktor's hands moved down to her hips. He held her a little tighter, and suddenly her fear got the better of her. "Maybe one of you can just," she said, trying to step away, "let him know I'm here." She took another breath. "You know what? I'll just be getting back. You can tell him I stopped by."

A voice coming down from the staircase said, "Let go of her." It was Alexander, who appeared in the doorway with his rifle. Tatiana breathed immediate relief.

Viktor quickly let go. "Nothing to it, Lieutenant. We were just checking her for weapons. She says she is your cousin from—"

"Private!" Alexander came up close to Viktor, towering over him. "We have standards, Private, even in the Red Army. These standards do not allow us to menace young girls. Unless you want to face disciplinary action, I suggest you don't let me catch you doing that again." He put his hand on Tatiana's back and said to his men, "You two, go back on the street where you belong. Corporal, you stay here until you're relieved by Petrenko and Kapov."

"Yes, sir," the three soldiers said in unison. The corporal took his post by the doorway.

Alexander was trying not to smile. "It's quite a hike up," he said, his hand on her back, prodding her to the staircase. "Come on." When they were around a column and not seen by anyone's eyes, Alexander smiled broadly. "Tania . . ." he said, "I'm *so* happy you came to see me."

Sighing, melting, warming, Tatiana said softly, "Me, too."

"Did they scare you? They're harmless," he said, stroking her hair.

"If they're so harmless, why did you come down?"

"I heard your voice and theirs. They're harmless, but you sounded scared." He was looking at her so . . .

"What?" Tatiana said shyly.

"Nothing." Alexander crouched in front of her. "Go on. Grab my neck. Remember how to do this?"

"You're going to carry me up two hundred stairs?"

"It's the least I can do after you came all this way. Can you hold my weapon?"

Holding on to the rails, he propelled himself up with her hands around his neck. Hoping he wouldn't notice, Tatiana silently kissed the back of his military tunic.

Alexander brought her into a glassed-in circular arcade with five columns that partially obstructed the view of the horizon and the sky. Setting her down, he took his rifle from her and propped it against the wall of the gold dome. "We have to go out on the balcony for a clearer view. Will you be all right?" He smiled. "We're very high up. You're not afraid of heights, are you?"

"I'm not afraid of heights, no," Tatiana said, looking up at him.

They walked out onto a narrow outdoor balcony deck circling the arcade above the rotunda. A short iron railing ran around the deck. The view from up here would have been quite striking, Tatiana thought, if only Leningrad weren't prepared for war. All the lights were extinguished, and in the black of night she could not make out even the white airships floating silently in the dark sky. The air was cool and smelled of fresh water.

"What do you think? Nice up here?" Alexander said, coming up to her. Tatiana couldn't move if she wanted to. She was between him and the railing.

"Mmm," she said, peering into the night, afraid to look at him, afraid to let him see her heart. "What do you do here all by yourself, night in and night out?"

"Nothing. Sit on the floor. Smoke. Think."

Alexander threaded his arms around her waist and closed his hands on her stomach, pressing her into him. She felt his lips at her neck whisper, "Oh, Tatia . . ."

How instant it was, desire. It was like a bomb exploding, fragmenting and igniting all her nerve endings.

Not desire.

Burning desire for Alexander.

Tatiana tried to move aside, but he held her too tightly. All she wanted was to sink to the ground. Why was that? Why, every time he touched her, did she want to lie down? "Shura, wait," she said, not recognizing her own voice, which, thick with longing, said, *Come here, come, come.* Tatiana closed her eyes, muttering, "I don't see any planes."

"Me neither."

"Are they coming?" She moaned softly.

"Yes. The placards are finally right. The enemy *is* at the gates." He continued to kiss her under the wisps of her hair.

"Do you think there is any chance we could get out?"

"Not a chance. You're trapped in the city." His hot breath and his moist lips on her neck were making her shiver.

"How will it be?"

He didn't answer.

"You said you wanted to talk to me . . ." Tatiana said hoarsely.

"Talk?" Alexander said, holding her stomach tight against him.

"Yes, talk . . . to me . . . about . . ." She couldn't remember what. "Dimitri?"

He pulled her blouse away and kissed her shoulder blade. "I like your blouse," he whispered, his mouth on her skin.

"Stop it, Shura, *please*."

"No," he said, rubbing against her back. "I can't stop." He breathed into her hair. "Any more than I can stop breathing."

Alexander's hands moved to rest below her breasts. Her healing ribs hurt slightly and exquisitely from his touch, and Tatiana couldn't help herself, she moaned. Squeezing her tighter, he turned her around to him, his mouth on her throat and whispered, "No, you can't make a sound. Everything carries downstairs. You can't let them hear you."

"Then take your hands off me," Tatiana whispered back. "Or cover my mouth."

"I'll cover your mouth, all right," he said, kissing her fervidly.

After three seconds Tatiana was ready to pass out. "Shura," she moaned, grasping on to him. "God, you need to stop. How do we stop?" The pulling in her stomach was fierce.

"We don't."

"We do."

"We *don't*," he repeated, his lips on her.

"I don't mean . . . I mean, *this*? How do we ever get relief from *this*? I can't go through my days like this, thinking of you. How do we get relief?"

Alexander pulled back from her lips. "The only thing I want in my *whole* life," he whispered hotly, "is to show you how we get relief, Tania." His hands held her to him in a vise.

Tatiana remembered Marina's words. *You are just a conquest to a soldier.* And despite herself, despite the unflappable certainty in the things she believed to be true, despite the shining moment with Alexander at the top of the sacred cathedral up in the Leningrad sky, Tatiana's worst got the better of her. Not trusting her own instincts, scared and doubting, she pushed Alexander away.

"What's the matter?" he said. "What?"

Tatiana fought for her courage, struggled for the right words, afraid of asking, afraid of hearing his answer, afraid of making him angry or upset. He didn't deserve it, and in the end she trusted and believed in him so much that it made her like herself less to think that she would give the cynical Marina any credit for her ill-chosen words. Yet the words sat in her chest and churned in her anxious, aching stomach.

Tatiana didn't want to burden Alexander. She knew he was already carrying plenty. At the same time she could not continue to let him touch her. His hands were tenderly caressing her from her hips up to her hair and back down again. "What's the matter?" Alexander whispered. "Tania, tell me, what?"

"Wait," she said. "Shura, can you—" She limped sideways from him. "Wait, just stop, all right?"

He didn't come after her, and she was a couple of meters away in the arcade when she sank to the floor and gathered her knees to her chest.

"Talk to me about Dimitri," she said, feeling slightly deflated.

"No," Alexander said, continuing to stand. He folded his arms. "Not until you tell me what's bothering you."

Tatiana shook her head. She just couldn't have this conversation with him. "I'm fine. Really." She smiled. Did she manage a good smile? Not according to his long face.

"Just—It's nothing."

"All the more reason to tell me."

Looking down at her long brown skirt, at her toes peeking out from the cast, Tatiana took a few deep breaths. "Shura, this is very, very difficult for me."

"I know," he said, crouching where he stood, his arms coming to rest on his knees.

"I don't know how to say this to you," she said without lifting her head.

"Open your mouth and speak to me," said Alexander. "Like always."

Tatiana couldn't find her nerve. "Alexander, there are too many more important things for us to resolve, to discuss—" Tatiana managed a quick glance at him. He was studying her with curiosity and concern. "I can't believe I'm wasting our minutes like this—" She stopped. "But . . ." He said nothing. "Am I . . . ?" It was so stupid. What did she know of these things? She sighed. "Listen, you know who helped me get out to see you tonight? My cousin Marina."

Alexander nodded, unsmiling. "Good. What does she have to do with us? Am I ever going to meet this girl?"

"You might not want to after I tell you what she told me . . ." Tatiana paused. "About soldiers." She lifted her eyes. Alexander's suddenly comprehending and upset face was filled with annoyance, and guilt.

That was not what she wanted to see. "She told me some interesting things."

"I bet she did."

"She wasn't talking about you—"

"That's a relief."

"She was trying to warn me about Dimitri, but she said that to soldiers all girls were just a big conquest party and notches in their belt." Tatiana stopped talking. She thought it was very brave of her to get out even this much.

Slowly Alexander moved over to Tatiana. He didn't touch her; he just sat by her quietly and finally said, "Do you have a question for me?"

"Do you want a question?"

"No."

"I won't ask you then."

"I didn't say I wouldn't answer it. I said I didn't want it."

Tatiana wished she could look into Alexander's face. She just didn't want to see the guilt there again. And she thought, what if, after our summer, after Kirov, after Luga, after all the unfathomable, breath-dissolving things that I have felt—what if after all that, I will right now find out that Marina was right about Alexander, too? Tatiana could not ask. Yet to have so much of what she felt be built on a lie . . . How could she not?

"What's your question?" Alexander repeated, so softly, so patiently, so *everything* of what he had been to her, that Tatiana, strengthened by him, as always, opened her mouth and in her smallest voice said, "Shura, is that what I am . . . just another conquest to you? Just more difficult? Am I, too, just another young, difficult notch in *your* belt?" She lifted her uncertain, vulnerable eyes to him.

Alexander enveloped her in his arms whole, all gathered together like a tiny bandaged package. Kissing her head, he whispered, "I don't know what I am going to do with you." Pulling away slightly, he cupped her face. His eyes sparkled. "Tatiasha," he said beseechingly, "what are you *talking* about? Have you forgotten the hospital? Conquest? Have you forgotten that if I wanted to, that night, or the following night, or any night that followed, I could have taken it from you standing?" He stared at her and said, even more quietly, "And you would have given it to me standing. Have you forgotten that it was I who put a stop to our senseless desperation?"

Tatiana shut her eyes.

Alexander held her face firmly in his hands. "Come on, open your eyes and look at me. Look at me, Tania."

She opened her mortified and emotional eyes to find Alexander gazing at her with unremitting tenderness. "Tania, please. You're not my conquest, you're not a notch in my belt. I know how difficult it is, what you are feeling. I wish you wouldn't worry yourself for a second with things you *know* to be plainly not true." He kissed her passionately. "Do you feel my lips?" Alexander whispered. "When I kiss you"—he kissed her tenderly—"don't you feel my lips? What are they telling you? What are my hands telling you?"

Tatiana closed her eyes and moaned. Why did she feel so helpless near him, why? It occurred to her that not only was he right, not only would she have given it to him *then*, but she would give it to him *now*, on the cold hard floor of the gilded rotunda. When she opened her eyes, Alexander was looking at her and smiling lightly. "Perhaps," he said softly, "what you should be asking me is not, *are* you another notch in my belt, but why *aren't* you another notch in my belt?"

Tatiana's hands were trembling as she held his sleeves. "All right," she whispered. "Why?"

Alexander laughed.

Tatiana cleared her throat. "Do you know what else Marina told me?"

"Oh, that Marina," said Alexander, sighing and moving away. "What else did Marina tell you?"

Tatiana curled back into her knees. "Marina told me," she said, "that *all* soldiers have it off with garrison hacks nonstop and never say no."

"My, my," said Alexander, shaking his head. "That Marina is trouble. It's a good thing you *didn't* get off the bus to go and see her that Sunday in June."

"I agree," said Tatiana, her face melting at the memory of them on that bus.

And his face melted back.

What was she even thinking? What was she even doing? Tatiana shook her head, upset at herself.

"Now, listen to me. I didn't want to tell you any of this, but . . ." Alexander drew a deep breath. "When I first got into the army, I saw that genuine relationships with women were going to be very difficult because of the nature of our confinement"—he shrugged—"and the realities of Soviet life. No rooms, no apartments, no hotels for the Soviet man and the Soviet woman to go to. You want the truth from me? Here it is. I don't want you to be afraid of it or afraid of me because of it. On our weekend furlough, it is true, we would go out for some beers and often find ourselves in the presence of all kinds of young women, who were quite willing to . . . knock around with soldiers without any strings attached." Alexander stopped.

"And did you"—Tatiana held her breath—"knock around?"

"Once or twice," Alexander replied. He didn't look at her. "Don't be upset by this, please."

"I'm not upset," Tatiana mouthed. Stunned, yes. Torn with self-doubt, yes. Entranced by you, yes again.

"We were all just having a bit of youthful fun. I kept myself extremely unattached and detached. I hated entanglements—"

"What about Dasha?"

"What about her?" Alexander said tiredly.

"Was Dasha . . . ?" Tatiana couldn't get the words out.

"Tatia, please," said Alexander, shaking his head. "Don't think about these things. Ask Dasha what kind of a girl she was. I'm not the one to tell you."

"Alexander, but Dasha is an entanglement!" Tatiana exclaimed. "Dasha does have strings attached to her. Dasha has her heart."

"No," he said. "She has *you*."

Tatiana sighed heavily. This was too hard for her—talking about Alexander and her sister. Hearing about Alexander and meaningless girls was easier than hearing about one Dasha. Tatiana sat with her hands around her knees. She wanted to ask him about the present time but couldn't get the words out. She didn't want to ask him about anything. She wanted to go back to how it was before the night in the hospital, before the wretched confusion of her body blinded her to the truth she felt about him.

Alexander rubbed her thighs. "I can feel you're afraid." Quietly, he added, "Tania, I beg you—don't let stupidity come between us."

"All right," she said with remorse.

"Don't let bullshit that has nothing to do with us keep you away from me. We already have so much keeping you away from me." He paused. "Everything."

"All right, Alexander."

"Let it all fall away, Tatiana. What are you afraid of?"

"I'm afraid of being wrong about you," she whispered.

"Tania, how could you of all people be wrong about me?" Alexander clenched his fists in frustration. "Can't you see," he said, "it's exactly because of who I had been that I came to you? What's the matter?" he asked. "You couldn't see my loneliness?"

"Barely," Tatiana replied, clutching her hands to her chest, "through my own." Falling back against the railing, Tatiana said, "Shura, I'm surrounded by half-truth and innuendo. You and I don't have a moment to talk anymore, like we used to, a moment to be alone—"

"A moment of privacy," said Alexander, speaking the last word in English.

"Of what?" She didn't know that word. She would have to look it up when she got home. "What about now? Besides Dasha, are you still—"

"Tatiana," said Alexander, "all the things you're worried about—they're gone from my life. Do you know why? Because when I met you, I knew that if I continued and a good girl like you ever asked me about them, I wouldn't be able to look you in the face and tell you the truth. I would have to look you in the face and lie." He was looking into her face. The wordless truth was in his eyes.

Tatiana smiled at him and breathed out, the tight, sick feeling in her stomach dissolving with her exhaled breath. She wanted him to come and hug her. "I'm sorry, Alexander," she whispered "I'm sorry for my doubt. I'm just too young."

"You're too much of everything," he said. "God!" he exclaimed. "How insane this is—never to have the time to explain, to talk anything out, never to have a minute—"

We've had a minute, Tatiana thought. We had our minutes on the bus. And at Kirov. We had our minutes in Luga. And in the Summer Garden. Breathless minutes, we had. What we want, she thought, keeping herself from welling up, is eternity.

"I'm sorry, Shura," Tatiana said, grasping his hands. "I didn't mean to upset you."

"Tania, if only we could have a moment of privacy," Alexander said, again speaking the last word in English, "you would never doubt me again."

"What is this privacy?" she repeated.

Alexander smiled sadly. "Being secluded from the view or from the presence of other human beings. When we need to be alone together to have intimacy, that's impossible in two rooms with six other people," he explained in Russian. "We say, we want some privacy."

"Oh." Tatiana blushed. So that was the word she had been searching for, ever since she met him! "There is no word for anything like that in Russian."

"I know," he said.

"And there is a word for this in America?"

"Yes," said Alexander. "Privacy."

Tatiana remained silent.

Alexander slid closer, putting both his legs around her. "Tania, when will we next have a moment alone?" he asked, peering into her eyes.

"We're alone now," she said.

"When will I next be able to kiss you?"

"Kiss me now," she whispered.

But Alexander didn't. He said grimly, "Do you know that it might be never? The Germans are here. Do you know what that means? Life, as you knew it, is over."

"What about this summer?" she asked. "Nothing's been quite the same since June 22."

"No, it hasn't," he agreed. "But before today we were simply arming ourselves. Now it's war. Leningrad will be the battleground for your freedom. And at the end, how many of us will be left standing? How many of us will be free?"

Oh, God. "Is that why you come every chance you get, even if it means dragging Dimitri with you?" Tatiana asked.

With a small nod and a large sigh, Alexander said, "I'm always afraid it'll be the last time I'm going to see your face."

Tatiana swallowed, curled into her knees. "Why . . . *do* you always drag him with you?" she asked. "Can't you ask him to leave me alone? He doesn't listen to me. What am I going to do with him?"

Alexander made no reply, and Tatiana anxiously tried to catch his eye. "Tell me about Dimitri, Shura," she said quietly. "What do you owe him?"

Alexander looked at his cigarettes.

Faintly Tatiana said, "Do you owe him . . . me?"

"Tatiana," Alexander said, "Dimitri knows who I am."

"Stop," she uttered almost inaudibly.

"If I tell you, you won't believe it," Alexander said. "Once I tell you, there will be no going back for us."

"There is no going back for us now," Tatiana said, and wanted to mouth a prayer.

"I don't know what to do about him," Alexander said.

"I will help you," said Tatiana, her heart scared and swelling. "Tell me."

Alexander moved away on the narrow balcony to sit diagonally across from her against the wall, stretching his legs out to her. Tatiana continued to sit against the railing. She sensed he didn't want her too close. Taking off her one shoe, Tatiana stretched her bare feet out to his boots. Her foot was half the size of his.

Shuddering as if trying to stave off a beast, Alexander began. "When my mother was arrested," he said, not looking at Tatiana, "the NKVD came for me, too. I wasn't even able to say good-bye to her." Alexander looked away. "I don't like to talk about my mother, as you can imagine. I was accused of distributing some capitalist propaganda when I had been fourteen, still in Moscow, and going to Communist Party meetings with my father. So at seventeen, in Leningrad, I was arrested and taken right to Kresty, the inner-city prison for nonpolitical criminals. They didn't have room for me at Shpalerka, the Big House, the political detention center. I was convicted *in camera* in about three hours," Alexander said with scorn. "They didn't even bother with an interrogation. I think all their interrogators were tied up with more important prisoners. I got ten years in Vladivostok. Can you imagine?"

"No," said Tatiana.

"You know how many of us finally got on that train headed for Vladivostok? A thousand. One man said to me, 'Oh, I just got out, and now this again.' He told me the prison camp we were going to had 80,000 people in it. Eighty thousand, Tania! One camp. I told him I didn't believe it. I had just turned seventeen." Alexander looked at her. "Like you are now." He continued, "What could I do? I couldn't spend *ten* years of my youth in prison, could I?"

"No," she said.

"I had always believed, you see, that I was meant to live a good life. My mother and father believed in me. I believed in myself—" He broke off. "Prison never entered into it. I never stole, I never broke windows, I didn't terrorize old ladies. I did nothing wrong. I wasn't going. So," he said, "we were crossing the river Volga, near Kazan, thirty meters up over a precipice. I knew it was either now or I was going to Vladivostok for what seemed to me like the rest of my life. I had too much hope for myself. So I jumped right into the river." Alexander laughed. "They didn't even stop the train. They thought for sure I had died in the fall."

"They didn't know who they were dealing with," said Tatiana, wanting to put her arms around him, but he was too far away. "When you jumped, was that when you found out you indeed could swim?" She smiled.

Alexander smiled back. The soles of his boots were touching the soles of her feet. "I could swim a little bit."

"Did you have anything on you?"

"Nothing."

"Papers? Money?"

"Nothing." Tatiana thought Alexander wanted to tell her something else, but he continued. "It was the summer of 1936. After I escaped, I made my way south on the Volga, on fishing boats, by foot, in the back of horse carriages. I fished, worked briefly on farms, and moved on south. From Kazan to Ulyanovsk, where Lenin was born—interesting city, like a shrine. Then to Saratov, downstream on the Volga, fishing, harvesting, moving on. Wound up in Krasnodar, near the Black Sea. I was headed down south into Georgia, and then Turkey. I hoped to cross the border somewhere in the Caucasus Mountains."

"But you had no money."

"None," Alexander said. "But I made some along the way, and I did think that my English, once I got into Turkey, would help me. But in Krasnodar, fate intervened." He glanced at her. "As always. It was a brutal winter, and the family I was staying with, the Belovs—"

"The Belovs?" exclaimed Tatiana.

Alexander nodded. "A nice farming family. Father, mother, four sons, one daughter." He cleared his throat. "Me. We all got typhus. The entire village of Belyi Yar—360 people—got typhus. Eight-tenths of the village population perished, including the Belovs, the daughter first. The local council from Krasnodar, with the help of the police, came and burned down the village, for fear that the epidemic would spread to the nearby city. All my clothes were burned, and I was quarantined until I either died or got better. I got better. The local *Soviet* councilman came to issue me new papers. Without a moment's hesitation I said I was Alexander Belov. Since they burned the village in its entire—" Alexander raised his eyebrows. "Only in the Soviet Union. Anyway, since they burned the village, the councilman could not confirm or deny my claim to be Alexander Belov, the youngest Belov boy."

Tatiana closed her mouth.

"So I was issued a brand-new domestic passport and a brand-new identity. I was Alexander Nikolaevich Belov, born in Krasnodar, orphaned at seventeen." He looked away.

"What was your full American name?" asked Tatiana faintly.

"Anthony Alexander Barrington."

"Anthony!" she exclaimed.

Alexander shook his head. "Anthony was for my mother's father. I myself was never anything but Alexander." He pulled out a cigarette. "You don't mind?"

Tatiana shook her head.

"Anyway," he said, "I returned to Leningrad and went to stay with relatives of the Belovs. I needed to be back in Leningrad—" Alexander hesitated. "I'll tell you why in a minute. I stayed with my 'aunt,' Mira Belov, and her family. They lived on the Vyborg side. They hadn't seen their nephews in a decade; it was ideal. I was like a stranger to them." He smiled. "But they let me stay. I finished school. And it was in this school that I met Dimitri."

"Oh, Alexander," said Tatiana. "I cannot believe what you lived through when you were so young."

"I'm far from finished. Dimitri was one of the kids I played with at school. He was spindly, unpopular, and never much fun. When we played war at recess, he was always the one taken prisoner. Dimitri POW Chernenko we used to call him. We said that for him alone the Soviet Union should have signed the 1929 Geneva Convention, because he was getting himself wounded or taken prisoner or killed every time we played, managing to get himself caught somehow without help from anyone."

"Please go on."

"But then I found out that his father was a prison guard at Shpalerka." Alexander stopped.

Tatiana stopped breathing. "Your parents were still alive?"

"I didn't know," Alexander said. "So I *chose* to become close to Dimitri. I hoped that maybe he could help me see my mother and father. I knew that if they were alive, they would be tortured by their worries about me. I wanted to let them know I was all right." He paused. "My mother particularly," he said, his voice controlled. "We had been very close once."

Tatiana's eyes filled with tears. "What about your father?"

With a shrug, Alexander said, "He was my father. We had some conflict in the last years. What can I say? He thought he knew everything. I thought I knew everything. So it went."

Tatiana did not blink as she stared at Alexander, transfixed. "Shura, they must have loved you so much." She swallowed hard.

"Yes," Alexander said, taking a deep, pained drag of the cigarette. "They did once love me."

Tatiana's heart was breaking for Alexander.

"Little by little," he continued, "I gained Dimitri's confidence, and we became better and better friends. Dima really liked the fact that I picked him out of many to be my closest friend."

"Oh, Shura," said Tatiana. She understood. Crawling to him, Tatiana wrapped her arms around Alexander. "You had to *trust* Dimitri."

With one arm he hugged her back. The other held his cigarette. "Yes. I had to tell him who I was. I had no choice but to trust him. Leave my parents to die, or trust him."

"You *trusted* Dimitri," Tatiana repeated incredulously, letting go of him and sitting close by his side.

"Yes." Alexander looked down into his large hands, as if trying to find the answer to his life in them. "I didn't want to trust him. My father, the good Communist that he was, taught me never to trust anyone, and though it wasn't easy, I learned that lesson well. But it's a hard way to live, and I wanted to trust just one person in my life. Just one. I really needed Dimitri's help. Besides, I was his friend. I said to myself that if he did this for me and I got to see my mother and father, I would be his friend for life. And that's exactly what I told him. 'Dima,' I said, 'I will be your friend for life. I will help you in any way that I can.'" Alexander lit another cigarette. Tatiana waited, the aching in her chest increasing.

"Dimitri's father found out that I was too late to see my mother." Alexander's voice cracked. "He told me what had happened to her. But my father was still alive, though apparently not for long. He'd already been in prison for nearly a year. Chernenko got Dimitri and me inside Shpalerka, and then we had five minutes with the foreign infiltrator, Harold Barrington. Me, my father, Dimitri, his father, and another guard. No *privacy* for me and my father."

Tatiana took Alexander's hand. "How was that?"

Alexander stared straight ahead. "Pretty much how you imagine it might be," he said, keeping his voice even. "And bitterly brief."

In the small gray concrete cell, Alexander looked at his father, and Harold Barrington looked at Alexander. Harold did not move from his bed.

Dimitri stood in the center of the small cell, Alexander to the side. The guard and Dimitri's father were behind them. A single lightbulb hung from the ceiling.

In Russian, Dimitri said to Harold, "We are here for only a minute, comrade. You understand? Just for a minute."

"All right," replied Harold in Russian, blinking back tears. "Thank you for coming to see me. I'm happy to see two Soviet boys. Your name, son?" he asked Dimitri.

"Dimitri Chernenko."

"And your name, son?" His body shaking, Harold looked at Alexander.

"Alexander Belov," said Alexander.

Harold nodded.

The guard said, "All right, enough gawking at the prisoner. Let's go."

Dimitri said, "Wait! We just wanted the comrade to know that despite his crime against our proletarian society, he will not be forgotten."

Alexander said nothing, his eyes on his father.

"It's because of his crime against our society that he will not be forgotten," said the guard.

Chewing his lips, Harold looked at Dimitri and Alexander, whose back was to the guard but whose face was to his father.

"Popov, can I shake their hands?" Harold asked the guard.

The guard shrugged, stepping forward. "I'm going to watch you do it. Make it quick."

Alexander said, "I've never heard English before, Comrade Barrington. Can you say something for us in English?"

Harold came up to Dimitri and shook his hand. "Thank you," he said in English.

Then he came up to Alexander and took his hand, holding it tightly between his. Alexander shook his head slightly, trying to will his father to stay calm.

In English, Harold whispered, "Would that I had died for thee, O Absalom, my son, my son!"

Alexander mouthed, Stop.

Letting go of Alexander's hand, Harold stepped slightly away, struggling not to cry and failing. "I'll tell you something in English," he said in Russian. "A few corrupted lines from Kipling."

"Enough," said the guard. "I have no time—"

"If you can bear to hear the truth you've spoken," Harold said loudly in En-

glish, "twisted by knaves to make a trap for fools . . ." *Tears rolled down his face.* "Or watch the things you gave your life to, broken . . ." *He was down to a whisper.* "Son!—stoop and build them up with worn-out tools." *Harold stepped back and made a small sign of the cross on Alexander.*

"*Let's go!*" *yelled the guard.*

Alexander mouthed to his father, in English, "I love you, Dad."

Then they left.

Tatiana was crying. Alexander put his arm around her, and said, "Oh, Tania . . ." He wiped her face. "From the effort to remain composed," he told her, "I cracked one of my side teeth. See?" He showed her an upper bicuspid. "Now you can stop asking me about it. So I did get to see my father once before he died, and I never would have been able to do it without Dimitri." With a heavy breath, he took his arm away.

"Alexander," said Tatiana, crouching beside him, "you did an unbelievable thing for your father." Her lips trembled. "You gave him comfort before his death." Feeling very shy, yet overwhelmed by her emotion, her throbbing heart overfilled with him, she took hold of Alexander's hand, bent her head to it, and kissed it. Blushing and clearing her throat, she let go of him and raised her eyes.

"Tania," he said with feeling, "who *are* you?"

She replied, "I am Tatiana." And gave him her hand. They sat silently.

"There is more."

She nodded. "The rest I know." Tatiana took Alexander's pack of cigarettes and pulled one out. She had needed just a little truth to see the whole. She knew the rest at the point Alexander told her that he gave Dimitri something Dimitri had never had before. It wasn't friendship, and it wasn't companionship, and it wasn't brotherhood. Tatiana's hands were shaking as she put the cigarette into Alexander's mouth, and reached for his lighter. Flicking it on, she brought it to his face, and when he inhaled, she kissed his cheek and extinguished the light.

"Thank you," Alexander said, smoking down half the cigarette before he continued. He kissed her. "You're not crazy about smoker's breath?"

"I'll take your breath any way you give it to me, Shura," said Tatiana, blushing again. Then she spoke. "Let me tell you the rest. You and Dimitri enrolled in university. You and Dimitri joined the army. You and Dimitri went to officers' school together. And then Dimitri didn't make it." She lowered her head. "At first he was all right with it. You remained best friends. He knew you would do anything for him." She paused. "And then," Tatiana said, raising her eyes, "he started asking."

"I see," said Alexander. "So you do know everything."

"What does he ask you for, Shura?"

"You name it."

They didn't look at each other.

"He asks you to transfer him here, to make exceptions for him there, he asks you for special privileges and for special treatment."

"Yes."

"Anything else?"

Alexander was mute for a few minutes. It was such a long time that Tatiana thought he had forgotten her question. She waited patiently. Finally Alexander said, his voice filled with *something*, "Very occasionally, girls. You'd think there was plenty for everyone, but every once in a while I would be with a girl Dimitri wanted to be with. He'd ask me, and I'd back off. I just went and found myself a new girl, and things went on as before."

Tatiana stared ahead, her eyes the clearest sea green. "Alexander, tell me something. When Dimitri asked you for a girl, he only asked for one you actually liked, right?"

"What do you mean?"

"He didn't want just any of your girls. He asked you for girls that he saw you liked. That's when he asked. Right?"

Alexander was pensive. "I guess."

Slowly Tatiana said, "So when he asked you for me, you just backed off."

"Wrong. What I did was show him my indifferent face, hoping that if he thought you didn't matter to me, he would leave you alone. Unfortunately, that has backfired."

Tatiana nodded, then shook her head, then started to cry. "Yes, you're not doing such a good job with your face, Shura. He won't leave me alone."

"Please." Alexander brought her into his arms. "I told you this was a dire mess. I can back off you now as far as Japan for all he cares. Because now Dimitri has fallen for you and wants you for himself." He stopped.

Tatiana studied Alexander for a few moments and then pressed herself into him. "Shura," she said quietly, "I'm going to tell you something right now, all right? Are you listening?"

"Yes."

"Don't hold your breath like that." She managed a smile. "What do you think I'm about to say?"

"I don't know. I'm ill equipped to guess at the moment. Maybe you have a small child living with a distant aunt?"

Tatiana laughed lightly. "No." She paused. "But are you ready?"

"Yes."

Tatiana said, "Dimitri has not fallen for me."

Alexander pulled away from her.

She shook her head. "No. Not at all. Not even remotely. Believe me when I tell you."

"How do you know?"

"I *know*."

"So what does he want with you then? Don't even suggest—"

"Not with me. All Dimitri wants—listen carefully—all he craves, all he desires, all he *covets* is power. That's the only thing that's important to him. That's the love of his life. Power."

"Power over you?"

"No, Alexander! Power over *you*. I'm just a means to an end. I'm just ammunition."

When he looked at her skeptically, she continued. "Dimitri doesn't have any. You have it all. All he has is what he has over you. That's his whole life." She shook her head. "How sad for him."

"Sad for him!" Alexander exclaimed. "Whose side are you on?"

Tatiana didn't speak for a moment. "Shura, look at *you*. And look at *him*. Dimitri needs you, he is fed and sheltered and grown by you, and if you're stronger, he becomes stronger, too. He knows that and depends on you blindly for so many things that you are glad to provide. And yet . . . the more *you* have, the more he hates you. Self-preservation may be his driving force, but all the same, every time you get a promotion, you go up in rank, you get a new medal, you get a new girl, every time you laugh with joy in the smoky corridor, it diminishes and lessens *him*. Which is why the more powerful you become, the more he wants from you."

"Eventually," said Alexander, glancing at Tatiana, "he is going to want from me something I can't give. And then what?"

"Coveting from you the best of what you have will eventually lead him into hell."

"Yes, but me into death." Alexander shook his head. "Unspoken underneath all his pleas and requests is that one word from him about my American past to the NKVD general at the garrison, one vague accusation, and I instantly vanish into the maw of Soviet justice."

Nodding sadly, Tatiana said, "I know it. But maybe if he *had* more, he wouldn't *want* so much."

"You're wrong, Tania. I have a bad feeling about Dimitri. I have a feeling he is going to want more and more from me. Until," Alexander said, "he takes it all."

"No, *you're* wrong, Shura. Dimitri will never take *all* away from you. He will never have that much power." He might want to. He just doesn't know who he is dealing with, Tatiana thought, raising her venerating eyes to Alexander. "Besides, we all know what happens to the parasite when something happens to the host," she whispered.

Alexander gazed down at her. "Yes. He finds himself a new host. Let me ask you," he finally said, "what do you think Dimitri wants the most from me?"

"What you want most."

"But, Tania," said Alexander intensely, "it's you that I want most."

Tatiana looked into his face. "Yes, Shura," she said. "And he knows it. As I said from the beginning—Dimitri has not fallen for me at all. All he wants is to hurt *you*."

Alexander was quiet for a spate of eternity under the August sky.

So was Tatiana until she whispered, "Where is your brave and indifferent face? Put it on and he will back away and ask you to give him what you wanted most before me."

Alexander did not move and did not speak.

"Before me." Why was he so silent? "Shura?" She thought she felt him shudder.

"Tania, stop. I can't talk to you about this anymore."

She could not steady her hands. "All of this—all this between us, and my Dasha, too, now and forever, and still you come for me every chance you can."

"I told you, I cannot stay away from you," said Alexander.

Flinching with sadness, Tatiana said, "God, we need to forget each other, Shura. I can't believe how not meant to be we are."

"You don't say?" Alexander smiled. "I will bet my rifle that your ending up on that bench two months ago was the most *unlikely* part of your day."

He was right. Most of all, Tatiana remembered the bus she had *decided* not to take so she could buy herself an ice cream. "And you would know this how?"

"Because," said Alexander, "my walking by that bench was the most unlikely part of mine." He nodded. "All this wedged between us—and when we do our best, and grit our teeth, and move away from one another, struggling to reconstruct ourselves, fate intervenes again, and bricks fall from the sky that I remove from your alive and broken body. Was that also not meant to be, perhaps?"

Tatiana inhaled a sob. "That's right," she said softly. "We can't forget that I owe you my life." She gazed at him. "We can't forget that I belong to you."

"I like the sound of that," Alexander said, hugging her tighter.

"Retreat, Shura," Tatiana whispered. "Retreat and take your weapons with you. Spare me from him." She paused. "He just needs to believe you don't care for me, and then he will lose all interest. You'll see. He'll go away, he'll go to the front. We all have to get through the war before we get to what's on the other side. So will you do that?"

"I'll do my best."

"Are you going to stop coming around?" she asked tremulously.

"No," said Alexander. "I can't retreat that far. Just stay away from me."

"All right." Her heart skipped. She clutched him.

"And forgive me in advance for my cold face. Can I trust you to do that?"

Nodding, Tatiana rubbed her cheek against his arm, pressing her head to him. "Trust me," she whispered. "Trust *in* me. Alexander Barrington, I will never betray you."

"Yes, but will you ever *deny* me?" he asked tenderly.

"Only in front of my Dasha," she replied. "And your Dimitri."

Lifting her face to him, with an ironic smile Alexander said, "Aren't you glad *now* that God stopped us at the hospital?"

Tatiana smiled lightly back. "No." She sat wrapped in his arms. They stared at each other. She put her palm out to him. He put his palm against hers. "Look," she said quietly. "My fingertips barely come up to your second knuckle."

"I'm looking," he whispered, threading his fingers through hers and squeezing her hand so hard that Tatiana groaned and then blushed.

Bringing his face to hers, Alexander kissed the skin near her nose. "Have I ever told you I adore your freckles?" he murmured. "They are very enticing."

She purred back. Their fingers remained entwined as they kissed.

"Tatiasha . . ." Alexander whispered, "you have amazing lips . . ." He paused and pulled away. "You are"—reluctantly she opened her eyes to meet his gaze—"you are oblivious to yourself. It's one of your most endearing, most infuriating qualities . . ."

"Don't know what you mean . . ." She had no brain left. "Shura, how can there be not a single place in this world we can go?" Her voice broke. "What kind of a life is this?"

"The Communist life," Alexander replied.

They huddled closer.

"You crazy man," she said fondly. "What were you doing fighting with me at Kirov, knowing all this was stacked against us?"

"Raging against my fate," said Alexander. "It's the only fucking thing I ever do. I just refuse to be defeated."

I love you, Alexander, Tatiana wanted to say to him, but couldn't. *I love you.* She bowed her head. "I have too young a heart . . ." she whispered.

Alexander's arms engulfed her. "Tatia," he whispered, "you do have a young heart." He tipped her back a little and kissed her between her breasts. "I wish with all of mine, I wasn't forced to pass it by."

Suddenly he moved away and jumped to his feet. Tatiana herself heard a noise behind them in the arcade. Sergeant Petrenko stuck his head out onto the balcony, saying it was time for a shift change.

Alexander carried Tatiana down on his back, and then, with his arm around her, they hobbled through the city streets, back to Fifth Soviet. It was after two in the morning. Tomorrow their day would begin at six, and yet here they both were, clinging to each other in the last remaining hours of night. He carried her in his arms down Nevsky Prospekt. She carried his rifle. He carried her on his back.

They were very alone as they made their way through dark Leningrad.

7

The next evening after work Tatiana found her mother moaning in the room and Dasha sitting in the hallway, crying into her cup of tea. The Metanovs had just received a telegram from the long-defunct Novgorod command, informing them that on 13 July 1941 the train carrying one Pavel Metanov and hundreds of other young volunteers was blown up by the Germans. There were no survivors.

A week before I went to find him, thought Tatiana, pacing dully through the rooms. What did I do on the day that my brother's train blew up? Did I work, did I ride the tram? Did I even think once of my brother? I've thought of him since. I've felt him not being here since. Dear Pasha, she thought, we lost you and we didn't even know it. That's the saddest loss of all, to go on for a few weeks, a few days, a night, a minute, and think everything is still all right when the structure you've built your life on has crumbled. We should have been mourning you, but instead we made plans, went to work, dreamed, loved, not knowing you were already behind us.

How could we not have known?

Wasn't there a sign? Your reluctance to go? The packed suitcase? The not hearing from you?

Something we could point to so that next time we can say, wait, here is the sign. Next time we will know. And we will mourn right from the start.

Could we have kept you with us longer? Could we have all hung on to you, held you closer, played in the park once more with you to stave off the unforgiving fate for a few more days, a few more Sundays, a few more afternoons? Would that have been worth it, to have you for one more month before you were claimed, before you were lost to us? Knowing your inevitable future, would it have been worth it to see your face for another day, another hour, another minute before you were *blink* and gone?

Yes.

Yes, it would have been worth it. For you. And for us.

Papa was drunk, spread out on the couch, and Mama was wiping the couch, crying into the bucket of water. Tatiana offered to clean up. Mama pushed her away. Dasha was in the kitchen, crying while she was cooking dinner. Tatiana was filled with an acute sense of finality, a sharp anxiety for the days ahead. Anything could happen in a future forged by the incomprehensible present in which her twin brother was no longer alive.

As they prepared dinner, Tatiana said to Dasha, "Dash, a month ago you asked me if I thought Pasha was still alive, and I said—"

"Like I pay any attention to you, Tania," snapped Dasha.

"Why did you ask me?" questioned a surprised Tatiana.

"I thought you were going to give me some comforting pat answer. Listen, I don't want to talk about it. You might not be shocked, but we all are."

When he came for dinner, Alexander raised his questioning eyebrows to Tatiana, who told him about the telegram.

No one ate the cabbage with a little canned ham that Dasha had made, except Alexander and Tatiana, who, despite a small hope, had been living with a lost Pasha since Luga.

Papa remained on the couch, and Mama sat by his side listening to the tick-tock, tick-tock of the radio's metronome.

Dasha went to put the *samovar* on, and Alexander and Tatiana were left alone. He didn't say anything, just bent his head slightly and peered into her face. For a moment they held each other's eyes.

"Courage, Alexander," she whispered.

"Courage, Tatiana."

She left and went out onto the roof, looking for bombs in the chilly Leningrad night. Summer was over. Winter wasn't far off.

Part Two

WINTER'S FIERCE EMBRACE

BESET AND BESIEGED

1

WHAT did it cost the soul to lie? At every step, with every breath, with every Soviet Information Bureau report, with every casualty list and every monthly ration card?

From the moment Tatiana woke up until she fell into a bleary sleep, she lied.

She wished Alexander would stop coming around. *Lies.*

She wished he would end it with Dasha. Alas. *More lies.*

No more trips to St. Isaac's. That was good news. *Lies.*

No more tram rides, no more canals, no more Summer Garden, no more Luga, no more lips or eyes or palpitating breath. Good. Good. Good. *More lies.*

He was cold. He had an uncanny ability to act as if there were nothing behind his smiling face, or his steady hands, or his burned-down cigarette. Not a twitch showed on his face for Tatiana. That was good. *Lies.*

Curfew was imposed on Leningrad at the beginning of September. Rations were reduced again. Alexander stopped coming every day. That was good. *More lies.*

When Alexander came, he was extremely affectionate with Dasha, in front of Tatiana and in front of Dimitri. That was good. *Lies.*

Tatiana put on her own brave face and turned it away and smiled at Dimitri and clenched her heart in a tight fist. She could do it, too. *More lies.*

Pouring tea. Such a simple matter, yet fraught with deceit. Pouring tea, for someone else *before* him. Her hands trembled with the effort.

Tatiana wished she could get out from the spell that was Leningrad at the beginning of September, get out from the circle of misery and love that besieged her.

She loved Alexander. Ah, finally. Something true to hold on to.

After news of Pasha, Papa worked sporadically, being frequently too intoxicated. His being home made it difficult for Tatiana to cook, to clean, to be in the rooms, to read. *More lies.* That's not what made it difficult. It's what made it unpleasant. Sitting on the roof was the only peace left to Tatiana, and even then peace was relative. There was no peace inside her.

While she was on the roof, she closed her eyes and imagined walking, without a cast, without a limp, with Alexander. They walked down Nevsky, to Palace Square, down the embankment, all around the Field of Mars. They meandered across the Fontanka Bridge, through the Summer Garden, and back out onto the embankment, and then to Smolny and then past Tauride Park, to Ulitsa Saltykov-Schedrin, past their bench, and on to Suvorovsky, and home. And as she walked with him, it felt as if she were walking into the rest of her life.

In her mind they had walked along the streets of their summer while she sat on the roof and heard the echo of gunfire and explosions. It was a small solace to think the gunfire wasn't as close as it had been at Luga. Alexander wasn't as close as he had been at Luga either.

Alexander's own visits became as truncated as Tatiana's rations. He was rationing himself the way the Leningrad Council was rationing food. Tatiana missed him, wishing for a second, a moment alone with him again, just to remind herself that the summer of 1941 had not been an illusion, that there had indeed been a time when she had walked along a canal wall, holding his rifle, while he was looking at her and laughing.

There was little laughing nowadays.

"The Germans aren't here yet, right, Alexander?" asked Dasha over tea— the damned tea. "When they come, will we repel von Leeb?"

"Yes," Alexander replied. Tatiana knew. *More lies.*

Tatiana would grimly watch Dasha nuzzling Alexander. She would avert her eyes and say to Dimitri, "Hey, want to hear a joke?"

"What, Tania? No, not really. Sorry, I'm a little preoccupied."

"That's fine," she would say, watching Alexander smile at Dasha. *Lies, lies, and lies.*

All that Alexander was doing wasn't enough. Dimitri wasn't leaving Tatiana alone.

Meanwhile, Tatiana hadn't heard from Marina about coming to live with them, and in the hospital Vera, along with the other nurses, was anxious about the war. Tatiana felt it herself—war was no longer something on the Luga River, something that had swallowed Pasha, something that was fought by the Ukrainians far away in their smoldering villages or by the British in their distant and proper London. It was coming here.

Well, something better come here, Tatiana thought, because I can't imagine continuing this way.

The city seemed to hold its collective breath. Tatiana certainly held hers.

For four nights in a row Tatiana cooked fried cabbage for dinner, with less and less oil each day.

"What the hell are you cooking for us, Tania?" asked Mama.

"You call this cooking?" Papa remarked.

"I can't even dip my bread in the oil. Where is the oil?"

"Couldn't find any," said Tatiana.

The radio offered only the *most* depressing news. Tatiana thought the announcers must deliberately wait until Soviet performance at the front was particularly awful and then begin broadcasting. After Mga fell at the end of August, Tatiana had heard that Dubrovka was under attack—her mother's mother, Babushka Maya, lived in Dubrovka, a rural town just across the river, right outside city limits.

And then Dubrovka fell on September 6.

Suddenly Tatiana got unexpectedly good news, and good news was becoming as hard to come by as oil. Babushka Maya was coming to live with them on Fifth Soviet! Sadly, Mikhail, Mama's stepfather, had died of TB a few days earlier, and when the Germans burned Dubrovka, Babushka Maya escaped to the city.

When Babushka came, she took one room, and Mama and Papa moved back in with Dasha and Tatiana. No more *please, Tania, go away.*

Babushka Maya had lived all her long life in Leningrad and said that it had never even occurred to her to evacuate. "My life, my death, all right here," she told Tatiana as she unpacked.

She had married her first husband back at the turn of the century and had Tatiana's mother. After her husband disappeared in the war of 1905, she never remarried, though she lived with poor tubercular Uncle Mikhail for thirty years. Tatiana had once asked Babushka why she never married Uncle Mikhail, and Babushka had replied, "What if my Fedor comes back, Tanechka? I'd be in quite a pickle then." Babushka painted and studied art; her paintings had hung in galleries before the revolution, but after 1917 she made her living by illustrating propaganda materials for the Bolsheviks. Everywhere in her house in Dubrovka, Tatiana would find sketchbooks filled with pictures of chairs and food and flowers.

After she arrived, Babushka told Tatiana that she didn't have time to get anything out of her house before it burned. "Don't worry, Tanechka. I'll draw you a nice new picture of a chair."

Tatiana said, "Maybe you can draw me a nice apple pie instead? It's the season for them."

The following evening, on September 7, Marina finally arrived—just before dinner. Marina's father had died in the fighting around Izhorsk, died as an untrained assistant gunner in a tank he had made himself. Uncle Boris was beloved by the Metanovs, and his death would have been a terrible blow, had the family not been reeling from their own nightmare of losing Pasha.

Marina's mother remained hospitalized; unrelated to the war, she was slowly dying of renal failure. Tatiana's naïveté surprised even herself. How could anything that happened nowadays be unrelated to the war? First Uncle Misha, now Aunt Rita. There was something universally unfair about that—for people to be dying of causes unrelated to the trenches Alexander had been digging.

Papa looked at Marina's suitcase. Mama looked at Marina's suitcase. Dasha looked at Marina's suitcase. Tatiana said, "Marinka, let me help you unpack."

Papa asked if she was staying for a while, and Tatiana said, "I think so."

"You think so?"

"Papa, her father is dead and your sister is dying. She can stay with us for a while, no?"

"Tania," Marina said, "have you not told Uncle Georg that you invited me? Don't worry, I brought my ration card, Uncle Georg."

Papa glared at Tatiana. Mama glared at Tatiana. Dasha glared at Tatiana.

Tatiana said, "Let's unpack you, Marina."

That night there was a small problem with dinner. The girls had left the food on the stove for a moment, and when they came back to the kitchen, they found that the fried potatoes, onions, and one small fresh tomato had disappeared. The frying pan had been left empty and dirty. A few of the potatoes had stuck to the bottom, and there they remained, encrusted and covered with a bit of oil. Dasha and Tatiana looked around the kitchen incredulously and vacuously, even coming back inside, thinking maybe they had already brought the dinner in and simply forgotten.

The potatoes were gone.

Dasha, because that was her way, dragged Tatiana with her, knocking on every door of the apartment, asking about the potatoes. Zhanna Sarkova opened the door, looking unkempt and haggard, almost as if she were related to crazy Slavin.

"Is everything all right?" Tatiana asked.

"Fine!" barked Zhanna. "Potatoes—my *husband's* disappeared! You haven't seen him in Grechesky, have you?"

Tatiana shook her head.

"I thought maybe he was wounded somewhere."

"Wounded where?" Tatiana gently wanted to know.

"How should I know? And no, I haven't seen your stupid potatoes." She slammed the door.

Slavin was lying on the floor, muttering. His small room reeked of everything *but* fried potatoes.

"How is he going to feed himself?" asked Tatiana as they walked by.

"That's not our problem," said Dasha.

222

The Iglenkos were not even home. After the loss of Volodya alongside Pasha, Petr Iglenko spent all his days and nights at the factory that melted down old scrap metal for ammunition. They had just got more bad news. Petka, their eldest son, had been killed in Pulkovo. Only their two youngest, Anton and Kirill, remained.

"Poor Nina," said Tatiana as they headed back down the corridor to their rooms.

"Poor Nina!" exclaimed Dasha. "What the hell are you talking about, Tania? She still has two sons. *Lucky* Nina."

When they returned to the door that led to their own hallway, Dasha said, "They're all lying."

"They're all telling the truth," said Tatiana. "Fried potatoes with onions are not easy to hide."

The Metanovs ate bread with butter for dinner that night and complained the whole time. Papa yelled at the girls for losing his dinner. Tatiana kept quiet, heeding Alexander's warning that she should be careful around people who were likely to hit her.

But after dinner the family wasn't taking any more chances. Mama and Babushka brought the canned goods, the cereals and the grains, soap and salt and vodka into the rooms, stacking it all in the corners and in the hallway behind the sofa. Mama said, "How fortunate we are that we have the extra door partitioning our corridor from the rest of the scavengers. We'd never keep our food otherwise, I see that now."

Later that night, when Alexander came by and heard about the potatoes, he told the Metanovs to keep the rear entrance to the kitchen locked.

Dasha introduced Alexander to Marina. They shook hands and both stared at each other for longer than was appropriate. Marina, embarrassed, stepped away, averting her gaze. Alexander smiled, putting his arm around Dasha. "Dasha," he said, "so *this* is your cousin Marina." Tatiana wanted to shake her head at him, while a perplexed Marina remained speechless.

Later on in the kitchen, Marina said to Tatiana, "Tania, why did Dasha's Alexander look at me as if he knew me?"

"I have no idea."

"He is adorable."

"You think so?" said Dasha, who was heading past the girls to the bathroom, leaving Alexander in the corridor. "Well, keep your hands off him," she added cheerfully. "He's mine."

"Don't you think?" Marina whispered to Tatiana.

"He's all right," said Tatiana. "Help me wash this frying pan, will you?"

Adorable Alexander stood in the doorway, smoking and grinning at Tatiana.

Papa continued to grumble about Marina's arrival. Her student rations would bring little to the family, and another mouth to feed would only drain their resources further. "She just came here to eat my father's cans of ham," he said to Mama, gazing at the cans. Tatiana couldn't tell if Papa wanted to eat the cans or to kiss them. "She is your niece, Papa," Tatiana whispered, so Marina wouldn't overhear. "She is your only sister's only daughter."

2

The following day, on September 8, there was unrest in the city from early morning. The radio said, "Air raid, air raid!"

At work, Vera grabbed Tatiana's hand and exclaimed, "Do you hear that noise?"

They walked out the front entrance of the hospital on Ligovsky Prospekt, and Tatiana heard distant heavy thundering that didn't get closer, just increased in frequency. Calmly, Tatiana said to Vera, "Verochka, it's just the mortars. They make that sound when they release the bombs."

"Bombs?"

"Yes. They set this machine in the ground—I don't know exactly how it works—but it fires big bombs, little bombs, explosive bombs, short-fuse, long-fuse. Fragmentation bombs are the worst," said Tatiana. "But also they have these little antipersonnel bombs. They fire them a hundred at a time. They're lethal."

Vera stared at Tatiana, who shrugged. "Luga. Wish I hadn't gone. But . . . Listen, can you saw my leg off?"

They went inside. Vera said, "How about if I just remove the cast? I think taking the leg off is a bit drastic."

It was the first time Tatiana had seen her leg in over six weeks. She wished she had more time to contemplate her peculiar, wilted limb without the cast, but as she was wobbling around, she heard a commotion down the hall at the nurses' station. All the nurses ran upstairs. Tatiana followed them limply. Her leg hurt when she put weight on it.

On the roof she watched two formations of eight planes each fly above her. Half a city away there was an explosion, followed by fire and black smoke. She thought, it's really happening. The Germans are bombing Leningrad. I thought I had left it all behind in Luga. I thought what I had seen there was the worst I was ever going to see. At least I was able to leave Luga and come back to peace. Where can I go now?

Tatiana smelled acrid acidity and thought, what is that? "I'm going home," she said to Vera. "To my family." But all she could think about was that smell.

By afternoon they knew. The Badayev storage warehouses supplying Leningrad with food had been bombed by the Germans and now lay in flaming ruins. The acrid smell was burning sugar.

"Papa," asked Tatiana while they were sitting solemnly at the dining table, "what's going to happen to Leningrad?"

Papa had no answers. "What happened to Pasha, I suspect."

Mama started to cry. "Don't talk like that!" she exclaimed. "You'll scare the children."

Dasha, Tatiana, and Marina looked at each other.

The bombing continued through late afternoon.

Anton came for Tatiana, and they both went out onto the roof. However odd it was to be walking without a cast, there was nothing odder than the sight of black smoky fragments in the sky over Leningrad.

Alexander was right, she thought, He has been right about everything. Everything that he told me would happen has come to pass. Her heart swelling with respect and affection, she made a mental note to listen to every word he uttered from now on, but then a tic of fear ran through her.

Hadn't Alexander told her there would be a battle to the death on the city streets?

Dimitri with his gun, Alexander with his grenade, and Tatiana with her rock.

Hadn't Alexander told her to buy food as if she were never going to see it again? Maybe he was exaggerating for effect, she thought, feeling only slightly relieved. Didn't he rail at her to get out of the city when he used to come to pick her up at Kirov? As the black smoke hung like a memorial canopy over Leningrad, Tatiana got a feeling of foreboding, a slight, aching darkness as she thought of her family's future.

Anton stood looking at the sky with expectant eyes. "Tania!" he exclaimed. "Earlier I did it. One fell, an incendiary, and I put it out with this!" He pointed to the stick in his hand, the bottom end of which was attached to a concrete half-circle that looked like a soldier's helmet.

Jumping up and down and waving his fist to the sky, Anton squealed, "I'm ready for you, come on, come again!"

"Anton," said Tatiana, laughing, "you're as crazy as Slavin."

"Oh, much crazier," said Anton happily. "He's not on the roof, is he?"

Tatiana could see fires in the direction of Nevsky, in the direction of the river.

Suddenly Mama stuck her head out the stairwell door, not daring to venture onto the roof herself, and yelled, "Tatiana Georgievna! Are you crazy? Come down this instant!"

"I can't, Mama, I'm on duty."

"I said, come! Come this instant."

"I'm going to come in about an hour, Mamochka. Go on, go downstairs."

Mama muttered angrily and left, but in ten minutes she returned, this time with Alexander and Dimitri.

Tatiana, standing high on the roof, shook her head. "What are you doing, Mama, bringing reinforcements?"

"Tatiana," Alexander said, striding out to her, "come downstairs with us." Dimitri remained near the landing with Mama.

When Tatiana didn't move, Alexander said, raising his eyebrows, "Immediately, Tania."

Sighing, she said, "I can't leave Anton here by himself, can I?"

"I'll be fine, Tania!" Anton yelled, waving his stick at the sky. "I'm ready for them."

As he was leaving, Alexander turned to Anton and remarked, "Put the helmet on your head, soldier."

Downstairs in the room, Dimitri said, "Tania, dear, you really shouldn't go on the roof during an air raid."

"Well, there's not much point going on the roof at other times," she retorted mildly. "Unless I wanted to get a suntan." She moved away from him.

"You live in the wrong city for a suntan," snapped Alexander. "But honestly, Tania, *what* are you thinking? Dimitri is right. Your mother is right. Do you want to leave your family without two of their three children? All bombs are not incendiaries; they don't land harmlessly at your feet like felled pigeons. Have you forgotten Luga? What do you think happens when a bomb explodes in midair? The explosive wave blows apart glass, wood, plastic. Why did we tape all the windows in the city? What do you think would happen to you if that wave hit you?"

"Maybe," Tatiana said dryly, "we can put a little tape on *me*, maybe a little palm tree."

"Stop it with your smart mouth!" said Dasha. "Don't cause more trouble. I'm not having our brave boys dig you out again." She squeezed Alexander.

"I really cannot take any credit for that," said Dimitri, his eyes flaring. "Can I, Alexander?"

"Tania, you know what?" said Mama. "Why don't you go and start dinner and leave us adults to talk a bit, all right? Marina, go help Tania with dinner."

Tatiana made potatoes with a little butter, and some beans and carrots on the side. That's really not enough food for everyone, she thought, and fried up one of Deda's cans of ham, which no one liked.

"Tania, your parents still don't like to talk in front of you, do they?" said Marina.

"No, not really."

"The soldiers are quite protective of you. Especially Alexander," Marina remarked.

"He is protective of everybody," stated Tatiana. "Can you go and get me more butter? I don't think this will be enough."

Dinner was a somber occasion that evening. Alexander and Dimitri were leaving for the front, and everyone was afraid to mention the unspeakable— Germans in the middle of their city and Alexander and Dimitri leaving for the front. Tatiana knew that, unlike Dimitri, Alexander was not going into front-line battle, but that was small comfort to her, imagining him commanding his artillery company.

Still somehow it was she who managed to ask brightly, "Well, what now?" as everyone was sipping black tea.

Alexander said, "All of you, use the bomb shelter you've got downstairs. You're lucky to have one. Many buildings don't. Use it every day. And, Dasha, make sure your sister doesn't go on the roof. Tell her to let the boys take care of the bombs. Do you hear me, Dasha?"

"I hear you, darling."

Tatiana heard him loud and clear.

"Alexander, was there much food in the burned-down warehouses?" she asked.

Alexander shrugged. "There was sugar, some flour. Perhaps a couple of days' supply. It's not the Badayev warehouses we have to worry about. It's the Germans surrounding the city."

Dasha said, "Oh, Alexander, I can't believe they're here, in Leningrad! All summer they seemed so far away."

"Now they're here. The circle around Leningrad is nearly complete."

"Hardly a circle," muttered Tatiana.

"Who the hell are *you* to argue with an army lieutenant!" yelled her intoxicated father.

Alexander lifted his hand and said calmly, "Your father is right, Tania. Don't argue with me. Even if you *are* right."

Tatiana kept herself from smiling.

Alexander continued, also not smiling, "Unfortunately, the Germans have geography on their side. We have too much water all around the city." Then he smiled. "I'll rephrase that. With the gulf, Lake Ladoga, the river Neva, and the Finns up north, the circle around Leningrad is nearly complete." Looking at Tatiana, he asked, "How is that? Is that better?"

She muttered unintelligibly and accidentally caught Marina's eye.

Dimitri sat closer to Tatiana, putting his arm around her and nuzzling in her hair. "Your hair is growing out, Tanechka," he said. "Grow it out all the way, will you? I loved it long."

Whatever Alexander is doing, Tatiana thought, is not enough. Whatever we're doing is not enough. How long can we continue? We need to stop talking to each other in front of Dima and Dasha and the rest of my family. Or soon there will be trouble. As if reading Tatiana's mind, Alexander moved his chair closer to Dasha's.

"Alexander," asked Dasha, "the Germans are not up the whole Neva, are they?"

"Around the city, yes. All the way up the river to Lake Ladoga, to Shlisselburg."

Shlisselburg was a small city built at the tip of Lake Ladoga, where the Neva spilled out of the lake and meandered seventy kilometers to Leningrad, emptying out into the Gulf of Finland.

227

"Is Shlisselburg under German control?" Dasha asked.

"No," Alexander said, sighing. "But tomorrow it will be."

"And then what?"

"Then we fight to keep the Germans out of Leningrad."

Tatiana's mother asked, "Now that the warehouses have burned down, how is food going to get into the city?"

Dimitri said, "Not just food, but kerosene, gasoline, munitions."

Alexander said, "First, we stop the Germans from getting inside, then we worry about everything else."

Dimitri laughed unpleasantly. "They can come inside if they want. Every major building in Leningrad has been mined. Every factory, every museum, every cathedral, every bridge. If Hitler enters the city, he will die in its ruins. We are not going to be stopping Hitler, just dying alongside him."

"No, Dimitri, we *are* going to be stopping Hitler," said Alexander. "*Before* the Germans get into the city."

"So Leningrad is now scorched earth, too?" asked Tatiana. "What about all of us?"

No one replied.

Shaking his head, Alexander finally said, "Dimitri and I are headed for Dubrovka tomorrow. We will stop them if we can."

"But why is it that it's me and you who have to stand between the Germans and this city?" Dimitri exclaimed. "Why can't we just give Leningrad up? Minsk gave up. Kiev gave up. Tallinn gave up, having burned to the ground first. The entire Crimea gave up. All of the Ukraine *happily* gave up!" He was getting himself into a terrible agitation. "What the hell are we doing killing all of our men to stop Hitler from coming here? Let him come."

"But, Dimochka," said Mama, "your Tania is here. And Alexander's Dasha."

"Oh, and let's not forget me," said Marina. "Even though I belong to nobody, I'm here, too."

"That's right, Dima," said Alexander. "Do you want to step out of Hitler's way so he can get to your girl?"

"Yes, Dima," exclaimed Dasha. "Haven't you heard what the Germans are doing to all the Ukrainian women?"

"I haven't heard; what are they doing?" asked Tatiana.

"Nothing, Tania," Alexander said gently. "Can I please have some more tea?"

Tatiana stood up.

Dimitri looked down into his empty cup. "I'll get you some tea, too, Dima," said Tatiana.

Marina said, looking down into her empty cup, "My poor Papa couldn't stop them. They seem unstoppable, don't you think?"

Alexander said nothing.

"They *are* unstoppable!" Dimitri exclaimed. "We have three pathetic army divisions. That's not going to be enough, even if every last man dies and if every last tank is destroyed!"

Alexander stood from the table and saluted everyone. "On that note," he said, "we must be going. Forget my tea, Tania." Turning to Dimitri, he said, "Soldier on, Private, and let's go. Your life stands between the Metanovs and Hitler." He did not glance at Tatiana.

"That's exactly what I'm afraid of," mumbled Dimitri.

As they were leaving, Dasha cried, clinging to Alexander. "Will you promise to come back alive?"

"I will do my best." And then he glanced at Tatiana.

Tatiana did not cry, nor did she extract the same promise from Dimitri. After they left, she had a piece of sweet biscuit, nursing it like a wound.

Marina said, "I really like your Dima, Tania. He is more honest than anyone I know. I like that in a soldier."

Puzzled, Tatiana looked at her cousin. "What kind of a soldier doesn't want to go and fight? You can have him, Marina."

3

The next morning, as they were getting dressed, the Metanovs heard on the radio that an incendiary bomb had fallen on the roof of a building on Sadovaya Ulitsa and the roof patrol wasn't able to put it out in time. It exploded, killing everyone there, nine people, all of them under the age of twenty.

My brother was under the age of twenty, Tatiana thought, putting on her shoes. Her shin was throbbing.

"You see? What did I tell you?" said Mama. "It's dangerous to be on the roof."

"We are in the middle of a city under siege, Mama," Tatiana said. "It's dangerous to be everywhere."

The bombing started at precisely eight in the morning. Tatiana hadn't even gone to get her rations yet. The family all piled downstairs to the bomb shelter. Restlessly Tatiana bit her nails to the quick and drummed and drummed a tune on her knees, but nothing helped. They sat for an hour.

Afterward Papa gave Tatiana his ration book and asked her to get his rations for him. Mama said, "Tanechka, can you get mine, too? I've got all this sewing to do before work. I'm sewing extra uniforms for the army." She smiled. "One uniform for our Alexander, ten rubles for me."

Tatiana asked Marina to come with her to the store. Marina declined, saying she was going to help Babushka get dressed. Dasha was in the kitchen washing clothes in the cast-iron sink.

Tatiana went by herself. She found a large store on the Fontanka Canal near the Theatre of Drama and Comedy. The theatre was showing Shakespeare's *Twelfth Night* at seven that evening. The line at the store spilled down the embankment.

She forgot all about *Twelfth Night* when she got to the counter and learned that after yesterday's burning of the Badayev warehouses the ration had been further reduced.

Papa got half a kilo of bread on his worker's ration card, but everyone else got only 350 grams each, and Marina and Babushka only 250 grams. Altogether they had about two kilos of bread for the day. Besides bread, Tatiana managed to buy some carrots, soybeans, and three apples. She also bought 100 grams of butter and half a liter of milk.

After running home, Tatiana told her family of the reduced rations. They weren't concerned. "Two kilos of bread?" Mama said, putting away her sewing. "That's more than enough. That's plenty. No need to stuff ourselves like pigs in times of war. We can tighten our belts a little bit. Plus we have all that extra food just in case. We'll be fine."

Tatiana divided the bread into two piles—one for breakfast, one for dinner—and then divided each of the piles into six portions. She gave Papa the most bread. She gave herself the least.

At the hospital gone was the pretense of training with Vera. Tatiana was reduced to cleaning the toilets and baths for the patients and then washing their soiled bedding. She served lunch and was herself able to eat. Sometimes soldiers came in to eat. While serving them, she always asked if they were stationed in Pavlov Barracks.

Intermittent bombing continued during the day.

That night Tatiana had enough time to make dinner and clean up before the air-raid siren sounded at nine. Back to the bomb shelter. Tatiana sat and sat and sat. It's been only two days, she thought. How many more days of this? Next time I see Alexander, I'm going to get him to tell me the truth about how long this is going to continue.

The shelter was long and narrow, painted gray, with two kerosene lamps for the sixty or so people, who sat on benches or stood leaning against the walls. "Papa," Tatiana asked her father, "how much longer do you think?"

"It will be over in a few hours," he said wearily. Tatiana smelled vodka heavy on his breath.

"Papa," Tatiana said in a tired voice, "I *meant* . . . the fighting, the war. How much longer?"

"How should I know?" he said, trying to stand up. "Until we're all dead?"

"Mama, what's the matter with Papa?" Tatiana asked.

"Oh, Tanechka, you can't be that blind. Pasha is the matter with Papa."

"I'm not blind," muttered Tatiana, moving away. "But his family needs him."

Edging closer to Dasha and Marina, Tatiana asked, "Dash, Marinka here told me that Misha in Luga had a crush on me. I told her she was crazy. What do you think?"

"She is crazy."

"Thank you."

Marina looked at Tatiana and Dasha. "You are both crazy," she said. "And *you*, Dasha, are one day going to eat your words."

"There you go, Tania," said Dasha, without even looking at her sister. "Maybe it's Misha you need and not Dimitri." She sighed.

The next day was the same. This time Tatiana brought a copy of Dostoyevsky's *Notes from the Underground* with her.

The next day she said to herself, I can't do this anymore. I can't sit and drum out my life on my knees. So as her family was heading downstairs, Tatiana fell a little behind and then ran back through the apartment and up the rear stairs to the roof, where Anton, Mariska, and Kirill and a few other people she didn't know were watching the sky. Tatiana thought that with a bit of luck her family might not even notice her absence.

The bursting and whistling noise from the shelling was fearful on the roof. Tatiana stayed for two hours. No bombs landed near them, much to everyone's disappointment.

Tatiana had been right. No one realized she hadn't gone to the shelter. "Where did you sit, Tanechka?" asked her mother. "On the other side next to the lamp?"

"Yes, Mama."

There was no word from Alexander or Dimitri. The girls were beside themselves. They could barely be civil to each other, much less to anyone else. Only Babushka Maya, unshakable to the last, kept quiet and continued to paint.

"Babushka, where do you get your peace of mind from?" asked Tatiana one evening, brushing Babushka's long hair that was just starting to go gray.

"I'm too old to care, sunshine," replied Babushka. "I'm not young like you." She smiled. "I don't want to live quite so much." She looked over her shoulder and touched Tatiana's face.

"Babushka, don't say that." She came around to the front and hugged her grandmother. "What if Fedor comes back?"

Stroking Tatiana's head, Babushka Maya said, "I didn't say I didn't want to live at all. I said not quite so *much*."

Tatiana was a little worried about Marina. She was gone from the apartment from early morning until night, going to Leningrad University and then faithfully visiting her mother at the hospital.

At night Mama sewed. At night Papa drank. And screamed, and slept. At night Dasha and Tatiana listened to the radio for news. At night, there was bombing, and Tatiana sneaked out to the roof.

And during the day she heard the sound of war. It was never quiet in Leningrad. Shell fire came in two sounds, distant and nearby, stopping briefly for lunch in the afternoon and a sleep in the evening.

Tatiana worked, got bread, healed her leg, and acted as if her life had not stopped dead like the tram near the white-night Obvodnoy Canal.

Babushka Maya had a room all to herself. Mama slept alone on the sofa, and Papa slept alone on Pasha's cot. Tatiana, Marina, and Dasha slept in the same bed. Tatiana was almost grateful for the buffer between her and Dasha, the buffer that allowed her to face the crisis of bombings by averting her eyes from the crisis of her sister, who had the *right* during war to love Alexander.

Not enough of a buffer. Dasha one night climbed over Marina and put her arms around Tatiana. "Tania, darling, are you asleep?"

"No. What's the matter?"

"Do you think about them dying?" Dasha asked in the dark.

"Girls, I have school tomorrow," said Marina. "Go to sleep."

"Of course." Tatiana heard Dasha's quiet whimpers.

"Do you think they're dead now?" asked Dasha, holding on to Tatiana.

Taking an aching breath, Tatiana inhaled for Alexander. "No," she said. "I don't think so." She did not want to be talking to Dasha about Alexander. Not now. Not ever. "Dasha, worry about yourself. Look at the conditions we're living in. Do you even see? In the hospital they asked me if I would mind leaving the kitchen and going upstairs to help with the bomb victims. I agreed, but then I saw what was left of them." Tatiana paused. "Did you see that today across Ligovsky a whole building collapsed?"

"I didn't see."

"A girl, seventeen . . ."

"Like you." Dasha squeezed her.

"Yes—was buried under the rubble. Her father was trying to help the firemen dig her out. All day they were digging. At six when I left the hospital, they had just succeeded. And she was already dead. Hole in her forehead."

Dasha didn't say anything.

Marina said, "Tania, did you just say you left the hospital at *six*? But there was bombing at six. You didn't go to the shelter?"

"Marinka," said Dasha. "Don't even talk about that with her." She whispered into Tatiana's hair, "If you don't start going to the shelter, I'm going to tell on you."

That night the sirens woke them up at three in the morning. The Germans obviously wanted to have a little fun. Tatiana turned to the wall and would have continued to sleep had her family not dragged her out of bed. They crowded on the landing behind the stairs, and Tatiana thought, it can't get much worse than this.

4

Alexander and Dimitri returned during the night of September 12, the first night and day there was no bombing at all. They had come back from Dubrovka for just one evening—to pick up more men from the garrison and more artillery weapons.

Alexander turned up, much to the tearful relief of Dasha, who would not let go of him for a second, refusing to help with dinner. Dimitri hung on to Tatiana in much the same way Dasha hung on to Alexander, but while Alexander was able to hug Dasha back, Tatiana stood like a skinned goose and looked helplessly around the room. "All right, now, all right," she said, trying very hard not to look at Alexander's black hair and large body, and failing. To see his shape in front of her eyes would have to be comforting enough. She would have to do without his arms around her.

When Dimitri went to wash and Dasha ran to make tea, Marina said, "You know, Tania, you could show a little more interest in the man who is fighting for you at the front."

I'm showing plenty of interest, thought Tatiana, barely able to glance away from Alexander.

"Your cousin is right, Tania," said Alexander, grinning at her. "You can show at least as much interest as Zhanna Sarkova, who, as we walked by her slightly ajar door, was lying on her bed with a glass to your wall."

"She was?"

Raising his voice, Alexander took his rifle, banged once very hard on the wall and said loudly, "Have you heard this joke? A man showed a friend his apartment. The guest asked, 'What's the big brass basin for?' And the man replied, 'Oh, that's the talking clock,' and gave a shattering pound with a hammer." Alexander banged the wall hard again. "Suddenly a voice on the other side of the wall screamed, 'It's 2 A.M., you *bastard!*' "

Tatiana laughed so loudly that Alexander put down his rifle and patted her gently on the back. "Thank you, Tania," he said, smiling. "I'm starved. What's for dinner?"

As Tatiana turned to go to the kitchen, she had to walk past Marina's eyes.

Tatiana fried two cans of ham with a bit of rice that Alexander had brought, and some clear broth, which once had chicken in it. While she was cooking, Alexander came out into the kitchen to wash. Tatiana held her breath. He came up to the stove and checked under all the lids. "Hmm, ham," he said. "Rice. What's this, water? Don't give me any of that."

"It's not water, it's soup," said Tatiana quietly. His bent head was very close to her arm. If she moved three centimeters, she could touch him.

Still holding her breath, she moved three centimeters.

"I'm so hungry, Tania," Alexander said, raising his eyes to her, but before he could say another word, Marina came out to the kitchen and said, "Alexander, Dasha wanted me to give you a towel. You forgot."

"Thanks, Marina," said Alexander, grabbing the towel and disappearing. Tatiana stared into her clear soup, perhaps for a reflection.

Marina came over to the stove, looked inside the pot, and said, "Anything interesting in there?"

"No, not at all." Tatiana straightened up.

"Mmm," said Marina, walking away. "Because there is plenty of interesting out here."

Over dinner Dasha asked, "Is the fighting terrible?"

Eating hungrily and happily, Alexander replied, "You know, strangely, no. It was the first two days, right, Dima? He knows. He was in the trenches for two days. The Germans were obviously trying to see if we would buckle. When we didn't, they stopped attacking, and our recon guys swore to us that it looked as if the Germans were building permanent trenches. Concrete trenches and bunkers."

"Permanent? What does *that* mean?" asked Dasha.

Slowly Alexander said, "It means that they are probably not going to invade Leningrad."

The family rejoiced at this—everyone except Papa, who was half asleep on the couch, and Tatiana, who saw an ominous hesitation in Alexander's face, a reluctance to tell the truth.

Biting her lip, Tatiana carefully asked, "Are *you* happy about it?"

"Yes," Dimitri replied instantly, as if she were talking to him.

"I'm not, no," Alexander replied slowly. "I thought we would fight," he stated. "Fight like men—"

"And die like men!" interrupted Dimitri, banging on the table.

"And die like men, if we had to."

"Well, speak for yourself. I'd rather the Germans sit in their bunkers for two years and starve Leningrad to death than endure their fire."

"Oh, come on!" Alexander said, putting down his knife and fork and staring at Dimitri. "This wasting away in the trenches, you don't think it's a bit unbecoming? It's almost like cowardice." He gave Dimitri one more cold glance, wiped his mouth, and reached for the vodka. Tatiana pushed the bottle toward him from the other side of the table.

"Not at all like cowardice," Dimitri declared. "It's smart. You sit and you wait. When the enemy weakens, you strike. It's called strategy."

Nervously picking at her ham, Mama said, "Dimochka, surely you don't mean *starve* Leningrad to death? Not in the literal sense, right?"

"Right, right," said Dimitri. "I meant figuratively."

Tatiana studied Alexander, who remained silent.

"Is there any more vodka?" Dimitri asked, lifting the nearly empty bottle. "I feel like becoming senseless tonight."

Everyone glanced at Papa and glanced away.

"Alexander," Tatiana said in her cheerful voice. She liked being able to say his name out loud. "Nina Iglenko came by today asking us if we could

234

spare some flour and some ham. We have plenty, so I gave her some. She said she wished she had been as forward-thinking as we were—"

"Tania," Alexander interrupted, and she sat heavily back in her chair. Her feelings had been right. He knew too much. And he wasn't telling. "Don't give a gram of your food away, for any reason, do you understand? Not even if Nina Iglenko seems more hungry than you."

"We're not that hungry," said Tatiana.

"Yes, Alexander," said Dasha, "we've had rations before. Where were you during the Finnish campaign of last year?"

"Fighting the Finns," he said grimly. Tatiana wondered why Dasha always had to euphemize war into a *campaign* or a *conflict*. Was she writing propaganda for the radio?

"Dasha, all of you, listen to me. Hang on to your food as if it's the last thing between you and death, all right?" Alexander said.

"Why do you have to be so serious?" Dasha asked sulkily. "Where's your famous sense of humor? We're not going to starve. The Leningrad council will get food in somehow, right? We're not completely surrounded by the Germans, are we?"

Alexander lit a cigarette. "Dasha, do me a favor, save your food."

"All right, dearest. You have my word." She kissed him.

Alexander turned to Tatiana. "You, too, Tania."

"All right." *Dearest.* "You have my word." She didn't kiss him.

"Alexander, how long was London bombed for in the summer of 1940?" asked Dasha.

"Forty days and nights."

"Do you think it's going to be as long here?"

There was the question Tatiana wanted. She didn't even have to ask it herself.

"Longer," said Alexander. "The bombing will continue until Leningrad either surrenders or falls, or we push the Germans away."

"Are we going to surrender?" asked Dasha. "I'll fight the Nazis on the streets of Leningrad if I have to."

Tatiana thought that was brave talk from Dasha, the girl who sat in the bomb shelter every night.

Shaking his head, Alexander said, "You don't want to fight them, Dasha. A street war is devastating, not only for the besieged but also for the attacker. The loss of life is enormous. And while our beloved great leader might not set much store by the lives of his own men, Hitler maintains a surprisingly healthy interest in the lives of the Aryan race. I don't think he will risk his men for Leningrad." He glanced at Tatiana. "I think Dima will get his wish after all," Alexander finished, with barely concealed contempt.

Tatiana looked at Dimitri—splayed on the couch, either asleep or in a stupor, next to her father—and went to get the cups for tea.

"Is it going to be like London?" Dasha said, throwing back her curly hair, her eyes gleaming. "London was bombed, but the people still went on with their lives, and there were clubs, and young people went dancing. We saw pictures. It all looked so gay." She smiled at Alexander, stroking his leg.

"Dasha, where are you living? London?" Alexander exclaimed, moving away from her. "London might as well be Mars as far as you're concerned. We don't have dance clubs in Leningrad *now*. Do you think they will build them just for the blockade?"

Dasha's face soured. "Blockade?"

"Dasha! London was not blockaded. Do you understand the difference?"

"Are *we* blockaded?" asked Dasha.

Alexander did not reply.

Mama, Dasha, Marina, and Babushka were squeezed around the table, all devouring Alexander with their eyes, all except Tatiana, who was standing in the doorway, her hands full of cups and saucers.

She did not look at him when she said, "We are indeed blockaded. That's why the Germans have entrenched. They're not going to lose their own men. They *are* going to starve us to death. Right, Alexander?"

Alexander said, "I've had enough questions for one evening. Just don't give your food away."

Mama said with disbelief, "Alexander, I heard the Germans are at Peterhof Palace. Is that true?"

"Remember we went to Peterhof, darling?" Dasha murmured, holding his hand. "Oh, Alexander, it was the happiest day! It was the last young, carefree day we had. Do you remember?"

"I remember," Alexander said, *not* glancing at Tatiana.

"Nothing's been the same since that wonderful day," Dasha said sadly.

Turning to Mama, Alexander said, "Irina Fedorovna, Peterhof is indeed in German hands. The Nazis have taken the carpets out of the palace and are lining their trenches with them."

"Darling," said Dasha, sipping her tea, "maybe Dimitri was right. There are three million people still left in Leningrad. That's too many to sacrifice, don't you think?" She paused. "Has the Leningrad command considered giving up?"

Alexander studied Dasha. Tatiana was trying to figure out what was in his eyes.

"I mean," Dasha continued, "if we give up—"

"Give up and then what?" Alexander exclaimed. "Dasha, the Germans have no use for us. Certainly they will have no use for *you*." He paused. "Have you read about what they have done to the Ukrainian countryside?"

"I'm trying not to," said Dasha.

"But now *I* have," said Tatiana quietly.

Alexander continued. "Dimitri for a while there thought it might be a good idea to become a prisoner in a German camp. Until he learned how the Nazis shot the prisoners, looted and burned the villages, slaughtered the cattle, razed the barns, killed all the Jews and then all the women and children, too."

"Not before they raped all the women," Tatiana said.

Dasha and Alexander stared at her, dumbstruck.

"Tania," said Dasha, "pass me the blueberry jam, will you?"

"Yes, and stop reading so much, Tania," said Alexander quietly. He stared into his teacup.

Spooning some blueberry jam into her mouth, Dasha asked, "Well, if we are blockaded, how is the food going to get into Leningrad?"

Mama said, "We have plenty. We've saved quite a lot."

Dasha stated firmly, "I don't know, Mama. I think I'm with Dimitri on this. I think we should hand over—"

Looking bleakly at Tatiana, Alexander shook his head. "No," he said. "Right, Tania? . . . *We shall not flag or fail. We shall go on to the end . . . We shall fight on the seas and the oceans. . . . In the air, we shall defend our island whatever the cost may be."*

"We shall fight on the beaches," continued Tatiana bravely, her eyes all over Alexander. *"We shall fight in the fields and in the streets . . . We shall fight in the hills."* She swallowed a lump in her throat. *"We shall never surrender,"* she finished, realizing her hands were trembling. "Churchill."

Dasha heaved herself up in frustration and said, "Can you just go and make us a little more tea, Churchill?"

Marina came out to the kitchen to help Tatiana clean up and whispered, "Tania, I have never in my life seen anybody more dense and dumb than your sister."

"Don't know what you mean," Tatiana said, pale and still.

A few days later Tatiana and Dasha counted what was left of their provisions, most of which Tatiana had purchased with Alexander's help on the first day of war.

Their ephemeral first day of war.

That day seemed so far away, as if it belonged in another life, in another time. Two months ago, and yet already so irretrievably in the past.

In the present the Metanovs had forty-three kilo cans of ham. They had nine cans of stewed tomatoes and seven bottles of vodka. Tatiana realized with a shock that they had had eleven bottles of vodka when the Badayev warehouses burned down eight days ago. Papa must be drinking more than they knew, she thought.

They had two kilos of coffee, four kilos of tea, and a ten-kilo bag of sugar divided into thirty plastic sacks. Tatiana also counted fifteen small cans of smoked sardines. They had a four-kilo bag of barley, six kilos of oats, and a ten-kilo bag of flour.

"Seems like plenty, doesn't it?" said Dasha. "How long can the siege possibly last?"

"According to Alexander, until the end," said Tatiana.

They had seven boxes of 250 matches each.

Mama said that they also had 900 rubles in cash, enough to buy food on the black market. "Let's go and buy some, Mama," said Tatiana. "Right now."

The sisters went with their mother to a commercial store, which had opened in August in Oktabrski Rayon, near St. Nicholas's Cathedral. It took them over an hour to walk there, and they stared with disbelief at the prices of the few products on the shelves. There were eggs and cheese and butter and ham and even caviar. But sugar cost seventeen rubles a kilo. Mama laughed, turning toward the door until Tatiana grabbed her arm, and said, "Mama, don't be cheap. Buy the food."

"Let go of me, idiot," said Mama roughly. "What kind of fool do you think I am, buying sugar for seventeen rubles a kilo? Look at the cheese, ten rubles for a hundred grams. Are they joking?" She yelled to the store clerk, "Are you joking? That's why you don't have lines in this store, you know, unlike the regular Russian stores! Who will buy the food at these prices?"

The young store clerk smirked and shook his head. "Girls, girls. Buy or leave the store."

"We're leaving," said Mama. "Let's go."

Tatiana didn't move. "Mama, do you remember what Alexander told us?" She took out the rubles she had saved from her job at Kirov and the hospital. There wasn't much. She received only twenty rubles a week, and ten of it went to her parents. But she had managed to save a hundred rubles, and with that money she bought a five-kilo bag of flour for an outrageous forty rubles ("What do we need *more* flour for?"), four packets of yeast for ten rubles, a bag of sugar for seventeen, and one kilo of canned ham for thirty. She had three rubles left and asked what she could get. The clerk said a box of matches, 500 grams of tea, or some old bread that she could toast and make into crackers. Tatiana thought carefully and opted for the bread.

She spent the rest of Saturday cutting the bread into small pieces and toasting it in the oven, while Mama and Papa, and even Dasha, laughed at her. "She spent three rubles on stale bread, and now she is toasting it. She thinks we're going to eat it!" Tatiana ignored them all, thinking only of Alexander's words in the *Voentorg* store. *Buy the food as if you're never going to see it again.*

That evening Alexander listened to the story and then said, "Irina Fedorovna, you should've spent every last kopeck of your nine hundred rubles buying up that stale bread." He paused. "Just like Tania."

Thank you, Alexander, thought Tatiana. She was on the other side of the room, and the room was filled with people. She hadn't touched him in days. She was trying so hard to stay away from him, as he had asked her to.

Mama waved him off. "I was not brought up to spend seventeen rubles on sugar. Right, Georgi?"

Georgi was already asleep on the couch. He'd had too much to drink again.

"Right, Mama?"

Babushka Maya was painting. "I guess, Irina," she said. "But what if Alexander is the one who is right?"

5

The Germans were virtuously punctual. Every evening at five the air-raid sirens went off and the radio's metronome pounded at 200 beats a minute.

The frightening monotony of the shells falling on Leningrad was surpassed only by the frightening monotony of the lies Tatiana was living with inside herself, and the unyielding fear for Alexander's life, and the frustration with Papa, who had so thoroughly left the family that he no longer even knew it was still September. "That's impossible," he said one evening as the siren sounded. "They've been bombing us for what seems like a thousand days."

"No, just eleven, Papa," said Tatiana quietly. "Just eleven."

Tatiana's frustration was not just with Papa these days. Mama had withdrawn into her work. Babushka painted as if the war were not going on. Marina was wrapped up in anxiety over her mother—and, besides, Tatiana didn't want to be talking too much to Marina. And Dasha . . . well, Dasha was wrapped up in Alexander.

Deda and Babushka were safely in Molotov. She had just received a letter from them. Pasha was gone.

Dimitri was brooding and unhappy, drinking more and more the few times he came over. One evening he had actually pushed Tatiana against the wall near the kitchen window, and if Dasha hadn't come out, Tatiana didn't know where that would have led.

Tatiana's only comfort were her friends on the roof and Alexander.

When she came out onto the roof, little Mariska was hopping around as usual, hoping for more planes, more bombs. The seven-year-old semi-abandoned child ran around happily, waving at the plane formations. "Here, here!" she kept squealing, her curly hair bouncing with her.

Anton stood at the ready with his cement cap on a stick to extinguish the incendiaries. "But, Anton," Tatiana said, sinking down onto the tar and pulling out a cracker, "what if the bomb falls on your head? You're holding the cap on your stupid stick, but if the bomb falls on your poor head, what are you going to do then? Why don't you just put a helmet on your head right now and sit down next to me?"

He wouldn't, as he continued to talk excitedly about the fragmentation bombs, which could slice you before you even lifted your head to see what was coming. Tatiana could swear Anton wanted to see someone sliced.

239

Tatiana watched Mariska—her little frame impossibly small—with tired amusement as she chewed her cracker.

Mariska ran up to Tatiana and said, "Hey, Tanechka, what are you chewing?"

"Just a bread cracker," replied Tatiana, sticking her hand in her pocket. "Want one?"

Mariska nodded fervently and then grabbed the cracker out of Tatiana's hand, and before Tatiana could say, "Don't snatch!" the little girl swallowed the thing whole and said, "Got any more?"

Suddenly Tatiana saw something in Mariska she had not seen before. She got up and took Mariska's hand. "Your mama and papa, where are they?" she asked, walking with the little girl to the stairs.

Shrugging, Mariska said, "Sleeping, I think."

Anton called after Tatiana, "Don't, Tania. Leave her be."

Tatiana took Mariska downstairs to her room. "Mama, Papochka, look, someone here to see you," the girl said.

Mama and Papochka did not move from the one bed in the room. Both were facedown in the filthy pillows. The room smelled like Tatiana's communal toilet. "Come upstairs with me, Mariska," she said. "I'll find you something to eat."

The next morning at six-thirty Tatiana, already washed and dressed, stood over her sister's sleeping body. "Dashenka," said Tatiana, "may I suggest that you don't use the eight o'clock air-raid siren as your own personal alarm clock? Get up with me right now and come to the store."

Dasha barely stirred. "Why, Tania?" she said. "You're doing so well by yourself."

"Come on," Tatiana said, pulling back the covers on Marina and Dasha. "Come and see the early show."

The girls didn't move.

"Or," said Tatiana, covering them back up, "you can just catch the main event promptly at five."

Dasha's and Marina's eyes didn't open.

"If you miss that, try for the late show," Tatiana said, leaving the room. "Nine o'clock sharp."

Maybe Alexander is in Leningrad, Tatiana thought. Maybe he will come by tonight and talk to me as if he is still alive, as if I am still alive. Can't somebody talk to me? No one feels me near them anymore; they've all disappeared inside themselves, as if I'm no longer here. Come by, Alexander, Tatiana thought, as she buttoned her coat and walked briskly down Nekrasova to the ration store. Come by and remind me I am still living.

That evening, between air raids, Alexander did come by, bringing his rations and a very moody Dimitri with him. The room was filled with people, as always. Tatiana went out to the kitchen to make a dinner of beans and rice. Alexander followed her, and her heart beat faster, but then Zhanna Sarkova came into the kitchen, and Petr Petrov, and then Dasha and Marina. And Alexander left the kitchen.

During dinner the entire family was around the table except for Papa, who was intoxicated in the next room. Tatiana could speak to Alexander, but she could not look at Alexander, with all those eyes, all those faces. She looked at her food, or at Mama. She could not look at Dasha, or Marina, or Babushka—who seemed to have a sense about everything.

While talking about how badly prepared the Soviet Army was to defend the Neva from the Germans, Alexander said, "Two days ago my battalion went up the Neva, across from Shlisselburg, to dig some trenches. We got some mortars up, but, you know, nothing was in place. Even the"—he lowered his voice a notch—"the *ubiquitous* NKVD barely had a presence there."

"They can't be everywhere at once," said Tatiana. "They have too many functions. Border troops, Kirov factory guards, street militia—"

"The Gestapo," finished Alexander. "Oh, and let's not forget the ministers of all internal affairs and the guardians of internal safety."

They managed a small smile, she into her food. Tatiana needed to touch his hand to ease him away from his past and into their present. She could not touch him· her family was around the table, and so was Dimitri. But Alexander *needed* to be touched. In a moment she was going to get up and give him what he needed, and let the rest of them who needed nothing from her be damned.

Standing up, she started clearing the table. Coming around to take his plate, she pressed her hip into his elbow for one slow moment and then quickly moved on.

"Tania, you know, if the Germans had attacked properly in the first two weeks of September," Alexander continued, "I think they would have been assured success. We had no tanks, no guns in place. The only armies we had across the river from Shlisselburg were remnants of the Karelian force, some underarmed People's Volunteers." He paused. "How well trained were the People's Volunteers in Luga, Tania? As we know, not everyone has Tania's presence of mind during a bombing."

Dasha interrupted, "What are you talking to *her* about war for? She couldn't be less interested. Talk to her about Pushkin or something. Maybe cooking. She likes to cook now. She thinks the war is not even going on."

With a serious face Alexander said, "All right, Tania. Would you like to talk about Pushkin?"

Flustered, Tatiana said, "Wait, speaking of cooking—of food, rather—where do you think a safe store for me to go to would be? No matter where I go to get rations, I'm getting bombed. It's . . . inconvenient," she finished, and Alexander laughed.

"That's one way of putting it," he said. "Don't go anywhere. Stay in the shelter during bombing."

No one said a word.

"My question is," Tatiana continued quickly in order *not* to let Dasha say a word, "where are they shooting at me from?"

"Pulkovo Heights," replied Alexander. "They don't even need to fly the planes. Have you noticed how comparatively few planes we've seen?"

"Well, no, there were about a hundred last night."

"Yes, at night, because it's harder for us to hit their planes at night. But they don't want to waste their precious airpower. They're sitting very nicely and comfortably at Pulkovo Heights, and their bombs reach all the way to Smolny. You know where Pulkovo is, don't you, Tania? It's right by Kirov."

She blushed—into the dirty dishes she was carrying. He had to stop that. No, don't stop it. I need it to continue breathing. When she came back from the kitchen, Mama said, "Well, thank God you don't work all the way in Kirov anymore, Tanechka."

Alexander suggested that Tatiana not go down Suvorovsky for her rations. Tatiana told him she didn't. "I go to a store on Fontanka and Nekrasova," she said pointedly. "I'm there every morning promptly at seven. Right, Dasha?"

"I wouldn't know," Dasha said. "I never go."

"Don't walk on any north-south roads if you can help it," Alexander repeated, glancing at Tatiana.

Dasha laughed. "But, darling! That's about half of the roads in Leningrad!"

"How would you know?" asked Tatiana mildly. "You don't go out until the bombing stops."

Putting her arms around Alexander's neck, Dasha stuck out her tongue at Tatiana. "That's because *I* have sense."

"Do *you*, Tania?" Alexander asked quietly, holding Dasha's arms away from his face. "Do *you* go out only when the bombing stops?"

Dasha said, "Are you joking? She's got absolutely *no* sense. Ask her how often she goes to the shelters."

There was a silence in the crowded room.

Alexander's eyes flashed.

"Oh, look," Tatiana said uncomfortably, "I go." She shrugged. "Yesterday I sat under the stairs."

"Yes, for three minutes. Alex, she can't sit still."

"She hasn't been out on the roof, has she?"

No one said anything. To avoid Alexander's gaze, Tatiana busied herself with the sewing machine. "Can I go on Nevsky Prospekt?" she asked him, not looking up.

"Never. They're bombing that the heaviest. But they are being very careful not to hit the Astoria Hotel. You know where the Astoria is, Tania. It's right by St. Isaac's."

Tatiana's whole face turned red.

Alexander went on hurriedly. "Never mind. Hitler booked the Astoria for his victory celebration after he marches with his flag down Nevsky. Stay away from Nevsky. And don't ever walk on the north side of an east-west street. You all understand?"

Tatiana was quiet. "When is the celebration in the Astoria scheduled for?" she asked at last.

"October," said Alexander. "He thinks the people of Leningrad are going to abandon their city by October. But I will tell you that Hitler is going to be late."

Marina said, "What would we all do without you, Alexander?"

Dasha went over and, hugging him tight, said to Marina, "Stop it. Go and flirt with Tania's soldier."

"Yes, Marina, go ahead," muttered Tatiana, looking over at Dimitri, half conscious on the couch.

But Marina said, "What do you think, Tania, should I go and flirt with your soldier?"

Not far enough of a retreat, Alexander, Tatiana thought. Not far enough.

As she was cleaning up after tea, Dimitri awoke and in a stupor pulled Tatiana on top of him. "Tanechka," he muttered, "Tanechka . . ."

Tatiana struggled to get up, but he was holding her to him. "Tania," he whispered. "When, when?" His breath reeked. "I can't wait any longer."

"Dima, come on, let me go," Tatiana said, starting to hyperventilate. "I'm holding a wet rag in my hands."

"Really, Dima," said Mama. "Tania, I think he is having too much to drink."

Tatiana felt Alexander right behind her. She heard Alexander's voice right behind her. "Yes," he said, pulling Dimitri's arms away from Tatiana, and helping her stand. "He is definitely drinking too much." His hand remained on her long enough for him to squeeze her arm and let go.

"What's the matter with him, Tania?" inquired Mama. "He seems peculiar these days. Grumpy. Not talkative. And not as nice to you."

Out of breath, Tatiana watched Dimitri for a moment. "He is getting less interested in me," she said to her mother, "the closer he is feeling to his own death." She turned and went to the kitchen without glancing at Alexander, but catching Marina's eyes and Babushka's. Dasha was in the next room, tending to Papa.

6

Tatiana thought she could take it. Tatiana thought she could take it all. But one night—two weeks after the burning of Badayev warehouses—when they all came home from work and instead of making dinner were sitting in the bomb shelter, hungry and tired, Dasha plopped down next to Tatiana and in a thrilled voice exclaimed, "Guess what, everybody? Alexander and I are getting married!"

The kerosene lamps gave too much light to hide what exploded inside Tatiana. Marina gasped. But the jubilant Dasha, who continued to smile while the bombs fell outside, remained oblivious to Tatiana's feelings.

Marina said, "That's great, Dasha. Congratulations!"

Mama said, "Dashenka, finally, one of my daughters is going to have a family of her own. When?"

Papa, sitting next to Mama, mumbled something.

"Tania? Did you hear me?" asked Dasha. "I'm getting married!"

"I heard you, Dasha," Tatiana said. Turning away, she was faced with Marina's sympathetic, pitying glance. Tatiana didn't know which was worse. She turned back to her smiling sister. "Congratulations. You must be so happy."

"Happy? I'm delirious! Can you imagine? I'm going to be Dasha Belova." She giggled. "As soon as he gets a couple of days' furlough, we'll go to the registry office."

"You're not worried?"

"I'm not worried," said Dasha with a wave of her healthy-looking arm. "Worried about what? Alexander is not worried. We'll make it."

"I'm glad you're so sure."

"What's the matter?" Dasha put her arm around Tatiana, who didn't know how she was still sitting. "I won't kick you out of your bed. Babushka will give us her room for a couple of days." Dasha kissed her. "Married, Tania! Can you believe it?"

"I can't believe it."

"I know!" Dasha exclaimed excitedly. "I can hardly believe it myself."

"It's war. He could die, Dasha."

"I know that. Don't you think I know that? Don't be flip about him dying."

"I'm not flip," said Tatiana, trembling. About him dying. She shut her eyes.

"Thank God, he's finally out of that awful Dubrovka and up across from Shlisselburg. It's quieter there." Dasha smiled. "You know, that's what I do now—I close my eyes and I feel for him out there somewhere, and I know he's still alive." She added with pride, "I have a sixth sense, you know."

Marina coughed loudly. Opening her eyes, Tatiana glared at Marina with an expression that instantly stifled Marina's coughing fit.

"What do you want, Dash?" she whispered. "You want to be a widow, instead of just a dead soldier's girl?"

"Tania!"

Tatiana said nothing. Where was relief going to come from? Not from the night, not from Mama or Papa, not from Deda and Babushka, far away, not from Babushka Maya, too old to care, not from Marina, who knew too much without knowing anything, not from Dimitri, who was mired in his own hell, and certainly not from Alexander, the impossible, maddening, unforgivable Alexander.

The absence of comfort was so compelling that Tatiana could no longer continue to sit. She left the shelter in the middle of the raid, hearing only Dasha's puzzled voice: "What is wrong with *her*?"

How did she spend the night next to her wall, next to Marina, next to Dasha? How did she do it? She didn't know. It was the worst night of Tatiana's life.

The next morning she got up late and, instead of going to her regular store on Fontanka and Nekrasova, went to one on Old Nevsky, near her former school. She'd heard they had good bread there. The air-raid siren sounded. She didn't even take cover.

Tatiana walked with her eyes to the ground. The whistling bombs, the wind-induced piercing shrieks, followed by the sound of brick exploding and then distant human cries were nothing compared to the screaming hurt inside her body.

Tatiana realized that war no longer scared her. This was new to her, the acknowledgment of the absence of fear. It was Pasha who had always been intrepid. Dasha was confident. Deda was ruthlessly honest, Papa was strict—and drunk—Mama bossy, and Babushka Anna arrogant. Tatiana carried everyone's hidden insecurities on her thin shoulders. Insecurities, yes. Timidity, yes. *Their* fears, yes again. But not her own. She wasn't afraid of random war. It was like being struck by lightning, even if the lightning did strike a thousand times a day. No, it wasn't war that terrified Tatiana. It was the resolute chaos of her broken heart.

She went to work, and when five o'clock came, she stayed at work, and when six came, she stayed at work, and when seven came, she stayed at work. At eight o'clock she was washing the floor in the nurses' station when she saw Marina come through the doors and head in her direction. Tatiana did not want to see Marina.

"Tania, what are you doing?" Marina said. "Everybody is worried sick about you. They think you've been killed."

"I haven't been killed," Tatiana said. "I'm right here, washing the floor."

"It's three hours past quitting time. Why aren't you home?"

"I'm washing the floor, Marina, can't you see? Step out of my way. Your shoes will get wet." Tatiana did not look up from the mop.

"Tania, they're all waiting. Dimitri is there, Alexander is there. You're being selfish. The family can't celebrate Dasha's betrothal, because they're so worried about *you*."

"All right," Tatiana said through her teeth as she pushed the mop back and forth. "You found me. I'm right here. Tell them not to worry and go and celebrate. I have work to do. I'm doing a double shift. I'll be home later."

"Tania," said Marina, "come on now, honey. I know it's hard. But you have to come home and raise a glass to your sister. What are you thinking?"

"I'm working!" Tatiana yelled. "Can you leave me alone, please!" And she looked back down at her soapy mop, blinded by her tears.

"Tania, please."

"Leave me alone!" repeated Tatiana. "Please."

Reluctantly Marina left.

Tatiana mopped the nurses' station, and the corridor nearby, and the bathrooms, and some of the patient rooms. And then a doctor asked her for help in bandaging five bomb victims, and Tatiana went with him. Four of the victims died within the hour. Tatiana sat with the last one, an old man of about eighty, until he died, too. He died holding her hand, and before he died, he turned to her and smiled.

By the time she came home, everyone was asleep, and Dimitri and Alexander were long gone. Tatiana slept on the small sofa in the hall, waking up before the rest of the family, washing, and again going to get their rations on Old Nevsky.

When she got home after work, Papa was in a fit. At first Tatiana couldn't figure out what it was that was making him upset, nor did she care to find out. As her father came into the room, still shouting, Tatiana concluded that he must be upset with *her*.

"What did I do *now*?" she said tiredly. She couldn't have cared less.

He was slurring his words, but Mama, who was also angry—but sober—came in from the hallway and told Tatiana that last night when she was God knows where while the family was celebrating Dasha's imminent marriage, a little girl named Mariska came by, asking for some food. "Mariska said that someone named Tania has been feeding her for a *week*!" Mama shouted. "A week with our food!"

"Oh." Tatiana looked at her parents. "Yes. Mariska's parents are both drunk, and they're not feeding her. She needed some food. I gave her a little. Mama, I thought we have plenty." She went into the kitchen to get a knife. Papa and Mama followed her, still shouting and shouting and shouting.

The following day Alexander and Dimitri came by after dinner to take the girls for a short walk before the air raid and curfew. Tatiana did not raise her eyes to Dimitri, nor to Dasha, and certainly not to Alexander.

"What happened to you yesterday?" Dimitri asked. "We were waiting forever for you."

"I was working yesterday," said Tatiana, grabbing her cardigan from the hook on the wall and walking out past Alexander, her eyes to the floor.

It was quiet in Leningrad that evening. The four of them walked in peace down Suvorovsky heading toward Tauride Park. Relative peace, for on Eighth Soviet a corner building was shattered and glass was spread like fractured ice all over the street.

Dimitri and Tatiana walked in front of Alexander and Dasha. Dimitri asked why Tatiana kept staring at the ground. Tatiana shrugged and said nothing, her growing-out blonde hair covering half her face.

"Isn't it fantastic about Alexander and Dasha?" Dimitri asked, putting his arm around Tatiana.

"Yes," said Tatiana coldly and loudly. "It's *fantastic* about Alexander and Dasha." She did not look up, nor did she look back. She could feel Alexander's eyes on her, and she simply did not know how she was going to continue walking straight.

Dasha giggled and said, "I sent Deda and Babushka a letter in Molotov. They'll be so happy. They've always liked you, Alexander." There were some chuckling noises from behind Tatiana. She stumbled on the curb. Dimitri grabbed her arm.

Dasha said, "Tania is a little glum these days, Dima. I think she wants you to propose, too."

Squeezing her arm, Dimitri said, "Should I, Tanechka? What do you think? Should I ask you to marry me?"

Tatiana did not reply. They stopped at an intersection to let a tram pass. Tatiana said, "Want to hear a joke?" She continued before anyone had a chance to speak. " 'Honey, when we get married, I'll be there to share all your troubles and sorrows,' says the man. 'But I don't have any, my love,' says the woman. 'I said, *when* we get married,' says the man."

"Oh, *nice*, Tania," said Dasha from behind.

Tatiana laughed mirthlessly, and when she laughed, her hair bobbed back just long enough to reveal a black swollen bruise over her eyebrow. Dimitri gasped. Tatiana lowered her head, brushing her hair back into her face. Alexander said, "What's the matter, Dima?"

Dimitri didn't reply, but Alexander walked around and stood in front of Tatiana. She looked down at the pavement. "It's nothing," she muttered.

"Can you look up, please?" Alexander demanded.

Tatiana wanted to look up and scream. But Dasha was standing on one side of her and Dimitri on the other, and she could not look up into the face she loved. Simply could not. The best she could do was repeat quietly that it was nothing.

"Ah, Tania," said Alexander, paling under the effort of keeping himself in check. "Ah, Tania."

"It's totally her fault," said Dasha, taking Alexander's arm. "She perfectly well knew that Papa was drunk. Yet she couldn't help talking back to him. He yelled at her a little bit for feeding a waif—"

"He yelled at me for Mariska, but he hit me for not washing his sheets," Tatiana said. "Which was *your* job."

"How did he open your brow like that?" Dimitri asked with concern.

"That was my fault," Tatiana said. "I lost my balance and fell. The kitchen drawer was open. It's not a big thing."

247

"Ah, Tania," Alexander repeated again.

"*What?*" said Tatiana, raising her livid, broken eyes at him.

He lowered his gaze.

"Hey, listen," Dasha said, defending herself, "I didn't care what Papa said. He was drunk. I wasn't going to get into a fight with him over nothing."

"You mean over *me?*" Tatiana said. "You mean you weren't going to come forward and say, 'Papa, I should've washed your sheets, and I'm sorry I didn't'?"

"What for? He was drunk!"

"He's always drunk!" yelled Tatiana. "Always, and it's war, Dasha! Have we not got enough trouble, you think?" She panted. "Believe me, we've got enough trouble." She stared at her sister. "Forget it. Let's cross."

As they crossed the street, Tatiana could hear Alexander's seething breaths. "Dasha, let's go," he said suddenly, pulling her quickly by the arm down the street, away from Tatiana. He started running with Dasha beside him.

Dimitri and Tatiana were left on Suvorovsky, and Tatiana said, trying to smile, "So, Dima, how are *you?* I hear the Germans are completely entrenched. Has the fighting stopped?"

"Tania, you don't want to be talking about the fighting," said Dimitri.

"No, I do, I do. Tell me, is it true that Hitler has issued a directive to his men that Leningrad is to be wiped off the face of the earth?"

Shrugging, Dimitri said, "You'll have to ask Alexander about that."

"I heard—" but then Tatiana stopped and realized something. "You know what, Dima? I think we better head back home."

"You know what?" he said. "I think I'm going to head back to the barracks. You don't mind, do you? I've got"—he paused—"things to do. All right?"

"Of course, Dima," said Tatiana, staring at him standing next to her in his helpless, distant, pointless proximity. Could other people have interested him *less?* Tatiana didn't think so.

"I don't know when I'm going to come by again," Dimitri said. "I hear my platoon is being sent over the river. I'll come by when I'm back. *If* I'm back. I'll write if I can."

"Of course." Tatiana said good-bye to Dimitri on the street corner, watching him as he walked away from her. She didn't think she would be seeing him again soon.

She went home by herself, and when she was near her apartment building, she saw Alexander run out the front doors. She was maybe ten meters away from him. He stood for a moment trying to get his breath, and then saw her stopped dead on the pavement. Tatiana's control over herself was so fragile that she knew she could not face him. She turned around and started walking quickly in the opposite direction. "Tania!" she heard him calling from behind, and in a moment he stood in front of her. Tatiana backed away and

248

put her arms up. "Leave me alone," she said in a faint voice. "Just leave me *alone*."

"Where have you been?" Alexander asked quietly. "I've been coming to the store on Fontanka and Nekrasova for three mornings in a row trying to catch you."

"Well, you caught me, all right," said Tatiana.

"Tania, look at you, how could you let him do that to you?"

"I ask myself that question over and over," Tatiana said. "And not just about him."

Alexander blinked. "Tania—"

"I don't want to talk to you right now!" Tatiana screamed. And then, taking another step back, her lip shaking and her eyes filled with tears, she said, much more quietly, "I don't want to talk to you *ever*."

"Tania, can I just explain—"

"No."

"Will you for a second—"

"No!"

"Tania . . ."

"NO!" She came up to him, her teeth gritted, and she couldn't believe herself: she wanted to hit him. She clenched her fists. She wanted to *hit* Alexander.

He stared at her fists and at her and said with upset incredulity, "You promised me you would forgive me—"

"Forgive you," Tatiana hissed through her teeth, tears streaming down her face, "for your brave and indifferent *face*, Alexander!" She groaned in pain. "Not your brave and indifferent *heart*."

Before he had a chance to respond or to stop her, Tatiana ran from him, through the doors, flying up three flights of stairs to her apartment.

At home Papa was lying on the floor in the hallway, still drunk, but also unconscious. Mama and Dasha were crying in the room. Oh, my God, thought Tatiana, wiping her own face. Will this never end?

Marina whispered to Tatiana, "Tania, what a mess! You cannot believe the things Alexander said when he stormed in here. Look what he did to the wall!" She pointed with a thrill to some broken plaster in the hallway. "Alexander said that with his drinking your Papa had turned his back on his family just when they needed him most. That he had failed in his responsibilities to the people he was supposed to protect, not harm. Alexander was like a growling tank!" Marina said, looking extremely impressed. "He said, 'Where can she go if outside the Nazis are bombing her, and inside her own father is trying to kill her?' Tania, he was unstoppable!" Marina exclaimed. "He told your mother to put your father in the hospital. He said, 'You are a *mother*, for God's sake—save your children!' " Tatiana lowered her eyes away from Marina. "Your father was very drunk and went to hit him, and Alexander grabbed him by both shoulders and shoved him against the wall and cursed and screamed and then stormed out. How he didn't kill him, I swear I don't know. Can you believe it?"

"I can believe it," Tatiana whispered. Alexander carried his own father with him wherever he went. He carried his own father, his own mother, his own self. Tatiana was the only person in the world he trusted, and so she bore some of that cross with him. Not much of it, but just enough to remember him at this time. For a moment—but it was all that she needed—Tatiana stopped feeling for herself and felt for Alexander, and when she did, she became less angry with him.

"Has he just passed out?" Tatiana said, sitting down on the sofa and looking at her father.

"No, I think he fell from fear. Tania, did you hear me? Alexander looked ready to kill him!"

"I heard you," said Tatiana.

"Oh, Tania," said Marina, lowering her voice to a whisper in the hallway, two meters away from one room, three meters away from another. "Tania, whatever are you two going to do?"

"I don't know what you're talking about," Tatiana said. "I, for one, am going to try to help Papa."

Papa remained unconscious, and the Metanovs became worried. Mama suggested that maybe they really should put Papa in the hospital for a few days to sober up. Tatiana thought it was a good idea. Papa had not been sober for many days.

Tatiana asked Petr Petrov down the hall for help with carrying Papa to the drunk ward at Suvorovsky Hospital. There were no beds available at Grechesky, where Tatiana worked.

The girls and Petr carried Papa to the hospital—on the north side of an east-west street—where he was admitted and put into a large room with four other drunk men. Tatiana asked for a sponge and some water and washed her father's face, and then sat with him for a few minutes, holding his flaccid hand. "I'm really sorry, Papa," she said.

She sat with him, holding his hand, every once in a while squeezing it and saying, "Papa, can you hear me?"

Finally he groaned in a way that told her maybe he could. He opened his unfocused eyes.

"Right here, Papa," she kept saying. "I'm right here. Look at me."

His head bobbed on the pillow. She continued to hold his hand. "You're in the hospital for just a few days. Until you get sober. Then you'll come home. Everything will be all right then." Tatiana felt him squeeze her hand. "I'm sorry I wasn't able to bring Pasha back for you. But you know, the rest of us are all still here."

She saw tears in his eyes. His mouth opened as he squeezed her hand again, whispering hoarsely, "It's all my fault . . ."

Tatiana kissed him on the head and said, "No, darling Papa. It's not. It's just war. But you do need to get sober." He closed his eyes, and Tatiana went home.

At home Dasha was upset at Tatiana and shouted at her while Marina mediated. Tatiana sat on the sofa in the room and remained silent, imagining herself sitting peacefully between Deda and Babushka. At one point Dasha got herself so worked up that she leaned forward to hit Tatiana and was pulled away by Marina, who said, "Dasha, this is ridiculous. Stop it!"

Dasha ripped herself from Marina's grasp, but Marina exclaimed, "Stop yourself. She is hurt enough! Can't you see she's hurt enough?"

Tatiana watched Marina with soft eyes and Dasha with harder ones, and then she got up wearily and went to walk past them to the other room. She needed to lie down and never have another day like this one. Or like the last one. Or the one before. Dasha grabbed her. Tatiana twisted away, raised her face to her sister, and said, "Dasha, in one minute I'm going to lose my patience. Stop and leave me alone. Can you do that?"

Her eyes remained unblinking on her sister, who let go of her and left Tatiana alone.

Later that night in bed Marina stroked Tatiana's back, whispering, "It's all right, Tania. It'll be all right."

"And you know this how?" Tatiana whispered. "We're bombed every day, we're blockaded, soon there will be no food, Papa can't stop drinking—"

"That's not what I'm talking about," whispered Marina.

"Then I don't know what you're talking about," Tatiana whispered back, "but before you tell me, stop talking."

Dasha was not in bed.

Tatiana slept with her face to the wall, her hand on Alexander's *The Bronze Horseman* book, her brow throbbing. But in the morning it felt a little better. She dabbed some diluted iodine on the cut and went to work, her face discolored by the sienna antiseptic.

During her lunch hour she left the hospital and slowly walked to the Field of Mars. It had been made unrecognizable by the trenches dug around it and the concrete emplacements for artillery weapons erected around the perimeter. The field itself was mined; she could not walk there. All the benches had been removed. The only thing Tatiana could do was stand several hundred meters from the archway that led to Pavlov Barracks and watch smoking, laughing soldiers loudly filtering out.

She stood for half an hour. Then she went back to the hospital, thinking, *not bombs nor my broken heart can take away from me walking barefoot with you in jasmine June through the Field of Mars.*

That evening during the post-dinner bombing show the Suvorovsky Hospital where Papa lay was hit.

Three bombs fell on the hospital, which caught fire and burned into the night, despite the efforts of the firefighters. The hospital was not made of brick, which resisted fire, but of wattle and daub, the early-eighteenth-century material out of which most of Leningrad was built. The whole building collapsed onto itself, then went up in flames. The few people who were able to move jumped from the windows, screaming as they fell.

Papa, at forty-three years old, having been born in the previous century, wasted on remorse, unable to sober up, never rose from his bed.

Dasha and Tatiana and Marina and Mama ran down Suvorovsky and watched with unsteady, horrified impotence as the inferno conquered the firemen, the water hoses, the building, the night.

The girls helped to throw useless buckets of water on the ground-floor windows. They got sand from the rooftops of the surrounding buildings, but it was all just meaningless movement sustained by inertia. Tatiana wrapped charred bodies in wet sheets provided by Grechesky Hospital. She stayed until morning. Dasha and Marina went back home with Mama.

Only a handful of people had made it out alive. The firemen could not even find Papa's body and made no apologies as they put out the last of the flames. They were not taking bodies out of that hospital. "Look at the building, girlie," said one fireman. "Does it look like we can get anything out? It's all cinder. Once it cools down, you'll be able to touch it and watch it turn to black ash." He patted her absentmindedly on the shoulder. "Time to let go. Your father, is it? Fucking Germans. Comrade Stalin is right. Don't know how, but we're going to bring it all home to them."

As Tatiana walked slowly home at dawn, she thought of herself being buried beneath Luga station, feeling life ooze out of the three people she had crawled under. She hoped Papa had never woken up, never suffered.

At home she silently got the family's ration cards—all except Papa's—and went out to get bread.

If life in the two communal rooms was difficult for Tatiana before, it became nearly impossible after the death of her father.

Mama was inconsolable and not talking to Tatiana.

Dasha was angry and not talking to Tatiana.

Tatiana wasn't sure if Dasha was angry because of Papa or if Dasha was angry because of Alexander. Dasha was certainly not saying. She wasn't talking to Tatiana at all.

Marina visited her mother daily in Vyborg and continued to level her understanding eyes on Tatiana.

And Babushka painted. She painted an apple pie that Tatiana said looked good enough to eat.

A few days after Papa's death Dasha asked Tatiana to come with her to the barracks to tell Alexander about what had happened. Tatiana dragged Marina along for strength. She wanted to see him, and yet . . . there was so little to say. Or was there too much to say? Tatiana wasn't sure, couldn't figure it out without Alexander's help, and was afraid to face him.

Alexander was not at the barracks, and neither was Dimitri. Anatoly Marazov came into the passageway and introduced himself.

Tatiana knew of him well from Alexander. "Isn't Dimitri under your command?" she asked.

"No, he is under Sergeant Kashnikov, who has one of the platoons under my command, but they've all been sent by powers higher than me to Tikhvin."

"Tikhvin? On the other side of the river?" said Tatiana.

"Yes, in a barge across Ladoga. Not enough men up in Tikhvin."

"And Alexander, too?" Tatiana said, short of breath.

"No, he's up at Karelia," Marazov replied, looking Tatiana over appreciatively. "So are you the girl?" Marazov smiled. "The girl he's forsaken all others for?"

"Not her," Dasha said rudely, coming up to Tatiana. "Me. I'm Dasha. Don't you remember? We met in Sadko back in early June."

"Dasha," mumbled Marazov. Tatiana paled, leaning harder against the wall. Marina stared at her.

Marazov turned to Tatiana. "And what's your name?"

"Tatiana," she said.

Marazov's eyes flared and then dimmed. Dasha asked, "Do you know each other?"

"No. We've never met," he said.

"Oh," said Dasha. "Just for a moment you looked as if you recognized my sister."

Marazov left his gaze on Tatiana. "Not at all," he said slowly, but his eyes flickered a confused familiarity at her. He shrugged. "I'll tell Alexander you stopped by. I'm going to join him in Karelia in a few days."

"Yes, please tell him that our father has died," Dasha said. Tatiana turned and walked out of the passageway, pulling Marina with her.

The family was split apart like faulted earth. Mama could not move from her bed. Babushka took care of her. Mama didn't want to have anything to do with Tatiana, or her apologies, or her pleas for forgiveness. Finally Tatiana stopped pleading.

The emptiness Tatiana felt overpowered her; the sense of guilt, the anchor of responsibility weighed her down. It wasn't my fault, it wasn't my fault, she kept repeating to herself in the mornings as she cut the bread, put some on her plate, and ate it silently. It would take her maybe thirty seconds to eat her share, and she would pick up all the little crumbs with her forefinger, and then she would turn the plate over and shake it onto the table. All that— thirty seconds. And thirty seconds of, it wasn't my fault, it wasn't my fault.

After Papa died, his half-kilo-a-day bread ration stopped. Mama finally thrust 200 rubles into Tatiana's hand and told her to go and buy some more food. She came back home, having spent the money on seven potatoes, three onions, half a kilo of flour, and a kilo of white bread, which was as rare as meat.

Tatiana continued to get the rations, and once or twice as she stood in line for their food, she thought with shame that if only they hadn't told the authorities immediately that Papa had died, they could still be getting his ration until the end of September.

She thought it with shame, but she did not stop thinking it.

Because when September turned into October, and the rawness of her sorrow dulled yet the emptiness remained, Tatiana realized that the emptiness was not sorrow but hunger.

Night Sank Down

1

Even during the warm months of the summer, the air in Leningrad carried a vague chill, as if the Arctic constantly reminded the northern city that winter and darkness were only a few hundred kilometers away. The wind carried ice in it, even in the pale nights of July. But now that October was here, now that the flat and forlorn city was shelled every day and stood barren and silent at night, the air wasn't just cold, and the wind carried on its breath more than the Arctic. It carried a distinct sense of desperation, a harried hopelessness. Tatiana bundled herself into a gray coat and put Pasha's old gray hat with earmuffs on her head and wrapped a ripped brown scarf around her neck and mouth, but she couldn't protect her nose from breathing in the icy daggers.

The bread ration had been reduced again, to 300 grams each for Tatiana, Mama, and Dasha and 200 grams each for Babushka and Marina. Less than a kilo and a half for all of them.

Besides bread, the stores weren't giving out or selling anything else. There were no eggs, no butter, no white bread, no cheese, no meat of any kind, no sugar, no oatmeal, no barley, no fruit, no vegetables. Once in early October, Tatiana bought three onions and made onion soup. It was fairly good. It would have been better with more salt, but Tatiana was very careful with her salt.

The family hung on to their supplies of food, but every night they had to open a can of ham, saying a short word of thanks to Deda. They had to stop cooking it outside in the kitchen because the smell from the ham would permeate the communal apartment, and frequently Sarkova and Slavin and the

255

Petrovs would come to the kitchen, stand near the stove, and say to Tatiana, "You think maybe there's a little for us?"

Slavin would emit cackling noises as Dasha sent them all back to their rooms, cackling noises simmering with unrepressed glee. "That's right, eat the ham, girlie-burlie. Eat that ham. Because I just got the latest report, straight from the Führer himself. Herr Hitler plans to coincide his troop withdrawal from Leningrad with your *last* can of ham." He laughed hysterically. "Or haven't you heard?"

The Metanovs bought a small freestanding cast-iron stove called a *bourzhuika,* which had an exhaust flue that Tatiana stretched to a small framed opening in the windowpane. The flat iron surface of the *bourzhuika* served as the cooktop. Only a little wood was needed to fire up the stove; the problem was that it only warmed up a small section of the room.

Alexander was still away in Karelia. Dimitri was in Tikhvin. No one had heard from either of them.

In the second week of October, Anton finally got his wish. A fragmentation bomb split over Grechesky, and a piece of metal flew from the sky, hitting Anton and slicing his leg. Tatiana wasn't on the roof. After Tatiana found out, she secretly brought a can of ham to Anton, and he ate the whole thing by himself in ravenous gulps. "Anton," Tatiana said, "what about your Mama?"

"She eats at work," he said. "She has soup. She has oatmeal."

"What about Kirill?"

"What about him, Tania?" Anton snapped impatiently. "Did you bring it for Kirill or for me?"

Tatiana didn't like the way Mariska was looking. Her curly hair started to fall out. Every day Tatiana secretly made Mariska oatmeal. But she knew she couldn't continue to feed Mariska; Tatiana's family was already unhappy with her. The oatmeal had a bit of salt and sugar, but it had no butter or milk. It wasn't oatmeal, it was gruel. Mariska would eat it as if it were her last meal. Finally Tatiana took her to the children's ward in Grechesky Hospital, carrying her for the last block.

When Tatiana was younger, she would sometimes forget to eat for half a day. And then suddenly remembering, she would say, "Oh, no, I'm STAR-ving." An empty rumbling stomach, a salivating mouth. She would devour soup or pie or mashed potatoes, gorge herself, fall away from the table, and then she wouldn't be STAR-ving anymore.

This feeling that Tatiana experienced, faintly at the end of September, more distinctly at the beginning of October, was similar in that she had the empty rumbling stomach, she had the salivating mouth. She would devour the clear soup, the black thick mud bread, the oats, and when she was done, she would fall away from the table and realize she was still STAR-ving. She would have some of the crackers she had toasted. But the cracker bag was diminishing in size by the hour. The nights were just too long after work. Dasha and Mama began to take some crackers with them in their coat pockets on the way to work. First a couple, then more and more. Babushka nibbled on crackers all day while she painted or read. Marina took some crackers to university and some for her dying mother.

After they bought the *bourzhuika*, Mama gave Tatiana the rest of her money—500 rubles—one cold morning and told her to go to the commercial store and buy anything she could get her hands on. The commercial store near St. Nicholas's Cathedral was far, and when Tatiana got there, she found a double irony. Not only was the store bombed out and abandoned, but there was a sign on the crushed window dated September 18—NO FOOD LEFT.

Slowly she went home. September 18, four weeks ago, Papa still alive, Dasha planning to marry.

Marry *Alexander*.

At home Mama didn't believe Tatiana about the store and went to hit her in frustration and stopped herself, which Tatiana found so miraculous that she went to her mother, hugged her and said, "Mamochka, don't worry about anything. I will take care of you." Tatiana gave Mama back her money, put the ration bread on the table, taking just a small piece for herself, and swallowed it ravenously while she walked slowly to the hospital, thinking about nothing but lunchtime, when she would get her soup and maybe some oatmeal, too. Tatiana thought about little else but food. The acute hunger she experienced from morning until night defeated most other feelings in her body. While walking to Fontanka she thought about her bread, and while she worked she thought about lunch, and in the afternoon she thought about dinner, and after dinner she thought about the piece of cracker she could have before she went to bed.

And in bed Tatiana thought about Alexander.

Once Marina offered to get the rations instead of Tatiana.

Puzzled, Tatiana gave her the ration cards. "Want my company?"

"No," Marina said. "I'll be glad to do it."

Marina came back to her waiting family and put the bread on the table. There was maybe half a kilo.

"Marina," said Tatiana, "where is the rest of the bread?"

"I'm sorry," Marina said. "I ate it."

"You ate a *kilo* of our bread?" Tatiana did not believe it.

"I'm sorry, I was very hungry."

Tatiana looked at Marina in sharp surprise. For six weeks Tatiana had been going to get her family rations, and it had never even entered her head to eat the bread five people were waiting for.

And through it all Tatiana was STAR-ving.

And through it all she missed Alexander.

257

2

One morning in the middle of October, as Tatiana neared the Fontanka embankment, feeling in her coat pocket for the ration cards, she saw an officer up ahead, and through her bleary, early-morning haze she wanted him to look like Alexander. She came closer. It couldn't be him, this man, looking much older, grimy, his trench coat and rifle covered in mud. Carefully she moved forward. It *was* Alexander.

When she came up to him and looked into his face, she saw sadness mixed with bleak affection. Tatiana came a little closer. Her gloved hand touched his chest. "Shura, whatever happened to you?"

"Oh, Tania," he said. "Forget about me. Look how thin you are. Your face, it's . . ."

"I've always been thin. Are you all right?"

"But your lovely round face," he said, his voice cracking.

"That was a different life, Alexander," Tatiana said. "How was—"

"Brutal," he said, shrugging. "Look. Look at what I brought you." He opened his black rucksack, from which he pulled out a hunk of white bread and, wrapped in white paper, cheese! Cheese and a piece of cold pork *meat*. Tatiana stared at the food, breathing shallowly. "Oh, my," she said. "Wait till they see. They'll be so happy."

"Well, yes," Alexander said, giving her the white bread and the cheese. "But before they see, I want you to eat it."

"I can't."

"You can and you will. What? Don't cry."

"I'm not crying," said Tatiana, trying very hard not to cry. "I'm just very . . . moved." She took the bread and the cheese and the pork and gulped down the food while he watched her with his molten copper eyes, warm, full of Alexander. "Shura," she said, "I can't tell you how hungry I've been. I don't even know how to explain it."

"Tania, I know."

"Are they feeding you better in the army?"

"Yes. They feed the front-line troops adequately. They feed the officers a little better. What they don't give me, I buy. We get the food before it gets to you."

"That's the way it should be," said Tatiana, her mouth so full, so happy.

"Shh," he said, smiling. "Slow down. You're going to give yourself a terrible stomachache."

She slowed down—a little. Smiling back—a little.

"For the family I brought some butter and a bag of white flour," Alexander said. "And twenty eggs. When was the last time you had eggs?"

Tatiana remembered. "September fifteenth. Let me have a little piece of butter now," she said. "Can you wait with me? Or do you have to go?"

"I came to see you," he said.

They stood looking at each other without touching.

They stood looking at each other without talking.

At last Alexander whispered, "Too much to say."

"Not enough time to say any of it," said Tatiana, looking at the long line of people in the store. She had stopped eating. "I've been thinking about you," she said, keeping her voice calm.

"Don't think about me again," said Alexander with resigned finality.

Tatiana backed away. "Don't worry. You've made it very clear that that's certainly what you want."

"What are you talking about?" He looked at her in confusion. "You have no idea what it's like out there."

"I only know what it's like in here," she said.

"We're all dying. Even the ranking officers." Alexander paused. "Grinkov died."

"Oh, no."

"Oh, yes." He sighed. "Let's get in line."

Alexander was the only man getting rations. They stood together for forty-five minutes. It was quiet in the crowded store; no one else spoke. And they couldn't stop. They talked about public things: the cold weather, the waiting Germans, the food. But they couldn't stop.

"Alexander, we have to get more food from somewhere. I don't mean me, I mean Leningrad. Where is it going to come from? Can't they fly some in?"

"They are already. Fifty tons a day of food, fuel, munitions."

"Fifty tons . . ." Tatiana thought. "That sounds like a lot."

When he didn't answer, she asked, "Is it?"

She could tell that Alexander was trying not to answer. "It's not enough," he replied at last.

"Not enough by how much?"

"Oh, I don't know," he said shortly.

"Tell me."

"I don't *know*, Tania."

"Well," she said with mock cheeriness, "I think that it must be good enough. Fifty tons. Sounds tremendous. I'm glad you told me, because Nina has nothing for her family—"

"Stop!" Alexander exclaimed. "What are you doing?"

"Nothing," Tatiana said sweetly. "Nina doesn't have—"

"Fifty tons sounds like a lot to you, does it?" he said. "Pavlov, our city food chief, is feeding three million people on a thousand tons of flour a day. How's that?"

"What he is giving us *now* amounts to a thousand tons?" Tatiana said, startled.

"Yes," Alexander replied, shaking his head and looking at her with uneasy dismay.

"And they're bringing only fifty tons by plane?"

"Yes again. Fifty tons of not just flour."

"How is the remaining nine hundred fifty tons getting here?"

"Lake Ladoga. Thirty kilometers north of the blockade line. Barges."

"Shura," said Tatiana, "but these thousand tons, if we didn't have our own supplies, we wouldn't be able to make it. We couldn't live on what they give us."

Alexander didn't say anything.

Tatiana stared at him and then turned her head away. She wanted to go home instantly and count how many cans of ham they had left.

"Why can't they fly more planes in?" she asked.

"Because all the planes in the army are being directed to the Battle of Moscow."

"What about the Battle of Leningrad?" Tatiana said faintly, not expecting an answer and not getting one.

"Do you think the blockade will be lifted before the winter?" she said in a small voice. "The radio reports keep saying we're trying to establish a foothold here, make a break there, pontoon bridges. What do you think?"

Alexander didn't answer, and Tatiana didn't look at him again until they left the store.

"Are you coming home with me?"

"Yes, Tania," said Alexander. "I'm coming home with you."

She nodded. "Come on then. With the butter you gave me, I'll make nice hot oatmeal for breakfast. I'll make you some eggs."

"You still have oatmeal left?"

"Hmm. I will say that it's getting harder and harder to keep them all away from the food between meals. I think Babushka and Marina are the biggest culprits. I think they eat the oatmeal uncooked right out of the bag."

"Do *you*, Tatia?" Alexander asked. "Do you eat oatmeal right out of the bag?"

"Not yet," replied Tatiana. She didn't mention how badly she wanted to. How she put her face inside the oat bag and smelled its sickly, slightly moldy aroma, wishing for butter and for sugar and for milk, and for eggs.

"You should," Alexander said.

They walked slowly along the misty Fontanka Canal. It reminded Tatiana a little of Obvodnoy Canal during their Kirov summer days. Her heart hurt. Three blocks away from home, they both slowed down, then stopped and leaned against the cold building. "I wish there were a bench," Tatiana said quietly.

Just as quietly, Alexander said, "Marazov told me about your father." When Tatiana didn't answer, he continued. "I am really sorry." Pause. "Will you forgive me?"

"There is nothing to forgive," she replied.

"It's my helplessness," Alexander continued, his eyes filling with loud frustration. "There's just nothing I can do to protect you. And I tried. I tried from the very beginning. Remember Kirov?"

Tatiana remembered.

"All I wanted then was for you to leave Leningrad. I failed there. Failed to protect you against your father." He shook his head. "How is your brow feeling?" He reached out and touched the healing bruise with his fingertips.

"It's all right," Tatiana said, moving away from him. Alexander put his hands down, looking at her with rebuke.

"How is Dimitri?" she asked. "Have you heard from him?"

Shaking his head, Alexander said, "What can I tell you about Dimitri? When I first went to Shlisselburg in mid-September, I said, come with me, come with my command. He refused. He said we were too unprotected there. All right, I said. Then I volunteered myself and a battalion of soldiers to go to Karelia and push the Finns back a bit." He paused. "To give our trucks breathing room as they brought food from Ladoga to Leningrad. The Finns were just too close. The skirmishes that flared up between them and the gun-happy NKVD border troops constantly resulted in the death of some poor hapless truck driver, who was just trying to get food into the city. I told Dimitri to come with me. Yes, it's dangerous, I said. Yes, it's attacking enemy territory, but if we succeed—"

"You will be heroes," Tatiana said. "Have you succeeded?"

Quietly Alexander said, "Yes."

Shaking her head in wonder, Tatiana gazed up at him. She hoped it was not blatantly obvious what she was feeling at that moment. "You *volunteered* for this?"

"Yes."

"Did they promote you at least!"

He saluted her lightly and said, "I'm now Captain Belov. And see my new medal?"

"No, stop it!" she exclaimed, her mouth melting into a smile.

"What?" Alexander asked, his eyes roaming all over her face. "What? Are you . . . proud?"

"Hmm," Tatiana said, trying to stop smiling.

"Which was my whole point with Dima," continued Alexander. "If it worked out, he could have become a corporal. The higher up you go, the farther from the front line you are."

Nodding, Tatiana said, "He is so shortsighted."

"And worse," said Alexander. "Because now he has been sent along with Kashnikov to Tikhvin. Marazov followed me. Became first lieutenant. But Dima was transported in a barge across Ladoga, and he is now part of tens of thousands of men, one and all cannon fodder for Schmidt."

Tatiana had heard about the town of Tikhvin. The Soviets took Tikhvin from the Germans in September and were now fiercely struggling to hold on to it, to allow themselves a continuous railroad passage to the Ladoga food barges. Without Lake Ladoga there would be no food getting into Leningrad at all.

She had long ago stopped smiling. Carefully she said, "I wish you had succeeded with Dimitri. A promotion would have been good for him."

"I agree."

"And maybe if he had become a hero," Tatiana went on evenly, "you wouldn't have to marry my sister."

His face falling, Alexander said, "Oh, Tatia—"

"But as it is," she continued loudly, interrupting him, "you're a captain, and he's in Tikhvin. You'll *have* to marry Dasha now, won't you?" She stared at him unremittingly.

Alexander rubbed his eyes with his blackened hands. Tatiana had never seen him so unclean. She had forgotten all about him, so busy was she thinking all about herself. "Oh, Shura. What am I *doing?*" Tatiana said. "I'm so sorry. Come home. Look at you. Come. You'll wash." She said softly, "You can have a hot bath. I'll boil the water for you. I'll make you nice oatmeal. Come on." She wanted to add *darling* but didn't dare. *Marry Dasha*, Tatiana *almost* wanted to say. *Marry her if it helps you live.*

Alexander didn't move from the wall.

"Please come, Shura."

"Wait." He bit his lip. "Are you upset with me because of your father?"

He didn't fight, he didn't argue, he didn't say it wasn't his fault. He just accepted responsibility and went on, as if it now was just another burden to be carried on his shoulders. Well, his shoulders were wide enough for several burdens, including some of Tatiana's, and, oddly, to see him square his chest made her own lighter. Relief came at Alexander's expense, but it was welcome relief nonetheless. She wanted comfort? There it was.

"No, Shura," Tatiana said. "No one is upset. They'll be overjoyed you're alive."

Alexander raised his eyes to her. "I didn't ask about them. Are *you* upset with me?"

Tatiana looked at him with compassion. Underneath his battle armor, the man who commanded an armored battalion needed *her*. If he was wounded, she could bandage him. If he was hungry, she could feed him. If he wanted to talk to her, there she was. But now her Alexander was sad. She wanted to tell him that it wasn't for her father she was upset with him. But she couldn't, because all she wanted was to give him comfort back. She didn't want him to be sad for another moment.

Reaching out, Tatiana took hold of his hand. He had dirt under his nails and bloody scratches, but his hand was warm and strong, and it squeezed hers gratefully.

"No, Shura," she said tenderly. "Of course, I'm not upset with you."

"I just want you to be safe," he said, his back to the wall. "That's all. Safe from everything."

Tatiana came into Alexander's arms. "I know. I'm going to be just fine," she said into his coat, feeling so happy to be hugging him that she was afraid of falling down. Brushing the hair away from her forehead, Alexander pressed his lips to her healing brow and whispered, "Don't back away from me like before when I touch you."

"All right," Tatiana murmured, her eyes closed and her arms tight around him.

3

"Look who I found!" Tatiana exclaimed as Alexander walked in behind her. Dasha shrieked, running to him.

Tatiana went to put the water on to boil for his bath. She found soap for him, and fresh towels, and a razor, and Alexander went and had a hot bath.

"Is it warm enough?" she called to him from the kitchen, boiling more water, just in case.

His laughing voice carried from the bathroom. "No, not at all. Come, bring me another jug. Come in here, Tania."

Blushing and smiling, Tatiana went and asked Dasha to bring Alexander another jug of boiling water.

He came inside the room all scrubbed and flushed and clean-shaven, so warm, his black hair so damp and shiny, his teeth so white, his mouth so moist that Tatiana didn't know how she kept from flinging her arms around him. While he sat in his long johns and thermal shirt, Dasha went to wash his uniform. Marina, Babushka, and Tatiana clucked around him; everyone did except surly Mama.

Tatiana didn't tell Mama she had eggs. She was going to, but when she saw that Mama was not prepared to forgive Alexander for yelling at her and Papa, Tatiana was not prepared to share eggs with her. Forgiveness had to come first.

Alexander had given them a kilo of butter. Tania hid it under the sack of flour on the windowsill. Mama had a weak cup of tea with some bread and butter, gruffly thanked Alexander, and went to work.

Babushka took some silverware, some silver candlesticks, some money, old blankets off the bed, and stuffed them all into a sack as she, too, got ready to leave.

Tatiana had to go and cook breakfast, but she remained in the room, sitting quietly in a chair, staring at Alexander.

"Where is she going?" Alexander inquired.

"Oh, across the Aleksandr Nevsky Bridge to Malaya Ochta," said Dasha, coming into the room. Tatiana quickly lowered her gaze. "She's got friends there," Dasha continued, "and she trades our things for potatoes or carrots. She was good to them when things were good, and now they're good to her when things are not. Your clothes won't dry for a while," she said to Alexander, smiling.

"That's all right," he said, smiling back. "I don't have to report to base for four days. Will they be dry by then?"

Tatiana's heart skipped with joy. Four days of Alexander!

"Tania, are you going to go and make breakfast?" Dasha asked, leaving again. Marina was in the other room, getting ready to go to university.

Alexander turned to Tatiana. "Tatiasha," he said, "can I have some tea?"

Instantly she got up from the table. What was she thinking, sitting around? He must be so tired, so hungry. "Of course." He was sitting and smoking, with his long legs stretching across the floor all the way to the couch. There was no room for Tatiana to walk past, and Alexander wasn't moving his legs. Tatiana stared at him. He was smiling.

"Excuse me, Alexander," Tatiana said quietly, trying *very* hard to keep a straight face.

"Step over them," he said, lowering his voice. "Just take care not to trip. Because then I'd have to catch you."

Turning red, Tatiana raised her eyes and saw Marina watching her from the door. "Excuse me, Alexander," Tatiana repeated, keeping her breathy voice even.

Reluctantly Alexander moved his legs. "Come here, Marina," he said with a sigh. "Let me take a look at you. How have you been keeping?"

Tatiana brought Alexander a cup of tea, making it nice and strong and sweet for him, just the way he liked it. "Thank you," he said, looking up at her.

"You're welcome." She gazed down at him.

"My legs still in your way?"

"Yes, you're too large for this room," Tatiana whispered.

Before he could reply, Dasha came back with some clean sheets. "Girls, how does your Babushka do across the Neva?" Alexander asked, taking his tea and looking away from Tatiana.

Folding sheets and putting them away, Dasha said, "Yesterday she brought five turnips and ten potatoes. But all of Mama's wedding dishes are now gone. After these candlesticks, I don't know what else she'll have to sell."

"How about those gold teeth you took from the dentist, Dasha?" Tatiana asked. "Would the farmers like some gold?" She sat down at the table next to the wall, her back to Dasha, her eyes to Alexander.

"What could they possibly do with gold?"

"What would they do with candlesticks?"

Alexander said, "Ah, have light. Have heat. Use them as weapons against the Germans." He turned to Tatiana. "Tania . . ." He smiled. "Where *is* this promised oatmeal? Where are those promised eggs?"

There was a knock at the front door, and Tatiana went to answer it. It was Nina Iglenko wanting to know if they had any extra anything she could give Anton. Tatiana knew that Nina was having a hard time sustaining him on a dependent's ration after he was wounded on the roof. Alexander came out to the hallway, enormous and imposing, standing next to her small, sweater-wrapped body. His arm pressing into Tatiana's arm, Alexander said, "Comrade Iglenko, everyone collects the same dependent ration. I'm sorry, we have nothing." And he shut the door, turning to Tatiana. "You didn't tell me that Anton got wounded on the roof." He was still very close to her. Not only could she smell him, breathe him, inhale him, but in one moment his chest would touch her face.

"He's fine," Tatiana said in a dismissive tone, trying not to breathe erratically. "It's just a scratch on his leg." She didn't want Alexander to worry.

"Tania, did you know that everyone collects the same dependent ration?" Alexander said pointedly, edging forward and scaring Tatiana into the coat-rack.

"I heard that."

"You don't have any more than Nina does."

"I know. Excuse me. I have to go and make you breakfast." Tatiana couldn't spend another second standing with him in the narrow hallway while he was wearing his long johns. She walked out and caught up with Nina in the corridor, handing her a hunk of the butter.

"God bless you, Tanechka," said Nina. "God bless you as long as you live. You'll see. He will protect you all your life for your kind heart."

Tatiana returned to the kitchen and was making eggs and oatmeal, when Alexander came in and leaned against the stove, facing her.

"Careful, your back will get burned," said Tatiana, not looking at him.

He didn't say anything at first, but then a fierce whisper came out of him. "Tania, better than anyone else, I know what you are. I know what you're doing—"

"What?" she said. "I'm making oatmeal. And eggs."

Alexander put his finger under her chin and turned her face up to him. "You cannot give your food away, do you understand? There isn't enough for you and your family."

Opening her mouth and pretending to bite his finger, Tatiana nodded. Alexander left his fingers on her for a moment.

Tatiana made the oatmeal with a couple of tablespoons of milk, some butter, and a few teaspoons of sugar. And water. She made enough for four small bowls and divided it into four uneven parts, the largest one for Alexander, the next for Dasha, then Marina, and the smallest for her. He had brought them twenty eggs. She scrambled five of them with butter and salt. It felt as if they were having a feast.

Alexander took one look at his bowl and said he would not eat it. Dasha had already finished her oatmeal by the time he had stopped speaking. Marina, too. And her eggs.

Only Tatiana gazed down into her bowl as Alexander gazed down at his. "What is the matter with you two?" Dasha said. "Alex, you need much more food than she does. You're a man. She is the smallest. She needs the least out of all of us. Now, eat. Please."

"Yes," said Tatiana, still not looking up. "You're a man. I am the smallest. I do need the least. Now, eat. Please."

Alexander switched his bowl with Tatiana's. "Now, *you* eat," he said. "I can get food at the barracks. Eat."

Gratefully Tatiana ate every last bite in seconds. Then she finished her eggs.

Dasha said, "Oh, Alexander, how different things are since the last time you were here. It's a lot harder now. People are harder. Everyone is now only for themselves, it seems." She sighed, glancing away.

Alexander and Tatiana silently stared at Dasha.

"We're getting only three hundred grams of bread a day," she continued. "How much worse can it get?"

"Much worse," said Tatiana, sparing Alexander an answer. "Because our provisions will soon be gone."

"How many cans of ham do you have left?" he asked.

"Twelve."

"Yes," said Tatiana, "but four days ago we had eighteen. We ate six cans in four days. We've been hungry at night." She wanted to add that they were hungry every waking and sleeping minute of every day but didn't.

The girls had to go to work. Tatiana watched Dasha come close to Alexander, who put his hands on her waist. "Oh, Alexander, I've gotten so thin," Dasha said. "You're not going to like me anymore, thin like this. Soon I'll start looking like Tania." She kissed him. "Are you going to be all right while we're gone? What are you going to do?"

Alexander smiled. "I'm going to fall down in your bed and not wake up until you come home."

Tatiana *ran* home at five o'clock, bombing or no bombing.

At home it was toasty warm. Alexander came out of the room grinning happily at her, and Tatiana, grinning happily back, said, "Hello, Alexander, I'm home!"

He laughed.

She wanted to kiss him.

He had gone and retrieved a dozen bundles of wood from the basement and brought them upstairs. Dasha came in from the kitchen. "Isn't it cozy in here, Tania?" she said, hugging Alexander.

"Girls," he said, "you will have to keep heating these rooms. It's getting too cold."

"We're getting heat from the central heating system, Alex," argued Dasha.

"Dash," he said, "the Leningrad Council is heating residential buildings to a maximum of ten degrees Centigrade. You think that's warm enough?"

"It hasn't been so bad," said Tatiana, taking off her coat.

Alexander patted Dasha's arm. "I'm going to bring you more wood from the basement and leave it for you. Heat your rooms with the big stove, not the little *bourzhuika* that can't warm up a penguin. All right, Tania?"

Suddenly shivering, Tatiana said nothing at first. "Alexander, these wood-burning stoves take a lot of wood," she said, and hurried out to make him dinner.

Babushka brought seven potatoes from Malaya Ochta. They ate one more can of ham and all of the potatoes. After dinner Alexander suggested that from now on they eat only half a can of ham a day. Dasha got upset. She said they could barely make it on the whole can. He said nothing.

When the air-raid siren sounded, he motioned for the family to go down into the shelter—everyone, including Tatiana. When Dasha asked him to come with them, Alexander looked at her thoughtfully and said, "Dasha, go on now, and don't worry about me." When she insisted, he said, more firmly, "What kind of a soldier would I be if I ran for shelter every time there was a little bombing? Now, go. And, Tania, you, too. You haven't been on the roof, have you?"

No one answered him as they filed out, certainly not Tatiana.

Later that night Dasha said, "Marinka, can you sleep with Babushka tonight? Please? It's warm in her room, not like ours. I want Alexander to sleep next to me. Mama, you don't mind, do you? We *are* getting married."

"Next to you and *Tania?*" Marina gave Tatiana a look that Tatiana did not return.

"Yes." Dasha smiled, getting clean bedding out of the dresser. "Alexander, you don't mind sleeping in the same bed as Tania?"

He grunted.

"Tanechka, tell me," Dasha said teasingly, as she started to make the bed, "should I put him in the middle, between us?" She laughed lightly. "It will be good for Tania. It'll be the first time she has slept with a man." Amused at herself, Dasha pinched Alexander's arm and said, "Though, darling, maybe she shouldn't start with *you.*"

Not looking at Tatiana, Alexander muttered that he really wouldn't be comfortable in the middle, and Tatiana, not looking at him, muttered that he was right, and Dasha said to him, "Relax, you don't think I was really going to put you next to my sister?"

At bedtime Tatiana climbed in next to her wall, Dasha climbed in next to her, and Alexander fitted in on the end in his thermals. There was no room to move, but it *was* warmer, and his presence so close, yet so far away, a whole heart away, softened Tatiana's eyes. Quietly they lay in bed listening to Mama as she cried on her sofa.

Then Tatiana heard Dasha whispering to Alexander, "You said before that we would get married—when, my love, when?"

He whispered back, "Let's wait, Dasha."

"No," she said. "Wait for what? You said we would do it when you got leave. Let's get married tomorrow. We'll go to the registry office and get married in ten minutes. Tania and Marina can be our witnesses. Come on, Alexander, we have nothing to wait for."

Tatiana turned to the wall.

"Dasha, listen to me. The fighting is too intense. And haven't you heard? Comrade Stalin has made it a crime to be taken prisoner. It's now against the law to fall into German hands. To prevent me further from *willingly* giving myself up to the Germans, our great leader has decided to take away family rations from the Soviet POW. If I get taken by the Germans and we're married, you will lose your rations. You. Tania. Your mother, grandmother. All of you. I will have to get killed to keep you getting your bread."

"Oh, Alexander. Oh, no."

"We'll wait."

"Wait for what?"

"For a better time."

"Will there be a better time?"

"Yes."

Then they fell quiet.

Tatiana turned away from the wall, to Dasha, and stared at the back of Alexander's head. She was remembering lying in his arms, naked and broken in Luga, with his breath in her hair.

In the middle of the night Dasha got up to go to the bathroom. Tatiana thought Alexander was asleep, but he turned around and faced her. In the dark she made out his liquid eyes. Under the blanket his leg moved sideways and touched hers; she was wearing socks and two layers of flannel pajamas. When she heard Dasha in the outside hallway, she closed her eyes. Alexander moved his leg away.

The following evening Tatiana cooked only half a can of ham for all of them. It was about a tablespoonful each, but at least it was ham. Dasha grumbled that it wasn't enough.

"Anton is dying," said Tatiana. "Eat the ham. Nina Iglenko has not had ham since August."

After dinner Mama went to her sewing machine. Since the start of September she had been bringing work home. The army needed winter uniforms, and the factory offered Mama a bonus if she made twenty uniforms a day instead of ten. A bonus of a few rubles and one extra ration. Mama worked until one in the morning for 300 grams of bread and some rubles. This evening she went to her sewing seat, sat down, took her materials, and said, "Where *is* my sewing machine?"

No one spoke.

"Where is my sewing machine? Tania, where is my sewing machine?"

"I don't know, Mama," said Tatiana.

Babushka limped forward and said, "Irina, I sold it."

"You *what?*"

"I traded it in for those soybeans and oil you had tonight. They were so good, Ira."

"Mama!" Irina screamed. She became hysterical. For minutes she sobbed into her hands. Tatiana stood and watched Alexander's pained expression as he went out into the hallway.

"Mama, how could you do that?" Irina cried. "You know that every night they offer me work, and every night I kill myself on that thing to make something for myself, to bring something for my family, something just for us! Don't you know they were telling me I could get some oats every day, too, if I managed to get up to twenty-five uniforms. Oh, Mama, what have you done?"

Tatiana left the room herself. Alexander was sitting on the hallway sofa, smoking. Taking a pen, she went behind the sofa, knelt on the floor, and started lifting the bag of oats so she could mark its level. The oatmeal, the flour, the sugar just kept disappearing. Behind her she heard Alexander say, "Come on, get up off the floor. It's too hard for you. Let me help." She moved out of his way, and he lifted the bag for her as she looked inside and drew a black line on the outside. "What do you think, Tatia?" Alexander said, calling her *Tatia* quietly. "Private enterprise for your mother? Who would've thought?"

"It's everywhere, though," said Tatiana. "'Socialism in one country' seems not to work so well when the country is fighting a war." She motioned to the bag of flour.

Picking it up, Alexander nodded. "Just like during the Russian civil war and right after. Have you noticed that during war, to preserve its own life, the beast subsides and lies low . . ."

"Just long enough to get strong again and rear its head. Wait, hold the flour a little lower." Her hand with the pen touched his hand holding the bag. She did not look up.

"What's your Mama going to do, Tania?"

"I don't know. What's Babushka going to do? She's got nothing left to sell." Taking her hand away, Tatiana went into the kitchen to wash the dishes from dinner.

As she headed back to the room, Alexander entered the kitchen. They were alone. She went to walk past him, and he moved in front of her; she tried to go the other way, and he moved in front of her. Tatiana looked up at him and saw that his eyes were twinkling.

Her own eyes twinkling, she stood still for a moment and then moved right, left, and was around him. Glancing back and smiling, Tatiana said quietly, "Got to be quicker than that, Shura," and he laughed loudly.

* * *

Alexander left after four days and went back to base. Everybody missed him when he went.

The good news was he was staying in Leningrad for another week or so, doing patrol work and base maintenance, building barricades and training new recruits. He couldn't stay over anymore, but he spent most evenings with them, and in the mornings he came at six-thirty and walked Tatiana to Fontanka to get her rations.

One morning when he came, he said, "I heard Dimitri's been shot!"

"No!"

"True." He paused.

"What happened? Did he go down in a blaze of glory?"

"He shot himself in the foot with his Nagant sidearm."

"Oh, I forget," Tatiana said. "He is not you."

Placing a hand on her coat, Alexander told her Dimitri was in a Volkhov hospital, indefinitely out of action. "On top of the foot wound, he's got dystrophy."

"What's that?"

Tatiana felt that Alexander almost did not want to tell her. "Dystrophy," he said slowly, "is a muscle-mass disease, degenerative. Brought on by acute malnutrition."

Patting him lightly, Tatiana said in a weak voice, "Don't worry, Shura. I won't get it. I have no muscles."

They waited patiently for her rations.

Alexander kept looking down at her, trying to get her to meet his expectant gaze. Tatiana strongly sensed that he wanted something from her, but what it was she didn't know and couldn't guess at.

Couldn't? Or didn't want to?

Alexander's rations helped them stretch their food supplies a little longer. He got a king's ration—800 grams of bread per day!—more than half of what they were getting for the five of them. He also received 150 grams of meat and 140 of cereals and half a kilo of vegetables.

Tatiana was elated when he came for dinner, bringing with him his food for the day. Was it because she was happy to see him or was it because she was happy to eat better? Alexander would hand her the food, telling her to divide it into six portions. "And, Tania," he would tell her every time, "six *equal* portions."

The meat in his ration was not beef but some kind of pasty pork or sometimes an aged chicken leg with thick skin. It took all of Tatiana's mental strength not to give him the largest cut. She did what she could and gave him the best.

There were no more candlesticks to trade and no more dishes, except for the six plates the Metanovs kept for themselves and Alexander. Babushka wanted to trade their old blankets and coats, but Mama put her foot down. "No. Winter is cold here in the city. We will need them." The temperature had dropped below freezing in the third week of October. Only six sheets remained for three beds, only six towels. Babushka wanted to trade one of the towels, but Tania put *her* foot down, remembering that Alexander needed a towel, too.

Babushka Maya stopped going across the Neva.

4

Tatiana was in the hallway when she heard Dasha, Alexander, Marina, Mama, and Babushka all arguing heatedly inside the room. She was about to open the door and walk in with the tea when she heard Alexander say, "No, no, you cannot tell her. This is not the time."

And Dasha's voice spilled through the crack in the door. "But, Alexander, she is going to have to know eventually—"

"Not now!"

"What's the point?" said Mama. "What does it matter? Tell her."

Babushka said, "I agree with Alexander. Why weaken her now when she needs her strength?"

Tatiana opened the door. "Tell me what?"

Everyone fell mute.

"Nothing, Tanechka," Dasha said quickly, glaring at Alexander, who lowered his gaze and sat down.

Tatiana was holding the tray of teacups, saucers, spoons, and a small teapot. "Tell me what?"

Dasha's face was streaked with tears. "Oh, Tania," she said.

"Oh, Tania, what?" said Tatiana.

No one said anything. No one even looked at her.

Tatiana looked from her grandmother to her mother to her cousin to her sister and stopped on Alexander, who was smoking and looking at his cigarette. Someone lift your eyes to me, Tatiana thought.

"Alexander, what don't you want them to tell me?"

He raised his eyes. "Your grandfather died, Tania," he said. "In September. Pneumonia."

The tray with the teacups fell from Tatiana's hands, and the cups broke on the wood floor, and the hot tea spilled on her stockings. Tatiana knelt on the floor and picked up all the shards without saying a word to anyone, which was just as well, because no one could say a word to her. And then she put all the broken pieces on the tray, picked the tray up and went back out to the kitchen. As she was closing the door, she heard Alexander say, "Happy now?"

Dasha and Alexander came out to the kitchen, where Tatiana was stand-

271

ing next to the window, numbly grasping the sill. Dasha went to Tatiana and said, "Honey, I'm sorry. Come here." She hugged Tatiana and whispered, "We all adored him. We are all devastated."

Tatiana hugged her sister back and said, "Dasha, it's a bad sign."

"No, Tanechka, it isn't."

"It's a bad sign," Tatiana repeated. "It's as if Deda died because he couldn't bear to see what was about to happen to his family."

Both girls looked at Alexander, who stood nearby watching them and said nothing.

The next morning Alexander and Tatiana walked in silence to the ration store and waited in silence for their bread. When they were outside by the Fontanka Canal, Alexander stuck his hand into his coat pocket and said, "I have to go back up tomorrow, Tania. But look. Look what I brought you." He held a small bar of chocolate. She took it from him and managed a weak smile. Her eyes filled up.

Alexander took hold of Tatiana's hand and said soothingly, patting his chest, "Come here."

She stood for a long time—her face pressed into Alexander's chest, his arms around her—and cried.

Anton's leg was not getting better. Anton was not getting better.

Tatiana brought him a piece of Alexander's chocolate. Anton ate it, but listlessly.

She sat by his bed. They didn't speak for a while.

"Tania," he said, "remember summer before last?" His voice was weak.

"No," said Tatiana. She only remembered last summer.

"In August when you came back from Luga, me, you, Volodya, Petka, and Pasha played soccer in Tauride Park? You wanted the ball so much, you kicked my shin to get it? I think it was the same leg." A faint smile passed over Anton's face.

"I think you're right," Tatiana said quietly. "Shh, Anton." She took his hand. "Your leg will heal, and maybe next summer we'll go to Tauride Park and play soccer again."

"Yes," he said, squeezing her hand and closing his eyes. "But not with your brother. Or my brothers."

"Just you and I, Anton," whispered Tatiana.

"Not even me, Tania," he whispered back.

They're waiting for you, Tatiana wanted to say to him. They're waiting to play soccer with you again.

And with me.

Tatiana used to leave at six-thirty to get the rations—herself as punctual as a German—so that even with waiting in line and the ration store being all the way on Fontanka, she could be back by eight when the bombing formations flew overhead and the air-raid sirens sounded. But she had noticed that either the raids were starting earlier or she was getting out later, because three mornings in a row she got caught in the shell fire while still on Nekrasova returning home.

Only because she had *promised, sworn* to Alexander that she would, Tatiana waited out the bombing in a shelter in someone else's building, holding her precious bread to her chest and wearing the helmet he had left her and made her *promise and swear* to wear when she went out.

The bread Tatiana was holding wasn't delicious bread; it wasn't white, and it wasn't soft, and it didn't have a golden crust, but still a smell emanated from it. For thirty minutes she sat while thirty pairs of eyes glared at her from all directions, and finally an old woman's voice said, "Come on, girlie, share with us. Don't just sit there holding the loot. Give us a bite."

"It's for my family," Tatiana said. "There are five of us, all women. They're waiting for me to bring it to them. If I give it to you, they will have no food today."

"Not much, girlie," the old woman persisted. "Just a bite."

The shelling stopped, and Tatiana was the first one out. After that she made sure she didn't lag behind anymore.

But despite her best efforts she could not seem to get to the ration store and back before the bombs came.

To go at ten was impossible. Tatiana had to be at work; people depended on her there, too. She wondered if Marina would do better, or maybe Dasha. Maybe they could move faster than Tatiana. Mama was sewing uniforms by hand in the morning and at night. Tatiana couldn't possibly send her mother, who practically never looked up from her sewing nowadays, trying to finish a few uniforms so she could get some extra oatmeal.

Dasha said she couldn't go because she had to do laundry in the morning. Marina also refused, which was just as well. She had nearly stopped going to university. Taking her ration card, she picked up her own bread and ate it immediately. At night when she came back to Fifth Soviet, she *demanded* more food from Tatiana. "Marinka, it's just not fair," Tatiana would say to her cousin. "We're all hungry. I know this is hard, but you have to keep yourself in check—"

"Oh, like you keep yourself in check?"

"Yes," Tatiana said, sensing that Marina was not talking about the bread.

"You're doing well," Marina said. "Very well, Tania. Keep it up."

But Tatiana didn't feel she was doing well.

She felt that she was doing worse than ever before, and yet her family was lauding her efforts. Something was not right with the world in which her family thought Tatiana was making a success out of a big botch. It wasn't that she felt herself to be slow that bothered her, but that she felt herself *slowing down*. All her efforts at haste, at deliberate speed, were met with an unknown resistance—resistance from her own body.

It wasn't moving as fast as it used to, and the inarguable proof of that lay with the German bombers, who at precisely eight o'clock flew their planes over the center of the city and for two hours sounded the mortar clarion call, the high-explosive bugle, to disrupt the rush hour of the morning.

Sunrise came at eight also. Tatiana walked to the store and back in near-dark.

One morning Tatiana was walking on Nekrasova and without much thought passed a man walking in the same direction. He was tall, older, thin, wearing a hat.

Only when she passed him did it occur to Tatiana that she hadn't passed anyone in a long time. People walked at their own pace, but it was never an overtaking pace. Either I'm walking faster, she thought, or he is even slower than me.

She slowed down, then stopped. As she turned around, she saw him drift down like a parachute by the side of the building and keel over to his side. Tatiana walked back to him, to help him sit up. He was still.

Nonetheless, she tried to straighten him up. She lifted his hat. His unblinking eyes stared at Tatiana. They remained open, as they were just minutes ago when he had been walking on the street. Now he was dead.

Horrified, Tatiana let go of the man and his hat and hurried on without turning around. On the way back with her rations, she decided to take Ulitsa Zhukovskogo instead so as not to walk by the corpse. The air raid had started, but she ignored it and walked on. If they wanted to take my bread in the shelter, there would be nothing I could do to stop them, Tatiana thought, pulling Alexander's helmet down over her head.

That morning she told her family she had seen a dead man on the street. They barely acknowledged it. "Oh?" said Marina. "Well, I saw a dead horse in the middle of the street, cut open, and a crowd of people helping themselves to the horse's flesh. And that's not the worst part. I walked up behind someone and asked if there was anything left for me."

The man's face, his walk, his silly hat stayed in Tatiana's mind as she closed her eyes at night. It wasn't his death that tormented her, because, unfortunately, Tatiana had seen death before—in Luga, in the abject absence of Pasha, as she watched her father burn. But it was this man's walking gait that Tatiana saw when she closed her eyes, because when *he* died, he had been walking, and though he was walking slower than Tatiana, he was not walking slower by *much*.

6

"How many cans of ham do we have left?" Mama asked.

"One," Tatiana replied.

"That can't be."

"Mama, we've been eating it every night."

"But it can't be," said Mama. "We had ten just a few days ago."

"About nine days ago."

The next day Mama asked, "Have we got any flour left?"

"Yes, we have about another kilo. I've been making pancakes with it every evening."

"Is that what those are? Pancakes?" Dasha said. "Tastes like flour and water to me."

"It is flour and water." Tatiana paused. "Alexander calls them sea biscuits."

"Can you make bread out of it?" demanded Mama. "Instead of silly pancakes?"

"Mama, *bread*? Out of what? We have no milk. We have no yeast. We have no butter. And we certainly have no more eggs."

"Just mix it with a little water. We must have some soy milk?"

"We have three tablespoons."

"Use it. Put some sugar in it."

"All right, Mama." For dinner Tatiana made unleavened bread with sugar and the remaining milk. They had the last can of ham. It was October 31.

"What's *in* this bread?" Tatiana asked, breaking off a piece of the black crust and looking inside. "What is this?" It was the start of November. Babushka was on the couch. Mama and Marina had already gone out for the day. Tatiana was procrastinating, trying to make her portion last. She didn't want to go to the hospital.

Dasha leaned over from her chair and shrugged. "Who knows? Who cares? How does it taste?"

"Actually, revolting."

"Eat it. What, maybe you'd like some white bread instead?"

Tatiana picked at a little piece of something in the bread, poked it with her fingers, then put it on her tongue. "Dash, oh my God, you know what it is?"

"I don't care."

"It's sawdust."

Dasha paused in her own chewing, but only for a second. "Sawdust?"

"Yes, and this here?" Tatiana pointed to a brown fleck between her fingers. "That's cardboard. We're eating paper. Three hundred grams a day, and they're giving us paper."

Finishing every last crumb of her piece and looking hungrily at the one Tatiana was kneading between her fingers, Dasha said, "We're lucky to have *that*. Can I open the can of tomatoes?"

"No. We have only two left. Besides, Mama and Marina are not here. You know if we open it, we'll eat it all."

"That's the idea."

"We can't. We'll open it tonight for dinner."

"What kind of dinner is that going to be? Tomatoes?"

"If you didn't eat all your cardboard in the morning, you'd have some left for dinner."

"I can't help it."

"I know," said Tatiana, putting the rest of the bread in her mouth and chewing it with her eyes closed. "Listen," she said when she had swallowed hard, "I've got some crackers left. Want to have some? Just three each?"

"Yes." The girls glanced at Babushka, who was sleeping.

They ate seven each. Only small remainders were left of what used to be whole pieces of toasted bread. Broken remainders with crumbs on the bottom.

"Tania, are you still getting your monthlies?"

"What?"

"Are you?" There was anxiety in Dasha's voice and anxiety in Tatiana's as she answered. "No. Why do you ask?"

"I'm not either."

"Oh."

Dasha was quiet. The sisters breathed shallowly.

"Are you *worried*, Dasha?" Tatiana said at last, with great reluctance.

Dasha shook her head. "I'm not worried about *that*. Alexander and I—" She glanced at Tatiana. "Never mind. I'm worried I'm not getting it. That it just ceased to be."

"Don't worry," said Tatiana, relieved and sad for her sister at the same time. "It'll come back when we start to eat again."

Dasha raised her eyes at Tatiana.

Tatiana looked away.

"Tania," Dasha whispered, "aren't you feeling it? Like your whole body is just shutting down?" She started to cry. "Shutting down, Tania!"

Tatiana hugged her sister. "Dearest," she said. "my heart's still beating. I'm not shutting down, Dasha. And you're not either."

The girls were silent in the cold room. Hugging Tatiana back, Dasha said, "I want that senseless hunger back. Remember last month when we were always starving?"

"I remember."

"You don't feel that anymore, do you?"

"No," admitted Tatiana faintly.

"I want it back."

"You'll get it back. When we start eating, it will all come back."

That night Tatiana came home with a pot of clear liquid they served in the hospital cafeteria. There was one potato floating in it.

"It's chicken soup," Tatiana said to her family. "With some ham hock."

"Where is the chicken? Where is the ham hock?" Mama asked as she looked into the small pot.

"I was lucky to get this."

"Yes, Tanechka, you were. Come, pour for us," Mama said.

It tasted like hot water with a potato. It had no salt, and it had no oil. Tatiana divided it into five portions because Alexander was still away.

"I hope Alexander comes back soon so we can have some of his food. He's so lucky to have such a good ration," said Dasha.

I hope Alexander comes back soon, too, thought Tatiana. I need to lay my eyes on him.

"Look at us," said Mama. "We've waited for this dinner since our one o'clock lunch. But someone has to help with the bombs, the fires, the glass, the wounded. We're not helping. All we want to do is eat."

"That's exactly what the Germans want," said Tatiana. "They want us to abandon our city, and we are ready to do it to have a potato."

"I can't go out there," said Mama. "I've got five uniforms to sew by hand." She glared at Babushka, who sat quietly, chewed her bread, and said nothing.

"We won't go out there," said Tatiana. "We will sit and work and sew. But we are not abandoning our Leningrad. No one is leaving here."

No one else spoke.

When the air raid began, they all descended to the shelter, even Tatiana, who tripped over a woman who had died sitting up against the wall and whom no one had bothered to move. Tatiana sank down and waited out the darkness.

7

Dasha wrote to Alexander each day; every single day she wrote him a short letter. How lucky she is, Tatiana thought. To be able to write to him, to have him receive her thoughts, how lucky.

They also wrote to their widowed Babushka in Molotov.

Letters back from her were rare.

The mail was terrible.

Then it stopped coming at all.

When the mail stopped coming to the building, Tatiana started going to the post office on Old Nevsky, where an old gray man with no teeth sat and gave her the mail only after asking her if she had any food for him. She would bring him a remainder of a small cracker. Finally she got a letter from Alexander to Dasha.

My dear Dasha, and everyone else,

The saving grace of war is that most women don't have to see it, only the nurses who tend to us, and they are immune to our pain.

Across from Shlisselburg we're trying to supply the island fortress Oreshek with munitions. A small group of soldiers has been holding that island since September, despite intense German shelling from the banks of Lake Ladoga just 200 meters away. You remember Oreshek? Lenin's brother Alexander was hanged there in 1887 for his part in the plot to assassinate Alexander III.

Now that war has started, the sailors and soldiers guarding the entrance to the Neva are lauded as heroes of the New Russia—the Russia after Hitler. We are all told that after we win, everything will be completely different in the Soviet Union. It will be a much better life, we are promised, but for that life we have to be prepared to die. Lay down your life, we are told, so your children can live.

All right, we say. The fighting doesn't end, even at night. Neither does the rain. We have been wet all day and all night for seven days. We can't dry out. Three of my men have died of pneumonia. It almost seems cosmically unfair to die from pneumonia, when Hitler is so intent on killing us himself. I'm glad I'm not in Moscow right now. Have you heard much about what's going on there? I think that's what's saving us. Saving you. Hitler diverted a large part of his Army Group Nord, including most of his planes and tanks, away from Leningrad for his attack on Moscow. If Moscow falls, we're done for, but right now it's our only reprieve.

I'm fine myself. I don't like being wet much. They still feed us officers. Each day I have meat I think of you.

Be well. Tell Tatiana to walk close to the sides of the buildings. Except when the bombs are falling; then tell her to stop walking and wait in a doorway. Tell her to wear the helmet I left.

Girls, under no circumstances give away your bread. Stay clear of the roof.

And use the soap I left you. Remember that you always feel slightly better about things when you're clean. My father told me that. I will add it's impossible to keep yourself clean on the winter front. But on the plus side, it's so cold here that the lice that spread typhus can't live.

Believe me when I tell you I think of you every minute of every day.

Until I see you again, I remain distantly

Yours,

Alexander

Tatiana wore the helmet. She used the soap. She waited in the doorways. But for some reason all she could think about with a peculiar and prolonged aching, as she didn't take off her felt boots, her felt hat, and her quilted coat, which Mama had made in the days when there was a sewing machine, was Alexander being wet all day and night in his uniform on the icy Ladoga.

PETER'S DARKENED CITY

THERE was no longer any denying that what was happening to Leningrad was nothing like what they could have ever imagined.

Marina's mother died.

Mariska died.

Anton died.

The shelling continued. The bombing continued. There were fewer incendiaries falling, and Tatiana knew this because there were fewer fires, and she knew this because as she walked to Fontanka, there were fewer places for her to stand and warm her hands.

As she was making her way to the store one November morning, Tatiana noticed two dead people lying in the street. On the way back two hours later there were seven. They weren't injured, and they weren't wounded. They were just dead. She made the sign of the cross as she walked past them, stopped and thought, what did I just do? Did I make the *sign of the cross* on dead people? But I live in Communist Russia. Why would I do that? She made the sign of the hammer and sickle as she slowly walked on.

There was no place for God in the Soviet Union. In fact, God clearly went against the principles by which they all lived their lives: faith in work, in living together, in protecting the state against nonconformist individuals, in Comrade Stalin. In school, in newspapers, on the radio, Tatiana heard that God was the great oppressor, the loathsome tyrant who had kept the Russian worker from realizing his full potential for centuries. Now, in post-Bolshevik Russia, God was just another roadblock in the way of the new Soviet man. The Communist man could not have an allegiance to God because that would mean his first allegiance was to something other than the state. And nothing could come before the state. Not only would the state provide for the Soviet people, but it also would feed them and it would give them jobs and protect them from the enemy. Tatiana had heard that in kindergarten, and through nine years of school and in the *Young Pioneer* classes she attended when she was nine. She became a Pioneer because she had no choice, but when it was time for her to join the *Young Komsomols* in her last year of school, she refused. Not because of God necessarily, but just because. Somewhere deep inside, Tatiana had always thought she would not make a very good Communist. She liked Mikhail Zoshchenko's stories too much.

As a child in Luga, Tatiana had known some religious women who were always trying to get their hands on her, to baptize her, to teach her, to make her believe. She would run from them, hiding behind the lilac tree in the neighbors' garden, and watch them shuffle down the village road, but not before they made airy crosses on her with benevolent smiles on their faces, every once in a while lovingly calling out to her, *Tatia, Tatia.*

Tatiana made another sign of the cross, this time on herself. Why was that so conspicuously comforting?

It's as if I'm not alone.

She went to sit inside the church across the street from her building. Do churches ever get bombed? she wondered. Did St. Paul's in London get bombed? If the Germans couldn't be smart enough to destroy the magnificently conspicuous St. Paul's, how were they ever going to find the little church she was in? She felt safer.

At the post office Tatiana had to step over a dead man to get inside. He had died on the doorstep. "How long has he been here?" she asked the postmaster.

Toothlessly he grinned. "I'll tell you for another cracker."

"I don't want to know that badly," she replied, "but I'll give you a cracker anyway."

In the dark no one could see what was happening to their bodies. No one could *face* what was happening to their bodies either. Dasha removed all the mirrors from their rooms and from the kitchen. No one wanted to catch even an accidental glimpse of themselves. They stopped looking at one another. No one wanted to catch even an accidental glimpse of someone they loved.

To hide her own body from herself and everyone else, Tatiana wore a flannel undershirt, a flannel shirt, her own wool sweater, Pasha's wool sweater, a pair of heavy stockings, long trousers, a skirt over them, and her quilted winter coat. She took off her coat to sleep.

Dasha mentioned that she had lost her breasts, and Marina said, breasts? I don't have a mother anymore, and you're talking about breasts? Wouldn't you trade breasts for your mother? I would. And Dasha apologized, but in the kitchen she broke down crying and said, "I want my breasts back, Tanechka."

Tatiana gently rubbed Dasha's back. "Come on, now," she said. "Courage, Dasha. We're not doing too badly. Look, we have some oatmeal left. Go inside. I'll make you some."

After Aunt Rita died, Marina still went out every morning to university, even though, as she told Tatiana, the professors taught nothing, there were no books and no lectures. But there was some heat, and Marina could sit in the library for a few hours until she could go to the canteen and get her clear soup.

"I hate soup," Marina said. "Hate it now. It's so meaningless."

"It's not meaningless. It's hot water," said Tatiana, as she crouched beside her dwindling bag of sugar. They still had some barley left. "Don't touch the barley," she said. "It will be our dinner for the next month."

"There is hardly a cupful in the bag!" Marina exclaimed in disbelief.

"It's a good thing you can't eat it raw," Tatiana said. But she was wrong. The next day there was less barley in the bag.

2

The leaflets rained down as they had in Luga. First the leaflets, then the bombs. The difference was, there had been food then, and it was warm. The difference was, back then Tatiana had believed in many things. She had believed she would find Pasha. She had believed the war would soon be over. She had believed Comrade Stalin.

Nowadays she believed in only one faint but immutable thing.

In one immutable man.

Now the leaflets that rained down from the Luftwaffe planes proclaimed to her in Russian: *Women! Wear your white dresses. Wear your white dresses so when you walk along Suvorovsky to get your 250 grams of bread, we can see you from 200 meters in the sky, and not shoot you and not throw bombs your way.*

Wear your white dress and live, Tatiana! was what the leaflets shouted to her.

Tatiana saved one, a few days before the twenty-fourth celebration of the Russian Revolution on November 7. She brought it home and carelessly dropped it on the table. There it stayed until the next day, when Alexander returned, thinner than he had been two weeks earlier, his face more gaunt. Gone was the twinkling glance, gone was the perpetual smile, gone the charm and the liveliness. Gone.

What was left was a man who hugged Dasha and even Mama, who hugged him back and said, "Good to see you, dearest. Good to see you. We can't bear to think about you in that wet and cold."

"It's drier, but not much warmer here," said the man, who hugged Babushka standing against the wall in the hallway, because she could not stand unsupported anymore, and who pecked Marina on the cheek, and who, when he turned to Tatiana standing awkwardly by the door, holding on to the brass handle, could not bring himself to come over and *touch* her. Couldn't, despite the fact that his dark eyes lingered on her. He waved to her. That was something. Waved, turned and walked inside the room, put down his rifle, took off his heavy coat, sat, and asked for his soap. The girls twittered around him. Dasha brought him a piece of bread, which he swallowed whole. Marina stared at the bread before he ate it.

"It's Revolution Day tomorrow, Alexander. Will there be a little extra to celebrate with?" Dasha asked.

"I'll get you some food when I go back to the barracks. I'll bring some tomorrow, all right?"

"What about now? Do you have anything now?"

"I came straight from the front, Dasha. I have nothing today."

Tatiana stepped forward. "Alexander, do you want a cup of tea? I'll make you some."

"Yes, please."

"*I'll* make it!" barked Dasha, and disappeared.

Taking out a cigarette, Alexander lit it and offered it to Tatiana. "Have a smoke," he said quietly. "Go ahead."

Shaking her head, Tatiana looked at him, puzzled. "You know I don't smoke."

"I know," Alexander said. "But it'll lessen your appetite." He paused. "What? What are you looking at me like that for?" He smiled faintly. "Keep looking," he whispered.

Staring at him with her clear, affectionate eyes, Tatiana couldn't help herself. She placed her glove-clad hand on the back of his uniform and patted him softly. "Shura," she whispered, "you're still months behind us, aren't you? I *have* no appetite." She took her hand away. He put the cigarette into his own mouth.

Standing behind Alexander, Babushka and Marina watched them. Tatiana didn't care. His face was to her. Marina said, coming up to them, "Alexander, offer me a cigarette, why don't you? To lessen *my* appetite."

Taking the cigarette out of his mouth, Alexander handed it to Marina, who took it and said to Tatiana, "Are you sure you don't want a smoke? It's just been in his mouth, Tania."

Alexander looked from Marina to Tatiana with a tired, slightly bemused expression. "Marinka," he said, "have the cigarette and leave Tania alone."

Picking up the Nazi leaflet off the table, he said, "To celebrate the glorious revolution, Leningrad Party chief Zhdanov is trying to get a couple of table-spoons of sour cream for the children. There might be—"

He stopped talking. Reading the leaflet more carefully, he said, "What's this?"

"Oh, nothing," said Tatiana, stepping closer to the table. Marina had sat down. Babushka continued to stand against the wall. Tatiana opened her coat and showed Alexander the white dress with the red roses she was wearing underneath.

Alexander paled. "Is that *your* dress?" he asked, his voice breaking.

Only Tatiana stood in front of Alexander, and only Tatiana could see what his eyes were filled with. Stepping away from him, she shook her head at him imperceptibly, to say, *no, stop, this room is too small for us, stop.*

"Yes, that's my dress," Tatiana said, looking at the dress hanging off her. She closed her coat.

Dasha came through, shutting the door behind her with her foot. "Alex, here, have some tea. It's weak, but tea is something we still have. Not much else, mind you, not much—" She broke off. "What's the matter?"

"Nothing." Alexander looked back down at the leaflet. "What's this?"

Dasha looked at Marina quizzically, and Marina just shrugged as if to say, *I'll be damned if I know.*

Tatiana remained standing. "That's why I'm wearing a white dress," she said to Alexander. "To avoid being hit."

Alexander shot up from his seat so fast that he spilled the hot tea all over himself. Holding the leaflet, he banged his fist hard on the table. "Are you crazy?" he yelled at Tatiana. "Have you lost your mind?"

Dasha grabbed him by the sleeve. "Alexander, are *you* crazy? What are you shouting at her for?"

"Tania!" he yelled again, taking a lunging step toward her. Tatiana did not back away; she blinked.

Dasha got between them, pushing Alexander away. "Sit down, what's the matter with you? Why are you shouting?"

Alexander sat down, never taking his eyes off Tatiana, who reached behind the sofa, got an old rag, came to the table, and started wiping up the spilled tea.

"Tania," Dasha said, "don't come so close to him. Or in a minute he'll—"

"In a minute I'll *what*, Dasha?" Alexander said.

"Forget it, Dash," Tatiana said quietly. Picking up the empty teacup, she started toward the door.

Alexander grabbed her arm. "Tania, put the cup down and go change your dress." He didn't let go of her arm, but added, "Please."

Tatiana put the cup down.

"Tania," said Alexander, his eyes boring into her. How she wished he would stop holding her arm and looking at her. "Tania, do you know what the Germans did in Luga? You were there, didn't you see? They rained these leaflets down on the volunteer women and young girls, who were digging the trenches and potatoes. Wear your white dresses and white shawls, they said, and we'll know you're civilian women and we'll avoid shooting at you. The women said, oh, all right, and happily went to change and put on their best whites, and the Germans, as they were flying overhead, saw their dresses from 300 meters in the sky and slaughtered them all right there in the trenches. It made targeting them so much easier."

Tatiana pulled her arm from him.

"Now, go and change. Put on something brown. And warm." Alexander got up. "I'll make my own tea." Looking at Dasha, he added coldly, "And, Dasha, do me a favor—don't ever confuse me with anyone who has hurt your sister."

"Can you stay?" Dasha asked.

He shook his head. "Have to report to the garrison by nine."

They ate soup with a bit of cabbage leaf. Black bread as heavy as brick, a few tablespoons of buckwheat kernels, and some unsweetened tea. They gave Alexander a shot of their precious vodka. He went and found wood in the basement and made a nice fire. It got warm in the room. How remarkable, Tatiana thought.

Alexander was at the table, with Dasha on one side and Mama on the other and Marina standing behind him. Babushka remained on the couch. And Tatiana was in the farthest corner, looking into her beige tea. Everyone was around Alexander, except for her. She couldn't even get close.

"Alexander?" Mama asked. "Dear, it must be so hard for you at the front thinking about food all the time, like us."

"Irina Fedorovna," said Alexander, "I'll tell you a little secret." He bent his head to her. "When I'm at the front, I don't think about food at all."

Rubbing his arm, Mama spoke again. "Is there any way you can get my girls out of Leningrad? We're almost out of food."

Shaking his head and trying to disentangle himself from the women, Alexander said, "It's impossible. Anyway, you know that I'm not on the Ladoga command. I'm below on the Neva, bombing the German positions across the river in Shlisselburg." He shuddered. "They're just relentless. But besides, the lake is not frozen over yet, and the barges—There are over two million civilians in Leningrad, and only a few thousand have been evacuated by barge out of the city, all of them children with their mothers."

"We are also children with our mothers," said Dasha.

"*Small* children with their mothers," Alexander corrected himself. "All of you work—who is going to let you go? You and Dasha are making uniforms for the army," he said to Mama, patting her. "Tania works in the hospital. How are you doing there, Tania?" His eyes were on her. She had moved near the window, away from the dining table.

Tatiana shrugged. "Today I sewed forty-two sacks. Still wasn't enough—seventy-eight people died. Mama, I wish I could bring a sewing machine home for you."

Mama turned around and glared at Babushka on the couch, who said in a defeated voice, "You used to like the potatoes I brought, daughter. Now I have nothing to give you."

"Tomorrow," said Alexander, "I will bring potatoes from the army store. I'll bring you a little white flour. I'll bring you everything I can. But I can't get you out. Did you hear about the gunboat *Konstructor*? It was crossing Ladoga with women and children on board, headed around the Ladoga horn to Novaya Ladoga, and it was hit. The captain avoided one bomb. The second one sank his ship, drowning all 250 people."

Dasha declared, "I would rather take my chances here in Leningrad than die in the cold sea like that."

"How have you all been holding up?" Alexander said. "Marina, are you hanging in there?"

"Barely," Marina said. "Look at us all."

"You've looked better," Alexander agreed, glancing at Tatiana, who said emptily, without glancing at him, "Anton died. Last week."

"Yes," said Dasha. "Maybe now Nina will stop coming around asking you for food for him."

"I'm sorry Anton died, Tania," Alexander said. "You're not giving away your food, are you?"

Tatiana didn't reply. "Have you heard from Dimitri?" she asked, changing the subject. "We haven't heard a word."

Lighting a cigarette and shaking his head, Alexander said, "Dimitri is in the Volkhov Hospital fighting for his life. I'm sure he doesn't have the energy to write." He and Tatiana glanced at each other.

The air-raid siren sounded. Alexander looked around the table. No one moved. "Does anyone go down to the shelter anymore, or has Tania corrupted each and every one of you?" he asked over the shrill wailing sound.

Wrapping her cardigan tighter around herself, Dasha replied, "Marina and I still go every once—"

"Tania, when was the last time you went to the shelter?" interrupted Alexander.

Tatiana shrugged. "I went just last week," she said. "I sat next to a woman who wasn't speaking to me. I struck up a conversation three times until I realized she was dead. And not *recently* dead either." Tatiana raised her eyebrows.

"Tania, tell the truth," said Dasha. "You were there for five seconds, and the bombing went on that night for three hours. And when was the time before that?"

"September," said Mama casually, getting up and going to get her sewing.

"Mama, you know what? You're a fine one to talk," exclaimed Dasha. "You haven't been there since September either."

"I have work to do. I'm trying to make extra money. You should do the same."

"I do, Mama! I just take my sewing to the bomb shelter."

"Yes, and I saw what you did to that uniform—attaching the arm upside down. Can't sew in the near-dark, Dasha."

While they were bickering, Tatiana watched Alexander, and he watched Tatiana.

"Tania," he asked, "you haven't taken off your gloves all night. Why? It's so warm in the room. Stop standing by the window where it's cold. Come and sit down with us."

"Oh, Alexander!" Marina exclaimed, putting her arm around him. "You're not going to believe what your Tanechka did last week."

"What did she do?" he asked, turning to Marina.

Dasha stepped in with, "*Your* Tanechka? No, Alexander, we mean, you *really* won't believe it."

"*I* want to tell it." Marina was petulant.

"*Somebody* tell it," said Alexander.

Tatiana groaned. "Do I *have* to stay for this?" she said, walking over to the table and collecting the cups. "Maybe Alexander can throw some more wood on the fire."

He immediately rose and went to the stove, saying, "I can throw wood on the fire *and* listen."

Dasha continued for Marina. "Last Saturday, Marinka and I were coming back from the public canteen on Suvorovsky. We had left Tania in the room, *we* thought peacefully sleeping, but as we're coming back, Kostia from the second floor is running toward us on the street, yelling, 'Hurry, your sister is on fire! Your sister is on fire!' "

Alexander came back to the table and sat down. His eyes were still on her, but Tatiana had noticed they had become considerably less warm.

"Tania, dear, why don't you tell Alexander the rest?" Dasha said. "I think it would be more fun coming from you. Tell him what happened."

Tatiana, her hair short, her eyes sunken, her frame withered away, her arms full of her family's dishes, said, "Nothing happened."

"Why don't you tell me, Tatiana?" said Alexander, glaring at her.

She tutted and stared at Marina with disapproval. "Kostia is too small to be on the roof by himself. I went up to help him. A very small incendiary exploded, and he couldn't put the fire out by himself. I helped him, that's all."

"You went out onto the roof?" Alexander said quietly.

"Just for an hour," she said, trying to be jovial, shrugging a little, managing a smile. "It was really nothing. There was a small fire. I used the sand, and in five minutes put it out. Kostia is a hysteric." She glared at Marina. "And he's not the only one."

"Really, Tania?" Dasha exclaimed. "Don't keep giving Marina the evil eye. A hysteric? Why don't you take off your gloves and show Alexander your hands."

Alexander was mute.

Tatiana moved toward the door with her load. "Like he wants to see my hands."

"You know what?" Alexander said, standing up. "I don't want to see anything. I'm leaving. I'm late."

He grabbed his rifle, his coat, his rucksack and was out the door without even brushing past Tatiana.

After he left, Dasha looked at Tatiana, at Marina, at Mama, at Babushka. "What was wrong with *him?*" she asked wearily.

No one spoke for a moment.

From the couch Babushka said, "Much, much fear."

"Marinka," said Tatiana, "why? You know he worries about all of us endlessly. Why worry him further with nonsense? I'm fine on that roof, and my hands will be fine, too."

"Tania is right! And what did you mean by '*your*' Tanechka anyway?" Dasha demanded, whirling round to Marina.

"Yes, Marina, what *did* you mean?" asked Tatiana, looking angrily at her cousin, who replied that it was just a figure of speech.

"Yes, a stupid figure of speech," said Dasha.

3

That night Tatiana dreamed that she did not sleep, that the night lasted all year, and that in the dark his fingers found her.

In the early morning there was a knock on the door as she was getting up. It was Alexander. He had brought them two kilos of black bread and a cupful of buckwheat kernels. Everyone besides Tatiana was still in bed. He waited for her in the kitchen with his arms crossed and his eyes cold while she brushed her teeth over the kitchen sink. He mentioned that the toilet smelled worse than ever. Tatiana was beyond noticing.

She was already dressed. She slept dressed.

"Shura," Tatiana said, "don't go out now. It's so cold. I can carry a kilo of bread. I think I can still do that. Give me your ration card, I'll get yours, too."

"Oh, Tatiana," Alexander said, "the day has not come when you'll be getting my rations."

"Really?" she snapped, moving toward him so quickly that he actually backed away a step. "If you can go to the front, Alexander—"

"Like I have any choice—"

"Like *I* have any choice. I can get your rations for you. Now, give me your card."

"No," he said. "Let me get your coat. How are your hands?"

"They're fine," she said, showing them. She wanted him to take hold of them, to touch them, but he didn't. He just stared at her with the same cold eyes.

They went out into the bitterness together. It was minus ten degrees. At seven o'clock the skies were still dark, and there was a shrieking wind that got underneath Tatiana's coat and into her ears, whistling its Arctic lament for ten blocks to the store. Inside the store was better, and there were only thirty people ahead of them. It might take only forty minutes this time, Tatiana thought.

"Amazing, isn't it?" Alexander said, his voice tinged with barely suppressed anger. "That here it is *November*, and you're still doing this by yourself."

Tatiana didn't reply. She was too sleepy to reply. She shrugged, pulling her scarf tighter around her head.

Alexander said, "Why do you do this? Dasha is perfectly capable of going. At the very least she can come with you. Marina, too. Why do you continue to go alone?"

Tatiana didn't know what to say. First she was too cold, and her teeth were chattering. After a few minutes she warmed up, but her teeth were still chattering, and she thought, why *do* I go on my own, during air raids, and cold, and dark? Why don't we ever switch? "Because if Marina goes, she eats the rations on the way home. Because Mama sews every morning. Because Dasha does laundry. Who am I going to send? Babushka?"

Alexander didn't reply, but the anger didn't leave his face.

Tatiana touched his coat. He moved away. "Why are you upset with me?" she asked. "Because I went out onto the roof?"

"Because you don't—" He broke off. "Because you don't listen to me." He sighed. "I'm not upset with you, Tatia. I'm angry at *them*."

"Don't be," she said. "It all just happened this way. I'd rather be out here than washing laundry."

"Oh, because Dasha is washing laundry so often? You could be sleeping late six days a week like she is."

"Listen, she is having a hard time with all this. I started going—"

"You started going because they told you to, and you said all right. They said, oh, and can you cook for us, too, and you said all right, broken leg and all."

"Alexander, what are you upset about? That I do what they tell me to? I also do what you tell me to."

Gritting his teeth, he said, "You do what I tell you to? Are you off the fucking roof? Are you in the shelter? Have you stopped giving your food to Nina? Yes, you do what I tell you."

"You think I listen to them *more*?" Tatiana said incredulously. It wasn't their turn yet. A dozen people still ahead of them in line. A dozen people listening to them. "I thought you said you weren't upset with me?"

"I'm not upset about *that*. You want to know what I'm upset about?"

"Yes," she said tiredly. She didn't really.

"Everything they ask of you, you do."

"So?"

"Everything," he said. "They say, go, you say, all right. They say, give me, you say, how much? They say, go away, you say, fine. They hit you, you defend them. They say, I want your bread, I want your milk, I want your tea, I want your—"

Suddenly seeing where he was going, Tatiana tried to stop him. "No, no," she said, shaking her head. "No, don't."

Through clamped teeth, trying to keep his voice quiet, Alexander continued. "They say, he's mine, and you say, all right, all right, he's yours, of course, take him. Nothing matters to me at all. Not me, not my food, not my bread, not my life, and not him either, *nothing* matters to me." He brought his face very close to hers and whispered angrily, "I, Tatiana, fight for *nothing*."

"Oh, Alexander," Tatiana said, looking at him with intense reproach.

They fell silent until they got their rations. Alexander received potatoes, carrots, bread, soya milk and butter. And sour cream.

On the street he carried the bag with the food, and she walked mutely beside him. He was walking too fast; she couldn't keep up. First Tatiana slowed down, and when she saw that he did not shorten his stride, she stopped.

Turning around, Alexander barked, "What?"

"You go ahead," Tatiana said. "Go ahead home. I can't walk that fast. I'll be along."

He came back and gave her his arm. "Let's go," he said. "To celebrate our Russian Revolution, the Germans are going to start bombing in a few minutes, and mark my words, they will not end until late tonight."

Tatiana took his arm. She wanted to cry, and she wanted to keep up, and she wanted not to be cold. Snow seeped inside her ripped boots that were tied together with twine. Sorrow seeped inside her ripped heart that was tied together with twine.

They trod through the snow looking at their feet.

"I didn't give you away, Shura," Tatiana said finally.

"No?" There was so much bitterness in his voice.

"How can you do that? How can you turn the right thing I did for my sister into a tragic flaw on my part? You should be ashamed of yourself."

"I *am* ashamed of myself," he said.

She held on tighter to his arm. "You're supposed to be the strong one. I don't see you fighting for me."

"I fight for you every day," said Alexander, walking faster again.

Pulling on him to slow down, Tatiana laughed soundlessly, the spirit taken away from her by the weakness of her body. "Oh, asking Dasha to marry you is fighting for me, is it?"

From above, Tatiana heard the thunderous burst of clapping followed by a high-pitched warble, becoming more insistent, but not nearly as insistent as the sirens of her heart. "Now that Dimitri is a wounded dystrophic and out of the picture, you're getting brave!" Tatiana exclaimed. "Now that you think you don't have to worry about him, you are allowing yourself all sorts of liberties in front of my family, and now you're getting angry with me over what's long passed. Well, I won't have it. You're feeling bad? Go and marry Dasha. That'll make you feel better."

Alexander stopped walking and pulled her into a doorway.

They got caught in the downpour. Bombs bombs bombs.

"I didn't *ask* her to marry me!" he yelled. "I *agreed* to marry Dasha to get Dimitri off your back! Or have you forgotten?"

Tatiana yelled, "Oh, so *that* was your grand plan! You were going to marry Dasha for *me*! How thoughtful of you, Alexander, how *humane*!"

The words were coming out angry, hurled at him between her frozen breaths, and Tatiana grabbed his coat as she pulled her body against him and pressed her face into his chest. "How could you!" she yelled. "How could you . . ." she whispered. "You asked her to marry you, Alexander . . ." Did she yell that or whisper it? Tatiana shook him—it was weak and pathetic—and she pounded his chest with her small mittened fists, but it wasn't pounding, it was tapping. Alexander grabbed her and hugged her to him so hard that the breath left her body.

"Oh, God," he whispered. "What are we doing?" He didn't let go. She closed her eyes, her fists remaining on his chest.

Waiting it out in the doorway, she said, looking up at him, "What's the matter, Shura? Are you afraid for me? Do you feel I'm close to death?"

"No," he said, not looking down at her.

"Do you have a clear picture of me dying?" she asked, pulling away and going to stand on the other side of the doorway.

When at last Alexander spoke, his choking voice revealed his emotion. "When you die, you'll be wearing your white dress with red roses, and your hair will be long and falling around your shoulders. When they shoot you, up on your damn roof or walking alone on the street, your blood will look like another red rose on your dress, and no one will notice, not even you when you bleed out for Mother Russia."

Trying to swallow the lump in her throat, Tatiana said, "I took the dress off, didn't I?"

Alexander stared onto the street. "It doesn't matter. Think about how little actually matters now. Look what's happening. Why are we even standing here? Let's walk home. Walk home, holding your 300 grams of bread. Let's go."

Tatiana didn't move.

He didn't move. "Tania, why are we still pretending?" he asked. "Why? For whose sake? We have minutes left. And not good minutes. All the layers of our life are being stripped away, and most of our pretenses, too, even mine, and yet we still continue with the lies. Why?"

"I'll tell you why! I'll tell you for whose sake!" Tatiana exclaimed. "For *her* sake. Because she loves you. Because you want to comfort her in the minutes she has left. That's why."

"What about you, Tania?" Alexander asked, his voice cracking. He didn't say anything else for a moment, staring at her as if he wanted her to say something. She said nothing.

At last he spoke. "Don't *you* want comfort in the minutes you have left?"

"No," she said weakly. "This isn't about me or you and me anymore." She lowered her head. "I can take it. She can't."

"I can't take it either," said Alexander.

Tatiana raised her eyes and said intensely, "You can take it, Alexander Barrington. And more. Now, stop it."

"Fine," he said, "I'll stop it."

"I want you to promise me something."

His weary eyes blinked at her.

"Promise me you won't . . ."

"Won't what?" Alexander asked from across the doorway. "Marry her or break her heart?"

A small tear ran down Tatiana's face. Gulping and pulling her coat tighter around herself, she whispered, "Break her heart."

He looked at her in disbelief. She couldn't believe herself either. "Tania, don't torture me," Alexander said.

"Shura, promise me."

"One of your promises or one of mine?"

"What is that supposed to mean?"

"Nothing."

"I'm not hearing a promise."

"Fine. I promise, if you will promise me . . ."

"What?"

"That you will never wear your white dress again, never give away your bread, never go out onto the roof. If you do, I will tell her everything instantly. Instantly, do you hear?"

"I hear," Tatiana muttered, thinking that really wasn't very fair.

"Promise me," Alexander said, taking her hand and pulling her to him, "that you will never do any less than your best to survive."

"All right," she said, looking up, her eyes pouring her heart into him. "I promise."

"Is that one of your promises or one of mine?"

"What is *that* supposed to mean?"

He took her face in his hands. "If you stay alive, then I swear to you," Alexander whispered, pressing her to him, "I won't break your sister's heart."

4

The following morning Tatiana went without him to the store. She had just gotten the family their kilo of bread, light even in her weak arms, and was about to walk out when suddenly she felt a blow to the back of her head and another blow to her right ear. She buckled and watched helplessly as a young boy of maybe fifteen grabbed her bread and before she could utter a sound, shoved it into his hyena mouth, his eyes wild and desperate. The other customers beat him with their purses, but under their blows he continued to swallow her bread until it was all gone, every last bite. One of the store managers came out and hit him with a stick. Tatiana yelled, "No!" but he fell, and his eyes from the floor were still wild, a destroyed animal's eyes. Blood dripping out of her ear where he had hit her, Tatiana bent down to help him up, but he shoved her away, got up, and ran out the door.

The salesclerk couldn't give her more bread. "Please," said Tatiana. "How can I go home with nothing?"

The clerk, her eyes sympathetic, said, "I can do nothing. The NKVD will shoot me for giving away bread. You don't know what it's like."

"Please," she begged. "For my family."

"Tanechka, I would give you bread, but I can't. The other day they shot three women for forging ration cards. Right on the street. And left them there. Go on, honey. Come back tomorrow."

"Come back tomorrow," muttered Tatiana as she left the store.

She could not go home. In fact, she did not go home, but sat in the bomb shelter and then appeared at the hospital to work. Vera was gone; Tatiana's punch card was gone; no one cared. She went and slept in one of the cold rooms, and in the cafeteria she received some clear liquid and a few spoonfuls of gruel, but there was no extra for her to take home. She looked for Vera to no avail. She sat at the nurses' station, then went into one of the rooms and sat with a dying soldier. As she held his hand, he asked if she was a nun. She said no, not really, but you can tell me anything.

"I have nothing to tell you," the man said. "Why are you bleeding?"

She began to explain, but really there was nothing to say, except "for the same reason you're lying here in the hospital."

Tatiana thought of Alexander, how he kept trying to protect her. From Leningrad, from Dimitri, from working at the hospital—the brutal, infectious, contagious place. From the bricks in Luga. From the German bombs, from the hunger. He didn't want her to do duty on the roof. He didn't want her to walk to Fontanka alone or without the absurd helmet he had given her, or to sleep without all her clothes. He wanted her to clean herself, even with cold water, and he wanted her to brush her teeth even though they had no food on them. He wanted just one thing.

He wanted her to live.

That brought a bit of relief.

A bit of comfort.

That would have to be good enough.

When she got home, around seven in the evening, she found her family frantic with worry. After she told them what had happened, they were upset that she hadn't just come home. "We would have understood," said Mama. "We don't care about the bread."

Dasha said she had sent Alexander out to look for her.

"You've got to stop doing that, Dasha," said Tatiana wearily. "You're bound to get him killed."

Tatiana was surprised her family was not *more* upset with her. Then she found out why. Alexander had brought them some oil—and soybeans—and half an onion. Dasha had made a delicious stew, adding a tablespoon of flour and a bit of salt. "Where is this stew?" Tatiana asked.

"There wasn't a lot, Tanechka," said Dasha.

"We thought you'd eat wherever you were," added Mama.

"You ate, right?" asked Babushka.

"We were so hungry," said Marina.

"Yes," Tatiana said, deeply discouraged. "Don't worry about me."

Alexander came back around eight. He had been out for three hours. The first thing he said was, "What happened to you?"

Tatiana told him.

"Where have you been all day?" he demanded, talking to her as if there were no one else in the room.

"I went to the hospital. To see if they had some food there."

"They didn't."

"Not much. I did have some oatmeal." White water.

"It's all right," Alexander said, taking off his coat. "There's some stew."

Coughs. Averted eyes.

Alexander didn't understand. He turned to Dasha. "I brought you soybeans. Dasha? You said you were making stew."

"We did, Alexander," said Dasha sheepishly. "But there was so little. We ate it."

"You ate it and didn't leave *her* any?" He turned red.

"Alexander, it's all right," said Tatiana anxiously. "They didn't leave you any either."

Dasha laughed nervously. "You can eat at the barracks, and she said she ate, dear."

"She is a liar!" he screamed.

"I did eat," Tatiana put in.

"You're a liar!" Alexander screamed at her. "I forbid you," he yelled to Tatiana, "I forbid you to get their food for them. Give them back their ration cards and tell them all to get their own damn food. I never want to see you getting their bread for them if they can't save you some of the food I bring!"

Tatiana stood quietly, her entire heart so full that for a moment she did not need any bread at all.

Turning to Dasha, Alexander said, out of breath, "Who is going to get your bread for you if she dies? Who is going to carry soup back home in a pail? Who is going to bring you porridge?"

Mama said disagreeably, "I bring porridge from the factory."

"You eat half of it before you set foot in the house!" yelled Alexander. "What, you think I don't understand? You think I don't know that Marina finishes her coupons before the month is out and then demands bread from Tania, who is getting beaten up while you're still sleeping?"

"I'm not sleeping. I sew," said Mama. "I sew every morning."

"Tania," Alexander stated, glaring at her, "you are not getting them their rations again. Understand?" Again he was talking to her as if there were no one else present.

Tatiana muttered that she was going to go and wash. When she came back, Alexander was sitting at the table smoking. He was calmer. "Come here," he said quietly.

Marina was in the other room with Mama. Babushka was down the hall with Nina Iglenko.

"Where is Dasha?" Tatiana said, moving slowly toward him. She saw his eyes.

"Getting a can opener from Nina. Come closer."

Standing in front of him, Tatiana said quietly, "Shura, please. Where is your indifferent face? You promised me."

He stared into her sweater.

"Don't worry," she whispered. "I'll be all right."

"You're making me feel worse," Alexander said. "Don't do it." Reaching out, he placed his hand on her hip. A small groan of anguish escaped him. Tatiana leaned into him and pressed her forehead to his forehead.

For a moment they stood still.

She took her forehead away.

He took his hand away. "Look what I have for you, Tania." He pulled out a small metal can from his coat.

Dasha came into the room, saying, "Here's the can opener. What do you need it for anyway?"

Alexander used it to open the small can and, taking a knife, cut the product inside into little morsels. He passed the can to Tatiana. "Go ahead, try it."

"What is it?" she asked, wanting to smile. It was the most delicious thing she had ever tasted. Not quite ham, not quite bologna, not quite pork, but all three, covered with lard and aspic. The can was small, maybe a hundred grams. "What *is* that?" she said, her eyes showing the delight that her body, her lips could not muster.

"Spam."

"Spam? What is Spam?"

"Like ham. In Russian it's *tushonka.*"

"Oh, it's much better than ham."

"Can I try it?" asked Dasha.

"No." Alexander didn't turn to Dasha. "I want your sister to eat the whole can. Dasha, you already ate. You can't possibly want more after all that stew."

"I just want a little bite," said Dasha. "To taste."

"No."

"Tania?" Dasha said. "Please? I'm sorry I ate your stew. I know you're upset."

"I'm not upset, Dasha."

"I am, though," said Alexander, turning to her. "You're a grown woman. I expect better from you."

Dasha said grumpily, "I said I was sorry."

Tatiana took another bite, and another. Half a can left. "Alexander?"

"No, Tatiana."

She had one more bite. Two small pieces left. Tatiana licked up all the lard and the aspic, and then she took one piece out of the can and handed it to Alexander. He shook his head. "Please," Tatiana said. "One for you, one for Dasha?"

Dasha snatched it out of Alexander's hand. Tatiana gave him the last piece, giving it one more glance. He ate it. Nodding, she licked out the can with her tongue. "This is the most wonderful thing. Where did you get it?"

"Americans, through Lend-Lease. A case of Spam for Leningrad and two of their army trucks."

"I'd rather have a case of this."

"I don't know. They're very good trucks." Alexander smiled.

Tatiana wanted to smile back. Looking away from him and to her sister, Tatiana said, "Dasha, honey, how is Nina holding up?"

"Terrible."

After a few minutes Alexander left to go back to the barracks. The next morning, when Tatiana got up to get the rations, Dasha came with her.

The following morning Dasha stayed in bed, but downstairs on the street a soldier was waiting for Tatiana. "Sergeant Petrenko!" she said, managing a smile. "What are *you* doing here?"

"Orders of the captain." He saluted, looking warmly at her. "He asked me to take you to the store."

The morning after that, Petrenko wasn't downstairs, but Alexander was waiting for Tatiana at Fontanka. He walked her home and went back to base. The next morning he came to the apartment.

On the way back from the store he had left her to help a lady struggling with two sleds that she was trying to pull by herself down Ulitsa Nekrasova. One had a body wrapped in a white sheet, and one had a *bourzhuika*. Alexander went to explain to the woman that she would have to come back for one or the other. He told Tatiana he was going to suggest taking the stove and coming back for the body.

Tatiana was waiting for him patiently and alone, leaning against a building, when she saw three boys approaching her with determined strides. She looked for Alexander, who was maybe a hundred meters away, with his back to Tatiana, pulling one of the sleds for the woman. "Alexander!" she yelled, but the wind was loud and her voice was weak. He didn't hear.

Tatiana turned to the boys. One of them she recognized as the boy who had taken her bread three days earlier. The street was deserted, and the snowdrifts were piled meters high on the road. In the snowdrifts lay dead bodies. There were no cars, no buses. Just Tatiana. She sighed. She thought of running across the street, but the effort, the effort. She couldn't move. She stood.

When they came close, she extended her and Alexander's bread to them without a word. Two of them grabbed her and pulled her into a doorway. She struggled, but there was nothing of her to struggle with. The third boy, the hyena from before, took her bread but then looked at her with his beastly eyes and said to the other two, "Ready? Let's go." A shiny metal blade flashed in front of Tatiana.

Without blinking or breathing, Tatiana looked the boy in the eye and said, "Go, get away while you have time. Go on, now. He is going to kill you."

The boy looked at her and said, "What?"

"Go!" Tatiana said, but in that instant a pistol handle came down hard on the boy's head and he dropped to the snow. The other two didn't have even a moment to let go of her. Alexander smashed his gun into one, then the other. In seconds they were all motionless on the ground.

Pulling Tatiana out of the doorway and behind him, he said, "Step away," and cocked his gun, aiming it at her assailants.

Her hand came up from behind and rested on the gun. "No," she said.

He pushed her hand away. "Tatiana, please. They are going to get up and terrorize someone else. Step back."

"Shura, please. No. I saw their eyes. They won't last till morning. Don't let their deaths be at *your* hands."

Alexander reluctantly put away his gun, then picked up their bag of bread off the ground and, with his arm around Tatiana, walked her back home in the blistering cold. "Do you know what would have happened to you if I hadn't been there?" he asked.

"Yes," she said, wanting to look up at his face but not having the energy to look anywhere but down at the ground. "Same thing that's happening to me when you are."

The next morning Alexander brought her a gun. Not his own standard-issue Tokarev, but a P-38 self-loading German pistol he had acquired near Pulkovo two months earlier.

"Remember the boys are all cowards; they will only pick on you because they think they can. You don't have to use the gun. Just flash it at them. They won't come up to you again."

"Shura, I've never used a—"

"It's war, Tania!" he exclaimed. "You remember how you played war with Pasha? Did you play to win? Well, play now. Just remember the stakes are higher."

Then he gave her a handful of rubles.

"What's this?"

"A thousand rubles," he said. "It's half my monthly pay. There is no food, but you can still get something on the black market. Go, and don't even think about the prices. Just buy what you have to. In Haymarket they're still selling flour, maybe some other things. I'm afraid to leave you, but I have to. Colonel Stepanov wants me to go with our trucks and men to Lake Ladoga."

"Thank you," she whispered.

Alexander's face was drawn. "The girls need to go with you to the store, Tatia. Please don't go by yourself. I won't be back for a week, maybe ten days. Maybe longer." The unspoken hung in the crushing cold. "Don't worry about me." He paused. "Bad news is we've lost Tikhvin," he said grimly. "Dimitri shot himself just in time. Tikhvin was—" He broke off. "Never mind."

"I can imagine."

Nodding, he continued. "There is no railroad going to the other side of the lake. The only way to bring food into Leningrad is by Ladoga, but now there's no way to get the food *to* Ladoga." He paused. "The bread you're getting—it's made from reserve flour. We have to get Tikhvin and the railroad back. Without them we have no realistic way of getting food into the city."

"Oh, no," she said.

"Oh, yes. Meanwhile, the council has issued a command that we have to build a road through the barely inhabited villages up north near Zaborye that lead to the other side of the lake. There's never been a road there, but we have no choice. Either build the road or die."

"How do you get food from there across a barely iced lake?" She shuddered.

Alexander's brown eyes were sadder than a calf's. "If we don't get Tikhvin back, there will be no food to bring no matter how well iced the lake is. We have no chance without it," Alexander said, not touching Tatiana. "No chance at all." Reluctantly he added, "Hang on to whatever provisions you've got left. The ration is going to be reduced again."

"There's not much left, Shura," she whispered.

As they were walking to the corner of Nevsky and Liteyniy where he was going to say good-bye to her, Alexander said, "Yesterday you called me Shura in front of your family. You have to be more careful. Your sister is bound to notice that."

"Yes," Tatiana said mournfully. "I will have to be more careful."

On Haymarket, Tatiana bought less than half a kilo of flour for 500 rubles. Two hundred and fifty rubles a cup. She bought half a kilo of butter for 300 rubles, some soy milk, and a small package of yeast.

At home they still had a bit of sugar. She made bread.

That's what a thousand rubles bought the Metanovs—half of Alexander's monthly salary for defending Leningrad bought them a loaf of bread with a smear of butter. Dinner for one night. At least Alexander had gotten them some wood for the stove, and even a little kerosene.

They broke the bread Tatiana made into five portions, put it on their plates, and ate it with a knife and fork, and afterward Tatiana didn't know about anyone else, but personally she thanked God for Alexander.

5

It was November, and the mornings were dark. They had covered their windows with blankets to keep out the cold, but in doing so they also kept out the light.

What light? thought Tatiana, as she slowly made her way from the bed to the kitchen with her toothbrush and peroxide one morning in the third week of November. She used to have peroxide *and* baking soda, but she had left the baking soda on the kitchen sill one evening, and someone had eaten it.

Tatiana turned on the tap. And turned. And turned.

There was no water.

Sighing, she shuffled back to her room with her toothbrush and her peroxide and got back into bed. Dasha and Marina groaned a little.

"There is no water," said Tatiana.

When it was nine in the morning and there was light, Tatiana and Dasha walked to the local council office. An emaciated woman with sores on her face told them that a few days ago power had been cut from the Fifth City Electric Plant because Leningrad had run out of fuel.

"What does it have to do with our water?" asked Dasha.

"What pumps the water?" asked the woman.

Dasha, slowly blinking, said, "I give up. Is this a test?"

Tatiana pulled her sister by the arm. "Come on, Dasha." She turned to the woman. "The power will be restored, but the pipes will have frozen for good." She spoke in an accusing tone. "We won't have water till the spring thaw."

"Don't worry," said the woman, going back to her business, "none of us will be alive in the spring."

Tatiana asked around the Fifth Soviet building and found out that the first floor had water—there just wasn't enough pressure to pump it all the way up

299

to the third. So the next morning Tatiana went down to the street and got a bucket of snow to carry upstairs. She melted the snow on the *bourzhuika* and used that water to flush the toilet. Then she went back down to the first floor and got a bucket of clean cold water to wash herself and Dasha and Mama and Marina and Babushka.

"Dasha, can you get up and come with me?" Tatiana said to her sister one morning.

Dasha was still in bed under the covers. "Oh, Tania," Dasha mumbled. "It's so cold. It's too hard to get up these days."

Tatiana couldn't get to the hospital before ten, sometimes eleven, by the time she was done with the water and the ration store.

They had no more oatmeal left, just a little flour, a little tea and some vodka.

And three hundred grams of bread a day each for Tatiana, Dasha, and Mama, and two hundred grams of bread each for Marina and Babushka.

Dasha said, "I'm gaining weight."

"Yes, me, too," mouthed Marina. "My feet are three times their normal size."

"And mine, too," said Dasha. "I can't fit them into my boots. Tania, I can't go with you today."

"That's fine, Dasha, my feet aren't swollen," said Tatiana.

"Why am I swelling up?" Dasha said in a desperate voice. "What's happening to me?"

"To you?" said Marina. "Why is it always about you? Everything is *always* about you."

"What is that supposed to mean?"

"What about me?" exclaimed Marina. "What about Tania? That's the trouble with you, Dasha—you never see other people around you."

"Oh, and you do, you bread-eater? You oatmeal-eater. Wait till I tell Tania how much oatmeal you stole from us, you thief."

"I may be hungry, but at least I'm not blind!"

"What the hell is *that* supposed to mean?"

"Girls, girls!" exclaimed Tatiana weakly. "What is the point of this? Who is swelling the most? Who is suffering the most? You both win. Now, get into bed and wait for me to come back. And be quiet, both of you, especially you, Marina."

6

"What are we going to do?" said Mama one evening when Babushka was in the other room and the girls were all in bed.

"About what?" asked Dasha.

"About Babushka," she said. "Now that she doesn't go across the Neva anymore, she's home all day."

"Yes," said Marina, "and now that she's home all day, she eats what's left of Alexander's flour one spoonful at a time."

"Marina, shut up," said Tatiana. "We have no flour left. Babushka eats the sweepings from the bottom of the bag."

"Oh?" Marina changed the subject. "Tania, do you think it's true? Have all the rats left the city?"

"I don't know, Marina."

"Have you seen any cats or dogs?"

"There aren't any left," Tatiana said. "That I know." She had looked.

Coming up to the girls' bed and crouching beside it, Mama shook her head. "Listen to me, all of you," she said. Mama's voice was not boisterous anymore; it was not strident, it was not loud. It was barely even a voice, certainly not a voice Tatiana recognized as being her mother's. The kerchief still tied Mama's hair back from her head. "I'm talking about the cold. She is here all day; do we have enough wood to heat the *bourzhuika* for her all day?"

"No," said Dasha, propping herself up on one elbow. "I know we don't. We need all the wood we have to heat the *bourzhuika* at night. We barely have enough for that. Look how long it's been since we properly heated our rooms from the big stove."

Since Alexander was here last, thought Tatiana. He always gets the wood and builds the fire and makes the room warm.

Wringing her hands, Mama said, "We're going to have to tell her to keep the *bourzhuika* on all day."

"We'll tell her that, Mama," said Tatiana, "but soon we will have no wood."

"Tania, she is freezing in the apartment. Do you see how slowly she is moving?"

Dasha nodded. "She used to go to the public canteen and spend all day there waiting for some soup, some porridge. Today I never saw her get up from the couch once, not even to eat dinner with us. Tania, can we get her into your hospital?"

"We can try," said Tatiana from her wall. "But I don't think there are any spare beds. The children have them all. And the wounded."

"Let's try tomorrow, all right?" said Mama. "At least in the hospital she'll be warmer. They're still heating the hospitals, right?"

"They've closed three wings of the hospital," Tatiana replied, crawling out of bed. "They're keeping just one open. And it's full."

She went to see her grandmother. The blankets had fallen off Babushka Maya, who lay on the sofa covered by just her coat. Tania picked up the blankets and covered Babushka thoroughly, up to her neck, tucking the blankets all around her. She knelt on the floor. "Babushka," she whispered, "talk to me."

Babushka groaned faintly. Tatiana put her hand on her grandmother's head. "No strength left?" she asked.

"Not much . . ."

Tatiana managed a smile. "Babushka, I remember sitting by you when you painted; the smells of the paint were very strong, and you were always covered with it, and I used to sit so close to you that I would become covered by it, too. Do you remember?"

"I remember, sunshine. You were the sweetest child." She smiled. Tatiana's hand remained on her.

"You taught me how to draw a banana when I was four. I had never seen a banana and couldn't draw one, remember?"

"You drew a very good banana," Babushka said, "even though you had never seen one. Oh, Tanechka . . ." She broke off.

"What, Babushka?"

"Oh, to be young again . . ."

"I don't know if you've noticed," Tatiana whispered, "but the young ones aren't doing so well either."

"Not them," Babushka said, opening her eyes briefly. *"You."*

The next morning Tatiana fetched the two buckets of water and then went to get the rations, and when she came back, Babushka was dead. She was lying on the couch, covered by Tatiana's blankets and a coat, still and cold. Marina, crying, said, "I went in to wake her, and she wasn't moving."

Tatiana and her family stood over Babushka.

Sniffling, shrugging, turning toward the dining table, Marina said, "Come on, let's eat."

And Mama, nodding her head and turning herself, agreed. "Yes, let's have the morning bread. I already made a little chicory to drink. Sarkova warmed up the kitchen stove for breakfast with her own wood. There was a little heat left for me."

They sat down at the table, and Tatiana cut their ration into two halves—just over half a kilo for now, just over half a kilo for later. She divided the half-kilo into four pieces, and they ate, 125 grams each. "Marina," Tatiana said firmly, "bring your bread home, you hear?"

"What about Babushka's share?" said Marina. "Let's divide it up and eat it now." And they did. And then Marina and Dasha and Mama ate the chicory grinds from which they had just made a liquid that looked and smelled like coffee. Tatiana said no to the grinds.

She told her mother she would go to the local Soviet council to notify them of Babushka's death so the burial crew could come and take her body. Mama placed her hand on Tatiana. "Wait," she said. "If the council comes, they'll know she is dead."

"Yes?"

"And her rations? They'll stop."

Tatiana got up from the table. "Mama, we'll still have the coupons until the end of the month. That's ten more days of her bread."

"Yes, but then what?"

Clearing the table, Tatiana said, "Mama, you know what? I'm not really thinking that far ahead."

"Stop clearing, Tania," said Dasha. "There is no water to wash anything with. Leave the dishes. All they had was bread on them. We'll reuse them tonight." Turning to her mother, Dasha said, "Besides, Mama, if not the council, then who? We can't move her ourselves. We can't leave her here. Can we?" She paused. "We can't continue to eat dinner and sew with our grandmother on the couch."

Mama stared at Babushka. "Better for her to be here than lying out in the street," she said faintly.

Tatiana stopped clearing the table and went to get a white sheet from the dresser. "Mama, no, we can't leave her here. A body needs to be buried. Even in the Soviet Union," she said sadly. "Dasha, help me, will you? We need to wrap her before they take her. We'll wrap her in this."

Taking the coat and the blankets off Babushka, Dasha said, "We'll keep the blankets. We'll need them."

Tatiana looked around the room. She saw pockets of disarray: books off the shelves, clothes on the floor, plates on the table. Where was the thing she was looking for? Ah, there. She went to the window and picked up a small drawing. It was a charcoal sketch of a latticed apple pie that Babushka had drawn back in September. Tatiana picked it up and placed it gently on Babushka's chest. "All right, let's go," she said.

After the girls wrapped Babushka in the sheet, Mama sewed up the top and the bottom, making a sack. Tatiana crossed herself, quickly wiped her tears, and went to the council.

Later that afternoon two men from the council came. Mama paid them with two shots of vodka each. "Can't believe you still have vodka, comrade," one of the men said. "You're the first one so far this month."

"Did you know vodka is the number-one trading item?" said the other man. "You can get yourself some nice bread if you've got any more."

The Metanov women exchanged looks. Tatiana knew they had two bottles left. After Papa died, and with Dimitri away, no one drank the vodka except Alexander when he came, and he drank only a little.

"Where are you taking her?" Mama asked. "We'll come with you." They had all stayed home from work.

The council men said, "We've got a full truck waiting outside. There is no room for you on this truck. We'll be taking her to the closest cemetery. That would be Starorusskaya. Go and see her there."

"What about a grave?" Mama said. "A casket?"

"Casket?" The man opened his mouth and silently laughed. "Comrade, give me the rest of your vodka and I still won't be able to get you a casket. Who is going to make them? And out of what?"

Tatiana nodded. She would take a casket and burn it for firewood herself before she used it to bury her grandmother. She shivered, buttoning up her coat.

"What about a grave?" asked Mama, her face ashen and her voice cracking.

"Comrade," the council man exclaimed, "have you seen the snow, the frozen ground? Come outside with us, come and take a look, and while you're at it, take a look at our truck."

Tatiana stepped forward, putting her hand on the man's arm. "Comrade," she said quietly, "just get her downstairs for us. That's the hardest thing. Get her downstairs and we'll take care of her from there."

She went to the attic, where once upon a time they used to hang their washing. There was no washing there now, but she did find what she was looking for—her childhood sled. It was a brightly painted blue sled with red runners. She carried it downstairs to the street, careful not to slip. Babushka's body had already been taken down and left on the snowy pavement. "Come on, girls, on one-two-three," Tatiana said to Marina and Dasha. Marina was too weak to help. Tatiana and Dasha lifted Babushka onto the sled and pulled her three blocks to Starorusskaya, with Mama and Marina following. Tatiana did reluctantly glimpse in the back of the open council truck. The bodies were piled three meters tall, one on top of another.

"These are all the people who died today?" she asked the driver.

"No," he said. "That's just what we picked up this morning." He bent toward her. "Yesterday we picked up fifteen hundred bodies off the streets. Sell your vodka, girl, sell it and buy yourself some bread."

The entrance to the cemetery was barricaded with corpses, some in white sheets, some without.

Tatiana saw a mother with a young child who had been pulling their dead father to the cemetery when they themselves froze in the entrance, in the snow. Closing her eyes, Tatiana shook the image out of her head. She wanted to get home. "We can't get through. We can't clear the path. Let's leave our Babushka," Tatiana said. "What else can we do?" She and Dasha took Babushka's body and laid it gently in the snow next to the cemetery gates. They stood over her for a few minutes.

Then they went home.

They sold their two bottles of vodka and received only two loaves of white bread for it on the black market. Now that Tikhvin had gone to the Germans, there was no bread even on the black market.

7

A week passed. Tatiana could not flush the toilet. She could not brush her teeth. She could not wash. Alexander would not be happy with that, she thought. They hadn't heard from Alexander. Was he all right?

"When do you think they will repair the pipes?" Dasha asked one morning.

"You should hope not too soon," said Tatiana. "Otherwise you're going to have to start doing laundry again."

Dasha came over to Tatiana and hugged her. "I love you. You're still making jokes."

"Not good ones," said Tatiana, hugging her sister back.

Living with small buckets of water was hard. The freezing of the water pipes was worse. But the worst was the spilling of the water that people carried upstairs from the first floor. The water splashed out of the buckets onto the stairs and froze. It was five to twenty degrees below zero every day, and the stairs remained perpetually covered with ice. Every morning, to get the water, Tatiana had to hold the bucket with one hand and the railing with the other, sliding down on her bottom.

Carrying the full bucket upstairs was much harder. She would fall at least once and have to go back for more water. The more water was spilled on the stairs, the more easily she fell and the thicker the ice on the stairs became. The back stairs were even more treacherous. A woman from the fourth floor fell down a flight, broke her leg, and could not get up. She froze on the stairs, into the ice. No one could move her, before or after.

Tatiana, Marina, Dasha, and Mama sat on the couch and listened to the radio's metronome pound its own relentless heartbeat over the airwaves, its frequencies open and occasionally interrupted by a steady stream of words, some sensible, like "Moscow is fighting the enemy for its very life," some nonsensical, like "The bread ration is cut once again to 125 grams a day for dependents, 200 grams for workers."

Other words sometimes followed: "losses," "damage," "Churchill."

Stalin talked of opening a second front in Volkhov. But not until Churchill opened a second one of his own to distract the Germans in the North European countries. Churchill said he had neither the men nor the resources to open a second front, but said he was prepared to repay Stalin for the material losses he had suffered. To which Stalin tartly replied that he would be presenting *that* bill straight to the Führer himself.

Moscow was in death throes, every last breath expended in the struggle against Hitler. The city was bombed as Leningrad was bombed.

"Haven't heard from Babushka Anna in a month," said Dasha one late November evening. "Tania, have you heard from Dimitri?"

"Of course I haven't," said Tatiana. "I don't think I'll be hearing from him again, Dasha." She paused. "We haven't heard from Alexander for a while either."

"I have," said Dasha. "Three days ago. I just forgot to tell you. Want to read his letter?"

Dear Dasha and all the girls,

I hope this letter finds you well. Are you waiting for me to return? I am waiting to come back to you.

My commander sent me up to Kokkorevo—a fishing village with no fishermen left. It's a bombed-out hole where the village used to be. We had practically no trucks on this side, certainly no fuel for the ones we do have. There were twenty of us standing around with a couple of horses. We were there to test the ice, to see if it could hold a truck with food and munitions, or at the very least a horse with a sledge filled with food.

We walked out onto the ice. It's so cold you'd think the ice would have formed by now, but no. It was surprisingly thin in places. We lost a truck and two horses right away, and then we just stood on the banks of Lake Ladoga and looked at the ice spreading before us, and I said, forget this, give me the damn horse. I hopped on it and rode the mare for four hours—on ice—all the way to Kobona! Temperatures were a dozen degrees below zero. I said this ice will suffice.

As soon as I came back—with a sledge full of food, I was instantly put in charge of a transport regiment—another name for a thousand People's Volunteers. No one would spare real soldiers for this.

Before the ice got thick enough for the trucks, the volunteers had to ride the horses with the sledges to Kobona to pick up flour and other supplies and ride the horses back. I tell you, your Babushka would have done better than some of those men. They had either never ridden horses or never been out in the cold, or both, because I can't tell you how many accidents we had with men falling off their horses, falling through the ice, drowning. First day we lost a truck and a load of kerosene right off. We were trying to bring fuel into Leningrad. The fuel shortage is almost as bad as the food shortage. There is no petroleum to fire up the kilns to bake the bread.

We said, let's forget the trucks for a few days, let's just use the horses. Little by little, the horses from Kobona made the thirty-kilometer journey to Kokkorevo. One day we brought in over twenty tons of food. It's not nearly enough, but it's something. I'm in Kobona now, loading food onto the sledges, having a hard time looking at flour and knowing you are in your apartment without any. The front-line troop rations have been reduced to half a kilo of bread a day. I heard the dependent ration fell to 125g. We'll try to get it back up.

I don't need to tell you that the Germans are not happy about our little ice road. They bomb it mercilessly, day and night. Less at night. During our first week we lost over three dozen trucks and much food with them. Finally it became clear that I couldn't be driving the trucks anymore; it was just not putting me to the best use. Now I'm on the Kokkorevo side, as an artillery gunner against the German planes. I'm behind a Zenith antiaircraft weapon. It shoots either machine-gun fire or bombs. It gives me a great feeling of satisfaction to know that I blew up a plane that was going to sink a truck that was bringing food to you.

The ice is thick now except for a few weak patches, and we have some good trucks. They can go as fast as forty kilometers an hour across the lake. The other soldiers and I are calling the ice road the Road of Life. Has quite a ring to it, don't you think?

Still, without Tikhvin, we're unable to bring much into Leningrad. We must recapture Tikhvin. What do you think, Dasha, should I volunteer my services for that? Charge the Germans on my starving gray mare, with my brand-new Shpagin machine gun in my arms? I'm just kidding, I think. The Shpagin is a superb gun, though.

I don't know when I'll be able to return to Leningrad again, but when I do, I'm bringing food with me, so hang on and keep going.

Courage, all.

Yours,

Alexander

Walk, walk, don't lift your eyes, Tatiana told herself. Pull that scarf over your face, pull it over your eyes if you have to, just don't look up, don't see Leningrad, don't see your courtyard where the bodies pile up, don't see the streets where the bodies are laid out on the snow, lift your foot and step over them. Walk around the corpse. Don't look—you don't want to see. That morning Tatiana saw a man freshly dead, lying in the street missing most of his torso. Not from a bomb. His flanks had been cut out with a knife. Feeling for Alexander's pistol in her coat pocket, Tatiana mutely moved through the snowdrifts, her gaze on the ground in front of her.

She had to brandish Alexander's pistol twice, out in the street by herself, in the dark of the early morning.

Thank God for Alexander.

At the end of November an explosive wave blew out the glass in the room where they ate. They covered the hole with Babushka's blankets. They had nothing else. The room temperature dropped by thirty degrees, from just above freezing to much below.

Tatiana and Dasha carried the *bourzhuika* into their room, placing it in front of Mama's couch, so when Mama sewed the uniforms she would be warm. Continuing to encourage private initiative, the factory paid her twenty rubles for every extra uniform she sewed above her norm. It took

Mama the whole of November to sew five uniforms. Then she gave Tatiana a hundred rubles and told her to go and find something in the stores.

Tatiana returned with a glass of black dirt. It was the dirt into which the sugar had melted when the Germans bombed the Badayev warehouses in September. As cheerfully as she could, Tatiana said, "Once the dirt settles to the bottom, our tea will be sweet."

Step over, don't lift your eyes, Tatiana, just stand in line and keep your place; if you lose your place they won't have any bread for you, and then you'll have to scavenge the city for another store. Stay, don't move, someone will come and clear this up. A bomb had fallen into the street, into the line Tatiana was in, right on Fontanka, fell and blew apart half a dozen women. What to do? Take care of the living? Of her family? Or move the dead? Don't lift your eyes, Tatiana.

Don't lift your eyes, Tatiana, keep them peeled to the snow, and look at nothing but your falling-apart boots. Mama once could have made you another pair. But Mama can't even hand-sew one extra uniform nowadays, with or without Dasha's help, with or without your help, when in October she was sewing ten a day by machine.

Alexander! I want to keep my promise to you. I want to stay alive—but I just don't see how even I with my small needs and stunted metabolism can make it on 200 grams a day, of which 25 percent is edible cellulose—sawdust and pine bark. Bread doused with cottonseed cake, previously thought to be poisonous to humans—not anymore. Bread that is not bread but hardtack—flour and water. Sea biscuit, you called it? Bread that is as dark and heavy as a cobblestone. I cannot make it on 200 grams a day of that bread.

I cannot make it on clear soup. I cannot make it on watery porridge.

Luba Petrova could not. Vera could not. Kirill could not. Nina Iglenko could not. Can Mama and Dasha? Can Marina?

Whatever I have been doing so far is not enough.

To live is going to require something more from me, something not of this world. Some other force is needed that can crowd out *want* with nothing, *cold* with nothing. *Hunger* with nothing.

The desire for food gave way to a terminal malaise, a poxy pallid loss of interest in everything and everybody. The shelling Tatiana completely ignored. She had no strength to run from it, no strength to drop down, no strength to help move bodies or lift victims. A pervasive numbness, an encompassing apathy like a fortress permeated and surrounded her, a fortress broken into by only a spattering of twinges that resembled feeling.

Her mother tweaked her heart; Dasha stirred her affections. Marina—even Marina, despite her miserable greed—moved something inside Tatiana, who didn't judge her but was disappointed. Nina Iglenko had aroused some pity as she waited for her last son to die before she died herself.

Tatiana had to stop *feeling*. Already she set her teeth to get through her day. She would have to set them harder. Because there was no food anymore.

I won't shudder, and I won't flinch from my short life, I won't lower my head. I will find a way to lift my eyes.

Keep everything out. Except for you, Alexander. Keep you *in*.

FORTRESS PIECES

1

T HE flip side of white nights—Leningrad's December. White nights—light, summer, sunshine, a pastel sky. December—darkness, blizzards, cloud cover, a hunkering sky. An oppressive sky.

Bleak light appeared at around ten in the morning. It hovered around until about two, then reluctantly vanished, leaving darkness once more.

Complete darkness. In early December the electricity was turned off in Leningrad not for a day but seemingly for good. The city was plunged into perpetual night. Trams stopped running. Buses hadn't run in months because there was no fuel.

The workweek was reduced to three days, then two days, then one day. Electricity was finally restored to a few businesses essential to the war effort: Kirov, the bread factory, the waterworks, Mama's factory, a wing in Tatiana's hospital. But the trams had stopped running permanently. There was no electricity in Tatiana's apartment and no heat. Water remained only on the first floor, down the icy slide.

These days brought a pall with the morning that blighted Tatiana's spirit. It became impossible to think about anything but her own mortality—impossible as it was.

At the beginning of December, America finally entered the war, something about the island of Hawaii and the Japanese. "Ah, maybe now that *America* is on our side . . ." said Mama, sewing.

A few days after news of America, Tikhvin was recaptured. Those were words Tatiana understood. Tikhvin! It meant railroad, meant ice road, meant food. Meant an increase in ration?

No, it didn't mean that.

A hundred and twenty-five grams of bread.

When the electricity went out, the radio stopped working. No more metronome, no more news reports. No light, no water, no wood, no food. Tick tock. Tick tock.

They sat and stared at each other, and Tatiana knew what they were thinking.

Who was next?

"Tell us a joke, Tania."

Sigh. "A customer asks the butcher, 'Can I have five grams of sausage, please?'

" 'Five *grams?*' the butcher repeats. 'Are you mocking me?'

" 'Not at all,' says the customer. 'If I were mocking you, I would have asked you to slice it.' "

Sighs. "Good joke, daughter."

Tatiana was coming back to the rooms dragging her bucket of water behind her through the hall. Crazy Slavin's door was closed. It occurred to Tatiana that it had been closed for some time. But Petr Petrov's door was open. He was sitting at his small table trying unsuccessfully to roll a cigarette.

"Do you need help with that?" she asked, leaving her bucket on the floor and coming in.

"Thank you, Tanechka, yes," he said in a defeated voice. His hands were shaking.

"What's the matter? Go to work, there'll be something there for lunch. They still feed you at Kirov, don't they?"

Kirov had been nearly destroyed by German artillery from just a few kilometers south in Pulkovo, but the Soviets had built a smaller factory inside the crumbled façade, and until a few days ago Petr Pavlovich took tram Number 1 all the way to the front.

Tatiana faintly remembered tram Number 1.

"What's the matter?" she asked. "You don't want to go?"

He shook his head. "Don't worry about me, Tanechka. You've got enough to worry about."

"Tell me." She paused. "Is it the bombs?"

He shook his head.

"Not the food, not the bombs?" She looked at his bald shrunken head and went to close the door to his room. "What is it?" she asked, quieter.

Petr Pavlovich told her that he was moved to Kirov only recently to fix the motors of tanks that had broken down. There were no shipments, no new parts, and no actual tank motors.

"I figured out a way to make airplane motors fit the tanks. I figured out how to repair them to use in the tanks, and then I fix them for airplanes, too."

"That sounds good," she said. "For that you get a worker's ration, right?" She added, "Three hundred and fifty grams of bread?"

He waved at her and took a drag of the cigarette. "That's not it. It's the Satan spawn, the NKVD." He spit with malice. "They were ready to shoot the poor bastards before me who couldn't fix the engines. When I was brought in, they stood over me with their fucking rifles to make sure I could fix the equipment."

Tatiana listened to him, her hand on his back, her bones chilled, her heart chilled. "But you did fix them, comrade," she breathed out.

"Yes, but what if I didn't?" he said. "Isn't the cold, the hunger, the Germans enough? How many more ways are there to kill us?"

Tatiana backed away. "I'm sorry about your wife," she uttered, opening the door.

That afternoon as she was coming back home, his door was still open. Tatiana glanced in. Petr Pavlovich Petrov was still sitting behind his desk, the half-smoked cigarette Tatiana had rolled for him in his hands. He was dead. With trembling fingers Tatiana made the sign of the cross and closed the door.

They stared at each other from the couch, from the bed, across the room. The four of them. They slept and ate in one room now. They would put the plates on their laps and they would have their evening bread. And then they would sit in front of the *bourzhuika* and watch the flames through the small window in the stove. That was the only light in the room. They had plenty of wick, and they had matches, but they had nothing to burn. If only they had some—

Nothing to burn. Oh, no. Tatiana remembered.

The motor oil. The motor oil Alexander had told her to buy on the Sunday in June when there was still ice cream, and sunshine, and a glimmer of joy. He had told her—and she hadn't listened.

And now look.

No tick tock, tick tock anymore.

"Marina, what are you doing?"

Marina was peeling the wallpaper off the wall one December afternoon. Ripping off a chunk, she went to the bucket of water, dipped her hand in it, and moistened the backing.

"What are you doing?" Tatiana repeated.

Taking a spoon, Marina started to scrape off the wallpaper paste. "The woman in front of me in line today said some of the wallpaper paste was made with potato flour." She was scraping frantically at the paper.

Carefully Tatiana took the paper away from Marina. "Potato flour and *glue*," Tatiana said.

Marina ripped the paper back from Tatiana. "Don't touch that. Get your own."

Tatiana repeated, "Potato flour and *glue*."

"So?"

"Glue is poison."

Marina laughed soundlessly, scraping off the damp paste and spooning it into her mouth.

"Dasha, what are you doing?"

"I'm lighting the *bourzhuika*." Dasha was standing in front of the stove window, throwing books onto the flames.

"You're burning *books?*"

"Why not? We have to be warm."

Tatiana grabbed Dasha's hand. "No, Dasha. Stop. Don't burn books, please. We haven't been reduced to that."

"Tania! If I had more energy, I would kill you and slice you open and eat you," Dasha said, throwing another book onto the fire. "Don't tell me—"

"No, Dasha," Tatiana said, holding on to her sister's wrist. "Not books."

"We have no wood," said Dasha matter-of-factly.

As quickly as she could, Tatiana went and checked under her bed. Her Zoshchenko, John Stuart Mill, the English dictionary. She remembered that on Saturday afternoon she had been reading Pushkin and had carelessly left the precious volume by the couch. She turned to Dasha, who kept relentlessly throwing more books onto the fire.

In horror, Tatiana saw *The Bronze Horseman* in her sister's hands. "Dasha, no!" she screamed, and lunged at her sister. Where did she find the strength to scream, to lunge? Where did she find the strength for emotion?

She grabbed it, YANKED it out of Dasha's hands. "No!" She clutched her book to her chest. "Oh, my God, Dasha," Tatiana said trembling. "That's my book."

"They're all our books, Tania," Dasha said apathetically. "Who cares now? To stay warm is everything."

Licking her lips, Tatiana couldn't speak for a while, she was so shaken. "Dasha, why books? We have the whole dining room set. A table and six chairs. It will last us the winter if we're careful." She wiped her mouth and stared at her hand. It was streaked with blood.

"You want to saw up the dining room set?" Dasha said, throwing Karl Marx's *Communist Manifesto* onto the fire. "Be my guest."

Something was happening to Tatiana. She didn't want to scare her mother or her sister. She knew that Marina was beyond fear. Tatiana waited for Alexander. She would ask him what was happening to her. But before he came back and she had a chance to ask him, she noticed that Marina, too, was bleeding from her mouth. "Let's go, Marina," she said. "Let's go to the hospital."

Finally a doctor came to take a look at them. "Scurvy," the doctor said flatly. "It's scurvy, girls. Everybody has it. You're bleeding from the inside out.

Your capillaries are getting too thin, and they're breaking. You need vitamin C. Let's see if we can get you a shot."

They both got a shot of vitamin C.

Tatiana got better.

Marina didn't.

In the night she whispered to Tatiana, "Tania, you listening?"

"What, Marinka?"

"I don't want to die," she whispered, and if she could have cried, she would have. She was barely able to emit a low wail. "I don't want to die, Tania! If I hadn't stayed here with Mama, I would be in Molotov right now with Babushka, and I wouldn't die."

"You're not going to die," said Tatiana, putting her hand on Marina's head.

"I don't want to die," whispered Marina, "and not feel just once what you feel." She struggled for her breath. "Just *once* in my life, Tania!"

As if from a distance, Dasha's voice came at them. "What does Tania feel?"

Marina didn't reply. "Tanechka . . ." she whispered. "What does it *feel* like?"

"What does *what* feel like?" asked Dasha. "Indifference? Cold? Wasting away?"

Tatiana continued to gently caress Marina's forehead. "It feels," she whispered, "as if you're not alone. Now, come on, where is your strength? Do you remember us with Pasha, me rowing and you and Pasha swimming alongside trying to keep up? Where is that strength, Marinka?"

The next morning Marina lay dead beside Tatiana.

Dasha said, "We have her rations until the end of the month," barely blinking at the sight of her dead cousin.

Tatiana shook her head. "As you know, she has already eaten them. It's the middle of the month. She's got nothing left until the end of December."

Tatiana wrapped her cousin in a white sheet, Mama sewed up the top and bottom, and they slid Marina down the stairs and onto the street. They tried to put her in the sled, but they couldn't lift her. After Tatiana made the sign of the cross on Marina, they left her on the snowy pavement.

2

One more day, another shot of vitamin C. Another two hundred grams of blackened bread. Tatiana pretended to go to work so she could continue to receive a worker's ration, but there was nothing for her to do at work, except sit by the dying.

A week after Marina died, Tatiana, Dasha, and Mama were sitting on the sofa in the quiet night in front of a nearly extinguished *bourzhuika*. All the books were gone, except for what Tatiana hid under her bed. The embers did not light up the room. Mama was sewing in the dark.

"What are you sewing, Mama?" Tatiana asked.

"Nothing," Mama said. "Nothing important. Where are my girls?"

"Here, Mama."

"Dasha, remember Luga?"

Dasha remembered.

"Dashenka, remember when Tania got a fish bone stuck in her throat, and we couldn't get it out for anything?"

Dasha remembered. "She was five."

"Who got it out, Mama?"

"Pasha. He had such small hands. He just stuck his hand in your throat and pulled it out."

"Mama," Dasha said, "remember when our Tania fell out of the boat in Lake Ilmen, and we all jumped after her, because we thought she couldn't swim, and she was already dog-paddling away from the boat?"

Mama remembered. "Tania was two."

"Mama," Tatiana said, "remember how I dug that big hole in our yard to trap Pasha and then forgot to fill it up, and you fell in?"

"Don't remind me," said Mama. "I'm still angry about that."

They tried to laugh.

"Tania," said Mama, her hands moving on her sewing work, "when you and Pasha were born, we were in Luga, and while the whole family was clucking around our new boy Pasha, saying what a great boy he was and what a fine boy, Dasha over here, all seven years of her, picked you up and said, 'Well, you can all have the black one. I'm taking the white one. This baby is mine.' And we all teased her and said, 'Fine then. Dasha, you want her? You can name her.' " Mama's voice cracked once, twice. "And our Dasha said, 'I want to name my baby Tatiana . . . ' "

One more day, one more shot of vitamin C for Tatiana, whose fingers trickled blood onto the two hundred grams of bread she cut up for her mother and sister.

One more day, a bomb fell in the corner of the Fifth Soviet roof. No Anton to put it out, no Mariska, no Kirill, no Kostia, and no Tatiana. It caught fire and burned through the fourth floor, which faced the church on Grechesky Prospekt. No one came to put it out. It smoldered for a day and then gradually burned itself out.

Was it Tatiana's imagination, or was the city quieter? Either she was going deaf or there was less bombing. There was still some every day, but shorter in duration, milder in intensity, almost as if the Germans were bored with the whole thing. And why not? Who was left to bomb?

Well, Tatiana.

And Dasha.

And Mama.

No, not Mama.

* * *

Her hands still held the white camouflage uniform she was sewing, and underneath her wool hat she wore her kerchief. In front of the frail fire from the small *bourzhuika*, Mama said, "I can't anymore. I just can't." Her hands stopped moving, and her head, too. Her eyes remained open. Tatiana could see short spasms of breath leaving her mouth, short, brief, then gone.

Tatiana and Dasha kneeled by their mother. "I wish we knew a prayer, Dasha."

"I think I know part of something called the Lord's Prayer," said Dasha.

Tatiana's back was to the fire, and her back was warm, but her front was cold. "Which part do you know?"

"Only the part with *Give us this day our daily bread*."

Tatiana placed her hand on her mother's lap. "We'll bury Mama with her sewing."

"We'll have to bury her *in* her sewing," Dasha said, and her voice was weak. "Look, she was sewing herself a sack."

"Dear Lord," said Tatiana, holding her mother's cold leg. "*Give us this day our daily bread* . . ." She paused. "What else, Dasha?"

"That's all I know. What about *Amen?*"

"Amen," said Tatiana.

For dinner they cut the bread into three pieces. Tatiana ate hers. Dasha ate hers. They left their mother's on her plate.

That night Tatiana and Dasha held each other in their bed. "Don't leave me, Tania. I can't make it without you."

"I'm not going to leave you, Dasha. We are not going to leave each other. We can't be left alone. You know that we all need one other person. One other person to remind us we are still human beings and not beasts."

"We're the only two left, Tania," said Dasha. "Just you and me."

Tatiana held her sister closer. You. Me. And Alexander.

3

Alexander returned a few days later. The dark circles around his eyes and his thick black beard gave him a robber baron look, but otherwise he seemed to be holding up. That made Tatiana warmer on the inside. Seeing him, in fact . . . well, what could she say? Dasha stood in the hallway, and his arms were around Dasha, while Tatiana stood back and watched them. And he watched her.

"How are you?" she said faintly.

"I'm fine," he said. 'How are my girls?'

"Not so good, Alexander," said Dasha. "Not so good. Come, look at our mother. She's been dead for five days. The council doesn't come anymore. We can't move her."

Behind Dasha, Alexander walked past Tatiana and glided his gloved hand across her face.

He placed their mother in the white camouflage uniform cape and carried her—taking care not to slip on the ice—down the stairs, put her on Tatiana's red and blue shiny sled, and pulled her to the cemetery on Starorusskaya as the girls walked beside him. He moved the frozen bodies at the entrance gate to make way for the sled and pulled Mama all the way inside, where he gently laid her in the snow. He broke off two small branches and held them in front of Tatiana, who with a piece of twine tied them together in a cross, which they laid on top of Mama.

"Do you know a prayer, Alexander?" asked Tatiana. "For our mother?"

Alexander stared at Tatiana, then shook his head. She watched him cross himself and mutter a few words under his cold breath.

As they were walking out, Tatiana asked, "You don't know a prayer?"

"Not in Russian," he whispered back.

Back in the apartment he was almost cheerful. "Girls," he said, "you won't believe what goodies I have for you." He paused. "Just for you."

He had brought them a sack of potatoes, seven oranges he had found God knows where, half a kilo of sugar, a quarter kilo of barley, linseed oil, and, smiling with all his teeth at Tatiana, three liters of motor oil.

If she could have, Tatiana would have smiled back.

Alexander showed her how to make light with the motor oil. After pouring a few teaspoons of the oil between two saucers, he placed a moistened wick inside, leaving the end out, and lit the wick. The oil illuminated an area big enough to sew or read by. Then he went out and returned half an hour later with some wood. He said he had found the broken beams in the basement. He fetched them water.

Tatiana wanted to touch him. But Dasha was taking care of that. Dasha was not leaving his side. Tatiana couldn't even meet his eyes. She got a pot and made some tea and put sugar in it; what a revelation. She cooked three potatoes and some barley. She broke their bread. They *ate*. Afterward she warmed up the water on the *bourzhuika*, asked Alexander for some soap, and washed her face and neck and hands.

"Thank you, Alexander," said Tatiana. "Have you heard from Dimitri?"

"You're welcome," he replied. "And no, I haven't. You?"

Tatiana shook her head.

"Alexander, my hair has started to fall out," said Dasha. "Look." She pulled out a black clump.

"Dash, don't do that," he said, turning back to Tatiana. "Has your hair begun to fall out, too?" His eyes on her were so warm, almost like a *bourzhuika*.

"No," she muttered softly. "My hair can't afford to fall out. I'll be bald tomorrow. I'm bleeding, though." She glanced at him and wiped her mouth. "Maybe an orange will help."

"Eat all seven of them, but slowly. And, girls, don't go out in the street at night. It's too dangerous."

"We won't."

"And always lock your doors."

"We always do."

"Then how come I waltzed right in?"

"Tania did it. She left it open."

"Stop blaming your sister. Just lock the damn doors."

After dinner Alexander retrieved a saw from the kitchen and sawed the dining-room table and the chairs into small pieces to fit into the *bourzhuika*. As he was working, Tatiana stood by his side. Dasha sat on the couch, bundled in blankets. The room was cold. They never went into this room anymore. They slept and ate and sat in the next room, where the windows weren't broken.

"Alexander, how many tons of flour are they feeding us on now?" asked Tatiana, taking the sawed pieces from him and stacking them in the corner.

"I don't know."

"Alexander."

Great sigh. "Five hundred."

"Five hundred tons?"

"Yes."

Dasha said, "Five hundred sounds like a lot."

"Alexander?"

"Oh, no."

"How many tons of flour did they give us during the July rations?" Tatiana wanted to know.

"What am I, Leningrad food chief Pavlov?"

"Answer me. How many?"

Great sigh. "Seventy-two hundred."

Tatiana said nothing, glancing at Dasha sitting on the couch. Dasha is withdrawing, Tatiana thought, her unblinking eyes focusing on Alexander. Putting on her most chipper voice, Tatiana said tremulously, "Look on the bright side—five hundred tons goes a lot further than it used to."

The three of them sat huddled on the couch in semidarkness in front of the *bourzhuika* that had just a bit of light coming out from its little metal door. Alexander was between Tatiana and Dasha. Tatiana wore her quilted coat that Mama had sewn for her and quilted trousers. She pulled her hat over her ears and her eyes. Only her nose and mouth were exposed to the air in the room. A blanket lay across their legs. At one point Tatiana thought she was going to sleep and leaned her head to the right—on Alexander. His hand came to rest on her lap.

Alexander spoke. "The saying goes, 'I'd like to be a German soldier with a Russian general, British armaments, and American rations.' "

"I would just like to have American rations," said Tatiana. "Alexander, now that the Americans are in the war, will it be easier for us?"

"Yes."

"You know this for a fact?"

"Absolutely. Now that the Americans are in the war, there is hope."

Tatiana heard Dasha's voice. "If we come out of this, Alexander, I swear we are leaving Leningrad and moving to the Ukraine, to the Black Sea, somewhere where it isn't ever cold."

"No place like that in Russia," he replied. He wore his quilted khaki coat on top of his uniform, and his *shapka* covered his ears. Dasha insisted. Alexander said, "No. We're too far north. Winters are cold in Russia."

"Is there a place on earth where it doesn't get below freezing in the winter?"

"Arizona."

"Arizona. Is that somewhere in Africa?"

"No." Mildly he sighed. "Tania, do you know where Arizona is?"

"America," Tatiana replied. The only warmth was coming from the little window in the stove. And from Alexander. She pressed her head into his arm.

"Yes. It's a state in America," he said. "Near California. It's desert land. Forty degrees in the summer. Twenty degrees in the winter. Every year. Never freezes. Never has snow."

"Stop it," said Dasha. "You're telling us fairy tales. Tell it to Tatiana. I'm too old for fairy tales."

"It's the truth. Never."

Her eyes closed, Tatiana listened to the resonant lilting of Alexander's voice. She never wanted him to stop talking. You have a good voice, Alexander, she thought. I can imagine myself drifting off, hearing only your voice, calm, measured, courageous, deep, spurring me on to eternal rest. Go, Tatia, go.

"That's impossible," said Dasha. "What do they do in the winter?"

"They wear a long-sleeved shirt."

"Oh, stop it," said Dasha. "Now I know you're making it up."

Tatiana pulled up her hat and stared into the flickering copper light of the stove.

"Tatia?" Alexander said quietly. "*You* know I'm telling the truth. Would *you* like to live in Arizona, '*the land of the small spring*'?"

"Yes," she replied.

Her voice flat and apathetic, Dasha asked, "What did you call her?"

"Tatiana," Alexander said.

Dasha shook her head. "No. The accent was in the wrong place for Tatiana. *Tátia.* I've never heard you call her that before."

"Really, Alexander," said Tatiana, pulling the hat over her face. "What's gotten into you?"

Dasha struggled up. "I don't care. Call her anything you want."

319

She stepped out to go to the bathroom.

Tatiana continued to sit next to Alexander, but her head was not resting on him anymore.

"Tatia, Tatiasha, Tania," he whispered, "can you hear me?"

"I can hear you, Shura."

"Press your head into me again. Go on."

She did.

"How are you holding up?"

"You see."

"I see." He took her mittened hand and kissed it. "Courage, Tatiana. Courage."

I love you, Alexander, thought Tatiana.

The following day Alexander came back in the evening and said happily, "Girls! You know what day today is, don't you?"

They looked at him blankly. Tatiana had gone to the hospital for a few hours. What she did there, she could not remember. Dasha seemed even more unfocused. They attempted to smile, and failed. "What day is it?" asked Dasha.

"It's New Year's Eve!" he exclaimed.

They stared.

"Come, look, I brought us three cans of *tushonka*." He grinned. "One each. And some vodka. But only a little bit. You don't want to be drinking too much vodka."

Tatiana and Dasha continued to stare at him. Tatiana finally said, "Alexander, how will we even know when it's New Year? We have only the wind-up alarm clock that hasn't been right in months. And the radio is not working."

Alexander pointed to his wristwatch. "I'm on military time. I always know *precisely* what time it is. And you two have *got* to be more cheerful. This is no way to act before a celebration."

There was no table to set anymore, but they laid their food out on plates, sat on the couch in front of the *bourzhuika*, and ate their New Year's Eve dinner of *tushonka*, some white bread and a spoonful of butter. Alexander gave Dasha cigarettes and Tatiana, with a smile, a small hard candy, which she gladly put in her mouth. They sat chatting quietly until Alexander looked at his watch and went to pour everyone a bit of vodka. In the darkened room they stood up a few minutes before twelve and raised their glasses to 1942.

They counted down the last ten seconds, and clinked and drank, and then Alexander kissed and hugged Dasha, and Dasha kissed and hugged Tatiana, and said, "Go on, Tania, don't be afraid, kiss Alexander on New Year's," and went to sit on the couch, while Tatiana raised her face to Alexander, who bent to Tatiana and very carefully, very gently kissed her on the lips. It was the first time his lips had touched hers since St. Isaac's.

"Happy New Year, Tania."

"Happy New Year, Alexander."

Dasha was on the couch with her eyes closed, a drink in one hand, a cigarette in the other. "Here's to 1942," she said.

"Here's to 1942," echoed Alexander and Tatiana, allowing themselves a glance before he went to sit next to Dasha.

Afterward they all lay down in the bed together, Tatiana next to her wall, turned to Dasha, turned to Alexander. Are there any layers left? she thought. There is hardly life left, how can anything be covering our remains?

The day after New Year's, Alexander and Tatiana slowly made their way to the post office. Every week Tatiana still went to check if there were any letters from Babushka and to send her a short note. Since Deda died, they had received just one letter from her, telling them she had moved from Molotov to a fishing village on the mighty Kama.

Tatiana's letters were brief; she could not get out more than a few paragraphs. She wrote to Babushka about the hospital, about Vera, about Nina Iglenko, and a little about crazy Slavin, who before his inexplicable disappearance two weeks earlier had spent the days and nights, as always, on the floor of the corridor, halfway in, halfway out, indifferent to the bombing and the hunger, his only nod to winter being a blanket over his sunken frame. Slavin, Tatiana could write about. Herself, she could not; even less about the family. She left that to Dasha, who always seemed to manage to write a bright sentence to tack onto Tatiana's grim paragraph. Tatiana didn't know how to hide the Leningrad of October, November, December 1941. Dasha, however, hid it all, constantly and cheerfully writing only about Alexander and their plans for marriage. Well, she was a grown-up. Grown-ups could hide so well.

The letter Tatiana was carrying today did not have an addendum from Dasha, who had been too tired yesterday to write.

Alexander and Tatiana made their careful way in the snow, their faces down and away from the choking wind. The snow was getting inside Tatiana's shredded boots and not melting. Holding on to Alexander's arm, she was thinking about her next letter. Maybe in the next letter she could write about Mama. And Marina. And Aunt Rita. And Babushka Maya.

The post office was on the first floor of the old building on Nevsky. It used to be on the ground floor, but high explosives blew out the windows on the ground floor, and the glass could not be replaced. So the post office moved upstairs. The problem with upstairs was that it was hard to get to. The stairs were covered with ice and bodies.

At the foot of the stairs Alexander said, "It's getting late, I have to go. I have to report back at noon."

"It's many hours till noon," said Tatiana.

"No, actually, it's eleven. It took us an hour and a half to get here."

Tatiana felt even colder. "Go, Shura, get out of the cold," she muttered.

Fixing her scarf, Alexander said, "Don't go to any stores. Go straight home. I already gave you my ration. And we spent all my money."

"I know. I will."

"Please."

"All right," she said. "Are you coming back tonight?"

Shaking his head, he said, "I'm leaving tonight. I'm going back up. My replacement gunner—"

"Don't say it."

"I'll come back as soon as I can."

"All right. You promise?"

"Tatia, I'm going to try to get you and Dasha out of Leningrad on one of the trucks. You hang on until I can do it, all right?"

They stared at each other. She wanted to tell him she was grateful to be able to look into his face but didn't have the energy. Nodding, she turned to walk up the stairs. Alexander remained at the bottom. She slipped on the second step and stumbled backward. Putting his hands out, Alexander caught her, straightening her up. She grabbed on to the railing and then turned around to him. Something resembling a smile passed over her face. "I really am all right without you," she said. "I can manage."

"What about the ravenous boys who follow you home?"

Tatiana warmed her eyes, so she could look at him with the truth that was inside her. "I really am not all right without you," she said. "I can't manage."

"I know," Alexander said. "Hold on to the rail."

Slowly Tatiana walked up the slippery stairs. At the top she turned around to see if Alexander was still there. He was, looking up at her. She pressed her gloved hand to her lips.

The morning after the post office Dasha could not get up. "Dasha, please."

"I can't. You go."

"Of course I will go, but, Dasha, I don't want to go by myself. Alexander is not here."

"No, he's not."

Tatiana fixed the blankets and coats on top of her. Even as she begged Dasha to get up, Tatiana knew that her sister wasn't going anywhere. Dasha's eyes were closed, and she was lying in the same position in which she had fallen asleep the night before. Dasha had also been very quiet the night before. Very quiet except for a cough. "Please get up. You need to get up."

"I'll get up later," said Dasha. "I just can't right now." Her eyes were closed.

Tatiana went to fetch water from downstairs. That took her an hour. She lit the fire in the *bourzhuika*, putting a chair leg in it, and when the fire was started, she made Dasha some tea.

After she had fed Dasha small spoonfuls of the barely brown, barely sweet liquid, she left by herself to go to the ration store. It was ten in the morning but still dark. At eleven it would be light, Tatiana thought. When I'm coming back with the bread it will be light. *"Give us this day our daily bread,"* she whispered to herself. I wish I had known that earlier. I could have said that prayer every day since September.

It's dark all the time now. Was it late? Was it early? Was it evening or night? She looked at the alarm clock. She couldn't make out the hands in the dark. I don't see light. In the morning it's dark, and when I drag the bucket of water up the stairs, it's dark, and when I wash Dasha's face and go to the store and the bombs fly, it's dark. Then a building explodes and burns brightly, and I can go and stand in front of it and warm up a bit. The fire reddens my face, and I stand—for how long? Well, today, I stood until around noon. I didn't get to the hospital until one. Tomorrow maybe I can go and find another fire somewhere. But at home it's dark. Alexander's oil and wick in the little plate help, I can sit and look at a book, maybe, or at Dasha's face.

Dasha—why is she staring at me like that? She has not been herself for five days. She hasn't gotten out of bed for the last three. Her eyes are darker—what's in them? She is staring as if she doesn't know who I am.

"Dasha? What's the matter?"

Dasha staring, not replying. Not moving.

"Dasha!"

"What are you screaming at?" Dasha said quietly.

"Why are you looking at me like that?"

"Come here."

Tatiana came and kneeled by Dasha's face. "What, honey?" she said. "What can I get you?"

"Where is Alexander?"

"I don't know. Up in Ladoga?"

"When is he coming back?"

"Don't know. Maybe tomorrow?"

Dasha staring.

"What's the matter?" Tatiana asked.

"Do you want me to die?"

"What?" Even in her own half-extinguished life, Tatiana was aghast. "Of course not. You're my sister. We all need a second person to remain human, Dasha, you know that."

"I know that."

"So what's the matter?"

"You're my second person, Tania."

"Yes."

"But *who* is yours?" whispered Dasha.

There it is.

Tatiana blinked. *"You,"* she said. Inaudibly.

323

Across That Formidable Sea

1

I saw you, Tatiana," said Dasha in the darkness. "I saw you and him together."

"What are you talking about?" Tatiana's heart stopped.

"I saw you. You didn't know I was watching you. But I saw you five days ago at the post office."

"What post office?"

"You went to the post office."

Tatiana, kneeling by Dasha's head, thought back. Post office, post office. What happened at the post office? She could not remember. "You know we went to the post office. We told you we were going."

"I'm not talking about that. He goes with you everywhere."

"He goes to protect us."

"Not *us*."

"Yes, Dasha, us. He is very worried about us. You know why he goes with me. Did you forget about the food he brings us?"

"I'm not talking about any of that," Dasha said.

"Because of him, no one takes our bread. No one takes our ration cards. How do you think I've fed you? He has kept the cannibals from me."

"I don't want to talk about that."

But Tatiana did. "Dasha, he brings me bread from dead soldiers to give to you, and when he can't find that, he gives me half of his ration to give to you."

"Tatiana, he brings it to you so you will love him."

Stunned, Tatiana said, "What?" Recovering quickly, she said, "Wrong again. He gives it to *you* so you will live."

"Oh, Tania."

"Oh, Tania, nothing. Why did you follow me to the post office?"

"I felt guilty for not writing to Babushka. She looks forward to my notes. You are too depressing for her. You just can't hide the truth like I can. Or so I thought," Dasha said. "I wrote her a cheery note. I didn't follow you. I saw you already at the post office."

"We went to the store first."

Tatiana got up to put another chair leg in the fire. The chair leg wasn't going to last all night, but they had to ration themselves. When Alexander sawed up the table for them, Tatiana didn't realize how much they wanted to be warm. The whole table was gone. Four chairs remained.

When Alexander brought them food, Tatiana didn't realize how much they wanted to be full. The potatoes were gone. The oranges were gone. Only a bit of the barley remained.

When Tatiana came back to bed, she pulled the blankets and coats higher over Dasha and climbed in herself, wanting to turn to the wall. She didn't.

They didn't speak for a few minutes. Dasha slowly turned around to face Tatiana. "I want him to die at the front," she whispered.

"Don't say that," said Tatiana, wanting to cross herself but unable to lift her cold arm out of the warm blanket. She was too weak for inflection. Soon the fire would go out. They would be plunged into black again. They were both spent and done. Tatiana thought they were too weak for heartbreak.

But when Dasha said, "I saw you and him, I saw the way you looked at each other," Tatiana realized, no, they weren't too weak.

"Dashenka, what are you talking about? There was no look. My hat was covering half my face. I don't even know what you mean."

"He stood at the bottom of the stairs. You stood two steps up. He stopped you from tripping on the ice. He said something to you, and you looked down and nodded. And then you looked at each other. You walked up the stairs. He stood at the bottom and watched you. I saw it all."

"Dasha, darling, you're worrying yourself over nothing."

"Am I? Tania, tell me, how long have I been *completely* blind?"

Shaking her head in the night, Tatiana whispered, "No."

"Have I been blind from the very beginning? From the day I walked into the room and saw him standing in front of you? Since then and through all the days that followed? Oh, God, tell me!"

"You're crazy."

"Tania, I may have been blind, but I'm not stupid. What do you think, I can't tell? I have *never* seen that look in his eyes. He watched you go up the stairs with such longing, such tenderness, such possessiveness, such *love*, I turned away and would have thrown up in the snow had I had something to throw up."

Weakly, Tatiana repeated, "You're wrong."

"Am I? And when you were looking at him at the post office, what was in your eyes, sister?"

"I don't know anything about the post office. He walked me there. We said good-bye. I walked up. Good-bye was in my eyes."

"It wasn't good-bye, Tania."

"Dasha, stop. I'm your *sister*."

"Yes, but *he* owes me nothing."

"He is just protective over me—"

"Not protective, Tania. Consumed."

"No."

"Have you been with him?"

"What are you asking?"

"Answer me. It's a simple question. Have you *been* with Alexander? Have you made love to Alexander?"

"Dasha, of course I haven't. Look, this is just—"

"You've lied to me for so long. Are you lying to me now?"

"I'm not lying."

"When? Then? Now?"

"Not then. Not now," Tatiana said, barely able to get the words out.

"I don't believe you." Dasha closed her eyes. "Oh, God, I can't take it," she whispered. "I can't take it. All those days, those nights, those hours we have spent together, slept in the same bed and ate out of the same bowl—how can all of that have been a lie, how?"

"It wasn't a lie! Dasha, he loves you. Look how he kisses you. How he touches you. Didn't he used to make sweet love to you?" Those words were difficult to get out.

"Kissed me. Touched me. We haven't been together since August. Why is that?"

"Dasha, please . . ."

"I'm not for touching these days," said Dasha. "You're not either."

"These days will be over."

"Yes, and me along with them." Dasha coughed.

"Don't talk like that."

"Tania, what are you going to do when I'm gone? Will it be easier for you?"

"What are you talking about? You're my sister . . ." Tatiana, if she could have, would have wept. "I haven't left, haven't gone away! I've stayed here with you. I'm not anywhere else. I'm not leaving you. And we are not dying. He loves *you*." Tatiana put her hands on her chest to stifle a lingering groan.

"Yes," Dasha said brokenly, "but what I want is for him to love me the way he loves *you*."

Tatiana said nothing. She was listening to the wood burning in the ceramic stove, estimating how long they had before the chair leg burned to ashes, her hands on her heart. "He doesn't love me," she said in a hollow voice. How can he love *me*, but plan to marry *you*?

"Tell me," Dasha said, "how long were you going to keep this from me?"

Until the end. "Nothing to keep from you, Dasha."

"Oh, Tania." Dasha fell quiet. "How is it possible that at a time like this, in the dark, so close to the other world, you still have the energy to lie and I still have the energy to be angry? I can't even get up anymore. But anger, yes; lies, oh, yes."

"Good," said Tatiana. "You're warmer for it. Feel it. Hate me if you need to. Hate me with all your might if it helps you."

"Should I hate you?" Dasha's mouth barely moved. "Is there reason for me to hate you?"

"No," said Tatiana, turning to the wall. *Lies to the last.*

2

The next day Dasha still could not get up. She wanted to, she just could not. Tatiana got the blankets off her and the coats. It was nine in the morning, and the girls once again had slept through the eight o'clock air-raid siren.

Tatiana finally left by herself and went to the store. She got there about noon and found there was no more bread. They had gotten a small shipment in, which had all gone by eight in the morning.

"Do you have anything at all you can give me? Is there anything you can do to help me?" asked Tatiana of the woman behind the glass counter. The woman could not even answer.

Tatiana left and walked to find the only one who could help her.

To the sentry at the gate to the barracks she said, "I'm looking for Captain Belov. Is he here?"

"Belov?" The guard, whom Tatiana had not seen before, looked at his roster schedule. "Yes, he's here. But I don't have anyone to go and fetch him."

"Please," said Tatiana. "Please. There was no bread today, and my sister is—"

"What do you think, the captain has bread for you? He doesn't have any bread. Get out of here."

Tatiana didn't move. "My sister is his fiancée," she said.

"That's very good," he said. "Why don't you tell me the rest of your life story?"

"What is your name?" she asked.

"Corporal Kristoff," he said. "*Corporal,*" he repeated.

"That's very good, *Corporal,*" Tatiana said. "I know you can't leave your post. Can you please let me go and see the *captain?*"

He said, "Let you go on base? You are crazy."

"Yes," said Tatiana, holding on to the gate. She felt as though she were about to fall down, having walked too far. But she wasn't going home without food for her sister. "Yes, I *am* crazy. But look at me. I'm not asking you to give me food out of your mouth. I'm not even asking you to move if you don't want to. All I'm asking you to do is let me see Captain Belov. Please help me in this small way. Small way," she repeated. "I'm not asking too much, am I?"

"Listen, girlie, I'm done talking to you," Kristoff said, taking the rifle off his shoulder. "You better move on out of here. You get what I'm saying?"

Clinging to the gate, Tatiana wanted to shake her head but couldn't. Only her lips moved. "Corporal Kristoff, I will wait right here. Sergeant Petrenko, Lieutenant Marazov, Colonel Stepanov—they all know me. Go on and tell them you are turning away Captain Belov's dying fiancée's sister."

"Are you threatening me?" Kristoff asked in disbelief, raising his weapon.

"Corporal!" An officer walked across the yard. "What's going on here? Is there trouble?"

"Just telling this girl to get the hell out of here, sir," said Kristoff.

The officer looked at Tatiana. "Who are you here for?" he asked her.

"Captain Belov, sir," Tatiana said.

The officer said to Kristoff, "Captain Belov is upstairs. Have you called him?"

"No, sir."

"Open the gate."

The officer pulled Tatiana through. "Come, what's your name?"

"I'm Tatiana."

"Tatiana . . ." the officer said. "Was Kristoff giving you trouble?"

"Yes, sir," she said.

"Don't worry about him. He is just overeager. I'll be right back."

The officer went into Alexander's quarters. Alexander was sleeping. He had been on barracks patrol all night. "Captain," the officer said loudly.

Alexander woke up with a start.

"There is a young lady waiting for you outside, sir," he said. "I know it's against the rules. Can I send her in? A girl named Tatiana."

Before he finished, Alexander was already up and getting dressed. "Where is she?"

"Downstairs. I brought her in, I thought you wouldn't mind."

"I don't mind."

"That bastard Kristoff was ready to fire at her. I barely—"

"Thank you, Lieutenant." He was out the door.

Tatiana was sitting on the bottom stair, her head pressed to the wall.

"Tatia?" He came to stand in front of her. "What's happened?"

"Dasha can't get up. There was no bread at the store." She couldn't even look up.

"Come." He extended his hand. She took it but couldn't pull herself up. He had to place both his arms around her to lift her. "You walked too far," he said gently.

She nodded.

"Come to the mess." Alexander found Tatiana a piece of black bread with a teaspoon of butter, half a cooked potato with some linseed oil, and even real coffee with a bit of sugar. She ate gratefully and drank. "What about Dasha?" she asked.

"Eat. I have food for Dasha."

He gave her another hunk of black bread, half a potato, and a handful of beans that she stuffed in her coat pocket. "I wish I could come with you," Alexander said. "But I can't. I can't leave the barracks today."

"That's fine," Tatiana said, and thought, I don't think I can make it back. I don't think I can. It was after lunch hour in the mess, and it was quiet. Only a few soldiers were sitting at the tables.

Tatiana wanted to ask Alexander about his week, about Petrenko, whom she hadn't seen in a long time, and about Dimitri. She wanted to tell him about Kristoff. She wanted to tell him Zhanna Sarkova had died. It was time to go to the post office again, but she couldn't walk there by herself anymore.

Tatiana wanted to tell him about Dasha. But the effort required to continue *that* conversation was too great even in Tatiana's head. To make the words come out of her mouth, and then follow them up with more words and more thoughts, was unimaginable to her now, when she couldn't find the energy to chew the bread she needed to live. She couldn't think past the black bread in front of her. I'll tell him another time.

They both remained utterly silent.

Alexander walked her to the gate. She stumbled on flat ground and nearly fell. "Oh, my God, Tatia," he said.

She didn't reply, but his calling her *Tatia* made her heart beat faster. She wanted to answer him. Straightening up, she leaned on his arm and said, "I'll be all right. Don't worry."

"Wait here." He sat her on a bench near the gate and strode off. A few minutes later he came back with a sled and said, "Come. I'll take you home. Stepanov let me have two hours." He put his arm around her. "Come. You won't have to do anything. I'll do everything. You just sit."

Alexander signed himself out in the roster at the sentry gate. "I'm very sorry about before," the corporal said to Tatiana, throwing a fearful look in Alexander's direction. Alexander opened his mouth to say something, but Tatiana pulled him by the sleeve of his coat. She didn't shake her head, didn't say a word, just pulled him, and he prodded her away a little, closed his mouth, clenched his fist, and punched Kristoff in the face. The corporal fell to the ground. "I'll be back in two hours, Corporal," he said, "and then I'll deal with you."

Alexander told Tatiana to sit. She lay down instead. She thought, I don't want to lie down. I'm not a corpse yet. Not yet. But she couldn't help it. She couldn't sit up.

Tatiana lay on her side, and Alexander pulled the sled through the snow, through the quiet, snowed-in streets of Leningrad in the middle of an afternoon. Tatiana thought, it's too heavy for him. It's always him. When we first met, he carried my food for me down these streets. And now he is carrying me. She wanted to reach out and touch the bottom of Alexander's coat. Instead she fell asleep.

When she opened her eyes, Tatiana saw Alexander crouching beside her, his warm bare hand on her cold bare cheek. "Tatia," he whispered, "come on, we're home."

I'm going to die with Alexander's hand on my face, Tatiana thought. That is not a bad way to die. I cannot move. I can't get up. Just can't. She closed her eyes and felt herself drifting.

Through the haze in front of her she heard Alexander's voice. "Tatiana, I love you. Do you hear me? I love you like I've never loved anyone in my whole life. Now, get up. For me, Tatia. For me, please get up and go take care of your sister. Go on. And I'll take care of you." His lips kissed her cheek.

She opened her eyes. He was very close to her, and his eyes looked true. Did she just hear him? Or did she dream that? She had dreamed of him saying he loved her for so many nights facing the wall, she had longed for those words, longed for them since Kirov. Was she just wishing for the white-night sun again?

Tatiana got up. He couldn't carry her up the slippery stairs on his back. But he put his arm around her, and by holding on to him and the railing she made it upstairs. They walked through the long apartment, but at the door to their hallway Tatiana stopped. "Go in," she said. "I'll wait here. Go and see if she's . . ." Tatiana couldn't finish.

Alexander brought her inside and then went into the bedroom. "Yes, Tania," she heard his voice. "Dasha is fine. Come in."

Tatiana came in and knelt by the bed. "Dasha," she said, "look, he brought you food."

Dasha, her eyes two large brown saucers, two large brown empty saucers, moved her lips soundlessly, her stilted gaze traveling from Tatiana's face to Alexander's and back again.

"I've got to go," said Alexander. "Go early tomorrow to get your bread. There is enough here for you until then. Have you girls already eaten all your barley?" He kissed Dasha on the head. "I'll bring you more tomorrow."

She lifted her arm to him. "Don't leave," said Dasha.

"I have to. You'll be all right. Just get your rations. I'll come and see you very soon. Tania, do you need help? Can you get up off the floor?"

"I can get up," she said.

"Right," he said, and put his hands under her arms. "Up we go."

She stood up. She wanted to look at him, but she knew that Dasha was watching, so instead she looked at Dasha. It was easier; her head was already bent down. "Thank you, Sh—Alexander."

They lay under their blankets in semiconsciousness. During the night Tatiana woke up hearing a knock on the door. It took her many minutes to get out of bed from under the coats and blankets. Unsteadily she walked through the dark hallway.

Alexander stood at the door dressed in his white battle uniform. Over his ears and head was a quilted hat, and in his hands he held a blanket.

"What's the matter?" she said, putting her hand on her chest. Seeing him, Tatiana's heart pulsed a beat faster, even in the middle of the night. Her eyes opened a bit wider; she was awake. "What's happened?"

"Nothing," he said. "Get yourself and Dasha ready; where is she? She needs to get ready."

"Where are we going? Dasha can't get up," Tatiana said. "You know that. She is coughing badly."

"She will get up," Alexander replied. "Come on. There is an armament truck leaving the garrison tonight. I will get you to Ladoga, and then you will go to Kobona. Tania! I will get you out of Leningrad."

He walked through the hallway and came into the bedroom. Dasha was lying under her blankets and coats. Her lips were not moving, her eyes would not open.

"Dasha," Alexander whispered. "Dashenka, dear, wake up. We've got to leave. Right now, we've got to go. Quick."

Without opening her eyes, Dasha muttered, "I can't get up."

"You can get up, and you will get up," he said. "An armament truck is waiting at the barracks. I will get you to Lake Ladoga. Then we will get you across the lake. Tonight. You'll get to Kobona, where there is food, and then you girls can go to your Babushka in Molotov. But you have to get up right now, Dasha. Now, let's go." He moved the blankets off her.

Dasha whispered, "I can't get to the barracks."

"Tania has a sled. And look!" He opened his coat and took out a piece of white bread with a crust. Breaking off a hunk of the soft inside, he put it to Dasha's mouth. "White bread! Eat. It will give you strength."

Dasha opened her mouth. She chewed listlessly without opening her eyes and then coughed. Tatiana stood nearby, wrapped in her own coat with a blanket over her shoulders, looking at the piece of bread the way she once used to look at Alexander. Maybe Dasha won't finish it all. Maybe there will be some left for me.

It was only a little piece. Dasha ate everything. "Is there more?" she asked.

"Only the crust," Alexander replied.

"I'll have it."

"You can't chew it."

"I'll swallow it whole."

"Dasha . . . maybe your sister can have it?" he asked with feeling.

"She's standing, isn't she?"

Alexander looked up at Tatiana, who was standing next to him. Shaking her head, she said, looking longingly at the crust, "Give it to her. I'm standing."

Breathing in deeply, Alexander gave the crust to Dasha and then, rising to his feet, said to Tatiana, "Let's get going. What do you need to do to get ready? Can I help you pack?"

Tatiana stared at him with empty eyes. "I have nothing. I'm ready now. My boots are on. My coat is on. We've sold everything and burned everything else."

"*Everything?*" he asked her in the darkness—one word, brimming with the past.

"I have . . . the books—" She broke off.

"Bring them," Alexander said and, leaning closer to her, continued, "Check out the *back* cover of Pushkin when you're feeling particularly down on your luck. Where are they?"

Alexander crawled under the bed to get her books, while Tatiana found Pasha's old backpack. Then he lifted Dasha and forced her to stand up. In the dark the three silhouettes struggled in silence, with only Dasha's intermittent moans and chesty coughing breaking the night into shards. Finally Alexander picked her up and carried her out of the apartment, and they slid down the stairs. Outside in the bitter night he laid Dasha across the sled, covering her with the blanket he had brought. Alexander and Tatiana picked up the reins and slowly pulled Dasha down the streets through the snow in the girls' childhood blue sled with bright red runners.

"What's going to happen to Dasha?" Tatiana said quietly.

"In Kobona there is food and a hospital. Once she is better, you will go to Molotov."

"She sounds bad."

Alexander didn't say anything.

"Why is she coughing like that?" Tatiana said, and coughed herself.

Alexander didn't say anything.

"I haven't heard from Babushka in so long."

"She is fine. She is better off than you," Alexander said. "Is it hard for you to pull? Just walk beside me. Let go of the sled."

"No." It was a tremendous effort. "Let me help you."

"Save your strength." He made her release the rope. Tatiana let go and walked alongside him.

"Hold on to my arm," Alexander told her. She did.

The night was so cold, Tatiana stopped feeling her feet. Leningrad was still and silent and almost completely dark. In the sky the translucent banded lights of the aurora borealis streaked green through the blackness. Tatiana turned around to look at Dasha, who lay motionless in the sled.

"She seems so weak," Tatiana said.

"She *is* weak."

"How do you manage?" she asked in a low voice. "How do you manage to carry your weapon, to stand guard, to go and fight, to be strong for all of us?"

"I give you," said Alexander, glancing at her, "what you need most from me."

They trod mutely through the snow. Alexander got slower. Tatiana took the second rope from his hands. He did not protest.

"I'll feel better knowing you two are out of Leningrad. I'll feel better knowing you're safe," he said. "Don't you think it will be better?"

Tatiana didn't reply. Better to eat, yes. Better for Dasha to eat, yes.

But not better for Alexander, not better for her. Not better to stop seeing him. She said none of these things. And then she heard his soft "I know." And wanted to cry, but she knew crying was impossible. Her eyes exposed to the black frost, sore from the wind, half shut from the cold, were dry.

When they finally got to the barracks an hour later, the army truck was minutes away from leaving. Alexander carried Dasha inside the covered vehicle. There were six soldiers sitting on the floor, and a young woman holding a small infant sitting next to a man who looked barely alive. He looks much worse than Dasha, Tatiana thought, but when she looked at Dasha, she saw that her sister could not even sit up by herself. Every time Alexander sat her up Dasha would tilt to one side. Tatiana needed help getting inside the truck. She could not jump up or pull herself up by her arms. She needed someone to lift her. All the people inside the truck were oblivious to her, including Alexander, who was trying anxiously and solicitously to get Dasha to open her eyes. Someone from the outside shouted, "Go!" And the truck started slowly moving forward in the snow. "Shura!" Tatiana cried.

Alexander crawled across the floor of the truck, grabbing Tatiana's arms and pulling her in.

"Did you forget about me?" she asked and saw Dasha's open eyes watching them.

The door closed, and it became very dark, and in the dark, on her hands and knees, Tatiana made her way to Dasha.

In silence they drove toward Lake Ladoga.

Alexander sat on the floor next to his rifle. Dasha lay on the sawdust-covered floor with her head in his lap. Tatiana picked up her sister's feet and slid under them, closer to Alexander. Dasha now lay nearly on top of them. Alexander had her head, Tatiana had her feet. Alexander leaned against the wall of the cabin, and Tatiana leaned against the wall of the truck. She picked up a piece of sawdust and put it in her mouth. It tasted like bread. She had another piece.

"Don't eat that, Tania," said Alexander. How could he see her? "It's filthy."

Time passed. In the occasional flicker of light, Tatiana would catch Alexander staring at her. Their eyes met and held until the light from the passing vehicle dimmed. Without saying a word, without touching each other, they sat on the floor and in every lit moment caught each other's gaze.

Endless minutes passed.

"What time is it, do you know?" Tatiana asked quietly.

Alexander said, "Two in the morning. We'll be there soon."

Tatiana wanted to eat, and she wanted to stop being cold. She wanted her sister to get better, to get up. At the same time, leaving for Molotov seemed so final.

She waited for another light so she could catch Alexander's eye for a second or two. Her eyes got used to the dark, and she could make out his silhouette, his head and hat, the shape of his arms that lay around Dasha to keep her warm. Tatiana squeezed Dasha's legs, first softly, then harder. She shook Dasha's legs, first softly, then harder. Dasha stirred a bit and coughed. Relieved, Tatiana closed her eyes, only to instantly open them again. She didn't want to close her eyes. In a little while she would be across the Ladoga ice, away from him. If I reach out, I can almost touch him, she thought.

"Tania?" she heard his voice.

"Yes—Alexander?"

"What's the name of the village your grandmother lives in?"

"Lazarevo." She stretched out her hand to him. He stretched out his hand to her.

"Lazarevo." Passing light. Alexander and Tatiana touched each other. Darkness again.

Alexander fell asleep. Dasha was asleep. All the people in the truck had their eyes closed, except for Tatiana, who could not take her eyes off Alexander's sleeping form. Maybe I'm dead, she thought. Dead people can't close their eyes. Maybe that's why I can't sleep. I'm dead. But she could not close her eyes. She watched him. Both his hands were on Dasha's head.

"Alexander, why didn't you buy yourself an ice cream, too?"

"I didn't want one."

"Then why are you looking so longingly at mine?"

"I'm not looking longingly at your ice cream."

"No? Would you like a taste?"

"All right." He bent and had a lick of her creamy ice cream.

"Isn't it good?"

"So good, Tania."

Finally the truck stopped. Alexander opened his eyes. The other people stirred. The woman with the baby got up first and whispered to her husband, "Leonid, come on, dear, time to get across, get up, darling."

Alexander moved out from under Dasha, stood, and gave his arm to Tatiana. "Get up, Tatia," he said softly. "It's time." He pulled her up. She swayed from weakness.

"Shura," she said, "what am I going to do with Dasha in Kobona? She can't walk. And I'm not you, I can't carry her."

"Don't worry. There will be soldiers and doctors to help you. Look at that woman," he whispered to her. "She carries her baby, but her husband can't hold himself up, just like Dasha. She'll manage. You'll see. Come, I'll help you down."

Jumping down, he extended his arms to Tatiana, who could not have jumped down if she wanted to. Alexander lifted her and brought her down to stand in front of him. He did not let go.

"Go get Dasha, Shura," Tatiana whispered.

"Come on! Let's move it!" a sergeant shouted behind them. Alexander let go of Tatiana and grimly turned around. The sergeant quickly apologized to the captain.

Tatiana saw four other trucks with their lights on, shining down on the snow-covered field ahead. She realized that it wasn't a field. It was Lake Ladoga. It was the Road of Life.

"Come on, come on, comrades! Walk down to the lake. There is a truck waiting there for you. Come on, the quicker you get inside, the quicker we can go. It's thirty kilometers, a couple of hours on the ice, but there's butter on the other side, and maybe even some cheese. Hurry!"

The woman with the baby was already walking down the hill with her husband limping beside her.

Dasha was in Alexander's arms. "Stand her up, Shura," said Tatiana. "Let's get her to walk."

He put Dasha down, but her legs buckled under her. "Come on, Dasha," said Tatiana. "Walk with me. There's butter on the other side, did you hear?"

Dasha groaned. "Where am I?" she whispered.

"You're at the Road of Life. Now, come on. In just a little while we're going to eat, and we're going to be all right. A doctor will look at you."

"Are you coming with us?" Dasha asked Alexander.

He supported her with his arm. "No, Dasha, I stay. My Zenith is just up ahead. But write to me as soon as you get to Molotov, and when I get furlough, I'll come and see you." Alexander said it without glancing at Tatiana, but Tatiana couldn't hear it without glancing at Alexander.

Dasha moved a few meters by herself and then sank to the snow. "I can't."

"You can, and you will," said Tatiana. "Come on. Show him your life means something. Show him you can walk to the truck to save yourself. Come on, Dasha." They lifted Dasha to her feet.

She walked another few meters and stopped. "No," she whispered.

Holding Dasha up between them, Alexander and Tatiana walked down the slope to the lake, where the army truck was waiting.

Alexander lifted Dasha and laid her on the floor of the truck. Then he hopped down to help Tatiana, who could barely stand. She leaned against the tarpaulin, heard shouts. The truck revved its engines.

"Come on, Tania, I'll help you inside," Alexander said. "You have to be strong for your sister." He came close to her.

"I will be," she thought she said.

"Don't worry about the bombing," Alexander said. "It's usually quieter at night."

"I'm not worried," Tatiana said, coming into his arms.

He hugged her. "Be strong for me, Tatiana," Alexander said hoarsely. "Save yourself for me."

"That's what I do, Shura," Tatiana said. "I save myself for you."

Alexander bent to her, but she couldn't even look up. He kissed the top of her hat. They held on for a few more seconds.

"Time!" someone shouted.

Alexander helped Tatiana inside the truck. He hopped in himself to get the two girls comfortable, moving Dasha's head to rest on top of Tatiana's lap.

"Is this all right?" he asked, and both sisters answered, "Yes."

Kneeling down in front of Dasha, Alexander said, "Now, remember, when they offer you food in Kobona, eat small bites. Don't gulp it down, it can tear your stomach. Eat small and eat slow. You'll get used to it, and then you can eat more. Drink soup in small spoonfuls. All right?"

Dasha took hold of his hand. He kissed her on the forehead. "So long, Dasha. I'll see you soon."

"Good-bye—" whispered Dasha. "What did my sister call you? Shura?"

Alexander glanced at Tatiana. "Yes, Shura."

"Good-bye, Shura," said Dasha. "I love you."

Tatiana closed her eyes so as not to look at him speak. If she could have covered her ears, she would have.

"I love you, too," Alexander said to Dasha. "Don't forget to write."

After he stood up, Dasha said, "Say good-bye to Tania. Or did you already say good-bye?"

"Good-bye, Tatiana," he said.

"Good-bye," she replied, staring at him.

"As soon as you get to Molotov, I want to hear from you. Promise?" Alexander said, hopping off the truck.

"Alexander!" Dasha called after him.

"Yes?" he leaned in.

"Tell me, how *long* have you loved my sister?"

Alexander glanced from Tatiana's face to Dasha's and back again. He opened his mouth to speak and then closed it with a shudder of his head.

"How long? Tell me. Look at us all—what secrets can we possibly have left? Tell me, darling. Tell me."

Setting his jaw, Alexander said forcefully, "Dasha, I *never* loved your sister. *Never*. I love *you*. You know what we have."

"You told me that next summer maybe we would get married," said Dasha weakly. "Did you mean it?"

Nodding, he replied, "Of course I meant it. Next summer I will come and we will get married. Now, go."

He blew Dasha a kiss and disappeared, not even glancing at Tatiana. And she desperately wanted just one small *last* glance, almost in the dark, his soft eyes on her, so she could see a bit of truth. But he didn't look at her. She didn't see any truth. She saw Alexander not even breathe her way. She saw Alexander *deny* her.

The tarpaulin was closed, the truck was off, and they were in the dark again. Except that now there was no Alexander between the darkness and the light, and no moon, just gunfire and the sound of bursting in the distance that Tatiana could barely hear, so loud was the sound of bursting inside her chest. Finally she closed her eyes, so that Dasha, who was lying with her eyes open, couldn't look up and see what must have been so plain on Tatiana's face.

"Tania?"

She didn't answer. Her nose was hurting from breathing the freezing air. She parted her lips and breathed through her mouth.

"Tanechka?"

"Yes, Dasha, dear?" she whispered at last. "Are you all right?"

"Open your eyes, sister."

Couldn't. Wouldn't.

"Open them."

She opened them. "Dasha, I'm very tired. You've kept your eyes closed for hours. Now it's my turn. I've pulled your sled and held your legs and helped you down the hill. Now you're lying on me, and I just want to close my eyes for a second, for a minute. All right?"

Dasha didn't say anything but looked at Tatiana with lucid clarity. Tatiana held her sister's face and closed her eyes, listening to Dasha's wet cough.

"How did it feel, Tania, hearing him say he *never* loved you?"

With the greatest effort Tatiana stopped herself from a groan of pain. "Fine," she said hoarsely. "As it should be."

"Then why did your body recoil as if he had hit you?"

"Don't know what you mean," Tatiana said faintly.

"Open your eyes."

"No."

Dasha spoke. "You love him unbearably, don't you? *How* did you manage to hide it from me, Tania? You couldn't love a man more."

I couldn't love a man more. "Dasha," said Tatiana with finality and grace, "I love you more." She never opened her eyes as she spoke.

"And you *didn't* hide it from me," said Dasha. "Not at all. You put your love for him on a shelf, not in a cupboard. Marina was right. I was just blind." She closed her own eyes, but her voice carried across the truck, to the woman with her baby and husband, to Tatiana, to the truck driver. "You left it for me to see in a thousand places. I see every bitter one of them now." She started to cry, breaking into a coughing fit. "But you were a child! How could a child love anyone?" Dasha fell quiet and then groaned.

I grew up, Dasha, thought Tatiana. Somewhere between Lake Ilmen and the start of war, the child had grown.

Outside there was a distant sound of cannons, of mortar fire. Inside the truck was silent.

Tatiana wondered about the baby that was held by the mother, a young woman with sallow skin and sores on her cheeks. Her husband was leaning on her shoulder; in fact, he was more than leaning, he was falling on his wife, and no matter how hard she pulled at him to sit upright, he would not sit up. The woman started to cry. The baby never made a sound.

Tatiana spoke to the woman. "Can I help you?"

"Listen, you've got your own problems," said the woman brusquely. "My husband is very weak."

Dasha said, "I'm not a problem. Pull me up, Tania, and lean me against the wall. My chest hurts too much to keep lying down. Go, help her."

Tatiana crawled across the truck to the woman and her husband. The woman was clutching her baby with both arms and not letting go.

Tatiana shook the man a bit, pulled him up briefly, but he fell back down, and this time he fell to the floor of the truck. He was heavily wrapped in a scarf, and his coat was buttoned to his neck. It took Tatiana ten minutes to unbutton him. The woman kept talking to her nonstop.

"He is not doing well, my husband. And my daughter is not much better. I have no milk for her. You know, she was born in October, what luck! Huh, what bad luck for a baby to be born in October. And when I got pregnant last February, we were so happy. We thought it was a sign from God. We just got married the September before. We were so excited. Our first baby! Leonid was working at the city public transportation department; he couldn't leave and his ration was quite good, but then the trams stopped, and there was nothing for him to do—why are you unbuttoning him?"

Without waiting for an answer, the woman continued. "I'm Nadezhda. My daughter was born, and I had no milk for her. What to give her? I've been giving her soy milk, but it gave her terrible diarrhea, so I had to stop. And my husband really needed the food. Thank God, we finally got on the truck. We've been waiting to get out for so long. Now it will all be all right. Kobona will have bread and cheese, someone said. What I would do to see a chicken, or something hot. I'll eat horsemeat, I don't care. Just something for Leonid."

Tatiana took her two fingers off the man's neck and very carefully buttoned him up again and wrapped the scarf around his neck. She moved him slightly so he was not lying on top of his wife's legs and went back to sit by Dasha. The truck was deathly quiet. All Tatiana could hear was Dasha's shallow breathing broken by bursts of coughing. That, and Alexander saying he never loved her.

Both sisters closed their eyes so as not to look at the woman and her dead baby and her dead husband. Tatiana put her hand on Dasha's head. Dasha did not push it away.

They got to Kobona at daybreak—daybreak, a purple haze on the dark horizon. The features on Dasha's face became dim instead of vague. Why was Tatiana noticing Dasha's rasping breathing all of a sudden?

"Can you get up, Dasha?" Tatiana asked. "We're here."

"I can't," she said.

Nadezhda was shouting for someone to help her and her husband. No one came. Rather, a soldier came, lifted the tarpaulin off the back of the truck, and grunted, "Everybody off. We've got to load up and drive back."

Tatiana pulled at Dasha. "Come on, Dasha, get up."

"Go and get help, Tania," Dasha said. "I can't move anymore."

Yanking at her sister, Tatiana pulled Dasha up on all fours. "You crawl to the edge, and I'll help you down."

"Can you help my husband down?" said Nadezhda plaintively. "Help him, please. You're so strong. You see he is sick."

Tatiana shook her head. "He's too big for me."

"Oh, come on, you're moving. Help us, will you? Don't be selfish."

"Just wait," said Tatiana. "I'm going to help my sister down, and then I will help you."

"Leave her alone," Dasha said to Nadezhda. "Your husband is dead. Leave my poor sister alone."

Nadezhda shrieked.

Dasha crawled, pulling herself like a soldier across the truck floor. At the edge Tatiana swung Dasha around, lowering her off the truck, legs first. Dasha's legs hit the ground, and the rest of her body followed and fell. She remained in the snow.

"Dasha, come on, please. I can't pull you up by myself," said Tatiana.

The driver of the truck came around and in one motion lifted Dasha to her feet. "Stand up, comrade. Stand up and walk to the field tent. They're giving you food and hot tea. Now, go."

From inside the truck Nadezhda shouted, "Don't you forget me in here!"

Tatiana didn't want to stay to hear Nadezhda discover the truth about her husband and baby. Turning to Dasha, she said, "Use me as a crutch. Put me under your arm and walk with me." She pointed up a shallow slope. "Look, we're at the river Kobona."

"I can't. I couldn't walk with you *and* Alexander downhill on the other side, I can't walk uphill with just you."

"It's not a hill. It's a slope. Use that anger you feel at me. Use it, and walk up the damn slope, Dasha."

"So easy for you, isn't it?" said Dasha.

"Is that what it is?" Tatiana shook her head.

"So easy. You just want to live, and that's all."

I do want to live. But that's not all. They stumbled through the snow, Dasha holding on to Tatiana.

"And you? Don't you want to live?"

Dasha made no reply.

"Come on," said Tatiana. "You're doing so well. There is nobody to help us." She squeezed her sister and whispered intensely, "It's just you and me,

Dasha! The soldiers are busy, the other people are all helping their own. Like I am. And you *do* so want to live. In the summer Alexander will come to Molotov, and you will get married."

Dasha summoned enough strength to laugh softly. "Tania, you never stop, do you?"

"Never," said Tatiana.

Dasha fell in the snow and would not get up.

Swirling around in despair, Tatiana spotted Nadezhda walking up the hill alone, no baby, no husband. She went up to her. "Nadezhda, please help me. Help me with Dasha. She's fallen in the snow."

Nadezhda ripped her arm away from Tatiana's hold. "Get away from me. Can't you see, I've got no one with me now."

Tatiana saw. "Please help me."

"You didn't help *me*. And now they're all dead. Leave me alone, will you?" Nadezhda walked away.

Suddenly Tatiana heard a familiar voice. "Tatiana? Tatiana Metanova?"

Turning in the direction of the voice, she saw Dimitri hobbling to her, supported by his rifle.

"Dimitri!" She walked up to him. He hugged her. "Help me, Dima, please. My sister! Look, she has fallen."

Dimitri quickly got to Dasha. "Come on," he said. "I'm still wounded. I can't carry her myself. I'll get you another soldier." He turned to Tatiana and gave her another long hug. "I can't believe we ran into each other like this." Smiling. "It must be destiny," he said.

Dimitri got someone else to lift Dasha and carry her to the hospital field tent as Tatiana trudged after them in the mauve light of the sky.

In the hospital tent near the Kobona River, a doctor came to see Dasha. He listened to her heart, to her lungs, felt her pulse, opened her mouth, shook his head, stood, and said, "Galloping consumption. Forget about her."

Tatiana took a step toward the doctor. "*Forget* about her? What are you talking about? Give her something, some sulfa—"

The doctor laughed. "You're all the same, all of you. You think I'm going to be giving away my precious sulfa on a terminal case? What are you, crazy? Look at her. She doesn't have an hour to live. I wouldn't waste a piece of bread on her. Have you seen how much mucus she's bringing up? Have you listened to her breathing? I'm sure the TB bacteria has traveled to her liver. Go and get some soup and porridge for yourself in the next tent. *You* might actually make it, if you eat."

Tatiana studied the doctor for a few moments. "Am *I* all right?" she asked. "Can you listen to *my* lungs? I don't feel all right."

The doctor opened Tatiana's coat and pressed the stethoscope to her chest. Then he turned her around and listened through her back. "You need some sulfanilamide yourself, girl. You've got pneumonia. Let me have the nurse take care of you. Olga!" Before he left, he turned to Tatiana and said, "Don't go near your sister anymore. TB is contagious."

Tatiana lay on the ground, while Dasha lay in the clean bed. After a while she became too cold. Tatiana lay down on her side in the narrow cot very close to her sister. "Dasha," she whispered, "all my life whenever I had nightmares, I would nestle like this with you, in our bed."

"I know, Tania," whispered Dasha. "You were the sweetest child."

Outside wasn't light so much as blue. Dark blue tints on Dasha's trembling face. She heard Dasha's hoarse voice. "I can't breathe . . ."

Tatiana knelt on the ground in front of the bed, opened Dasha's mouth, and blew into it, blew into it cold, brusque, stunted, pitiful breath, breath without soil, without roots, without food. She breathed from her own lungs into her sister's. Tatiana tried to breathe deeply, but she couldn't. For endless minutes Tatiana breathed into Dasha's mouth, into Dasha's lungs, the shallow whisper of life.

A nurse came up to them and pulled Tatiana away. "Stop it," she said in a kind voice. "Didn't the doctor tell you to leave her alone? Are you the sick one?"

"Yes," whispered Tatiana, holding Dasha's cold hand.

The nurse gave Tatiana three white pills, some water, and a hunk of black bread. "It's dipped in sugar water," she said.

"Thank you," gasped Tatiana between pain-soaked breaths.

The nurse put her arm on Tatiana's back. "Do you want to come with me? I'll try to find you a place to lie down before breakfast."

Tatiana shook her head.

"Don't give her any of the bread. Eat it yourself."

"She needs it more than I do," said Tatiana.

"No, darling," the nurse replied. "No, she doesn't."

As soon as the nurse left, Tatiana crushed the sulfa tablets against the bed frame, crumbling them into her hand and then into the water, and after taking a small gulp, lifted Dasha's head slightly off the pillow and made her drink the dissolved medicine.

Tatiana broke off a little piece of the bread and fed it to Dasha, who swallowed with obvious pain and choked. Spluttering, she coughed up blood onto the white sheet. Tatiana wiped Dasha's mouth and chin and then blew her breath into Dasha's mouth again.

"Tania?"

"Yes?"

"Is this dying? Is this what dying feels like?"

"No, Dasha" was all Tatiana could reply.

She stared into Dasha's muted, blinking eyes.

"Tania . . . darling, you're a *good* sister," whispered Dasha.

Tatiana continued to breathe into Dasha's mouth.

She couldn't hear her sister's painful labored breathing, only her own.

341

Tatiana felt a warm hand on her back, and a voice behind her said, "Come. You won't believe what I have for you. It's breakfast time. I have buckwheat *kasha* and bread and a teaspoon of butter. You will have tea with some sugar, and I will even find you some real milk. Come. What's your name?"

"I can't leave my sister," said Tatiana.

The nurse said in a sympathetic voice, "Come, my dear. My name is Olga. Come, breakfast won't last forever."

Tatiana felt arms lifting her. She stood up, but one look at Dasha and she sank back down on the floor.

Dasha's mouth remained open as Tatiana had left it open. Her eyes were open, too, staring upward to the violet sky beyond the cloth of the tent, beyond Tatiana.

Bending and broken, Tatiana kissed Dasha's eyes closed and made the sign of the cross on her forehead. She struggled up, took Olga's hand, and left.

In the adjoining mess she sat down at a table and looked into an empty plate. Olga brought her some buckwheat. Tatiana ate half the small bowl. When Olga asked her to eat more, Tatiana said she couldn't because she was saving the rest for Dasha, and fainted.

Tatiana awoke in a bed.

Olga came, offering her a piece of bread and some tea. Tatiana refused.

"If you don't eat, you will die," said Olga.

"I'm not going to die," said Tatiana weakly. "Give it to Dasha, my sister."

"Your sister is dead," said Olga.

"No."

"Come with me. Let me take you to her."

Tatiana walked to a back room with Olga, where she saw Dasha lying on the floor next to three other bodies.

Tatiana asked who was going to bury them. Olga said with a laugh, "Oh, girl, what *are* you thinking? Nobody, of course. Did you take the drugs the doctor gave you?"

Shaking her head, Tatiana said, "Olga, can you bring me a sheet? For my sister."

Olga brought Tatiana a sheet, some more medicine, a cup of black tea with sugar, and bread with a chunk of butter. This time Tatiana took the drugs and ate, sitting in a low metal chair in a room full of corpses. After she finished, she laid the sheet on the ground and rolled Dasha into it.

Tatiana held her sister's head in her hands for a long time.

After wrapping Dasha tightly with the sheet, ripping the tattered ends and tying them together, Tatiana left the tent and went to find Dimitri. In Kobona, the small seaside town in the dark of January, Tatiana found many soldiers, but not him. She needed to find him. She needed his help. She went back to the Kobona River. Stopping an officer, she asked him where Dimitri

Chernenko might be. He did not know. She asked ten soldiers, but none of them knew. The eleventh one looked at her and said, "Tania? What the hell is the matter with you? I *am* Dimitri."

She did not recognize him. Without emotion she said, "Oh. I need your help."

"Don't you recognize me, Tania?"

"Yes, of course," she said flatly. "Come with me."

He limped with her, his arm lightly around her shoulder. "Aren't you going to ask me about my leg?"

"In a bit, all right," Tatiana said, leading him to the partitioned room and showing him Dasha's body wrapped in a sheet surrounded by uncovered corpses. "Will you help me bury Dasha?" she asked, the strands of her voice barely holding together.

Dimitri sucked in his breath. "Oh, Tania," he said, shaking his head.

She continued. "I can't take her with me. But I can't leave her here either. Please help me."

"Tania," he said, opening his arms. She backed away from him. "Where are we going to bury her? The ground is frozen solid. An earthmoving machine couldn't dig this dirt."

Tatiana stood and waited. For sunshine, for a solution.

"The Nazis are bombing the Road of Life, yes?"

"Yes."

"The ice on the lake gets broken, yes?"

"Yes." His face registered gradual understanding.

"Then, let's go."

"Tania, I can't."

"Yes, you can. If I can, you can."

"You don't understand—"

"Dima, *you* don't understand. I can't let her lie in the back room, now, can I? I won't be able to leave her, and I won't be able to save my own life." Tatiana came up to stand in front of him. "Tell me, Dimitri, when *I'm* dead, will you even know how to sew a sack for me? When I'm dead, will you put me in the back room on top of the other bodies? What will you do with me?"

Banging his rifle on the ground, he said, "Oh, Tania."

"Please. Help me."

Sighing, he barely shook his head. "I can't. Look at me. I've been in the hospital for nearly three months. They just let me out, put me on the Kobona detail, and now I have to walk around for hours. It hurts my foot, and the Germans bomb the lake all the time. I'm not going out there. I can't run if the shelling starts."

"Get me a sled, will you? Can you do *that* for me?" she said coldly, going to sit by Dasha.

"Tania—"

"Dimitri, just a sled. Surely you can do that?"

He came back after some time with a sled. Tatiana got up off the ground. "Thank you. You can go," she said.

"Why are you doing this?" Dimitri exclaimed. "She is dead. Who cares now? Don't worry about her anymore. This fucking war can't hurt her."

Raising her eyes at him, Tatiana said, "*Who* cares? *I* care. My sister did not die alone. I'm still here. And I will not turn from her until I bury her."

"And then what are you going to do? You don't sound too good yourself. Are you going to go ahead to your grandparents? Where were they again? Kazan? Molotov? You probably shouldn't go, you know. I keep hearing horror stories about the evacuees."

"I don't know what I'm going to do." She added, "Don't worry about me."

As he was leaving, she called after him. "Dimitri?"

He turned around.

"When you see Alexander, tell him about my sister."

He nodded. "Of course, I will, Tanechka. I'm going to see him next week. I'm sorry I couldn't be of more help."

Tatiana turned sharply away.

After he left, she got Olga to help her lift Dasha's body onto the sled and then pushed the sled down the slope and walked after it. On the Kobona River she took the reins, and under the seeping silent gray sky, Tatiana pulled Dasha, wrapped in a white hospital sheet, on Lake Ladoga. It was early afternoon and nearly dark. There were no German planes overhead. About a quarter of a kilometer out, Tatiana found a water hole. She kept tugging at Dasha's body until it slid down onto the ice.

Tatiana knelt next to it and put her hand on the white sheet.

Dasha, do you remember when I was five and you were twelve, teaching me how to dive into Lake Ilmen? You showed me how to swim underwater, saying you loved the feeling of water all around you because it was so peaceful. And then you taught me to stay under longer than Pasha, because you said that girls always had to beat boys. Well, you go and swim underwater now, Dasha Metanova.

Tatiana's wet face was turning to ice in the Arctic wind. She whispered, "I wish I knew a prayer. I need a prayer right now, but I don't know one. Dear God, please let my only sister Dasha swim in peace and not ever be cold again, and please . . . can you let her have all the daily bread she can eat, up in Heaven . . . ?"

On her knees Tatiana pushed Dasha's body into the ice hole. In the waning light the white sack looked blue. Dasha went in reluctantly, as if unwilling to part with life, and then disappeared. Tatiana continued to kneel on the ice. Eventually she got up and, coughing into her mittens, slowly pulled the empty sled back to shore.

Book Two

THE GOLDEN DOOR

Part Three

LAZAREVO

SCENTING SPRING

1

ALEXANDER went to Lazarevo on faith.

He had nothing else. Literally nothing else, not a letter, not a *single* piece of correspondence from either Dasha or Tatiana to let him know they had arrived in Molotov. He had grave doubts about Dasha, but he had seen Slavin survive the winter, so anything was possible. It was the *absence* of letters from Dasha that worried Alexander. While she was in Leningrad, she wrote to him constantly. Here the rest of January and February sped on, and not a word.

A week after the girls had left, Alexander had driven a truck across the ice to Kobona and searched for them among the sick and dispossessed on the Kobona shores. He found nothing.

In March, anxious and depressed, Alexander wrote a letter to Dasha in Molotov. He also had telegraphed the *Soviet* office in Molotov asking them for information on a Daria or a Tatiana Metanova but did not hear back until May and by regular post. A one-sentence letter from the Molotov *Soviet* informed Alexander that there was no information on a Daria or a Tatiana Metanova. He telegraphed again, asking if the Lazarevo village *Soviet* could receive telegraphs. Here the two-word telegram came the next day: NO. STOP.

Every off-duty hour he got, Alexander went back to Fifth Soviet, letting himself in with the key Dasha had left him. He cleaned the rooms, swept and washed the floors, and washed the linen when the city council repaired the pipes in March. He installed new glass panes in the second bedroom. He found an old photo album of the Metanovs and started looking through it,

349

then suddenly closed it and put it away. What was he thinking? It was like seeing ghosts.

That's how Alexander felt. He saw their ghosts everywhere.

Each time he was back in Leningrad, Alexander went to the post office on Old Nevsky to see if there were any letters *to* the Metanovs. The old postmaster was sick of the sight of him.

At the garrison, Alexander constantly asked the sergeant in charge of the army mail if there was anything for him *from* the Metanovs. The sergeant in charge of the army mail was sick of the sight of him.

But there was nothing for Alexander, no letters, no telegrams, and no news. In April the Old Nevsky postmaster died. No one had been notified of his death, and, in fact, he remained in his chair behind the desk, with mail on the floor, and on the counter, and in boxes, and in unopened mail sacks.

Alexander smoked thirty cigarettes as he searched through all the mail. He found nothing.

He went back to Lake Ladoga, continued protecting the Road of Life—now a water road—and waited for furlough, seeing Tatiana's ghost everywhere.

Leningrad slowly came out of the grip of death, and the city council became afraid—with good reason—that the proliferation of dead bodies, of clogged sewers, of raw sewage on the streets would result in a mass epidemic once the weather warmed up. The council initiated a full frontal assault on the city. Every living and able person cleared the debris from the bombing and the bodies from the streets. The burst pipes were fixed, the electricity restored. Trams and then trolleybuses began running. With new tulips and cabbage seedlings growing in front of St. Isaac's Cathedral, Leningrad seemed to be temporarily reborn. Tania would have liked to see the tulips in front of St. Isaac's, Alexander thought. The civilian ration was increased to three hundred grams of bread for dependents. Not because there was more flour. Because there were fewer people.

At the start of war, on June 22, 1941, the day Alexander met Tatiana, there were three million civilians in Leningrad. When the Germans blockaded the city on September 8, 1941, there were two and a half million civilians in Leningrad.

In the spring of 1942 a million people remained.

The ice road over Ladoga had so far evacuated half a million people from the city, leaving them in Kobona to their dubious fate.

And the siege was not over.

After the snow melted, Alexander was put in charge of dynamiting a dozen mass graves in Piskarev Cemetery, to which nearly half a million corpses were transported on Funeral Trust trucks and eventually buried. Piskarev was just one of seven cemeteries in Leningrad to which the bodies were carried like cordwood.

And the siege was not over.

American foodstuffs—courtesy of Lend-Lease—were slowly making their twisted way into Leningrad. A few times during spring, Leningraders received dehydrated milk, dehydrated soup, dehydrated eggs. Alexander picked up some items himself, including an English-Russian phrase book he bought from a Lend-Lease truck driver in Kobona. Tania might like a new phrase book, he thought. She had been doing so well with her English.

The city rebuilt Nevsky Prospekt with false fronts to cover up the gaping holes left by German shells, and Leningrad went on slowly, neatly, and mostly quietly, into the summer of 1942.

German shelling and bombing continued daily and unabated.

January, February, March, April, May.

How many months could Alexander not hear? How many months of no news, of not a word, of not a breath? How many months of carrying hope in his heart and of admitting to himself that the inevitable and the unimaginable could have happened, might have happened, and—finally—must have happened? He saw death everywhere. At the front most of all, but hopeless death on the streets of Leningrad, too. He saw mutilated bodies and mangled bodies, frozen bodies and famished bodies. He saw it all. But through it all Alexander still believed.

2

In June, Dimitri came to see him at the garrison. Alexander was shocked and hoped his face didn't show it. Dimitri looked older by years, not just by months. He walked with a distinct limp, hunched over a little on his right side. His body looked wearied and thin, and there was a tremor in his fingers Alexander had not seen before.

And when Alexander stared at Dimitri, he thought, Dimitri survived, why not Dasha and Tania, too? If he could, why not them? If I could, why not them?

"My only good foot is now the left foot," Dimitri told him. "What stupidity on my part, don't you think?" He smiled warmly at Alexander, who reluctantly invited him to sit on one of the bunks. He had been hoping he was done with Dimitri. No such luck, he could see. They were alone, and Dimitri had a thoughtful flare in his eye that Alexander did not care for.

"At least," Dimitri said cheerfully, "I'll never have to see real combat again. I much prefer it this way."

"Good," said Alexander. "It's what you wanted. To work in the rear."

"Some rear," Dimitri snorted. "Do you know that first they put me on evacuation detail in Kobona—"

"Kobona!"

"Yes," Dimitri drew out slowly. "Why? Does Kobona have some special significance other than the American Lend-Lease trucks that come through there?"

Alexander studied Dimitri. "Yes. I didn't know you worked in Kobona."

"We had fallen a little out of touch."

"Were you there back in January?"

"I can't even remember anymore," said Dimitri. "That was such a long time ago."

Alexander got up and came toward him. "Dima! I got Dasha and Tatiana out through the ice—"

"They must be so grateful."

"I don't know if they're grateful. Did you see them, perhaps?"

"You're asking me if I saw two girls in Kobona, through which thousands of evacuees came?" Dimitri laughed.

"Not two girls," Alexander said coldly. "*Tania* and Dasha. You'd recognize *them*, wouldn't you?"

"Alexander, I would—"

"Did you see them?" He raised his voice.

"No, I didn't," said Dimitri. "Stop shouting. But I must say . . ." He shook his head. "To put two helpless girls in a truck to try to make it to—Where were they headed again?"

"East, somewhere." He wasn't about to tell Dimitri where they had been headed.

"Somewhere deep in the country? I don't know, Alexander, *what* were you thinking?" Dimitri chuckled. "I can't imagine you wanted them to die."

"Dimitri, what are you talking about?" Alexander snapped. "What choice did I have? Have you not heard what happened to Leningrad last winter? What's still happening now?"

Dimitri smiled. "I heard. Wasn't there something else you could have done? Couldn't Colonel Stepanov do anything for you?"

"No, he couldn't." Alexander was fed up. "Listen, I've got—"

"I'm just saying, Alexander, the evacuees that came our way were all at death's door. I know Dasha is made of strong stuff, but Tania? I'm surprised she made it long enough for you to get her across the ice." Dimitri shrugged. "I thought she'd be the first to— I mean, even *I* got dystrophy. And most of the people coming through Kobona were sick and starved. Then they were forced to get on more trucks to be transported sixty kilometers to the nearest trains, which were all cattle trains." Lowering his voice, Dimitri said, "I don't know if it's true, but I heard through the grapevine that seventy percent of all the people we put on the trains died of either cold or disease." He shook his head. "And you wanted Dasha and Tania to go through that? Some future husband you are!" Dimitri laughed.

Alexander clenched his teeth.

"Listen, I'm glad I'm out of there," Dimitri said. "Didn't like Kobona much."

"What?" said Alexander. "Was Kobona too dangerous?"

"No, that wasn't it. The trucks were usually backed up onto the Ladoga ice, because the evacuees were so damn slow. We were expected to go out and help unload them. But they couldn't walk. They were all near death." Staring at Alexander, Dimitri said, "Just last month the Germans blew up three of the six trucks on the ice." He sighed. "Some rear. Finally I asked to be transferred into supplies."

Turning his back to Dimitri, Alexander began folding his clothes. "Supplies is not the safest thing either. On the other hand," he said, thinking to himself, *what am I saying? Let him go into fucking supplies,* "supplies might be good for you. You'll be the guy selling the cigarettes. Everybody will love you." The yawning chasm between what had been between them and what was now was too great. There were no boats and no bridges. Alexander waited for Dimitri either to leave or to ask after Tatiana's family. He did neither.

Finally Alexander couldn't take it anymore. "Dima, are you even remotely interested in what happened to the Metanovs?"

Shrugging, Dimitri said, "I figured the same thing that happened to most of Leningrad. Everybody died, no?" He could have been saying, *everyone went shopping, no?* Alexander lowered his head.

"This is war, Alexander," Dimitri said. "Only the strongest survive. That's why I finally had to give up on Tania. I didn't want to, I quite liked her, and I still do; I have fond memories of her, but I had barely enough strength to keep myself going. I couldn't be worrying about her, too, without food or warm clothes."

How clearly Tatiana saw right through Dimitri. He never did care for her at all, Alexander thought, putting his clothes into his locker and avoiding Dimitri's gaze.

"Alexander, speaking of surviving, there is something I wanted to talk to you about," Dimitri began.

Here it comes. Alexander did not look up while he waited for it.

"Since the Americans have joined the war—it's better for us, yes?"

Nodding, Alexander replied, "Certainly. Lend-Lease is a great help."

"No, no." Getting up off the bed, Dimitri said in an excited and anxious voice, "I don't mean for *us,* I mean for you and me. For our plans."

Getting up off the floor, Alexander faced Dimitri. "I haven't seen too many Americans on this side," he said slowly, pretending not to understand.

"Yes," exclaimed Dimitri, "but they're all over Kobona! They're trucking and shipping supplies, tanks, jeeps, boots, through Murmansk and down the whole east coast of Lake Ladoga, to Petrozavodsk, to Lodeinoye Pole. There are dozens of them in Kobona."

"Is that true? Dozens?"

"Maybe not dozens. But Americans!" He paused. "Maybe they can help us?"

Alexander came up closer to Dimitri. "In what way?" he said sharply.

Smiling, and keeping his thin voice low, Dimitri said, "In what way? In that *American* way. Perhaps you can go to Kobona—"

"Dima, go to Kobona and what? Who am I going to talk to? The truck drivers? You think if a Soviet soldier starts talking English to them, they'll just say, oh, sure, come with us on our steamer. We'll take you back home." Alexander paused, taking a drag on his cigarette. "And even if somehow that were not impossible, how do you suggest we get *you* out? Even if a stranger *was* willing to risk his neck for me because of what you perceive as some American bond, how do you think that would help *you?*"

Taken aback, Dimitri said hastily, "I'm not saying it's a good plan. But it's a start."

"Dima, you're injured. Look at you." Alexander looked him up and down. "You are in no condition to fight, nor are you in any condition to . . . run. We need to forget our plans."

In a frantic voice, Dimitri said, "What are you talking about? I know you still want to—"

"Dimitri!"

"What? We have to do *something*, Alexander," Dimitri said. "You and I had plans—"

"Dimitri!" Alexander exclaimed. "Our plans involved fighting through NKVD border troops and hiding out in the mined swamps in Finland! Now that you've shot yourself in the foot, how do you think *that* will be possible?"

Alexander was grateful that Dimitri did not have any immediate answers. He backed away.

Dimitri said, "I agree, maybe the Lisiy Nos route is harder, but I think we have a good chance of bribing the Lend-Lease delivery boys."

"They're not delivery boys!" Alexander said angrily. He paused. It was not worth it. "These men are trained fighters, and they subject themselves to submarine torpedoes every day as they trudge 2,000 kilometers through the Arctic and North Russia to bring *you tushonka*."

"Yes, and they are the very men who can help us. And, Alexander"— Dimitri stepped closer—"I need somebody to help me." He stepped closer still. "And very soon. I have no intention whatsoever of dying in this fucking war." He paused, his slit eyes on Alexander. "Do *you?*"

"I will die if I have to," said an unyielding Alexander.

Dimitri studied him. Alexander hated to be studied. He lit a cigarette and stared icily at Dimitri, who retreated. "Do you still have your *money* on you?" Dimitri asked.

"No."

"Can you get to it?"

"I don't know," said Alexander. He took out another cigarette. This conversation was over.

"You have an unsmoked one in your mouth," Dimitri remarked dryly.

Alexander received a generous furlough of thirty days. He asked Stepanov for more time. He got a little more time, from June 15 until July 24.

"Is that enough time?" asked Stepanov, smiling lightly.

"It's either too much time, sir," replied Alexander, "or not enough."

"Captain," said Stepanov, lighting a cigarette and giving one to Alexander, "when you come back . . ." He sighed. "We can no longer stay at the garrison. You see what has happened to our city. We cannot spend another winter like the last one. It simply *cannot* happen." He paused. "We are going to have to break the blockade. All of us. This fall."

"I agree, sir."

"Do you, Alexander? Have you seen what's happened to our men at Tikhvin and Mga last winter and this spring?"

"Yes, sir."

"Have you heard what's been happening to our men in Nevsky Patch across the river from Dubrovka?"

"Yes, sir," Alexander said. Nevsky Patch was a Red Army enclave inside enemy lines—a place the Germans used for daily target practice. Russian soldiers were dying there at a rate of 200 a day.

Shaking his head, Stepanov said, "We're going to move across the Neva in pontoon boats. We have limited artillery—you. We have single-shot rifles—"

"Not me, sir, I have a Shpagin machine gun. And my rifle is an automatic." Alexander smiled.

Smiling himself, Stepanov nodded. "I'm making it sound brutal."

"It is, sir."

"Captain, don't get scared off by the good fight, an unequal fight though it may be."

Alexander, raising his eyes to Stepanov and squaring his shoulders, said, "Sir. When have I ever?"

Coming up to him, Stepanov said, "If we had more men like you, we would have won this war long ago." He shook Alexander's hand. "Go. Have a good trip. Nothing will be the same when you come back."

3

Alexander thought as he traveled halfway across the Soviet Union: Dasha, Tania—wouldn't they have written to him if they were alive?

His doubt attacked him like shell fire.

To go sixteen hundred miles east, across Lake Ladoga, over the Onega River and the Dvina River, over the Sukhona River and the Unzha River, to the Kama River and the Ural Mountains, to go having heard nothing for six months, for half a year, for all those minutes in between, having heard not a sound from her mouth or a word from her pen, was it lunacy?

Yes, yes, it was.

During his four-day journey to Molotov, Alexander recalled every breath he took with her. Sixteen hundred kilometers of the Obvodnoy Canal, of coming to see her at Kirov, of his tent in Luga, of her holding on to his back, of the hospital room, of St. Isaac's, of her eating ice cream, of her lying in the sled as he pulled her, nearly out of life. Sixteen hundred kilometers of her giving her food to everyone, of her jumping up and down on the roof under German planes. There were some memories of last winter from which Alexander flinched, recalling them all nonetheless. Her walking alongside him after burying her mother. Her standing motionless in front of three boys with knives.

Two images continually sprang to his mind in a restless, frantic refrain.

Tatiana in a helmet, in strange clothes, covered with blood, covered with stone and beams and glass and dead bodies, herself still warm, herself still breathing.

And

Tatiana on the bed in the hospital, bare under his hands, moaning under his mouth.

If anyone could make it, would it not be the girl who every morning for four months got up at six-thirty and trudged through dying Leningrad to get her family their bread?

But if she had made it, how could she not have written to him?

The girl who kissed his hand, who served him tea, and who gazed at him, not breathing as he talked, gazed at him with eyes he had never seen before—was that girl gone?

Was her heart gone?

Please, God, Alexander prayed. *Let her not love me anymore, but let her live.*

That was a hard prayer for Alexander, but he could not imagine living in a world without Tatiana.

Unwashed and undernourished, having spent over four days on five different trains and four military jeeps, Alexander got off at Molotov on Friday, June 19, 1942. He arrived at noon and then sat on a wooden bench near the station.

Alexander couldn't bring himself to walk to Lazarevo.

He could not bear the thought of her dying in Kobona, getting out of the collapsed city and then dying so close to salvation. He could not face it.

And worse—he knew that he could not face himself if he found out that she did not make it. He could not face returning—returning to what?

Alexander actually thought of getting on the next train and going back immediately. The courage to move forward was much more than the courage he needed to stand behind a Katyusha rocket launcher or a Zenith antiaircraft gun on Lake Ladoga and know that any of the Luftwaffe planes flying overhead could instantly bring about his death.

He was not afraid of his own death.

He was afraid of hers. The specter of her death took away his courage.

If Tatiana was dead, it meant God was dead, and Alexander knew he could not survive an instant during war in a universe governed by chaos, not purpose. He would not live any longer than poor, hapless Grinkov, who had been cut down by a stray bullet as he headed back to the rear.

War was the ultimate chaos, a pounding, soul-destroying snarl, ending in blown-apart men lying unburied on the cold earth. There was nothing more cosmically chaotic than war.

But Tatiana was order. She was finite matter in infinite space. Tatiana was the standard-bearer for the flag of grace and valor that she carried forward with bounty and perfection in herself, the flag Alexander had followed sixteen hundred kilometers east to the Kama River, to the Ural Mountains, to Lazarevo.

For two hours Alexander sat on the bench in unpaved, provincial, oak-lined Molotov.

To go back was impossible.

To go forward was unthinkable.

Yet he had nowhere else to go.

He crossed himself and stood up, gathering his belongings.

When Alexander finally walked in the direction of Lazarevo, not knowing whether Tatiana was alive or dead, he felt he was a man walking to his own execution.

4

Lazarevo was ten kilometers through deep pine woods.

The forest wasn't just pine; it was mixed with elms and oaks and birches and nettles and blueberries all drifting their pleasing way into his senses. Alexander walked carrying his rucksack, his rifle, his sidearm and ammunition, his large tent and blanket, his helmet, and a sack filled with food from Kobona. He could hear the nearby rush of the Kama River through the trees. He thought of going and washing, but by this point he needed to keep moving forward.

He picked a few blueberries off the low bushes as he walked. He was hungry. It was very warm, very sunny, and Alexander was suddenly filled with a pounding hope. He walked faster.

The woods ended, and in front of him was a dusty village road, flanked on both sides by small wooden huts, overgrown grasses, and old falling-down fences.

To the left, past pines and elms, he could see the glimmer of the river, and past the river, past more voluminous, voluptuous forest, the round-topped, evergreen-covered Ural Mountains.

He inhaled deeply. Did Lazarevo smell of Tatiana? He smelled firewood burning and fresh water and pine needles. And fish. Alexander saw the smokestack of a fishing plant on the outskirts of the village.

He continued down the road, passing a woman sitting on the bench outside her house. She stared at him; he understood. How often did these people see a Red Army officer? The woman got up and said, "Oh, no! You're not *Alexander*, are you?"

Alexander didn't know how to answer that. "Oh, yes," he finally said. "I *am* Alexander. I'm looking for Tatiana and Dasha Metanova. Do you know where they live?"

The woman started to cry.

Alexander stared at her. "I'll just ask someone else," he muttered, walking on.

The woman ran after him in small steps. "Wait, wait!" She pointed down the road. "On Fridays they have a sewing circle in the village square. Straight ahead, over there." Shaking her head, she walked back.

"So they are alive?" Alexander said in a weak voice, flooded with relief.

The woman could not answer. Covering her face, she ran back to her house.

She said *they*? *They* meaning . . . he asked for two sisters; she replied *they*. Alexander slowed down, lighting a cigarette and taking a drink out of his flask. He walked on but stopped before he got to the village square thirty meters ahead.

He couldn't come straight up the road. Not yet.

If *they* were alive, then in a moment he was going to have different problems from the ones he had imagined, and he thought he had imagined them all. He would deal with this one as he dealt with everything, but first—

Alexander walked through someone's garden, apologizing hastily, opened the back gate, and was on the village back path. He wanted to come a roundabout way to the square. He wanted to see Tatiana for a moment without her seeing him. Before there was Dasha, he wanted an instant of being able to look at Tatiana the way he wanted to look at her, without hiding.

He wanted proof of God before God looked upon the man with His own eyes.

The elms were standing tall in a green canopy around the small square. A group of people sat beneath the trees at a long wooden table. Most were women; there was, in fact, only one young man. It was a *sewing* circle, thought Alexander, moving nearer to the table to get a better look.

He was obstructed from their view by a fence and a sprawling lilac tree. The flowers got into his face and nose. Breathing in their ripe fragrance, he peeked out. He did not see Dasha anywhere. He saw four old women seated around the table, a young boy, an older girl, and a standing Tatiana.

At first Alexander could not believe it was his Tania. He blinked and tried to refocus his eyes. She was walking around the table, gesturing, showing, leaning forward, bending over. At one point she straightened out and wiped her forehead. She was wearing a short-sleeved yellow peasant dress. She was barefoot, and her slender legs were exposed above her knee. Her bare arms were lightly tanned. Her blonde hair looked bleached by the sun and was parted into two shoulder-length braids tucked behind her ears. Even from a distance he could see the summer freckles on her nose. She was achingly beautiful.

And *alive*.

Alexander closed his eyes, then opened them again. She was still there, bending over the boy's work. She said something, everyone laughed loudly, and Alexander watched as the boy's arm touched Tatiana's back. Tatiana smiled. Her white teeth sparkled like the rest of her. Alexander didn't know what to do.

She was alive, that was obvious.

Then why hadn't she written him?

And where was Dasha?

Alexander couldn't very well continue to stand under a lilac tree.

He went back out onto the main road, took a deep breath, stubbed out his cigarette, and walked toward the square, never taking his eyes off her braids. His heart was thundering in his chest, as if he were going into battle.

Tatiana looked up, saw him, and covered her face with her hands. Alexander watched everyone get up and rush to her, the old ladies showing unexpected agility and speed. She pushed them all away, pushed the table away, pushed the bench away, and ran to him. Alexander was paralyzed by his emotion. He wanted to smile, but he thought any second he was going to fall to his knees and cry. He dropped all his gear, including his rifle. God, he thought, in a second I'm going to *feel* her. And that's when he smiled.

Tatiana sprang into his open arms, and Alexander, lifting her off her feet with the force of his embrace, couldn't hug her tight enough, couldn't breathe in enough of her. She flung her arms around his neck, burying her face in his bearded cheek. Dry sobs racked her entire body. She was heavier than the last time he felt her in all her clothes as he lifted her into the Lake Ladoga truck. She, with her boots, her clothes, coats, and coverings, had not weighed what she weighed now.

She smelled incredible. She smelled of soap and sunshine and caramelized sugar.

She felt incredible. Holding her to him, Alexander rubbed his face into her braids, murmuring a few pointless words. "Shh, shh . . . come on, now, shh, Tatia. Please . . ." His voice broke.

"Oh, Alexander," Tatiana said softly into his neck. She was clutching the back of his head. "You're alive. Thank God."

"Oh, Tatiana," Alexander said, hugging her tighter, if that were possible, his arms swaddling her summer body. *"You're* alive. Thank God." His hands ran up to her neck and down to the small of her back. Her dress was made of very thin cotton. He could almost feel her skin through it. She felt very soft.

Finally he let her feet touch the ground. Tatiana looked up at him. His hands remained around her little waist. He wasn't letting go of her. Was she always this tiny, standing barefoot in front of him?

"I like your beard," Tatiana said, smiling shyly and touching his face.

"I love your hair," Alexander said, pulling on a braid and smiling back.

"You're messy . . ."

He looked her over. "And you're *stunning.*" He could not take his eyes off her glorious, eager, vivid lips. They were the color of July tomatoes—

He bent to her—

With a deep breath Alexander remembered Dasha. He stopped smiling, letting go of Tatiana and stepping slightly away.

She frowned, looking at him.

"Where's Dasha, Tania?" he asked.

What Alexander saw pass through her eyes then . . . there was hurt and sadness and grief and guilt, and anger—at him?—all of it, and in a blink it was all gone, and then an icy veil clouded her eyes. Alexander watched something in Tatiana shut against him. She looked at him coolly, and though her hands were still trembling, her voice was steady and low. "Dasha died, Alexander. I'm sorry."

"Oh, Tania. *I'm* sorry." Alexander reached out to touch her, but she backed away from him. She didn't just back away from him. She *staggered* away from him.

"What?" he said, perplexed. "What?"

"Alexander, I'm really sorry about Dasha," Tatiana said, unable to meet his eyes. "You came all this way . . ."

"What are you talking—"

But before he had a chance to continue or Tatiana a chance to respond, the other members of her sewing circle surrounded them. "Tanechka?" said a small, round salt-and-pepper woman with small, round eyes. "Who is this? Is this Dasha's Alexander?"

"Yes," said Tatiana. "This is Dasha's Alexander." Glancing at him, she said, "Alexander—meet Naira Mikhailovna."

Naira started to cry. "Oh, you poor man." She didn't just shake Alexander's hand, she hugged him. Poor man? He stared at Tatiana.

"Naira, please," Tatiana said, backing farther away from him.

Sniffling, Naira whispered to Tatiana, "Did he *know?*"

"He didn't know. But he does now," replied Tatiana. That provoked a sustained wail out of Naira.

Tatiana made further introductions. "Alexander, meet Vova, Naira's grandson, and Zoe, Vova's sister."

Vova was precisely the kind of strapping lad Alexander hated to think about. Round-faced, round-eyed, round-mouthed, a dark-haired version of his small and compact grandmother, Vova shook Alexander's hand.

Zoe, a large, black-haired village girl, hugged him, shoving her big breasts into his uniform tunic. She held Alexander's hand in hers and said, "We're so pleased to meet you, Alexander. We've heard so much about you."

"Everything," said a bright, curly-haired woman, whom Tatiana introduced as Naira's older sister, Axinya. "We've heard everything about you," Axinya said energetically and vocally. She hugged Alexander, too.

Then two more women moved front and center. They were both gray-haired and frail. One of them had a shaking disorder. Her hands shook, her head shook, her mouth shook as she spoke. Raisa was her name. Her mother's name was Dusia, who was taller and broader than her daughter and wore a large silver cross over her dark dress. Dusia made the sign of the cross on Alexander, and said, "God will take care of you, Alexander. Don't you worry."

Alexander wanted to tell Dusia that having found Tatiana alive, he had nothing to worry about, but before he could say anything, Axinya asked Alexander how he was feeling, which was followed by a second round of hugs and a second round of tears.

"I'm feeling fine," said Alexander. "Really, there is no need to cry."

He might as well have been speaking English. They continued to cry.

Alexander looked at Tatiana perplexed. But not only did she stand off to the side, but Vova stood by her.

"You are just the—oh, I can't, I can't, I just can't," cried Naira.

"Then don't, Naira Mikhailovna," Tatiana said mildly. "He is all right. Look. He'll be fine."

"Tania is right," Alexander said. "Really."

"Oh, dear man," said Naira, grabbing his sleeve. "You've traveled so far. You must be exhausted."

He wasn't until five minutes ago. He looked at Tatiana and said, "I am a little hungry." And smiled.

She did not smile back when she said, "Of course. Let's go eat."

Nothing was making any sense to a tired and hungry Alexander, who found himself suddenly losing his patience. "Excuse me, please," he said, extricating himself from Axinya, who was standing in front of him, and making his way through the sea of people to Tatiana. "Can I talk to you for a second?"

Tatiana backed away from him, averting her face. "Come on. I'll make you dinner."

"Can we"—Alexander found himself having trouble getting the words out—"just for a moment, talk, Tania?"

"Alexander, of course," said Naira. "We'll talk. Come, dear, come to our house." She took him by the arm. "This must be the worst day of your life."

Alexander didn't know what to think about this day.

"Let us take care of you," Naira continued. "Our Tania is a very good cook."

Their Tania? "I know," Alexander said.

"You'll eat, you'll drink. We'll talk. We'll talk plenty. We'll tell you everything. How long are you here for?"

"I don't know," Alexander said, not even trying to catch Tatiana's eye anymore.

They started walking, amid all the commotion forgetting their sewing. "Oh, yes," said Tatiana blankly and went back to the table. Alexander followed her. Zoe ran alongside him, and he said, "Zoe, I need a moment alone with Tania," and without even waiting for a response, hurried to catch up with Tatiana.

"What's the matter with you?" he said to her.

"Nothing."

"Tania!"

"What?"

"Talk to me."

"How was your trip here?"

"That's not what I mean. It was fine. Why didn't you write to me?"

"Alexander," she said, "why didn't you write to *me?*"

Taken aback, he said, "I didn't know you were alive."

"I didn't know you were alive either," she replied, *almost* calmly, if only he didn't see through the veil. Under it there was a storm she was not letting him near.

"You were supposed to write to me and tell me you made it here safely," Alexander said. "Remember?"

"No," Tatiana said pointedly. "*Dasha* was supposed to write to you and tell you. Remember? But she died. So she couldn't." She gathered up the material—the needles, the thread, the beads and buttons and paper patterns—stuffing it all into a bag.

"I'm so sorry about Dasha, I'm so sorry. Please." Alexander touched her back.

Tatiana flinched from him and blinked back tears. "Me, too."

"What happened to her? Did you make it out of Kobona?"

"I did," Tatiana said quietly. "She didn't. She died the morning we got there."

"Oh, God."

They didn't look at each other, and they were silent.

Dragging Dasha down the slope to Ladoga, begging her to hold on, to walk, while Tania herself could not keep upright, yet pushing her sister forward, willing her to live.

"I'm sorry, Tatia," Alexander whispered.

"Seeing you," Tatiana said, "brings it all back, doesn't it? The wounds are

362

still so raw." That's when she raised her eyes and looked at him. And Alexander saw the wounds.

Slowly they walked back to everyone else.

Vova slapped Alexander on the shoulder and asked, "So how's the war going?"

"The war is good, thanks."

"We hear our guys are not doing so great. The Germans are near Stalingrad."

"Yes," Alexander said. "The Germans are very strong."

Vova slapped Alexander's shoulder again. "I see they have to keep you fit in war. I'm joining. I'm seventeen next month."

"I'm sure the Red Army will make a man out of you," Alexander said, trying to sound more cheerful. He watched Tatiana carry the large bag of sewing. "Want me to carry that?" Alexander asked her.

"No, it's all right. You've got enough of your own things."

"I brought you something."

"*Me?*" Tatiana didn't look at him when she said it.

What was going on? He said quizzically, "Tania . . . ?"

"Alexander," Naira said, "tomorrow is our day to go to the *banya*. Can you wait until then?"

"No. I'll wash tonight in the river."

"Surely you can wait one day?" said Naira.

He shook his head. "I've been on trains for four days. I haven't had water on me for too long."

"Four days!" exclaimed Raisa, shaking. "The man has been on trains for four days!"

"Yes," cried Naira, wiping her face, "and for what, for what? Oh, what a wasteland this war is, what waste, what tragedy." The other ladies sniffled in agreement.

Alexander heard a small muffled groan escape Tatiana. He wanted her to look at him. He wanted to look into her face. He wanted her to tell him what was wrong. He wanted to touch her bare arms. He wanted to touch her so badly that . . . but his hands were full of his things. "Tatia . . ." he whispered, leaning deeply into her, nearly touching her hair with his mouth.

He heard her breath stop for a moment, and then she moved away.

In slight frustration he straightened up, noticing that Vova did not stray far from Tatiana's side, and she did not appear to move away from him.

They ambled down the road. From the small village houses, neighbors poured out in milky lines, some shaking their heads, some pointing, some dabbing their eyes. Many saluted him. One middle-aged lady came over and gave Alexander a sympathetic hug. One old man said, "You make us all proud." Why did Alexander think it wasn't for his effort in the war? "The way you came here for your Dasha." The man pumped his hand. "Anything you need, anything at all, you come to me. I'm Igor."

Alexander asked quietly, "Tania, why do I feel as if everybody knows me here?"

"Oh, because they all do," Tatiana said flatly, staring straight ahead. "You are the captain in the Red Army, who has come to marry my sister. They all know that. Unfortunately, she has died. And they all know that, too. And everyone is very sorry." Her voice remained almost steady.

Sobs from Dusia from behind and Naira from the front. "Alexander," Naira said, "at home we'll give you plenty of vodka, and we'll tell you everything."

"*We?*" He glanced at Tatiana. He was hoping the *we* wasn't going to be more than two. Why did he suspect it might be?

"Tania, how have you been?" Alexander asked. "How did—"

"Oh, she's been great," Vova interrupted, putting his arm around Tatiana. "She's much better now."

Alexander stared straight ahead, his gaze clouding. The tick inside him was multiplying.

It was at that moment—when he set his teeth and turned his face away—that Tatiana moved away from Vova to Alexander and put her hand on him. "You must be exhausted, hmm?" she said gently, peering into his face. "Four days on trains. Have you eaten today?"

"In the morning," he replied, not looking at her.

Tatiana nodded. "You'll feel better once you're clean and fed," she said, smiling. "And shaved." She squeezed his arm.

He felt better and smiled back. He was going to have to talk to her about Vova. Alexander saw unresolved things in Tatiana's eyes. The last time they had peace or energy to resolve *anything* was St. Isaac's. A moment with her alone and things would get better, but first he had to talk to her about Vova.

"Alexander," Axinya echoed, "we pulled our Tanechka right out from the jaws of death." There was a loud wail.

Alexander looked at Tatiana walking next to him, feeling a liquid warmth ooze through him. "Please, let me carry that," he said.

She was about to give him her sewing bag when Vova intercepted it, saying, "I'll carry it."

"Tania," Alexander asked, "you didn't by any chance run into Dimitri in Kobona, did you?"

Naira quickly turned around and hissed at Alexander, her eyes bright imploring cups. "Shh. We don't talk about Dimitri."

"That *bastard!*" exclaimed Axinya.

"Axinya, please!" said Naira, turning to Alexander and nodding. "She is right, though. He *is* a bastard," she whispered.

Alexander stared at them all, wide-eyed. "Tania," he said, "am I to assume that you did run into Dimitri in Kobona?"

364

"Hmm," she said, and nothing else.

Alexander shook his head. He *was* a bastard.

Zoe on his left leaned in and said in a conspiratorial whisper, "Another reason we don't talk about Dimitri is because our Vovka's got a *big* thing for Tania."

Moving away from Zoe and toward Tatiana, Alexander muttered, "Really?"

Naira's house at the top end of the village toward the river was white, wooden, and square. And small. "You all live here?" Alexander asked, glancing at Tatiana, who walked ahead.

"No, no," Naira said, "just us and our Tania. Vova and Zoe live with their mother on the other side of Lazarevo. Their father was killed in the Ukraine last summer."

"Babushka," said Zoe, "I don't think there's going to be room in your house for Alexander."

Alexander looked at the house. Zoe may have been right. In the front garden there were two goats, and three chickens in a wire coop. It looked as if *they* had plenty of room.

Following Tatiana inside, Alexander walked up a couple of wooden steps into a roomy glassed-in porch that had two small couches at one end and a long, rectangular wooden table at the other. Coming through the porch, he stood in the doorway looking into the darkened parlor room in the middle of which stood a wood-burning stove.

Taking up nearly the entire back of the room, the stove had a long cast-iron hearth and three compartments—the center for burning wood and two side ones for baking. The chimney went up and to the left. Above the stove was a flat surface covered with quilts and pillows. In many village huts across the Soviet Union, the top of the stove was frequently used as a bed. After the fire below went out, it was very warm up there.

In front of the hearth stood a high table for food preparation, and at the back was a sewing machine on a desk, and a black trunk. On the right were two doors, leading to what Alexander guessed were bedrooms.

Tatiana was by his side. "Let me guess," he said to her. "You sleep up there?"

"Yes," she replied without meeting his eyes. "It's comfortable. Come inside for a minute." She walked through to the desk on the side of the stove.

"Wait, wait," said Naira from behind. "Zoechka is right. We really don't have much room."

"That's all right, I have my tent," said Alexander, following Tatiana.

"No, no tent," said Naira. "Why don't you stay with Vova and Zoe? They have room for you; they have a nice bedroom they could put you in. With a proper bed and everything."

"No," said Alexander, turning around to Naira. "But thank you."

"Tanechka, don't you think it would be more comfortable for him? He could—"

"Naira Mikhailovna," said Tatiana, "he already said no."

"We know," said Axinya, walking through the porch. "But it really would be more—"

"No," repeated Alexander. "I will sleep in my tent, right outside. I'll be fine."

Tatiana motioned him to her. He couldn't get to her fast enough. They were alone long enough for her to say, "Sleep here, on top of the stove. It's very warm."

He kept his voice even when he said, "And where are *you* going to sleep?"

Her face turned red, and he couldn't help himself—he burst out laughing and kissed her cheek. That made her even more red.

"Tania," he said, "you're the funniest girl."

She backed away practically into the porch.

Smiling at her, he said, "Listen, I'm going to go—"

"Go with Zoe and Vova?" said Naira, coming into the room. "That's a great idea. I knew our Tanechka could convince you. She can talk the devil into a new dress. Zoe!"

"No!" exclaimed Tatiana.

Alexander wanted to kiss her.

"Naira Mikhailovna, he's not going," Tatiana said. "He didn't come all this way to stay with Vova and Zoe. He'll stay here. He'll sleep up here."

"Oh," Naira said, her breath taken out of her a bit. "And you?"

Could she keep herself from blushing? No, she couldn't. "I'll sleep on the porch."

"Tania, if he's staying, why don't you change the linen on your bed so he'll have fresh sheets."

"I will," agreed Tatiana.

"Don't you *dare* touch them," whispered Alexander.

Saying she was going to get Alexander fresh towels, Naira disappeared to her room.

Instantly they turned to each other. She couldn't manage to look up at him, but she was turned to him and close to him, and—was she smelling him?

"I'm going to go and wash, and I will be right back," said Alexander, smiling. He didn't know what to do with his hands. He wanted to take hold of hers. "Don't go anywhere."

"I'm right here. Do you need soap?"

He shook his head. "Got plenty."

"I'm sure you do. But look what else I've got." Out of her desk drawer she pulled out a small bottle of shampoo. "Found it in Molotov. Cost me twenty rubles." She handed it to him. "Real shampoo for your hair."

"You spent *twenty* rubles on a bottle of shampoo?" he said, mock aghast, taking it from her and grabbing her fingers.

"Better than two hundred and fifty rubles on a cup of flour," she replied, quickly pulling her fingers away and trying to change the subject.

"Was that twenty of *my* rubles?"

"Yes," she said quietly. "The rubles in your book came in very handy. Thank you." She did not look at him. "Thank you for everything."

"I'm glad they did, and you're welcome. For everything." He could not tear his eyes away from her. "Tatiasha, you've gotten so blonde."

She shrugged casually. "It's the sun."

"And so freckled—"

"The sun."

"And so—"

"Let me point you to the river."

"Wait. Look what I've brought for you." Crouching near his bag, he showed her many cans of *tushonka*, some coffee, a large bag of lump sugar, rock salt, cigarettes, and bottles of vodka. "And I got you another English-Russian book," he said. "Have you been practicing your English?"

"Not really," Tatiana replied. "I haven't had time. I can't believe you carried all that. It must have been so heavy." Pausing, she said, "But thank you. Come on outside."

Taking a towel from Naira, they walked through the porch and down the steps to the back garden. Alexander stood as close to Tatiana as possible without his body actually touching hers. He knew that six pairs of eyes were on them from the porch. Tatiana pointed. Alexander wasn't even looking at where she was pointing. He was looking at her blonde eyebrows. He wanted to touch them with his fingers.

He wanted to touch *her* with his fingers.

Missing a breath, he touched the faint scar above the brow where she had been injured during the fight with her father. "That's almost gone," he said quietly. "Can't even see it."

"If you can't see it," Tatiana said lightly, "then why are you touching it?" She didn't look at him. "Alexander," she said, "can you look where I'm pointing? It's right through the pines. Will you look? Just cross the road, and there's a path between the trees. Walk down a hundred meters into the clearing. I do the laundry there. You can't miss it. The Kama is a big river."

"I'll get lost, for sure," said Alexander, bending to her ear and lowering his voice. "Come and show me."

"Tania has to cook dinner," said Zoe, coming up to them. "Why don't *I* show you?"

"Yes," Tatiana said, backing away. "Why doesn't Zoe show you? I really do have to start cooking if we're to eat tonight."

Alexander said, "No, Zoe. Excuse us," and he pulled Tatiana away. "Come with me to the river," he repeated. "You can tell me what's upsetting you, and I'll—"

"Not now, Alexander," Tatiana whispered. "Not *now*."

Sighing, he let go of her and went by himself. When he returned, clean and shaven, dressed in his Class-Bs, he saw that Zoe was shamelessly inter-

367

ested in him. Alexander wasn't surprised. In a town with no young men, he could have had one eye and no teeth and Zoe would have been interested. Tatiana was another story. She obstinately avoided meeting his eyes. While leaning over the hearth and her frying pans, she said, "You've shaved."

"How would *you* know?" He was staring at her back and hips as she leaned over in her yellow dress. Her waist tapered into her tight, round-as-a-moon hips, and the backs of her bare thighs peeked out below the short hem. He was pulsing inside. "Tania, this village life agrees with you," Alexander said after a few moments.

Straightening up, she was about to walk to the porch when he grabbed her hand and put it to his cheek. "Do you like it better smooth?" He rubbed her hand back and forth against his face and then kissed her fingers.

Gently she pulled her hand away. "I haven't seen much of you clean-shaven," she muttered. "Either way is fine. I'm covered in onions, Alexander," she said. "I don't want to get you all messy. You just got so nice and . . . clean." She cleared her throat and averted her eyes.

"Tatia," he said, not letting go of her floury hand, "it's *me*. What's the matter?"

She raised her eyes to him and blinked, and he saw hurt in her eyes, hurt, and warmth, and sadness, but hurt foremost, and he started to say, "What—"

"Alexander, dear, come in here with us. Let Tania finish making dinner. Come, have a drink."

He went out to the porch. Naira handed him a shot of vodka. Shaking his head, Alexander said, "I'm not drinking without Tatiana. Tania! Come."

"She'll drink the next one with us."

"No," he said. "She'll drink the first one with us. Tania, come out here."

She came out, smelling sweetly of potatoes and onions, and stood next to him.

Naira said, "Our Tanechka doesn't even drink."

"I'll drink to Alexander," Tatiana said. Alexander handed her his vodka glass, his fingers touching hers. Naira poured him another. They raised their glasses. "To Alexander," said Tatiana, her voice breaking. Her eyes were filled with tears.

"To Alexander," they echoed. "And to Dasha."

"And to Dasha," Alexander said quietly.

They drank, and Tatiana went back inside.

A dozen people from the village came by before dinner, all wanting to meet Alexander, all bringing small gifts. One woman brought an egg. One old man a fishhook. Another man a fishing line. One young girl a few hard candies. Every one of them shook his hand, and some bowed, and one woman got on her knees, crossed herself, and kissed the glass he was holding. Alexander was moved and exhausted. He took out a cigarette.

Vova said, "Why don't we take that outside? Our Tania has a hard time with smoke in the house."

Alexander put away his cigarette, swearing under his breath. To have Vova look out for Tania's welfare was too much. But before he could say another word, he felt Tatiana's hand on his shoulder and her face right in front of him as she put an ashtray on the table. "Smoke, Alexander, smoke," she said.

Petulantly Vova said, "But, Tania, the smoke bothers you. That's why we all go outside."

"I know I said that, Vova," Tatiana declared. "But Alexander didn't come all the way from the war to smoke outside. He'll smoke where he pleases."

Shaking his head, Alexander said, "I don't need to smoke." He wanted her hand on his shoulder and her face in front of him again. "Tania, do you need help?"

"Yes, you can help by getting up and eating my food. It's dinnertime."

The four ladies sat on one side of the long table that was flanked by two benches. "Usually Tatiana sits on the end. So she can get up and get stuff, you know?" Zoe smiled.

"Oh, I know," said Alexander. "I'll sit next to her."

"Usually I sit next to her," said Vova.

Shrugging and not interested in dealing with Vova, Alexander looked at Tatiana and raised his eyebrows.

She wiped her hands on a towel and said, "How about if I sit between Alexander and Vova."

"Fine," said Zoe. "And I'll sit on the other side of Alexander."

"Fine," said Alexander.

Tatiana had made a cucumber and tomato salad and cooked some potatoes with onions and *tushonka*. She opened a jar of marinated mushrooms. There was white bread, some butter, milk, cheese, and a few hard-boiled eggs.

"What can I get you, Shu—?" asked Tatiana, sliding in next to him. "Do you want some salad?"

"Yes, please."

She stood up. "What about some mushrooms?"

"Yes, please."

Tatiana spooned food onto his plate, standing near him. The only reason Alexander let her continue and didn't get the food himself was because her bare leg was touching his trousers and her hip was pressing into his elbow. He was going to have her get him seconds and thirds to keep her standing this close to him. His urge was to put his arm around her waist. He took his fork instead. "Yes, please, some potatoes, too. Yes, that's plenty. Some bread, yes, that's good, butter, yes."

Alexander thought she would sit down, but no, she walked around the table and ladled out food for the old ladies.

And then she served Vova. Alexander's heart tightened when he saw her serve Vova with casual familiarity. Vova thanked her, and she smiled lightly, looking right at him.

At Vova she looked. At Vova she smiled. For God's sake, thought Alexander. The only thing that prevented him from feeling worse about it was that in Tania's eyes he saw nothing for Vova.

Finally she sat down.

"Tania," he said, "I'm so glad to see food in front of you again."

"Me, too," she replied.

The rooms were so dark that he could not see her well, but he could see blood trickling from her mouth as she cut the black bread for him, for Dasha, and, last, for herself. Now she was eating white bread, and butter, and eggs. "Much better, Tatia," he whispered. "Thank God."

"Yes," she said, and nearly inaudibly, "Thank *you.*"

Zoe's annoying elbow intermittently and purposefully rubbed against Alexander's. Zoe played the game very well. Alexander wondered if Tatiana even noticed Zoe.

Moving away from Zoe, Alexander scooted closer to Tatiana. "Just to give you a bit more room, Zoe," he said with an indifferent smile.

"Yes, but look," said Naira, who was sitting across from them, "now poor Tanechka is all squished."

"I'm fine," said Tatiana. Under the table her leg was flush with his. He nudged her once.

"So," Alexander said, eating hungrily, "have I had enough to drink for you to tell me what happened to you?"

Tears. Not from Tatiana, from the four ladies. "Oh, Alexander! We don't think you've had enough to drink to hear it all."

"Can I hear some of it?"

Naira said, "Tania doesn't like us to talk about it, but, Tanechka, for Alexander, can we tell him what happened?"

"For Alexander, yes, tell him what happened." Tatiana sighed.

"I want Tania to tell me what happened," Alexander said. "Do you want more vodka?"

"No," she replied, pouring one for him. "Alexander, there is really not much to tell. Like I told you, we got to Kobona. Dasha died. I came here and was sick for a while—"

"Near death, I tell you!" exclaimed Naira.

"Naira Mikhailovna, please," said Tatiana. "I was a little sick."

"Sick?" Axinya cried. "Alexander, that child got to us in January and was at death's door until March. What didn't she have? She had scurvy—"

"She was bleeding from the inside out!" mouthed Dusia. "Just like our former Tsarevich Alexis. Just like him. Bled and bled."

"That's scurvy for you," said Alexander gently.

"The Tsarevich did not have scurvy," said Tatiana. "He had hemophilia."

370

"Have you forgotten about her double pneumonia?" cried Axinya. "Both her lungs collapsed!"

"Axinya, please," said Tatiana. "It was only one lung."

"It was the pneumonia that almost killed her. She couldn't breathe," Naira stated, sticking her hand across the table for Tatiana to pat.

"It wasn't pneumonia that nearly killed her!" Axinya exclaimed. "It was TB. Naira, you're so forgetful. Don't you remember her coughing up blood for weeks?"

"Oh, my God, Tania," whispered Alexander.

"Alexander, I'm fine. Really," said Tatiana. "I had a mild case of TB. They cured it even before I got out of the hospital. The doctor said soon I should be as good as before. The doctor said by next year the TB would be all gone."

"And you were going to let me smoke inside."

"So what?" she said. "You always smoke inside. I'm used to it."

"So what?" cried Axinya. "Tania, you were in an isolation tent for a month. We sat by her, Alexander, as she lay, coughing, spitting blood—"

"Why don't you tell him how you got TB?" said Naira loudly.

Alexander felt Tatiana shudder next to him. "That I'll tell him later."

"When later?" whispered Alexander out of the corner of his mouth. She did not whisper back.

"Tania!" exclaimed Axinya. "Tell Alexander about what you had to go through to get here. Tell him."

"Tell me, Tania," he said, looking at her with feeling. The food she made was so good; otherwise he would have lost his appetite.

As if it was a great effort to her, Tatiana said, "Look, me and hundreds of others were piled on into trucks and then driven to the train, near Volkhov . . ."

"Tell him about the train!"

"It wasn't the best of trains. There were a lot of us . . ."

"Tell him how many!"

"I don't know how many," said Tatiana. "We were . . ."

"What happened when the people died on the trains?" said Dusia, crossing herself.

"Oh, they just threw them out. To make more room."

Naira said, sniffling, "There was more room when they got to the Volga River."

Axinya exclaimed, "Alexander, the railroad bridge across the Volga had been blown up, and the train couldn't get across. All the evacuees, including our Tanechka, were told they had to cross the ice on foot in their frightful condition. What about that?"

Alexander blinked and blinked again. He didn't take his eyes off Tatiana's bemused and slightly wearied face.

"How many people crossed that, Tania? How many people died on the ice? Tell him."

"I don't know, Axinya. I wasn't counting . . ."

"Nobody," said Dusia. "I'm sure nobody survived it."

"Well, Tania survived it," said Alexander, his elbow pressing into Tatiana's arm, his leg pressing into hers.

"And other people survived it," said Tatiana. Lowering her voice, she added, "Not many."

"Tania, tell him," Axinya exclaimed, "how many kilometers you had to walk, tubercular, pneumatic, in the snow, in the blizzard, to the next rail station because there weren't enough trucks to carry all of you sick and starving to the train. Tell him how many." She widened her eyes. "It was, like, fifteen!"

"No, dear," Tatiana corrected. "It was maybe three. And there was no blizzard. It was just cold."

"Did they give you anything to eat?" Axinya demanded. "No!"

"Yes," said Tatiana. "I had a little food."

"Tania!" cried Axinya. "Tell him about the train, tell him how there was no place for you to lie down, how you stood for three days from Volkhov to the Volga!"

"I stood for three days," said Tatiana, stabbing her food with a fork. "From Volkhov to the Volga."

Wiping her eyes, Dusia said, "After the Volga crossing, so many people died that Tatiana had a shelf on the train to lie down on, right, Tania? She lay down—"

"And never got up again!" stated Axinya.

"Dear," said Tatiana, "I did eventually get up." She shook her head.

"No," said Axinya. "There I'm not exaggerating. You didn't. The conductor asked where you were going, and he couldn't wake you to ask you . . ."

"But finally he woke me."

"Finally, yes!" cried Axinya. "But he thought you were dead."

Raisa added, "She got off the train at Molotov and asked how far Lazarevo was, and when she heard it was ten kilometers, she . . ."

Loud crying from all four ladies.

Tatiana said to Alexander, "Sorry you have to hear all this."

Alexander stopped eating. He placed his hand on her back, patting her gently. When he saw she didn't move away and didn't flinch and didn't blush, he left his hand on her for another long moment. Then he picked up his fork again.

"Alexander, do you know what she did when she heard Lazarevo was ten kilometers from Molotov?"

"Let me guess," said Alexander, smiling. "She fainted."

"Yes! How did *you* know?" asked Axinya, studying him.

"I faint all the time," said Tatiana. "I'm a big wimp."

Naira said, "After she came out of isolation, we sat next to her hospital bed, holding her oxygen mask to her face to help her breathe." Wiping her face, she said, "When her grandmother died—"

The fork dropped from Alexander's hand. Involuntarily. Mutely he sat and looked into his plate, unable to turn his head even to Tatiana. It was she who turned her head to him, gazing at him with softness and sorrow. "Where is that vodka, Tania?" Alexander said. "Clearly I haven't had enough."

She poured it for him and poured a small glass for herself, and then they lifted their glasses, clinking lightly, and stared at each other, faces full of Leningrad, and Fifth Soviet, and her family and his family, and Lake Ladoga, and night. Tatiana whispered, "Courage, Shura."

He couldn't reply. He swallowed the vodka instead.

The rest of the people at the table fell quiet until Alexander asked, "How did she die?"

Naira wiped her nose. "Dysentery. Last December." She leaned forward. "Personally, I think that after she lost Tania's grandfather, she just didn't want to go on." Naira glanced at Tatiana. "I know Tania agrees with me."

Tatiana nodded. "She wanted to," she said. "She just couldn't."

Naira poured Alexander another drink. "When Anna was dying, she said to me, 'Naira, I wish you could see all my granddaughters, but you're probably never going to see our baby Tania. She'll never make it here. She is so frail.'"

"Anna," said Alexander, downing the vodka, "was not such a good judge of her granddaughters."

"She said to us," Naira continued, "'If my granddaughters come, please make sure they're all right. Keep my house for them.'"

"House?" asked Alexander, instantly perking up. "What house?"

"Oh, they had an *izba*—"

"Where is this *izba*?"

"Just in the woods a bit. By the river. Tania can show you. When Tania got better and came to Lazarevo with us, she wanted to live in that house," Naira said, widening her eyes meaningfully, "*all by herself*."

"What *was* she thinking?" questioned Alexander.

Beaming, the ladies all loudly agreed, scoffing and snorting in unison. Naira said, "No granddaughter of our Anna is going to live by herself. What kind of nonsense is that? Who lives by themselves? We said, you are our family. Your beloved Deda was my first husband's cousin by marriage. You come and live with us. It's so much better for you here. And it is, isn't it, Tanechka?"

"Yes, Naira Mikhailovna." Tatiana served Alexander some more potatoes. "Are you still hungry?"

"To tell you the truth, I'm not sure what I am anymore," said Alexander. "I will certainly continue to eat."

Naira said, "Our Tania is better now, but she has to watch herself. She still goes to Molotov every month to get checked out. TB can come back at any time. That's why we all smoke outside—"

"Gladly," piped up Vova, putting his arm on Tatiana's shoulder.

Alexander was going to have to talk to Tatiana about Vova, *and soon.*

Axinya said, "Alexander, you have no idea how thin she was when she came to us . . ."

"I have *some* idea," said Alexander. "Don't I, Tania?"

She whispered, "Some idea, Shura."

"She was skin and bones," said Dusia. "Christ Himself almost could not save her."

"It's good that we don't live in a collective farming village like our cousin Yulia, right, Naira?" said Axinya. "Yulia lives in Kulay near Archangelsk, and though she is fifty-seven, she works in the field all day, and then the *Kolkhoz* takes her food away. Here they just take our fish, but we can barter our eggs and goat milk for some butter or cheese or even some white flour."

"Poor Yulia," sniffed Naira. "But look at our Tanechka."

Axinya smiled and looked affectionately at Tatiana. "We've fattened you up, haven't we, honey? Eggs every day. Milk. Butter. We've fattened her up good, don't you think, Alexander?"

"Hmm," said Alexander, reaching underneath the table and lightly squeezing Tatiana's thigh.

"She's like a *warm bun,*" added Axinya.

"A warm bun?" Alexander repeated, his grinning face turning to Tatiana, who was a deep red. Her short dress wasn't long enough to cover her thighs. His bare hand caressed her bare leg, under the table, during dinner, in front of six strangers. Alexander had to take his hand away. *Had* to. He lost his breath, along with his reserve, and his self-control.

"Alexander, want more?" Tatiana said, standing and picking up the frying pan. Her hands were unsteady. "There is plenty." She smiled at him, breathing through her parted mouth. "Plenty." Her face was flushed.

"I think I'll have a drink instead," Alexander said, unable to look up at *her* for a change.

Axinya said, "Alexander, we want you to know that we weren't happy with Tanechka. We want you to know we were on your side."

"Tania, what did you do to upset these nice women?" said Alexander lightly.

Why did Tania stop smiling and glare at Axinya?

Naira, mouth full of fried potatoes, said, "We told her to write to you and tell you what happened to Dasha so you wouldn't come all this way expecting to marry your longtime love and be devastated. We told her. Spare him a trip to the middle of the country. Write to him and tell him the truth."

"And she refused!" Axinya exclaimed.

Alexander, the fire in his heart unsubsided, but the temper in his heart also unsubsided, stared at Tatiana. "Why did she refuse, Axinya?"

"She wouldn't say. But let me tell you, the thought of you coming here for your Dasha was killing us. We could talk about nothing else."

"*Nothing* else, Alexander," Tatiana said. "More drink?"

"Maybe if you had written to me, they would have stopped talking," he said, less friendly. "And yes, more drink."

She poured it for him so fast she nearly spilled it.

Alexander's head was swimming.

"We read all of Dasha's letters to Anna," said Naira. "The way that girl raved about you." She shook her head. "You were her shining knight, you know."

He finished his glass of vodka in two swallows.

"Tania, we told you to write to him!" Dusia exclaimed. "But our Tania can be very stubborn sometimes."

"Sometimes?" Alexander took the glass from Tatiana and finished her vodka, too.

Dusia crossed herself. "I said, you can do it, you can write that letter. But she said no. Not even with God's help she couldn't." She looked at Tatiana with disapproving eyes. "Alexander, we were hoping maybe God would spare you pain and let you die at the front."

Alexander raised his eyebrows. "You were *hoping* I would die at the front!"

"Tania and I prayed for your soul every day," said Dusia. "We didn't want you to suffer."

"Thank you, I think," Alexander said. "Tania, were *you* praying for my death every day?"

"Of course not, Alexander," she replied quietly, unable to be cold, unable to be insincere, unable to lie, or to look at him, or to touch him. Unable. Whatever sat inside her rendered her unable to deal with him. He looked around the crowded table.

"Oh, Alexander!" exclaimed Axinya. "That was some letter you wrote to Dasha. You're a poet. It was so full of love! When we read that nothing was going to stop you from coming and marrying her this summer, you just about broke our hearts."

"Yes, Alexander," said Tatiana. "Remember that poetic letter?"

Suddenly when he looked into her face—

He studied her. He was starting to lose focus in his brain. "Yes," he said. He had written that letter wanting to reassure Dasha. He didn't want Tatiana to face her sister by herself. "Should've written back, Tania," he said with reproach. "And told me about Dasha."

Bolting up, Tatiana started clearing the table.

"Never mind," Alexander said with a shrug. "Perhaps Tania was too busy? Who's got time to write nowadays? Especially during village life. There are sewing circles, there is cooking—"

She grabbed his plate. "How was your dinner, Alexander?" she asked. "Did you enjoy it?"

Too many things to say.

Nowhere to say them.

Just like before.

"Yes, thank you. More drink?"

"No," she snapped. "No, thank you."

Vova asked, "Alexander, so now what are you going to do? Are you going back?"

Another sharp intake of breath from Tatiana. Alexander held his own breath for a moment. "I don't know."

"You stay as long as you like," declared Naira. "We love you like family. You might as well already be Dasha's husband, that's how we feel about you."

"But he is not," said Zoe adamantly and flirtatiously, placing her hand on Alexander's arm and smiling. "Don't worry, Alexander. We'll cheer you up around here. How long is your furlough?"

"A month."

"Zoe," said Tatiana, "how is your good friend Stepan? Are you seeing him later tonight?"

Zoe took her arm away from Alexander, who, smiling and amused, glanced at Tatiana. So she is not *entirely* oblivious to Zoe, he thought.

She was clearing the table. Alexander looked around. No one else moved. Not even Zoe or Vova. As he started to stand up, Tatiana asked, "Where are you going? Smoke at the table."

"To help you clear up."

"No, no, no!" cried a chorus of voices. "What are you thinking? No. Tatiana does it."

"I know she does," said Alexander. "But I don't want her to do it by herself."

"Why?" asked Naira with genuine surprise.

"Honestly, Alexander," Tatiana said. "You didn't travel all this way to clear the table."

Alexander sat back down, turned to Zoe, and said, "I admit I'm a little tired. Could *you* help her?" He didn't smile at her. Zoe seemed to like that even better, giving him a large smile, as big as her breasts, and reluctantly going to help.

Tatiana made tea and poured a cup for Alexander first, and then for the four ladies and then for Vova and then for Zoe, and then for herself. She brought out the blueberry jam and was just climbing in to sit next to Alexander when Vova said, "Tanechka, before you sit, pour me another cup of tea, will you?"

Tatiana, legs straddling the bench, took Vova's cup when Alexander grabbed her wrist. The cup rattled on the saucer. "You know what, Vova?" Alexander said, lowering Tatiana's hand to the table. "The kettle of water is on the hearth, the teapot is right in front of you. Sit down, Tania. You've done plenty. Vova can pour his own tea."

Tatiana sat down.

Everybody at the table stared at Alexander.

Vova went and poured his own tea.

Finally it was time for Zoe and Vova to go home. The time couldn't come fast enough for Alexander, until Vova said, "Tania? Walk me out?"

Without acknowledging Alexander, Tatiana went outside with Vova. Alexander pretended to listen to Zoe and to Naira, but he watched Tatiana outside.

He wished he had had less vodka. He really needed to talk to Tania. When she came back, Alexander wanted her to look at him. She did not.

Zoe said, "Alexander, want to go for a smoke and a walk?"

"No."

"Tomorrow a group of us are going swimming down in the hole. You want to come?"

"We'll see," he said noncommittally. He didn't even look up. Soon she left.

"Tania, come and sit down," Alexander said. "Sit down next to me."

"I will. You want something else?"

"Yes. You to sit."

"What about something else to drink? We have a little cognac."

"No, thanks."

"What about—"

"Tania. Sit down."

Carefully she sat down on the bench next to him. He moved over to her. "You must be so tired," he said gently. "Want to come outside with me? I need a smoke."

Before Tatiana could reply, Naira said, "I'll tell you, Alexander, it was very hard for our Tania at first."

Tatiana got up with a sigh and disappeared into one of the bedrooms.

"She doesn't want us to talk about it," said Axinya in hushed tones.

"Of course not," Alexander said. He didn't either.

They continued unheeded. "She was in a bad way. She was just an apparition." The women all bent their heads toward him, clucking with tears in their eyes. He would have been almost amused by them, if only they weren't stopping him from getting two words alone with his horse and cart. Naira said, "No, but can you just imagine, losing your whole—"

"I can imagine," Alexander interrupted. He did not want to be talking to these women about it. He stood up, about to excuse himself and go after Tatiana.

"Alexander, and that's not even the half of it," Naira whispered. "Tania really doesn't like us to talk about what happened in Kobona. We didn't want to tell you before, but—"

"Oh, but that Dimitri is a right bastard!" Axinya exclaimed again.

Alexander sat back down. "Tell me quickly."

Tatiana came back with a slam of the door.

"I'm sorry, Tanechka," Axinya said, "but I just want to beat that man with a stick."

"Please stop talking about Kobona," Tatiana said.

Dusia said, "Woe betide Dimitri. Someday he is going to fall alone, and no one will be there to help him up."

Rolling her eyes, Tatiana left again with another slam of the door.

Axinya said, "I think that bastard broke her heart. I think she loved him."

Alexander was finding it difficult to remain upright.

Dusia shook her head vehemently. "Absolutely not," she said. "He never would have fooled her for a second. Our Tania sees through people right from the start."

"She does, doesn't she, Dusia?" said Alexander.

Axinya lowered her voice and said, "We still think there's another story to this, maybe some kind of *love* thing."

"Not a *love* thing," said Alexander, widening his eyes.

Naira shook her head. "*You* think so, Axinya. But *I* say no. I disagree. The girl lost everyone. She was devastated. There was no love."

"I think there was," said Axinya firmly.

"You're wrong," Naira said.

"Oh? Then why does she keep going to the post office to see if there is any mail for her?" Axinya asked triumphantly. "She's got no one left, who is she waiting for mail from?"

"Good point," said Alexander. Was he about to go do something? He couldn't remember. The day had been too long. Right now he couldn't remember the last thing anyone had said.

Axinya said, "And have you noticed how during the sewing circle at the square she always picks a place to sit so she can see the road?"

"Yes, yes!" agreed the other three ladies. "Yes, she does do that. She watches that road obsessively, as if she is waiting for somebody."

Alexander lifted his gaze. Tatiana stood behind the old ladies, her expressive, eternal eyes on him.

"Are you, Tatiasha?" he asked emotionally, his voice full. "*Are* you waiting for somebody?"

"Not anymore," she replied emotionally, her voice just as full.

"You see?" said Naira with satisfaction. "I told you there was no love thing!"

Tatiana sat down next to Alexander.

Naira said, "Tanechka, you don't mind that we gossip about you, do you? You know you're the most interesting thing that's happened to Lazarevo in years. Vova certainly thinks so." She laughed and to Alexander said, "My grandson has quite a crush on Dasha's little sister, you know."

Without a word Alexander blinked at Tatiana. He would have said a word, if he could have found one in his head.

All Alexander wanted was two seconds, maybe *one* conscious second alone with Tatiana—why was that too much to ask? Maybe conscious was out of the question, but why was putting his two hands somewhere on her repaired, fed, warm body out of the question?

He went outside to smoke, to wash. When he returned, he wanted to undress, to take off his boots. Instead he heard a constant stream of "Tanechka, darling, can you get me my medicine?" "Tanechka, dear, can you come and fix my blankets?" "Tanechka, sweetheart, can you get me a glass of water?" Finally he couldn't wait anymore. He took off his boots. "Tania, honey," he said, and then put his head down on the table and was instantly asleep. He woke up to feel himself being lightly shaken, lightly stroked. It was dark. "Come on, Shura," her voice whispered. She was trying to get him to stand up. "Come on, can you make it up? Please, wake up and go lie down. Please."

He got up on the hearth, hopped up onto the bed on top of the warm stove, and was asleep in his uniform. Through semiconsciousness he felt her taking off his socks, unbuttoning his tunic, unbuckling his belt and pulling it out from the loops. He felt her soft lips on his eyes, on his cheek, on his forehead. He felt fine feathers on his face. It must have been her hair. He wanted to wake up, but it was impossible.

5

The next morning Alexander opened his eyes and looked at his watch. It was late—eight in the morning. He looked around for Tatiana. She was nowhere, but he was covered by her quilt and he was lying on her pillow. Smiling, he turned on his stomach and pressed his face into the pillow. It smelled of soap and fresh air and her.

He went outside. It was a chirping and sunny rural morning; the air was as still as peacetime; the cherry tree blossoms and the lilacs filled the yard with their overripe scent. The lilacs made Alexander especially cheerful—the Field of Mars was full of lilacs in late spring. He could smell them all the way from the barracks. It was one of his favorite smells, lilacs in the Field of Mars. Not his favorite smell: of an alive Tatiana's breath as she kissed his unconscious face last night. Lilacs could not compete with that smell.

The house was quiet. After quickly washing, Alexander went to look for her, finding her on the road, returning home carrying two pails full of warm cow's milk. Alexander knew it was warm because he stuck his fingers in the pail. Tatiana's shiny white-blonde hair was left down, and she was wearing a blue wraparound skirt and a small white shirt that came up above her navel, exposing her stomach. The round outlines of her high breasts were clearly visible. Her face was a lovely flushed pink color. Alexander's heart stopped in his chest when he saw her. He took the milk pails from her. They walked for a minute in silence. He felt himself getting short of breath.

"I suppose after this you're going to go and fetch water from the well," he said.

"*Going* to?" Tatiana said. "And what did you shave with this morning?"

"Who shaved?"

"Did you brush your teeth?" She smiled lightly.

He laughed. "Yes, with your water from the well. Tania, after breakfast," he said, lowering his already husky voice, "I want you to show me your grandparents' house. Is it far?"

"It's not too far," she said and her face was inscrutable.

Alexander was not used to Tatiana being inscrutable. His job was to make her *scrutable*. He smiled. "Hmm."

"What do you want to see it for? It's all padlocked shut."

"Bring the key. Where did you sleep?"

"On the couch in the porch," she replied. "Were you comfortable? I didn't think so. You were in all your clothes. But I couldn't wake you up for anything—"

"Did you *try*?" asked Alexander in a measured tone.

"I had to practically shoot your pistol in the air to get you to climb up onto the stove."

"Tania, don't shoot it up in the air," Alexander said. "The bullet has to come down." Remembering her lips on his face, he added, "You removed my socks and my belt." He grinned. "You should have gone the extra step."

"Couldn't lift you," Tatiana said, blushing. "How are you feeling this morning? After all that vodka?"

"Great. How about you?"

"Hmm," she said, surreptitiously looking him over. "Do you have any clothes to wear besides your uniforms?"

"No."

"I'll wash your Class-As for you today," she said. "But if you're planning to stay for a little while, I have some regular clothes for you."

"Do you *want* me to stay for a little while?"

"Of course," Tatiana replied, her voice measured. "You came all this way. No point in going back so soon."

"Tania," Alexander said, walking close to her, knocking into her gently, "now that I'm lucid again, tell me about Dimitri."

"No," she said. "I can't. I will, but—"

"Tania, do you know that I saw him two weeks ago, and he didn't tell me he saw you in Kobona."

"What did he say?"

"Nothing. I asked him if he saw you or Dasha, and he said, no, he had not."

Shaking her head, Tatiana gazed straight ahead and faintly said, "Oh, he saw me and Dasha, all right."

Some of the milk spilled to the ground.

As they walked, Alexander told her about Leningrad, about Hitler and his losses. He told her about the vegetables growing all over the city. "Tania," he said, "they've planted cabbage and potatoes right in front of *St. Isaac's*." He smiled. "And yellow tulips. What do you think of that?"

"I think that's great," she said in a tone that conveyed no connection to St. Isaac's whatsoever. Inscrutable.

Alexander didn't want her to feel sad this morning. Were there just too many things for them to get past before he could get a morning smile out of her?

"What's the ration up to now?" Tatiana asked, her eyes to the ground.

"Three hundred grams for dependents. Six hundred for workers. But soon there might be white bread. The council promised white bread this summer."

"Well, it's certainly easier to feed one million people than it is to feed three."

"Fewer than a million now. They're being evacuated by barges across the lake." He changed the subject. "I see you have plenty of bread here in Lazarevo." Alexander eyed her. "Plenty of everything here in—"

"Everybody been buried?"

He sighed imperceptibly. "I supervised the excavation of graves at Piskarev Cemetery myself."

"Excavation?"

She didn't miss a thing. "We used military mines to dynamite—"

"Mass graves?" she finished.

"Tania . . . come on."

"You're right, let's not talk about it. Oh, look, we're home." She rushed ahead.

Disappointed they were already home, Alexander caught up with her. "Can you show me those clothes? I'd like to put something else on."

Inside the house she pulled out her trunk from near the stove and was about to open it when Dusia's voice sounded from one of the bedrooms. "Tanechka? Is that you?"

Naira came out and said, "Good morning, dear. I didn't smell the coffee this morning. I woke up, sweetheart, because I *didn't* smell the coffee."

"I'll make it now, Naira Mikhailovna."

Raisa came out of her bedroom and said, "When you have a minute, dear, could you help me to the outhouse?"

"Of course." Tatiana started to close the trunk. "I'll show you later," she whispered to Alexander.

"No, Tatiana," Alexander said impatiently. "You will show me *now*."

"Alexander, I can't *now*," she said, pushing the trunk back against the wall. "Raisa has a hard time going to the bathroom by herself. You see how she shakes. But you can sit for five minutes, can't you?"

What, he hadn't been patient enough? "I can sit for longer than that," he said. "I sat all night yesterday with you and your new friends."

She chewed her lip.

He sighed. "All right, all right. Do you have a mortar and pestle?" Alexander couldn't help himself; his spirits were too high, and he was too crazed by her to remain exasperated for long. Trying to keep the double meaning out of his voice, he asked, "Would you like me to grind your coffee beans for you?"

"Yes, thank you," Tatiana replied. She was not playing. "That will be a big help. I'll get you the cheesecloth, too." She paused. "Could you fire up the stove, please? So I can make breakfast?"

"Of course, Tania."

Tatiana took Raisa to the outhouse and then gave her her medicine.

She dressed Dusia.

She made all the beds, and then she fried some eggs with potatoes. Alexander watched it all. As he was sitting on the bench outside and smoking, Tatiana came up to him with a cup of coffee in her hands, and asked, "How do you like it?"

His eyes twinkling, Alexander looked up at her standing in front of him, so lavender fresh and young and alive. "How do I like *what*?"

"Your coffee."

"I like my coffee," said Alexander, "with thick, warm cream and lots of sugar." He paused. "Get the cream right from the pail, Tatiasha, right off the top. But warm. And lots of it."

The cup in her hands started to shake.

Scrutable.

It was all Alexander could do not to laugh out loud, not to grab her, not to pull her to him.

After breakfast he helped her clear the table and wash the dishes. Her hands were immersed in a pan of sudsy water when Alexander, having watched her for a while, put his own hands in and felt for hers.

"What are you doing?" she said in a hoarse voice.

"What?" he said innocently. "I'm helping you with the dishes."

"You are not a very good helper, I'm afraid," Tatiana said, but she did not take her hands away, and as Alexander watched her face, he finally saw something dissolving against her wall of pain. He rubbed intently between her fingers, getting fixated and inflamed by the fine blonde down on her forearms and by her blonde eyebrows. "I think the dishes are going to be very clean," he said, glancing at the four women, who were sitting in the morning sunshine and chatting within a few meters of them. In the warm, soapy water, Alexander stroked Tatiana's fingers one by one, from the first knuckle down to the fingertip, and with his thumbs circled the palms of her slippery hands, while Tatiana stood, barely breathing through her parted lips, her eyes glazed over.

The fire raged in Alexander's stomach.

"Tatia," he said quietly, "your freckles are *so* pronounced. *And*," he added, "very enti—"

Axinya came up to Tania, pinching her bottom. "Our Tanechka is freck-led as if she's been kissed by the sun." Damn it. Alexander couldn't even *whisper* to her without them overhearing. But when Axinya turned her back, Alexander leaned forward and softly kissed Tatiana's freckles. He let her pull her fingers away from him and walk off, wet hands and all. Without drying his own hands, he followed her. "Is *now* a good time for you to show me those clothes?"

Going inside and opening her trunk, Tatiana pulled out a large white cot-ton button-down shirt with short sleeves, a knitted cotton shirt, a cream linen shirt, and three pairs of drawstring trousers made out of bleached linen. She also had a couple of sleeveless tops for him, and some drawstring cotton shorts. "To go swimming in," she said. "What do you think?"

"These are great." He smiled. "Where did you get them?"

"I made them."

"You made them?"

She shrugged. "Mama taught me how to sew. It wasn't hard. What was hard was trying to remember how big you were."

"I think you remembered quite well," Alexander said slowly. "Tania, you . . . *made* clothes for me?"

"I didn't know for sure you were coming, but if you were, I wanted you to have something comfortable to wear."

"Linen is expensive," he said, very pleased.

"There was a lot of money in your Pushkin book." She paused. "I bought a few things for everybody."

Ah. *Less* pleased. "Including Vova?"

Tatiana guiltily glanced away.

"I see," Alexander said, dropping the clothes into the trunk. "You bought Vova things with my money?"

"Just some vodka, and cig—"

"Tatiana!" Alexander took a deep breath. "Not here. Let me change," he said, turning away from her. "I'll be right out."

She went outside while he changed into the trousers and the white cotton shirt that was slightly tight around his chest but otherwise fit fine.

When Alexander stepped down from the house, the old women clucked at how nice he looked. Tatiana was gathering clothes into a basket. "I should have made it a little bigger. You do look nice." She swallowed and lowered her eyes. "I haven't seen you often in civilian clothes."

Alexander looked around. Here it was, his second day with her, and they were still clucking around four old women, and he was still unable to get to whatever was bothering her, to all the things that were bothering him, much less to her ample blondeness. That was it. "You've seen me in civilian clothes once," he said. "In Peterhof. Perhaps you've forgotten Peterhof." He extended his hand. "Come on, let's go for a walk."

Tatiana stepped up to him but did not take his hand. He had to reach down and take hold of her hand himself. Being so close to her made him a little light-headed. "I want you to show me where the river is."

"You know where the river is," she replied. "You went there yesterday." She took her hand out from his. "Shura, I really can't. I've got to hang yesterday's laundry and then wash today's."

He pulled her with him. "No. Let's go."

"No."

"Yes."

"Shura, no, please!"

Alexander stopped. What the hell *was* that in her voice? What did that sound like? That wasn't anger. Was that . . . *fear?* He peered into her face. "What's wrong with you?" he said. She was flustered, and her hands were shaky. She couldn't look at him. Letting go of her hand, he took hold of her face, lifting it to him. "What—"

"Shura, please," Tatiana whispered, trying to look away from his eyes, and then Alexander saw, and he knew.

Letting go of her, he backed away and smiled. "Tania," he said, in a soothing voice, "I want you to show me your grandparents' house. I want you to show me the river. A field, a fucking rock, I don't give a shit. I want you to take me to two square meters of space where there is no one around us, so we can talk. Do you understand? That's all. We need to talk, and I'm not talking—I'm not doing anything—in front of your new friends." He paused, keeping the smile away. "All right?"

Deeply flushed, she did not raise her eyes.

"Good." He pulled her by the hand.

Naira said, "Tanechka, where are you going?"

"We're going to pick some blueberries for tonight's pie," Tatiana yelled back.

"But, Tanechka, what about the clothes?"

Raisa yelled, "Will you be back at noon to give me my medicine?"

"When will we be back, Alexander?"

"When you're fixed, Tatiana," he said. "Tell her that. When Alexander fixes me, then I'll be back."

"I don't think even you can fix me, Alexander," said Tatiana, and her voice was cold.

He was walking with all deliberate speed away from the house.

"Wait, I have to—"

"No."

"Just one more . . ." She tried to pull her hand away. He wasn't having any of it. She tried again.

Alexander wasn't letting go. "Tania, you can't win this," he said, staring at her and squeezing her hand harder. "You can win a lot of things, but you can't win a physical struggle with me. Thank God. Because then I'd *really* be in trouble."

Naira yelled after them, "Tania, but Vova is coming for you soon! When shall I tell him you'll be back?"

Tatiana looked at Alexander, who stared back coldly, shrugged indifferently, and said, "It's me or the laundry. You're going to have to decide. I know the choice is tough. Or it's me or Vova." He let her hand drop. "Is that choice tough, too?" He'd just about had enough. They had stopped walking and were standing facing each other, a meter apart. Alexander folded his arms across his chest. "What's it going to be, Tania? The choice is yours."

Tatiana yelled back to Naira, "I'll be back in a while! Tell him I'll see him later!" Sighing, she motioned for Alexander to come.

He was walking too quickly, and she couldn't keep up.

"Why so fast?"

Temper was flaring up in Alexander, like the sizzle of an antipersonnel grenade before it exploded. He breathed in and out deeply to calm himself, to shove the pin back up the hole. "I'm going to tell you something right now," he said. "If you don't want trouble, you will have to tell Vova to leave you alone."

When she didn't reply, Alexander stopped walking and pulled her to him. "Do you hear me?" he said, raising his voice. "Or perhaps you'd like to tell *me* to leave you alone? Because you can do that right now, Tatiana."

Not raising her eyes and not trying to get away from him, Tatiana said quietly, "I'm sorry about Vova. Don't be upset. You know perfectly well I just don't want to hurt his feelings."

"Yes," Alexander said pointedly, "nobody's but mine."

"No, Alexander," Tatiana said, and this time she looked up at him with sullen reproach. "I don't want to hurt yours most of all."

He was not letting go of her. "What the hell is *that* supposed to mean?" He squeezed her arm. "One way or another, he will have to leave you alone—permanently—" Alexander said, "if we're to fix what's wrong between us."

Weakly prying his fingers off her, Tatiana said, "I don't know why you worry about him . . ."

"Tania, if I've got nothing to worry about, then show me. But I'm not playing these games anymore. Not here. Not in Lazarevo. I will not do it here for strangers, do you understand? I will not be guarding Vova's feelings the way I guarded Dasha's. Either you tell him, which would be best, or I tell him, which would be worst."

When Tatiana, biting her lip shut, didn't say anything, Alexander continued. "I don't want to grapple with him. And I don't want to have to pretend to Zoe as she brushes her tits against me. I won't do it just to keep peace in *this* house."

That made Tatiana look up. "Zoe does *what?*" Shaking her head, she muttered, "Vova doesn't go around brushing anything against *me*."

385

Standing very close against her, Alexander said, "No?" He paused. His breath quickened. Tatiana's breath quickened. And very lightly Alexander brushed against Tatiana. "You will tell him to leave you alone, do you hear me?"

"I hear you," she said faintly. He let go of her, and they resumed walking.

"But frankly," she continued, even more faintly, "I think Vova is the least of our problems."

Alexander walked faster down the village road. "Where are we going?"

"I thought you wanted to see my grandparents' house."

Alexander let out his breath and laughed without much humor.

"What's funny?" Tatiana did not sound amused herself.

Neither was Alexander. "I didn't think it was possible," he said, shaking his head. "I didn't, after what I had seen at Fifth Soviet, but somehow you managed to do it."

"Do *what?*" Tatiana said, no longer faintly.

"Explain to me how," he snapped. "How did you manage to find and surround yourself with people even more needy than your family?"

"Don't talk about my family that way, all right!"

"Why does everyone flock around you, why? Can you explain it?"

"Not to you."

"Why do you submerge yourself in their life this way?"

"I'm not discussing this with you. You're just being mean."

"Do you even have a moment to yourself in that fucking house?" Alexander exclaimed. "A moment!"

"Not a moment!" Tatiana retorted. "Thank God."

They walked in resentful silence the rest of the way, through the village, past the *banya* and the village *Soviet*, past the tiny hut that said "Library" and a small building with a gold cross on top of a white *kupola*.

They walked into the woods and down the path leading to the Kama. Finally they came to a wide, slightly sloping clearing surrounded by tall pines and clusters of leaning white birches. Willows and poplars framed the sparkling, streaming river.

On the left side of the clearing under the pines stood a boarded-up *izba*, a wooden cabin. It had a small covering on the side that served as a woodshed, but there was no wood.

"This is it?" Alexander said, walking around the cabin in thirty long strides. "It's not very big."

"There were only two of them," said Tatiana, walking around with him in fifty short ones.

"But they were waiting for three grandchildren. Where would you all have fit?"

"We would have fit," said Tatiana. "How do we fit in Naira's house?"

"*Extremely* tightly," declared Alexander, reaching into his rucksack. He pulled out his trench tool and started to break off the boards on the windows.

"What are you doing?"

"I want to see what's inside."

Alexander watched her walk to the sandy riverbank, sit down, and take off her sandals. He lit a cigarette and continued to break off the boards.

"Did you bring a key for the padlock?" he called to her.

He didn't hear her response. Fed up, he strode over and said loudly, "Tatiana, I'm speaking to you. Did you bring the key for the padlock, I asked?"

"And I replied to you," she snapped without glancing up. "I said no."

"Fine," he said, getting out his semiautomatic from his belt and pulling back the breechblock. "If you didn't bring the key, I will shoot the fucking padlock off."

"Wait, wait," she said, tutting and taking a rope from her neck on which the key hung. "Here. Don't snatch!" She turned away. "You're not at war, you know. You don't have to bring that gun everywhere."

"Oh, yes, I do." He started to walk away and glanced back—at her blonde hair, at her back exposed at the waist, at her shoulders. Alexander dropped the padlock key into his trouser pocket and, holding his pistol in one hand and his trench tool in the other, strode into the water, still in his boots, stood in front of her with his feet apart, and said in a determined voice, "All right, let's have it."

"Have what?" Still sitting down, she backed away from him slightly on her haunches.

"Have *what?*" he exclaimed. "Why are you upset? What did I do, or not do! What did I do too much of, or not enough of? Tell me. Tell me now."

"Why are you talking to me like that?" Tatiana said, jumping to her feet. "You have no right in the world to be upset with me."

"You have no right in the world to be upset with *me!*" he said loudly. "Tania, we are wasting our precious breath. And you're wrong—I have plenty of right to be upset with you. But unlike you, I'm too grateful you're alive and too happy to see you to be too upset with you."

"I have more reason to be upset with you." Tatiana paused. "And I *am* grateful you are alive." She couldn't look at him when she spoke. "I *am* happy to see you."

"It's hard for me to tell, your wall against me is so thick." When she didn't reply, Alexander said, "Do you understand that I came all the way to Lazarevo without hearing from you once in six months?" He raised his voice. "Not once in six months! I should have just thought you both were dead, no?"

"I don't know what you thought, Alexander," said Tatiana, looking past him at the river.

"I'm going to tell you what I thought, Tatiana. In case it's not clear. For six months I didn't know if you were alive or dead, because you couldn't be bothered to pick up a fucking pen!"

"I didn't know you wanted me to write to you," Tatiana said, grabbing a couple of pebbles and tossing them past him into the water.

"You didn't know?" he repeated. Was she mocking him? "What are you talking about? Hello, Tatiana. I'm Alexander. Have we met before? You didn't know I would have wanted to hear that you were all right, or perhaps that Dasha had died?"

He saw her recoil from his words, and from him.

"I am not talking about Dasha with you!" She walked away.

He followed her. "If not with me, then with who? With Vova, perhaps?"

"Better with him than with you."

"Oh, that's charming." Alexander was still trying to be rational, but if she kept saying things like that, all reason was going to leave him.

Tatiana said, "Look, I didn't write to you because I thought Dimitri would tell you. He said he definitely would. So I thought for sure you knew." Something unspoken remained in her after that, but Alexander's temper didn't let him get to it.

"You thought *Dimitri* would tell me?" Alexander repeated in disbelief.

"Yes!" she said challengingly.

"Why didn't you just write me yourself?" he yelled, coming close and looming over her. "Four thousand rubles, Tatiana, you'd think I'd deserve a fucking letter from you, no? You'd think my four thousand rubles would buy you a pen to write *me* and not just vodka and cigarettes for your village lover!"

"Put your weapons down!" she yelled back. "Don't you dare come near me with those things in your hands!"

Hurling away his gun and his trench tool, he came for her, making her back away, and came for her again, without touching her, making her back away once more. "What's the matter, Tania?" he said. "Am I crowding you? Getting too close?" He paused, leaning into her face. "*Scaring* you?" he added bitingly.

"Yes and yes," she said. "And *yes*."

Alexander picked up a handful of pebbles and threw them hard into the water.

For a minute, maybe two, maybe three, neither of them spoke, getting their breath. He waited for her to say something, and when she didn't, Alexander tried again to lure her back into what they felt when it was just the two of them, at Kirov, at Luga, at St. Isaac's. "Tania, when you first saw me here . . ." He trailed off. "You were so happy."

"What gave my happiness away?" she asked. "Was it my sobbing?"

"Yes," he said. "I thought you were crying from happiness."

"Have you seen *much* of that, Alexander?" Tatiana asked, and for a second, just for a moment, he wondered if there was a double meaning behind her words, but he was too confounded to think carefully.

"What did I say?" he asked.

"I don't know. What did you say?"

"Do we *have* to play these guessing games?" he said in exasperation. "Can't you just tell me?" When she didn't say anything, Alexander sighed. "All I asked was where Dasha was."

Tatiana almost curled into herself.

"Tania, if you're unhappy because I'm making you remember things you want to forget then we will deal with that—"

"If only—"

"Wait!" he said loudly, raising his hand. "I said *if* that's what it is. But if it's something else—" He stopped. Her face looked so upset. Lowering his voice back to calm, opening his hands to her, looking at her with everything he felt for her, Alexander said, "Listen. How about this? I will forgive you for not writing me, if you will forgive me for one thing that's bothering you." He smiled. "Is there only one?"

"Alexander, there are so many things that are bothering me, I don't even know where to begin."

He saw that she really didn't. And through it all, the hurt remained in her eyes.

It was Tatiana's eyes that Alexander reacted to now: they were the same eyes he had seen on the Fifth Soviet pavement when she yelled to him that she could forgive him for his indifferent face but not for his indifferent heart. Weren't they past that? He wore his heart for her as a medal on his chest; weren't they beyond all the lies?

How much was there beyond that Fifth Soviet pavement?

Alexander realized, only death was beyond that. They had never fixed that fight. And all the things that preceded it. And all the things that surpassed it.

And through all those things ran Dasha, whom Tatiana had tried to save and could not. Whom Alexander had tried to save and could not.

"Tania, is all this because Dasha and I were planning to get married?"

She didn't reply.

Aha.

"Is all this because of the letter that I wrote to Dasha?"

She didn't reply.

Aha.

"Is there more?"

"Alexander," Tatiana said, shaking her head, "how petty you manage to make it all sound. How trivial. All my feelings have now been reduced to your contemptuous '*all this.*'"

"I'm not contemptuous," he said, with surprise. "It's not trivial. It's not petty, but it's all in the past—"

"No!" she cried. "It's all right here, right now, all around me and inside, too! I live here now. And here," she said raising her voice even more, "they have been waiting for you to come to marry my sister! And I don't mean just the old women. I mean everybody in the village. Since I came to live here, it's all I've heard, and not just every day but every dinner, every lunch, every sewing circle. Dasha and Alexander. Dasha and Alexander. Poor Dasha, poor Alexander." She shuddered. "Does that seem like the past to you?"

Alexander tried to reason with her. "How is that my fault?"

"Oh, did *they* perhaps ask Dasha to marry you?"

"I told you, I didn't ask her to marry me—"

"Don't play this game with me, Alexander, don't toy with me! You told her you would be married this summer."

"And I did this why?" he said sharply.

"Oh, just stop it! At St. Isaac's we agreed to keep away from each other. Except you couldn't keep away from me, so you made plans to marry my sister."

"He left you alone after that, didn't he?" Alexander declared grimly.

"He would have left me alone if you'd never come to the apartment again, too!" she yelled.

"Which would you have preferred?"

She stopped moving for a moment. "Are you really asking me," she said, panting, "what I would have preferred?" Her eyes were wide. "Are you in all honesty asking me if I would have preferred your marrying my sister to not seeing you again?"

"Yes! At St. Isaac's you were ready to *beg* me not to stay away from you. So don't give me this shit. It's only easy to say now, in retrospect."

"Oh, is that what this is—easy?" Tatiana was walking around the clearing in such furious circles she was almost spinning. With his long strides Alexander kept up with her, but she was making him dizzy.

"Stop moving!" he shouted. She stopped. "I see, so you set the rules and then you don't like that I play by them. Well, live with it."

"I *am* living with it," Tatiana retorted. "Every single damned day since the day I met you."

"Oh, *this* is the fight you want?" Alexander yelled. "This fight? You won't win this one, because this one goes right back to you—"

"I don't want to hear it!"

"Of course you don't!"

Breathing hard, Tatiana said, "You told Dasha you would get married, she told my grandmother, my grandmother told the village. You wrote her a letter saying you were coming to marry her. Words have meaning, you know." Tatiana fell briefly quiet. "Even words you don't mean."

Why did he think she wasn't talking about Dasha now?

"If you felt so strongly about this," he said, "then why didn't you write me a letter back, saying, 'You know what, Alexander, Dasha didn't make it, but I'm right here.' " I would have come sooner. And I wouldn't have lived the six months I lived not knowing if you had survived!"

"After the letter you wrote her," Tatiana said incredulously, "you think I'd be writing you and asking you to come here? You think after that letter I'd be asking you for anything? I'd be an idiot to do that, wouldn't I? An idiot, or—" She stopped.

"Or what?" he demanded.

"Or a child," she said, not looking at him.

Alexander took a deep breath. "Oh, Tania—"

"These games you grown-ups play," she said, backing away from him. "These lies—you're just too good at them." She lowered her head. "Too good for me."

All Alexander wanted that instant was to touch her. Her lips, her anger, her face—he wanted to touch it all. "Tania . . ." he whispered, holding out his hands to her. "What are you talking about? What games, what lies?"

"Why did you come here, why?" she said coldly.

He felt himself about to choke on his words. "How can you even ask me that?"

"How? Because the last thing you wrote was that you were coming to marry Dasha. How much you loved her. How she was the woman for you. The *only* woman for you. I read that letter. That's what you wrote. Because one of the last things I heard you say on Lake Ladoga was that you never—"

"Tatiana!" Alexander screamed, the pin falling to the ground. "What the hell are you talking about? Did you forget you made me promise to lie till the last? *You* made me promise. As late as November I was still saying, let's tell the truth. But you! Lie, lie, lie, Shura, marry her, but promise me you won't break my sister's heart. Do you remember?"

"Yes, and you did commendably well," Tatiana said acidly. "But did you have to be so convincing!"

Running his hand through his hair, Alexander shook his head. "You know I didn't mean it."

"Which part?" she said loudly, stepping up close and looking up at him, angry and unafraid. "The marrying Dasha part? The loving her part? Which part of all those lies do I know you didn't mean?"

"Oh, for God's sake," he exclaimed. "What answer did you want me to give her as she lay dying in your arms?"

"The only answer you could give her," she replied. "The only answer you meant to give, living your life of lies."

"We both live that life of lies, Tatiana—because of you!" he yelled, wanting to tear her hair out. "But you know I didn't mean what I said."

"I thought you didn't mean it," Tatiana said. "I hoped you didn't mean it. But can you understand that it was the only thing I heard all the way on the train to Molotov and all the way across the Volga ice and for two months in the hospital as I struggled for my breath, can you understand that?"

She struggled for her breath now as Alexander stood and watched her, feeling unbearable remorse.

"I wouldn't have cared," Tatiana continued. "I told you, I don't need much, I don't need much comfort." She clenched her fists again. And the hurt was in her eyes. "But I do need a little bit," she said, her voice unsteady. "I need a little bit for me, and then you could have said what you needed to say to Dasha, as you absolutely had to!" She took a breath. "I wanted your eyes on me for a second to let me know that I wasn't nothing, so I could have a little faith. But no," she said. "You treated me like you always do—as if I weren't there."

"I don't treat you as if you aren't there," Alexander said, paling with confusion. "What are you talking about? I hide you from everyone. That's not the same thing."

"Ah, that's a fine difference for a girl like me," said Tatiana. "But if you can hide your heart so well even from my eyes, then maybe you can hide your heart for Dasha, too—the same way. And maybe for Marina and for Zoe, and for every girl you've ever been with. Maybe that's what you grown men do—in private look at us one way and then blatantly deny us in public, as if we mean absolutely nothing." She stared at the ground.

"Are you crazy?" asked Alexander. "Are you forgetting that the only one who did not see the truth was your blinded sister? Private, public, Marina saw it in five minutes." He paused. "On second thought, the only two people who seem not to have seen the truth are your sister and you, Tatiana."

"What truth?" She stood a stride away from him, and her fists were shaking. "I couldn't have done it," she said. "Lied so well. But you are a man. You did. You denied me in your last words, and you denied me in your last glance. And for a while it almost seemed right. How could you feel for me? I thought. Who could feel for anything after that Leningrad . . ." Tatiana paused, panting hard. "But still I wanted to believe in you so much! So when we got your letter to Dasha, I ripped it open, hoping I was wrong, praying that maybe there was a word in it for me—" Tatiana raised her voice. "A single word, a single syllable that I could keep for my own, needing it so desperately, to show me that my entire life had not been a complete lie!" She broke off. "A single word!" she yelled, hitting Alexander with both fists in the chest. "Just one *word*, Alexander!"

He tried to remember what he had written. He could not. But it was her hurting eyes he wanted to heal most of all. He took her into his arms, fighting with him, clutching him, and then crying. "Tania, please. You knew I was in agony—"

But she was so upset and volatile that she wrested herself out of his arms and cried, "I knew this? How did I know this?"

"You are supposed to just know," Alexander said, coming toward her. "That's the whole point of you."

"Well, what's the point of *you*?" she yelled, backing away.

"The point of me," he yelled back, "is that I stood with my arms around you and my whole heart in my eyes in the back of that fucking Ladoga truck and pleaded with you to save yourself for me!"

"How do I know you don't ask every girl you send across the Road of Life to save herself for you with those eyes of yours?"

"Oh, my God, Tatiana."

In a broken voice she said, "I don't know anything other than you. Not how to act, or how to play games, or how to lie, or *anything*." She lowered her head. "You show me one thing in private, and then suddenly you plan to marry my sister. On Ladoga you tell her you never felt for me, you tell her you love only her, you don't look at me as you leave me to face death, and then you don't send a word my way. How in the world do you expect someone like *me* to know what the truth is without a little help from you? All I've ever known in my life is your damn lies!"

"Tatiana!" he cried. "Have you forgotten St. Isaac's?"

"How many other girls went to visit you there, Alexander?"

"Have you forgotten Luga?"

"I was just a damsel in distress," she said bitterly. "Dimitri himself told me how much you liked to help us girls out."

Alexander was about to lose control completely. "What did you think I was doing coming to Fifth Soviet every chance I got, bringing you all my food?" he shouted. "Who did you think I was doing that for?"

"I never said you didn't feel pity for me, Alexander!"

"*Pity?*" he exclaimed. "For fuck's sake, *pity?*"

Folding her arms across her chest, Tatiana said, "That's right."

"You know what?" he said, nearly right up against her. "Pity is too good for you. That's the price you pay for living your life as a lie. Don't like it much, do you?"

"No, I hate it," Tatiana said, looking up and not backing away one centimeter. "And knowing that I hate it, why in the hell did you come here? Just to torture me further?"

"I came because I didn't know Dasha had died!" he yelled. "*You* couldn't be bothered to fucking write me!"

"So you *did* come to marry Dasha," Tatiana said in a calm voice. "Why didn't you just say so?"

Growling helplessly, Alexander clenched his fists and stepped quickly away from her.

"Can't keep all the lies straight in your head, can you?"

"Tatiana, you are completely out of line," he said. "I told you from the first day we met, let's come clean, let's not live this life. Let's choose a different one. I told you that from the start. Let's tell them the truth and live with the consequences. You were the one who said no. I didn't like it. But I said fine."

"No! You did not say fine, Alexander! Had you said fine, you would not have been coming to Kirov every single day against my wishes."

"*Against* your wishes?" he said, staggering back.

Tatiana shook her head at him. "You are unbelievable. What, whose head do you think you won't sway, Alexander Barrington, with your rifle and your height and your life? You think that just because I, a seventeen-year-old child, opened my mouth and my eyes and gaped at you as if I'd never seen anything quite like it, you had the right to ask my sister to marry you? You think because I'm so young that wouldn't break me? You think I need *nothing* from you, while you just take and take and take from me—"

"I don't think you need nothing from me, and I have not taken and taken and taken from you," Alexander said through his own clenched teeth.

"You've taken everything *but* that!" she screamed. "And that you don't deserve!"

He came up close to her and hissed, "I could have taken that, too."

"That's right," she said, furiously shoving him away. "Because you haven't broken me enough."

"Stop shoving me!"

"Stop menacing me! Stay away from me!"

He stood back. "None of this would be happening if you had listened to me from the beginning. None of it! Let's tell them, I told you."

"And I told *you*," Tatiana said vehemently, "that my sister was more important to me than some need of yours I couldn't comprehend. She was more important to me than some need of my own I couldn't understand either. All I wanted was for you to respect my wishes. But you! Oh, you kept coming at me and coming at me and coming at me, and little by little you tore me apart, and when it wasn't enough, you came for me in the hospital and tore me apart some more, and when that wasn't enough, you got me up on the roof of St. Isaac's with you to finish me off—"

"I have not finished you off," he said.

"To finish off my heart for good," continued Tatiana with clenched *everything*. "And you knew it. And when you had it all, and had me, and knew it, that's when you showed me how much I really meant to you by planning to marry my sister!"

"Well, what do you think?" Alexander shouted. "What do you think happens when you can't be fucking bothered to fight from the start for what you want? What do you think happens when you give the people you want away? That's what happens! They go on with their lives, they get married, they have children. You wanted to live that lie!"

"Don't tell me I wanted to live that lie! I was living the only truth I knew. I had a family I did not want to sacrifice for you! That's what I fought for."

Unsteady on his feet, Alexander could not believe the words that were coming out of her. "That was your only truth, Tatiana?"

She blinked and lowered her eyes.

"No," she said. "You came for me, and I did not push you away far enough. How could I? I was—" She broke off. "I was in this with my eyes open, and my eyes were only for you. I hoped you were smarter, but I saw you were not smarter by much, and so I continued with you, knowing that I would stand by you and believe in you. I would give you anything and everything you needed, wanting so little back for myself." She couldn't look at him bravely anymore. "Give me a glance at the end of your proclamation of love to someone else," Tatiana said, "and that would have been enough for me. Give me one word in your letter of love for someone else, and that would have been enough for me. But you didn't feel enough for me to know I might need even so little—"

"Tatiana!" he screamed into her face. "I will stand here and be accused of anything, but don't you dare tell me I didn't feel enough for you! Don't even pretend to yourself you can speak that lie and have it come out of your mouth as the truth. Everything I have fucking done with my life since the day I met you was because of how I felt about you, so if you continue to give me your bullshit now, I swear to God—"

"I won't," she said faintly, but it was too late then.

Alexander grabbed her and shook her. Tatiana felt so vulnerable, so soft in his arms. Utterly defeated by his anger and his remorse and his desire, he pushed her hard away, cursed, picked up his things off the ground, and ran up the hill and through the path.

6

Tatiana ran after him, yelling, "Shura, please stop! Please!"

She couldn't catch up. He disappeared through the woods. She ran all the way home. His things were still there, but he was not.

"What's the matter, Tanechka?" Naira asked, carrying a basket of tomatoes.

"Nothing," Tatiana replied, panting. She took the basket from Naira.

"Where is Alexander?"

"Still at the old house," she said. "Taking the boards off the windows."

"I hope he nails them back," Dusia said, looking up from the Bible, "when he is done. What's he doing that for anyway?"

"I don't know," Tatiana said, turning away so they wouldn't see her face. "Do you need your medicine, Raisa?"

"Yes, please."

Tatiana gave Raisa her medicine for the shakes, medicine that didn't help at all, and then she folded the sheets she had washed yesterday, and then—so afraid he was going to come, take his things, and leave—she hid his tent and rifle in the shed behind the house, and then she went down to the river and washed all his uniforms by hand on the washboard.

Alexander still had not come back.

Tatiana took his helmet into the woods and picked a whole helmetful of

395

blueberries. Returning home, she made a blueberry pie and blueberry *compôte*, a thick fruit drink.

Alexander still hadn't come back.

Tatiana went and caught some fish and made *ukha*, fish soup, for dinner. He once said he really liked *ukha*.

Alexander still hadn't come back.

Tatiana peeled some potatoes, grated them, and made potato pancakes.

Vova came and asked if she wanted to go swimming. She said no and got out some ribbed cotton material and made Alexander a new, larger sleeveless top.

And still he hadn't come back.

Why couldn't he just have stayed and finished their fight? She wasn't going anywhere; she was staying until the end, why couldn't he? The pit of her stomach was so empty and scared. Well, she wasn't going to let him go until they finished it. She didn't care how he lost his temper.

Now it was six o'clock and time to go to the *banya*. She left him a note. *Dearest Shura, If you're hungry, please eat the soup and the pancakes. We're at the bathhouse. Or you could wait for us and we will eat together. On your bed is a new top for you. I hope it fits better. Tania.*

In the bathhouse she scrubbed herself for him until she was glistening pink.

Zoe asked her if Alexander was going to join them by the fire this evening.

"I don't know," said Tatiana. "You'd have to ask *him*."

Zoe said, flinging her great big breasts, "He is quite delicious. Do you think he is feeling awful over Dasha?"

"Yes."

Zoe smiled. "Maybe he needs a little comfort."

Tatiana looked Zoe straight in the face. As if Zoe had any idea about what comfort Alexander needed. "I don't know what you mean," she said coolly.

"No, you wouldn't. Never mind." Zoe laughed and went to get changed.

Tatiana dried off and dressed, brushing her wet hair and leaving it down past her shoulders. She put on a blue print cotton dress she had made; it was thin and sleeveless with a half-open back and a short hemline. When they all came out of the bathhouse, Alexander was waiting for them outside. Tatiana locked her relieved eyes on him for a moment and then, unable to take his expression, looked away.

"There he is!" Naira said. "Where have you been all day?"

Dusia asked, "How are the windows in the house?"

"Windows? What house?" he asked gruffly.

"Vasili Metanov's house. Tania said you were taking the boards off the windows."

"Oh," he said, never taking his darkened eyes off Tatiana. She stood next to Raisa, hoping to hide behind Raisa's shaking.

"Are you hungry? Have you eaten?" Tatiana asked him in her smallest voice. She couldn't find a bigger one.

Mutely he shook his head.

They all started walking home. Axinya took Alexander's arm. Zoe came up close on the other side of him, took his other arm and asked if Alexander wanted to go to the fire.

"No," he replied, pulling away from Zoe and toward Tatiana, bending down to her and whispering, "What did you do with my things?"

"Hid them," she whispered back, her heart throbbing. She wanted to put her hand on him, but she was afraid he'd lose his control, and they would have to have it out in front of everyone.

"Tania makes very good fish soup, Alexander," Naira said. "You like fish soup?"

Dusia piped up, "And her blueberry pie is out of this world. I'm so hungry."

"Why?" Alexander whispered.

"Why what?" Dusia asked.

"Never mind," Alexander said, moving away from them all.

When they got home, Tatiana busied herself with setting the table. She looked up on her bed to see if he had read the note and taken the shirt. The note was gone. The shirt remained where she had left it.

Alexander came inside. The four ladies were out on the porch. "Where are my things?" he asked.

"Shura—"

"Stop it," he snapped. "Give me my things so I can leave."

"Alexander, can you come here?" Naira stuck her head in. "We need your help opening this bottle of vodka. The cap seems to be stuck."

He went out on the porch. Tatiana's hands were trembling as badly as Raisa's. She dropped one of the dishes. The metal plate made quite a clang when it hit the wooden floor.

Vova arrived. The porch was filled with laughing voices.

Alexander came inside and opened his mouth to speak. Tatiana motioned to the back of him. Vova stood in the doorway. "Tanyusha, do you need help? Can I carry something to the table for you?"

"Yes, Tanyusha," said Alexander bitingly, "can Vova carry something for you?"

"No, thank you. Can you give me a minute, please?"

"Come on," said Vova to Alexander, who hadn't moved. "You heard her. She wants a minute."

"Yes," said Alexander, without turning around. "A minute with me."

Vova reluctantly left the room.

"Where are my things?"

"Shura, why are you leaving?"

"Why? There is no place for me here. You've made that abundantly clear.

I can't believe you haven't packed for me, the way you feel. I don't need to be told twice, Tania."

Her lips were trembling. "Stay and have dinner with us."

"No."

"Please, Shura," she said, her voice breaking. "I made you potato pancakes." She took a step to him.

"No," he said, blinking.

"You can't leave. We haven't finished."

"Oh, we've finished."

"What can I say to make it better?"

"You've said it all very clearly. Now good-bye would be good."

The food table was between them. Tatiana came around on his side. "Shura," she said quietly, "please let me touch you."

"No." He backed farther away.

Naira stuck her head through the open door. "Is dinner ready?"

"Almost, Naira Mikhailovna," said Tatiana.

"I thought you weren't going to leave until you fixed me?" she said faintly. "Fix me, Shura."

"You told me yourself there isn't enough of me to fix what's wrong inside you. Well, you've made a believer out of me. Now, where are my things?"

"Shura—"

Coming closer to her, Alexander said through gritted teeth, "What do you want, Tania? You want a scene?"

"No," she said, trying very hard not to cry.

His face was near her. "A loud, ugly scene like the kind you're used to?"

"No," she whispered, not looking at him.

"Just give me my things, and I'll go quietly, and you won't have to explain a single word to your friends and your lover."

When she didn't move, Alexander said, much louder, "Now!"

Embarrassed and upset, Tatiana led him outside to the shed behind the house, out of everyone's view.

"Where are you going, Tanechka? Are we going to eat soo—"

"I'll be right back!" Tatiana yelled, her shoulders shaking. When they were behind the house, Tatiana tried to take hold of Alexander's hand, but he roughly ripped his arm away from her. She staggered but did not back off. Coming in front of him quickly, she wrapped her arms around his waist. He tried to push her away. "Please don't go," she said, looking up at him with pleading eyes. "Please. I beg you. I don't want you to go. I waited for you every minute of every day since I left the hospital. Please." She put her forehead on his chest.

Alexander didn't say anything. Tatiana didn't look up. His hands remained on her bare arms.

Holding him tightly, Tatiana said, "God, Alexander! How can you be so thick? Can't you see why I didn't write you?"

"Not at all. Why?"

She inhaled his smell, her face still in his chest. "I was so afraid that if I told you about Dasha, you wouldn't come to Lazarevo at all." She wished she were braver and could look at him, but she didn't want to see him be angry with her anymore. Taking his hand, she placed it on her cheek, and when his warmth gave her strength, she looked up at him. "Leningrad nearly finished us all off. I thought that maybe if you didn't know about her and came anyway, and I got healthy again, like last summer, maybe your feeling for me would come back—"

"Come *back?*" Alexander said hoarsely. "What are you thinking?" His hand remained on her cheek. His other hand, though, wrapped itself on her bare back, his fingers fanning her, grasping her, and moving on her flesh, pressing him to her. "Can't you see . . ." he said and broke off. He couldn't say any more. She felt it. And he didn't need to. She felt that, too.

At last Alexander spoke. "Tatia, I will earn your forgiveness. I will fix everything. I will do right by you, but you have to let me. You can't shut me out like this—you just can't."

"I'm sorry," Tatiana said. "Please understand." She hugged him tighter. "Just too many lies for me, too much doubt."

"Look at me."

She lifted her eyes to him.

His arms around her, Alexander said, "Tania, what doubt? I am here only for you."

"Then please stay," she said. "Stay for me."

Breathing hard, Alexander bent his head to her, and she gave him her wet hair to kiss. His lips stayed on her for a few moments, and then he said, "What is this, Lake Ladoga?"

"Shura," Tatiana said, "there is a houseful of people."

His fingertips were pressing into her bare shoulder blades so emphatically they were making her feeble.

"Lift your face to me this instant."

She lifted her face to him that instant.

"Tania, could we eat, please?" Naira's loud voice from the porch was hungry and irritated. "Everything is burning!"

Alexander kissed her so fiercely that for a moment Tatiana became supported only by his arms around her. Her numb legs could not hold her up.

"What is she doing out there? We're all starving. Tatiana!"

They heaved themselves away from each other, Tatiana didn't know how, retrieved his things from the shed, and went inside.

Tatiana poured soup for Alexander first, placing the bowl right in front of him and handing him the spoon. Then she served everyone else while Alexander waited for her to sit down before he took his first bite.

"So, Alexander," said Vova, "what does a captain in the Red Army do?"

"Well, I don't know what a captain in the Red Army does. I know what *I* do."

"Alexander, do you need some more fish?" Tatiana asked.

"Yes, please."

"What do *you* do?" asked Vova.

"Yes, tell us, Alexander," said Axinya. "The village is dying to know."

"I'm in heavy weapons, in a destroyer brigade. Do you know what that is?" Everybody but Tatiana shook their heads.

"I command an armored company of men. We provide extra support for the rifle guards." Alexander swallowed his soup. "At least, we're supposed to."

"What's extra support?" asked Vova. "Tanks?"

"Tanks, yes. Armored cars. Tania, are there more pancakes? We also operate antiaircraft machine guns called Zeniths, and mortars, and other field artillery. Cannons, howitzers, heavy machine guns. I myself stand behind a Katyusha, a rocket launcher."

"Impressive," said Vova. "So it's the best job. Less dangerous than the rifle *frontovik?*"

"More dangerous than anything. Who do you think the Germans are trying to knock out of position first—a guy with a slow, bolt-action Nagant or me with a mortar that pummels them with fifteen bombs a minute?"

Tatiana said, "Alexander, you want some more?"

"No, Tatiasha—" He stopped. She stopped. "I'm full, Tania, thank you."

"Alexander," said Zoe, "we hear Stalingrad is going to fall."

"If Stalingrad falls, we lose the war," said Alexander. "Any more vodka?" Tatiana poured him a shot.

Dusia said, "Alexander, how many men are we prepared to lose in Stalingrad to stop Hitler?"

"As many as it takes."

She crossed herself.

Red-faced, Vova said excitedly, "Moscow was quite a bloodbath."

Tatiana heard Alexander suck in his breath. Oh, no, she thought. No scene, please.

"Vova," said Alexander, leaning in front of Tatiana—who pressed into his side—to glare at Vova. "Do you know what a bloodbath is? Moscow had 800,000 troops before the battle for the capital started in October. Do you know how many were left when they stopped Hitler? Ninety thousand. Do you know how many men were killed just in the first six months of the war? How many young men were killed before Tania left Leningrad? Four million," he said loudly. "One of those young men could be you, Vova. So don't go around calling it a bloodbath, as if it were a game."

Everyone at the table was quiet. Tatiana, nested into Alexander, said, "You want more to drink?"

"No," he said. "I'm done."

"Well, I'll just go and clear—"

Alexander lowered his arm under the table and placed his hand on Tatiana's leg, shaking his head ever so slightly and keeping her in place.

Tatiana remained in place. Alexander did not take away his hand. At first her cotton dress was between his hand and her thigh, but Alexander obviously did not like that, because he moved the dress up, just enough to grasp her bare thigh with his bare hand. The aching in her stomach intensified.

Naira said, "Tanechka, aren't you going to clear up, dear? We can't wait for your pie. And some tea."

Alexander's hand squeezed her a little harder and moved up.

Tatiana clenched her teeth. In exactly one second she was going to moan right at the dinner table, in front of four old women.

Alexander said, "Tatiana cooked wonderfully for us. She's outdone herself. She's tired. Why don't we give her a break. Zoe, Vova—maybe you could clear up?"

Naira said, "But, Alexander, you don't understand—"

"I understand *extremely* well." Alexander's hold on Tatiana's leg did not abate.

Tatiana grabbed the edge of the table with her fingers. "Shura, please," she said hoarsely.

His hand gripped her thigh harder. Her hands gripped the table harder.

"No, Tania," Alexander said. "No. It's the very least they can do." He stared across to Naira. "Don't you think, Naira Mikhailovna?"

Naira said, "I thought Tanechka enjoyed doing the small things she does."

Dusia agreed. "Yes. We thought it brought her pleasure."

Alexander nodded. "Dusia, it does bring her pleasure. Next she'll be bending down and washing your feet. But don't you think the disciples need to pour drink for Jesus every once in a while?"

Dusia stammered, "What does Jesus have to do with anything?"

Alexander's steel grip tightened.

Tatiana opened her mouth and—

"Fine," snapped Zoe, "we'll clear up."

With a gentle pat, Alexander let go of Tatiana's thigh.

Tatiana breathed out. After a few moments her fingers managed to let go of the table. She not only could not look at Alexander but couldn't meet anyone else's eyes either.

"Zoe, Vova, thank you," said Alexander, grinning at Tatiana, who remained motionless.

"I'm going for a smoke," he said. Tatiana could not even acknowledge him.

After he left, the old ladies leaned in to Tatiana and lowered their voices. "Tania, he is very aggressive," said Naira.

Dusia said, "There is no God in the Red Army, that's the trouble. The war has made him hard, I tell you, hard."

Axinya said, "Yes, but look how protective he is of our Tanechka. It's adorable."

Tatiana looked at them with incomprehension. What were they saying? What were they talking about? What just happened?

"Tania, did you hear us?"

She stood up. Her sole defender in the world, her rifle guard, her battle brigade would have her unqualified support. "Alexander is not hard, Dusia. He is completely right. I should not be doing everything around here."

They had tea and blueberry pie, which was so good that soon there wasn't any pie left. After the old women went out for a smoke, Zoe, squeezing Alexander's arm and smiling coyly, asked once again if he wanted to go to the fire. Alexander took his arm away and said no once again.

Tatiana wanted Zoe to go away.

"Oh, come on," said Zoe. "Even Tania goes. With Vova," she added with emphasis.

"Not anymore," whispered Alexander, looking at Tatiana, who was putting sugar in his tea.

"Tania, tell Alexander that awful joke you told last week. No, it was so awful, we nearly died," said Vova.

"I thought I'd heard all of Tania's awful jokes," said Alexander. There was something so achingly familiar and comforting about sitting pressed against his large arm that Tatiana felt a need to put her head on him. She didn't.

"Tell him the joke, Tania."

"I don't think so."

Vova tickled Tatiana. "Come on! He is going to die."

"Vova, stop," said Tatiana, glancing at Alexander, who intently sipped his tea and said nothing.

"I'm not telling him," Tatiana said, suddenly embarrassed. She knew that Alexander would not be pleased with the joke. She did not want to displease him—not even for a single stupid moment.

"No, no." Alexander turned to her and put down his cup. "I love your jokes." He smiled. "I want to hear."

Sighing and looking at the table, Tatiana said, "Chapayev and Petka are fighting in Spain. Chapayev says to Petka, 'Why are the people screaming? Who are they welcoming?' 'Oh, some Dolores Ebanulli,' replies Petka. 'Well, what's she yelling?' asks Chapayev. Petka replies, 'She yells, "It's better to do it on your feet than on your knees." ' "

Vova and Zoe roared with laughter.

Alexander sat stonily, tapping on his teacup. "These are the kinds of jokes you now tell at the fire on Saturday nights?"

Tatiana didn't reply and didn't look at him. She knew he wouldn't like that joke.

Vova shoved her lightly. "Tania, we're going tonight, aren't we?"

"No, Vova, not tonight."

"What do you mean? We always go."

Before Tatiana had a chance to say anything, Alexander, with his hands still around his teacup, looked at Vova and said, "She said not tonight. How many more times will she have to say it before you hear it? Zoe, how many more times will *I* have to say it before you hear it?"

Vova and Zoe stared at Alexander and at Tatiana.

"What's going on?" Vova said in a confused voice.

"Go on," Alexander said. "Both of you. Go to your fire. But quick."

Vova opened his mouth to speak, but Alexander stood up from the table, leveled a look at Vova, and said calmly and slowly, "I said go on," in a voice that invited no argument. He got none. Vova and Zoe left.

Tatiana shook her head in amazement, staring at the table. Alexander bent to her, saying huskily, "*Like* that?" And kissed her on the head and went out to smoke.

After laying out her bedding on the porch, Tatiana helped the old ladies into bed. When she was done, Alexander was still sitting on the bench outside the house. The crickets were noisy tonight. Tatiana could hear the distant howl of a coyote, the murmuring hoot of an owl. She went to wash the dessert dishes.

"Tania, will you stop fussing and come here."

Her hands still wet, she nervously stepped up to him. The relentless throbbing in the pit of her stomach would not subside, not for dinner or the dishes, not for the old women or the laundry, not for *anything*.

"Closer," Alexander said, watching her for a few seconds. He dropped his cigarette on the ground and put his hands on her hips, bringing her between his open legs.

Tatiana was barely standing.

Holding on to her, Alexander looked up for a moment and then pressed his head into her rib cage just below her breasts.

Tatiana, not knowing what to do with her hands, placed them carefully on Alexander's head. His hair was short and thick, straight and dry. Tatiana liked how it felt. She closed her eyes, trying to breathe normally. "Are you all right?" she asked in a whisper.

"I am, yes," Alexander replied. "Tatia, instead of thinking about yourself, couldn't you have once thought about me? Couldn't you have just imagined me for five seconds, and what I was going through for six months?"

"I could have. I'm sorry," she said.

"Had you done that, thought of me for five seconds, and written to me, you would have gotten letters back that would have eased every single one of your fears. And you would have eased mine."

"I know. I'm sorry."

"I honestly thought that there could be only two explanations for your silence. One, you were dead. Two, you had"—he paused—"found someone else. I never imagined that any of the lies I spoke would get under your skin. I thought you had the ability to see clear to the truth."

"*I* had that ability?" Tatiana said softly, caressing his head. "Where is *your* ability?" Found someone else? she thought. "Honestly."

He rubbed his forehead from side to side against her. "What did Axinya call you? A warm bun?"

Tatiana couldn't breathe. "Yes," she muttered. "A warm bun."

Alexander's hands on her hips tightened. "A small warm bun," he whispered.

Very, very gently, Tatiana stroked his hair with her shaking fingers. Her breath was so shallow it was not getting air into her lungs.

"This is too close, even by Fifth Soviet standards," Alexander said at last.

"What?" she whispered, trying not to disturb the night. "Us? Or this house?"

"Us?" he said with surprise, looking up at her. "No. This house."

Tatiana shivered.

"Cold?"

She nodded, hoping he wouldn't touch her *burning* skin.

"Want to go in?"

Reluctantly Tatiana nodded again. All she wanted was for his hands to remain on her, tight around her hips, tight around her waist, around her back, around her legs, anywhere, everywhere, but tight and on her and permanent.

Alexander lifted his head to her. Parting her mouth, she was about to bend—

Suddenly Tatiana heard the shuffling of Naira Mikhailovna on the porch. Alexander lowered his hands and his head. Against her will she stepped away from him, just as Naira descended the steps, mumbling, "Forgot to go one last time."

"Of course," said Alexander, not even bothering to smile.

Naira stared at Tatiana for a moment. "Tanechka, what are you doing? Go get ready for bed, dear. It's so late already, and you know how early we wake up."

"I will, Naira Mikhailovna."

When Naira went around the corner, Tatiana let her glance stop at Alexander, who was looking at her unhappily. She shrugged, also unhappily. They went inside. Getting a big white shirt out of her trunk, Tatiana thought, where to change? Alexander had no such reservations. He took off his shirt right in front of her, leaving on his linen trousers as he hopped up onto the bed. Tatiana had never seen Alexander without his uniform, his shirt, his long johns; she had never seen Alexander bare. He was very muscled. Was she ever going to get her breath back? She did not think so.

She couldn't take off her dress and put on her nightshirt. She decided to leave the dress on.

"Good night," she said, dimming the kerosene lamp. Alexander did not reply.

Naira walked through the house to her bedroom saying, "Good night."

Tatiana said good night. Alexander didn't make a sound.

Still in her dress, Tatiana was under the blanket on the porch sofa when she heard Alexander's deep voice from inside call for her. "Tatia."

She got up and stood shyly in the doorway.

"Come here," Alexander said, his muted voice cracking.

All she wanted was to go to him. But she was so afraid. She walked around the table.

"Stand on the hearth," Alexander told her.

Tatiana stood, her face next to his, and before he had a chance to whisper or open his mouth, she kissed him, her hands clutching his head.

"Come here," he breathed out. She felt him trying to pull her up.

"Oh, Shura, I can't . . . There will be the biggest fuss . . ." She couldn't stop kissing him either.

"Tania, I don't give a shit if it's in tomorrow's papers. Right now come here to me." He pulled her up by her arms, and once she was up, he entwined her with all his limbs, his whole enormous body swallowing her as they kissed ravenously.

"God, Tatia," Alexander whispered. "Oh, God, I've missed you so much."

"Me, too," she replied, her lips open, her hands stroking his back. "So much." For a moment he stopped kissing her and moving against her, as he embraced her in a nest inside him. Tatiana could not believe how remarkable it felt to touch Alexander's naked back and hard shoulders and hard arms.

He was crushing her to him, his lips more demanding, his insistent hands all over her. He had only two hands? Then why were they everywhere at once? She was enveloped in him, unable to keep her eyes open, yet all she wanted was to see him, to not miss a second of him. Pulling up her dress to her waist, Alexander touched her bare leg. Involuntarily her legs spread apart slightly, and Tatiana moaned into his lips.

Smiling, Alexander whispered, "Oh, Tania. Moan, but not too loud. Wait, not so loud."

Her legs opened a little more. His hand caressed the inside of her thigh.

"No," she groaned. *Stop, please.*

He licked her lips. "Tania, your thighs . . ." Alexander whispered. His hand climbed on her.

Tatiana tried to pull away from him, but there was nowhere for her to go. "Shura," she whispered. "Please. *Stop.*"

"I can't," he said. "Are they sound sleepers?"

"No, not at all," she whispered. "They wake up at the sound of a cricket in the house. They come outside five times to go to the outhouse. Please. I can't keep quiet. You'd have to suffocate me to keep me quiet."

They kept whispering into each other's wet mouths.

"Stop," she whispered. "Stop." They could not stop.

Alexander's hand reluctantly came away from her leg, resting on her bare stomach under her dress. "I like the dress," he whispered.

"You're not touching the dress."

"No? Feels nice. Soft. Take it off."

"No," she said, pushing him away slightly.

They lay relatively quiet for a few minutes as they got their breath back.

Alexander's fingers went back to rubbing her leg. "Stop rubbing my leg," Tatiana whispered. She throbbed from her thighs to her navel. "Stop touching me."

"Can't. I've waited too long for you." Bending over her, he pressed his lips to her throat. "You don't want me, Tania?" he whispered. "Tell me you don't want me." His hands were tugging the dress down from her shoulders. "Take it off."

"Please," she panted. "Shura, come on, I can't keep quiet. You *have* to stop."

He wouldn't stop. The dress came off one arm, then off the other.

Alexander took her hand and put it on his chest. "Tania, feel my heart! Don't you want to lie against my chest?" he said imploringly. "Your bare breasts on my chest, your heart next to my heart. Come on, just for a second. Then you can put the dress back on."

Tatiana silently stared at him in the dark, at his blazing bronze eyes, at his moist mouth. How could she say no to Alexander? She lifted her arms. Alexander slipped the dress over her head. She went to cover her breasts, and his hands stopped her. "Keep your hands down."

He lay on his back and said, "Come, lie on top of me."

"You don't want to lie on top of *me?*" Tatiana asked softly.

He pulled her to him. "Not if you want me to stop."

Groaning, Tatiana lay down carefully against his chest.

"Oh, Tania," Alexander said intensely, his arms around her. "Do you feel that?"

"I do," she whispered, her own heart ready to burst.

His hands ran over her back down to her hips, caressing her through her panties, pulling them down a little, caressing her bare bottom. Pushing her up from him, Alexander fondled her breasts. "I have been dreaming of your beautiful breasts for a year," he said, smiling, breathing through his parted mouth. Tatiana wanted to tell him that she had been dreaming of his beautiful, unstoppable hands on her for a year but couldn't speak. She wanted to tell him that she had been dreaming of his beautiful, unstoppable mouth on her nipples for a year but couldn't speak. What she wanted to do was lean over him and put her nipple into his mouth. She was too shy to do that. All she could do was watch his face and pant.

Alexander closed his eyes. "Tatia, *please*, keep quiet. I can't wait any longer." He pulled at her nipples. She moaned so loudly that he stopped, but not for long. Pushing her off him, Alexander lay her down onto her back. "Look at you," he whispered. He sucked her nipples for a moment. Tatiana's hands were grasping at the sheet. One of Alexander's hands went around her mouth, the other went on her thigh. "Tania," he said, "you think I'm hungry?"

"Hmm . . ." she panted into his palm.

"I'm not hungry," Alexander whispered. "I'm *famished*. Watch out for me. Now, don't make a single sound," he said, getting on top of her. "Tania, God . . . I'll cover your mouth, just like this, and you hold on to my arms, just like this, and I'm going to—just like this—"

Tatiana cried out so loudly that Alexander stopped, fell back on the bed, put his arm over his face, and groaned.

They lay next to each other, only their legs touching, hers bare, his still in his trousers. His arm remained around his face.

Reluctantly Tatiana put her dress back on.

"I'm going to die," he whispered to her. "*Die*, Tatiana."

You're going to die? she thought, beginning to crawl to the edge to get down.

Alexander stopped her. "Where are you going? Sleep with me."

"No, Shura."

"What!" He smiled, still panting. "You don't trust me?"

"Not for a second." She smiled back.

"I promise I'll be good."

"No, they'll come out, they'll see."

"See what? What are they going to do?" He wasn't letting go of her arms. "Tatia, right here," he whispered, tapping on his chest, "just like you did in Luga. Remember? You called me over, you said, come near me. Well, now I'm telling you to come."

Tatiana crawled to him and put her head into the crook of his arm. Alexander pulled the blankets over them and hugged her. She placed her hand on his smooth bare chest, feeling his rapid heart. "Shura, darling . . ."

"I'll be all right," he said, sounding as if he wouldn't be.

"Just like in Luga." She rubbed his chest gently.

"Maybe a little lower? Just kidding, just kidding," he quickly said when Tatiana stopped. "Love your hair against me," Alexander whispered, stroking her head, kissing her temple. "Love everything of yours against me."

"Don't, Shura, please," Tatiana muttered, kissing his chest and closing her eyes. She felt infinite comfort lying in his arms. His fingers caressing her head were forcing her eyes shut. "That feels nice," she murmured.

Minutes passed. Minutes or—

Maybe seconds.

Moments.

Blink.

"Tania," Alexander said, "are you asleep?"

"No," she said, and then they looked at each other and smiled. She parted her mouth to kiss him, and he shook his head and said, "No. Keep your lips away, if you want me away."

Tatiana kissed his shoulder and stroked him while he stroked her. "Shura," she whispered, "I'm so happy you came for me."

"I know. Me, too."

She rubbed her lips against his skin.

"Tania," whispered Alexander, "want to talk?"

"Yes," she replied.

"Tell me. Start at the beginning. Don't stop until you finish."

Tatiana started at the beginning but couldn't get past the sled near the ice hole in the lake.

Neither could Alexander.

Then she was asleep and woke up when the rooster crowed.

7

"Oh, my," she said, trying to extricate herself from him. "Let go. I have to go, quick."

Alexander was profoundly asleep and not moving. She noticed that about him. He was a good sleeper. She managed to move out from under his arm and jump down from the side of the stove.

Tatiana put on a clean dress and ran to get the water from the well, and ran to milk the goat, and ran to exchange goat's milk for some cow's milk. When she came back to the house, Alexander was already up and shaving. "Good morning," he said to her, smiling.

"Good morning," she said, too embarrassed to look at him. "Here, let me help." She sat in the chair in front of him, holding a small broken mirror to her chest as he shaved. He kept cutting himself every few seconds, as if the knife he was using weren't sharp. "You're going to kill yourself with that thing," said Tatiana. "What do they issue you in the army? Maybe you should grow your beard back."

"It's not the knife," he said. "The knife is very sharp."

"What is it, then?"

"Nothing, nothing."

She saw him staring at her breasts.

"Alexander . . ." she said, putting the mirror down.

"Oh, now that it's daylight, I'm suddenly Alexander again?" he said.

Tatiana couldn't look at him but couldn't help smiling either. She felt so exhilarated this morning, she had practically skipped home carrying the two pails of milk.

Alexander made coffee. He poured her a cup, and they sat silently outside in the breathy morning and drank the hot liquid, their bodies lightly touching. "It's a nice morning," she said quietly.

"It's a glorious morning," he said, turning to her and beaming.

Naira called her, and Tatiana went to attend to her chores while Alexander collected his things. "What are you doing?" she asked with a twitch of anxiety when he came outside.

"We're getting out of here," he said. "Right now."

"We are?" A smile lit up her face.

"Yes."

"I can't, I have to do laundry. I have to make breakfast."

"Tania, that's my point exactly. I have to come before laundry. I have to come before breakfast." Alexander stared at her.

She backed away. "Look," she said, "help me. I'll be done so much faster if you help me."

"And then you'll come with me?"

"Yes," she said, almost inaudibly. But Alexander smiled at her. She knew he had heard.

She made eggs and potatoes for everyone. Alexander gulped down his food and said, "Let's go do the laundry."

Quickly he carried the basket of clothes to the river. Tatiana carried the washboard and soap. She could hardly keep up.

"So since when do you make rude jokes in the presence of a whole group of young people?" Alexander asked.

Tatiana shook her head. "Shura, it was just a stupid joke. I didn't realize it was going to upset you."

"Yes you did. That's why you didn't want to tell it in front of me."

She ran alongside him. "I didn't want you to be upset."

"Why would I be upset? Have I ever been upset by your other jokes?"

Tatiana kept quiet before she answered him because she wanted to figure out what it was that was obviously still niggling him. That the joke was inappropriate? That it was rude? That she told the joke to Vova? To strangers Alexander didn't know? That it was out of her character? That it didn't fit in with what he knew about her? Yes, Tatiana decided. It was the last. He brought it up now because he was worried about something. She said nothing until they got to the river. "I barely know what the joke means," she said.

He glanced at her. "But you know just enough what it means?"

Aha, thought Tatiana. He *is* worried about me. She didn't reply, stepping into the water and wetting the washboard and the soap.

Alexander watched her while he smoked. "So how do you keep your white dress from getting wet?"

"The bottom gets a little wet. What?" She blushed. "What are you looking at?"

"The whole dress doesn't get wet?" He was grinning.

409

"Well, no. I don't stand and wash clothes in water up to my neck."

Stubbing out his cigarette and taking off his shirt and boots, Alexander said, "Here, let me. Just hand me the clothes, will you?"

There was something so endearing and incomprehensible about him, a captain in the Red Army standing knee deep in the Kama, shirtless, his big soapy arms immersed in women's work, while Tatiana stood dry as gin and handed him dirty clothes. She found it so amusing, in fact, that when she saw him drop a pillowcase in the river and bend to pick it up, she tiptoed up to him and gave him a great shove. Alexander toppled over into the water.

When he came back up, Tatiana was laughing so hard it took her a few seconds to run up the riverbank away from him. Alexander caught her in three strides.

"Not very good balance, big man," Tatiana said, laughing. "What if I were a Nazi?"

Saying nothing, he carried her to the river.

"No, instantly put me down," she said, "I'm wearing a nice dress."

"You are," he said, flinging her into the water.

She came up soaked. "Now look what you've done," she said, splashing him. "I have nothing to go back in."

Alexander caught her in his arms and kissed her, lifting her into the air. Tatiana felt them both slipping back, back, back, and they fell in, and when they came up for air, all decorum gone, Tatiana jumped on him to dunk him, but she just didn't weigh enough to push him down. He threw her off him and held her head for a few seconds underwater while she grabbed for his leg. "Do you give up?" he asked, pulling her head out.

"Never!" she yelped, and he pushed her back down.

"Do you give up?"

"Never!"

Alexander pushed her back down.

After the fourth time, all out of breath, she said, "Wait, the clothes, the clothes!"

The laundry—undergarments, pillowcases—was all floating cheerfully by.

Alexander went after them. Dripping and laughing, Tatiana went back on shore.

He walked out of the water, dropped the clothes on the ground, and came for her. "What?" she said, dizzied by his expression. "What?"

"*Look* at you," he said hotly. "Look at your nipples, look at your body in that dress."

He lifted her. "Wrap your legs around me."

"What do you mean?" she said, wrapping her arms around his neck and kissing him.

"I mean, open your legs and wrap them around me." Holding her with one hand under her bottom, he moved her leg around his waist with the other hand. "Like this."

"Shura, I . . . put me down."

"No."

Their wet lips would not stop.

When they opened their eyes, Alexander *had* to put Tatiana down, because six women from the village were standing at the clearing, holding their clothes baskets, staring at them with a look of perplexed and frankly disapproving confusion.

"We were just leaving," Tatiana muttered as Alexander draped something wet over her shoulders to cover her see-through dress. She never wore a bra, didn't own one, and for the first time in her life she was aware of her nipples poking out and being seen through a sheer item of clothing. It was as if suddenly she saw herself with Alexander's eyes.

"Well, that will be all over Lazarevo tomorrow," she said. "Could it be any more humiliating?"

"I would say yes," said Alexander, leaning into her. "They could have come three minutes later."

Turning bright red, Tatiana didn't respond. Laughing, he put his arm around her.

When they got to the house, Tatiana in a wet dress and Alexander in wet trousers and nothing else, the old ladies looked mortified. "The clothes floated away," Tatiana explained—unsatisfactorily, she felt. "We had to dive in and rescue them."

"Well, I've never heard of such a thing happening," mumbled Dusia, crossing herself. "In all my years of living."

Alexander disappeared into the house, emerging five minutes later dressed in his khaki army trousers, black army boots, and the white ribbed sleeveless top Tatiana had sewn for him. She peered at him through the sheets she was haphazardly hanging. He was crouching as he rummaged through his rucksack. She watched Alexander in profile, his bare muscled arms, his soldier's body, his spiky wet black hair, a cigarette in the corner of his lips—Tatiana's breath was taken away from her, he looked so beautiful. He turned his head to her and smiled.

"I have a dry dress for you," he said, and out of his rucksack he produced her white dress with red roses.

He told her how he had retrieved it from Fifth Soviet.

"I don't think it'll fit me anymore," she said, very moved. "But maybe I'll try it on another day?"

"Fine," Alexander said, stuffing it back into his rucksack. "You can wear it for me another day." He picked up his rifle and all his belongings. "You don't need anything. You're done here. Let's go."

"Where are we going?"

"Away from here," he said, lowering his voice. "Where we can be uninterrupted and alone."

They stared at each other.

"Bring money," he said.

"I thought you said we didn't need anything?"

"And bring your passport. We might go to Molotov."

The immense excitement Tatiana felt vanquished all guilt as she told the four ladies she was leaving. Naira said, "Are you going to be back for dinner?"

Slinging his rifle on his back and taking Tatiana by the hand, Alexander said, "Probably not."

"But, Tania, our sewing circle is today at three."

"Yes . . ." Alexander drew out. "Tania won't be joining you today. But you ladies have a great session."

They ran down to the river. Tatiana never even looked back.

"Where are we going?"

"Your grandparents' house."

"Why there? It's such a mess."

"We'll see about that."

"And we had such a fight there yesterday."

"No." He gazed at her. "You know what we had there yesterday?"

Tatiana knew. She made no reply but held his hand tighter.

When they got to the clearing, Tatiana walked inside the *izba*, which was empty but spotless. It was a one-room cabin with four long windows and a great big furnace stove in the center that took up half the room. There was not an item of furniture, but the wooden floor had been mopped, the windows were clean, and even the sheer white curtains had been washed and dried and no longer smelled moldy. Tatiana peeked out. Alexander was on his knees driving a tent stake into the ground. His back was to her. She put her hand on her heart. Come on, calm down, she told herself.

Walking outside, she collected some twigs into a bundle in case he wanted to make a fire.

Tatiana was paralyzed by fear and love, walking around the sandy pine-needle banks of the river Kama during a sunlit noon in June.

She took off her sandals and put her feet into the cool water. She could not go near Alexander now, but maybe later they could go swimming. "Watch out!" she heard from behind her. Alexander sprinted into the water and dove in, wearing just his army skivvies.

"Tania, want to go swimming?" he called to her.

Her heart pounding, she shook her head. "I see you know how to swim very well," she said, watching him do the backstroke.

He lifted his face to her from the water. "I know how to swim," he said. "Come in, I'll race you." He grinned. "Underwater. All the way to the other side."

If she weren't so nervous, she would have grinned back and then taken him up on it.

Alexander came out, pulling back his wet hair. His naked chest, his naked arms, his naked legs glistened. He was laughing; to Tatiana he appeared to be glowing from the inside out. She couldn't tear her eyes away from his taut, magnificent body. His wet skivvies clung to him—

No, she was not going to make it.

"Feels good," Alexander said, coming up to her. "Come on, let's swim."

Tatiana shook her head, backing away on unsteady legs to the edge of the clearing, where she picked some blueberries off the low bushes. Please, calm down, she kept repeating to herself. Please.

"Tatia," he called quietly from right behind her, and she turned around. He was drying himself off. She handed him some blueberries; he took them but didn't let go of her hand, gently pulling her down to the grass. "You sweet girl, sit down for a minute."

Tatiana sat on the grass, and Alexander knelt in front of her. Leaning forward, he very softly kissed her lips. Tatiana stroked his arms. She could barely breathe.

"Tatia . . . Tatiasha," he said huskily, taking her hands and kissing them, kissing her wrists and the insides of her forearms.

"Yes?" she said, just as huskily.

"We're alone together."

"I know," she replied, suppressing a moan.

"We have *privacy*."

"Hmm."

"*Privacy*, Tania!" Alexander said intensely. "For the first time in our life you and I have real *privacy*. We had it yesterday. And we have it today."

She couldn't take the emotion in his crème brûlée eyes. She lowered her gaze.

"Look at me."

"I can't," she whispered.

Alexander cupped her small face in his massive hands. "Are you . . . scared?"

"Terrified."

"No. Please, don't be scared of me." He kissed her deeply on the lips, so deeply, so fully, so lovingly, that Tatiana felt the aching pit inside her open up and flare upward. She tottered, physically unable to continue sitting upright. "Tatiasha," he said, "why are you so beautiful? Why?"

"I'm a rag," she said. "Look at you."

He hugged her. "God, what a blessing." Pulling away, Alexander took her hands. "Tania, you are my miracle, you know that, don't you? You are the one God sent me to give me faith." He paused. "He sent you to redeem me, to comfort me, and to heal me—and that's just so far," he added with a smile. "I'm barely able to hold myself together right now, I want to make love to you so much . . ." Here he stopped. "I know you're afraid. I will never hurt you. Will you come into my tent with me?"

"Yes," Tatiana said, softly but audibly.

Alexander carried her in his arms to his tent, setting her down on his blanket and closing the tent flaps behind them. It was subdued and dusky inside, with only the barest sunlight filtering in through the open ties. "I would have brought you inside the nice, clean house," he said, smiling, "but we have no quilts, no pillows, and it's all wood and a hard furnace top."

"Mmm," Tatiana muttered. "Tent is good." She could have been on a marble floor of the Peterhof Palace for all she cared.

Alexander was hugging her to him, but all she wanted was to be lying down in front of him. How did he do that? "Shura," she whispered.

"Yes," he whispered back, kissing her neck.

But he wasn't . . . he wasn't doing anything else, as if he were waiting, or thinking, or . . .

Alexander pulled away from her, and she saw by the reserve in his eyes that something was troubling him.

"What's the matter?"

He couldn't look at her. "You said so many upset things to me yesterday . . . not that I don't deserve all of them . . ."

"You don't deserve *all* of them." She smiled. "What?"

He took a deep breath.

"Ask me." She knew what he wanted from her.

His eyes remained lowered.

Shaking her head, Tatiana said, "Lift your head. Look at me." He did. Kneeling in front of him, Tatiana held his face between her hands, kissed his lips, and said, "Alexander, the answer is yes . . . yes . . . of course I've saved myself for you. I belong to you. What are you even thinking?"

His happy, relieved, excited eyes flowed into her. "Oh, Tania." For a moment he didn't speak. "You have no idea . . . what that means to me—"

"Shh," she whispered. She knew.

He closed his eyes. "You were right," he said emotionally. "I don't deserve what you have to give me."

"If not you, who?" said Tatiana, hugging him. "Where are your hands? I want them."

"My *hands?*" He kissed her ardently. "Lift your arms." He took off her sundress and laid her down on the blanket, kneeling over her, roaming over her face and throat with his hungry lips, roaming over her body with his hungry fingers.

"Now I need you completely naked before me, all right?" he whispered.

"All right."

He took off her white cotton panties, and Tatiana in her weakness watched him in his weakness, staring at her and then uttering, "No, I can't take it . . ."

He put his cheek against her breast. "Your heart is pounding like gunfire . . ." He licked her nipples. "Don't be scared."

"All right," Tatiana whispered, her hands in his damp hair.

Bending over her, Alexander whispered, "You tell me what you want me to do, and I'll do it. I'll go as slow as you need me to. What do you want?"

Tatiana couldn't reply. She wanted to ask him to bring her instant relief from the fire but could not. She had to trust in Alexander.

His palm pressing into her stomach, Alexander whispered, "Look at you, your wet, erect nipples standing up, pleading with me to suck them."

"Suck them," Tatiana whispered, moaning.

He did. "Yes. Moan, moan as loud as you want. No one can hear you but me, and I came sixteen hundred kilometers to hear you, so *moan*, Tania." His mouth, his tongue, his teeth devoured her breasts as her back and chest and hips arched into him.

Lying down on his side next to her, Alexander eased his hand between her thighs.

"Wait, wait," she said, trying to keep her legs together.

"No, open," Alexander said, his hand pushing her legs apart. With his fingers he traced her thigh upward. "Shh," he whispered, wrapping his free arm around her neck. "Tania, you're trembling." His fingers touched her. Her body stiffened. Alexander's breath stopped. Tatiana's breath stopped. "Do you feel how gently I rub you," he whispered, his lips on her cheek. "You . . . so blonde all over."

Her hands were clenched on her stomach under his forearm. Her eyes were closed.

"Do you feel that, Tatia?"

She moaned.

Alexander stroked her up and down and then in small circles. "You feel unbelievable . . ." he whispered.

Her hands clenched tighter.

He rubbed her a little firmer. "Want me to stop?" He groaned slightly.

"No!"

"Tania, do you feel me against your hip?"

"Hmm. I thought that was your rifle."

His hot breath was in her neck. "Whatever you want to call it is fine with me." He bent over her and sucked her nipples as he rubbed her and rubbed against her—

In circles, in circles—

As she moaned and moaned—

And—

He pulled his fingers away and his mouth away and himself away.

"No, no, no. Don't stop," Tatiana murmured in a panic, opening her eyes. In the palpitating tension of her flesh she had begun to feel combustion, and when he stopped, she started to quiver so uncontrollably that Alexander lay on top of her briefly to calm her, pressing his forehead to her forehead. "Shh. It's all right." He paused for a second and got off her. "Tell me what you want me to do."

415

Unsteadily, Tatiana said, "I don't know. What else have you got?"

He nodded. "All right, then." He pulled off his shorts and knelt in front of her.

When Tatiana saw him, she sat straight up. "Oh, my God, Alexander," she muttered incredulously, backing away.

"It's all right," he said, smiling from ear to ear. "Where are you going?" His hands held on to her legs.

"No," she said, shaking her head, staring at him in astonishment. "No, no. Please."

"Somehow, and in His infinite wisdom," Alexander said, "God has ensured that it all works the way it's supposed to."

"Shura, it can't be possible. It'll never—"

"Trust me," Alexander said, staring at her with lust. "It will."

He lay her down flat, and said, "I cannot wait a second longer. Not another second. I need to be inside you *right now*."

"Oh, God. No, Shura."

"Yes, Tania, yes. Say that to me. Yes, Shura."

"Oh, God. *Yes*, Shura."

Alexander climbed on top of her, supporting himself on his arms. "Tania," he whispered passionately, "you are naked and underneath me!" As if he could not believe it himself.

"Alexander," she said, still trembling, "you are naked and above me." She felt him rubbing against her.

They kissed. "I can't believe it," he said, his breath shallow. "I didn't think this day would ever come." He paused and then whispered, "Yet I couldn't imagine my life without it. You alive, under me. Tania, touch me. Put your hands on me."

Instantly she reached down and took hold of him.

"Do you feel how hard I am," he whispered, ". . . for you?"

"God, yes," she said in crazed disbelief. Seeing him was a profound shock to her. *Feeling* him was entirely too much. "It's impossible," she muttered, stroking him gently. "You will *kill* me."

"Yes," Alexander said. "Let me. Open your legs."

She did.

"No, wider." Alexander kissed her and whispered, "Open yourself for me, Tania. Go ahead . . . open for *me*."

Tatiana did. She continued to stroke him.

"Now, are you ready?"

"No."

"You are, you *are* ready. Let go of me." He smiled. "Hold on to my neck. Hold on tight."

Slowly Alexander pushed himself inside her, little by little, little by little. Tatiana grasped at his arms, at the blanket, at his back, at the grass above her head. "Wait, wait, please . . ." He waited as best he could. Tatiana felt as she had imagined she would—that she was being torn open. But something else, too.

An intemperate hunger for Alexander.

"All right," he said at last. "I'm inside you." He kissed her and breathed deeply out. "I'm inside *you*, Tatiasha."

Softly she moaned, her hands around his neck. "Are you really inside me?"

"Yes." He pulled up slightly. "Feel."

She felt. "I can't believe you . . . fit."

Smiling, Alexander whispered, "Only just, but yes." He kissed her lips. Took a breath. Left his lips on her. "As if God Himself joined our flesh . . ." He took another breath. ". . . Me and you together, and said, they shall be one."

Tatiana lay very still. Alexander was very still, his lips pressed against her forehead. Was there more? Tatiana's body was aching. There was no relief. Her hands went around to hold him a little closer. She looked up into his flushed face. "Is that it? Is that all there is to it?"

Alexander paused a moment. "Not quite." He inhaled her breath. "I'm just—Tania, we've been so desperately longing for this . . ." he whispered into her mouth, "and the moment will never come again." He gazed into her face. "I don't want to let it go."

"All right," she whispered back. She was throbbing. She tilted her hips up to him.

Another moment.

"Ready?" He pulled slowly and slightly out and pushed himself back in. Tatiana gritted her teeth, but through the gritted teeth a moan escaped.

"Wait, wait," she said.

Slowly he pulled halfway out and pushed himself back in.

"Wait . . ."

Alexander pulled all the way out and pushed himself all the way in, and Tatiana, astounded, nearly screamed, but she was too afraid he would stop if he thought she was in pain. She heard him groan, and less slowly he pulled all the way out and pushed himself all the way in. Moaning, she gripped his arms.

"Oh, Shura." She was unable to breathe.

"I know. Just hold on to me."

Less slowly. Less gently.

Tatiana was feverish from the pain, from the flame.

"Am I hurting you?"

Tatiana paused, dizzy and lost. "No."

"I'm going as slow as I can."

"Oh, Shura." Breath, breath, where is my breath . . .

Short panting pause. "Tania . . . God, I'm done for, aren't I?" Alexander whispered hotly. "Done for, *forever*."

Less, less gently.

Speechlessly Tatiana clung to him, her mouth open in a mute scream.

"You want me to stop?"

"No."

Alexander stopped. "Wait," he said, shaking his head against her cheek. "Hang on tight," he whispered. He was still for another moment.

Through his parted lips he breathed, "Oh, Tania . . ." and suddenly he thrust in and out of her so hard and so fast that Tatiana thought she was going to pass out, crying in tumult and pain and gripping his head buried in her neck.

A breathless moment.

And another.

And another.

The heart was wild, and the throat was parched, and the lips were wet, and breath was slowly coming back, and sound, and sensation, and smell.

And her eyes were open.

Blink.

Alexander pulsed to a gradual stop, took a deep relieved breath, and lay on top of her for a few panting minutes.

Her hands continued to grip him.

A bittersweet tingle remained where he had just been. Tatiana felt regret; she wanted him inside her again; it had felt so excessive and absolute.

Lifting himself off her, Alexander blew on her wet forehead and chest. "Are you all right? I hurt you?" he whispered, tenderly kissing her freckles. "Tania, honey, tell me you're all right."

She couldn't answer him. His lips on her face were too warm.

"I'm fine," Tatiana finally replied, smiling shyly, holding him to her. "Are you all right?"

Alexander lay down by her side. "I'm fantastic," he said, his fingers running down the length of her body from her face to her shins and slowly back up again. "I have never been better." His shining smile was so full of happiness that Tatiana wanted to cry. She pressed her face against his face. They didn't speak.

His hand stopped moving and rested on Tatiana's hip. "You were surprisingly more quiet than I had anticipated," he said.

"Mmm, I was trying not to faint," Tatiana said, making him laugh.

"I thought you might be."

She turned on her side to him. "Shura, was it . . . ?"

Alexander kissed her eyes. "Tania," he whispered, "to be inside you, to come inside you . . . it was magic. You know it was."

"What did you think it was going to be like?" she asked, nudging him.

"This was better than anything my pathetic imagination could conjure up."

"Have you been imagining this?"

"You could say that." He held her to him. "Forget me. Tell me—what did *you* expect?" He grinned, kissed her, and laughed with delight. "No, I'm going to burst," he said. "Tell me everything." Huskily he added, "Have you been imagining this?"

"No," she said, nudging him again. Certainly not *this*. Her fingers floated down from Alexander's throat to his stomach. All she wanted was permission to touch him again. "Why are you looking at me like that? What do you want to know?"

"What were you expecting?"

Tatiana thought about it. "I really don't know."

"Come on, you must have been expecting something."

"Mmm. Not this."

"What then?"

Tatiana was quite embarrassed and wished Alexander wouldn't look at her with such mouthwatering adoration. "I had a brother, Shura," she said. "I knew what you all looked like. Sort of quiet . . . and down . . . and very . . . hmm . . ." Tatiana searched for a proper word. "Unalarming."

Alexander burst out laughing.

"But I've never seen one . . ."

"That was alarming!"

"Hmm." Why was he laughing like that?

"What else?"

Tatiana paused. "I guess I thought this unalarming thing would . . . I don't know . . . quietly sort of . . ." She coughed once. "Let's just say the movement was also quite a surprise to me."

Alexander grabbed her, kissing her happily. "You're the funniest girl. What am I going to do with you?"

Tatiana lay quietly facing him, the aching inside her thoroughly unsubsided. She was fascinated with his body. Her fingers lightly stroked his stomach. "So what now?" She paused. "Are we . . . done?"

"Do you want to be done?"

"No," she said at once.

"Tatiana," Alexander said, his voice filled with emotion, "I love you."

She closed her eyes. "Thank you," she whispered.

"Don't give me that," he said, lifting her face to him. "I have never heard you say it to me."

That couldn't be true, thought Tatiana. I've felt it every minute of every day since we met. Spilling over—"I love you, Alexander."

"Thank you," he whispered, gazing at her. "Tell me again."

"I love you." She hugged him. "I love you breathlessly, my amazing man." With affection she smiled into his face. "But you know, I have never heard you say it to me either."

"Yes, you did, Tatiana," said Alexander. "You heard me say it to you."

A moment passed.

She didn't speak, or breathe, or blink.

"You know how I know?" he whispered.

"How?" she mouthed inaudibly.

"Because you got up off that sled . . ."

Another mute moment passed.

The second time they made love, it hurt less.

The third time Tatiana experienced a floating, incandescent moment of such pain-infused exquisite pleasure that it caught even her by surprise. She cried out.

Crying out, she moaned, "God, don't stop. Please . . ."

"No?" Alexander said, and stopped.

"What are you doing?" she said, opening her eyes, parting her lips, looking up at him. "I said don't stop."

"I want to hear you moan again," he murmured. "I want to hear you moan for me not to stop."

"*Please* . . ." she whispered, milling her hips against him, her hands around his neck.

"No, Shura, no? Or yes, Shura, yes?"

"Yes, Shura, yes." Tatiana closed her eyes, "I beg you . . . don't stop."

Alexander moved in and out of her deeper and slower. She cried out.

"Like this?"

She couldn't speak.

"Or . . ."

Faster and faster. She cried out.

"Like this?"

She couldn't speak.

"Tania . . . is it so good?"

"It's so good."

"How do you want it?"

"Any which way." Her tense hands clenched around him.

"Moan for me, Tania," Alexander whispered, changing his rhythm and his speed. "Go ahead . . . moan for me."

Alexander didn't have to ask twice.

"Don't stop, Shura . . ." she said helplessly.

"I won't stop, Tania."

He didn't stop, and there it was—finally Tatiana felt her entire body stiffen and explode in a convulsive burn, then a lava melt. It was some time before she was able to stop moaning and quivering against Alexander. "What *was* that?" she uttered at last, still panting.

"That was my Tania discovering what is so fantastic about making love. That was . . . relief," he whispered, pressing his cheek to her cheek.

Tatiana clasped him to her, turning her face away and murmuring through her happy tears, "Oh, my God, Alexander . . ."

* * *

"How long have we been here?"

"I don't know. Minutes?"

"Where's your 'precise' watch?"

"Didn't bring it. Wanted time to stop moving forward," said Alexander, blinking and closing his eyes.

"Tania? You're not sleeping?"

"No. My eyes are closed. I'm very relaxed."

"Tania, will you tell me the truth if I ask for it?"

"Of course." She smiled. Her eyes were still closed.

"Have you ever touched a man before? *Touched* a man."

Tatiana opened her eyes and laughed quietly. "Shura, what are you talking about? Besides my brother when we were younger, I've never even *seen* a man before."

Tatiana was nestled in his arms, her fingers touching his chin, his neck, his Adam's apple. She pressed her index finger to the vividly pulsing artery near his throat. She moved up a little and kissed the artery and then left her mouth on it, feeling it beat against her lips. Why is he so endearing? she thought. And why does he smell so good?

"What about those hordes of young beasts you told me about, chasing you in Luga? None of them?"

"None of them what?"

"Did you touch any of them?" asked Alexander.

She shook her head. "Shura, why are you so funny? No."

"Maybe through clothes?"

"What?" She didn't take her mouth away from his neck. "Of course not." She paused. "What are you trying to get out of me?"

"What kind of things you got up to before me."

Teasingly, Tatiana said, "*Was* there life before Alexander?"

"You tell *me*."

"All right, what else do you want to know?"

"Who has seen your naked body? Other than your family. Other than when you were seven, doing your naked cartwheels."

Is this what he wanted? The complete truth? She had been so afraid to tell him. Would he want to hear it? "Shura, the first time any man saw me even *partly* naked was you in Luga."

"Is that true?" He moved away a little to see her eyes.

She nodded, returning to rubbing her mouth against his neck. "It's true."

"Has anyone touched you?"

"Touched me?"

"Felt your breasts, felt—" His fingers searched for her.

"Shura, please. Of course not."

421

Through his artery she felt his heart quicken its beat into her mouth. Tatiana smiled. She would tell it all to him right now, if that's what he wanted from her. "Do you remember the woods in Luga?"

"How can I forget?" he said huskily. "It was the sweetest kiss of my life."

Her lips in his neck, Tatiana whispered, "Alexander . . . it was the first kiss of mine."

He shook his head and then turned on his side, peering into her face in skeptical emotional disbelief, as if what she had been giving him were less than the total truth. Tatiana turned on her side to him. "What?" she asked, smiling. "You're embarrassing me. What now?"

"Don't tell me that—"

"All right, I won't tell you."

"Will you tell me, please?"

"I told you."

His stupefied eyes unblinking, Alexander said shallowly, "When I kissed you in Luga . . ."

"Yes?"

"Tell me."

"Shura . . ." She pressed her body flush against his. "What do you want? You want the truth from me or something else?"

"I don't believe you." He shook his head. "I just don't believe you."

"All right," Tatiana said, lying on her back and putting her hands under her head.

Alexander bent over her. "I think you're just telling me that because you think it's what I want to hear," he said, running his fingers over her breasts and stomach. His hands on her were unremitting. They never stopped moving.

"*Is* it what you want to hear?"

Alexander didn't reply at first. "I don't know. No. Yes, God help me," he said with difficulty. "But I want the truth more."

Tatiana patted him cheerfully on the back. "You have the truth." And smiled. "In my whole life I have never been touched by anyone but you."

But Alexander wasn't smiling. His bronze eyes melting right in front of her, he asked haltingly, "How can that be?"

"I don't know how it can be," she said. "It just is."

"What did you do, walk straight from your mother's womb into my arms?"

Tatiana laughed. "Very nearly." She gazed into his face. "Alexander, I *love* you," she said. "Do you understand? I never wanted to kiss anyone before you. I wanted you to kiss me so much in Luga I didn't know what to do. I didn't know how to tell you. I stayed up half the night trying to figure out a way to get you to kiss me. Finally in the woods, I wasn't going to give up. If I can't get my Alexander to kiss me in the woods, I thought, I have no hope of ever being kissed by anyone." Her hands were on him.

His face was over hers. "What are you doing to me?" he whispered intensely. "You need to stop right now. What are you doing to me?"

"What are you doing to *me?*" Her fingertips pressed into his back.

When Alexander made love to her, his lips did not leave hers, and in his impassioned climax, which she barely heard through her shattering own, Tatiana was almost sure he groaned as if he were stopping himself from crying. He whispered into her mouth, "I just don't know how I'm going to survive you, Tatiana."

"Honey," Alexander murmured, his body over her, as she lay underneath him. "Open your eyes. Are you all right?"

Tatiana didn't speak. She was listening to the loving cadence of his voice.

"Tania . . ." he whispered, his shimmering fingers circling her face, her throat, the top of her chest. "You have newborn skin," he said quietly. "Do you know that?"

"Well, no," she murmured.

"You have newborn skin and the sweetest breath, and your hair is silk upon your head." Kneeling over her, Alexander tenderly sucked her nipple. "You are divine through and through."

Listening, comforted, she held his head in her hands. He stopped talking and lifted his face to her. There were tears in his eyes.

"Please forgive me, Tatiana," said Alexander, "for hurting your perfect heart with my cold and indifferent face. My own heart was always overflowing with you, and it was never indifferent. You didn't deserve any of what you've been given, of what you've had to bear. None of it. Not from your sister, not from Leningrad, and certainly not from me. You don't even know what it took me not to look at you one last time before I closed the tarpaulin on that truck. I knew that if I did, it would all be over. I would not have been able to hide my face from you or from Dasha. I wouldn't have been able to keep my promise to you for your sister. It wasn't that I didn't look at you. I *couldn't* look at you. I gave you so much when we were alone. I hoped it would be enough to carry you forward."

"It was, Shura," said Tatiana, with tears in her own eyes. "I'm here. And it will be enough in the future." She pressed his head to her chest. "I'm sorry I ever doubted you. But now my heart is light."

Alexander kissed her between her breasts.

"You have fixed me." And Tatiana smiled.

Murmuring and whispering, Tatiana lay happily under Alexander, having been once again loved and relieved, and relieved . . . "Oh, and I thought I loved you before."

His lips pressed into her temple. "This does add a whole new dimension, doesn't it?" His hands did not leave her body. Nothing of him left her body. He was holding her from underneath, still moving inside her.

Turning her face up to him, a smile coming to her lips, a smile of youth and ecstasy, Tatiana said, "Alexander, you are my first love. Did you know that?"

He squeezed her bottom, pressed himself into her, licked the salt off her face, and nodded. "That I know."

"Oh?"

"Tatia, I knew it even before you yourself knew it." He grinned. "Before you finally found the word to describe to yourself what you were feeling, I knew it from the start. How else could you have been so shy and guileless?"

"Guileless?"

"Yes."

"Was I that obvious?"

"Yes." Alexander smiled. "Your inability to look at me in public, yet your total devotion to my face when we were together—like now," he said, kissing her. "Your embarrassment at the smallest things—I couldn't even keep my hand on you in the tram without you blushing . . . your fingers on me when I was telling you about America . . . your smile, your *smile*, Tania, when you ran to me from Kirov." Alexander shook his head at the memory. "What a prison you have set up for me with your first love."

She put her arms tighter around him and said teasingly, "Oh, so the first love part you believe, but the first kiss part you have a problem with? What kind of girl do you think I am?"

"The nicest girl," he whispered.

"Are you ready for more?"

"Tania . . ." Alexander shook his head in smiling disbelief. "What's gotten into you?"

She laughed, her hands caressing his stomach. "Shura . . . am I wanting too much?"

"No. But you are going to kill *me*."

Tatiana craved something, but she just couldn't find a way out of her timidity to ask him. Quietly, thoughtfully, she stroked his stomach and then cleared her throat. "Honey? Can I lie on top of you?"

"Of course." Alexander smiled, opening his arms. "Come and lie on top of me."

She lay down on him and softly, wetly kissed his lips. "Shura . . ." she whispered, "do you like that?"

"Mmm."

Her lips were on his face, on his throat, on the top of his chest. She whispered, "You know what your skin feels like to me? The ice cream that I love. Creamy, smooth. Your whole body is the color of caramel, like my crème brûlée, but you're not cold like ice cream, you're warm." She rubbed her lips back and forth against his chest.

"So—better than ice cream?"

"Yes." She smiled, moving up to his lips. "I love you better than ice cream." After kissing him deeply, she gently, gently sucked his tongue. "Do you like *that*?" she whispered.

He groaned his assent.

"Shura, darling . . ." she asked very shyly, "is there . . . anywhere else you might like me to do that?"

Pulling away, he gaped at her. Silent and tantalized, Tatiana watched his incredulous face.

"I think," Alexander said slowly, "there is a place where I might like you to do that, yes."

She smiled back, trying to hide her excitement. "You'll just—you'll just have to tell me what to do, all right?"

"All right."

Tatiana kissed Alexander's chest, listened to his heart, moved lower, lay her head on his rippled stomach. Moving lower still, she brushed her blonde hair against him and then rubbed her breasts against him, feeling him already swollen underneath her. She kissed the arrow line of his black hair leading down from his navel and then grazed her lips against him.

Kneeling between Alexander's legs, Tatiana took hold of him with both hands. He was extraordinary. "And now . . ."

"Now put me in your mouth," he said, watching her.

Her breath leaving her body, she whispered, *"Whole?"* and took what she could of him into her mouth.

"Move up and down on me."

"Like this?"

There was a thickening pause. "Yes."

"Or . . ."

"Yes, that's good, too."

Tatiana felt him hard against her fervent lips and rubbing fingers. When Alexander gripped her hair, she, stopping for a moment, looked into his face. "Oh, yes," she whispered, hungrily putting him deeper inside her mouth and moaning.

"You're doing so well, Tatia," he whispered. "Keep going, and don't stop."

She stopped. He opened his eyes. Smiling, Tatiana said, "I want to hear you groan for me not to stop."

Alexander sat up and kissed her wet mouth. "Please don't stop." Then he gently pushed her face down on him, falling back on the blanket.

Right before the end he pulled her head away and said, "Tania, I'm going to come."

"So come," Tatiana whispered. "Come in my mouth."

Afterward, as she lay cradled in his chest, Alexander said, gazing at her in stark amazement, "I've decided that I like it."

"Me, too," she said softly.

For a long time she lay next to him, feeling his tender fingers feather her.

"Why did we spend two days fighting when we could have been doing this?"

Alexander ruffled her hair. "That wasn't fighting, Tatiasha. That was fore-play."

They kissed each other. "I'm sorry again," Tatiana whispered.

"Me, too, again," he whispered back.

Then Tatiana fell quiet.

"What's the matter?" he asked. "What are you thinking?"

How does he know me so well? she thought. All I have to do is blink, and he knows I'm thinking, or fretting, or anxious. She took a breath. "Shura . . . have you loved many girls before?" she asked in a small voice.

"No, my angel face," Alexander said passionately, caressing her. "I have not loved many girls before."

Tears forming at the base of her throat, she asked, "Did you love Dasha?"

He was silent for a moment. "Tania, don't do this."

She was silent herself.

"I don't know what answer you want me to give you," Alexander said. "I'll give you whatever answer you want."

"Give me only the truth."

"No, I did not love Dasha," Alexander said. "I cared for her. We had some good times."

"How good?"

"All right," he said.

"The truth."

"Just all right," he repeated. He tweaked her nipple. "Haven't you figured out yet," Alexander said, "that Dasha was not my type?"

"What will you say about me to your next girl?"

He grinned. "I'll say that you had perfect breasts."

"Stop it."

"That you had young, perky, incredible breasts with the biggest, most sensitive cherry nipples . . ." he said, climbing on top of her and holding up her legs high against his arms. "And lips for the gods, and eyes for kings. I will say," Alexander whispered hotly, pushing himself inside her and groaning, "that you *felt* like nothing else on this earth."

"What time is it, do you think?"

"I don't know," he replied sleepily. "Toward evening."

"I don't want to go back to them."

"Who's going back?" said Alexander. "We're not moving from here." He paused. *"Ever."*

"We're not?"

"Try to leave."

Before night set, they crept out of the tent, and Tatiana sat on a blanket with Alexander's uniform tunic around her shoulders while he built a fire with the twigs and dry branches she had found earlier. The fire was a raging blaze in five minutes.

"You build a good fire, Shura," Tatiana said quietly.

"Thank you." He pulled out two cans of *tushonka*, some dry bread and water.

"Look what else I've got." In a piece of aluminum foil he had a few squares of chocolate.

"Wow," Tatiana mouthed, staring at him in wonder, not even looking at the chocolate.

They ate.

"Are we going to sleep in the tent?" Tatiana asked.

"If you want, I can build a fire in the house." He smiled. "Do you see how I cleaned it for you?"

"Yes, and when did you do this?"

"Yesterday, after our fight. What do you think I did all afternoon?"

"After our fight?" More surprised. "But before you came back and told me to give you your things so you could leave?"

"Yes."

Tatiana shoved him in the ribs. "You just wanted to hear me . . ."

"Don't say it," Alexander whispered. "Or right here, right now, I'll have to make love to you again, and you won't live through it."

And she almost didn't.

In front of the fire, in his arms, Tatiana was crying against Alexander's chest.

"Tania, why are you crying?"

"Oh, Shura."

"Please don't cry."

"All right. I miss my sister."

"I know."

"Did we treat her right, you think? Did we do right by her?"

"We did as well as we could. You did the best you could. What do you think, we asked for this? To break each other's hearts, to hurt other people, to fall in love like this? I struggled against my feelings. I wanted to love your sister, God bless her. I couldn't help that it was impossible."

Turning away from him, toward the fire and the Kama behind it and the full moon above it, Tatiana said, "I tried not to love you for her."

"But it was impossible."

"Yes." Then tentatively, "Shura . . . are you . . . in love with me?"

"Turn to me," Alexander said. She turned. "Tatia, I worship you. I'm crazy in love with you. I want you to marry me."

"What?"

"Yes. Tatiana, will you marry me? Will you be my wife?" Pause. "Don't cry." Pause. "You didn't answer me."

"Yes, Alexander. I will marry you . . . I will be your wife."

"Now why are you crying?"

8

The next morning at dawn Tatiana stumbled out to the water, barely able to walk. She felt raw.

Alexander followed her in. The Kama was cold. They were both naked.

"I brought soap," he said.

"Oh, my."

Alexander washed her entire body. "With this soap I thee wash," he sleepily murmured. "I wash you of the horrors that befell you, and I wash you of your nightmares . . . I wash your arms and your legs and your love-giving heart and your life-giving belly—"

"Give me the soap," Tatiana said. "I'll wash you."

"Wait, how does it go? What did God say to Moses—"

"Have no idea."

"Thou shall not be afraid for the terror by night; nor for the arrow that flieth by day . . ." Alexander broke off. "I can't remember the rest of it. Certainly not in Russian. Something about ten thousand falling at your right hand. I've got to brush up on my Bible and tell it to you. I think you'd like it. But you get my meaning."

"I get your meaning," Tatiana said. "I won't be afraid." She gazed at him. "How can I be afraid now?" she whispered. "Look what I've been given. Give me the soap," she repeated.

"I can't stand up," Alexander muttered. "I'm finished."

Her hands with the soap moved lower. "Not quite finished."

He fell backward in the water.

"Done for, certainly," Tatiana said, falling on top of him. "But not finished."

Tatiana was clinging to Alexander in the cold Kama, her feet not touching bottom, her arms wrapped around his neck. "Look at the sunrise over the mountains. It's pretty, isn't it?" she murmured. He was standing in the water.

She saw he was oblivious to the sunrise, holding her to him with one hand and stroking her face with the other. "I found my true love on the banks of the river Kama," whispered Alexander, staring at her.

"I found my true love on Ulitsa Saltykov-Schedrin, while I sat on a bench eating ice cream."

"You didn't find me. You weren't even *looking* for me. I found you."

Long pause. "Alexander, were you . . . looking for *me?*"

"All my life."

428

"Shura, how can we have such a closeness? How can we have such a connection? Right from the start."

"We don't have a closeness."

"No?"

"No. We don't have a connection."

"No?"

"No. We have communion."

Alexander built a fire in the foggy cool morning on the shore of the quietly flowing river. They had some bread from his rucksack and some water. He smoked.

"We didn't really come prepared," Tatiana said. "Wish we had a cup. A spoon. Some plates. Coffee." She smiled.

"I don't know about you," Alexander said, "but I brought everything *I* needed."

She blushed.

"No, no, don't do it," he said, his hands on her. "We'll never leave here."

"Are we leaving here?"

"Let's get dressed. We're going to Molotov."

"We are?" Last night, was that just a dream? What he said to her under the moon and the stars of night? "What for?" Holding her breath.

"We need to buy a couple of things."

"Like what?"

"Blankets, pillows. Pots, pans, plates. Cups. A laundry basket. Some food. Rings."

"Rings?"

"Rings, yes. To put on our fingers."

9

They walked slowly to Molotov. Her arm was through his. The sunlight peeked through above the pines.

"Shura, I've been practicing my English."

"You have? You told me you haven't had time. Seeing your life, I believed you."

Tatiana cleared her throat and said in English, "*Alexander Barrington, I want forever love in you.*"

Bringing her close, Alexander laughed and replied in English, "*Yes, me, too.*" He paused, looking down at her.

She looked up at him. "What?"

"You're walking slowly. Are you all right?"

"I'm fine." She blushed. She was not. "What?"

429

Alexander smiled. "Want me to carry you for a bit?" he asked huskily.

Her face melted. "Yes," Tatiana replied. "But this time in your arms."

"Someday," Alexander said, lifting her, "you'll have to explain to me why you took bus Number 136 clear across Leningrad to the bus terminal."

Tatiana pinched him. "Someday," she said, "you'll have to explain to me why you followed me."

"A *what*?" Tatiana asked in disbelief, getting down and walking beside him.

"A church. We have to find one."

"What for?"

Alexander looked at her askance. "Where do *you* intend to get married?"

Tatiana thought about it. "Like everybody in the Soviet Union—at the registry office."

Laughing, he said, "What's the point? Why don't we go back and continue as we were?"

"That's an idea," Tatiana muttered. The mention of a church unsettled her.

Alexander took her hand and said nothing.

"Why church, Shura?"

"Tania," said Alexander, looking at the road ahead, "who do you want this covenant of marriage to be made with? The Soviet Union? Or God?"

She had no answer.

"What do you believe in, Tatiana?" he asked.

"You," she replied.

"Well, I believe in God *and* you. We're getting married in a church."

They found a small Russian Orthodox church close to the center of town, St. Seraphim's. The priest inside studied them after Alexander told him what they wanted, and said, "Another war wedding. Hmm." He glanced at Tatiana. "Are you even old enough to be a bride?"

"I'm eighteen tomorrow," she said, sounding about ten.

"Do you have witnesses? Do you have rings? Did you register your marriage at the registry office?"

"None of the above," said Tatiana, pulling Alexander by the arm, but he freed himself from her hold and asked the priest where they could buy some rings.

"Buy?" the priest asked with surprise. His name was Father Mikhail. He was tall and bald, with penetrating blue eyes and a long gray beard. "Buy rings? Well—nowhere, of course. We have a jeweler in town, but he has no gold."

"Where is the jeweler?"

"Son, let me ask you, why do you want to get married in a church? Just go to the registry office. Like everybody. They'll give you a certificate in thirty seconds. I think you can use the court clerk as your witness."

Tatiana stood still next to Alexander, who after taking a deep breath, said,

430

"Where I come from, marriage is a public and *sacred* ceremony. We're only going to do this once, so we would like it done right."

We? thought Tatiana. She couldn't understand her misgivings.

Father Mikhail smiled. "All right, son," he said sincerely, "I'll be glad to marry two young people starting out in life. Come back tomorrow with rings and witnesses. Come back at three. I'll marry you then."

As they descended the church steps, Tatiana said dismissively, "Oh, well. We don't have the rings." And breathed a small sigh of—

"We will," said Alexander, producing four gold teeth out of his rucksack. "That should be enough for two rings."

Tatiana stared dumbfounded at the teeth.

"Dasha gave them to me. Don't look so horrified."

But she was, she was horrified. "We're going to make ourselves rings out of the teeth Dasha stole from her dental patients?"

"Do you have another idea?"

"Maybe we should wait."

"Wait for what?"

Tatiana had no answer to that. Wait for what indeed? With a heavy heart she followed Alexander down the street.

The jeweler lived in a small house in town and worked out of his home. He looked at the teeth, looked at Alexander and Tatiana, and told them he could make gold rings out of the teeth—for the price of two more gold teeth.

Alexander said he didn't have two more gold teeth, but he had a bottle of vodka. The jeweler, creaking refusal, returned the four teeth to Alexander, who sighed loudly and produced two more teeth out of his ruck.

Alexander asked if there was anywhere in Molotov they could buy some housewares.

"They'll probably want gold teeth for a blanket, Shura," whispered Tatiana. The jeweler introduced them to his overlarge wife Sofia, who sold them two down quilts, pillows, and sheets all for 200 rubles.

"Two hundred rubles!" exclaimed Tatiana. "I made ten tanks and five thousand flamethrowers and I did not get as much as that."

"Yes, but I," said Alexander, "blew up ten tanks and used up five thousand flamethrowers and got two *thousand* rubles for that. Never think about the money. Just spend it on what you have to."

They also bought a pot, a pan, a kettle, some plates, utensils and cups, and a soccer ball. Alexander also managed to talk two metal buckets out of Sofia.

"What's that for?" Tatiana asked, looking at the two metal buckets—one that fit inside the other.

"You'll see." He smiled. "A surprise for your birthday."

"How are we going to carry all this back home?"

Kissing her nose, Alexander said fondly, "When you're with me, don't worry—I will take care of everything."

Sofia sold them two kilos of tobacco but couldn't help them with produce.

She sent them to a stand where they picked up apples, tomatoes, and cucumbers, bread and butter, and with one of the *tushonka* cans they had a feast for lunch on a blanket in a secluded spot on the outskirts of town down by the Kama.

"What amazes me," Tatiana said, breaking the bread, "is that you gave me the Pushkin book for my birthday *last* year."

"Yes?"

"How did you get the rubles in there?" She poured Alexander a cupful of *kvas*, a beverage made from bread products.

"I gave you the book with the money already there."

She looked at Alexander thoughtfully. "Really?" she said.

"Of course."

"But you barely knew me. Why would you give me a book *full* of money?" She wanted him to tell her about all the money she had found in that book. But he said nothing. Tatiana knew this about Alexander: unless *he* wanted to, he didn't speak about anything. Tatiana stared at him. She wanted him.

"What?"

"Nothing, nothing," she said, glancing away.

Crawling over to her on the blanket, Alexander took the drink and the bread out of her hands and said, smiling, "I'll teach you this, too: whenever you want something from me and are too shy to ask, blink three times quick."

10

They had spent the night in his tent by the river. After swimming, they fell into unconscious sleep hours before the sun set at eleven and slept for fifteen hours straight.

In the late morning they left all their new purchases in the woods before going back into town to be married.

Tatiana put on her white dress with red roses. "I told you I was too big for this dress now." She smiled at Alexander lying on the blanket watching her. She knelt, turning her back to him. "Can you tie my straps, please? Just not tight. Not like before, on the bus." He wasn't budging behind her. She glanced at him. "What?"

"God, that dress on you," Alexander said, his fingers through the crisscross laces pressing on her bare back. He tied the straps for her, kissing her shoulder blades, telling her she looked so good the priest was going to want to marry her himself. She unbraided her hair and left it down, brushed behind her ears. Alexander put on his dress uniform and his cap. Saluting her, he asked, "What do you think?"

Shyly she saluted him back. "I think you're the most handsome man I ever saw."

Kissing her, his voice condensed with love, he said, "And in two hours I'm going to be the most handsome *husband* you ever saw. Happy birthday, my eighteen-year-old child bride." The joy was plain on his face.

Tatiana hugged him. "I can't believe we're getting married on my birthday."

Alexander hugged her back. "This way you'll never forget me."

"Oh, yes, because that's likely," Tatiana said, groping for him gently. "Who could ever forget *you*, Alexander?"

The judge behind the small desk in one of the rooms at the registry office indifferently asked them if they were both of sound mind and were entering into this contract willingly, then shrugged and stamped their passports.

"And you wanted to get married in front of *him*," Alexander whispered as they walked out.

Tatiana was quiet. She wasn't sure about the "sound mind" part.

"Alexander," she said. "But now our domestic passports are stamped, 'Married, June 23, 1942.' Mine states your name. Yours states my name."

"Yes?"

"Alexander, what about Dimi—"

"Shh," he said, putting two fingers against her lips. "Is that what we're going to do? Let that bastard stop us?"

"No," she agreed.

"I don't give a shit about him. Don't mention his name, understand?"

Tatiana understood.

"But we have no witnesses," she said.

"We'll get come."

"We could go back and ask Naira Mikhailovna and the rest to stand as witnesses."

"Is your intention to ruin this day completely, or is your intention to marry me?"

Tatiana didn't reply.

Putting his arm around her, Alexander said, "Don't worry. I'll get us perfectly good witnesses."

Alexander offered the jeweler and his wife Sofia a bottle of vodka to come with them to the church for half an hour. The couple readily agreed, and Sofia even brought a camera as an afterthought.

"You two are something," said Sofia as they walked down the street headed for St. Seraphim's. "You must really want to be married to go through all this trouble." She frowned at Tatiana, eyeing her suspiciously. "You're not in the family way, are you?"

"Yes, she is," said Alexander unabashedly, pulling Tatiana away. "Is it that obvious?" He patted her stomach. "This will actually be our third child." He smiled broadly. "But the first one who's not a bastard."

They walked more quickly down the street, and Tatiana, red in the face, pulled out one of Alexander's forearm hairs. "Why do you do that?"

"What?" he said, laughing. "Embarrass you every step of the way?"

"Yes," she said, trying not to smile.

"Tatia, because I don't want them to know anything about us. I don't want to give away a drop of you and me to anyone. Not to strangers, not to the old women you lived with. To nobody. This has nothing to do with them. Just you, me. And God," he added.

Tatiana stood by Alexander's side. The priest was not at the church yet. "He's not coming," she whispered, looking around. The jeweler and Sofia were standing at the back of the small church, close to the door, holding their bottle of vodka.

"He'll be here."

"Doesn't one of us have to be baptized?" Tatiana wanted to know.

"*I* am," he replied. "A Catholic, thanks to my thoughtful, once-Italian mother. And didn't I baptize you yesterday in the Kama?"

She blushed.

"That's my good girl," he whispered. "Hang on. We're almost there." Alexander faced the altar, his gaze unwavering, his head strong, his mouth closed. He stood and waited.

Tatiana thought it was all a dream.

A nightmare from which she could not wake up. But not her nightmare. Dasha's.

How could Tatiana be marrying Dasha's Alexander? Just last week she could not have imagined a moment in her life when that would have been possible. She couldn't help it, she felt as if she were living a life that was not meant for her.

"Shura, some integrity I have," Tatiana said quietly. "Pined after my sister's lover long enough for her to die and for me to claim him as my own."

"Tania, what are you thinking? Where are you?" he asked, puzzled, turning to her slightly. "I was never Dasha's. I was always yours." He took her hand.

"Even through the blockade?"

"Especially then. What little I had was all for you. It was you who was everybody else's. But I was only yours."

Alexander and Tatiana had had an impossible love. Suddenly marriage. A proclamation to the world, a banner. They met, they fell in love, now they were getting married. As if it were always meant to be. As if betrayal, deceit, war, hunger, death—and not just death but the death of everyone else she had ever loved—had been their courtship.

Tatiana's fragile resolve was weakening by the second.

There had been other lives and other people's hearts, deep and abiding hearts. There was her Pasha, losing his life before it even began, and Mama, trying so hard to keep going after the death of her favorite child. There was

Papa, under a cloud of alcohol-fueled guilt no war could fix, and there was Marina, missing her own mother, missing her home, unable to find a small place for herself in their cramped rooms.

There was Babushka Maya, painting away her life, half hoping her first love would return. There was her Deda, dying away from his family, and Babushka, dying because there was no point in living through war without him.

And then there was Dasha.

If things were as they were supposed to be, why did Dasha's death feel so unnatural, why did it seem to break the order of things in the universe?

Was Alexander right and Tatiana wrong? Was *she* to blame, with her misplaced integrity, her inexplicable commitment to her sister? Should Tatiana have let Alexander say to Dasha, *I like Tania best.*

Should Tatiana have said to Dasha from day one, *I want him for myself.*

Would that have been the *right* thing, maybe?

To come out with the truth, instead of hiding behind her fear?

No, Tatiana thought, as they waited for the priest. No. He was too much for me then. I was jaw-droppingly smitten, like I was twelve. It was only right that Dasha should have him. On the surface she seemed right for him, not me.

I was right for kindergarten, for Comrade Perlodskaya, who used to kiss me every day and hold me in her lap. I was right for Deda, because when he said, *Tania, you have to be this way,* I said, yes, I *will* be this way.

"Selfish!" she exclaimed in the church. Alexander looked at her. Nodding, she repeated, "Selfish, to the end. Dasha is dead, and I'm stepping in. Gingerly, I step in, careful not to disturb Vova's crush on me, or Naira's illusions about me, or Dusia's and my churchgoing. I step in but say, wait, just make sure my love for you doesn't interfere with my sewing circle at three."

"Tatiana, I guarantee," Alexander said, the light in his eyes flickering *off* for a moment, "your love for me will interfere with everything."

She stared up at him standing tall next to her. Tatiana was still jaw-droppingly smitten. Alexander was still too much for her. Now more than ever. "Shura," she whispered.

"Yes, Tatia?"

"Are you sure about this? Are you sure? You don't have to do this for me."

"Oh, but I do." He smiled, bending to her. "As a husband, I will have certain . . . inalienable rights that no one can assail."

"I'm serious."

He kissed her hand. "I've never been more sure of anything."

Tatiana knew: had Alexander told Dasha the truth from the beginning, he would have *had* to go his own way. He never then could have been part of Tatiana's life in the drab apartment with all those grand betrayals and hurts.

Tatiana would have lost him, and Dasha, too. She could not have contin-

435

ued to live with her sister, knowing that Dasha—with her breasts, her hair, her lips, and the fullness of her heart—was not enough for the man she loved. The chasm that cheap knowledge would have wreaked in Tatiana's family no bridge could have spanned, not even the bridge of sisterly affection.

No, Tatiana could not have claimed him for herself. She knew that.

But this was the thing: she didn't lay claim to Alexander. She was not reclaiming him now. She was not going to a warehouse of love and saying, I think he is mine, I'll take him. He'll do. Tatiana did not drive in her stake for the possession of his heart.

It was Alexander who came to her, while she was nothing but absorbed in her own small, lonely life, and showed her that larger than life was possible. Alexander was the one who crossed the street and said, *I'm yours*.

Alexander was the one.

Glancing at him, Tatiana saw that he was waiting patiently, confident and whole and perfect. The sun filtered in through the church's stained glass windows. She breathed in the faint smell of long-gone incense. Dusia had introduced her to the church in Lazarevo, and every evening after dinner Tatiana went willingly, ready to pray as Dusia had taught her, ready to part with her crushing sadness and her crushing doubt.

When Tatiana had been a child in Luga, her beloved Deda, seeing her depressed one summer and unable to find her way, said to her, "Ask yourself these three questions, Tatiana Metanova, and you will know who you are. Ask: *what do you believe in? What do you hope for?* But most important—ask: *what do you love?*"

She looked up at Alexander. "What did you call it, Shura?" she said quietly. "Our first night, you said you and I had something, you called us . . ."

"The life force," he replied.

I know who I am, she thought, taking his hand and turning to the altar. I am Tatiana. And I believe in, and hope for, and love Alexander for life.

"Are you ready, children?" Father Mikhail walked through the church. "Did I keep you waiting?"

He took his place in front of them at the altar. The jeweler and Sofia stood nearby. Tatiana thought they might have already finished that bottle of vodka.

Father Mikhail smiled. "Your birthday today," he said to Tatiana. "Nice birthday present for you, no?"

She pressed into Alexander.

"Sometimes I feel that my powers are limited by the absence of God in the lives of men during these trying times," Father Mikhail began. "But God is still present in my church, and I can see He is present in you. I am very glad you came to me, children. Your union is meant by God for your mutual joy, for the help and comfort you give one another in prosperity and adversity and, when it is God's will, for the procreation of children. I want to send you righteously on your way through life. Are you ready to commit yourselves to each other?"

"We are," they said.

"The bond and the covenant of marriage was established by God in creation. Christ himself adorned this manner of life by his first miracle at a wedding in Cana of Galilee. A marriage is a symbol of the mystery of the union between Christ and His Church. Do you understand that those whom God has joined together, no man can put asunder?"

"We do," they said.

"Do you have the rings?"

"We do."

Father Mikhail continued. "Most gracious God," he said, holding the cross above their heads, "look with favor upon this man and this woman living in a world for which Your Son gave His life. Make their life together a sign of Christ's love to this sinful and broken world. Defend this man and this woman from every enemy. Lead them into peace. Let their love for each other be a seal upon their hearts, a mantle upon their shoulders, and a crown upon their foreheads. Bless them in their work and in their friendship, in their sleeping and in their waking, in their joys and their sorrows, in their life and in their death."

Tears trickled down Tatiana's face. She hoped Alexander wouldn't notice. Father Mikhail certainly had.

Turning to Tatiana and taking her hands, Alexander smiled, beaming at her unrestrained happiness.

Outside, on the steps of the church, he lifted her off the ground and swung her around as they kissed ecstatically. The jeweler and Sofia clapped apathetically, already down the steps and on the street. "Don't hug her so tight. You'll squeeze that child right out of her," said Sofia to Alexander as she turned around and lifted her clunky camera. "Oh, wait. Hold on. Let me take a picture of the newlyweds."

She clicked once.

Twice.

"Come to me next week. Maybe I'll have some paper by then to develop them." She waved.

"So you still think the registry office judge should have married us?" Alexander grinned. "He with his 'of sound mind' philosophy on marriage?"

Tatiana shook her head. "You were so right. This was *perfect*. How did you know this all along?"

"Because you and I were brought together by God," Alexander replied. "This was our way of thanking Him."

Tatiana chuckled. "Do you know it took us less time to get married than to make love the first time?"

"Much less," Alexander said, swinging her around in the air. "Besides, getting married is the easy part. Just like making love. It was the getting you to make love to me that was hard. It was the getting you to marry me . . ."

"I'm sorry. I was so nervous."

"I know," he said. He still hadn't put her down. "I thought the chances were twenty-eighty you were actually going to go through with it."

"Twenty *against*?"

"Twenty *for*."

"Got to have a little more faith, my husband," said Tatiana, kissing his lips.

11

They walked back home down the forest road, carrying their purchases on their backs. Alexander carried nearly everything. Tatiana carried the two pillows.

"We should go to Naira Mikhailovna's," she remarked. "They must be out of their minds with worry."

"There you go, thinking about other people," he said in a slightly irritated tone. "People other than me. You want to go back to that house on our wedding day? On our *wedding night*?"

Alexander was right. Why did she always do that? What was she thinking? She didn't like making people feel bad, that was all. She told him that.

"I know. But it's all right. You can't make everyone feel good. I tell you what. Start with me. Feed me. Nurture me. Love me. Then we'll move on to Naira Mikhailovna." She walked slowly alongside him. "Tatiasha, we'll go and see them tomorrow if you want. All right?" said Alexander, sighing.

They arrived at their cabin in the clearing by six in the evening. There was a note on the door from Naira Mikhailovna that said, *Tania, where are you? We're worried sick. N. M.*

Alexander tore the note off the door.

"Aren't we going in?" she asked.

"Yes, but . . ." He smiled. "Just a minute. I have to do something, and then we'll go in."

"What?"

"Wait a minute, and you'll see."

Alexander took the housewares, the pillows, and the heavy quilts and disappeared inside. While Tatiana waited for him, she made them sandwiches out of bread, butter, *tushonka* and cheese. He was still inside.

Tatiana began to glide around the clearing in small circles, dancing to a tune in her head. "Someday we'll meet in Lvov, my love and I." She saw her dress twirl up, and, smiling, she spun faster and faster with extravagant delight, watching the roses float into the air under her hands. When she looked up, Alexander was standing by the door of the cabin, his enraptured eyes all over her.

She smiled. "Look," she said, pointing. "I made you a sandwich. Are you hungry?"

Alexander shook his head, walking to her. She ran to him and, throwing her arms around his neck, whispered, "I can't believe we're *married*, Shura."

Lifting her into his arms, he carried her to the door. "Tania, in America we have a custom. The new husband carries his new wife over the threshold of their new home."

She kissed his cheek. He was more beautiful than the morning sun.

Alexander carried her into the house and kicked the door closed behind them. Inside was shadowy like a dream. They needed a kerosene lamp. Forgot to buy one. Tomorrow they'd have to get one in Lazarevo.

"Now what?" she said, rubbing her cheek against his. "I see you've made the bed. Very thoughtful." His stubble was already growing in from this morning.

"I do what I can." He carried her to the bed he had made for them above the stove, stepped onto the hearth, and set her down, opening her legs and standing between them, nuzzling his head in her chest. He lifted her dress.

All Tatiana wanted to do was watch him, but desire kept gluing her eyes shut. "Aren't you going to come up here?" she asked.

"Not yet," he said. "Lie back. Like this." Pulling off her panties, Alexander brought her hips to his face.

For a moment all Tatiana heard was his rapid breathing. Reaching down, she touched his head. "Shura?" His eyes on her, his hands on her, his breath on her were weakening her.

His fingers stroked her. "All this underneath your white dress with red roses . . ." Alexander whispered. "Look at you . . ." He kissed her softly. "Tania, you are such a lovely girl." She felt his warm, wet lips on her. His hair and stubble rubbed against the insides of her thighs. It was too much. The burn and the melt were near-instant.

She was still quaking with aftershocks when Alexander climbed onto the bed, placing his soothing hand on her trembling lower stomach.

"Dear God, Alexander," she said breathlessly. "What are you doing to me?"

"You're unbelievable."

"I am?" Tatiana murmured, nudging him downward. "Please? . . . Again?" She glanced at him and closed her eyes when she saw his grin. "What?" She smiled herself. "Unlike you, I don't need a rest period."

Her hands clasped his head.

"Tatia . . . you're very blonde . . . have I mentioned how much I love that?"

She moaned in a whisper; his mouth, his tongue felt so tenderly, exceedingly arousing. "Oh, Shura . . ."

"Yes?"

Tatiana couldn't ask for a moment, unable to stop her soft exultation. "What did you think the first time you saw me in this dress?"

"What did I think?"

She moaned.

"I thought—Can you hear me?"

"Oh, yes . . ."

"I thought—"

"Oh, Shura . . ."

"If there is a God, I thought . . . Please someday let me make love to this girl while she wears that dress."

"Oh . . ."

"Tatiasha . . . isn't it nice to know there is a God?"

"Oh, yes, Shura, yes . . ."

"Alexander," she panted, lying on her side, her eyes half closed, her mouth dry, unable to get a decent breath out of her lungs, "I need you this minute to tell me that you have shown me everything there is. Because I'm just about done for."

Alexander smiled. "Can I surprise you?"

"No! Tell me there's nothing more." She saw the look in his eyes.

Flipping her onto her back, Alexander descended on top of her. "Nothing more?" Hungrily kissing her, he parted her legs. "I haven't even begun, do you understand?" he whispered. "I have been going easy on you."

"You've been going *easy* on me?" she repeated in disbelief, crying out as he entered her, clutching at him, moaning under his weight, her molten insides starting to burn again.

"Is it too much? You're clutching me as if . . ."

"Yes, it's too much . . ."

"Tania . . ." Alexander's mouth was on her shoulders, on her neck, on her lips. "It's our wedding night. Watch out for me . . . there will be nothing left of you. Only the dress will remain."

"Promise, Shura?" she whispered.

Kneading her hand, touching her ring, Alexander said, "In America, when two people get married, they say their vows. Do you know what those are?"

Tatiana was hardly listening. She had been thinking of America. She wanted to ask Alexander if there were villages in America, villages with cabins on the banks of rivers. In America where there was no war, and no hunger, and no Dimitri.

"Are you listening? The priest says, 'Do you, Alexander, take this woman to be your lawfully wedded wife?' "

"Lawfully *bedded?*"

He laughed. "That too. No, lawfully *wedded*. And then we say our vows. Do you want me to tell you what they are?"

"What what are?" Tatiana brought his fingers to her lips.

"You have to repeat after me."

"Repeat after me."

"I, Tatiana Metanova, take this man to be my husband—"

"I, Tatiana Metanova, take this *great* man to be my husband." Kissing his thumb and forefinger and middle finger. He had wonderful fingers.

"To live together in the covenant of marriage—"

"To live together in the covenant of marriage." Kissing his ring finger.

"I will love him, comfort him, honor and keep him—"

"I will *love* him, comfort him, honor and keep him." Kissing the ring on his ring finger. Kissing his little finger.

"And obey him."

Tatiana smiled, rolling her eyes. "And obey him."

"And, forsaking all others, be faithful to him until death do us part—"

Kissing the palm of his hand. Wiping tears from her face with the palm of his hand. "And, forsaking all others, be faithful to him until death do us part."

"I, Alexander Barrington, take this woman to be my wife."

"Don't, Shura." Sitting on top of him, rubbing her breasts into his chest.

"To live together in the covenant of marriage—"

Kissing the middle of his chest.

"I will *love* her"—his voice cracked—"*love* her, comfort her, honor, and keep her—"

Pressing her cheek to his chest and listening for the iambic rhyme of his heart.

"And, forsaking all others, be faithful to her until—"

"Don't, Shura." His chest wet from her tears. "Please."

His hands above his head. "There are things worse than death."

Her heart full, overwhelmed. Remembering her mother's body tilted over her sewing. Remembering Marina's last words, to the end saying, *I don't want to die . . . and not feel just once what you feel.* Remembering a laughing Dasha braiding her young hair already a lifetime ago. "Oh, yes? Like what?"

He didn't reply.

She understood anyway. "I'd rather have a bad life in the Soviet Union than a good death. Wouldn't you?"

"If it was a life with you, then yes."

Nodding into his chest, Tatiana said, "Besides, I haven't seen a good death."

"You've seen it. What did Dasha say to you before she died?"

Pressing herself into him. Wanting to be inside him, wanting to touch his magnanimous heart. "She said I was a good sister."

441

Alexander's hands holding her head gently to him. "You were a very good sister. She left you well." Pausing. "She died a good death."

Kissing the skin over his heart. "What will you say to me, Alexander Barrington, when you leave me alone in the world?" Tatiana whispered. "What will you say so I know, so I can hear it?"

Alexander lay her down on the bed, leaning over her. "Tania," he whispered, "there is no death here in Lazarevo. No death, no war, no Communism. There is only you and only me, and only life." He smiled. "Married life. Let's go and live it." He jumped off the bed. "Come outside with me."

"All right," she said.

"Put on your dress." He threw on his army trousers. "*Just* your dress."

She smiled and hopped down. "Where are we going?"

"We're going dancing."

"Dancing?"

"Yes. Every wedding day has to have dancing."

He took her out into the chilly clearing. Tatiana heard the rushing river, the crackling of pine, smelled pinecones. "Look at that moon, Tatia . . ." said Alexander, pointing into the distant valley between the Ural Mountains.

"I'm looking," she said, her eyes on him. "But we have no music." She stood smiling in front of him, her hands in his hands.

Alexander pulled her to him. "Under a wedding moonrise, a dance with my wife in her wedding dress . . ."

They waltzed in the clearing under a haloed rising round crimson moon. He sang:

> *Oh, how we danced*
> *On the night we were wed . . .*
> *We found our true love*
> *Though a word wasn't said . . .*

He sang in English. Tatiana understood most of it. "Shura, darling," she said, "you have such a good voice. I know that song. In Russian we call it 'The Danube Waltz.' "

"I like it better in English," said Alexander.

"Me, too," she said, pressed against his naked chest, looking up at him. "You have to teach me how to sing it, so I can sing it to you."

Taking her hand, he whispered, "Come, Tatiasha."

They did not sleep that night. Their sandwiches lay untouched on the ground by the trees where she had sat and made them.

Alexander.

Alexander.

Alexander.

Her *dacha* years, her boat, her Lake Ilmen, on which she once was queen, fell forever away into the cleft of vanished childhood as Tatiana in tremulous awe surrendered herself to Alexander, who, by turns voracious and tender, lavished her starving flesh with miracles she had not dreamed of . . . *as if pervaded with his deathless leaven . . . All earthly stuff—emotions, anguish, passion—had been transmuted to the stuff of heaven.*

12

In the groggy early morning Tatiana sat on the blanket in front of a blue crystal river, cradling Alexander's head in her hands. "Honey," she whispered, "want to go swimming?"

"I would," replied Alexander, his head in her lap, "if only I could move my body."

After they slept for a few hours and swam for a few hours, they got dressed and went to Naira's house. The women were inside on the porch, drinking tea and clucking.

"They're talking about us," Tatiana said to him, taking one step away as they walked.

"Wait till we give them something to really gossip about," Alexander said, nudging her forward and grabbing her bottom.

The women were upset with Tatiana. Dusia cried and prayed. Raisa shook even more than usual. Naira stared at Alexander reprovingly. Axinya twitched with excitement, as if unable to wait until she could tell her friends later in the afternoon.

"Where have you been? We didn't know what happened to you. We thought you had been killed," said Naira.

"Tania, tell them. *Have* you been killed?" Alexander said, trying not to smile.

The women—including Tatiana—all glared at Alexander, who saluted them and went outside to shave. Tatiana thought he must have looked like a pirate with his black stubble. What to do? To pretend? To own up? The explanations, though. Was it something she could stand? Could she explain to these well-meaning women the workings of her life? They believed their world with her to be one thing, and now she was about to tell them it was something else. Just a few days ago they were aflutter over Alexander's traveling 1,600 kilometers to marry his fiancée, supposedly heartbroken, and suddenly *this.* It didn't look very good for her, nor for him.

"Tatiana, will you tell us please where you were?"

"Nowhere, Naira Mikhailovna. We went to Molotov. We bought a few things, some food, some . . . We . . ."

What was she going to say?

"Where did you sleep? You've been gone for three days! We honestly didn't know what happened to you."

443

Alexander walked up the stairs, onto the porch, and said without ceremony, "Did you tell them we got married?"

Most of the oxygen on the porch was sucked into the lungs of the four old women who collectively went, "Aahhhhhh!"

Tatiana rubbed her eyes, shaking her head. Leave it to him. She sat down on a chair by the sofa and sighed.

"I'm starved," he said, walking into the parlor room. "Tatia, is there anything to eat?" He came out chewing a hunk of bread. He sat down next to Dusia on the sofa, put his arm around her, and said, "Ladies, you love newlyweds in small villages, don't you? Maybe we could have a little party." He grinned.

Losing her composure, Naira said tersely, "Alexander, I don't know if you've noticed, but we are upset. Saddened and upset."

"Married!" exclaimed Axinya.

"What do you mean, *married?*" cried Dusia, crossing herself. "Not my Tanechka. My Tanechka is pure—"

Coughing loudly, Alexander got up. "Tania? Please, let's go eat."

"Shura, wait."

He sat back down.

Dusia said, "Tatiana Georgievna, tell me it isn't true. Tell me he is just kidding. Just playing jokes on us, trying to get four old women older before their time."

Naira Mikhailovna said, "I don't think he is kidding, Dusia."

Tatiana, shaking her head at Alexander, said, "Dusia, please don't be upset—"

"Wait," Alexander interrupted, turning to Dusia sitting next to him. "Why should you be upset? We're married, Dusia. It's a good thing."

"Good?" she cried. "Tania, what about God?"

"What about your *sister?*" asked Naira sternly.

"What about decorum, propriety?" asked Axinya in a thrilled voice, as if decorum and propriety were the two *last* things she wanted here in Lazarevo.

Raisa shook. "Tania, your sister's memory is not yet cold."

Naira said sharply, "Alexander, we thought you had come to marry Dasha, God rest her soul."

One glance at Alexander told Tatiana that he was losing his patience. Hurriedly she said, "Look, look, let me explain—"

But it was too late. Alexander got up and said, "No. Let *me* explain. I came to Lazarevo for Tatiana. I came to marry *her.* We're done here. Tania, let's go. I'll take your trunk. We'll come back for the sewing machine."

"Take her trunk? No, she is not leaving here!" cried Naira.

"Yes," said Alexander. "She is."

"She doesn't have to go!"

"Ladies," Alexander said, his arm around Tatiana's neck, "we're *newlyweds.*" He raised his eyebrows. "Do you really want us in your house?"

Naira gasped. Dusia crossed herself. Raisa shook, and Axinya clapped her hands once in glee.

Tatiana squeezed Alexander's arm. "Shh," she whispered. "Please. Go outside. Let me talk to them for a second. All right?"

"I want to go."

"We will. Go outside."

Naira said, "I don't know why you have to go. You can have my bedroom. I will sleep on the stove."

Before Tatiana could stop him, Alexander leaned forward and said, "Naira Mikhailovna, trust me, you don't want us in your house—Ouch!"

"Alexander! Go outside. Please," Tatiana said, rubbing his arm where she had pinched him.

Turning back to Naira, Tatiana sat down. "Look, it will be better for us in the cabin." She wanted to say "more private" but she knew they wouldn't understand. "If you need anything, let us know. Alexander wants to come over and fix your fence. If you want us to come for dinner, let us know, too."

"Tanechka, we are so worried about you," said Naira. "You, of all people, with a *soldier*!"

Dusia muttered Christ's name.

Naira continued. "I just don't know about him. We would have thought you'd want someone a little more like yourself. More your match."

Smiling, Axinya said, "I'm beginning to suspect that's exactly what she got."

"Don't worry about me," Tatiana said. "I'm safe with him."

"Of course we want you to come for dinner," said Naira. "We love *you*."

Dusia said, "God spare you from the horrors of the marriage bed."

Keeping her face straight and glancing outside at Alexander, Tatiana said, "Thank you."

Outside, Alexander was doubled over.

He was carrying her big heavy trunk, so he was fairly helpless, which was the way she liked it, because she was yelling at him. "Why can't you let me handle things my own way, why?"

"Because your own way would entail milking a cow for hours and washing their clothes and then sewing them all new ones and God knows what else!"

"I don't understand," she said. "I would've thought after we got married you would calm down a bit, be less protective, less . . . you know. You. That American way that makes you stand out like a black peg among white nails."

Alexander laughed. "You don't understand anything," he said, panting a bit. "Why would you think *that*?"

"Because we're married."

"To shatter your illusions, I'll warn you right now that everything you've seen will increase a hundredfold now that you're my wife. Everything."

445

"Everything?"

"Yes. Protectiveness. Possessiveness. Jealousy. All of it. A hundredfold. That's the nature of the beast. Didn't want to tell you beforehand, thought it might scare you off."

"*Might?*"

"There you are. You can't get the marriage annulled." Alexander glanced at her, his eyes burning. "Not after it's been so . . . *thoroughly* consummated."

They couldn't even wait to get home. He carried the trunk into the pines and sat down on it. Tatiana climbed on top of him. "Don't be too loud in the woods," he told her, lifting her onto himself and kissing her.

Afterward Alexander said, "That's like asking you to shed your freckles for a day, isn't it?"

The four women came to see them at the house later in the afternoon. Alexander and Tatiana were playing soccer. Actually Tatiana had just gotten the ball away from him and, squealing, was trying to hold on to it, while he was behind her, trying to kick it from under her. He had lifted her off the ground and was pressing himself hard into her while she was shrieking. All he was wearing was his skivvies, and all she was wearing was his ribbed top and her underwear.

Flummoxed, Tatiana stood in front of Alexander, trying to shield his near-naked body from four pairs of wide eyes. He stood behind her, his arms on her shoulders, and Tatiana heard him say, "Tell them— No, forget it, *I* will," and before she could utter a sound, he came forward, walked up to them, twice their size, bare and unrelentingly himself, and said, "Ladies, in the future you might want to wait for us to come and see *you*."

"Shura," Tatiana muttered, "go and get dressed."

"Soccer is probably the least of what you'll see," Alexander said into the women's stunned faces before going inside the house. When he came back out, suitably covered, he told Tatiana he was going to the village to get a couple of things they needed, like ice and an ax.

"What an odd combination," she remarked. "Where are you going to get ice from?"

"The fish plant. They have to refrigerate their fish, don't they?"

"Ax?"

"From that nice man Igor," Alexander yelled, walking up the clearing, blowing her a kiss.

She gazed after him. "Hurry back," she called.

Naira Mikhailovna apologized hastily. Dusia was mouthing a prayer. Raisa shook. Axinya beamed at Tatiana, who invited them all for a bit of *kvas*. "Come inside. See how nicely Alexander cleaned the house. And look, he repaired the door. Remember, the top hinge was broken?"

The four women looked around for a place to sit.

446

"Tanechka," said Naira nervously, "there is no furniture in here."

Axinya whooped.

Dusia crossed herself.

"I know, Naira Mikhailovna. We don't need much." She looked down on the floor. "We have some things, we have my trunk. Alexander said he will make us a bench. I'll bring my desk with the sewing machine . . . we'll be fine."

"But how—"

"Oh, Naira," said Axinya, "leave the girl alone, will you?"

Dusia glared at the rumpled bedsheets on top of the stove. A flustered Tatiana smiled. Alexander was right. It *was* better to go and visit *them*. She asked when would be a good time to come for dinner.

Naira said, "Come tonight, of course. We'll celebrate. But you come every night. Look, you won't be able to eat here at all. There's nowhere even to sit or cook. You'll starve. Come every night. That's not too much to ask, is it?"

"Yes, it's too much to ask," Alexander said when he returned with no ice ("Tomorrow") but with an ax, a hammer and nails, a saw, a wood plane, and a kerosene-burning Primus stove. "I didn't marry you so we could go over there every night." He laughed. "You invited them inside? That's very brave of you, my wife. Did you at least make the bed before they came in?" He laughed harder.

Tatiana was sitting down on the cool iron hearth, shaking her head. "You're just impossible."

"I'm impossible? I'm not going there for dinner, forget it. Why don't you just invite them here afterward then, for the post-dinner *vaudeville*—"

"*Vaudeville?*"

"Never mind." He dropped all of his goods on the floor in the corner of the cabin. "Invite them here for the entertainment hour. Go ahead. As I make love to you, they can walk around the hearth, clucking to their hearts' content. Naira will say, 'Tsk, tsk, tsk. I told her to go with my Vova. I know he could do it better.' Raisa will want to say, 'Oh, my, oh, my,' but she'll be shaking too much. Dusia will say, 'Oh, dear Jesus, I prayed to You to spare her from the horrors of the marriage bed!' And Axinya will say—"

" 'Wait till I tell the whole village about his horrors,' " said Tatiana.

Alexander laughed and then went to the water to swim.

Tatiana nested inside the cabin, arranging their things, neatening up, and making the bed. She got herself ready to go to Naira's and was sitting by the iron hearth waiting for the water to boil on the little Primus stove so she could make some tea when Alexander came back inside. He took off his wet shorts and came close to her. She glanced up, her heart giving out at the sight of him. He nudged her with his leg. "What?"

"Nothing," she said, quickly turning her gaze back to the kettle. But he nudged her again, and she wanted to look at him so much.

Wanted to *taste* him so much.

Overcoming her shyness, Tatiana knelt on the wide-plank wood floor in front of Alexander, taking him into her tender hands. "Are all men this beautiful," she whispered fondly, "or just you?"

"Oh, just me," replied a grinning Alexander. "All other men are repellent." He lifted her off the floor. "Too hard on your knees on the wood."

"In America do they have carpets?"

"Wall to wall."

"Get me a pillow, Shura," whispered Tatiana.

They went over to Naira's for dinner. Tatiana cooked while Alexander fixed the broken fence. Vova and Zoe came, too, ostensibly confounded by the twisted hand of fate that had allowed their little, unassuming, innocent Tania to be married to a soldier in the Red Army.

Tatiana saw that everyone was watching her and Alexander's every move and interaction. So when she served Alexander and stood close against him as he looked up at her, she could *not* look down at him, her body throbbing with remembrance. She was afraid that every person at the table would know instantly what she was remembering.

After dinner Alexander didn't ask anyone to help her. He helped her himself, and when they were outside, bent over the dishpan, he turned her chin to him and said, "Tatia, don't turn your face away from me again. Because now you're mine, and every time I look at you, I need to see you're mine in your eyes."

Tatiana gazed at him, adoring him.

"There I am," he whispered, kissing her, their hands entwined in the warm, soapy water.

13

The following tranquil afternoon a barebacked and barefooted Alexander was crouching and fiddling with two metal bowls while Tatiana danced in little steps behind him, jumping up and down and asking him what he was doing. It occurred to her that she didn't like surprises. She liked to know things up front. Finally he had to get up, take her by the shoulders, and lead her away, asking her to go and cook something, read, practice her English—something, *anything* other than bother him for the next twenty minutes.

Tatiana could not. She stopped jumping but tiptoed near him, bending over his back to see.

Alexander put milk, heavy cream, sugar and eggs into the smaller metal bowl and mixed the ingredients briskly.

She lifted her shirt and rubbed her breasts against his bare back.

"Hmm," he said. "What I need right now, though, is a cup of blueberries."

Tatiana got those for him, glad to help. After filling the large bowl with ice and rock salt, Alexander put the small metal bowl inside the large metal bowl and with a long wooden spoon started stirring the milk and sugar mixture.

"What are you doing? When will you tell me?"

"Very soon you'll know."

"How soon? Just tell me now."

"You're impossible. You'll know in thirty minutes. Can you wait thirty minutes?"

"Thirty minutes? What are we going to do for thirty minutes?" She was bouncing up and down.

"You're too much." He laughed. "Look, I have to mix this. Come back in thirty minutes."

Tatiana walked around the clearing in circles, watching him.

She was deliriously happy. She was speechlessly, wordlessly, infinitely happy.

"Shura, are you watching? Look!" She cartwheeled and then balanced herself upside down on one hand.

"Yes, sweet girl," he said. "I'm watching."

Thirty minutes later Alexander called her over.

Tatiana skipped up and looked at the thick, blue-colored mixture in the bowl. "What is it?"

He handed her a spoon. "Try it."

She tasted it. "Ice cream?" she said incredulously.

He nodded with a grin. "Ice cream."

"You made me *ice cream?*"

"Yes. Happy birthday." Pause. "Now, *why* are you crying? Eat. It'll melt."

Tatiana sat on the ground with the bowl between her legs and ate her ice cream and cried. Alexander opened his hands with perplexed incomprehension and went to wash.

"I saved you some ice cream. Have some," Tatiana said tearfully when he returned.

"No, have it all," he said.

"It's too much for me. I had half of it. Have the rest. Otherwise what are we going to do with it?"

"I was thinking," Alexander said, kneeling by her, "that I'd like to undress you, spread the ice cream *all* over your body, and lick it off you."

Dropping the spoon, Tatiana said hoarsely, "Sounds like a waste of perfectly good ice cream."

Though she didn't think so when he was done with her.

Afterward they swam, and then he sat and smoked. "Tatia, show me your naked cartwheels."

"What, here? No, this isn't a good place."

"If not here, where? Go on, right into the river."

Tatiana stood up, smiling and sparkling naked, lifted her arms, and said, "Are you ready?" And then catapulted herself upside down in jubilant rainbow somersaults one two three four five six seven times into the Kama.

"How was that?" she called to him from the water.

"Spectacular," he replied, sitting on the ground, smoking and watching her.

14

Even without his watch, Alexander, still on military time, woke first in the early blue morning and went to wash and smoke, while Tatiana sleepily waited for him, curled into a ball like a warm bun, as if she had just come out of the oven. When he jumped into bed, he immediately pressed his ice-cold body into her. She yelped and futilely tried to get away. "Please, no! That's just merciless. I hope they fine you for that in the army. I bet you never did that to Marazov twice."

"I bet you're right," he replied, "But I don't have inalienable rights to Marazov. You're my wife. Now, turn to me."

"Let go and I'll turn."

"Tania . . ." whispered Alexander. "I don't need you to turn to me." He continued to press himself into her. "But I'm not letting go until I've had enough of you. Until you've warmed me from the inside out and the outside in."

After they made love, Tatiana made Alexander breakfast. Twelve potato pancakes, and then she sat on the blanket next to him in the crisp sunrise, every glittering day warmer than before. Alexander ate ravenously. She watched him.

"What?"

"Nothing." She smiled. "You're always so hungry. How did you survive last winter?"

"How did *I* survive last winter?"

She gave him the rest of her own pancakes. He protested, but not for long when she scooted closer to him, a breath away, and fed him herself, unable to look away from his face. She felt melted before him.

"What, Tatia?" Alexander asked softly, taking the last bite from the fork in her hands. He smiled. "Did I do something you liked?"

Blushing and shaking her head once, she emitted a small excited sound and kissed him on his unshaven cheek. "Come on, husband," she murmured. "Let's go and shave you."

While she was shaving him, she said, "Did I tell you that Axinya offered to fire up the *banya* tomorrow morning if we want to have a hot bath, and to stand guard by the door to make sure no one comes in?"

"Hmm. You told me," Alexander replied. "I like that Axinya, but you know she'll be standing at the door to hear us."

"You'll have to be quieter, then, won't you?" Tatiana said, wiping the soap off his smooth cheek.

"*I'll* have to be quieter?"

She blushed, and he smiled.

"What are we going to do today?" Tatiana asked as she finished the other cheek and dried his face. "We should go pick some blueberries later, so I can make blueberry pie."

"We should. But first I'm going to drag that log into the water so we can have a place to sit and brush our teeth, and then I'm going to build us a table to clean our fish," Alexander replied. "You will go to your damn sewing circle. To your women. I won't be happy."

"I'll be back in a couple of hours," she told him.

"I'll be happy."

"Your job is to be happy."

"I have only one job here in Lazarevo," Alexander said, catching her around the waist. "To make love to my nubile wife."

Tatiana almost moaned out loud. "I see a lot of talking and not a lot of—"

"*How is my English?*" Tatiana asked Alexander in English.

"*It's good,*" Alexander replied in English. It was late morning. They were walking through the dense deciduous riverbank woods a few kilometers from home, with two buckets for blueberries, and they were supposed to be talking only in English, but Tatiana backtracked and said in Russian, "I'm reading much better than I'm talking, I think. John Stuart Mill is simply unreadable now instead of unintelligible."

Alexander smiled. "That's a fine distinction." He yanked up a couple of mushrooms. "Tania, can we eat these?"

Taking them out of his hands and throwing them back on the ground, Tatiana said, "Yes. But we will only be able to eat them once."

Alexander laughed. She said, "I have to teach you how to pick mushrooms, Shura. You can't just rip them out of the ground like that."

"I have to teach you how to speak English, Tania," said Alexander.

In English, Tatiana continued, "*This is my new husband, Alexander Barrington.*"

And in English, Alexander replied with a smile of pleasure on his face, "*And this is my young wife, Tatiana Metanova.*" He kissed the top of her braided head and in Russian said, "Tatiana, now say the other words I taught you."

She turned the color of a tomato. "*No,*" she stated firmly, in English. "*I am not saying them.*"

"Please."

"No. Look for blueberries." Still in English.

She saw that Alexander couldn't have been less interested in blueberries. *"What about later? Will you say them later?"* he asked.

"Not now, not later," Tatiana replied bravely. But she was not looking at him.

Alexander drew her to him. *"Later,"* he continued in English, *"I will insist that you please me by using your English-speaking tongue in bed with me."*

Struggling slightly against him, Tatiana said in English, *"It is good I am not understand what you say to me."*

"I will show you what I mean," said Alexander, putting down his bucket.

"Later, later," she acquiesced. *"Now, pick up your backet. Collect blueberries."*

"All right," he said in English, not letting go of her. "And it's *bucket.* Come on, Tania. Say the other words." He held her. "Your shyness is an aphrodisiac to me. Say them."

Tatiana, breathless inside and out, said, *"All right,"* in English. *"Pick up your bucket. Let us go house. I will practice love with you."*

Alexander laughed. *"Make love to you, Tania. Make love to you."*

It was a dazzling and peaceful summer afternoon. Alexander was sawing a tree into short logs. Tatiana was by his side.

"What?"

She was nudging him.

"What? You're like my tiny shadow. Let me finish. I have to make a bench so we can sit and eat."

"Want to play something?"

"No. I've got to do this."

"We can play *Alexander Says.*" She smiled invitingly.

"Later."

"What about war-hide-and-seek?"

"Later."

"What? Afraid of losing again, Captain?" She grinned.

"Oh, you . . ."

"You want to . . . cavort?"

Alexander glanced at her. She blushed and said, "I meant really cavort. Frolic in the water. I want to stand in the palm of your hand and have you lift me above your head—"

"Only if I can fling you after."

"Never heard it called *that* before, but all right, you got yourself a game."

Laughing, not letting go of the saw, Alexander said, "We will do all that and twice, but first I have to finish sawing this damn wood."

Tatiana was silent a second. "Do you want to show me how you do your military push-ups?" She paused. "Fifty in a row?"

452

"Only if you give me an incentive."

"Fine. Now?"

"You're too much. Later."

She was silent another second. "Do you want to arm wrestle?"

"Arm wrestle?" Alexander said with a disbelieving grin. "You're joking, right?"

"Come on, big man, what are you, afraid?" She tickled him.

"Stop."

Tatiana tickled him again, croaking like a chicken. "Croak, croak, croak."

"That's it." He put down his saw, but she was already halfway across the clearing, running away and shrieking. He ran after her, yelling, "You better not let me catch you!"

She let him catch her with joy in the woods. Whirling her to him and panting, he said, "You're not allowed to tickle me when I have a saw in my hand!"

Tatiana was laughing. "But, Shura, you always have something in your hand. If it's not a saw, it's a cigarette, or an ax, or—"

He grabbed her bottom.

"Yes, or—"

He grabbed her breasts.

"Do you see what I mean?" she said, panting herself. "So wrestle me to the ground." She paused. "Like you want." She couldn't get her breath back as he hugged her. Either he didn't know his own strength or he was afraid of not being able to hold her close enough. Tatiana hoped it was the first one. "I'm here, Shura, I'm here," she panted, gently patting him. "Come on now."

He let her go, and she stood in front of him for a moment.

"All right." Alexander grinned. "You got me away from my work, now what? Push-ups now, cavort now, what now?"

They stood without moving. Tatiana's eyes twinkled. Alexander's eyes twinkled. She moved left, right—

But he was quicker this time. "Got to be quicker than that," he said, grabbing her and then setting her back down. "Try again?"

She moved right, right, left—

Still not quick enough. "Try again?"

Motionlessly she stood, stood, lunged left, and was around him on the right before he even straightened up.

Squealing, Tatiana jumped into his arms as he ran for her, and then hugging him and kissing his face, she said, "Let's do this. Let me blindfold you. I'll spin you around, and then you have to stumble around the clearing and find me." She giggled. "Stop tickling me."

"I'm tired of you blindfolding me," Alexander replied, continuing to tickle her. "How about instead if I blindfold *you* and feed you and you tell me what I'm putting in your mouth?"

Tatiana was laughing even before he finished. Alexander looked at her innocently. "What?"

"Shura!" she exclaimed. "How about if even *before* you blindfold me, I tell you what you're going to put in my mouth?"

Alexander laughed himself, carrying her to the house. "You have yourself a game," he said, "But only if you call what I'm putting in your mouth by name—in English." He put his hands under her dress, caressing her.

"Shura?"

"Yes?"

"Let go of me. I have to go and hide. You have to find me."

"Why should I have to find you? You're already right here." He fondled her bottom.

"Shura, you're holding me too tight. I can't move."

"I know. I don't want you to go anywhere."

"What kind of game is this?"

"The same game we play all day long."

"Which is . . ."

"Get up, make love. Wash, make love. Cook, eat, make love. Swim, make love. Play soccer, play dominoes, play blindfold, make love."

"Yes, but here we're going straight to making love. Where's the fun in that?"

15

After they had woken early and caught some trout and swum, Tatiana was crouching by the hearth showing Alexander how to make pancake batter. She didn't know what it was with him, but he was not paying any attention. "Shura! I'm not going to keep teaching you how to make pancakes. Do you just refuse to learn?"

"I'm a man. I'm physically unable to learn how to cook for myself," he said. He was lying on the wood floor very close to her as Tatiana mixed together the thick warm milk, flour, and sugar.

"But you made me ice cream."

"That was for you. I said, cook for *myself*."

"Shura!"

"What!"

"Why are you looking at me and not my batter?" He was sprawled on the floor, looking up at her with the sweetest face.

"I can't take my eyes off you," he said calmly, "because I find it profoundly arousing that you cook for me with such abandon. Anything I want. I can't take my eyes off you," he continued, less calmly, "because I am no longer hungry for pancakes."

"Stop looking at me," Tatiana said, trying to stay calm herself. "What are you going to do when you're in the woods by yourself and need to eat?"

"Do I *have* to learn how to make batter? I'll eat bark, berries, mushrooms."

"Do yourself a favor—don't eat the mushrooms," Tatiana said. "Will you watch, please?"

He looked away from her and into the pot. "So? Milk, flour, sugar? Is that it? Am I done? Can I look at you again?"

With a twitch of the wooden spoon, Tatiana flicked a bit of batter into his face. "Hey!" she exclaimed. "Watch, I said."

Shaking his head in disbelief, Alexander stuck his hand into the batter and threw a handful into Tatiana's face. "Who do you think you're dealing with around here?"

"I don't know," she slowly replied, wiping the batter from her eyes and proceeding to stir. "But I don't think you know who *you're* dealing with around here," Before he could move, Tatiana took the whole pot and poured it on him, then jumped up and ran outside.

When he caught her in the clearing, Alexander was dripping with batter. Hoisting her up, he rubbed his messy self all over her, into her, holding her mouth closed to stop her from laughing, but she wouldn't stop, feeling desperate delight and desire. Tatiana's whole body was shaking from laughter, and she could tell that it reminded her husband too much of her whole body shaking from pleasure, because he was already on to the next thing, but she was still laughing. Trembling, quickening, and sticky, their chests pressed together, they were poured like thick cream and warm sugar over one another, licking each other, stuck together and slippery, and afterward a panting and sated Alexander joyously asked, "If we don't cook the pancakes but eat the batter raw, does that still count as breakfast?"

"I'm almost sure of it," panted back Tatiana.

The sun was at full noon. Alexander was cleaning the trout at the small table he had built. He was using his army knife to scale the fish and cut off their heads. Tatiana stood by his side with a bag to catch the remnants and a pot of water to put the cleaned fish into. She was about to make fish soup with potatoes. They had only one sharp knife, and Alexander was very proficient with it. "As long as you don't have to cook the food you catch, you'll never starve, will you, Shura?" Tatiana said, watching him with admiration.

"Tania, if I had to, I would cook this fish on the fire that I build." He glanced at her. "What?"

"Alexander, you fish, you build fires, you make furniture, you fight, you log. Is there anything you can't do?" Tatiana blushed even as she was saying it.

"You tell *me*." Alexander leaned over and kissed her deeply, not stopping until she moaned into his mouth. "Don't be so delicious," he whispered.

Clearing her throat, she murmured, "I've got to stop turning red."

"Please don't. And yes, there is one thing I can't do. Can't make pancakes." He smiled at her.

"When are we going to go to Molotov to get our wedding pictures from the jeweler?"

"He's going to want our gold rings for those pictures, I know it."

Tatiana gazed at him, kissing his arm, pressing her face against him. "Do we have enough kerosene for the Primus stove?"

"Plenty, why?"

"After I put the *ukha* on, can we leave it for a little while?" She took a deep breath. "Shura?... Dusia asked me to come and help her at the church." She looked at Alexander. "Please? I feel bad because I haven't been over there much—"

"You're over there way too much." He stopped smiling.

"I thought I was your shadow?"

"Except when you're over there way too much." Alexander sighed. "What does she need this time?"

Relieved, Tatiana said, "One of the windows fell out. She was wondering if you could fix it. It's her only stained glass window."

"Oh, so she needs *me* this time."

"I'll come with you. She says she'll give you some vodka for your trouble."

"Tell her to leave you alone, and she's got herself a deal."

Leaving for a moment, Tatiana returned with a cigarette and a lighter. "Here," she said. "Open your mouth."

"How you talk," Alexander said, opening his mouth. She watched him take a few puffs. Then, not knowing what to do with the cigarette, she smelled it, brought it to her mouth, took a drag, and immediately broke into a cough. Alexander motioned for the cigarette back, took three or four deep drags, and said, "I'm done. And don't put it in your mouth again. I hear you breathing in the night—your lungs are struggling."

"That's not the TB," she said, stubbing out the cigarette. "That's you holding me." She looked away.

Glancing at her, Alexander said nothing.

At the church Tatiana helped Alexander hold the small stained glass window. She stood on a stepladder while he caulked the edge of the window with a gooey mixture of water, pulverized limestone, and clay. "Shura?"

"Hmm."

"Can I ask you a hypothetical question?"

"No."

"What would we have done if Dasha were still alive? Do you ever think about that?"

"No."

Tatiana paused. "Well, I do. Sometimes."

"Like when do you think of that?"

"Like now."

When he made no reply, Tatiana persisted. "Can you think about it? What would we have done?"

"I don't want to think about it."

"Do."

Alexander sighed. "Why do you enjoy torturing yourself? Do you feel life has been too good to you?"

Tatiana stared at him. "Life has," she said slowly, "been too good to me."

"Hold the window steady," he said. "It's Dusia's only stained glass window. I don't think she'll forgive even you for breaking it. Is it too heavy for you?"

"No, it's fine. Here, let me come closer to the frame."

"Just a minute longer. I'm almost done."

Tatiana moved on the ladder, lost her footing, and came toppling down, letting go of the glass, which fell out of the frame and was caught by Alexander, who grabbed it, laid it down, and went to help Tatiana off the ground. She was shaken but not hurt. She had a scrape on the back of her ankle. She was, however, frowning at her husband.

"What?" Alexander said. "Like my reflexes? Dusia will now be praying for my *life* every day." He tried to dust Tatiana off but just made her messier. "Look at my hands. I'm going to cement myself to you if I'm not careful." He smiled, kissing her collarbone.

Still Tatiana frowned at him.

"What?"

"Love your reflexes," she said. "Lightning quick. Good job. I just want to point out," she added, "that given the choice between the glass and your wife, you chose the glass, admirably quick though you were."

Laughing, Alexander helped Tatiana back onto the ladder, standing behind her on the ground. He didn't touch her with his messy hands, but he softly bit her bottom through her dress. "I didn't choose the glass," he said. "You were already on the ground."

"I didn't see your legendary reflexes reach for me while I was being propelled downward like a rocket."

"Oh? And what would have happened to you if that glass fell on top of you?" he asked. "You wouldn't have been very happy with me then."

"I'm not very happy with you now," she said, but she was smiling, and he bit her bottom again and went to the window to finish caulking. Finally the glass was solidly back in. Dusia, who was inside the church, thanked Alexander up and down and even kissed him, telling him he was not a bad man.

Alexander bowed his head slightly, nodding at Tatiana. "What did I tell you?"

Tatiana pulled him by his shirt. "Come on, not-a-bad-man," she said. "Let's go. I'll wash you." They walked back home through the sap-smelling woods. At the house Tatiana went inside to get soap and towels.

"Tania, can you feed me first?"

"Shura, you can't eat covered in muck like you are."

"Watch me," he said. "I know how the washing-me thing goes. I won't be eating for two hours, and I'm starving now. Just put the soup in a bowl, take a spoon, and feed me."

"Well, if you wouldn't take two hours . . ." Tatiana muttered under her breath, the flame pit in her stomach opening up.

"Just feed me, Tatia. Rail at me later." Alexander raised his brows, his eyes warming her like the fire. Her glad heart swelling, Tatiana obliged, and as she was feeding him, she resumed. "You didn't answer my hypothetical question."

"Blissfully, I forgot it."

"About Dasha."

"Oh, that." He chewed and swallowed a mouthful of potato and fish, and said in a serious tone, "I think you know the answer to that."

"I do?"

"Of course. You know if she were still alive, I would have had to marry her, as I had promised, and you would have had to go and have a bang with good old Vova."

"Shura!"

"What?"

She shoved his leg. "I'm not going to talk to you about this if you're not going to be serious."

"Oh, good. Can I have some more soup?"

After lunch, when they were in the water and he was scrubbing his hands while Tatiana was soaping his back, Alexander said, "I could never have married Dasha if you were still alive. You know that. My truth would have had to come out here in Lazarevo. What about yours?"

Tatiana didn't reply.

They were sitting in the river near the shore. Alexander took the bottle of shampoo and turned Tatiana's back to him to lather her hair. Running his fingers through her soapy strands, he said, "You miss her."

She nodded. "I wonder what being here in Lazarevo would have been like had she lived." Leaning back into him, she said, "I miss my family." She paused as her voice broke. "Like you must have missed your mother and father."

"I didn't have time to miss them," said Alexander. "I was too busy saving my fucking life." He tilted her head back to rinse her hair.

But Tatiana knew the truth. "You know, sometimes I get a funny feeling about Pasha."

"What funny feeling?"

She stood up and took the soap from him. "I don't know. A train blew up, no bodies were retrieved. As if the not knowing for certain what had happened to him makes his death somehow less real."

He stood up, too, and led her deeper into the water. "You're saying you only believe it if you *see* the people you love die?"

458

"Something like that. Does that make sense?"

"Not at all," said Alexander. "I didn't see my mother die. I didn't see my father die. They're dead all the same."

"I know." She soaped him comfortingly. "But Pasha is my *twin*. He is like half of me. If he is dead, what about me?" She lathered her breasts and rubbed her hard, soapy nipples against his chest.

"I can answer that. You're very much alive," said Alexander. "I tell you what: you want to play this hypothetical game? I'll play. I have a question for *you*," he said, taking the soap out of her hands and pitching it onto the shore. "Say Dasha were still alive, and you and I had not yet married, but"— Alexander stopped talking while he lifted Tatiana onto himself—"but I had made love to you standing"— he paused between breaths—"like *this*—" They both groaned. "Here, in our Kama River . . . tell me, oh, my very alive wife, what would you have done? Would you have let me go then, knowing—"

She cried out.

"—this?" whispered Alexander.

As if Tatiana could answer. "I don't want to play this game anymore," she moaned, wrapping her legs loosely around his waist and her arms tightly around his neck.

"Good," said Alexander.

Afterward Tatiana sat collapsed in the shallow water against a boulder jutting out of the river, and Alexander lay before her, the back of his head against her chest. They were murmuring and looking out onto the Kama and the mountains when Tatiana noticed that Alexander had become quieter. He had fallen asleep, his legs stretched out in the gentle lap of the river, his bare upper body pressed against her. Smiling and holding him to her, Tatiana softly kissed his sleeping head, leaving her lips in his wet hair.

Blinking, blinking, she sat for a long time not moving, until at last she soaked in a breath, an afternoon breath of sap and fresh water and cherry blossoms nearby. Wet grass, old leaves, sand, earth, Alexander, and she whispered, "Once upon a time there lived a man, a shining prince among peasants, who was worshipped by a frail maiden. The maiden escaped into the land of lilacs and milk and waited *impatiently* for her prince, who came and handed her the sun. They had nothing to run to and everything to run from; they had no refuge and no salvation; they had nothing but their tiny kingdom, in which lived but two people—the master, the mistress, and two slaves." Pausing for breath, Tatiana squeezed Alexander. "Each glorious day was a miracle from God. And they knew it. Then the prince had to leave, but that was all right because the maiden—" Tatiana stopped. She thought she heard him hold his breath. "Shura?"

"Don't stop," he murmured. "I'm very interested in what happens next. Why was it all right? What was the maiden going to do?"

"How was I doing so far?"

"Not bad. My favorite part was something about a master . . . ?"

Tatiana kissed his cheek.

"I reserve final judgment till the end." Alexander rubbed the back of his head against her chest. "Tell me why it was all right."

"It was all right," Tatiana continued, trying to think quickly, "because the maiden *patiently* waited for him to come back."

"Well, this is a fairy tale. And?"

"And he did."

"And?"

"There's an *and* after that? And . . . they lived happily ever after."

After the longest mute minute Alexander asked, "Where?"

Tatiana stared at the Ural Mountains and made no reply.

Grunting, Alexander got up and turned to her. "That wasn't a bad story, Tania."

"Wasn't bad? Why don't you try?"

"I'm not much for making up stories."

"Yes, you prefer to blow things up. Go ahead, try."

"Fine." Sitting with his legs crossed, he splashed water on his face, splashed water at her, and began. "Let's see . . . Once upon a time there lived a fair maiden—" He looked at her. "A maiden like no other. And one rene-gade mercenary knight had the fortune to be loved by her." He smiled. "Over and over."

Tatiana nudged him with her foot, but her own pleased smile was, if any-thing, broader than his.

"The knight left to protect the kingdom against marauders," Alexander paused. "And did not come back." He stopped looking at her, staring at the riverbank instead. "The maiden waited for her knight for a suitable period—"

"What would that be?"

"I don't know. Forty years?"

"Be reasonable." Tatiana pinched his leg.

"Ouch. But finally she couldn't wait anymore and gave herself to the liege of the local manor."

"After forty years who'd want her?"

Alexander turned his gaze back to Tatiana. "But lo and behold, surprise! Her knight came back, only to find his maiden running the manor and romp-ing with someone else—"

"Just like in Pushkin's *Evgeny Onegin*," said Tatiana.

"Oh, except unlike Onegin, this knight, feeling like an idiot, challenged the liege to a duel, fought for the maiden's honor, such as it was, and lost. He was then drawn and quartered right in front of her very eyes, which she dabbed with her silken handkerchief, vaguely remembering the land of lilacs they had once lived in, and then shrugged nonchalantly and went in for tea." Alexander laughed. "Now, *that's* a story!"

"Yes," Tatiana said, rising to her feet and walking to the cabin. "A stupid story."

As she was getting ready to leave, Alexander sat and smoked. "Why do you *always* have to go to your stupid sewing circle?"

"Not always. It's just for an hour." Tatiana smiled, wrapping her arms around him. "You can wait an *hour*, can't you, Captain?" she whispered huskily.

"Mmm," he said, holding her with one arm. His cigarette was in the other hand. "Can't they manage without you, for God's sake?"

She kissed his damp forehead. "Shura, have you noticed the days have been getting hotter?"

"I noticed. Can't you just sew here? I brought your sewing machine, your desk. I've made you a stool. I see you sewing; just the other day you were sewing all those dark clothes. What was that?"

"Nothing, just something silly."

"Well, continue sewing something silly here."

"I'm teaching them how to fish, Alexander."

"What?"

"Give a man a fish and he'll eat for a day," said Tatiana. "Teach him how to fish and he'll eat for a lifetime."

Shaking his head and sighing, Alexander said, "All right. I'll come with you."

"Stop it. Church is one thing, but no soldier husband of mine is going to a sewing circle. It'll unman you. Besides, you already know how to fish. Stay home. Play with your rifle or something. I'll be back in an hour. Do you want something delicious to eat before I go?"

"Yes, and I know exactly what I want," he said, laying her down on the blanket in the grass. The sun burned over their heads.

"Shura, I'm going to be late."

"Tell them your husband was starving and you had to feed him."

16

"So what do you have in your bags, big man?" Tatiana said one parched summer afternoon as she sat on the blanket in the clearing with his rucksack and the map case between her legs and painstakingly took out all of his things one by one. Tatiana was thirsty. It had been very hot in Lazarevo. Hot in the morning, sweltering in the afternoons, quite warm at night under the new moon. They slept naked under thin sheets with the windows open. They swam constantly. Still, they were always hot.

Alexander was sawing two long logs down to size. "Nothing at all of interest," he replied, his back to her.

Tatiana took out his semiautomatic, his pen and paper, a pack of cards, rolling papers, two books, two boxes of ammunition, his military knife, all his maps, and two hand grenades.

She became immediately interested in the maps, but before she had a chance to open them up, Alexander walked across the clearing to her, saw in his hand, cigarette in his mouth, and took the grenades from her. "Tell you what," he said. "Why don't we *not* play with explosive devices?"

"All right," she said, jumping to her feet. "You taught me how to shoot from the P-38, can you teach me how to fire from your rifle?" She stared at the maps on the blanket. "How many rounds can it fire one after another?"

"Thirty-five," replied Alexander, smoking down his cigarette.

"You could teach me how to shoot from your mortar, but you don't have a mortar in your ruck." She smiled.

He laughed. "No, I don't carry my mortar around with me in my ruck."

"You carry all your maps, though." Tatiana glanced at them again.

"So?"

"Shura, I wish you wouldn't stay on heavy weapons," Tatiana said, hugging him. "Can't Colonel Stepanov make you a runner or something? Can't you tell him you've married a nice girl who can't live without her soldier?"

"All right, I'll do that," he said.

Tatiana led him by the hand inside their house, taking his saw and throwing it on the ground.

"I haven't finished," he said, pointing to his logs.

"So? You're my husband, aren't you?"

"Yes? So?"

"Don't I have some inalienable rights, too?"

Tatiana was sitting naked on top of Alexander, pressing the palms of her hands into his chest.

"How does a *what* work?"

"A mortar. Didn't you tell Vova you operated a mortar? How does it work?"

"A mortar is one of the things I operate. What do you want to know?"

"Does it have a short barrel like a cannon or a long barrel?"

"It's got a long barrel."

"I see. So you have a long barrel, and what do you do?"

"You point it up at a forty-five-degree angle—"

"And then?"

"Then you pop a bomb into the barrel. It drops to the bottom, hits the firing pin, the propellant charge explodes, and—"

"I know what happens next. The bomb flies out at seven hundred meters a second."

"Something like that."

"So let me see if I've got it straight. Long barrel. Point up. Drop. Fire. Pop."

"I knew you'd understand."

"Again. Long. Up. Drop. Fire. Pop. I'm a quick learner."

"That you are."

"Shura?"

"Mmm?"

"Why does the mortar barrel have to be so long?"

"To improve muzzle velocity. Do you know what that is?"

"I have some idea."

Back outside, Tatiana had a quick drink and went straight to Alexander's relief maps. He went back to his logs. She was even hotter now; she needed to dunk her body in the Kama. Fascinated, Tatiana studied the maps. "Shura, why are all your maps only of Scandinavia? Look, there is one of Finland and one of Sweden and one of the North Sea between Norway and England. Why?"

"They're just campaign maps."

"But why of Scandinavia?" She looked over at him. "We're not fighting Scandinavia, are we?"

"We're fighting Finland."

"Oh, and here's a map of the Karelian Isthmus."

"So?"

"Didn't you fight in the Karelian Isthmus, near Vyborg, in the Winter War of 1940?"

Alexander came over and lay on his stomach next to her, kissing her shoulder. "I did, yes."

Tatiana was quiet for a moment. "At the start of the war last year, didn't you send Dimitri on several reconnaissance missions to the Karelian Isthmus, to Lisiy Nos?"

Taking the maps away from her, he said, "Do you ever forget anything I say to you?"

"Not a word," she replied.

"I wish you would have told me that sooner."

"Why all those maps?" she asked again.

"It's just Finland, Tania," Alexander replied, getting up and pulling her up. "Are you hot?"

"And Sweden, Shura. I am hot, yes."

"A little of Sweden." He blew on her forehead and her neck.

"And Norway and England, Shura." She closed her eyes, leaning against him. "Your breath is hot."

"What's your question?"

"Sweden is neutral in the current war, isn't it?" she asked.

Alexander led her inside their house. "Yes. Sweden is trying to stay neutral in the current war. Anything else?"

"I don't know." Tatiana smiled, her throat dry. "What else have you got?"

"You've seen it all, you've had it all—in spades," Alexander said softly, lifting her to their bed. "What do you want?" He smiled. "What can I do for you?"

"Hmm," she purred, her hands caressing him, feeling the droplets of heat all over her body. "Can you do that thing where you make us come together?"

"All right, Tatiasha," Alexander said, bending over her. "I'll do that thing where I make us come together."

Scorched and soaked, they fell away from each other. Breathless, they lay on their backs, and then they panted, and then they turned their faces to one another and smiled happily.

Alexander went to get them a drink, and when some time had passed and Tatiana was able to breathe normally again, she gently pleaded with him to tell her how he received his first medal of valor.

For a few minutes Alexander was mute. Tatiana waited. There was a breeze coming in through the curtains, but the breeze was hot. Alexander's body was wet. Tatiana's body was wet. They needed that Kama River to cool off in. But Tatiana wasn't getting off the bed until she heard about Karelia.

Finally he shrugged. "It was not much." His voice was even. "We had fought all through the swamps near the gulf, from Lisiy Nos practically to Vyborg. We pushed the Finns back to the city but then got bogged down in the swamps in the woods. The Finns were very well entrenched and had munitions and supplies, and we were in the mud and had nothing. In the terrible battle near Vyborg we lost more than two-thirds of our men. We were forced to stop and retreat."

Alexander paused. "It was really stupid. This was in March, just days before the armistice on March 13, and here we were, losing hundreds of men for no reason. I was in the rifle corps then. We had nothing but single-bolt rifles on us." He smiled. "And one or two mortars."

Tatiana smiled back. Her hand was on his chest.

"My platoon had thirty men when we started out. I had four left by the end of two days. Four plus me. When we returned out of the marshes to post at Lisiy Nos, we learned that one of the men left in the swamps near the defense line at Vyborg was Colonel Stepanov's young son, Yuri. He was eighteen and had just joined the army."

Alexander paused.

Paused or stopped?

Her hand on his chest, Tatiana waited. She felt his heart speed up.

And then Alexander moved her hand *away* from his heart.

Tatiana did not put it back.

He said, "So . . . I went back, spent a few hours looking for him, and found him still alive but hit. We brought him back to camp." Alexander tightened his mouth. "He didn't make it." He wasn't looking at Tatiana.

But she was looking at him. "Oh, no."

"For Yuri Stepanov I got my medal of valor."

The bones in Alexander's face were set, and his eyes were expressionless. Tatiana knew: he was making them expressionless.

She replaced her gentle hand on his chest and watched Alexander slowly blink away his life.

"The colonel was grateful to you for bringing his son back?"

"Yes," said Alexander, his voice flat. "Colonel Stepanov has been very good to me. He transferred me out of the infantry division and into the motorized. And when he became commander of the Leningrad garrison, he took me with him."

Tatiana was very, very quiet. She was barely breathing. She didn't want to know. She didn't want to ask. But she couldn't not ask.

"You didn't go into the swamps by yourself," she said at last, and sighed deeply. "Who did you take with you?"

Carefully Alexander replied, "Dimitri."

It was a long time before Tatiana spoke.

"I didn't know he was in your platoon."

"He wasn't. I asked him if he wanted to come on the mission with me, and he said yes."

"Why?"

"Why what?"

"Why would he say yes?" asked Tatiana. "I find it difficult to believe that Dimitri would go on a dangerous mission near enemy lines to find a wounded soldier."

Alexander didn't reply for a few moments. "Well, he did."

"So let me understand. You and Dimitri went into the swamps alone to retrieve Yuri Stepanov?" Tatiana tried to keep her voice even. She couldn't do it as well as Alexander. Her voice shook.

"Yes."

"Did you expect to find him?" She sounded pained.

"Well, I don't know," Alexander said. "Are you looking for a specific answer, Tatia? Something I'm not telling you?"

Tatiana paused, trying not to swallow. "Is there something you're not telling me?"

He was looking not at her but at the ceiling. "I told you. We went in, we looked for a couple of hours. We found him. We brought him back. That's all."

"Is that when Dimitri was promoted to private first class?"

"Yes."

Quietly with her fingers Tatiana drew large circles, small circles, medium circles on Alexander, her head on his chest. "Shura?"

"Oh, no."

"After the armistice of 1940, Vyborg was where the Soviet border with Finland was, right?"

"Right."

"How far is Vyborg from Helsinki?"

Alexander was silent. "I don't know."

Tatiana bit her lip. "Doesn't look far on the map."

"It's a map. Nothing looks far on it," he said impatiently. "Maybe 300 kilometers."

"I see. How far—"

"Tania."

"What? How far from Helsinki to Stockholm?"

"Oh, for God's sake! Stockholm?" But Alexander was still not looking at Tatiana. "Maybe another 500 kilometers. But across water. There is the Baltic Sea and the Gulf of Bothnia in between."

"Yes, there is the gulf, there is the sea," Tatiana said. "I have one more question."

"What?" He did not sound amused.

"Where is the border now?"

Alexander didn't reply.

"The Finns came down from Vyborg to Lisiy Nos, right? Where you sent Dimitri last year for reconnaissance?"

"Tatiana, is there a point to your questions?" he asked abruptly. "That's enough already."

She sat up abruptly and moved away, starting to climb down.

Alexander caught her by the arm. "Where are you going?"

"Nowhere," she said. "We were done, right? I'm going to cool off, and then I've got to start on dinner."

"Come here."

"No. I've got to—"

"Come here."

Tatiana closed her eyes. Alexander had that voice. He had that voice, those eyes, those hands, that mouth. He had that everything.

She came.

"What are you thinking?" he asked, laying her next to him, caressing her. "What are you asking me?"

"Nothing. I'm just thinking."

"You asked me about my medal, I told you. You asked me about the borders, I told you. You asked me about Lisiy Nos, I told you. Now, stop all that thinking," he said, gently kneading her nipple between his thumb and forefinger.

Alexander kissed her. They were still damp from before, still parched from before, and thirsty, and hot. "Do you have any more questions? Or are you finished?"

"I don't know."

He kissed her again, longer, warmer, deeper, kissed her tenderly, endlessly.

"I might be finished," she whispered. That's what he did to her: kissed her until the liquid flame dissolved her flesh. And he knew it. Everything he did to her he did unceasingly until he dissolved her. She was helpless before him. And he knew it. His mouth still on hers, Alexander prodded her thighs apart and slid two fingers inside her . . . pulled them out . . . slid them back in . . .

"I think I'm finished now," whispered Tatiana.

17

A few blistering summer days later, Tatiana was jumping up and down again. "What are you making now?" she asked. "You already made a bench. Stop all this building. Let's go swimming. Swimming! Come on, even the Kama is warm nowadays. Let's dive in, and I'll try to stay under longer than you."

Alexander was inside the house, having just brought in the two logs he had been working on, each about a meter tall. They came up to just below his hips.

"Later. I've got to make this."

"What are you making?" Tatiana repeated.

"Wait and you'll see."

"Why can't you just tell me?"

"A countertop."

"What for? What we need here is a table." She jumped up and down again. "We keep eating dinner on our laps. Why don't you make a table? Better yet, come swimming with me." She pulled on him.

"Maybe later. Is there anything to drink? God, this heat."

Tatiana left and came back instantly with water and a cut cucumber. "Do you want a cigarette?"

"Yes."

She brought him a cigarette. "But, Shura, we don't need a countertop. We need a table."

"I'll make a high table. Or we'll use this as a high bench."

"Why don't you just make it lower?"

"Wait and you'll see. Tatia, did anyone ever tell you that patience is a virtue?"

"Yes!" she said impatiently. "Tell me what you're making."

Alexander led her out of the house. "Can you go and get me some bread? I'm hungry. Please?"

"All right," she said. "I'll have to go to Naira's. We haven't got any."

"Good. Go to Naira's. Just be back soon."

Soon she came back with the bread, some butter, eggs, and cabbage. "Shura! I'm going to make cabbage pie tonight."

"Can't wait. I'm starving now."

"You're always starving. I can't keep you fed." She smiled. "Are you hot? You took off your shirt."

"So hot."

Tatiana beamed. "Are you done yet?"

"Almost. I'm just planing it."

Coming up to the bench, Tatiana looked at it, looked at him, and said, "Planing?"

"Making it smooth. We don't want to get splinters."

She was puzzled. "We don't? Shura, do you know what Dusia told me?"

"No, sweet girl. What did Dusia tell you?"

"That this is the hottest summer they've had in Lazarevo in seventy-five years, since 1867! Since she was four years old."

"Really?" said Alexander. Tatiana held out a flask of water for him. He drank it down whole and asked for more. He left the refilled flask on the countertop next to him as he continued to plane the flat top.

Tatiana watched him. "I don't understand," she said. "It comes up to my ribs. Why did you build it so high?"

Shaking his head, Alexander put down his wood plane and went to wash his hands and face in the bucket of water. "Come here," he said. "I'll help you up."

He lifted her to the countertop and stood in front of her. "Well? How do you like it?"

"I feel high," Tatiana said, looking at him. His eyes were peaceful, his lips were happy. "But I'm not afraid of heights." She paused. "And my face almost comes up to your face. I like *that*. Come closer, soldier."

Alexander opened her legs and stood between them. For a moment, their eyes nearly level, they gazed at each other, and then they kissed. He ran his hands under her dress up her thighs to her hips. She wasn't wearing any underwear.

"Hmm." He played with her and then untied his drawstring shorts. "Tell me, Tatiasha," Alexander murmured, guiding himself inside her and tugging her forward. "Is this close enough?"

"I think so," she said hoarsely, gripping the countertop.

Holding her hips up to him, he moved in and out of her and then yanked her sundress down to her waist, bent, and sucked her nipples. "I want your wet nipples against my chest," he said. "Grab my neck."

She couldn't.

"Grab my neck, Tania," he said, increasing his pace. "Do you still think the countertop is too high?"

She couldn't reply.

"That's what I thought," Alexander murmured, pressing her to him, enfolding her bare body in his avid hands. "Suddenly—it seems just the right height . . . doesn't it, my impatient wife, doesn't it—"

And afterward, as Alexander stood in front of her, panting and drenched, Tatiana, also panting and drenched, kissed his wet throat and asked, "Tell me, did you build it just for this?"

"Well, no," Alexander said, taking a long drink from the flask and then pouring the rest of the water over her face and breasts. "We can put potatoes on it."

Laughing, Tatiana said, "But we don't have any potatoes."

"That's a shame."

"Shura, you were right, this countertop *is* the perfect height! I finally have a place to knead the dough for my pies." Tatiana smiled at him while flouring her hands. The yeast dough had risen at last, and she was about to make them cabbage pie.

Alexander was sitting on top of the counter, swinging his legs back and forth. "Tatiana, don't try to change the subject! Are you honestly telling me," he said, "that Peter the Great should not have built Leningrad and modernized Russia in the process?"

"*I'm* not saying that," Tatiana replied. "Watch it—your leg is in my flour. Pushkin is saying that. Our Pushkin was of two minds about it when he wrote 'The Bronze Horseman.' "

"How long is this pie going to take?" Alexander asked, not moving a centimeter away. He flicked a bit of flour in Tatiana's face. "And Pushkin was not of two minds about it. The point of 'The Bronze Horseman' was that Russia needed to be brought into the New World—even if it was to be kicking and screaming."

Tatiana said, "Pushkin did not think Leningrad was built at a fair price. And don't start the flicking game," she said, throwing a *handful* of flour at Alexander. "You know you'll lose." She smiled. "The pie will take forty-five minutes."

"Yes, after you put it in the oven." Alexander brushed the flour off his face and swung his legs harder, not taking his eyes off Tatiana. "Look at what Pushkin wrote. *Was it not thus, a towering idol, hard by the chasm, with iron bridle, you reared up Russia to her fate?* Fate, Tania. Destiny. Can't fight against destiny."

"Shura, move a bit, can you?" said Tatiana, taking a rolling pin to roll out the dough. "Pushkin also wrote, *The emperor's generals went speeding,*" she continued, "*to save the people, who unheeding, with fear were drowning where they dwelled.* Fear, Alexander, drowning! That's what I mean about ambivalence. The people did not want to be saved or modernized, Pushkin wrote."

Alexander did not move away, his thigh deliberately bumping the rolling pin. "Tania, but there is a city where there was none before. There is a *civilization* where before there were marshes!"

"Stop bumping! Tell that to Pushkin's Eugene. He went mad. Tell that to Pushkin's Parasha. She drowned."

"Eugene was weak. Parasha was weak. I don't see a statue built to them." He did not stop bumping.

"Maybe," Tatiana said. "But, Shura, there is *no* denying that Pushkin himself was ambivalent. Was the human cost too high a price to pay for building Leningrad? he was asking."

"There is *yes* denying," said Alexander adamantly. "I don't think he was ambivalent at all. Is this pie going to have a filling, or are you just going to bake the crust in the oven?"

Tatiana stopped rolling out the dough and stood still, staring at him. "Shura, how can you say that?"

"How can I say that? There is no filling."

She tapped his leg lightly with the rolling pin. "Go and get me my frying pan off the hearth. How can you say he was not ambivalent?" Tatiana repeated, watching Alexander. "Look what Pushkin writes. Why, it's the point of his whole poem!" She took a breath:

> *"And in the moonlight's pallid glamour,*
> *Rides high upon the charging brute,*
> *Hand outstretched 'mid echoing clamor,*
> *The Bronze Horseman in pursuit."*

And another breath. "Pushkin doesn't end his poem as he began it, with the gorgeous granite parapets and golden spires of Leningrad and white nights and the Summer Garden." Her heart swelling at the mention of the *Summer Garden*, Tatiana smiled at Alexander, who smiled back. She continued. "Pushkin ends the poem by telling us that yes, Leningrad was built, but the statue of Peter the Great came to life as if in a nightmare and is chasing Eugene—our frantic wretch—for eternity through those beauteous Leningrad streets:

> *And all through that long night, no matter,*
> *What road the frantic wretch might take,*
> *There would pound with ponderous clatter,*
> *The Bronze Horseman in his wake."*

Tatiana shivered slightly. Why did she shiver? It was so hot.

Alexander held the cast-iron pan in front of her. "Tania, can you argue with me *and* put the filling in the dough at the same time? Or am I going to have to agree with you so you can make dinner?"

"Shura, that's the price of Leningrad! Parasha dead and drowned. Eugene pursued by the Bronze Horseman for eternity," Tatiana said as she spooned the filling inside the dough shell and started to seal up the edges. "I think Parasha would have liked to have her life. And Eugene didn't want to pay with his sanity, certainly. He would have preferred living in a swamp."

Alexander hopped back up onto the counter, his legs parted wide. "*Here lay asprawl my luckless knave, and here in charity they buried, the chill corpse in a pauper's grave.*" He shrugged casually. "Whatever. I say Eugene is a fair price to pay for the free world."

Tatiana paused, thought, looked up at him. "Is Eugene a fair price to pay to create '*socialism in one country,*' too?" she asked quietly.

"Oh, come on now!" Alexander exclaimed. "Surely you're not equating Peter the Great with Stalin!"

"Answer me."

Alexander jumped off the counter. "Kicking and screaming, Tatiana, but into the *free* world! Not kicking and screaming into *slavery*. It's a vital, essential, crucial difference. It's the difference between dying *for* Hitler and dying to stop him."

"Still dying, though, right, Shura?" said Tatiana, coming close to him. "Still dying."

"I'm going to be dying myself soon if I don't get fed," Alexander muttered.

"It's going in the oven now." She put the pie in and crouched to wash her hands and face in the bucket. The cabin was too hot with the stove on. The open doors, the open windows, nothing helped. Straightening up, Tatiana glanced at Alexander and said, "We have forty-five minutes. What do you want to do? No, wait. Forget I said that. God, all right, but can we clean the counter first? Look, I'm getting covered in flour. You like that, don't you? Oh, Shura, you're insatiable. We can't do this all the time . . .

"Oh, Shura, we can't . . .

"Oh, Shura . . .

"Oh . . ."

"And I know that you're just being contrary," Tatiana said to Alexander as they sat outside in the last light under the waxing crescent moon and ate their cabbage and onion pie with a tomato salad and black bread with butter. "I know you think that dying for Hitler and dying for Stalin amounts to the same thing."

Alexander swallowed his bite of pie. "I do, yes, but dying to *stop* Hitler does not. I am America's ally. I am fighting on the side of America." Resolutely he nodded once. "I'll take that fight."

Tatiana looked into her cabbage pie. "I think it wasn't cooked long enough," she said quietly.

"It's nine o'clock at night. I'd have eaten it raw four hours ago."

Not wanting to let their discussion go—because she thought she was right—Tatiana resumed. "Back to Pushkin, though. Russia, as represented by

Eugene, didn't want to be modernized. Peter the Great should have left well enough alone."

"Well enough?" exclaimed Alexander. "There *was* no Russia! While the rest of Europe was forging into the age of enlightenment, Russia was still in the dark ages. After Peter built Leningrad, suddenly there was French language and culture and education and travel, there was a market economy, an emerging middle class, a sophisticated aristocracy. There was music, and books. Books, Tania, that you love. *Happy families* that Tolstoy wrote about. Tolstoy could never have written his books had it not been for what Peter the Great built a hundred years before him. Eugene and Parasha's sacrifice meant that a better world order prevailed." He paused. "That light triumphed over darkness."

Tatiana said, "Yes, well, easy for you to talk about *their* sacrifice. You're not being chased by a block of bronze."

"Look at it another way," Alexander said, eating his bread. "What are we having for dinner tonight, dinner that's turned into a late-night supper? Cabbage pie. Bread. Why? Do you know why?"

She tutted. "I don't see—"

"Be *patient*, and you'll see in a minute. We're eating rabbit food because you did not want to get up at five this morning. I said, we have to go now if we're going to have some trout. Otherwise the fish will leave. Did you listen?"

She grunted. "Sometimes I listen . . ."

"Yes." He nodded. "And on the days you listen, we have fish. Was I right? Of course. Certainly it's terrible to get up so early. But afterward we have real food." Alexander ate the pie happily. "And that's my point: all great things worth having require great sacrifice worth giving. That's how I feel about Leningrad. It was worth it."

Tatiana paused. "Stalin?"

"No! No, no, and no!" He put his plate on the blanket. "I said *great* things worth having. Sacrifice for Stalin's world order is not only execrable, it's meaningless. What if I made you get up, *made* you, told you, you had no choice, you *had* to get up, bleary-eyed and exhausted, and go out into the cold, not for fish but for mushrooms? And not just for mushrooms but the kind of mushrooms *I* pick, the poisonous mushrooms I keep yanking from the ground, the ones that singe your liver upon contact, with death following in three to five minutes?" Alexander laughed. "Tell me—would you want to get up then?"

"I don't want to get up now," Tatiana grumbled, pointing to his plate. "Eat your food. It's not fish—"

He picked up his plate. "It's lovely Tania pie," said Alexander, his mouth full, cheerfully blinking at Tatiana. "There are some battles, no matter how much you don't want to fight them, that you just have to fight. That are worth giving your life for."

"I guess . . ." she said, looking away.

Alexander swallowed his food and set down his plate. "Come here."

Tatiana crawled to him on the blanket. "Let's not talk about this anymore," she said, hugging him tightly.

"*Please* let's not," said Alexander. "Let's go and dive into the evening Kama."

The next morning Tatiana was screaming from inside the cabin. Her shrieks carried to Alexander through the pines, over the sound of his ax falling down on the cracking wood. He dropped the axe and ran to the house to find her crouching on top of the high counter. Her legs were drawn up to her neck.

"What?" he exclaimed, panting.

"Shura, a mouse ran by my feet as I was cooking."

Alexander stared at the eggs on the hearth, at the small pot of bubbling coffee on the Primus stove, at the tomatoes already on their plates, and then at Tatiana, ascended a meter from the floor. His mouth reluctantly, infectiously drew into a wide grin. "What are you"—he was trying to keep from laughing—"what are you doing up there?"

"I told you!" she yelled. "A mouse ran by and brushed his"—she shivered—"his tail against my leg. Can you take care of it?"

"Yes, but what are you doing up *there?*"

"Getting away from the mouse, of course." She frowned, looking at him unhappily. "Are you just going to stand there, or are you going to catch it?"

Alexander walked to the counter and picked her up. Tatiana grabbed his neck but did not put her feet down. He hugged her, kissed her, kissed her again with enormous affection, and said, "Tatiasha, you goose, mice can climb, you know."

"No they can't."

"I've seen mice climb the pole of the commander's tent in Finland, trying to get to the piece of food at the very top."

"What was food doing at the top of the tent pole?"

"We put it there."

"Why?"

"To see if mice could climb."

Tatiana almost laughed. "Well, you're not getting breakfast, or coffee, or me in this house until that mouse is gone."

After carrying her outside, Alexander went back for the breakfast plates. They ate on the bench, side by side. Alexander turned and stared at her incredulously. "Tania, are you . . . afraid of mice?"

"Yes. Have you killed it?"

"And how would you like me to do that? You never told me you were afraid of mice."

"You never asked. How would I like you to kill it? You are a captain in the Red Army, for goodness' sake. What do they teach you there?"

"How to kill human beings. Not mice."

473

She barely touched her food. "Well, throw a grenade at it. Use your rifle. I don't know. But do something."

Alexander shook his head. "You went out into the streets of Leningrad while the Germans were throwing *five-hundred-kilo* bombs that blew arms and legs off the women standing ahead of you in line, you stood fearless in front of cannibals, you jumped off a moving train to go and find your brother, but you are afraid of *mice?*"

"Now you got it," Tatiana said defiantly.

"It doesn't make sense," Alexander said. "If a person is fearless in the big things—"

"You're wrong. Again. Are you done with your questions? Anything else you want to ask? Or add?"

"Just one thing." Alexander kept his face serious. "It looks like," he said slowly, his voice calm, "we've found *three* uses for that too-high potato countertop I built yesterday." And he burst out laughing.

"Go ahead, laugh," Tatiana said. "Go ahead. I'm here for your amusement." Her eyes twinkled.

Putting his own plate on the bench, Alexander took the plate out of her hands and brought her to him to stand between his legs. Reluctantly she came. "Tania, do you have any idea how funny you are?" He kissed her chest, looking up at her. "I adore you."

"If you really adored me," she said, trying to twist herself out of his arms, unsuccessfully, "you wouldn't be sitting here idly flirting when you could be militarizing that cabin."

Alexander stood up. "Just to point out," he said, "it's not called flirting once you've made love to the girl."

After Alexander went inside, a smiling Tatiana sat on the bench and finished her food. In a few minutes he emerged from the cabin holding his rifle in one hand, his pistol in the other, and a bayonet attachment between his teeth. The dead mouse was swinging at the end of the bayonet.

He spoke out of the corner of his mouth. "How did I do?"

Tatiana failed to keep a straight face. "All right, all right," she said, chortling. "You didn't have to bring out the spoils of war."

"Ah, but I know you wouldn't believe in a dead mouse unless you saw it with your own eyes."

"Will you stop quoting me back to me? Shura, you tell me, I will believe it," said Tatiana. "Now, go on, get out of here with that thing."

"One last question."

"Oh, no," said Tatiana, covering her face, trying not to laugh.

"Do you think this dead mouse is worth the price of a . . . killed mouse?"

"Will you just go?"

Tatiana heard his boisterous laughter all the way to the woods and back.

18

They were sitting on their rock fishing. Rather they were attempting to fish. Tatiana was holding her fishing line in the water, but Alexander had put his down and was lying on the rock, rubbing her bare back. Ever since she had sewn herself a new blue cotton sundress, which was open from the nape of her neck to the small of her back, Alexander seemed unable to concentrate on small tasks at hand, such as hunting and gathering. He didn't want her to wear anything else, but he couldn't *do* anything else either.

"Shura, please. We haven't caught a thing. I don't want Naira Mikhailovna to go hungry because you won't catch her a fish."

"Hmm. Because that's what I'm thinking of right now—Naira Mikhailovna. And I told you we should have gotten up at five."

Tatiana sighed, smiling, looking out onto the shimmering river. "You said you were going to read to me. You brought the Pushkin book out here. Read to me from 'The Bronze Horseman.'" She began, "*There was a time, our memories keep its horrors fresh and near us . . .*"

"I'd rather—"

"Read, *I'll* hunt and gather."

Alexander was kissing her back. "Put the fishing line down. I can't take it."

"It's nearly six in the evening, and we have no dinner!"

"Come on," he said, taking the fishing line out of her hands. "When *do* you ever *deny* me?" Alexander lay down on his back. "Pull up your dress and sit on me." Groaning slightly, he paused and said, "No, not like that. Turn around. Sit facing the river, away from me."

"*Away* from you?"

"Yes," Alexander said, closing his eyes. "I want to see your back when you're on top of me."

Afterward, as she was still facing away from him, a released and confined and perplexed Tatiana said inaudibly, "Perhaps I could have continued to fish. After all, I'm facing the right way."

Softly stroking the small of her back, Alexander said nothing.

Tatiana got off him. "Do you want to kiss me?" she asked.

He lay with his eyes closed. "Yes." But he did not move. "*How many days left, Tatiana?*" he asked in a gutted voice.

Turning quickly away from him and to the Kama, she picked up her fishing line. "I don't know," she whispered, staring at the water. "I'm not keeping time."

Then Tatiana heard Alexander's voice from behind. "Why don't I read to you now? Oh, here. Here's a passage you'll like:

> "*Get married? I? And yet why not?*
> *Of course it won't be easy sailing.*
> *But what of that? I'm young and strong,*

Content to labor hard and long,
I'll build us soon, if not tomorrow,
A simple nest for sweet repose
And keep—"

He paused. Tatiana knew that the name of the woman in Pushkin's poem was Parasha. She waited, her eyes glazing over from the ache in her heart. Alexander resumed reading, his cracked voice lower.

"And keep Tatiana free of sorrow,
And in a year or two, who knows,
I may obtain a snug position,
And it shall be Tatiana's mission
To tend and rear our children . . . yes,
So we will live, and so forever
Will be as one, till death us sever
And grandsons lay us both to rest . . ."

He stopped. Tatiana heard him slam the book shut. *"Like* that?"

"Read on, soldier," she said, her trembling hands gripping the fishing line. "Read bravely on."

"No," Alexander said from behind her. Tatiana did not turn to look at him. Instead, staring out onto the languid river, she continued from memory:

"Thus ran his reverie. Yet sadly
He wished that night the wind would still
Its mournful wail, the rain less madly
Be rattling at the windowsill . . ."

Alexander and Tatiana did not speak again until they returned to the cabin.

After coming back from Naira's in the late evening, Alexander built a fire, Tatiana made some tea, and they sat, Tatiana in a lotus position, Alexander next to her. He was very quiet, she thought, quieter than usual.

"Shura," she said softly, "come here. Put your head on me. Like always."

He lay down, his head in her lap. Gently, tenderly, full of aching affection, Tatiana stroked his face. "What's the matter, soldier?" she whispered, bending to smell him. Tea and cigarettes. She cradled his head between her thighs and her breasts, kissing his eyes. "What's bothering you?"

"Nothing," he replied. And said nothing else.

Tatiana sighed. "Want to hear a joke?"

"As long as it's one you haven't told Vova."

Tatiana said, "The paratroopers go to the parachute packer. 'Hey,' they ask, 'are your parachutes any good?' 'Well,' he replies, 'I've had no complaints.' "

Alexander almost laughed. "Funny, Tania." He jumped up away from her and took her cup. "I'm going to smoke."

"Smoke here. Leave the cups. I'll take care of them later."

"I don't want you to take care of them later," he said. "Why do you *always* do that?"

She chewed her lip.

Before he walked away, Alexander said, "And why do you *always* have to serve Vova? What? Are his hands broken? He can't serve himself?"

"Shura, I serve everybody." She paused and said quietly, "You first." She looked up at Alexander. "How would it look if I served everybody but him?"

"I don't give a shit how it would look, Tania. I just need you not to do it."

She didn't answer. Was he displeased with her?

Tatiana continued to sit in front of the flickering flame with her legs crossed. It was dark except for the circle around the fire and the waxing half-moon in the sky. The air smelled of fresh water and burning wood and night. She knew that Alexander was sitting on the bench by the house, slightly behind her, and that he was watching her. He was doing that more and more often. Watching her as he smoked. And smoked. And smoked.

She turned to him. Alexander was watching her, and smoking.

Rising, Tatiana walked to him and stopped at his legs. Stepping on his feet, she asked shyly, "Shura . . . want to go inside?"

He shook his head. "You go ahead. I'll sit here for a while and wait for the fire to burn out."

Tatiana looked him over, studied him, searched his eyes, his lips, his slightly unsteady hands.

Chewing her lip again, she didn't move.

"Go ahead," Alexander repeated.

Coming closer to him, she pulled his legs apart and knelt on the ground in front of him. His shallow breathing became more rapid. Looking up into his face and rubbing his legs, Tatiana said, "What do I love?"

Alexander didn't reply.

Tatiana prodded him again. "What do *you* love?"

"Your soft mouth on me," he said thickly.

"Mmm," she said, undoing the ties on his trousers. "Is it too dark? Or can you see?"

"I can see," he said, taking hold of her head as she took hold of him.

"Shura?"

"Mmm?"

"I love you."

19

Alexander was in the darkening woods collecting kindling. Tatiana called for him, but he did not answer. She wanted to see him before she ran quickly to Naira's. On the bench she set out for him a plate of warm fried potatoes, two tomatoes, and a cucumber. When he came back from the woods, he was always hungry. Near his plate she left a cup of sweet black tea, and next to it a cigarette and a lighter.

Tatiana's funny husband had lost interest in funny things. He had interest in smoking and in chopping wood. That's all he did now. Smoked for himself, chopped wood for her. They continued to occasionally wake before dawn and go fishing when the Kama was still as glass, the air dewy and blue, go silently and sleepily to their rock in the secluded river pool, just to the side of their clearing. Alexander was right, of course. It was the best time to go fishing. They would catch half a dozen trout in four or five minutes. He would leave them alive in the net basket lowered from a poplar branch into the river. Then he would smoke, and Tatiana would brush her teeth and go back to bed.

After he smoked and swam, Alexander would come back to bed, and Tatiana, as always, would receive him, having waited for him, listened for him, prayed for him. She was immoderately excited by him. He owned her. However Alexander wished to offer her his remarkable crown, Tatiana would take, even if it was with ice at dawn.

But whereas before, Alexander had been delighted in his perceived mistreatment of freezing her with his limbs, recently he had begun to touch her as if she were scalding hot, as if he were burning himself on her. He was drawn to the fire, he could not help but touch her, yet he touched her now as if he knew that the burns he was inflicting on himself would scar him for life, if they didn't kill him first.

What happened to the Shura who used to chase her and grab her and knock her down to the ground and lick her and tickle her? What happened to the Shura who needed to make love to her in broad daylight so he could look at her? Where was he, the laughing man, the joking man, the brash man, the careless man? Gradually he seemed to have been drowned and resurrected as the Alexander who did little but smoke and chop wood and watch her.

Sometimes when Tatiana was abundantly asleep, all tucked in to him, comforted and at peace, she would suddenly be woken up in the darkest night by Alexander. She wouldn't move or acknowledge him. She felt him lying awake, unable to breathe, suffocating her, embracing the breath out of her body. She would hear his broken gasps, feel his lips rubbing against her hair, and wish she could stop breathing permanently.

Tatiana was slicing his tomatoes as the tears were silently flowing down her cheeks.

Behind her she heard him say, "Going somewhere?"

Alexander was too stealthy a soldier. Quickly she wiped her eyes, cleared her throat, and said, "Hang on, I'm almost done." The light was waning; maybe he wouldn't see her wet face.

Turning her head to him and smiling, she saw he was perspiring and covered with wood chips. "Collecting more kindling?" Tatiana asked, her heart beginning to pound. "How much wood am I going to need?" She stood and stepped up to Alexander. "Mmm . . . you're so delicious-smelling," she murmured, short of breath at the scent of him, at the sight of him.

"Why is your face all red?"

"I was cutting onions for the potatoes. You know onions."

"I see only one plate. Are you going somewhere, I asked?" He was not smiling.

"Of course, not," said Tatiana, clearing her throat.

"Let me go and wash."

"Don't bother," she said, coming up barefoot to Alexander, feeling vulnerable and aroused. "I always feel so tiny when you're in your boots," she whispered, gazing up at him.

Alexander's whole body clamped her motionless. His left hand held her head, his right hand gripped her bottom, his body was on her and in her, around her and over her. She could not twitch without him letting her. Submitting to him completely, Tatiana could feel Alexander with every thrust struggling through his love for her, struggling through his need for her. By now she understood: Alexander knew his own strength very well.

Underneath him Tatiana pressed her lips to his collarbone. "Oh, Shura . . . I need you so much." Trying hard not to cry.

His voice cracked. "I'm here. Feel me."

"I'm feeling, soldier," she whispered. "I'm feeling."

Too soon Tatiana felt the burning wave start to flood her, and she bit her mouth shut, suppressing her crying moans. But she knew that Alexander felt it, too, holding her as taut as he did, for he stopped moving and pulled himself away. There it starts, Tatiana thought, opening her hands and pleading for him. There it starts and lasts all night until he finally, gentle and bruising, rhythmic and broken, releases his hunger and longing onto me, until he exhausts himself and me, until we both can't crawl away from his aching regret.

It was evening. Tatiana was looking unblinking at Alexander lying on his stomach, his face to her, his eyes closed. She was quietly by him, listening to his breath, trying to determine if he was asleep. She didn't think so. Every fourth breath or so, Alexander would shudder, as if he were thinking. Tatiana didn't want him to be thinking. Slowly she drew small circles on his back with her fingers. Alexander murmured and turned his face away from her.

479

What does he need? she thought. What can I give him?

"Want a massage?" she asked, kissing his upper arm, running her palm over his hard shoulders. She squeezed him. "Can you hear me?"

He turned to her, opening one eye. "You know how to give a massage?"

"Yes." She smiled. He was wearing only his skivvies. She hopped on top of him.

"Tatia, what do you know about massages?"

"What do you mean?" she said teasingly, pinching his behind. "I've given lots of massages."

"*Have* you?"

She knew that would get his attention. "Yes. Ready? Rail tracks, rail tracks," Tatiana began, with her fingertips tracing two long parallel lines down his spine, moving from his neck to the top of the elastic on his shorts.

"Rail ties, rail ties." She drew short perpendicular lines across.

"Here comes the late train . . ." A zigzagging line down.

"And it spills *all* the grain." Her hands tickled his back.

Alexander laughed, his head on his hands.

Tatiana had an urge to kiss him. But that wasn't part of the game.

"The chickens come, and they peck at it." She poked him with her fingers.

"The geese come, and they pinch it." She pinched him all over.

"What kind of a massage is this?"

"The children come, and they step on it!" She pounded his back with the palms of her hands.

"Hey," he said. "Why are you pounding me?"

"The robbers come, and they salt it, and they pepper it, and they eat it," she squealed, tickling him. He wriggled. I love that he is ticklish, Tatiana thought with pleasure. She couldn't resist, she bit his back. He was just too gorgeous lying under her, twitching from being tickled. As she bit him, he purred.

"Here comes Dedushka, he collects some grain," Tatiana said, pecking at Alexander with her fingers. "Here comes the zookeeper . . ."

"Oh, no, not the *zookeeper*," said Alexander.

"He sits down, and he begins to write." Tatiana drew a table and a chair. She made squiggly writing lines on Alexander's back.

"Please admit my daughter to the zoo, and please collect all the grain. He puts down a period . . . he places a stamp . . ." She slapped Alexander lightly.

"Trrrrr." She poked him in the ribs. He jumped. She laughed.

"Time to mail it!" Tatiana popped the elastic on his shorts. It snapped against his lower back. She pulled down his shorts a little and caressed his behind.

Alexander lay there not moving. "Is it over?" he asked in a muffled voice.

Laughing, Tatiana lay down flat on top of him. "Yes," she said, kissing him between his shoulders. "How did you like it?" She loved how his bare back felt under her body, like a firm bed. He carried me on his back, she thought.

Carried me nine kilometers, me and his rifle. Tatiana rubbed her cheek against his very tanned shoulder blade. All month out in the hot sun. She blinked.

"Hmm. Interesting. Was that some kind of a *Russian* massage?"

Tatiana told him she and the kids at Luga used to do that to each other twenty times a day, each time harder and more ticklish than the last. She didn't mention that she and Dasha, too, used to do it endlessly to each other.

Alexander moved out from under Tatiana. "My turn," he said.

"Oh, no," she squealed. "You better be nice."

"Turn over."

Tatiana turned over, still in her sundress.

"Wait. Up, up. Take the dress off." He helped her.

Tatiana lay down on her stomach in front of Alexander, her hair tied with white ribbons by the sides of her head, her neck exposed, her back exposed, smooth, cream-colored, satin. She had freckles on her shoulders from the sun, but the rest of her was ivory. Bending to her, Alexander traced a line from her shoulder blade to her neck with his tongue. He pulled the ribbons from her hair. His breath shallow, he said, "Wait, let's remove these, too," tugging at her blue silk panties.

Tatiana lifted her hips. "Shura," she said, "how are you going to do the elastic pop at the end if you remove my underwear?"

Lost as always at the sight of her hips moving *up*, Alexander took the skin near her shoulder into his mouth. "Since we don't have a train with grain or bears stomping on your back, maybe we can imagine the elastic on your underwear, too?" He saw she was smiling, her eyes already closed. He removed his own shorts with one hand.

As he continued to kiss her between her shoulder blades, she moaned softly and said, "You're not playing by the rules of the game."

Supporting himself on his knees, he sat astride her and began. "All right, how does it go?"

"Rail tracks, rail tracks," Tatiana said helpfully.

Alexander drew two lines from her neck all the way to her bottom.

"That's good," Tatiana said. "But you don't have to go so far down."

"No?" he said, his fingers, his hands remaining on her bottom.

"No," she repeated, but her voice quickened.

"The chickens," said Alexander. "What did they do?"

"They pecked," she said. Alexander lightly pecked her with his fingers. He pressed his palms into her back, fanning her from her spine to her ribs. His hands slipped around to her breasts. "What about the geese?" he asked, fondling her.

"They pinched." Gently he squeezed her nipples. "Shura, you're going to have to do better than that," Tatiana said, lifting her chest slightly off the bed. He squeezed her nipples less gently. "Mmm," she murmured.

"The robbers came . . ." Alexander said, moving off her, spreading her legs and kneeling between them. "They salted," he said, lifting her hips up to him, "they peppered," he continued, sliding himself fully inside her. Tatiana cried out, grasping the sheet with both hands. "And they ate it . . . once . . . and again . . . and again . . ."

Not stopping, Alexander bent over her, pressing his palm into her back, edging up to touch her glowing golden hair. He closed his eyes and straightened up, his hands like a vise clamping her hips.

Afterward, Tatiana muttered, "Was that some sort of an *American* massage? Because that was definitely not in the rules."

He laughed, but his eyes were still closed.

"You know, don't you, that I'm never going to feel the same way about that game now?" she said.

"Good," said Alexander. "Like you don't feel the same way about warhide-and-seek?"

"Yes, you've ruined that also," she murmured.

Alexander leaned forward and hugged her from behind, still inside her, feeling himself unable to hold her close enough.

20

Late at night Tania and Shura were playing strip poker. Tania, Tania, Tania. Death-defying, life-affirming, star-making, indomitable, ridiculously beautiful Tania hated to lose at anything. And she was splendidly losing at poker. Alexander needed to focus on the cards and not her.

Having just lost her shirt, his moaning wife was sitting halfway up, leaning back on her arms while Alexander was kneeling forward, lingeringly sucking her nipples. They were outside in the clearing in front of the fire below the waxing gibbous moon. "Take me inside," she whispered.

"Not until you lose one more hand." But he couldn't back away from her. "Look at me, Tania. I'm in a gaseous state when I'm with you . . ."

"Not all of you is in a gaseous state," she said, grabbing hold of him and falling back onto the blanket. "And I'm not losing one more hand for anything."

Things weren't going well for Tatiana in their poker game but very well for Alexander. She had only her underwear left. "My underwear and my wedding ring," she pointed out. "I think I can win in two tries."

"You take that wedding ring off, and you can keep it off for good," Alexander told her as he dealt the cards.

He watched her as she examined her hand; Alexander could barely pay attention to his own. By the fire, Tatiana's poetic face was focused on the cards she kept in front of her chest to cover herself from his prying eyes.

Alexander wanted her to put down the cards. He took a breath. He would get to her soon enough.

In English, she said, "*How do you say . . . hit me.*" She smiled. "*Twice.*"

She concentrated diligently. Suddenly her face cleared. Eyes flickering, she turned her gaze to him and said, back to Russian, "All right, I'll raise you two kopecks."

Trying to be serious, Alexander said, "I'll see your two. Come on, Tatia." He smiled. "Show me what you've got."

"Aha!" She threw down a full house, beaming at him.

"Aha nothing," Alexander said, putting down his cards. He had four kings.

"What?" She frowned.

"I win. Four kings." He pointed to her underwear. "Go on—off."

"What do you mean?"

"Four of a kind beats full house."

"Oh, you're such a liar," she fumed, throwing her cards at him and covering her breasts with her hands.

He pulled her hands away. "This isn't Luga, I've seen them." He grinned. "I've—"

She covered herself again. "I finally understand how you win all the time. You cheat."

Alexander could not stop laughing. He couldn't shuffle anymore. "How many times do I have to explain it, Comrade I-remember-everything-you-ever-tell-me? Huh?" He reached over and pulled at her panties. "Rules are rules. Off."

Tatiana scooted away from him on the blanket. "Yes, cheating rules," she declared defiantly. "Let's play again."

"We'll play again, but you'll be playing buck naked. Because you lost this game."

"Shura! Just the other day you told Naira Mikhailovna that your full house beat her four of a kind. You are just the biggest cheater. I'm not going to play with you if you cheat."

"Tania, the other day Naira Mikhailovna had three of a kind, not four of a kind, and I had a straight, and a straight *does* beat three of a kind." Alexander stared at her, grinning broadly. "I don't need to cheat to beat you in poker. Dominoes, yes. But not poker."

"If you don't need to cheat, then why do you?" Tatiana demanded.

"That's it," Alexander said, putting down the cards. "Your panties are coming off, Tania, one way or another. I won fair and square."

"Cheated fair and square," she said.

Alexander was wearing his army trousers. He was naked to the waist. Tatiana's hands were still up at her breasts, but her lips were moist and slightly parted, and her eyes were roaming over his exposed body. "Tania," he said, staring at her intently, "do you want me to enforce the rules?"

"Yes," she said, jumping up. "I want to see you try."

Alexander liked her fighting spirit. He was only seconds behind her when he jumped up off the blanket, but Tania was going to stop at nothing to get away. By the time he was up and running, she was already in the Kama.

Alexander stopped at the waterline. "You're out of your mind!" he yelled to her.

"Yes, and you cheat at poker just to get me to take my clothes off!" she yelled back from the river.

Crossing his arms on his chest, Alexander said, "Do I really need to cheat at poker to get you to take your clothes off? I can't keep them *on* you."

"Oh, you . . ." he heard from the river.

He laughed. "Come out." But he couldn't see her. She was a dark space in the river. "Come on, come out."

"Come in and get me if you're so clever."

"I'm clever but not crazy. I'm not going into the river at night. Come."

He heard her cluck like a chicken.

"Fine," Alexander said and turning around walked away from the shoreline. He went back to the fire, collected their cards, his cigarettes, their teacups. He brought everything, including the blanket, into the house and then came back out. The clearing was quiet. The river was quiet, too. It was cooler at night now.

"Tania!" Alexander called.

Nothing.

"Tania!" he called, louder.

Nothing.

Alexander walked quickly to the river. He could see nothing, not even a dark space. The moon was pale; the stars did not reflect in the water.

"Tatiana!" he shouted loudly.

Silence.

Suddenly Alexander remembered the swift midriver current of the Kama, the rocks they sometimes stumbled on, the drifts of wood that floated by. Panic like adrenaline shot through him.

"Tania!" he yelled. "This is not funny at all!" He listened for a splash, a breath, a stirring.

Nothing.

He ran into the water in his trousers. "You won't want to get near me if this is another one of your jokes!"

Nothing.

Alexander swam against the current, yelling for her. "Tania!"

He turned his gaze back to the shore.

And there she was—

Standing, already dry, wearing a long shirt, wiping her hair, watching him. He couldn't see her expression because the fire was behind her, but when she spoke, he could tell she was wearing a big smug smile on her face. "I thought you didn't want to go into the Kama with your trousers on, you big cheater?"

He was speechless. Relieved but speechless.

Running out of the water, Alexander came at her so quickly that she backed away and stumbled to the ground, looking up at him, the smile on her face evaporating.

He stood over her for a few moments, breathing hard and shaking his head. "Tatiana, you are impossible." He gave her his hand to pull her up but didn't look at her again as he let go and, dripping wet, walked to the cabin.

He heard her say behind him, "It was just a joke . . ."

"Not fucking funny!"

"Someone doesn't know how to take a little joke," she muttered.

"What do you think would be so funny to me about you drowning?" he shouted, whirling around to face her. "What part of that do you think I would find particularly funny?" Alexander grabbed her, let go, and went inside. He heard her behind him, and then she was in front of him. Longingly looking up at him, she whispered, "Shura . . ." She took his hand and placed it under her shirt. She had taken off her underwear. Alexander held his breath. She was *impossible*. His hand remained between her thighs.

"You were supposed to come into the water and rescue me," Tatiana said contritely, feeling for him, unbuttoning his trousers. "You forgot the part where the knight rescues the frail maiden."

His fingers caressed her. "Frail?" Alexander said, bringing her closer. "You must be thinking of someone else. And you forget that your sole job as a maiden is to make love to, not terrorize the knight."

"I didn't mean to terrorize the knight," she murmured as Alexander picked her up and laid her atop their bed. She opened her arms to him.

In the flickering light of the kerosene lamp, Alexander gazed at his Tatiana lying naked, flat on her back, quivering for him, open for him, moaning for him. They had been making love for a long while, and he knew she nearly had no more, having burned and burned through the wave. Tania, was all he could think. *Tania.* He placed his hand on her toes and ran it up her legs, between her open thighs, gently, so she wouldn't jump out of her skin, up her stomach to her chest, spanning her from one side to the other, pressing his palm into her breasts, and then slowly moving his hand up to encircle her throat.

"What, Alexander? What, darling?" she whispered.

Alexander made no reply. His hand remained on her throat.

"I'm here, soldier," said Tatiana, placing her own hand on top of his. "Feel me."

"I'm feeling, Tania," Alexander whispered, bending over her. "I'm feeling."

"Please come to me," she moaned. "Please . . . come, take me like you want . . . take me like I love . . . go ahead . . . but like I *love*, Shura . . ."

He took her like she loved, and afterward, when they were warm under the covers, spent, murmuring, clasped and saturated in each other, ready to go to sleep, Alexander opened his mouth to speak, and Tatiana said, "Shura, I know it all. I understand it all. I feel it all. Say nothing."

They were enveloped in a fierce embrace, their naked bodies not just pressed hard against each other but in a trance, attempting a Bessemer smelt, in which they would be alloyed and conjoined by heat and perhaps in their cooling, grieving bliss eventually be tempered.

Alexander didn't feel tempered. He felt as if he were being daily blown out of sand into a still-warm glass.

21

So they lived. From morning until night, from the first swell of the river to the last song of the lark, from the smell of the nettles to the scent of the pinecones, from the peaceful morning sun to the pale blue moon in the clearing, Alexander and Tatiana so spent their lilac days.

Alexander cut wood for her and made it into small bundles tied together with twigs. She made him blueberry pie and blueberry *compôte* and blueberry pancakes. The blueberries were plentiful that summer.

He built things for her, and she made bread for him.

They played dominoes. They sat on Naira's porch and played dominoes on the days it rained, and Tatiana beat Alexander every time, and no matter how hard he tried, he could not win. Alone they played strip poker. Tatiana always lost.

They played war-hide-and-seek, Alexander's favorite.

Tatiana sewed him five more tops and two new pairs of army skivvies. "So you feel me under your uniform," she told him.

They went mushroom picking together.

He taught her English. He taught her poems in English that he still remembered, some by Robert Frost: *The woods are lovely, dark, and deep, but I have promises to keep* . . .

And some by Emma Lazarus: *Here at our sea-washed sunset gates shall stand a mighty woman* . . .

After building a fire in the cabin, Alexander would read Pushkin to her while she cooked dinner on their hearth, though eventually he stopped reading "The Bronze Horseman." It was too much for them both.

In the book he had found a picture of himself that he had given to Dasha the year before. The photo was of him getting his medal of valor for Yuri Stepanov. "Is my wife proud of her husband?" he asked, showing Tatiana the picture.

"Hopelessly," she replied with a grin. "Think about this, Shura," she said. "When I was still a kid rowing on Lake Ilmen, you had already lost your father and mother, joined the army, and become a hero."

"Not a *kid* rowing on Lake Ilmen," he said, grabbing her. "A *queen* rowing on Lake Ilmen. Waiting for me."

"You know we still haven't gotten those wedding photos," Tatiana said.

"Who has time to go to Molotov?" remarked Alexander.

They did not speak about his leaving, but just the same the days sped on. By the end they didn't just speed on, they seemed to race ahead of them in triple time, as if the spring had broken on the hands of the pitiless clock.

Alexander and Tatiana did not speak about the future.

No, not *did* not.

Could not.

Not after the war, not during the war, not after July 20. Alexander found himself barely able to speak to Tatiana about the next day. They had no past. They had no future. They just *were*. Young in Lazarevo.

As they ate and played, and talked and told jokes, as they fished and wrestled, as they walked in the woods practicing Tatiana's English and swam naked across the river and back, as he helped her with their laundry and the laundry of four old women, as he carried the water from the well for her and her milk pails, as he brushed her hair each morning and made love to her many times a day, never tiring, never ceasing to be aroused by her, Alexander knew that he was living the happiest days of his life.

He held no illusions. Lazarevo was not going to come again, neither for him nor for her.

Tatiana held those illusions.

And he thought—it was better to have them.

Look at him.

And look at her.

Tatiana so ceaselessly and happily did for him, so constantly smiled and touched him and laughed—even as their twenty-nine moon-cycle days spun faster around the loop of grief—that Alexander had to wonder if she ever even *thought* about the future. He knew she sometimes thought about the past. He knew she thought about *Leningrad*. She had a stony sadness around her edges that she had not had before. But for the future, Tatiana seemed to harbor a rosy hope, or at the very least a sense of humming unconcern.

What are you doing? she would ask him when he was sitting on the bench and smoking. Nothing, Alexander would reply. *Nothing but growing my pain.*

He smoked and wished for her.

It was like wishing for *America* when he was a few years younger.

Wishing for a life with her, a life that was full of nothing else but her, a

487

simple, long, married life of being able to smell her and taste her, to hear the lyre of her voice and see the honey of her hair. To feel her staggering comfort. All of it, every day.

Could he find a way to turn his back on Tatiana and have her faithful face free him? Would she forgive him? For leaving her, for dying, for killing her?

He felt punched in the gut when he watched her skip stark naked out of the cabin in the morning, and throw herself squealing into the river, and then get out and head across the clearing to him, sitting on his stump of a heart. Watching her nipples hard from the cold, her flawless body trembling to be held by him, Alexander gritted his teeth and smiled and thanked God that when he pressed her to him, she could not see his contorted face.

Alexander smoked and watched her from his tree stump bench.

What are you doing? she would ask him.

Nothing, he would reply. *Nothing but growing my pain into madness.*

His temper flared up constantly.

It irritated him to no end seeing her fetch and carry for other people. Tatiana, seeing his displeasure, would only sublimate herself further to him, fetching and carrying for him until he couldn't breathe. "What can I get you? What else can I get you? What do you need?" came out of her mouth with heartbeat regularity.

He would say, no, I don't need anything. And she would come, carrying his cigarette, put it in his mouth, light it, and kiss the corner of his lip, her loving eyes centimeters away from his tortured ones. Alexander wanted to say, *stop, back away.* What will happen to you after I'm gone and you're left without me? What will be left of you after I'm gone when you have given me everything?

Alexander knew that Tatiana didn't know how to give to him any other way. She had one way—and that's what he got. Her devotion to him was indelible; her inability to hide her true self was the reason he fell in love with her in the first place. Soon she would have to learn, Alexander thought, as he swung his ax and crashed it down hundreds of times a day. Learn how to hide him even from her true self.

Alexander grew upset with her over the pettiest things. Her constant cheeriness vexed him constantly. She was always singing and bouncing around with a little spring in her step. He didn't understand how she could be so carefree when she knew he was leaving in fifteen days, ten days, five days, three days.

He grew bitterly jealous of her; even he was surprised at himself. He could not stand to see anyone looking at her. He could not stand to see her smiling at anyone. He could not stand to see her talking to Vova, much less serving him. He lost his temper with heartbeat regularity, but he couldn't stay upset with her for five minutes. The arsenal Tatiana carried to ease Alexander out of his bottomless hole had too many weapons.

Alexander could never get close enough to her. Not when they walked, not when they ate, not when they slept, not when they made love. His feelings teetering between intense tenderness and unrestrained lust, he needed her many times a day. His body would begin to physically ache when he remained without her while she went to her sewing circle or to help the old women. Tatiana's shy eagerness, her engulfing sweetness, her unconcealed vulnerability tore at Alexander's heart. All he hungered for was to feel her velvet flesh surround him as she cried out, whispering, *Oh, Shura.*

He grew unable to bear coming on top of her and watching her face and seeing her watch his. To finish, he would repeatedly have to turn her over, because when he was behind her, she could not see him.

It was all about making him feel better about leaving her.

To leave her was unthinkable.

The question Alexander had asked himself many times, he had started to forget the answer to.

At what price Tatiana?

In the beginning the answer was clear.

Tatiana *was* the answer.

But this wasn't the beginning anymore. This was the end.

She had gone to the fish plant, having heard there might be herring, while Alexander remained at the clearing, walking around numbly waiting for her to come back. He went to the house and was looking in her trunk for something to hold when he found something at the very bottom, almost as if that something had been hidden. The trunk had belonged to Tatiana's grandfather, so Alexander didn't give it much thought at first, but when he removed the top layer of sheets and clothes and some papers and three books, he pulled out a black canvas backpack. Immediately curious, he opened it. Inside he found his old P-38 pistol, bottles of vodka, winter boots, cans of *tushonka*, dried crackers, a flask, and rubles. There were warm clothes, too, all dark-colored.

Alexander smoked ten unhappy cigarettes waiting for her to return.

He heard Tatiana before he saw her. She was humming the waltz tune he had sung for her. "Shura!" she called out to him joyfully. "You won't believe it. Herring! Real herring. We're going to have a feast tonight."

She skipped to him and lifted her arms up to his neck. Breaking in two, Alexander kissed her, thinking that her face felt a bit wet, and then showed her the backpack. "What's this?"

She stared at it. "What?"

"This? What's this?"

"Are you going through my things? Come and help me with the herring."

"I'm not touching the herring until you tell me what this is."

"Whether or not I tell you, we still have to eat. It'll take me thirty—"

"Tatiana!"

She sighed loudly. "It's a pack for me."

489

"For what? Are you planning to go camping?"

"No . . ." She put the herring down and sat on the bench.

Alexander pulled out the drab, all-brown clothing and a brown hat. "Why so attractive?" He saw how she tensed.

"Just to make myself more inconspicuous."

"More inconspicuous? You'd better hide those take-me lips of yours then. Where are you going?"

"What's gotten into you?" she asked.

Alexander raised his voice. "Where are you going, Tania?"

"I just want to be ready for anything."

"For what?"

"I don't know," she said, lowering her gaze. "To go with you."

"Go with me *where*?" he gasped.

"Anywhere." She turned her eyes up. "Anywhere you go," Tatiana said, "I will go with *you*."

Alexander tried to speak but couldn't; he found himself without words. "But, Tania . . . I'm going back to the *front*."

She was looking down at the ground. "*Are* you, Alexander?" she asked quietly without looking up.

"Of course. Where *else* would I be going?"

Her eyes stared at him with profound emotion. "You tell *me*."

Blinking and stepping away from her, as if being too close to her left him unprotected, Alexander said, still holding her backpack, "Tania, I'm going back to the front. Colonel Stepanov gave me extra time to come here. I gave him my word I would return."

"And that's one thing about you Americans," she said, "you always keep your word."

"Yes, that's one thing about us," Alexander said bitterly. "It's no use talking about it. You know I have to go back."

Shivering, Tatiana raised her seaweed eyes to him and in a small voice said, "Then I'll go back with you. I'll go back to Leningrad." She must have taken his speechlessness to mean he was relieved, and continued, "I thought if you were back at the barracks—"

"Tatiana!" he shouted, aghast. "Are you joking? Are you fucking joking?"

Alexander was so upset that he had to walk away into the woods for a few minutes until reason got hold of him again. When he came back, she was cleaning the herring. Typical. He was mortified, she was cleaning herring. He walked up to her and knocked the fish hard out of her hands.

"Ouch!" she yelled. "Stop! What's the matter with you?"

Alexander went back into the woods to calm down and watched her pick up the herring, wash the sand and dirt off it, and proceed to clean it again.

Returning, he took the damned herring, put it down on the paper on the ground, stood Tatiana up in front of him, and took her by the shoulders. "Look at me, Tania. I'm trying to stay calm, all right? Do you see what an effort it is?" He paused. "What the hell are you thinking? You are not coming back with me."

She shook her head, but the soft words that came out of her were "I am."

"No!" Alexander said. "You're absolutely not. Not while there is breath in my body. You'll have to kill me to come with me. Forget it. I will come and see you on my next furlough."

"No," she said. "You will never come back. You will die out there without me. I can feel it. I'm not staying here."

"Tania, who will let you go back? *I* won't. Did you forget that Leningrad is under full blockade? You can't get back into Leningrad. We're still getting people *out*! Have you forgotten? Have you forgotten what Leningrad was? I can't imagine you have, because it was only six months ago, and you still wake up in the middle of the night. Leningrad is a city under siege. Leningrad is still bombed every single fucking day. There is no life in Leningrad. It's very dangerous, and you are not going back there." He was panting.

"Well, if you have another idea, let me know. I have to clean this herring."

Alexander picked up the herring and was going to throw the whole damn thing into the Kama, but Tatiana grabbed his arm, and said, "No! It's our dinner, and the old women are looking forward to it."

"You are *not* coming with me. And I'm done talking about it." Turning her backpack upside down, he threw all of her supplies onto the ground.

Tatiana watched him calmly and then said, "And who's going to pick all that up?"

Without a word, Alexander picked up the clothes and shredded them into pieces with his army knife.

Her eyes set yet frightened, Tatiana watched him from the bench. "Oh, *this* is calm?" she said. "Shura, I can make myself new clothes."

Cursing, Alexander clenched his fist and bent down to her. "God, are you deliberately trying to provoke me?"

Picking up the backpack, he was about to rip it to shreds when Tatiana grabbed his arm and the knife, her hand right on the blade, and said, "No. No. Please." She hung on to him, wrestling for the knife, pulling on the backpack. She was no match for him, and Alexander was about to shove her away, but what stopped him was that she still continued to struggle knowing she was outmatched. To stop her, Alexander would have had to hurt her. He let her have the knife and the backpack.

Out of breath, she went to clean the herring. With his knife.

Over at Naira's for dinner, Alexander didn't talk much; he was too upset. When Tatiana asked him if he wanted some more blueberry pie, he snapped at her, "I said *no*!" and saw the reproach in her eyes. He wanted to apologize but couldn't.

They didn't speak as they walked through the woods, but at home, as they undressed and got into bed, Tatiana said, "You're not still angry, are you?"

"No!" Alexander said. He left his shorts on as he got under the covers and turned away from her.

"Shura?" She stroked his back and kissed his head. "Shura."

"I'm tired. I'm going to sleep."

He didn't want her to stop touching him, and she, of course, didn't.

What was wrong with her?

"Come on," Tatiana whispered. "Come on, big man. *Feel*, I'm naked. Do you feel?"

He felt. Turning onto his back without meeting her eyes, Alexander said, "Tatiana, I want you to promise me you will stay right here where it's safe for you."

"You know I can't stay here," she said quietly. "I can't be without you."

"Of course you can, and you will. Just like before."

"There is no before."

"Stop. You don't understand anything."

"Then tell me everything."

Alexander didn't reply.

"Tell me," she pleaded, her small, warm hand on his arms, on his stomach, moving lower.

Pushing it away, he said, "We have only three days left. I'm not ruining them this way."

"No, but you're willing to ruin them with your sulkiness and bad behavior." Her forgiving hand returned to caressing him.

Pushing her hand away again, Alexander said, suddenly understanding, "Oh, so that's why you've been so damn chipper, as if you couldn't care less I was leaving? Because you thought you were coming *with* me?"

She pressed her body softly against his side, kissing his arm. "Shura," Tatiana whispered, "how do you think I've been able to live out these days with you? I couldn't continue if I thought you were leaving me. Husband," she said, her voice like a black pit, "everything I have I gave to you. If you leave, you're going to take it all."

Alexander had to get off the bed before he lost his mind. He jumped down to stand on the floor. "Well, you'd better get more from *somewhere*, Tania!" he exclaimed. "Because I *am* leaving, and I'm leaving without you."

Silently she shook her head.

"Don't shake your head at me!" Alexander yelled. "There is a war on, for fuck's sake! A war! Millions of people are already dead. What do you want, to be just another dead body without an ID tag in a mass grave?"

She started to convulse. "I have to come with you," she said in her smallest whisper. "Please."

"Look," he said, "I'm a soldier. This country is at war. I *have* to go back. But

492

you are safe here. I came to get away from the fighting, and you and I had a good time—" Was it possible to actually choke on words? "But now it's over, do you understand? Over," he said loudly. "I have to go back, and you can't come." He paused, panting. "I don't want you to come. I'm not even going to be at the garrison. I've been moved."

"Moved where?"

"I can't tell you. But Leningrad cannot have another winter like we had last year."

"You're breaking the blockade? Where?"

"Can't tell you."

"You tell me everything." She paused. "Don't you, Alexander?" Tatiana asked pointedly. "Don't you tell me everything?"

What *was* that in her voice? God. He wasn't about to ask. "Not this."

"Oh," Tatiana said, sitting on the bed, looking down at him. "On the third day after we met, you told me you were from America, just like that. You poured out your entire life to me on our third day. But now you can't tell me where you're *posted?*"

Tatiana jumped down. Alexander backed away. He couldn't be far enough from her eyes and her body and her open palms.

"Tell me, Shura," she said pleadingly. "You didn't marry me to keep secrets."

"Tania, I'm not having this with you! Do you understand?"

"No!" she yelled. "Why in the world did you marry me then, if all you wanted was to continue to lie!"

"I married you," Alexander yelled in a breaking voice, "so I could *fuck* you anytime I felt like it! Don't you get it by now? Anytime, Tania! What else do you think a soldier on furlough could possibly want? And if I hadn't married you, all of Lazarevo would now be calling you my whore!"

Alexander could see by Tatiana's sunken face she could not believe the words that had just come out of his mouth. She staggered back against the wall, not knowing what to cover on herself, her face or her body. "You married me so you could *what?*"

"Tatia . . ."

"Don't Tatia me!" she screamed. "First your insults, then Tatia? Your whore, Alexander?" She groaned helplessly and put her face into her hands.

"Tania, please . . ."

"You think I don't know what you're doing? That I don't know you're trying to make me hate you? Well, you know what," she said through gritted teeth. "After trying for days, I think you've finally succeeded!"

"Tania, please—"

"For days you've been trying to push me away so you could leave me easier!"

"I'm coming back," Alexander said hoarsely.

"Who'll have you!" she cried. "And are you really? Are you sure you haven't come here for this?" She ran to her trunk, rummaged through it, found the *Bronze Horseman* book, and tore from it a handful of hundred- and thousand-*dollar* bills.

"What's this?" she yelled, throwing the money at him. "Did you come for this, for your *American* money? For your ten thousand American dollars I found in your book? Did you come for this, so you could run to *America* without me? Or were you going to leave me some, as a kind of a *thank you for opening your legs, Tatiana?*"

"Tania . . ."

Grabbing his rifle by the barrel, she went up to Alexander and furiously shoved the butt of the gun into his stomach, pointing the muzzle at herself. "I want back what you took from me." She nearly couldn't continue. "I'm sorry I ever saved myself for you, but now shoot me, you liar and *thief*—that's what you want anyway. Take your damn hand away from my throat and pull the trigger." She jabbed him again, high in the solar plexus, putting the barrel between her breasts. "Go ahead, Alexander," she said. "Thirty-five rounds, right here in my heart."

He took the weapon from her without saying a word.

Tatiana raised her hand and slapped him hard on the face. "I want you to leave right now," she said, a tear rolling down her cheek. "We had some good times. We're certainly not going to have them again. You *fucked* me," she said, "anytime you felt like it. I get it by now. It's the only thing you wanted from day one. Well, you got what you wanted, you're done, so go." Tatiana ripped the wedding ring off her finger and flung it at him. "There—you can give it to your next whore!"

Her shoulders hunched and quaking, she climbed onto the bed, wrapping herself in a white sheet, like a body dead from the hunger.

Alexander went outside and went swimming in the cold Kama waters, wishing for his pain, his remorse, his love, for his whole life to be washed away into the tundra. The blue moon was three nights from full. If I stay in the water, maybe I can float in the river, down to the Volga, into the Caspian Sea, and no one will find me. I will float on my pain and my heart; I will float and feel no more. That's all I want. To feel no more.

Eventually he came back inside.

Climbing onto the bed, Alexander lay silently next to his Tania, listening for her breath. Every few minutes her breathing would break into the shudder of someone who had been crying for a long time. She lay in a fetal position, turned away from him to the wall.

Finally he unraveled her from the sheet and rubbed against her. Slightly parting her legs, he entered her, pressing his mouth to the nape of her neck and then to the top of her head. His left hand slipped under her to hold her to him, his right hand embraced her hip. He cradled her in himself, like always, as she cradled him in herself, like always.

Tatiana barely stirred. She did not pull away from him, but neither did she make a single sound. She is punishing me, Alexander thought, closing his eyes. I deserve much worse. Still, it was unbearable to hear her silence. Alexander kissed her head, her hair, her shoulders. He could not be deep enough in her enslaving warmth to find peace. At last she couldn't help herself, she groaned and shuddered and clutched his hand, and he did not stop himself from release this time. Afterward he remained inside her and then heard her crying.

"Tatiasha, I am so sorry," he whispered. "I'm sorry I said those heartless things. I didn't mean them." He held her stomach into him.

"You meant them," Tatiana said emptily. "You're a soldier. You meant them all."

"No, Tania," Alexander said, hating himself. "I didn't. I'm your husband first." He held her close. "Feel me, Tania, feel my body, feel my hands, my lips on you, feel my heart. I didn't mean them."

"Shura, I wish you would stop saying things you don't mean."

He breathed in her smello, rubbing his face in her hair. "I know. I'm sorry." She didn't reply, but her hand remained on his. "Turn to me?" he asked, pulling himself away.

"No."

"Please. Turn to me, and tell me you forgive me."

Tatiana turned, lifting her swollen eyes to Alexander.

"Oh, honey . . ." He paused, closing his eyes. He could not endure her expression. "Breathe on me," he whispered. "I want to smell your blueberry breath on my face."

She did. Alexander inhaled the warm spirit out of her lungs into his mouth and into his lungs. He hugged her. "Please tell me you forgive me, Tania."

"I forgive you." Her voice was flat.

"Kiss me. I want to feel your lips forgive me."

She kissed him. He watched her close her eyes.

"You have not forgiven me. Again."

Tatiana kissed him again softly. She kissed him, and then her mouth parted, and she made a small forgiving moaning sound. Her hands drifted down to take hold of him. Quietly she caressed him and caressed him. And caressed him.

"Thank you," Alexander said, gazing at her. "Say to me, Shura, I know you didn't mean it. You were just angry."

Sighing, she said, "I know you didn't mean it."

"Say to me, I know you love me to insanity."

"I know you love me."

"No, Tania," he said, raw emotion in his voice. "I love you to insanity." He ran his lips back and forth against her silken eyebrows, unable to breathe, afraid he would exhale her breath out of him.

"I'm sorry I hit you," Tatiana whispered.

"I'm surprised you didn't kill me."

"Alexander," she said, "is that why you came here?" She couldn't keep her voice from breaking. "For your . . . *money?*"

Crushing her with his arms, he said, looking at the wall, "Tania, stop it. No, I did not come for my money."

"Where did you get the American dollars from?"

"My mother. I told you my family had money in America. My father decided he was going to come to the Soviet Union with nothing, and my mother agreed, but she brought this money with her just in case and hid it from him. This was the last thing my mother left me, a few weeks before she was arrested. We carved out the inside covers of the Pushkin book. We hid the money together. Ten thousand dollars on one side, four thousand rubles on the other. She thought that maybe it could help me get out."

"Where did you put it when you were arrested in 1936?"

"I hid it in the Leningrad Public Library. And there it remained until I gave the book to you."

"Oh, my prescient Alexander," said Tatiana, "you gave it to me just in time, didn't you? The library shipped out most of its priceless items, including the entire Pushkin collection, way back last July and moved the rest of its books down to the cellar. Your money would have been long lost."

Alexander said nothing.

"Why did you give it to me? You wanted it to be in a safe place?"

Alexander turned his gaze back to her. "Because I wanted to trust you with my one life," he said.

Tatiana was quiet.

"The book wasn't in the library the whole time, though, was it?"

He made no reply.

"In 1940, when you went to fight Finland, you took the money with you, didn't you?"

He made no reply.

"Oh, Alexander." Tatiana buried her face in his chest.

Alexander wanted to speak. He just could not.

It was Tatiana who spoke. "One more thing for Dimitri not to forgive you for, as if there weren't enough already. When you went back for Stepanov's son, you took Dimitri with you because you two were going to escape through Finland, weren't you?"

Nothing moved on Alexander.

"You were going to run, through the swamps, right to Vyborg, and then to Helsinki, and then to *America!* You had brought your money, you were ready. It was the moment you had dreamed about for years." She kissed his chest. "Wasn't it, my husband, my heart, my Alexander, my entire life right here in this cabin, wasn't it, tell me?" She was crying.

Alexander had lost his powers of speech. He was very nearly losing his powers over everything. He never wanted to have *this* out with Tatiana.

Her voice trembled. "It was a great plan. You would have disappeared, and no one would have ever gone to look for you—they would just have assumed you had died. You didn't count on Yuri Stepanov being alive. You thought he'd be dead. It was just an excuse to return to the woods. Suddenly he was alive!" Tatiana emitted a low laugh. "Oh, Dimitri must have been *extremely* surprised when you said you were going back with Yuri. What are you thinking, he must have said. Are you crazy? You've wanted to go back to America for years. Here's your chance, here's my chance." She paused. "How close am I?"

Nuzzling into her blonde head, Alexander finally said in a stunned whisper, "As if you were there. How do you know this?"

She cupped his face in her hands. "Because I—better than anybody—know who you are." Tatiana paused, leaving her hands on his face. "So you returned to the Soviet Union with Stepanov's son, thinking you would have another chance to run. What did you have to do, Shura?" she asked. "Promise Dimitri that if you didn't die, one way or another you would get him to America?"

He pushed away her hands and turned on his back, shutting his eyes. "Tania, stop. I can't continue this anymore. I just can't."

She stopped only to get control of her faltering speech.

"So now what?"

"Now nothing," Alexander said darkly, looking up at the beamed ceiling. "Now you stay here and I go back to the front. Now Dimitri is crippled. Now I fight for Leningrad. Now I *die* for Leningrad."

"God! Don't say that!" Tatiana grabbed his arms, turning him to her and, crying, clutched at his chest. He held her as close as he could, but it wasn't close enough, not for her, not for him. "Don't say that, Shura!" She was sobbing uncontrollably. "Shura, please," she barely whispered. "Please don't leave me by myself in the Soviet Union."

Alexander had never seen Tatiana so upset. He didn't know what to do. "Come on," he said, his voice breaking, his heart breaking. *Come on, Tatiana, love me less, let me go, free me.*

Hours went by. In the deepest night, Alexander made love to her again. "Go on, Tatiasha," he whispered, "spread your legs for me like I love."

She tasted as if she were crying tears of nectar into his throat.

"Promise me," he said, kissing her blonde downy hair, licking the soft inside of her thighs, "promise me you will not leave Lazarevo."

There was no answer from her, just stifled moans.

"Are you my good girl?" he whispered, his fingers more tender, more persistent. "Are you my lovely girl?" he whispered, his mouth more gentle, more persistent, his hot breath imploring into her. "*Swear* to me you will stay here and wait for me. Promise me you'll be a good wife and wait for your husband."

"I promise, Shura. I will wait for you."

Then, later, "I'll be waiting a long time," Tatiana said brokenly, lying relieved and unrelieved in his arms, "here alone in Lazarevo."

Hugging her to him so hard she could barely breathe, an utterly unrelieved Alexander whispered, "Alone, but safe."

How they spent the next three days Alexander did not know. Awash in a flood of hostility and despair, they battled and railed and shattered their bodies on one another, unable to find one strand, one sobering swallow of solace.

22

The morning Alexander was leaving, they could not touch.

Tatiana sat on the bench outside while he packed. Alexander put on his dress uniform that she had washed and ironed for him with an iron warmed on the hearth, brushed his hair, and put on his sidecap. He made sure he had his helmet tied to him and his tent on his back. He had his pistol, his ammunition, his passport, his grenades, and his rifle.

He left her all of his money save for the few rubles it was going to cost him to get back.

When he came out of the house, Tatiana, who had been sitting, got up and disappeared into the house, appearing a few minutes later with a cup of coffee, full of milk and sugar, and a plate of food. Some black bread, three eggs, a sliced tomato.

Alexander took the plate from her. He was choking. "Thank you," he said.

Holding her stomach, she sat down heavily. "Of course," she said. "Eat. You have a long journey ahead of you."

Listlessly he ate as they sat almost side by side, if only she weren't turned one way and he another.

"Do you want me to come to the train station with you?"

"No," he said. "I can't."

Tatiana nodded. "I can't either."

Finishing his food, Alexander put the plate on the ground. "I've left you plenty of wood, don't you think?" he said, turning to her and pointing to the woodshed at the side of the cabin.

"Plenty," she said. "It should last me a good long while."

Gently Alexander pulled the white satin ribbons from her braids. Taking his comb, he brushed out her smooth blonde hair, rubbing the silken strands between his fingers. "How do I arrange for my money to come to you here?" Alexander asked. "I get two thousand rubles a month. That's a lot of money for you. I can send you fifteen hundred. I'll keep five hundred for cigarettes."

She shook her head. "Don't do it. You'll only get yourself into further trouble. Leningrad isn't Lazarevo, Shura. Protect yourself. Don't tell anyone we're married. Take the ring off your finger. You don't want Dimitri to find out somehow. We don't need more trouble for you. You already have plenty. I don't need your money."

"Yes, you do."

"Then send it to me when you write to me."

"Can't. The censors will steal it immediately."

"Censors? So I should avoid writing to you in my English?"

"If you want me to live, yes."

Tatiana didn't turn around when she said, "It's the only thing I want."

"I will send the money to the local *Soviet* in Molotov," said Alexander. "Go there once a month and check, all right? I'll say I'm sending it to Dasha's family." Closing his eyes, Alexander pressed his lips to her gleaming hair. "I'd better go. There is only one train a day."

Tatiana said in a stricken voice, "I'll walk you to the road. Have you got everything?"

"Yes."

All this without looking at each other.

They left together and walked up the path through the woods. Before the clearing disappeared from view, Alexander turned around one last time to look at the blue river and the deep green pines, at their wood cabin and their bench, at their log in the water, at the place where his tent had stood just yesterday. At their fire.

"Write to me," Alexander said to Tatiana, "and let me know how you're doing." He paused. "So I don't worry."

"All right." Her arms were twisted around her stomach. "You, too."

They got to the road. The pine needles smelled strong, the woods were quiet, the sun was warm overhead. They stood in front of each other, Tatiana in her yellow dress, looking at her bare feet, Alexander in his army uniform, rifle on his shoulder, looking down the road.

Her hand came up and patted him gently on the chest, pressing into his heart. "You keep yourself alive for me, soldier, you hear?" Tears were running down her face.

Alexander took her hand and brought it to his lips. She was wearing his ring. He couldn't speak, couldn't say her name aloud.

Tatiana placed her trembling palm on Alexander's face. "It'll be all right, my love," she whispered. "It'll be all right."

She let go of his face. He let go of her hand. "Turn around and go home," he said. "Don't watch me. I can't walk away with you standing here."

Tatiana turned away. "Go ahead. I won't watch you."

Alexander couldn't come near her. "Please," he said. "I can't leave you like this. Please go home."

"Shura," she said. "I don't want you to go."

"I know. I don't want to go, but please let me. Knowing you're safe is the only chance I have of staying alive. I will make my way back to you, but you have to be safe." He stopped. "Now I must go. Come on, lift your head to me. Lift your head to me, and smile."

Turning around, Tatiana lifted her crying face to him and smiled.

They stared at each other for a long moment. Tatiana blinked. Alexander blinked.

"What's that in your eyes?"

"I'm watching all my wooden crates descend the ramp from the Winter Palace," she whispered.

"Got to have a little more faith, my wife." Alexander raised his shaking right hand to his temple, to his lips, to his heart.

DESOLATE WAVES

1

TATIANA went back to their house, lay down on their bed, and did not get up.

During her semiconscious sleep Tatiana kept hearing the four old women in the room. They were talking quietly while fixing her blankets, adjusting the pillows under her head, stroking her hair.

Dusia said, "She needs to trust in the Lord. He will get her out of this."

Naira said, "I told her it wasn't a good idea to fall in love with a soldier. All they do is break your heart."

Raisa tremulously said, "I think the problem isn't that he's a soldier. The problem is she loves him too much."

Axinya whispered, patting Tatiana's back, "Lucky girl."

"What's lucky?" Naira said indignantly. "If only she had listened to us and stayed at our house, none of this would have happened."

"If only she came to church with me more often," said Dusia. "The Lord's rod and His staff, they would comfort her."

"What do you think, Tanechka?" Axinya said, standing close to Tatiana. "You think the Lord's rod and staff would comfort you right now?"

Naira said, "This is no good. We are not helping her."

Dusia: "I never liked him."

Naira: "Me neither. Never understood what Tania saw in him."

Raisa: "She is too good for him."

Naira: "She is too good for anybody."

Dusia: "She can be even better, closer to the Lord."

Naira: "My Vova is such a kind, gentle boy. He cared for her."

Raisa: "I bet you Alexander's not going to come back for her. He's left her here for good."

Naira: "I'm sure you're right. He married her—"

Dusia: "Soiled her—"

Raisa: "And discarded her."

Dusia: "I always suspected he was godless."

Axinya whispered to Tatiana, "The only thing that will keep him away is death."

Thank you, Axinya, thought Tatiana, opening her heavy eyes and lifting her body out of bed. But that's exactly what I'm afraid of.

The old girls convinced Tatiana without much effort to come back and live with them. Vova helped her to carry the trunk and sewing machine back to Naira's house.

At first Tatiana could not get through her day without physically holding herself together. There was no comfort inside her, and she knew it. There was nowhere she could turn to inside herself to leave the darkness. No memory she could fondly think of, no gentle joke, no musical refrain. There was no part of her body she could touch without shuddering. Nowhere she could look without seeing Alexander.

This time she didn't have the hunger to dull her sorrow. She didn't have infected lungs. There was nothing for her healthy body to do but grit its teeth and lift the buckets that went on her shoulders every morning, and milk the goat and pour the warm milk for Raisa, who could not pour it herself, and hang the clothes on the line and have the women say at night how wonderful the clothes smelled, having been hung by Tania in the sunshine.

Tatiana sewed for them and for herself, she read to them and to herself, she bathed them and herself, she tended their garden and looked after their chickens and took the apples off the trees, and little by little, bucket by bucket, book by book, shirt by shirt, their need enveloped her again, and Tatiana was comforted.

Just like *before*.

2

After two weeks came the first letter from Alexander.

Tatiasha,

Can there be anything harder than this? Missing you is a physical aching that grips me early in the morning and does not leave me, not even as I draw my last waking breath.

My solace in these waning empty summer days is the knowledge that you're safe, and alive, and healthy, and that the worst that you have to go through is serfdom for four well-meaning old women.

The wood piles I've left are the lightest in the front. The heaviest ones are for the winter. Use them last, and if you need help carrying them, God help me, ask Vova. Don't hurt yourself. And don't fill the water pails all the way to the top. They're too heavy.

Getting back was rough, and as soon as I came back, I was sent right out to the Neva, where for six days we planned our attack and then made a move in boats across the river and were completely crushed in two hours. We didn't stand a chance. The Germans bombed the boats with the Vanyushas, their version of my rocket launcher, the boats all sank. We were left with a thousand fewer men and were no closer to crossing the river. We're now looking at other places we can cross. I'm fine, except for the fact that it's rained here for ten days straight and I've been hip deep in mud for all that time. There is nowhere to sleep, except in the mud. We put our trench coats down and hope it stops raining soon. All black and wet, I almost felt sorry for myself until I thought of you during the blockade.

I've decided to do that from now on. Every time I think I have it so tough, I'm going to think of you burying your sister in Lake Ladoga.

I wish you had been given a lighter cross than Leningrad to carry through your life.

Things are going to be relatively quiet here for the next few weeks, until we regroup. Yesterday a bomb fell in the commandant's bunker. The commandant wasn't there at the time. Yet the anxiety doesn't go away. When is it going to come again?

I play cards and soccer. And I smoke. And I think of you.

I sent you money. Go to Molotov at the end of August.

Don't forget to eat well, my warm bun, my midnight sun, and kiss your hand for me, right in the palm and then press it against your heart.

Alexander

Tatiana read Alexander's letter a hundred times, memorizing every word. She slept with her face on the letter, which renewed her strength.

My love, my dear, dear Shura,

Don't talk about my cross—first heave your own off your shoulders.

How did I live last winter? I don't know, but I think almost longingly of it now. Because I moved. There was movement inside me. I had energy to lie, to pretend to Dasha, to keep her alive. I walked, I was with Mama, I was too busy to die myself. Too busy hiding my love for you.

But now I wake up and think, how am I going to go through the rest of my day until sleep?

To ease myself back into life, I've surrounded myself with the villagers. You think it was bad before. I'm from morning till night helping Irina Persikova, who had to have her leg cut off in Molotov, infection or something. I think I like her because she carries my mother's name.

I think of Dasha. I grieve for my sister.

But her face is not the last face I see before I sleep. Yours is.

You are my hand grenade, my artillery fire. You have replaced my heart with yourself.

Are you thinking of me with your rifle in your hands?

What do we do? How do we keep you from dying? These thoughts consume my waking minutes. What can I do from here to keep you alive?

Dead or wounded, those Soviets will leave you in the field.

Who is going to heal you if you fall?

Who is going to bury you if you die? Bury you like you deserve—with kings and heroes.

Yours,
Tatiana

Tatia,

You ask how I keep myself from dying. Poorly, I say. Though still better than Ivan Petrenko.

My commander tells me—choose the best men you have, and I salute him, and do. And then they die. What does that make me?

We came under the worst unprotected fire today. I can't believe I'm alive to write you these words. We were supplying the men across the river at the Nevsky Patch. We row the boats with food and arms and munitions and new men to the other side. But the Germans are relentless from Sinyavino Heights, we can't get past them or to them; they sit on their hills like vultures and hurl their metal at us. Usually I don't go—there's not enough of me to go on these suicide missions, and the commander knows it, but today we just didn't have enough soldiers to man the boats.

Petrenko died. We were in the boat coming back to our side, and a piece of artillery shell hit him. Took his arm off. I threw him on my back, and, you know, in my insanity I bent down to pick up his arm. I picked it up and he fell off my back, and as I looked at him lying in the boat I thought, what am I doing? Who is going to sew that arm back on?

I didn't want him and his arm reunited, I realized. I just wanted them to be buried together. There is no dignity in the man being ripped apart. The body has to be together so the soul can find it. I buried him and his arm by the woods, near a small birch. He had once said he liked birches. Had to take his rifle—we barely have enough weapons as it is—but I left him his helmet.

I liked him. Where is the justice that a good man like Petrenko dies and yet Dimitri, infirm and hobbled, still lives?

You want to know what I thought of in that boat?

I thought, I have to stay alive. Tatiasha will never forgive me.

But this war is unjust, as you've seen. A good man has as much chance of dying as a bad one. Maybe more so.

I want you to know that should something happen to me, don't worry about my body. My soul isn't going to return to it, nor to God. It's flying straight to you, where it knows it can find you, in Lazarevo. I want to be neither with kings nor heroes, but with the queen of Lake Ilmen.

Alexander

3

There were no more letters from Alexander.

August passed quietly into September, and still no letters. Tatiana did the best she could, drowning herself with the old women, with her village, with her books, with her English, with John Stuart Mill, whom she read out loud to herself in the woods, almost understanding everything.

Still nothing from him, and her soul wasn't quiet anymore, and it wasn't comforted.

One Friday at the knitting circle, Tatiana, her head buried in the sweater she was making for Alexander, heard Irina Persikova ask if she had received any letters from him.

"Not for a month now," said Naira quietly. "Shh. We don't talk about it. The Molotov Soviet has no news. She goes every week to check. Shh."

Dusia said, "Either way, God is with him."

Axinya jovially said, "Don't worry, Tanechka. The post is terrible. You know that. Letters take a long time to come."

"I know, Axinya," said Tatiana, looking at her knitting needles. "I'm not worried."

"I'll tell you a story that'll make you feel better. A woman named Olga lived in the village here a few months before you came, and her husband was at the front, too. She waited and waited for letters from him. Nothing. Like you she fretted and waited, and then she got ten letters all at once!"

Tatiana smiled. "Wouldn't that be great?" she said. "To get ten letters from Alexander all at once."

"Absolutely, darling." Axinya smiled. "So don't worry."

Dusia said, "Oh, that's right. Olga put the letters in chronological order and started reading them. She read nine of them, and the tenth letter was from the commandant, saying her husband had been killed at the front."

Tatiana paled. "Oh" was all she could get out.

"Dusia!" Axinya exclaimed. "For God's sake, have you no sense? Next you're going to tell her how Olga drowned herself in the Kama."

Tatiana put down her knitting needles. "You ladies finish up here without me, all right? I'm going to go and start on our dinner. I'm making cabbage pie."

She stumbled home and immediately got the Pushkin book out of the trunk. Alexander had told her he put the money back. Looking at the cover, looking and looking, Tatiana took a deep breath and carefully cut off the paper with a razor blade. The money was there. Breathing out a small sigh, she took it into her hands.

Then she counted it.

Five thousand dollars.

Without alarm she counted the crisp new bills again, taking care to separate each one. Ten one-hundred-dollar bills. Four one-thousand-dollar bills.

Five thousand dollars.

She counted it again.

Five thousand dollars.

Tatiana started doubting herself; for a moment she thought maybe it had always been five thousand dollars, that she had just mistaken the amount.

If only Alexander's voice in the kerosene-lamp-filled night didn't carry from her brain to her heart: *This was the last thing my mother left me, a few weeks before she was arrested. . . . We hid the money together. Ten thousand American dollars . . . four thousand rubles.*

Tatiana climbed on top of her bed and lay on her back, facing the beamed ceiling.

He had told her he was leaving her all the money.

No, he didn't say that. He said, *I'm leaving you the money.* She had watched him glue the cover back together.

Why would he take only five thousand dollars?

To mollify her? To have her not worry, not make another scandalous scene? Not return to Leningrad with him?

She held the money to her chest and tried to fathom Alexander's heart.

He was the man who, a few meters away from freedom, from *America*, had chosen to turn his back on his lifelong dream. Feel one way. Behave one way, too. Alexander may have hoped for *America*, but he believed more in himself. And he loved Tatiana most of all. Alexander knew who he was.

He was a man who kept his word.

And he had given it to Dimitri.

Part Four

In Live Defiance

Worn Out with Terror and Misgiving

1

Tatiana wasn't staying another second in Lazarevo by herself.

She wrote Alexander ten letters, relaxed, upbeat, comfortable letters. She made her news chronological and seasonal. She enlisted Naira Mikhailovna's help in sending them to Alexander one by one, at an interval of one every week.

She knew that if she just left without a word, the old ladies would write to Alexander or, worse, find a way to telegraph Alexander a frantic missive telling him of her disappearance, and if he were still alive to hear it, his uncontrolled reaction might cost him his life. So Tatiana told the women that to avoid having to get a job at the Lazarevo fish plant, where most of the villagers worked, she was going to Molotov to work in the hospital. Tatiana invited no argument, and after the first few muttered questions from Dusia, got none.

Naira Mikhailovna wanted to know why Tatiana couldn't send the letters straight from Molotov. Tatiana replied that Alexander didn't want her to leave Lazarevo, and he would be upset if he found out she was working in town. She didn't want to upset him while he was fighting. "You know how protective he can be, Naira Mikhailovna."

"Protective and unreasonable," Naira said, vigorously nodding. She was more than willing to enlist as a co-conspirator in what she saw as a plot to circumvent Alexander's impossible character. She agreed to send him the letters.

Having sewn herself all new clothes, and having packed as many bottles of vodka and *tushonka* as she could carry, Tatiana set out early one morning after saying good-bye to the four old women. Dusia said a prayer over her head. Naira cried. Raisa cried and shook. Axinya leaned in and whispered, "You are crazy."

Crazy for him, thought Tatiana. She left wearing dark brown trousers, brown stockings, brown boots, and a brown winter coat. Her light hair was tied in a plaid brown kerchief. She wanted to draw as little attention to herself as possible. She had sewn the dollars into an inseam flap on her trousers. Before she left, she took off her wedding ring and threaded it through a braided rope she had made. As she kissed it before tucking it inside her shirt, she whispered, "You're just closer to my heart this way, Shura."

As she was walking through the woods out of Lazarevo, Tatiana passed the path that led to their clearing. Stopping briefly, she thought about going down to the river and glancing . . . one last time. The thought alone—the imagining—was too much for her. Shaking her head, she continued onward.

There were some things she could not do.

She had watched Alexander steal one look; she could not. Since Vova had carried her trunk up the path over two months ago, Tatiana had not returned to the place where she had lived with Alexander. Vova boarded up the windows, put the padlock back on, and carried all of Alexander's cut wood to Naira's house.

In Molotov, Tatiana first went to the local *Soviet* to see if there was any money from Alexander for September.

Surprisingly, there was!

She asked if there was any telegram or letter with the money. There wasn't.

If he was still getting soldier's pay, it meant that he had neither died nor deserted. Taking the 1,500 rubles, Tatiana wondered what would make Alexander send her *ring money* but not write? Then she remembered the months it had taken for her grandmother's letters to reach them in Leningrad. Well, she didn't care if she got thirty letters from Alexander all at once, one for each day of September.

At the train station in Molotov, Tatiana told the Party domestic passport inspector that Leningrad was experiencing a dire shortage of nurses, what with the war and the hunger, and she was returning to help. She showed him the employment stamp from Grechesky Hospital in her passport. He didn't have to know she had washed floors and toilets and dishes and sewed body bags. For his help Tatiana offered him a bottle of vodka.

He asked for the letter from the hospital inviting her to return to Leningrad. Tatiana replied that the letter got burned, but here were her credentials from the Kirov factory, from the Grechesky Hospital, and here was a citation for valor in the Fourth People's Volunteer Army, and here was another bottle of vodka for his trouble.

He stamped her passport, and she bought her ticket.

Before she boarded her train, she went to see Sofia, who was so excruciatingly slow, Tatiana felt herself aging as she waited. Tatiana thought she would miss her train for sure, but Sofia finally managed to procure the two photographs she had taken of Alexander and Tatiana on the steps of St. Seraphim's church on their wedding day. Tatiana stuffed them in her backpack and ran to catch her train.

The train she was departing on was much better than the one on which she had arrived. It was a semblance of a passenger train, and it was going southwest to Kazan. Southwest was the wrong direction for Tatiana, who needed to be heading north. But Kazan was a big city, and she would be able to catch another train. Her plan was to somehow make her way back to Kobona and to catch a barge across Lake Ladoga to Kokkorevo.

As the train was pulling out, Tatiana looked across the road at the Kama in the far distance, obscured by pines and birches, and thought, will I ever see Lazarevo again?

She did not think so.

In Kazan, Tatiana got on a train headed to Nizhny Novgorod—not the Novgorod of her childhood and of Pasha, another Novgorod. She was now less than 300 kilometers east of Moscow. She caught another train, this one a freight train heading northwest to Yaroslavl, and from there a bus north to Vologda.

In Vologda, Tatiana found that she could take the train to Tikhvin, but that Tikhvin was under constant and oppressive German fire. And from Tikhvin getting to Kobona was apparently impossible. The trains were being knocked out of operation three to four times a day, with heavy loss of life and supplies. Thank God for the train inspector, who sold her the ticket to Tikhvin and who was more than willing to chat with her.

She asked the inspector how the food was getting into the blockaded Leningrad if the Kobona route was blocked by German fire.

After she found out, Tatiana decided to follow the food. From Vologda she took a train headed for Petrozavodsk, far north on the western shores of Lake Onega, and simply got off early, in Podporozhye, and walked fifty kilometers to Lodeinoye Pole, which was ten kilometers from the shores of Lake Ladoga.

In Lodeinoye Pole, Tatiana felt the earth rumbling underneath her feet and knew she was close.

While stopping at a canteen to have some soup and bread, Tatiana overheard four transport drivers talking at the next table. Apparently the Germans had practically stopped bombing Leningrad, diverting all their air power and artillery to the Volkhov front—where Tatiana was headed. The Soviet general Meretskov's 2nd Army was only four kilometers away from the Neva, and the German field marshal Manstein was determined not to let Meretskov push him from his positions along the river. Tatiana heard one of the men say, "Did you hear about our 861st division? Could not move the Germans at all, spent all day under their fire, and lost 65 percent of its men and 100 percent of its commanding officers!"

"That's nothing!" another exclaimed. "Did you hear how many men Meretskov lost in August-September in Volkhov? How many dead, wounded, missing in action? One hundred and thirty thousand!"

"Is that a lot?" said another. "In Moscow—"

"Out of one hundred and fifty thousand men!"

Tatiana had had quite enough of listening to other people's discussions. But she needed just a little bit more information. After striking up a conversation with the truck drivers, she found out that food barges departed on Lake Ladoga just south of a small town called Syastroy, about ten kilometers north of the Volkhov front. Syastroy was about a hundred kilometers south from where Tatiana was at the moment.

Tatiana was going to ask the men for a ride but didn't like the sound of them. They were staying in Lodeinoye Pole overnight, and the way one of them looked at her, even with her brown plaid kerchief . . .

She wiped her mouth, thanked them, and left. She felt better knowing she was carrying Alexander's loaded P-38.

It took Tatiana three days to walk the hundred kilometers to Syastroy. It was early October and cold, but the first snow had not fallen yet, and the road was paved. Many other people walked along with her—villagers, evacuees, itinerant farmers, occasionally soldiers returning to the front. She walked for half a day next to one who was returning from furlough. He looked as forlorn as Alexander must have felt. Then he caught a ride from an army truck, and Tatiana kept walking.

The bursting roar of heavy bombs exploding in the near distance never stopped shaking the earth underneath her feet as she walked, her pack on her back, her eyes to the ground. No matter how bad this seemed, it was better than running through the potato field in Luga. It was better than sitting in the train station in Luga, realizing that the Germans weren't leaving until Tatiana was dead. It was better than that, but not much. She kept walking, her eyes to the ground.

She walked even at night—it was calmer at night, and after eleven there were no bombings. She would walk for another few hours and then find a barn to sleep in. One night she stayed with a family who offered her dinner *and* their oldest son. She ate the dinner, passed on the son, offering money instead. They took it.

Ten kilometers west of Syastroy, right on the Volkhov River, Tatiana found a small barge about to take off across the lake around the horn of Novaya Ladoga. The longshoreman was untying the rope. She waited as the plank was just about to go up and then ran up to the man and told him she had food for the war effort, for the blockade, taking out five cans of ham and a bottle of vodka. The longshoreman stared longingly at the vodka. Tatiana asked him to keep the vodka for himself and let her go to see her dying mother in Leningrad. Tatiana knew this was a dire time for local people. Most of their relatives who had lived in Leningrad were either dead or dying. The dockhand gratefully kept the vodka and waved her on. "Warning you, though—it's a bad passage. Too long in the water, and the Germans bomb the barges all day long."

"I know," she said. "I'm ready." She crossed without incident.

The barge came to Osinovets, north of Kokkorevo, where Tatiana offered the rest of her *tushonka*—four cans—and another bottle of vodka to the truck driver who was taking food to Leningrad. He let her sit in the front with him and even shared some bread with her as they drove.

Tatiana stared out the window. Was she really going to be able to go back to her Fifth Soviet apartment? As if she had much choice.

But to go back to *Leningrad*?

She shivered. She didn't want to think about it. The driver dropped her off at Finland Station in the north of the city. She took a tram back to Nevsky Prospekt and walked home from Insurrection Square.

Leningrad was sad and empty. It was nighttime, and the streets were poorly lit, but at least there was electricity. Tatiana must have come at a good time, because it was quiet; there was no shelling. But as she walked, she saw three smoldering fires and many broken shambling gaps where windows and doors had once been.

She hoped her building on Fifth Soviet was still standing.

It was. Still green, still drab, still filthy.

Tatiana stood for a few minutes at the double front doors. She was searching for the thing Alexander called courage.

The courage to go back up the stairs that led to the two empty rooms where six other hearts had once lived. Rooms filled with jokes and vodka and dinners and small dreams and small desires and life.

She looked up and down the street. Across Grechesky the church still stood, untouched and unbombed. Turning her head to Suvorovsky, she saw a few people going into their buildings, coming home from work. Just a few people, maybe three. The pavement was clear and dry. The cold air was hurting her nose.

It was for him.

His heart was still beating, and it called to her.

He was going to be her courage.

She nodded to herself and turned the handle. The dark green hallway smelled of urine. Holding on to the railing, Tatiana slowly walked up three flights of stairs to her communal apartment.

Her key worked in the glossy brown door.

The apartment was quiet. There was no one in the front kitchen, and the doors to the other rooms were closed. All closed, except for Slavin's, whose door was slightly ajar. Tatiana knocked, looked in.

Slavin was on his floor, listening to the radio.

"Who are *you*?" he said in a shrill voice.

"Tania Metanova, remember? How *are* you?" She smiled. Some things never changed.

"Were you here during the War of 1905? Oh, did we give those Japs hell." He pointed his finger to the radio. "Listen, listen carefully."

Just the sound of the metronome, beat beat beat.

Quietly she backed away. The Russians lost that war. Slavin looked up from the floor at her and said, "You should have come last month, Tanechka—only seven bombs fell on Leningrad last month. You would have been safer."

"Don't worry," she said. "If you need anything, I'm right down the hall."

There was no one in her kitchen either. To her surprise, the door to her hallway and her two rooms was unlocked. In the hallway on her sofa she found two strangers, a man and a woman drinking tea.

Tatiana stood for a moment staring at them. "Who *are* you?" she asked at last.

They said they were Inga and Stanislav Krakov. They were both in their forties; he was paunchy and spottily balding, she was small and wizened.

"But who *are* you?" she asked again.

"Who are *you*?" demanded Stanislav, not even looking at her.

Tatiana put down her backpack. "These are my rooms," she said. "You're sitting on my sofa."

Inga quickly explained that they had lived on Seventh Soviet and Suvorovsky. "We had a nice apartment, our own apartment," she said. "Our own bathroom, and kitchen, and a bedroom." Apparently their building was bombed to the ground in August. With the shortage of housing in Leningrad because of so many demolished buildings, the Soviet council placed Inga and Stanislav in the Metanov rooms, which were unoccupied. "Don't worry," said Inga. "They'll find us our own apartment soon; they said, maybe even a two-bedroom. Right, Stan?"

"Well, I'm back now," said Tatiana. "The rooms are no longer unoccupied." She looked around the hallway. Alexander had cleaned the place so well, she thought with sadness.

"Yes? And where are we supposed to go?" asked Stan. "We are registered with the council to stay here."

"What about the other rooms in the communal apartment?" she asked. The other rooms—where *other* people had died.

"They're all taken," said Stan. "Listen, why are we still talking about this? There's enough space here. You can have a whole room to yourself. What's to complain about?"

"Both rooms are mine, though," she said.

"Actually, no," said Stan, continuing to drink his tea. "Both rooms belong to the state. And the state is at war." He laughed joylessly. "You are not being a good proletarian, comrade."

Inga said, "Stan and I are Party members in the Leningrad corps of engineers."

"That's great," said Tatiana, suddenly feeling very tired. "Which room can I take?"

Inga and Stan had taken her old room, where she had slept with Dasha, with Mama, with Papa, with Pasha. It was also the only room with heat. Deda and Babushka's old room had a broken stove in it.

Even if the stove weren't broken, Tatiana had no wood to heat it.

"Could I at least have my *bourzhuika* back?" she asked.

"And what will we use?" said Stan.

"What's your name anyway?" asked Inga.

"Tania."

Sheepishly Inga said, "Tania, why don't you move the little cot to the wall near where the stove is on our side? The wall is warm. Do you want Stan to help you?"

"Inga, stop, you know my back is bad," snapped Stan. "She can move it herself."

"Yes," said Tatiana. She moved Deda's sofa just far enough to sandwich Pasha's little cot in between the back of the sofa and the wall.

The wall was warm.

Tatiana slept for seventeen hours covered by her coat and three blankets.

After waking, she went to the Soviet council housing committee to register herself once again as a resident of Leningrad. "What did you come back for?" the woman behind the desk asked her rudely, filling out documents for a new ration card. "We're still under blockade, you know."

"I know," said Tatiana. "But there's a shortage of nurses. The war is still on." She paused. "Someone has to take care of the soldiers, right?"

The older woman shrugged, not lifting her eyes. Is anyone in this city going to lift their eyes and look at me? thought Tatiana. Just one person. "Summer was better," the woman said. "More food. Now you won't be able to get potatoes."

"That's all right," Tatiana said, twinging with pain, remembering the potato counter Alexander had built in Lazarevo.

With her ration card in hand, she went to the Elisey food store on Nevsky. She couldn't bear to go back to the store on Fontanka and Nekrasova where she used to get the family rations a year ago. In Elisey it was too late for bread, but she did get some real milk, some beans, an onion, and four tablespoons of oil. For a hundred rubles she bought a can of *tushonka*. Since she wasn't working yet, her bread ration was only 350 grams, but for workers it rose to 700. Tatiana planned to get a job.

Tatiana looked for a *bourzhuika* but had no luck. She even went to Gostiny

Dvor shopping center, across from Elisey on Nevsky, but couldn't find anything there. She had 3,000 rubles left of Alexander's money, and she would have gladly spent half of it on a *bourzhuika* to keep her warm, but there was none to be found. With her bag of food Tatiana walked across Nevsky, past the European Hotel, down Mikhailovskaya Ulitsa, crossed the street into the Italian Gardens, and sat on the bench where Alexander had told her about *America.*

She didn't move, not even when the bombing started, not even when she saw shelling down Mikhailovskaya and across Nevsky. She watched a bomb fall on the pavement and explode in a black flame. Alexander will be so angry when he finds out I'm here, Tatiana thought, finally getting up and heading home. But she wanted him alive; she didn't care if he killed her. She had seen Alexander's temper—he had lost his mind during their last days in Lazarevo. How Alexander got sane—if Alexander got sane—after he left her, Tatiana did not know.

She went back to work at Grechesky Hospital. She had been right. The hospital *was* in dire need of help. The administration officer saw her former Grechesky employment stamp, asked if she had been a nurse, and Tatiana replied that she had been a nurse's aide and that it would take her no time at all to brush up on her skills. She asked to be placed in the critical care unit. She was given a white uniform and followed a nurse named Elizaveta for one nine-hour shift and then a nurse named Maria for another nine-hour shift. The nurses did not lift their eyes to Tatiana.

But the patients did.

After two weeks of working eighteen-hour days, Tatiana was finally given her own rounds and a Sunday afternoon off. She got up her courage to go to Pavlov barracks.

2

Tatiana needed just a word that Alexander was all right and where he was stationed.

The sentry at the gate was no one she knew; his name was Viktor Burenich. The young soldier was friendly and eager to help. She liked that. He checked the roster of all the soldiers currently at the barracks and told her that Alexander Belov was not there. She asked if he knew where the captain was. The guard replied with a smile that he did not. "But he's all right as far as you know?" she asked.

The guard shrugged. "I think so, but they don't tell me these things."

Holding her breath, Tatiana asked if Dimitri Chernenko was still alive.

He was. Tatiana exhaled. Burenich said Chernenko wasn't at the garrison at present, but that he constantly came and went with supplies.

Tatiana tried to think of who else she knew. "Is Anatoly Marazov here?" she asked.

He was, what luck.

In a few minutes Tatiana saw Marazov through the gate.

"Tatiana!" He seemed glad to see her. "What a surprise to see you here. Alexander had told me you evacuated with your sister." He paused. "I'm sorry about your sister."

"Thank you, Lieutenant," she said, her eyes welling up involuntarily. She was extremely relieved. If Marazov mentioned Alexander so offhandedly, it meant that everything was all right.

"I didn't mean to upset you, Tania," Marazov said.

"No, no, you haven't upset me." They stood in the passageway.

"You want to walk around the block?" Marazov asked her. "I have a few minutes."

They strolled with their coats buttoned to Palace Square.

"Are you here to see Dimitri? He's not in my unit anymore."

"Oh, I know," she said, and stammered. Could she keep all the lies in her head? How would she have known about Dimitri? "I know he was injured. I saw him at Kobona a few months back." And if she wasn't here to see Dimitri, who was she here to see?

"Yes, he's now on this side. Running. Unhappy about that, too. I just don't know what he wants the war to give him."

"Are you still in— Alexander's destroyer company?"

"No, Alexander doesn't have a company anymore. He was wounded—" Marazov broke off as Tatiana stumbled. "Are you all right?"

"I'm sorry. Yes, of course. I tripped," she said, crossing her arms around her stomach. She thought that any minute she was going to faint. She had to keep herself together at all costs. She had to. "What happened to him?"

"His hands were burned in an attack in September."

"His hands?" *His hands.*

"Yes. Second-degree burns. Couldn't hold a cup of water for weeks. He's better now."

"Where is he?"

"Back at the front."

Tatiana couldn't continue anymore. "Lieutenant, maybe we should go back. I really must get back."

"All right," Marazov said, puzzled, as they turned around. "Why did you come back to Leningrad anyway?"

"There's a shortage of nurses. I came back to be a nurse." She quickened her step. "Are you posted to Shlisselburg?"

"Eventually, yes. We have a new base of operations for the Leningrad front, up in Morozovo—"

"Morozovo? Listen—I'm glad you're all right. What's next for you?"

He shook his head. "We've lost so many men trying to break the blockade, we're constantly regrouping. But next time out I think I'm with Alexander again."

"Oh, yes?" she said, her legs weakening. "Well, I hope so. Listen, it was good to see you."

"Tania, are you all right?" Marazov stared at her, that look of sad familiarity creeping into his eyes again. Tatiana remembered his face when he met her for the first time, last September. He had looked at her as if he already knew her.

She managed a small smile. "Of course. I'm fine." Stiffly she came up to him and laid her hand on his sleeve. "Thank you, Lieutenant."

"Should I tell Dimitri you stopped by?"

"No! Please don't."

He nodded. Tatiana was nearly down the street when he yelled, "Should I tell Alexander?"

She turned around. "Please don't," she called back faintly.

The following night when Tatiana came home from the hospital, she found Dimitri waiting for her in the hallway with Stan and Inga.

"Dimitri?" said a shocked Tatiana. "What—how—what are you *doing* here?" She glared at Stan and Inga.

"We let him in, Tanechka," said Inga. "He said you used to see each other last year?"

Dimitri came up to Tatiana and put his arms around her. She stood with her own arms at her side. "I heard you came asking for me," he said. "I was so touched. You want to go inside your room?"

"Who told you I stopped by?"

"Burenich, the sentry guard. He said a young girl stopped by asking for me. You didn't leave your name, but he described you. I'm very touched, Tania. These have been very hard months for me."

He was lopsided and hollow-eyed.

"Dimitri, this is not a good time for *me*," she said, casting an angry glance toward Inga and Stan. She turned her face away from him. "I'm very tired."

"You must be hungry. You want to have dinner?"

"I ate at the hospital," Tatiana lied. "And I have almost nothing here." How to get him to go, just go? "I have to wake up tomorrow at five. I have two nine-hour shifts back to back. I'm on my feet all day. Another time, perhaps?"

"No, Tania. I don't know if there will be another time," Dimitri said. "Come on. Maybe you can make me some tea. A little something to eat? For old times?"

Tatiana could not even imagine Alexander's reaction when he found out that Dimitri was in the room with her. This was not in her plans—to deal with him. She didn't know what to do about him. But then she thought, Alexander still has to deal with him. So *I* have to deal with him. He is not just Alexander's. He is ours.

Tatiana fried Dimitri some soybeans on a Primus stove that she had borrowed from Slavin in return for occasionally cooking for him. She threw in a few small carrots with the beans and a piece of old onion. She gave him some black bread with a spoonful of butter. When Dimitri asked for vodka, Tatiana told him she was all out, not wanting him to get drunk while she was alone with him. The room was poorly illuminated by a kerosene lamp; there was electricity, but Tatiana couldn't find any light-bulbs in the stores.

He ate with the plate on his lap. She sat on the far end of the couch and realized she had not taken off her coat yet. She took off her coat, and while he ate, she went and made herself a cup of tea.

"Why is it so cold in this room?" Dimitri asked.

"No heat," replied Tatiana. She was still wearing her nurse's uniform, and her hair was tied back in a nurse's white head kerchief.

"So, Tania, tell me—how have you been? You look good," Dimitri said. "You don't look like a girl anymore." He smiled. "You look like a young woman. You look older."

"Enough things happen to you," said Tatiana, "and you almost can't help it."

"You look very good. This war agrees with you." Dimitri smiled. "You've gained weight since I saw you last—"

Tatiana leveled a look at him that stopped him. "Dimitri," she said quietly, "last time you saw me, I was in Kobona, asking for your help to bury my sister. Maybe you've forgotten. But I haven't."

"Tania, oh, I know," he said, with a casual drift of his hand. "We just completely lost touch. But I never stopped thinking about you. I'm glad you made it out of Kobona. Many people didn't."

"My sister, for one." Tatiana wanted to ask how in the world could he have looked Alexander in the face and lied about Dasha, but Tatiana could not bear to say her husband's name in front of Dimitri.

"I'm sorry about your sister," Dimitri said. "My parents died, too. So I know how you feel." Dimitri paused. Tatiana waited. Waited for him to finish eating and leave.

"How did you get back to Leningrad?" Dimitri asked her.

Tatiana told him.

But she didn't want to talk about herself. She didn't want to talk about anything. Where was Dasha, where was Alexander, where were Mama and Papa, surrounding Tatiana so she wouldn't have to sit in the room alone with Dimitri?

Taking a deep breath, Tatiana asked him what he was doing with himself, now that he looked to be permanently injured.

"I'm a runner. Do you know what that is?"

Tatiana knew what a runner was. But she shook her head. If he was talking about himself, he was not asking her questions.

"I get supplies for the front lines and for the rear units from trucks, from planes, from ships, and I distribute them around—"

"Where do you distribute them? Here in Leningrad?" she asked.

"Here, yes. Also to various delivery points on this side of the Neva. And to the Karelian side near Finland." Glancing at her sideways, Dimitri said, "Do you see why I'm so unhappy?"

"Of course I do," Tatiana said. "The war is dangerous. You don't want to be in this war."

"I don't want to be in this country," Dimitri mumbled, barely heard.

But heard.

"Did you say you deliver to the Finnish line?" she asked, her voice fading with her strength.

"Yes, to the border troops on the Karelian Isthmus. I also deliver to our new headquarters for the Neva operations in Morozovo. The command post was built there, while we plan our next move—"

"Where on the Karelian Isthmus?"

"I don't know if you've ever heard of a place called Lisiy Nos . . ."

"I've heard of it," Tatiana said, holding on to the arm of the couch.

"There." Dimitri smiled. "I also bring supplies on foot from quarters to quarters. Do you know, Tania, I even bring in supplies for the *generals!*" he said, raising his eyebrows.

"Oh, yes?" she said, barely listening. "Anyone interesting?"

Lowering his voice, Dimitri said, "I'm getting to be quite friendly with General *Mekhlis.*" He laughed with satisfaction. "I bring him paper, pens, plus if I get anything extra—if you get my meaning—I bring it to him. Never ask him to pay me. Cigarettes, vodka, all goes to him. He quite looks forward to my visits."

"Oh?" Tatiana said. She had no idea who Mekhlis was. "Mekhlis . . . what army does he command?"

"Tania, are you joking?"

"No. Why would I joke?" Tatiana was exhausted.

In a gleeful whisper Dimitri said, "Mekhlis commands the NKVD army!" Lowering his voice, he said, "He is Beria's right-hand man!" Lavrenti Beria was Stalin's People's Commissar of the NKVD.

Tatiana had been afraid of bombs once, and of hunger, and of death. She was afraid once of being lost in the woods. And once she was afraid of a human being wanting to do her harm for no reason other than to do her harm.

The harm was the means *and* the end.

Tonight Tatiana wasn't afraid for herself.

But studying Dimitri's depraved, ominously insinuating face, she was afraid for Alexander.

Before tonight she had felt twinges of remorse about leaving Lazarevo and reneging on what had been a heartfelt promise to her husband. But now she became convinced that Alexander didn't just need her closer to him, he needed her more than even she herself had thought possible.

Someone had to protect Alexander—not just from random death, no, but from deliberate destruction.

Without moving, without blinking, without flinching, Tatiana studied Dimitri.

She watched him put down his cup and move closer on the couch to her. Then she blinked and came out of her thoughts. "What are you doing?"

"I can tell, Tania," Dimitri said. "You are not a child anymore."

She did not move a muscle as he moved closer still.

"Inga and Stan out there told me you are working so much that they are convinced you are seeing a doctor at the hospital. Is that true?"

"If *Inga and Stan* told you, then it must be," Tatiana said. "The Communists never lie, Dimitri."

Nodding, Dimitri moved closer.

"What are you doing?" Tatiana got up off the couch. "Listen, it's getting late."

"Tania, come on. You're lonely. I'm lonely. I hate my life, hate every minute of every day of it. Do you feel like that sometimes?"

Only tonight, Tatiana thought. "No, Dima. I'm fine. I have a good life, all things considered. I'm working, the hospital needs me, my patients need me. I'm alive. I have food."

"Tania, but you must be so lonely."

"How can I be lonely?" she said. "I'm constantly surrounded by people. And I thought I was seeing a doctor? Listen, let's stop this. It's late."

He got up and made a move toward her. Tatiana put out her hands. "Dimitri, that's all over. I'm not the one for you." She stared at him pointedly. "And you've always known that, yet you've always been quite persistent. Why?"

With an easy laugh, Dimitri said, "Maybe I had been hoping, dear Tania, that the love of a good young woman like yourself would redeem a rogue like me."

Tatiana leveled her cold gaze on him. "I'm glad to hear," she said at last, "that you don't think you're beyond redemption."

He laughed again. "Oh, but I am, Tania," he said. "I am. Because I didn't have the love of a good young woman like you." He stopped laughing and raised his eyes to her. "But who did?" he said quietly.

Tatiana didn't reply, standing in the place where the dining room table used to be, before Alexander sawed it to pieces for her and Dasha to use as firewood. So many ghosts in one small, dark room. It was almost as if the room were still crowded with feeling, with want, with hunger.

Dimitri's eyes flashed. "I don't understand," he said loudly. "Why did you

521

come to the barracks asking for me? I thought this was what you wanted. Are you just trying to lead me on? To tease me?" He raised his voice, far beyond the levels these walls could contain. He came closer. "Because in the army we have a word for girls who tease us." He laughed. "We call them mothers."

"Dima, is that what you think? That I'm a tease? You think that's me, the girl who wants one thing and pretends she wants another? Is that me?"

He grumbled without replying.

"I thought so," said Tatiana. "I've been very clear with you right from the start. I came to the barracks asking for you, for Marazov. I just wanted to see a familiar face." Tatiana wasn't going to back down, though inside she was cold and far away from him.

"Did you ask for Alexander, too, perhaps?" Dimitri asked. "Because if you did, you know, you wouldn't find him at the garrison. Alexander would be either up in Morozovo, if he was on duty, or in every knocking joint in Leningrad, if he wasn't."

Feeling herself pale inside and out, and hoping Dimitri didn't see and didn't hear the paling of her voice, Tatiana said, "I asked for everybody I knew."

"Everybody except Petrenko," Dimitri said, as if he knew. "Even though you were quite friendly with him, coming around as often as you used to last year. Why didn't you ask for your friend, Ivan Petrenko? Before he got himself killed, he told me that he sometimes used to walk you to the ration store. On orders of Captain Belov, of course. He was quite helpful to you and your family. Why wouldn't you ask about him?"

Tatiana was stunned. She felt herself to be so ridiculously in need of Alexander, so ridiculously in need of protection against this specter of a man in her room that she didn't know what to say.

Tatiana hadn't asked about Petrenko because she knew that Petrenko was dead. But she only knew he was dead from Alexander's letters, and Alexander could not be writing to her.

What to do, what to do, to end this revolting lie enveloping her life.

Tatiana was so fed up, so frustrated, so tired, so desperate, that she nearly opened her mouth and told Dimitri about Alexander. Truth was better than this. Tell the truth and live with the consequences.

It was the consequences that stopped her.

Straightening her back and staring coldly at Dimitri, Tatiana said firmly, "Dimitri, what the hell are you trying to get out of me? Stop trying to manipulate me with your questions. Either ask me outright or keep quiet. I'm too tired for your games. What do you want to know? Why I didn't ask for Petrenko? Because I asked for Marazov first, and once I knew he was at the garrison, I stopped asking. Now, enough!"

Dimitri stared at her with uneasy surprise.

There was a knock on the door. It was Inga. "What's going on?" she said sleepily, standing in her tattered gray bathrobe. "I heard so much noise. Is everything all right?"

"Yes, thank you, Inga," Tatiana said, slamming the door. Tatiana would deal with Inga later.

Dimitri came up to her and said, "I'm sorry, Tania. I didn't mean to upset you. I just misunderstood your intentions."

"That's fine, Dimitri. It's late. Let's say good night."

Dimitri tried to come near her, and Tatiana backed away.

Stepping away himself, he shrugged. "I always wished it had worked out for us, Tania."

"Did you, Dimitri?" said Tatiana.

"Of course."

"Dimitri! How—" Tatiana exclaimed and broke off.

Dimitri stood in a room in which he had once spent many evenings being fed and watered. He had sat with Tatiana's family, who had invited him into their home and made him a part of their life. He had been in this room now for an hour. He had talked freely about himself, accused Tatiana of she didn't know what. He'd told her things that sounded like lies. She didn't know. What he did not do was ask her what had happened to the six people who had once been in this room with him. He did not ask about her mother, or her father, or her grandparents, or Marina, or her mother's mother. He did not ask her in Kobona in January, he did not ask her now. If he knew about their fate, he did not utter a single commiserating word, he did not make a single comforting wave of his hand. How did Dimitri think it could have worked out for him and anyone, but especially for him and Tatiana, when he could not look for a second beyond himself into anyone else's life or heart? Tatiana didn't care that he didn't ask after her family. What she wanted was for him not to pretend to her, as if *she* didn't know the truth.

Tatiana wanted to say this to Dimitri. But it wasn't worth it.

Though she suspected that the truth was plain in her eyes, because bowing his head and appearing even more hunched, Dimitri stammered, "I just can't seem to say the right thing."

"We'll say good night," Tatiana said coldly. That will be the right thing.

He went to the door, and she followed him. "Tania, I think this is goodbye. I don't think we're going to see each other again."

"If we're meant to, we will." Tatiana swallowed hard, numb inside, her legs weak.

Dimitri lowered his voice, and whispered, "Where I'm going, Tatiana, you will never see me again."

"Oh, yes?" she mouthed, her strength gone.

He left at last, leaving black turmoil behind for Tatiana, who lay on her cot between the wall and the back of the couch, lay in all her clothes clutching her wedding ring to her chest, not moving or sleeping until morning.

3

In Morozovo, Alexander was sitting behind a table in his officer's tent when Dimitri stepped inside with some cigarettes and vodka. Alexander was wearing his coat, and his injured hands were numb from the cold. He was thinking of going to the mess tent to get some warmth and some food, but he couldn't leave his tent. It was Friday, and he had a meeting with General Govorov in an hour to talk about their preparations for an assault on the Germans across the river.

It was November, and after four failed attempts to cross the Neva, the 67th Army was now impatiently waiting for the river to freeze. Finally the Leningrad command concluded that it would be easier to attack with the foot soldiers in line formations on ice instead of being clustered in easy-to-destroy pontoon boats.

Dimitri placed the bottles of vodka and the tobacco with the rolling papers on the table. Alexander paid him. He wanted Dimitri to leave. He had just been reading a letter from Tatiana that was puzzling him. He hadn't written to her for the few weeks that he'd been hurt, even though he could have had a nurse write the letter for him. Alexander knew that if Tatiana saw a letter in someone else's handwriting, she would go insane reading between the lines into how badly he was *really* injured. Not wanting her to worry, he had sent her his September money and waited until he could hold a pen, writing to her himself toward the end of the month.

He wrote that his burn wounds were just God's way of protecting him. Unable to function at his weapons, Alexander had missed two disastrous assaults on the Neva in September, which had decimated the first and second line armies so utterly that all reserves had to be brought in from the Leningrad garrison. The Volkhov front would have been glad to supply the Leningrad front with men—if only they had some. But after Hitler's directive to Manstein to hold the Neva and the blockade around Leningrad at all costs, there were hardly any men left in Meretskov's 2nd Army in Volkhov.

Elsewhere, Stalingrad was being razed to the ground. The Ukraine was Hitler's. Leningrad was barely holding. The Red Army was thoroughly debilitated. Govorov was planning another attack on the Germans across the Neva. And Alexander was sitting at his desk, trying to figure out what the hell was wrong with his wife.

Here it was November, and none of her letters that came with steady and conversational regularity, though without some of her usual candid fervor, mentioned a word about his injuries. He was driving himself to distraction trying to read between the lines of *her* letters when Dimitri had come in with the supplies. And now Dimitri wasn't leaving.

"Alexander, can you pour me a drink? For old times' sake?"

Reluctantly Alexander poured Dimitri a drink. He poured himself a smaller one. He sat behind his desk, Dimitri in a chair opposite him. They talked about the impending invasion and about the frightful battles with the Germans across the Neva on the Volkhov side.

"Alexander," Dimitri said quietly, "how can you sit there so calmly knowing what's ahead of you? Four attempts to cross the Neva, most of our men dead, and I hear that the fifth attack once the ice freezes is going to be our last one, that not a single man will be allowed to return until the blockade is broken; did you hear that, too?"

"I heard something about it, yes."

"I can't be here anymore. I can't. Just yesterday I was delivering supplies to the Neva for the Nevsky Patch troops, and a rocket bomb flew all the way from Sinyavino across the river and blew up yet another fucking squadron getting ready to ferry. I was maybe a hundred meters away from the explosion. But look"—he showed Alexander the cuts on his face—"it doesn't end."

"No, Dimitri, it doesn't."

Lowering his voice a notch, Dimitri said, "Alexander, you will not believe how unprotected the Lisiy Nos area is right now! I deliver to our border troops there and see the Finns in the woods. There are maybe a dozen men in all. It's providential. You can come with me in my delivery truck, and before we get to the border, we can dump the truck, and then—"

"Dima!" whispered Alexander. "Dump the truck? Look at you. You can barely walk on straight ground. We talked about this in June—"

"Not just in June. We talked this to death. I'm tired of talking. Tired of waiting. I can't wait anymore. Let's just go, we'll go, and we'll make it, and if we won't make it, they'll shoot us. What's the difference? At least this way we stand a chance."

"Listen to me—" Alexander said, getting up from his desk.

"No, you listen to *me*. This war has changed me—"

"Has it?"

"Yes!" said Dimitri. "It has shown me that I have to fight for my own life to survive. By whatever means necessary. Everything I've done so far just hasn't worked. Not the moving from platoon to platoon, not the foot wound, not the months in the hospital, not the Kobona interlude—nothing! I've been trying to save my life until we make our move again. But the Germans are determined to kill me. And I'm determined not to let them." Dimitri paused and lowered his voice. "Makes your little stunt with the now deceased and forgotten Yuri Stepanov even *more* infuriating in retrospect." His voice barely audible, Dimitri said, "He's dead, and we're still here. All because you had to bring him back. We'd be in *America* right now, if it weren't for you."

Fighting with himself for control, Alexander came around on Dimitri's side of the desk, bent down to him, and said through his teeth, "And I told you then the same thing I am telling you now. Over and over then. Over and over now. Go! Leave. Go ahead. I will give you half of my money. You know how to get to Helsinki and Stockholm like the back of your hand. Why don't you just go?"

Dimitri pulled away on his chair from Alexander. "You know very well I can't go on my own. I don't speak a word of English."

"You don't need to speak English! Just get to Stockholm and claim refugee status. They'll take you, Dimitri, even without English," Alexander said coldly, backing slightly away.

"And now with my leg—"

"Forget your leg. Drag it behind you if you have to. I'll give you half of the money—"

"Give me half of the money? What the fuck are you talking about? We are supposed to be going together, remember? That was our plan, right. Together?" Dimitri paused. "I'm not going alone!"

"If you're not going alone," Alexander hissed, "then you will wait until *I* say the time is right." He unclenched his fists. "The time is not right. In the spring it will be—"

"I'm not waiting till the fucking spring!"

"What choice do you have? Do you want to succeed, or do you want to fail in a hurry? You know the NKVD border troops shoot deserters on the spot."

"I'll be dead by the spring," said Dimitri, getting up from the chair and attempting to square off against Alexander. "You'll be dead by the spring. What's the matter with you? What the fuck has gotten into you? Do you not want to run anymore? What would you rather do—*die?*"

Keeping the torment out of his eyes, Alexander did not reply.

Dimitri glared at him. "Five years ago, when you were nobody, had nobody, when you needed me, I did you a favor, Captain of the Red Army."

Alexander took one stride and stood so close to Dimitri that Dimitri not only backed off but fell into his chair, glancing up at Alexander with anxiety.

"Yes, you did," Alexander said. "And I have never forgotten it."

"All right, all right," Dimitri said. "Don't get all—"

"Have I made myself clear? We will wait for the right time."

"But the border at Lisiy Nos is unprotected *now!*" Dimitri exclaimed. "What the fuck are we waiting for? Now is an ideal time to go. Later the Soviets will bring more troops in, the Finns will bring more troops in, the war will continue there. Now it's a stalemate. I say let's go now—before the battle for Leningrad kills you."

"Who's stopping you?" said Alexander. "Go!"

"Alexander," said Dimitri, "for the last time, I'm not going without you."

"Dimitri," said Alexander, "for the last time, I'm not going now."

"When then?"

"I will tell you when. First we will break the blockade. Yes, it will take all we have, but we will do it, and then in the spring—"

Dimitri chuckled. "Maybe we should just send Tania to do it."

For a moment Alexander thought he had misheard.

Did Dimitri just mention Tatiana?

"What did you just say?" he asked quietly and slowly.

"I said, maybe we should just send Tania. She is quite the little blockade runner."

"What are you talking about?"

"That girl," Dimitri said with admiration, "I am convinced, could get to Australia by herself if she wanted to!" Howling, he threw his head back. "Before we know it, she'll be making regular food runs between Molotov and Leningrad."

"What the fuck are you talking about?"

"I'm telling you, Alexander," Dimitri continued, "instead of wasting two hundred thousand of our men, including you and me, we should have Tatiana Metanova break the blockade."

Stubbing out his cigarette, Alexander said, "I have no idea what you're talking about." Hoping Dimitri wouldn't notice, he clenched his hands around the chair posts,

"I said to her, I said, 'Tania, you ought to enlist. You'll be a general in no time.' And she said she actually was thinking of joining —"

"What do you mean—" Alexander interrupted, finding it hard to continue. "What do you mean, you *said* to her?"

"A week ago. She made me dinner on Fifth Soviet. They finally had their pipes fixed. The apartment, well, some complete strangers are living there, but . . ." Dimitri smiled. "She is getting to be quite the little cook."

It took most of what Alexander had to remain impassive.

"Are you all right?" Dimitri said with an amused look on his face.

"I'm fine. But what are you talking about, Dima? Is this another one of your little white lies? Tatiana is not in Leningrad."

"Alexander, believe me, I'd know Tania anywhere." He smiled. "She looks good. She told me she was seeing a doctor." He laughed. "Can you believe it? Our little Tanechka. Who would have thought that she would be the only one left standing?"

Alexander would have liked to say *stop it*, but he did not trust his voice. He said nothing, his hands remaining on the posts of the chair.

He had just gotten a letter from her yesterday. A letter!

"Tania came looking for me at the barracks. Made me dinner. She said she'd been in Leningrad since the middle of October. No, and how she got there, too!" Dimitri laughed. "Literally walking through the Volkhov front, as if Manstein and his thousand-kilo bombs did not exist." Dimitri shook his head. "When I get into the good fight, I want her with me."

Keeping himself under barest control, Alexander said, "And when is it, Dimitri, that you think *you'll* be going into the good fight?"

"Very clever—"

"Dimitri, I don't give a shit. This doesn't matter. But I just realized I'm late. I have a meeting with General Govorov in a few minutes. You will have to excuse me."

After Dimitri left, Alexander became so upset in his tent that in his stricken fury he broke apart the wooden chair he had been sitting on.

Now he knew what was wrong with her letters. Alexander was weak from anger, and he didn't have enough time to calm down before his meeting with Govorov, or after. Anger continued to cloud his judgment. After his meeting he went to Colonel Stepanov.

"Oh, no," said Stepanov, coming from around his desk. "I see that look in your eyes, Captain Belov." He smiled.

With his hat in his hands, Alexander nodded and said, "Sir, you have been very kind to me. I haven't had a day off since I came back in July."

"But, Belov, you had over five weeks off in July!"

"All I'm asking for is a few days, sir. If you like, I can drive a supply truck into Leningrad. That way it will be partly for army business, too."

"What's going on, Alexander?" Stepanov said, coming closer and lowering his voice.

Alexander gave a small shake of his head. "Everything is fine."

Stepanov studied him. "Does it have anything to do with the money you're sending out of here to Molotov every month?"

"You're right, sir, maybe we should stop the money transfers to Molotov."

Stepanov lowered his voice another notch. "Does it have anything to do with the stamp from a registry office in Molotov that I saw in your passport when I was signing you in?"

Alexander kept silent. "Sir, I am urgently needed in Leningrad." He paused, trying to collect himself. "It's just for a few days."

Stepanov sighed. "If you don't come back by ten o'clock roll call on Sunday . . ."

"Sir, I will be here. It's more than enough time. Thank you. I've never let you down. I won't forget this."

As Alexander was leaving, Stepanov said, "Take care of your personal business, son. Forget the supplies. You won't have another chance for personal business until we break the blockade."

Tatiana was dragging her feet. She was hanging around her last patients even though it was long past her sign-out time. She was a little hungry, but cooking for herself was such a displeasure, she wished she could nourish her body intravenously, like some of the wounded. Working with critically injured men and women was preferable to being in her room by herself.

Finally she left and, not lifting her head, slowly walked home down Grechesky in the dark.

She walked through the communal apartment. Inga was sitting on the couch in the hallway and casually drinking tea. Why was she in Tatiana's home? It was so incongruous that she and Stan should remain. "Hello, Inga," said Tatiana tiredly as she took off her coat.

"Hmm. Someone was here for you."

She squared her shoulders. "Did you do as I asked and not let anyone in?"

"Yes, I did as you asked," Inga replied shortly. "He wasn't too pleased, though. Another soldier —"

"What soldier?"

"I don't know."

Coming up to Inga and lowering her voice, Tatiana whispered, "Who was it? It wasn't the same soldier, was it—"

"No. Different. Tall "

Tatiana's heart jumped. Tall!

"Where—" she stammered. "Where did he go?"

"I don't know. I told him he couldn't come in. He didn't want to hear anything after that. You have quite a contingent of soldiers following you around, don't you?"

Without even grabbing her coat, Tatiana swirled around the small hallway, swung open the door, and there in front of her stood Alexander.

"Oh," she gasped, her knees buckling. "Oh, God." Seeing the expression in his darkened eyes, she knew what he was feeling. She didn't care. Her eyes filling with tears, she leaned her head into his coat.

He didn't even put his arms around her. "Come on," he said coldly, taking her by the arm. "Let's go inside."

Inga said, "Tania told me not to let anyone in, Captain— Tania, aren't you going to introduce us?" She had put down her cup.

"No," said Alexander, pushing Tatiana into the room and kicking the door shut behind him. She came to him instantly, her shaking arms open, her face overflowing. She could barely get his name out of her emotional mouth. "Shura . . ."

He put his palms out. "Don't come near me."

Not listening, Tatiana came to him, and said, "Shura, I am so happy to see you. How are your hands?"

He pushed her hard away, saying loudly, "No, Tatiana! Stay away from me."

He walked through the room to the window. It was cold by the window. Tatiana followed him. Her need to lay her hands on him and to have him touch her was so desperate that she forgot the pain left by Dimitri's visit, by the missing five thousand dollars, by her own twisted feelings. "Shura," Tatiana said, her voice breaking. "Why are you pushing me?"

"What have you done?" Alexander's eyes were bitter and angry. "Why are you here?"

"You know why I'm here," Tatiana said to him. "You needed me. I came."

"I don't need you here!" he yelled. Tatiana flinched but did not move away. "I don't need you here," he repeated. "I need you safe!"

"I know," she said. "Please let me touch you."

"Stay away from me."

"Shura, I told you, I cannot be away from you. I didn't think you could feel me all the way in Lazarevo. You need me close to you."

"Close to me? Not close to *me*, Tatiana," he said nastily, standing against the windowsill. It was dark in the room, the only light coming from the street. Alexander's face was dark, his eyes were dark.

"What are you talking about?" Her voice was trembling in supplication. "Of course, close to you. Close to who?"

"What the fuck were you thinking," he yelled, "going to the barracks and asking for Dimitri?"

"I didn't ask for Dimitri!" she exclaimed faintly. "I went to find *you*. I didn't know what happened to you. You stopped writing to me."

"You didn't write to me for six months!" he said loudly. "You could have waited two weeks, no?"

"It was over a month, and I couldn't have, no," she said. "Shura, I'm here for you." Tatiana came a step closer. "For *you*. You told me never to look away from you. Here I am. Look into my eyes and tell me what I feel." Pleadingly she opened her hands to him. "What do I feel, Shura?" she whispered.

Alexander blinked, his teeth grinding. "Look into *my* eyes and tell me what *I* feel, Tatiana."

She clasped her hands together.

"You promised me!" Alexander said. "You *promised* me. You gave me your *word!*"

Tatiana remembered. She looked into his face. She was so weak and wanted him so much. And she could see that he needed her, if anything, even more. He just couldn't see past his anger. Like always. "Alexander, husband, it's me. It's your Tania." She almost cried as she opened her palms to him. "Shura, please . . ."

When he didn't reply, Tatiana took off her shoes and came to stand in front of him at the window. She felt more vulnerable than ever, standing in her white uniform in front of him, with his black hair, black boots, and black trench coat looming over her, so emotional, so upset. "Please, let's not fight. I am so happy to see you. I just want . . ." She would not lower her eyes from him, would not. "Shura," she said, her body trembling, "don't . . . push me away."

He turned his face from her. Tatiana unbuttoned the front of her uniform and took hold of Alexander's hand. "*Kiss the palm of your hand and press it against your heart,* you wrote to me," she whispered, kissing the palm of his hand and then putting it on her bare breast, his large, warm, dark hand, the hand that had carried her and caressed her, and she closed her eyes and moaned.

"Oh, my God, Tatiana . . ." Alexander said, pulling her to him, his hands attacking her body. He pushed her down on the couch, his incensed lips not leaving her mouth, his hands in her hair. "What do you *want* from me?" He yanked off her uniform, vest, and underwear, leaving her naked except for her garters. Gripping her bare thighs above the stockings, he whispered, "Tania, God, what do you want from me . . . ?"

Tatiana couldn't even answer. His body on hers was making her speechless.

"I'm furious with you." He was kissing her as if he were dying. "You don't care I'm furious with you?"

"I don't care . . . take your anger out on me," Tatiana groaned. "Go ahead, take it out on me, Shura . . . now."

He was inside her in seconds.

Her hands clutching his head, Tatiana whispered, "Cover my mouth," ready to scream.

Alexander hadn't taken off his coat, nor his boots.

There was a knock on the door. "Tania, are you all right?" Inga's voice sounded.

His hand over Tatiana's mouth, Alexander yelled, "Get the hell away from the door!"

"Cover my mouth, Shura," Tatiana whispered, crying from happiness. "Oh, God, cover it."

"No, don't get off me, don't get off me, please," she murmured, holding on to his coat, to his head, grasping on to any part of him. "How are your hands?" In the dark, she couldn't see them. They felt scabbed.

"They're fine."

Tatiana was kissing his lips, his chin, his stubble, his eyes—she couldn't take her lips away from his eyes—holding his head close to her. "Shura, darling, don't get off me, please, I've missed you so much, stay right here. Stay where you are . . ." For a few dark moments Tatiana pressed herself against Alexander. "Don't pull away from me, feel how warm I am? Don't pull out into the cold . . ." She lay underneath him and tried not to cry. And failed. "Is that why you hadn't written to me? Because of your hands?"

"Yes," Alexander said. "I didn't want you to worry."

"You didn't think the absence of your letters would make me crazy?"

"You know," he said, getting off her, "I had hoped you would just wait."

"Darling, lovely husband, are you hungry?" Tatiana murmured to him. "I can't believe I'm touching you again. I can't be this lucky. What can I make for you? I have some pork, some potatoes. Do you want food?"

"No," Alexander said, helping her sit up. "Why is it so cold in here?"

"Stove's broken. *Bourzhuika* is in the other room, remember? Slavin lets me use his Primus stove in the kitchen." She smiled, her hands running up and down his coat. "Honey, Shura, do you want me to make you some tea?"

"Tania, you'll freeze. Do you have anything else to wear? Something warm?"

"I'm burning," she said, her hands on his coat. "I'm not cold." She hung on to him.

"Why is the sofa in the middle of the room?"

"My bed is behind the couch."

Alexander looked over the back of the couch to see Tatiana's cot. Pulling a blanket off it, he covered her. "Why are you sleeping between the sofa and the wall?"

When she didn't answer, Alexander reached over and touched the wall with his hand. They stared at each other in the dark. "Why did you give them the warm room, Tania?"

"I didn't give it to them. They took it. There are two of them, only one of me. They're sad. He's got a bad back. Shura, how about a hot bath? I'll run you one."

"No. Get dressed. Right now." Alexander buckled his belt and walked out of the bedroom, still in his coat. Disheveled and barely buttoned, Tatiana followed him. He walked past Inga in the hallway into the bedroom, where Stan was sitting reading the newspaper, and asked Stan to switch rooms with Tatiana. Stan said he wasn't switching. Alexander replied that indeed Stan was, and he and Tatiana started moving all of Inga and Stan's things into the cold room and all of Tatiana's things into the warm room.

For fifteen minutes Tatiana heard Stan grumbling, standing with Inga in the hallway, and at one point as she passed him, she whispered, "Stanislav Stepanich, shh. Please. Don't provoke him."

Stan did not heed her warning. As Alexander was walking past carrying Stan's trunk, Stan seethed, "Who do you think you are? You don't know who you're dealing with. You've got no right to treat me this way."

Dropping the trunk, Alexander grabbed his rifle and jammed Stan against the wall with the barrel under his throat. "Who the fuck do you think *you* are, Stan?" Alexander said loudly. "You don't know who *you're* dealing with! What, you think I'm going to be scared of you, too, you bastard? You've come to the wrong man. Now, get into the other room, and don't fuck with me, because I'm not in the mood." He gritted his teeth. "And don't *ever* upset her again, you hear me?" Giving Stan a last jolt under the chin, Alexander stepped away from him and kicked his heavy trunk, rolling it over. "Here, carry your own fucking trunk."

Tatiana, who watched Alexander, did not come to Stan's rescue, even though she thought Alexander looked angry enough to really hurt Stan. Inga mumbled, "What kind of sick people come and see you here, Tania? Come on, Stan, let's go."

Rubbing his throat, Stan started to stay something, and Inga yelled, "Come on, Stan. Shut your mouth and let's go!"

In the warm room Tatiana quickly stripped off Inga and Stan's bedding, throwing it out into the hall, and put clean sheets on her old bed.

"That's better, don't you think?" Alexander said, sitting on the sofa and motioning Tatiana to him.

Tatiana shook her head. "Oh, you, Alexander. Do you want some food?"

"Later. Come here."

"Will you take off your coat this time?"

"Come here and I'll let you know."

She fell into his arms. "Leave your coat on. Leave everything on."

Tatiana ran a hot bath for Alexander, took him by the hand into the small bathroom, undressed him, and soaped him and scrubbed him and rinsed him, and cried over him, and kissed him. "Your poor hands," she kept saying. His red fingers looked pretty bad to her, but Alexander assured her they would heal almost without scarring. His wedding ring was not on his finger but on a rope around his neck—just like hers.

"Is the water warm enough for you?"

"It's fine, Tania."

"I can boil another pot." She smiled. "And then I'll come in here and pour the boiling water over you. Remember?"

"I remember," he said, and did not smile.

"Oh, Shura . . ." she whispered, kissing his wet forehead, turning his face to her as she knelt beside the bath. "I know," she said, brightening. "We can play a game."

"No games right now," he said.

"You'll like this one," she murmured. "Let's pretend we're in Lazarevo, and I'm you, stroking my fingers in the dishpan. Remember?" She immersed her arms up to her elbows in the soapy hot water.

"I remember," said Alexander, closing his eyes and reluctantly smiling.

While he was drying and dressing, Tatiana went outside into the kitchen and made him dinner, cooking him almost all the food she had—potatoes, carrots, and a bit of pork meat—and then took him into the bedroom and breathlessly sat by him on the couch, watching him eat. "I'm not hungry," she said. "I ate at the hospital. Eat, darling, eat."

* * *

During their senseless, sleepless night, Tatiana told Alexander about everything Dimitri had told her—the NKVD general, Lisiy Nos, and the other allusions. Alexander stared at the ceiling. "Are you waiting for me to answer you before you ask me?"

"No," Tatiana said. "I'm not asking you anything." She was lying in his arms, playing with his wedding ring.

"I'm not talking to you about Dimitri here."

"That's fine."

"Because the walls have ears." Alexander banged loudly on the wall with his fist.

"Well, then, they've already heard everything."

He kissed her forehead. "Everything else he told you—about me—it's not true."

"I know." She laughed lightly. "But, Shura, tell me, how many knocking joints are there in Leningrad, and why would you have to go to all of them?"

"Tania, look at me."

She gazed at him.

"It's not true. I—"

"Shura, darling—I *know*." She kissed his chest and covered them both up with two wool blankets. "There is only one thing true nowadays, Alexander."

"Only one," he whispered, staring at her intensely in the dark. "Oh, Tatia."

"Shh."

"Do you have a picture of yourself here? A picture I can take with me?"

"Tomorrow I'll find you one. I'm afraid to ask. When are you leaving?"

"Sunday."

Her heart squeezed shut. "So soon."

"My commander puts his head on the butcher block every time he lets me have special leave."

"He is a nice man. Thank him for me."

"Tatiana, someday I will have to explain to you the concept of keeping a promise. You see, when you *give* your word, you have to *keep* your word." He was stroking her hair.

"I know what keeping a promise means."

"No, you only know what *making* a promise means," Alexander said. "You are very good at making the promise. It's *keeping* the promise you have a problem with. You promised me you would stay in Lazarevo."

Thoughtfully Tatiana said, "I promised because that's what you wanted me to do." She squeezed tighter into the crook of his arm. "You didn't give me much choice." She couldn't lie close enough to him. "At the point you were asking for my promise, I would have promised you anything." Under his arm was no good. She climbed on top of him. "And did." She kissed him softly. "You wanted me to promise. I promised. I always do what you want me to do."

His hands tenderly moving down her back, Alexander said, "No, you always do as you please. You certainly *make* the right noises."

"Mmm," she said, rubbing herself into him.

"Yes, *that* you do," Alexander said, his hands more insistent. "You certainly say the right things. Yes, Shura; of course, Shura; I promise, Shura; maybe even, I love you, Shura, but then you just do as you please."

"I love you, Shura," Tatiana said, her tears falling into his face.

All the agonizing words Tatiana had meant to say to Alexander, she kept inside, slightly surprised that he kept his own agonizing words to her under control, and she could tell he had plenty. But she knew—the endless November Leningrad night was too short for misery, too short for what they were feeling, too short for them. Alexander wanted to hear her moan, she moaned for him, indifferent to Inga and Stan just centimeters of thin plaster away. Under the flickering light of the open *bourzhuika* Tatiana made love to her Alexander, yielding to him, clutching him, clinging to him, unable to keep herself from crying each time she came, each time he came, each time they came together. She made love to him with the abandon of the skylark's last flight south when the bird knows he is going to either make it to the warmth or die.

"Your poor hands," she was whispering as she kissed the scars on his fingers and wrists. "Your hands, Shura. They'll heal, right? They won't scar?"

"Your hands healed," he said. "Yours didn't scar."

"Hmm," she said, remembering putting out the fire on the roof last year. "I don't know how."

"I know how," Alexander whispered. "You healed them. Now heal mine, Tania."

"Oh, soldier." Tatiana was on top of him, desperately pressing his head to her naked breasts.

"I can't breathe."

She was embracing him the way he used to embrace her in Lazarevo. And for the same reason. "Open your mouth," she whispered, leaning into his face. "I'll breathe for you."

5

The next morning, before they came out into the corridor, Tatiana hugged Alexander and said, "Be *nice*," as she opened their bedroom door.

"I'm always nice," said Alexander.

Stan and Inga were sitting in the hallway. Stan stood up, extended his hand to Alexander, introduced himself, apologized for yesterday, and asked Alexander to sit and have a smoke. Alexander did not sit, but he took a cigarette from Stan.

"This kind of living is hard on everyone, I know. But it's not forever. You know what the Party says, Captain—" said Stan, smiling ingratiatingly.

"No, what does the Party say, comrade?" Alexander asked, glancing down at Tatiana, who stood beside him holding his hand.

"Being determines consciousness, doesn't it? We live like this long enough, and we'll all get used to it. Soon we'll all become changed human beings."

"But, Stan," Inga said plaintively, "I don't want to live like this! We had a nice apartment. I want that back."

"We'll get it back, Inga. The council promised us a two-bedroom."

Alexander said, "How long do you think, Stan, we'll have to live like this before we're changed? And changed into what?" He stared bleakly at Tatiana, who said, peering up into his face, "Shura, I have some *kasha*. Darling, I'll make you some?" Smoking as if it were his breakfast, Alexander nodded. She didn't like the look in his eyes.

When she came back inside with two bowls of *kasha* and a cup of coffee for him, Tatiana overheard Stan telling Alexander that he and Inga, married for twenty years, were both engineers and long-standing members of the Communist Party of the Soviet Union.

Alexander barely excused himself before he went to eat his *kasha* inside the room, not even asking Tatiana to follow him.

Tatiana ate her *kasha* with Inga and Stan, refusing to answer Inga's curious questions about Alexander. Then she washed the dishes from the night before, cleaned the kitchen, and finally and reluctantly joined him inside the room. Tatiana knew she was procrastinating. She did not want to face Alexander alone.

He was collecting her things into her black backpack. Glaring at her, he said, "You wanted to come back for this? You missed this? Strangers, *Communist Party* strangers, listening to your every word, your every moan? You missed all this, Tania?"

"No," Tatiana said. "I missed *you*."

"There is no place for me here," he said. "There is hardly a place for you."

After watching him for a moment she asked, "What are you doing?"

"Packing."

"Packing?" she repeated quietly, closing the door behind her. Here it starts, Tatiana thought. I didn't want it. I wished we didn't have to have it. But here it is. "Where are we going?"

"Across the lake. I can get you across easily to Syastroy, and then I'll take you in an army truck to Vologda. From there you'll catch a train. We have to go now. It'll take me a while to get back, and I must return to Morozovo tomorrow evening."

Vigorously Tatiana shook her head.

"What?" Alexander snapped. "What are you shaking your head for?"

She shook her head.

"Tatiana, I'm warning you. Don't provoke me."

"All right. But I'm not going anywhere."

"Yes you are."

In a small voice she said, "No. I'm not."

Alexander raised his voice. "You are!"

In the same small voice Tatiana said, "Don't raise your voice to me."

Dropping her backpack with a thud to the wooden floor, Alexander came up to her and, leaning down, said into her face, "Tatiana, in a *second* I'm going to raise more than my voice to you."

Tatiana felt so sad inside. But she squared her shoulders and did not look away. Quietly she said, "Go ahead, Alexander. I'm not afraid of you."

"No?" he said, gritting his teeth. "Well, I'm terrified of you." He stepped away and picked up the backpack. Tatiana remembered the first day of the war, she remembered Pasha telling her father, no, I don't want to go, and being sent away anyway, and dying.

"Alexander, stop it, I said. I'm not going anywhere."

"Oh, you are, Tania," he said, whirling to her, his face distorted by anger. "You are. I will take you to Vologda, if have to carry you there myself, kicking and screaming."

Tatiana backed away from him, just a little bit, half a step, and said, "Fine. But I will not be kicking, I will not be screaming. As soon as you leave, I will come back."

Alexander threw the backpack against the wall, close to Tatiana's head. He came at her with clenched fists and smashed the wall near her so hard that the plaster crumbled and his hand went through the hole.

Her legs trembling, her eyes closed, Tatiana backed away another half a step and stopped moving.

"For fuck's sake!" Alexander screamed in a rage, punching the wall next to her face. "What will it take for you to listen to me, just once, just fucking once, what will it take for you to do as I say?" He grabbed her by the arms and pinned her roughly against the wall.

"Shura, this is not the army," Tatiana whispered tremulously, afraid to look at him.

"You are not staying here!"

"I am," she said faintly.

There was a knock. Alexander went to the door, ripped it open, and shouted, "What?"

Inga, her face red, muttered, "I just wanted to see if Tania was all right. Tania? I heard yelling—banging—"

"I'm fine, Inga," Tatiana said, stepping away from the wall on unsteady legs.

"You'll hear a lot more before we're done," Alexander said to Inga. "Just put the fucking glass to the wall," and slammed the door shut. Whirling around, he came for Tatiana, who backed away from him, her hands up, whispering, "Shura, please . . ." but, unstoppable and crazed, he came at her just the same and shoved her down onto the couch. She fell back and covered her face. Bending over her, Alexander knocked her hands away. "Don't cover your face!" he shouted, grabbing her cheeks between his fingers and shaking her. "Don't make me more crazy!"

Tatiana cried out and tried to push him away, but it was useless. "Stop!" she panted. "Stop . . ."

"Safe or dead, Tania?" he yelled. "Safe or dead? What will it be?"

Clutching helplessly at his arms, she wanted to answer him but couldn't speak. *Dead*, she wanted to say. *Dead, Shura.*

"You can see what it's doing to me, your being here!" Alexander squeezed her face harder and harder as she struggled to break free. "You can *see*. But you just don't give a shit."

She ceased fighting him, placing her hands over his. "Please," Tatiana whispered, trying to catch his eye. "Please . . . stop. You're *hurting* me."

Alexander eased his hold on her but did not let go of her face, nor did Tatiana pull away, even though she could hardly breathe. Underneath him, she lay on the couch, panting. Covering her with his body, he lay on top of her, panting. Through the crashing noise in her head Tatiana remotely heard the air-raid siren and explosive sounds outside her windows. She moved her mouth away from his hands a little. She was suffocating. Her own hands went around his back to clasp him. "Oh, Shura," she whispered.

Alexander got off Tatiana, stood miserably before her, and then dropped to his knees. "Tatiana," he said in a broken voice, "this frantic wretch *begs* you, please leave. If you feel any love for me at all, please go back to Lazarevo. Be safe. You just don't know what kind of danger you're in."

Still short of breath, her body trembling, her face aching, Tatiana sat up at the edge of the couch and pulled Alexander to her. She couldn't bear to see him so upset. "I'm so sorry you're angry," she said, holding his face. "Please don't be angry with me."

Alexander moved her hands off him. "Do you hear the bombs? Do you hear, or are you deaf? Do you see there is no food?"

"There's food," she said quietly, putting her hands back on him. "I get 700 grams a day. Plus my lunch and dinner at the hospital. I'm doing well." She smiled. "It's much better than last year. And I don't care about the bombs."

"Tatiana . . ."

"Shura, stop lying to me. It's not the Germans or the bombs that frighten you. What are you afraid of?"

Outside, the whistling shells whizzed nearby. One sounded close. Tatiana pulled Alexander to her. "Listen to me," she whispered, clutching his head to her breasts. "Do you hear my heart?"

He surrounded her. She sat for a moment holding on to him, closing her eyes. Dear God, she prayed. Please let me be strong for him. He needs my strength so much, don't let me weaken right now. Gently pushing him away, she went to her dresser. "You left something behind in Lazarevo, Shura. Besides me."

Alexander got up and sat heavily on the couch.

Ripping open the inseam on her trousers, Tatiana took out Alexander's five thousand dollars. "Look. I returned to give you this." She stared at him. "I see you took only half. Why?" Stop. Breathe.

Alexander's bronze eyes were toffee pools of pain. "I'm not talking about this with Inga at our door," he said, barely moving his lips.

"Why not? We do everything else with Inga at our door."

They looked away from each other. Tatiana could tell they were both splintering. Who was going to pick up their fragmented pieces? She. She was going to pick them up. Leaving the money on the dresser, Tatiana went to him, straddling him, holding his head to her. "This isn't Lazarevo, is it, Shura?" she whispered into his hair.

His voice breaking, his arms encircling her, Alexander whispered back, "What *is*, Tatia?"

She made love to him, kneeling on top of him, pressing her fragile self into him, bearing down on him, praying to him, wanting him to swallow her, to impale her, to save her and to kill her, wanting from him everything and yet for herself nothing, only to give *back* to him, *only to give his life back to him*. At the end she was crying again, all her strength gone, panting and melting and burning and crying.

"Tatiasha," Alexander whispered, still unceasing, "stop crying. What's a man to think when every time he makes love to his wife, she cries*!*"

"That he is his wife's only *family*," Tatiana replied, cradling his head. "That he is her *whole* life."

"As she is his," said Alexander. "But you don't see him crying." He was turned away from her. Tatiana couldn't see his face.

After the air raid was over and they were finished, they bundled up and went out. "Too cold to be out," Tatiana said, clinging to him.

"Why didn't you wear a hat?"

"So you can see my hair. I know you like it." She smiled.

Taking off his glove, he ran his hand across her head. "Put on your scarf," he said, tying it around her. "You'll be cold."

"I'm fine." She took his arm. "I like your new coat. It's big, like a tent." In sadness, she lowered her eyes. She shouldn't have said the word *tent*. Too many Lazarevo memories. Some words were like that. Whole lives attached to them. Ghosts and lives and ecstasy and sorrow. The simplest words, and suddenly she couldn't continue to speak. "It looks warm," she added quietly.

Alexander smiled. "Next week I will have better than a tent. I'll have a room in the main headquarters, just five doors away from Stepanov. There is heat in the building. I'll actually be warm."

"I'm glad," said Tatiana. "Do you have a blanket?"

"My coat is my blanket, and I have another one, yes. I'm all right, Tania. It's war. Now, where do you want to go?"

"To Lazarevo—with you," she said, unable to look at him. "Barring that, let's walk to the Summer Garden."

He sighed heavily. "To the Summer Garden it is, then."

They walked silently for many minutes. With her arm through his, Tatiana kept pressing her head into Alexander's sleeve. Finally she took a deep breath. "Talk to me, Alexander," Tatiana began. "Tell me what's going on. We're alone now. We have a little *privacy*. Tell me. Why did you take half the money?"

Alexander said nothing. Tatiana listened. Still nothing. She put her face on his woolen coat. Still nothing. She looked at the slushy snow at her feet, at the trolleybus that went by, at the policeman on a horse that trotted by, at the broken glass they stepped over, at the red traffic light up ahead. Nothing. Nothing. Nothing.

She sighed. Why was this so difficult for him? More difficult than usual. "Shura, why didn't you take *all* of the money?"

"Because," he let out slowly, "I left you what was mine."

"It's all yours. All the money is yours. What are you talking about?"

Nothing.

"Alexander! What did you take five thousand dollars for? If you're running, you need all of it. If you're not running, you don't need any of it. Why did you take half?"

No reply. It was like Lazarevo. Tatiana would ask, he would answer, tight-lipped and thoughtful, and she would spend an hour trying to decipher what was between the single words. Lisiy Nos, Vyborg, Helsinki, Stockholm, Yuri Stepanov, all multisyllables with Alexander hidden in the middle of them, saying nothing.

"You know what?" Tatiana said, exasperated, detaching herself from him. "I'm tired of this game. In fact, I'm done with it. You either tell me everything without holding back, without stupid guessing games where I'm trying to figure things out and getting them wrong, you tell me everything right now, or just turn around, go and get your things, and get away from me. Go on. *The choice is yours.*" Tatiana stopped walking near the Fontanka Canal, folded her arms, and waited.

Alexander stopped walking, too, but didn't reply.

"Are you thinking it over?" she exclaimed, pulling on his arm, trying to look deeper—behind his constricted face. Letting go of him, her voice unable to hide her anguish, she said, "I know, Alexander, that when you're wearing these clothes, your army clothes, you wear them as armor against me, so you don't have to tell me anything. Because I also know that when you're naked and making love to me, you're completely defenseless, and if only I were stronger, I could ask anything then, and you would tell me. Trouble is . . ." Her voice broke. "I'm not stronger. I'm just as defenseless against you. So you, afraid I'm going to see the truth and your agony, afraid I'll see that you're saying good-bye to me, you turn me over because you think if I don't see it, I can't feel it." She started to cry. I'm not doing so well, she thought. Where is my strength?

"Please, stop," Alexander whispered, not looking at her.

"Well, I *can* feel it, Shura," Tatiana said, wiping her face and grabbing his hand. He pulled it from her. "You came here, angry, yes, upset, yes, because you thought you had said good-bye to me for good in Lazarevo—"

"That's not why I was angry and upset."

"As it turns out," Tatiana continued, "you're going to have to say good-bye to me in Leningrad. But you'll have to do it to my *face*, all right?"

Tatiana saw Alexander's tormented eyes.

She stepped up. He backed away. What a waltz they danced in the stark morning. But Tatiana's heart was strong; she could take it. "Alexander. I know—you think I don't know? I've got nothing to do but think about the things you tell me. You have wanted to escape to America all your Soviet life. It was the only thing that had kept you going the years before me, those years in the army. That someday you might return home." She stretched out her hand to him. He took it. "Am I right?"

"You're right," Alexander said. "But then I met you."

Then I met you. Stop, stop. *Oh, the summer last year, the white nights by the Neva, the Summer Garden, the northern sun, his smiling face.* Tatiana looked at his heartbreaking face. She wanted to speak. Where were all those words she once knew? Where were they now when she needed them most?

Alexander shook his head. "Tania, it's too late for me. From the moment my father decided to abandon the life we had in America, he doomed us all. I knew it first—even then. My mother second. My father third, last, but most heartfelt. My mother could ease her pain by blaming him. I thought I could ease mine by joining the army and by being young, but who did my father have to point a finger to?"

Tatiana came up to him and held on to his coat. Alexander put his arms around her. "Tania, when I found you, I felt for that hour or two we were together—before Dimitri, before Dasha—that somehow I was going to right my life." Alexander smiled bitterly. "I had a sense of hope and destiny that I can neither explain nor understand." He wasn't smiling anymore. "Then our Soviet life interfered. You saw, I tried to stay away. I thought, I must stay away. I must keep away. Before Luga. After Luga. Look how I tried after I came to see you at the hospital. I tried to put distance between us after St. Isaac's, after the Germans closed the ring around Leningrad." He paused. He shook his head. "I should have, somehow . . ."

"I didn't want you to," Tatiana said faintly.

"Oh, Tania," Alexander said. "If only I hadn't come to Lazarevo!"

"What are you talking about?" she gasped. "What are you saying? How can you regret—" She didn't finish. How could he be regretting *them*? She stared at him, perplexed and ashen.

Alexander didn't respond. "Some destiny. I've done nothing since the day I met you but hurt your heart and—worse—drag you into my own destruction." He shook his head so hard his cap fell off.

Tatiana picked up his cap, brushed off the slush, and gave it back to him.

"What are you talking about? Hurt my heart? Forget all that, it's done with. Alexander . . . and I came willingly." She paused, frowning. "What destruction? I'm not doomed," said Tatiana slowly, not understanding. "I'm lucky."

"You're blind."

"Then open my eyes." *Like you did once before.* She pulled the scarf tighter around her neck, wanting to bundle up, wanting to be near a fire, wanting to be in Lazarevo.

Tatiana watched Alexander gulp down his fear. He turned his face away and started to walk along the canal pavement. Not looking at her, Alexander said, "I took the five thousand dollars because I was going to give it to Dimitri. I've been trying to convince him to run by himself—"

Tatiana laughed without feeling. "Stop it." She shook her head. "I suspected that was why you took half the money. The man who wouldn't go half a kilometer out onto the ice with me? Is that the man you think is going to *America* by himself? Honestly." They stopped for a red light just past Engineers Castle, last winter used as a hospital and now nearly unrecognizable after repeated bombings. "Dimitri would never go by himself," Tatiana went on. "I already told you. He is a coward and a parasite. You are his courage and his host. What are you even thinking? As soon as Dimitri realizes you're not going, he won't go either, and if he remains in the Soviet Union and sees suddenly that he's got no hope of escape, then he's going straight to his new friend Mekhlis of the NKVD, and you will be instantly—"

Tatiana broke off, staring at Alexander. Something dawned on her. His face was too miserable. "You know all this. You know he'll never go without you. You know this already."

Alexander didn't reply.

They began walking again, over the crippled-by-shelling Fontanka Bridge, stepping over the granite pieces. "So what are you even talking about, then?" Tatiana said, nudging him slightly and looking up into his face, full of incomprehensible fear. She could not imagine that Alexander was afraid for himself. Whom was he afraid for?

"You're not thinking of me—" Tatiana wanted to continue, but the words got stuck in her throat.

Her eyes opened; her heart opened.

Truth flowed in, but not the truth she had known with Alexander. No. Truth illuminating terror. Truth lighting up those hideous corners of an ugly room, with the rotting wood and the broken plaster and the ratty furniture. Once Tatiana saw it, once she saw what was left—

She came around and stood in front of Alexander, stopping him from walking. Too many things were making themselves clear on this desolate Leningrad Saturday. Alexander *was* thinking of her. He was thinking *only* of her.

"Tell me . . ." Tatiana said faintly, "what do they do to wives of Red Army officers arrested on suspicion of high treason? Arrested for being foreign infiltrators? What do they do to wives of American men who jumped out of trains on the way to prison?"

Alexander said nothing, closing his eyes.

And suddenly—the flip side. His eyes were closed. Hers were open.

"Oh, no, Shura . . ." she said. "What do they do to wives of deserters?"

Alexander did not reply. He tried to go around her, but Tatiana stopped him, putting both her hands on his chest. "Don't turn your face from me," she said. "Tell me, what does the Commissariat of Internal Affairs do with wives of soldiers who desert, soldiers who run into the woods in marshy Finland, what do they do with the Soviet wives who remain behind?"

Alexander didn't answer her.

"Shura!" she cried. "What is the NKVD going to do with me? The same thing they do to wives of MIAs? Or POWs? What did Stalin call it, *protective custody*? What is that a euphemism for?"

Alexander was silent.

"Shura!" Tatiana wasn't letting him off the bombed-out bridge. "Is that a euphemism for being *shot*? Is it?" She was panting.

Tatiana stared at Alexander in disbelief, inhaling the cold wet air, her nose hurting from the frost, and she thought back to the river Kama—the icy water every morning on *her* naked body as it touched *him*, thought back to all Alexander had tried to hide from her in the corners of his soul where he hoped she would not peek. But in Lazarevo, Tatiana's eyes saw only the Kama sunrise. It was only here in dreary Leningrad that all was exposed, the darkness and the light, the day and the night. "Are you telling me," she breathed out, "that whether you go or stay, I am done for?"

Turning his agonized face away from her, Alexander said nothing.

Tatiana's scarf fell off her head. Numbly she picked it up and held it in her hands. "No wonder you couldn't tell me. But how could I not have seen?" she whispered.

"How? Because you never think of yourself," Alexander said, grabbing his rifle, moving from foot to foot, not looking at her. "And that's why," he said, "I wanted you to stay in Lazarevo. I wanted you to stay as far away from here, as far away from *me*, as possible."

Tatiana shivered, putting her hands inside the pockets of her coat. "What did you think?" she said. "If you kept me in Lazarevo, you'd keep me safe?"

She shook her head. "How long do you think it would take the village *Soviet* right next to the bathhouse to receive the order by that long Lend-Lease telegraph line to have me come in for a few questions?"

"That's why I liked Lazarevo so much," he said, not looking at her. "The village *Soviet* didn't have a telegraph line."

"Is *that* why you liked Lazarevo so much?"

Alexander lowered his head to his chest, his warm eyes cooling off, his breath a vapor. His back to the stone wall, he said, "Now do you see? Now do you understand? Are your eyes opened?"

"Now I see." *Everything.* "Now I understand." *Everything.* My eyes are opened.

"Do you see there is only one way out before us?"

Narrowing her eyes at him, Tatiana stopped talking, backing away from Alexander, tripping over her scarf, and falling on the bombed, deserted bridge under the liquid sky. Alexander went to help her up and then let go. He could not continue to touch her, Tatiana saw that. And for a moment she could not touch him. But it was just a moment. At first it was black, but the clearing inside her own head made her breathless. Suddenly, through the darkness, there was light, light! She saw it up ahead and she flew to it, knowing what it was, and before she opened her mouth to speak, she felt such relief as if her weight—and his—had been lifted.

Tatiana looked at Alexander with her clearest eyes.

Perplexed, he stared at her. She stretched out her arms to him and said quietly, "Shura, look, look here."

He looked at her.

"All around you is darkness," she said. "But in front of you I stand."

He looked at her.

"Do you see me?" she said faintly.

"Yes." Just as faintly.

She came closer to him, stepping over the broken granite. Alexander sank to the ground.

Tatiana studied him for a few moments and then descended to her knees. Alexander put his face into his shaking hands.

Tatiana said, "Darling, soldier, husband. Oh, God, Shura, don't be afraid. Will you listen to me, please? Look at me."

Alexander would not.

"Shura," Tatiana said, clenching her fists to keep her composure. Stop. Breathe. Beg for strength. "You think your death is our only choice? Remember what I told you in Lazarevo? Do you not remember me in Lazarevo? I cannot bear the thought of you dying. And I will do everything in my pathetic, powerless life to keep that from happening. You have no chance here in the Soviet Union. No chance. The Germans or the Communists *will* kill you. That's their sole objective. And if you die at war, your death will mean that for the rest of my life I will be eating poisoned mushrooms in the Soviet Union, alone and without you! And you know it. Your greatest sacrifice will be for my life in darkness." Come on, Tania, be strong. "You wanted me to let you go? You wanted my faithful face to free you?" Her voice could not keep from breaking. "Well, here I am! Here is my face." She wished he would look at her. "Go, Alexander. Go!" she said. "Run to America, and *never* look back." Stop. Breathe. Breathe again. She couldn't even wipe her eyes. All right, I cried, but I think I did well, Tatiana thought. And besides, he wasn't looking at me.

Taking his hands away from his face, Alexander *glared* at her for several moments before he spoke. "Tatiana, are you out of your mind? I need you right now," he said slowly, "to stop being ridiculous. Can you do *that* for me?"

"Shura," Tatiana whispered, "I never imagined that I could love anyone like I love you. Do this for me. Go! Return home, and don't think about me again."

"Tania, stop it, you don't mean a word of that."

"What?" she exclaimed, still on her knees. "Which part don't you think I mean? Have you be alive in America or dead in the Soviet Union? You think I don't mean that? Shura, it's the only way, and you know it." She paused when he did not speak. "I know what I would do if I were you."

Alexander shook his head. "What would you do? You would leave me to die? Leave me in the Fifth Soviet apartment, living with Inga and Stan, orphaned and alone?"

Frantically Tatiana chewed her lip. It was love or truth.

Love won.

Steeling herself, she said, "Yes," in a fragment of a voice. "I would choose *America* over you."

Alexander broke down. "Come here, you lying wife," he said, bringing her close, encompassing her.

The ice on the Fontanka Canal was just forming where they were crumbled against the granite parapets.

"Shura, listen to me," Tatiana said into Alexander's chest, "if no matter which way we twist in this world, we are faced with this impossible choice, if no matter what we do, *I* cannot be saved, then I beg of you, I *beg* of you—"

"Tania! God, I will not listen to this anymore!" he shouted, pushing her away and jumping to his feet, holding the rifle in his hands.

She stared at him pleadingly, still on the ice. "You can be saved, Alexander Barrington. *You*. My husband. Your father's only son. Your mother's only son." Tatiana extended her hands to him in supplication. "I am Parasha," she whispered. "And I am the cost of the rest of your life. Please! There was once a time I saved myself for you. Look at me, I'm on my knees." She was weeping. "Please, Shura, please. Save your *one* life for me."

"Tatiana!" Alexander pulled her up to him so hard, he lifted her off her feet.

She clung to him, not letting go. "You are not going to be the cost of the rest of my life!" he said, setting her down. "Now, I need you to stop this."

She shook her head into his chest. "I won't stop."

"Oh, yes, you will," he said, squeezing her to him.

"You'd rather we *both* perish?" she cried. "Is that what you would prefer? You'd prefer *all* the suffering, *all* the sacrifice, and no Leningrad at the end of it?" She shook him. "Are you out of your mind? You must go! You *will* go, and you will build yourself a new life."

Alexander pushed her away and walked a few strides from her. "If you don't keep quiet," he said, "I swear to God, I am going to leave you here and go"—he pointed down the street—"and I will *never* come back!"

Tatiana nodded, pointing in the same direction. "That's exactly what I want. Go. But far, Shura," she whispered. "*Far.*"

"Oh, for God's sake!" Alexander yelled, slamming his rifle on the ice. "What kind of crazy world do you live in? What, you think you can come here, fly in on your little wings, and say, all right, Shura, you can go, and I just go? How do you think I can leave you? How do you think it'll be possible for me to do that? I couldn't leave a dying stranger in the woods. How do you think I can leave *you?*"

"I don't know," Tatiana said, crossing her arms. "But you better find a way, big man."

They fell quiet. What to do? She watched him from a distance.

"Do you see how impossible it is what you're saying?" Alexander said. "Do you even see, or have you completely lost your senses?"

She saw how impossible it was what she was saying. "I've completely lost my senses. But you must go."

"Tania, I'm not going anywhere without you," he said, "except to the wall."

"Stop it. You must go."

He yelled, "If you don't stop—"

"Alexander!" Tatiana screamed. "If *you* don't stop, I am going back to Fifth Soviet and I'm going to hang myself over the bathtub, so you can run to America free of me! I'm going to do it on Sunday, five seconds after you leave, do you understand?"

They stared at each other for a mute, unspeakable moment.

Tatiana stared at Alexander.

Alexander stared at Tatiana.

Then he opened his arms, and she ran into them; he lifted her off her feet, they hugged and did not let go. For many silent minutes they stood on the Fontanka Bridge, wrapped around each other.

At last Alexander spoke into her neck. "Let's make a deal, Tatiasha, all right? I will promise you that I'll do my best to keep myself alive, if you promise me that you'll stay away from bathtubs."

"You got yourself a deal." Tatiana looked into his face. "Soldier," she said clutching him, "I hate to point out the obvious at a time like this, but still . . . I need to point out that I was completely right. That's all."

"No, you were completely wrong. That's all," Alexander said. "I said to you that *some* things were worth a great sacrifice. This is just not one of those things."

"No, Alexander. What you said to me—your exact words to me—was that all great things worth having required great sacrifices worth giving."

"Tania, what the hell are you going on about? I mean, just for a second, step away from the world in which you live and into mine, for a millisecond, all right, and tell me, what kind of life do you think I could build for myself in America knowing that I left you in the Soviet Union—to die—or to rot?" He shook his head. "The Bronze Horseman would indeed pursue me all through that long night into my maddening dust."

"Yes. And that would be your price for light instead of darkness."

"I'm not paying it."

"Either way, Alexander, my fate is sealed," Tatiana said without acrimony or bitterness, "but you have a chance, right now, while you are still so young to kiss my hand and to go with God because you were meant for great things." She took a breath. "You are the best of men." Her arms were around his neck, and her feet were off the ground.

"Oh, yes," said Alexander, clamping her to him. "Running to America, abandoning my wife. I'm just fucking priceless."

"You're just impossible."

"*I'm* impossible?" Alexander whispered, setting her down, "Come on, let's walk a bit before we freeze." She held on to him as they stepped slowly through the trampled snow down Fontanka to the Field of Mars. Silently they crossed the Moika Canal and walked into the Summer Garden.

Tatiana opened her mouth to speak, but Alexander shook his head. "Don't say a word. What are we even thinking, walking through here? Let's go. Quick."

Their heads bent and his arm around her, they walked quickly down the path among the tall, bare trees, past the empty benches, past the statue of Saturn devouring his own child. Tatiana remembered that the last time they were here in the warmth, she had yearned for him to touch her, and now in the cold she *was* touching him and feeling that she did not deserve what she had been given—a life in which she was loved by a man like Alexander.

"What did I tell you then?" he said. "I told you that was the best time. And I was right."

"You were wrong," Tatiana said, unable to look at him. "The Summer Garden was not the best time."

She was sitting on his bare shoulders in the water, waiting for him to throw her over into the Kama. He wasn't moving. "Shura," she said, "what are you waiting for?" He wasn't moving. "Shura!"

"You're not going anywhere," he said. "What kind of man would throw off a girl sitting naked around his neck?"

"A ticklish man!" she shouted.

Exiting through the gilded iron gates on the Neva embankment, they headed mutely upriver. Weakening by minutes, Tatiana took Alexander's arm and slowed him down. "Can't walk our streets with you anymore," she said hoarsely.

From the embankment they turned to Tauride Park. They passed their bench on Ulitsa Saltykov-Schedrin, walked a little farther along the wrought-iron fence, stopped, stared at each other and turned around. They sat down in their coats. Tatiana sat for a minute next to Alexander, then got up and climbed into his lap. Pressing her head to his, she said, "That's better."

"Yes," he said. "That's better."

Silently they sat together on their bench in the cold. Tatiana's whole body struggled with heartbreak. "Why," she whispered into his mouth, "why can't we have even what Inga and Stan have? Yes, in the Soviet Union, but together twenty years, still *together*."

"Because Inga and Stan are Party spies," replied Alexander. "Because Inga and Stan sold their souls for a two-bedroom apartment, and now they don't have either." He paused. "You and I want too much from this Soviet life."

"I want nothing from this life," said Tatiana. "Just you."

"Me, and running hot water, and electricity, and a little house in the desert, and a state that doesn't ask for your life in return for these small things."

"No," Tatiana said, shaking her head. "Just you."

Moving her hair back under her scarf, Alexander studied her face. "And a state that doesn't ask for *your* life in return for me."

"The state," she said with a sigh, "has to ask for something. After all, it protects us from Hitler."

"Yes," Alexander said. "But, Tania, who is going to protect you and me from the state?"

Tatiana held him closer. One way or another she had to help Alexander. But how? How to help him? How to save him?

"Don't you see? We live in a state of war. Communism is war on you and me," Alexander said. "That's why I wanted to keep you in Lazarevo. I was just trying to hide my artwork until the war was over."

"You're hiding it in the wrong place," said Tatiana. "You told me yourself there was no safe place in the Soviet Union." She paused. "Besides, this war is going to be a long one. It's going to take some time to reconstruct our souls."

Squeezing her, Alexander muttered, "I have to stop talking to you. Do you ever forget anything I tell you?"

"Not a word," she said. "Every day I'm afraid that's all I'll have left of you."
They sat.

Tatiana brightened. "Alexander," she said, "want to hear a joke?"

"Dying to."

"When we get married, I'll be there to share all your troubles and sorrows."

"What troubles? I don't have any troubles," said Alexander.

"I said *when* we get married," replied Tatiana, her tearful eyes twinkling.
"You have to admit that you getting killed at the front so I can live in the
Soviet Union, and me hanging myself over a bathtub so you can live in
America is an ironic tale quite well told, don't you think?"

"Hmm. But since we are not leaving a scrap of family behind," said
Alexander, "there will be no one to tell it."

"There is that," said Tatiana. "But still . . . how *Greek* of us, don't you
think?" She smiled and squished his face.

Alexander shook his head. "How do you do that?" he asked. "Find comfort? Through anything. How?"

"Because I've been comforted by the master," she said, kissing his forehead.

He tutted. "Some master I am. Couldn't even get one tiny tadpole of a
wife to stay in Lazarevo."

Tatiana watched him stare at her. "What, husband?" she said. "What are
you thinking?"

"Tania . . . you and I had only *one* moment . . ." said Alexander. "A single
moment in time, in your time and mine . . . one *instant*, when another life
could have still been possible." He kissed her lips. "Do you know what I'm
talking about?"

*When Tatiana looked up from her ice cream, she saw a soldier staring at her
from across the street.*

"I know that moment," whispered Tatiana.

"Regret that I crossed the street for you?"

"No, Shura," she replied. "Before I met you, I could not imagine living a
life different from my parents, my grandparents, Dasha, me, Pasha, our children. Could not have conceived of it." She smiled. "I didn't dream of someone like you even when I was a child in Luga. You showed me, in a glimpse,
in our tremor, a beautiful life . . ." She peered into his eyes. "What did *I* ever
show you?"

"That there is a God," whispered Alexander.

"There is!" exclaimed Tatiana. "And I felt your *need* for me clear across
the steppes. I'm here for you. And one way or another we will fix this." She
squeezed him. "You'll see. You and I will fix this together."

"How? And now what?" came Alexander's voice at her head.

Taking a frigid breath, Tatiana spoke, trying to sound as cheerful as possible. "How, I don't know. What now? Now we go blindly into the thick forest
at the other side of which awaits the rest of our short but oh-so-blissful time

on this earth. You go and fight me a nice war, Captain, and you stay alive, as promised, and keep Dimitri off your back—"

"Tania, I could kill him. Don't think I haven't thought about it."

"In cold blood? I know you couldn't. And if you could, how long do you think God would look after you then in war? And me in the Soviet Union?" She paused, trying to get hold of her departing senses. It wasn't as if she herself hadn't thought about it . . . but Tatiana had the feeling that it was not the Almighty who was keeping Dimitri alive.

"And what about you?" asked Alexander. "What now for you? I don't suppose you might consider going back to Lazarevo?"

Smiling, Tatiana shook her head. "Don't worry about me. You must know that having survived last winter's Leningrad, I'm ready for the worst." She traced her glove along Alexander's cheeks, thinking, *and the very best, too*. "And though I do sometimes wonder," she continued, "what's ahead of me if I needed Leningrad to pave my way into it . . . it doesn't matter. I'm here for the long haul, or the short haul. I'm here to stay. And I'm paved and ready for it all." Her heart throbbing, Tatiana hugged him to her. "Regret crossing the street for me, soldier?"

Taking her hand into both of his, Alexander said, "Tania, I was spellbound by you from the first moment I saw you. There I was, living my dissolute life, and war had just started. My entire base was in disarray, people were running around, closing accounts, taking money out, grabbing food out of stores, buying up the entire Gostiny Dvor, volunteering for the army, sending their kids to camp—" He broke off. "And in the middle of my chaos, there was *you*!" Alexander whispered passionately. "You were sitting alone on this bench, impossibly young, breathtakingly blonde and lovely, and you were eating ice cream with such abandon, such pleasure, such mystical delight that I could not believe my eyes. As if there were nothing else in the world on that summer Sunday. I give you this so that if you ever need strength in the future and I'm not there, you don't have to look far. You, with your high-heeled red sandals, in your sublime dress, eating ice cream before war, before going who knows where to find who knows what, and yet never having any doubt that you would find it. That's what I crossed the street for, Tatiana. Because I believed that you would find it. I believed in *you*."

Alexander wiped the tears from her eyes and, pulling off her glove, pressed his warm lips to her hand.

"But I would've come back empty-handed that day if it weren't for you."

He shook his head. "No. You didn't start with me. *I* came to you because you already had yourself. You know what I bring you?"

"What?"

His voice choking with emotion, he said, "Offerings."

Alexander and Tatiana sat a long time with their wet, cold faces pressed against each other, his arms around her, her hands cradling his head, while the wind blew the last dead leaves off the trees, while the sky was a leaky November gray.

A tram went by. Three people walked down the street at the end of which Smolny Monastery stood, concealed with scaffolding and camouflage. Down by the granite carapace the river was icy and still. And past the empty Summer Garden the Field of Mars lay flat under blackened snow.

A WINDOW TO THE WEST

1

AFTER Alexander left, Tatiana wrote to him every day until her ink ran out. When her ink ran out, she went across the street to Vania Rechnikov's apartment. She had heard he had ink he lent sometimes. Vania was dead at his writing table. He had put his head down on the letter he had been writing and died. Tatiana couldn't pry the pen from his stiff fingers.

Tatiana went to the post office every day in hopes of hearing from Alexander. She couldn't take the silence in between the letters. Alexander wrote her a stream, but the stream would come in a flood instead of a steady trickle. The damn mail.

She stayed in her room when she was not working and practiced her English. During air raids she read her mother's cookbook. Tatiana started cooking dinner for Inga, who was sick and alone.

One afternoon the postmaster wouldn't give her any of Alexander's letters, offering her not only his letters but a bag of potatoes, too, in return for something from her.

She wrote to Alexander about it, afraid that none of his future letters would get through.

Tania,

Please go to the barracks and ask for Lieutenant Oleg Kashnikov. He is on base duty, I think from eight to six. He has three bullets lodged in his leg and can't fight anymore. He is the one who helped me dig you out in Luga. Ask him for some food. I promise he won't ask for anything in return. Oh, Tatia.

Also, give him your letters, and he will bring them to me in a day. Please don't go to the post office.

What do you mean, Inga is alone? Where is Stan?

Why are you still working such crazy hours? The winter is getting harsher.

I wish you knew how much solace I have thinking of you not too far from me. I'm not going to tell you that you were right to come back to Leningrad, but . . . Did I mention that we were promised ten days off after we broke the blockade?

Ten days, Tania!

I wish until then there were a place you could be comforted. But you hang on until then.

Don't be worried about me, we're not doing anything but bringing troops and munitions in for our assault on the Neva sometime very early in the new year.

Wait till you hear this! I don't even know what I did to deserve it, but I've received not only another medal but a promotion to go with it. Maybe Dimitri is right about me—somehow I manage to turn even a defeat into a victory, don't know how.

We're testing the ice on the Neva. The ice doesn't seem strong enough. It'll hold up a man, a rifle, maybe a Katyusha, but will it hold a tank?

We think yes. Then no. Then yes. Then one general engineer who had been designing the Leningrad subway gets the idea to put the tank on a wooden outrigger, flat wood boards on ice, sort of a wooden railroad, to distribute the pressure from the treads evenly. The tanks and all the armored vehicles would use this outrigger to cross. All right, we say.

We build the outrigger.

Who is going to drive the tank out on the water to test it?

I step up and say, sir, I'll be glad to do it.

The next day my commander is not pleased at all when all five generals show up for our little demonstration. Including Dimitri's new friend. Commander motions to me: don't blow it.

So here I go, I get into our best and heaviest, the KV-1—you remember them, Tatia? And I drive this monster out onto the ice with my commander walking beside the tank and the five generals right behind us, saying, well done, well done, well done.

I went about 150 meters, and then the ice started to crack. I heard it and thought, oops. The generals from the back yelled at my commander, run, run!

So he ran, they ran, the tank broke a canyon in the ice and sank into it, like a, well, like a tank.

Me with it.

The turret was open, so I swam up.

The commander pulled me out and gave me a swig of vodka to warm me up.

One general said, give this man the order of the Red Star. I've also been made a major.

Marazov says I have become really insufferable. He says I think everyone should listen only to me. You tell me—does that sound like me?

Alexander

Dearest MAJOR Belov!

Yes, Major, it does sound like you.

I'm *very* proud of you. You'll be a general yet.

Thank you for letting me give my letters to Oleg. He is a very nice, polite man and yesterday even gave me some dehydrated eggs, which I found amusing and didn't know quite what to do with. I added water to them, they're kind of—oh, I don't know. I cooked them without oil on Slavin's Primus. Ate them. They were rubbery.

But Slavin liked them and said Tsar Nicholas would have enjoyed them in Sverdlovsk. Sometimes I don't know about our crazy Slavin.

Alexander—there *is* one place I'm comforted. I wake up there, and I go to sleep there; I am at peace there, and loved there: your subsuming arms.

Tatiana

2

In December the International Red Cross came to Grechesky Hospital.

There were too few doctors left in Leningrad. Out of the 3,500 that were there before the war, only 2,000 remained, and there was a quarter of a million people in various city hospitals.

Tatiana met Dr. Matthew Sayers when she was washing out a throat wound on a young corporal.

The doctor came in, and before he opened his mouth, Tatiana suspected he was an American. First of all he smelled clean. He was thin and small and dark blond, and his head was a little big for the rest of his body, but he radiated confidence that Tatiana had not seen in any man but Alexander and now this man, who entered the room, swung up the chart, looked at the patient, glanced at her, glanced back to the patient, clicked his tongue, shook his head, rolled his eyes, and said, in English, *"Doesn't look so good, does he?"*

Though Tatiana understood him, she remained mute, remembering Alexander's warnings.

In heavily accented Russian, the doctor repeated himself.

Nodding, Tatiana said, "I think he'll be all right. I've seen worse."

Emitting a good, non-Russian laugh, he said, "I bet you have, I just bet you have." He came up to her and extended his hand. "I'm with the Red Cross. Dr. Matthew Sayers. Can you say Sayers?"

"Sayers," Tatiana said perfectly.

"Very good! What's Matthew in Russian?"

"Matvei."

Letting go of her hand, he said, "Matvei. Do you like it?"

"I like Matthew better," she told him, turning back to the gurgling patient.

Tatiana was right about the doctor, he was competent, friendly, and instantly improved the conditions in their dismal hospital, having brought miracles with him—penicillin, morphine, and plasma. Tatiana was also right about the patient. He lived.

3

Dear Tania,

I haven't heard from you. What are you doing? Is everything all right? Oleg told me he has not seen you in days. I cannot worry about you, too. I've got enough craziness on my hands.

They're getting better, by the way.

Write to me immediately. I don't care if your own hands have fallen off. I forgave you once for not writing to me. I don't know if I can be so charitable again.

As you know, it's almost time. I need your advice—we're sending out a reconnaissance force of 600 men. It's actually more than a reconnaissance force, it's a stealth attack with the rest of us waiting to see what kind of defense the Germans put up. If things go well, we will follow them.

I have to decide which battalion goes.

Any ideas?

Alexander

P.S. You haven't told me what happened to Stan.

Dear Shura,

Don't send your friend Marazov.

Can you send any supply units? Ah, a bad joke.

On that note, we must bear in mind that our own righteous Alexander Pushkin challenged Baron George d'Anthes to a duel and did not live to write a poem about it. So instead of seeking revenge, we will simply stay away from those who can hurt us, all right?

I'm fine. I'm very busy at the hospital. I'm hardly ever home. I'm not needed there. Shura, dear, please don't go insane worrying about me. I'm here, and I'm waiting—impatiently—until I can see you again. That's all I do, Alexander—wait until I can see you again.

It's dark from morning until night with an hour off in the afternoon. Thinking of you is my sunshine, so my days are perpetually sunny. And hot.

Tatiana

P.S. The Soviet Union happened to Stan.

Dear Tania,

Pushkin never needed to write again after *The Bronze Horseman*—and never did, having died so young. But you're right—the righteous do not always forge a path to glory. But often they do.

I don't care how busy you are, you need to write me more than a couple of lines a week.

Alexander

P.S. And you wanted to have what Inga and Stan have.

Dearest Tatiasha,

How was your New Year? I hope you had something delicious. Have you been to see Oleg?

I'm not happy. My New Year was spent in the mess tent with a number of people, none of whom was you. I miss you. I dream sometimes of a life in which you and I can clink our glasses on New Year's. We had a little vodka and many cigarettes. We hoped maybe 1943 would be better than 1942.

I nodded, but thought about the summer of 1942.

Alexander

P.S. We lost all 600. I did not send Tolya. He said he will thank me after this war is over.

P.S.S. Where are you, damn it? I haven't heard from you in ten days. You haven't gone back to Lazarevo, have you, now that I've finally grown accustomed to your strengthening spirit from only seventy kilometers away? Please send me a letter in the next few days. You know we're going and we're not coming back until the Leningrad front and the Volkhov front shake hands. I need to hear from you. I need one word. Don't send me out on the ice without a single word from you, Tatiana.

Darling Shura!

I'm here, I'm here, can't you feel me, soldier?

I myself spent New Year at the hospital, and I just want you to know that I clink my glass against yours every day.

I've been working I cannot tell you how many hours, how many nights I sleep in the hospital and don't come home at all.

Shura! As soon as you're back, you must come and see me instantly. Other than for the obvious reasons, I've got the most amazing wonderful fantastic thing I desperately need to talk to you about—and soon. You wanted a word from me? I leave you with one—the word is HOPE.

Yours,
Tania

In Storied Battles

1

ALEXANDER looked at his watch. It was the early morning of January 12, 1943, and Operation Spark—the Battle for Leningrad—was about to begin. There was going to be no further attempt. This was it. On the orders of Comrade Stalin, they were going to break the German blockade, and they weren't returning until they did.

Alexander had spent the last three days and nights hidden in the wooden bunker on the banks of the Neva with Marazov and six corporals. The artillery encampment was right outside, hiding from view their two 120-millimeter breech-loading mortars, two portable 81-millimeter muzzle-loading mortars, one Zenith antiaircraft heavy machine gun, a Katyusha rocket launcher, and two portable 76-millimeter field guns. On the morning of the attack Alexander was not just ready to fight, he would have fought Marazov if it meant getting out of the confinement of the bunker. They played cards, they smoked, they talked about the war, they told jokes, they slept—he was done with it all after six hours, and they had stayed in it for seventy-two. Alexander thought about Tatiana's last letter. What the hell did she mean by "HOPE"? How was that going to help him? Obviously she couldn't tell him in the letter, but he wished she wouldn't go firing up his imagination when he didn't know when he would be able to get to her.

He needed to get to her.

Wearing white camouflage, he peeked out of the encampment. The river was disguised like Alexander, the south shore barely visible in the gray light. He was on the northern bank of the Neva just west of Shlisselburg. Alexander's artillery unit was covering the outermost flank of the river crossing and the most dangerous—the Germans were extremely well entrenched and defended in Shlisselburg. Alexander could see the fortress Oreshek a kilometer in the distance at the mouth of Lake Ladoga. A few hundred meters before Oreshek lay the bodies of 600 men, who had made a surprise attack six days ago and failed. Alexander wanted to know if they had failed gloriously or vainly. Bravely and without support, they went across the ice and were laid down one by bloody one. Will history remember them? wondered Alexander as he turned his gaze straight ahead.

He was on air detail today. Marazov was launching Katyusha's solid-fuel rockets. Alexander knew this was it. He *felt* it. They were going to break the blockade or die in the process. The 67th Army was forcing the river along an eight-kilometer stretch at whatever the cost. The strategy for the attack was to close ranks with Meretskov's 2nd Army in Volkhov that was simultaneously attacking Manstein's Army Group Nord from the rear. The plan was for the rifle guard divisions and some light tanks to cross the river, four guard divisions in all. Two hours later three more rifle divisions with heavy and medium tanks would follow, including six of the men under Alexander's immediate command. He would remain behind the Zenith on the Neva. He would cross in the third wave, with another heavily armored platoon, commanding a T-34, a medium tank that had a chance of crossing the river without sinking.

It was just before nine, barely sunrise, the morning sky a dark lavender.

"Major," said Marazov, "is your phone working?" He put out his cigarette and stepped up to Alexander.

"Phone's working fine, Lieutenant. Back to your post." He smiled. Marazov smiled back.

"How many miles of field phone wire did Stalin demand from the Americans?" Marazov asked.

"Sixty-two thousand," replied Alexander, taking the last deep drag of his cigarette.

"And your phone is not working already."

"Lieutenant!"

Marazov saluted Alexander. "I'm ready, Major." He stepped aside to the Katyusha. "I've *been* ready. Sixty-two thousand miles is a bit excessive, don't you think?"

Alexander threw his cigarette butt in the snow, wondering if he had time to light another one. "It's not nearly enough. The Americans will supply us with five times that much before this war is over."

"You'd think they could supply you with a working telephone," Marazov mumbled, looking away from Alexander.

"Patience, soldier," said Alexander. "Phone is working fine." He was trying to figure out if the Neva was wider than the Kama. He decided it was, but not by much. He had swum the Kama to the other shore and back in heavy current in about twenty-five minutes. How long would it take him to cross the 600 meters of the Neva ice under German fire?

Alexander concluded he would have to take less than twenty-five minutes. The phone rang. Alexander smiled. Marazov smiled. "Finally," he said.

"All good things come to those who wait," said Alexander, his heart soaring to Tatiana and away. "All right, men," he called. "This is it. Be ready," he said, standing slightly behind them, his arms positioning the barrel of the Zenith upward. "And be brave."

He picked up the phone and flagged the go-ahead command to the corporals on the mortars. The men fired three slow-emission smoke bombs that flew across the river and exploded, temporarily obscuring the Nazi line of sight. Instantly Red Army soldiers poured out onto the ice in long, snakelike formations, one right in front of Alexander, and ran across.

For two hours the heavy fire from 4,500 rifles did not cease. The mortars were deafening. Alexander thought the Soviet soldiers did better than expected—remarkably better. With his binoculars he spotted a number of downed men on the other shore, but he also spotted many running up the bank and hiding in the trees.

Three German planes flew low overhead, firing at the Soviet soldiers and breaking holes in the ice—more danger zones for trucks and men to avoid. A little lower, a little lower, Alexander thought, opening machine-gun fire on the aircraft. One plane exploded; the other two quickly gained altitude to avoid being hit. Alexander loaded a high-explosive shell into the Zenith and fired. Another of the planes burst into flames. The last one gained more altitude and was now unable to fire at the ice; it flew back to the German side of the Neva. Alexander nodded and lit a cigarette. "You're doing well," he yelled to his men, who were so busy loading the shells and firing they didn't hear him. He hardly heard himself: his ears were muffled to prevent hearing loss.

At 11:30 A.M. a green flash went off as a signal for the motorized division to move across the Neva in the second wave of attack.

The go-ahead was too early, but Alexander hoped the element of surprise would work in their favor—it might if they could move across the ice quickly. Alexander motioned for Marazov to take his men and run. "Go," Alexander yelled. "Stay covered! Corporal Smirnoff!" One of the men turned around. "Take your weapons," said Alexander.

Marazov saluted Alexander, grabbed the handles of the 76-millimeter field gun, yelled to his men, and they started down the short slope and onto the ice. Two other corporals were running holding the 81-millimeter mortars. The 120-millimeter guns were left behind. They were too heavy to transport without a truck. Three soldiers in the front were running with their Shpagins.

Alexander watched Marazov knocked down by fire, barely thirty meters onto the ice. "God, Tolya!" he shouted and looked up. The German plane was making one pass over the Neva, firing at the men on the ice. Marazov's soldiers dropped. Before the plane had a chance to reverse and return, Alexander swung the barrel of the Zenith, aimed, and fired a high-explosive impact shell. He did not miss. The plane was low enough; it burst into flames and dead-spiraled into the river.

Marazov continued to lie motionless on the ice. Watching him helplessly, Marazov's men hovered by the field gun. The river was being pummeled by shell fire. "Oh, for fuck's sake!" Alexander ordered Ivanov—the remaining corporal—to man the Zenith, grabbed his machine gun, jumped off the slope, and ran to Marazov, yelling for the rest of the soldiers to continue across the river. "Go! Go!" They grabbed the field gun and the mortars and ran.

Marazov was splayed on his stomach. Alexander saw why his men had watched him with such helplessness. Kneeling by him, Alexander wanted to turn him over, but the soldier was breathing so painfully that Alexander was afraid to touch him. "Tolya," he said, panting. "Tolya, hang on." Marazov had been hit in the neck. His helmet had fallen off. Alexander desperately looked around to see if he could find a medic to give him some morphine.

Alexander saw a man appear on the ice, carrying not a weapon but a doctor's bag. The man wore a heavy woolen overcoat and a woolen hat—not even a helmet! He was running to the right of Alexander to a group of downed men near a hole in the ice. Alexander had just enough time to think, what a fool, a *doctor* on the ice, he is *insane*, when he heard soldiers behind him screaming at the doctor, "Get down! Get down!" But the gunfire was too loud, black smoke was clouding all, and the doctor, standing erect, turned around and yelled in *English*, "What? What are they saying? What?"

It took Alexander an instant. He saw the doctor on the ice, in the middle of enemy fire but—more important—on the edge of the trajectory path of shells from the German side. Alexander knew he had one quarter second, a splinter of time to think. He jumped up and screamed at the top of his lungs in English, "GET THE FUCK DOWN!"

The doctor heard immediately and dropped. Just in time. The conical shell flew a meter over the man's head and exploded on impact just behind him. The doctor was propelled like a projectile across the ice and landed head first in the water hole.

With clear eyes Alexander glanced at Marazov, who, with fixated pupils, was spurting blood from his mouth. Making the sign of the cross on him, Alexander picked up his machine gun and ran twenty meters across the ice, fell on his stomach, and crawled another ten to the water hole.

The doctor was unconscious, floating in the water. Alexander tried to reach him, but the man was facedown and too far away. Alexander threw his weapons, ammo, and ruck down onto the ice and jumped in. The water was a piercing, frozen deluge and then an instant whole-body anesthetic, numbing him like morphine. Grabbing the doctor by the neck, Alexander pulled him to the edge of the hole and with all his strength hurled him out with one hand while holding on to the ice with the other. Crawling out himself, he lay breathing heavily on top of the doctor, who came to and groaned. "God, what happened?" In English.

"Quiet," said Alexander in English. "Stay down. We have to get you to that armored truck on the wooden boards, do you see it? It's twenty meters. If we can get behind it, we'll be safer. We're out in the open here."

"I can't move," said the doctor. "The water is freezing me from the outside in."

Feeling the wet bitter cold himself, Alexander knew what the doctor meant. He scanned the immediate ice. The only cover was the three bodies near the water hole. Crawling across on his stomach, he pulled one body to the doctor and lay it on top of him. "Now, just lie still, keep the body on you, and don't move."

Then he crawled and retrieved another body, throwing it over his back, and picked up his ruck and his weapons. "You ready?" he said to the doctor, in English.

"Yes, sir."

"Hold on to the bottom of my coat *for your life*. Don't let go. You're going for an ice skate."

As quickly as he could with one dead man on top of him, Alexander dragged the doctor and the additional corpse twenty meters to the armored truck.

Alexander felt as though he were losing his hearing, the bursting noise around him filtering in and out in fits through his helmet and his conscious mind. He had to make it. Tatiana made it through the blockade, and she didn't have a dead man covering her. I can do this, he thought, pulling the doctor faster, faster, faster amid the black, snarling clatter. He thought he heard the whiz of a low plane and wondered when Ivanov was going to shoot the fucker down.

The last thing Alexander remembered was a whistling noise closer than he'd ever heard before, an explosion, then painless but severe impact, as he was propelled with frightening force helmet first into the side of an armored truck. Lucky I have a dead man on top of me, thought Alexander.

2

Opening his eyes took too much energy out of him. It was such an effort that as soon as he opened them, he closed them again and slept for what felt like a week or a year. It was impossible to tell. He heard faint voices, faint noises; faint smells trickled in: camphor, alcohol. Alexander dreamed of his first roller coaster, the stupendous Cyclone on the shores of Revere Beach in Massachusetts. He dreamed of the sand on Nantucket Sound. There was a short wooden boardwalk, and on this boardwalk they sold cotton candy. He bought three *red* cotton candies and ate them in his dreams, and every once in a while something would smell not like cotton candy and not like the salt water, and instead of looking forward to a roller coaster, or swimming, or playing cops and robbers under the boardwalk, Alexander started trying to place the smell.

There were other memories, too—of woods, of a lake, of a boat. And other images—collecting pinecones, stringing together a hammock. Falling into a bear trap. They were not his own.

Through his closed eyes and closed brain he heard soft female voices, over him, and male voices, too; once he heard something fall loudly to the floor; once the noise of a heartbeat: must be the metronome. Then he was thinking of driving through the desert as a child, sandwiched between his mother and father. It was the Mojave; it wasn't pretty, but it was hot and the car was stuffy, yet he felt cold. Why was he cold?

But the desert. For some reason that smell again in the desert. Not cotton candy, not salt, just the smell of—

A river rushing morning in.

He opened his eyes again. Before he closed them, he tried to focus. Blurry vision and all, he made out no faces. Why couldn't he see any faces? All he saw was hazy glimpses of white. But there was the smell again. A shape bending over him. He closed his eyes and could have sworn he heard someone whisper, *Alexander*. Then metal clanging. Felt his head being held. Held.

Held.

Suddenly his brain came awake. He willed his eyes open. He was on his stomach. That's why he couldn't see any faces. Blurry again. The shape of something small and white. A voice whispering. What? What? he wanted to say. He couldn't speak. That smell. It was breath, sweet breath, close to his face. A distinct smell of comfort, the kind of comfort he had known only once in his life.

That brought his eyes into alertness. Not focus, just a steady Gaussian white blur.

"Shura, please wake up," the voice whispered. "Alexander, open your eyes. Open your eyes, my love." He felt pillow lips on his cheek.

Alexander opened his eyes. His Tatiana's face was next to him.

His eyes filling with tears, he shut them, mouthing, no. No.

He *had* to open his eyes. She was calling him. "Shura, right now open your eyes."

"Where am I?"

"At the field hospital in Morozovo," she replied.

Trying to shake his head. Couldn't move. "Tatia?" he whispered. "It can't be you."

He slept.

Alexander was on his back. A doctor was standing in front of him, talking to him in Russian. Alexander concentrated on the voice. Yes. A doctor. What was he saying? It wasn't clear. The Russian, he couldn't understand it.

A little while later, more clear, more comprehensible. Russian suddenly wasn't foreign.

"I think he's coming out of it. How are you feeling?"

Alexander tried to focus. "How have I been?" Slowly.

"Not too good."

Alexander looked around. He was in a rectangular wooden structure with a few small windows. The beds, full of white- and red-bandaged people, were in two rows with a passageway in between.

He tried to look at the nurses in the distance. The doctor was calling his attention back to him. Alexander reluctantly returned his gaze to the doctor, not wanting to answer any questions. "How long?"

"Four weeks."

"What the hell happened?"

"Do you not remember?"

"No."

The doctor sat by the bed and spoke very quietly. "You saved my life," he said in comforting, grateful English.

Dimly Alexander remembered. The ice. The hole. The cold. He shook his head. "Russian only. Please," he added. "Don't want to be trading your life for mine."

Nodding, the doctor said, "I understand." He squeezed his hand. "I'll come back in a few days when you're a little better. You can tell me more then. I'm not here for long. But you can be sure I wasn't going to leave you until you were out of the woods."

"What were you thinking . . . going out on the ice?" Alexander asked. "We have medics for that."

"Yes, I know," said the doctor. "I was going out to save the medic. Who do you think you put on my back as you dragged us to the truck?"

"Oh."

"Yes. It was my first time at the front. Could you tell?" The doctor smiled. A good American smile. Alexander wanted to smile back.

"Has our sleepy patient come awake?" said a cheery nurse with black hair and black button eyes, coming up to his bed, smiling, bustling, and feeling his pulse. "Hello there. I'm Ina, and aren't you a lucky one!"

"Am I?" said Alexander. He did not feel lucky. "Why is my mouth full of cotton?"

"It's not. You've been on morphine for a month. We've just begun to cut you back last week. I think you were getting hooked."

"What's your name?" Alexander asked the doctor.

"Matthew Sayers. I'm with the Red Cross." He paused. "I was an idiot, and for that you nearly paid with your life."

Alexander shook his head. He looked around the ward. It was quiet. Maybe he had dreamed it. Maybe he had just dreamed *her*.

Dreamed her *whole*.

Wouldn't that be something? She was never in his life. He had never known her. He could go back to the way it had been. To the way *he* had been.

What *was* that way? That man was dead. Alexander did not know that man.

"A shell exploded right behind us, and a fragment hit you." Dr. Sayers said. "You rammed into the truck and fell. I couldn't move you myself." His Russian wasn't very good, but he continued. "I was waving for help. I didn't want to leave you, but . . ." The doctor glanced at Alexander. "Let's just say we needed a stretcher for you immediately. One of my nurses came out onto the ice to help." Sayers shook his head. "She is something, that one. Actually crawled out. I said to her, 'Well, you're three times smarter than me.' " Sayers leaned into Alexander. "And not only that, she crawled out pushing the box of plasma in front of her!"

"Plasma?"

"Blood fluid without the blood. Lasts longer than whole blood, freezes great, especially in your Leningrad winter. A miracle for wounded like you— it replaces fluid you lose until we can get a transfusion into you."

"Did I . . . need fluid replacement?" Alexander asked.

The nurse patted him cheerfully on the arm. "Yes, Major," she said, "you could say you needed fluid replacement."

"All right, nurse," said Dr. Sayers. "The rule we have in America is that we don't upset the patient. Are you familiar with that rule?"

Alexander stopped the doctor. "How bad was I?"

Sayers said jovially, "You weren't looking your best. I left the nurse with you while I went—crawled," the doctor corrected himself, smiling, "to get the stretcher. I don't know how, but she helped me carry it. She carried the end with your head. After we got you to shore, she looked as if she could have used some plasma herself."

Alexander, wanting to make the doctor feel better, said, "Crawling or not, if the shell hits you, you're done for."

The nurse said, "You *were* almost done for. A shell hit you."

"Did *you* crawl out onto the ice?" Alexander asked, feeling grateful, wanting to pat her hand.

She shook her head. "No, I stay far from the front line. I'm not with the Red Cross."

Sayers said, "No, I brought my nurse with me from Leningrad." He smiled. "She volunteered."

"Oh," said Alexander. "What hospital were you with?" He felt himself starting to fade again.

"Grechesky."

Alexander couldn't help it, he groaned in pain. He couldn't stop until Ina gave him another dose of morphine. The doctor, watching carefully, asked if he was all right.

"Doctor, the nurse who came with you?"

"Yes?"

"What is her name?"

"Tatiana Metanova."

A wretched sound escaped Alexander.

"Where is she now?"

Shrugging, Sayers replied, "Where isn't she? Building the railroad, I think. We broke the blockade, you know. Six days after you were hit. The two fronts joined together. Immediately eleven hundred women started to build that railroad. Tania is helping out on this side."

"Well, she didn't start right away," said Ina. "She was with you, Major, for most of the time."

"Yes, but now that he's better, she's gone to help." Dr. Sayers smiled. "They're calling it the railroad of victory. Too soon if you ask me, seeing the state of the men that are brought in here."

"Can you bring the nurse in here when she returns from the railroad?" Alexander paused. He wanted to explain but felt shattered. He *was* shattered. "Where did you say I was hit?"

"Your back. Your right side got blown out. But the shell fragment cut open the body on top of you, so it's a good thing you had him." Dr. Sayers paused. "We worked very hard to save your kidney." He leaned forward. "Didn't want you to be taking on the Germans in the future with just one kidney, Major."

"Thank you, Doctor. How did you do?" Alexander tried to think about what hurt. "My back doesn't feel great."

"No, Major, it wouldn't. You've got a third-degree burn around the periphery of the wound. That's why we kept you on your stomach for so long. We just started rolling you over on your back." Sayers patted him on the shoulder. "Feel your head? You hit that truck quite hard. But, listen, you're going to be as good as new, I figure, once the wound and the burn heal and we wean you off the morphine. Maybe in a month you'll be out of here." The doctor hesitated, studying Alexander, who did not want to be studied. "We'll talk another time, all right?"

"Fine," Alexander muttered.

Brightening, the doctor said, "But on the plus side, you've been given another medal."

565

"As long as it wasn't posthumously."

"As soon as you can stand up, they're going to promote you, I've been told," Sayers said. "Oh, and some supply guy keeps coming around asking about you. Chernenko?"

"Bring the nurse to me, won't you?" said Alexander, closing his eyes.

3

A night passed before he saw her again. Alexander woke up, and there she was, sitting by his side. They sat and stared at each other. Tatiana said, "Shura, now, don't be upset with me."

"Oh my God" was all Alexander could manage. "You are just relentless."

Nodding, Tatiana quietly said, "Relentlessly married."

"No. Just relentless."

Leaning toward him, she whispered, "Relentlessly in love." She added, "You needed me. I came."

"I didn't need you here," Alexander said. "How many times do I have to tell you? I need you safe."

"And who is going to keep *you* safe?" She took his hand and smiled. Looking around to make sure there were no nurses or doctors close by, she kissed his hand and then pressed it to her face. "You're going to be all right, big man. You just hang on."

"Tania, after I'm out of here, I'm getting a divorce." He was not letting go of her face. For anything.

Shaking her head, she said, "Sorry. Can't. You wanted a covenant with God? You got it."

"Tatiasha . . ."

"Yes, darling, yes, Shura? I'm so happy to hear your voice, to hear you talking."

"Tell me the truth. How bad was I hurt?"

"Not too bad," she replied in a low voice, smiling at him, her face white.

"What was I thinking running out after Marazov like that? I should have let his men take care of him. They were stuck, though. They couldn't move forward, they weren't bringing him back." He paused. "Poor Tolya."

Her smile never leaving her mouth, Tatiana said, slightly glazed over with sadness, "I said a prayer for Tolya."

"Did you say one for me, too?"

"No," she said. "Because you weren't dying. I said a prayer for me. I said, dear God, please help me heal him." She held his hand. "But, Alexander, you could no more help running after Marazov than you could help yelling in English at the doctor, or jumping into the water after him, or pulling him behind you to safety. You could no more help that than you could help returning with Yuri Stepanov. Remember, Shura, we are all a sum of our parts. And what do your parts say about you?"

"That I'm a fucking lunatic. My back feels like it's on fire." He smiled, remembering Luga. "Is it just glass cuts, Tania?"

Hesitating for a moment, she said, "You got burned. But you'll be fine." She pressed her cheek harder into his hand. "Tell me the truth, tell me you're not happy to see me."

"I could say it, but I'd be lying." He rubbed her freckles, gazing at her without blinking.

She took out a small vial of morphine from her pocket and attached it to the entry point in his IV drip.

"What are you doing?"

She whispered, "Giving you a small intravenous morphine push. So your back doesn't feel like it's on fire." In seconds he felt better. She leaned her head back into his hand.

Alexander looked her over up and down. Tatiana exuded a porous, evanescent, yet everlasting warmth; her very presence, her satin face in his palm made his back hurt less. Her radiant eyes, her flushed cheeks, her slightly parted loving lips . . . Alexander stared at her, his eyes wide open, his soul wide open, his adoring heart hurting exquisitely. "You are an angel sent from heaven, aren't you?"

An electric smile lit up her face. "And you don't know the *half* of it," she whispered. "You don't know what your Tania has been cooking up here." In her delight she nearly squealed.

"What have you been cooking up? No, don't sit up. I want to feel your face."

"Shura, I can't. I'm practically on top of you. We need to be very careful." The smile faded an octave. "Dimitri walks around here all the time. Walks in, out, checks on you, leaves, comes back. What's he worried about? He was quite surprised to find me here."

"He's not the only one. How did you get here?"

"All part of my plan, Alexander."

"What plan is this, Tatiana?"

She whispered, "To be with you when I die of old age."

"Oh, *that* plan."

"Shura, I have to talk to you. I need to talk to you when you're lucid. I need you to hear me very carefully."

"Tell me now."

"I can't now. I said *lucid*." She smiled. "Besides, I have to go now. I was sitting for an hour waiting for you to wake up. I'll come back tomorrow." She looked around his bed. "See how I put you here in the corner, so that we can have a wall next to you and a little *privacy*." She pointed to the window next to his bed. "I know it's high, but you can see a bit of sky and two trees, northern pines, I think. *Pines*, Shura."

"*Pines*, Tania."

She got up. "The man next to you can't hear or see. If he can speak, it's a mystery how." She smiled. "Plus, do you see the isolation tent around him so he can breathe clearer air? I put the tent around him, to help him, but it blocks you from half the ward. This is almost more private than Fifth Soviet."

"How *is* Inga?"

Pausing, chewing her lip, Tatiana said, "Inga is not at Fifth Soviet anymore."

"Oh, finally she moved?"

"Yes," said Tatiana, "she's *been* moved."

They stared at each other and then slowly nodded. Alexander closed his eyes. He did not, *could not* let go of her. "Tania," he whispered, "is it true you went out on the ice? In the middle of a ferocious battle for Leningrad, you crawled out onto the ice?"

Bending over him, she quickly kissed him and whispered, "Yes, the bravest soldier of my heart. For *Leningrad*."

"Tatia," said Alexander, his nerve endings aching, "tomorrow don't wait an hour to wake me up."

4

Alexander thought of nothing else but when he would see her again the following day. She came around lunchtime, bringing him his food. "I'll feed him, Ina," she said brightly to the regular nurse. Ina didn't look too pleased, but Tatiana paid no attention.

"Nurse Metanova thinks she owns my patient," Ina said, signing Alexander's chart.

"She does own me, Ina," said Alexander. "Isn't she the one who brought me the plasma?"

"You don't know the half of it," mumbled Ina sulkily, glaring at Tatiana and walking away.

"What did she mean by that?" Alexander asked.

"Don't know," Tatiana replied. "Open your mouth."

"Tania, I can feed myself."

"You *want* to feed yourself?"

"No."

"Let me take care of you," she said tenderly. "Let me do what you know I ache to do for you. Let me *do for you*."

"Tania, where is my wedding ring?" he asked. "It was hanging on a rope around my neck. Did I lose it?"

Smiling, she pulled the braided rope out of her uniform. Two rings hung next to each other. "I'll keep it until we can wear them again."

"Feed me," he said, his voice deepening with emotion.

Before she could feed him, Colonel Stepanov came to see Alexander. "I heard you'd awakened," he said, glancing at Tatiana. "Is this a bad time?"

Tatiana shook her head, put the spoon back on the tray, and stood up. "Are you Colonel Stepanov?" she asked, looking from Alexander to the colonel.

"Yes," he replied, puzzled. "And you are—"

Tatiana took the colonel's hand in both of hers and held it. "I'm Tatiana Metanova," she said. "I just want to thank you, Colonel, for all you have done for Major Belov." She did not let go of his hand, and he did not pull away. "Thank you, sir," she repeated.

Alexander wanted to hug his wife. "Colonel," he said, grinning, "my nurse knows that my commander has been good to me."

"Nothing you don't deserve, Major," said Stepanov. He did not pull his hand away from Tatiana's until she released him. "Have you seen your medal?"

The medal hung on the back of the chair by Alexander's bed.

"Why didn't they wait until I was conscious to give it to me?" Alexander asked.

Stepanov said, "We didn't know if—"

"Not just a medal, Major," interrupted Tatiana. "The highest medal of honor there is. *A Hero of the Soviet Union* medal!" she added breathlessly.

Stepanov looked from Tatiana to Alexander and back again and said, "Your nurse is very proud of you, Major."

"Yes, sir." He was trying not to smile.

Stepanov said, "Tell you what, why don't I come back another time, when you're less busy?"

"Wait, sir," Alexander said, looking away from Tatiana for a moment. "How are our troops doing?"

"They're fine. They had their ten days off, and now they're trying to push the Germans out of Sinyavino. Big problems there. But you know, little by little." Stepanov paused. "Better news—von Paulus surrendered in Stalingrad last month." Stepanov chuckled. "Hitler made von Paulus a field marshal two days before surrender. He said no German field marshal in history had ever surrendered."

Alexander smiled. "Von Paulus obviously wanted to make history. That *is* great news. Stalingrad held. Leningrad broke the blockade. We may yet win this war." He fell quiet. "It will be a Pyrrhic victory indeed."

"Indeed." Stepanov shook Alexander's hand. "The kinds of losses we're suffering, I don't know who'll be left to enjoy even a Pyrrhic victory." He sighed. "Get better soon, Major. Another promotion is waiting for you. Whatever else happens, we'll get *you* away from the front line."

"Don't want to be away from the action, sir."

Tatiana shoved him in the shoulder.

"I mean, *yes*, thank you, sir."

Again Stepanov stared at Alexander and Tatiana.

"It's good to see you in better spirits, Major. I don't remember the last time I saw you so . . . cheerful. Near-fatal injury agrees with you."

Stepanov left.

"Well, you've completely flummoxed the colonel," said Alexander, grinning at Tatiana. "What did he mean by near-fatal injury?"

"Hyperbole. But you were right. He *is* a nice man." Tatiana looked at Alexander with teasing rebuke. "I can see you forgot to thank him for me, though."

"Tania, we're men. We don't go around slapping each other on the shoulder."

"Open your mouth."

"What food did you bring me?"

She had brought cabbage soup with potatoes and white bread with butter.

"Where did you get all this butter from?" There was a quarter of a kilo.

"Wounded soldiers get extra butter," she said. "And you get extra *extra* butter."

"Like extra *extra* morphine?" he asked, smiling at her.

"Mmm. You need to get better quick."

Every time the spoon moved to his mouth, bringing her fingers closer to him, Alexander breathed in deeply, trying to smell her hands behind the soup.

"Have you eaten?"

Tatiana shrugged. "Who's got time to eat?" she said breezily. She pulled up her chair closer to his bed.

Alexander said, "Do you think the other patients will object if my nurse kisses me?"

"Yes," she said, pulling away a bit. "They're going to think I kiss everybody."

Alexander looked around. There was a man across the room from them, dying, his legs gone. Nothing could be done for him. In the isolation tent next to Alexander's bed, he heard a man struggling for his every breath. Like Marazov.

"What's wrong with him?"

"Oh, Nikolai Ouspensky? He's lost a lung," Tatiana said. She cleared her throat. "He'll be fine. He is a nice man. His wife lives in a village nearby, keeps sending him onions."

"Onions?"

Tatiana shrugged. "Villagers, what can I tell you."

"Tania," he said quietly, "Ina told me I needed fluid replacement. How badly—"

Tatiana quickly said, "You're going to be fine. You lost a little blood, that's all." She paused, then shook something off. "Listen," she said, lowering her voice to a whisper, "listen carefully—"

"Why aren't you here with me all the time? Why aren't you my nurse?"

"Wait. Two days ago you told me to go away, and now you want me here all the time?"

"Yes."

"Dearest," she whispered, smiling, "*he* is here all the time. Did you not hear me? I'm trying to keep a professional distance. Ina is a good critical care nurse. Soon you'll get better, and maybe we can move you to a convalescent bed if you want."

"Is that where you are? I'll get better in a week."

"No, Shura. I'm not there."

"Where are you?"

"Listen, I need to talk to you, and you keep interrupting."

"I won't interrupt," said Alexander, "if you hold my hand under the blanket."

Tatiana stuck her hand under the blanket and took hold of his hand, intertwining her little fingers through his. "If I were stronger, bigger, like you," she said softly, "I would have picked you up and carried you off the ice myself."

Squeezing her hand tight, he said, "Don't make me upset, all right? I'm too happy to see your lovely face. Please kiss me."

"No, Shura, will you listen—"

"Why do you look so fucking incredible? Why are you oozing happiness? I don't think you've ever looked better."

Tatiana leaned toward him, parting her lips and lowering her voice to a husky whisper. "Not even in Lazarevo?"

"Stop, you're making a grown man cry. You're just shining from the inside out."

"You're alive. I'm ecstatic." She looked ecstatic.

"How did you get to the front?"

"If you would listen, I'd tell you." She smiled. "When I left Lazarevo, I knew I wanted to become a critical care nurse. Then after you came to see me in November, I decided to enlist. I was going to the front where you were. If you were going into battle for Leningrad, so was I. I was going to go on the ice with the medics."

"That was your plan?"

"Yes."

He shook his head. "I'm glad you didn't tell me then, and I certainly don't have the strength for this now."

"You're going to need a lot more strength when you hear what I'm about to tell you." She could barely contain her excitement. His heart pounded. "So when Dr. Sayers came to Grechesky," Tatiana continued, "I immediately asked him if he needed an extra pair of hands. He came to Leningrad at the Red Army's request to help with the anticipated flow of the wounded in this attack." She lowered her voice. "I have to tell you, I think even the Soviets underestimated the number of wounded. There is simply no place to put anyone. Anyway, after Dr. Sayers told me he was going to the Leningrad front, I asked him if there was anything I could do to help . . ." Tatiana smiled. "I learned that question from *you*. As it turned out, he did need my help. The only nurse he had brought with him took ill. Not a surprise is it, in wintry Leningrad? Poor thing caught TB." Tatiana shook her head. "*Imagine*. Now she's better, but she remained in Grechesky. They need her there. Since I hadn't enlisted yet, I came here with Dr. Sayers as his temporary assistant instead. Look," Tatiana said proudly, showing Alexander her white armband with the Red Cross symbol on it. "Instead of a Red Army nurse, I'm a Red Cross nurse! Isn't this great?" She beamed.

"I'm glad you're enjoying being at the front, Tania," Alexander said.

"Shura! Not at the front. Do you know where Dr. Sayers came from?"

"America?"

"I mean, where he drove his Red Cross jeep from to come to Leningrad?"

"I give up."

In a thrilled whisper, she said, *"Helsinki!"*

"Helsinki."

"Yes."

"All right . . ." Alexander drew out.

"And do you know where he is going back to in a little while?"

"No, where?"

"Shura! *Helsinki!*"

Alexander didn't say anything. Slowly he turned his head away and closed his eyes. He heard her calling him. He opened his eyes and turned back to her. Her eyes were dancing, and her fingers were tapping his arm, her warm face flushing red, her breathing rapid.

He laughed.

A nurse on the other side of the hall turned around.

"No, don't laugh," Tatiana said. "Keep quiet."

"Tatia, Tatia, stop. I beg you."

"Will you listen to me? As soon as I met Dr. Sayers, I started thinking and thinking."

"Oh, no."

"Oh, yes."

"What are you thinking?"

"In Grechesky I thought and thought, trying to come up with a plan—"

"Oh, no, not another plan."

"Yes, plan. I asked myself, *can* Dr. Sayers be trusted? I thought he could be, yes. I thought I could trust him because he seemed like a good American. I was going to trust him and tell him about you and me, and beg him to help you get back home, beg him to help get us to Helsinki somehow. Just to Helsinki. After that you and I could make it to Stockholm ourselves."

"Tania, I can't take any more of this."

"No, listen to me!" she whispered. "If only you knew how God is with us. In December a wounded Finnish pilot came to Grechesky. They come in all the time—to die. We tried to save him, but he had severe head wounds. Crashed his plane into the Gulf of Finland." She was barely audible. "I kept his uniform and his ID tag. I hid them in Dr. Sayers's jeep, in a box of bandages. That's where they are now—waiting for you."

In astonishment Alexander gaped at Tatiana.

"The only thing I was afraid of was asking Dr. Sayers to risk himself for total strangers. I didn't know quite how to do that." Tatiana leaned over and kissed his shoulder. "But *you*, my husband, you had to intervene. You had to save the doctor. Now I'm sure he will help get you out if he has to carry you on his back."

Alexander was speechless.

"We will put you in a Finnish uniform, you'll become Tove Hanssen for a few hours, and we will drive you across the Finnish border in Dr. Sayers's Red Cross truck to Helsinki. Shura! I will get you out of the Soviet Union."

Alexander was still speechless.

Laughing soundlessly but happily, Tatiana said, "We have amazing luck, don't you think?" Pointing to the Red Cross badge on her arm and squeezing his hand under the covers, Tatiana said, "Depending on when you'll be strong enough, from Helsinki we will take either a merchant vessel, if the ice on the Baltic has broken, or a truck with a protective convoy to Stockholm. Sweden is neutral, remember?" She smiled. "And no, I don't forget a single word of anything you ever tell me." Letting go of him, she clapped her hands. "Is that not the best plan you ever heard? Much better than your idea of hiding out in the gulf swamps for months."

He looked at her with delirium and dizzy disbelief. "Who *are* you, this woman sitting in front of me?"

Tatiana got up. Bending over him, she kissed him deeply on the lips. "I'm your beloved wife," she whispered.

Hope was an amazing healer.

Suddenly the days stretching out weren't long *enough* for Alexander to try to get up, to walk, to move. He couldn't get out of bed, but he tried supporting himself on his arms, and he sat up finally, and fed himself, and lived for the minutes when Tatiana could come and see him.

His idleness was making him crazy. He asked Tatiana to bring him pieces of wood and an army knife, and while waiting for her he sat for hours carving the coarse wood into palm trees, into pine trees, into knives and stakes and human forms.

She would come, every day, many times a day, and sit by him, and whisper. "Shura, in Helsinki, we can take a sleigh ride, a *drozhki* ride. Wouldn't that be something? And we could actually go to a real church! Dr. Sayers told me Helsinki's Emperor Nicholas church looks a lot like St. Isaac's. Shura, are you listening?"

Smiling, he would nod and whittle.

And she would sit by him and whisper. "Shura, did you know that Stockholm is all built out of granite, just like Leningrad? Did you know that our very own Peter the Great took the hotly contested Karelia from Sweden in 1725? Ironic, don't you think? Even then we were fighting over the land that will now set us free. By the time we get to Stockholm, it'll be spring, and apparently right on the harbor they have a morning market where they sell fruits and vegetables and fish—oh, and Shura, they have smoked ham and something called bacon, Dr. Sayers told me. Have you ever had bacon? Shura, are you listening?"

Smiling, he would nod and whittle.

"And in Stockholm we'll go to this place, called, I can't remember right now—oh, yes, called, Sweden's Temple of Fame, the burial place for her kings." Delight was all over her face. "Her kings and heroes. You'd like that. We'll go and see it?"

"Yes, sweet girl," Alexander said, putting down his knife and his wood, reaching for her, bringing her to him. "We'll go and see it."

5

"Alexander?" Dr. Sayers said, sitting in the chair next to him. "If I talk quietly, can I speak in English? Russian is so hard for me day in and day out."

"Of course," Alexander replied, also in English. "It's good to hear the language again."

"I'm sorry I haven't been able to come by sooner." He shook his head. "I can see I'm getting myself mired in the hell that is the Soviet front. I'm running out of all my supplies, the Lend-Lease shipments can't come quickly enough, I'm eating your Russian food, sleeping without a mattress—"

"You should have a mattress."

"The wounded have a mattress. I have thick cardboard."

Alexander wondered if Tatiana also had thick cardboard.

"I thought I'd be out of here already, but look at me. Still here. My days are twenty hours long. Listen, I have a bit of time finally. You want to talk?"

Alexander shrugged, studying the doctor. "Where are you from, Dr. Sayers? Originally?"

Sayers smiled. "Boston. Familiar with Boston?"

Alexander nodded. "My family was from Barrington."

"Ah, well," Sayers exclaimed. "We're practically neighbors." He paused. "So tell me. Long story with you?"

"Long."

"Can you tell me? I'm dying to know how an American ended up as a major in the Red Army."

In response Alexander studied the doctor, who said gently, "How long have you lived not being able to trust anyone? Trust *me*."

Taking a deep breath, Alexander told him. If Tatiana trusted this man, it was good enough for him.

Dr. Sayers listened intently and then said, "That's some mess."

"You're not kidding," said Alexander.

Now it was Sayers's turn to study Alexander. "Is there anything I can do to help?"

Alexander did not reply at first. "You owe me nothing."

Sayers paused. "Do you . . . want to come home?"

"Yes," said Alexander. "I want to come home."

"What can *I* do?"

Alexander looked at him. "Talk to my nurse. She'll tell you what to do." Where *was* his nurse? He needed to lay his eyes on her.

"Ina?"

"Tatiana."

"Ah, Tatiana." The doctor's face eased into affection. "*She* knows about you?"

Alexander did a double take at the doctor's expression and then laughed softly, shaking his head. "Dr. Sayers, I am indeed going to trust you with everything. You will hold two lives in your hands. Tatiana . . ."

"Yes?"

". . . is my wife." Those words trickled warmth all over his insides.

"She's what?"

"My wife."

The doctor stared at him incredulously. "She *is?*"

With quiet amusement Alexander watched the doctor's reaction as he blanked, then cleared, then thought back, then understood with a spark of mixed sadness and comprehension. "Oh, how stupid of me," he said. "Tatiana *is* your wife. I should've known. So many things are suddenly clear." Breathing hard, Dr. Sayers said, "Well, well. Lucky you."

"Yes—"

"No, Major. I mean, you're a *lucky* man. But never mind."

"No one knows but you, Doctor. Talk to her. She is not on morphine. She is not injured. She'll tell you what she wants you to do."

"Of that I have no doubt," said Dr. Sayers. "I can see, I'm not leaving anytime soon. Anyone else you'd like me to help?"

"No, thank you."

As he stood up, Dr. Sayers shook Alexander's hand.

"Ina," Alexander asked the nurse, who took care of him between Tatiana's visits, "when am I going to be moved to the convalescent wing?"

"What's your hurry? You've just regained consciousness. We will take care of you here."

"All I lost is a little blood. Let me out of here. I'll walk there myself."

"You've got a hole in your back, Major Belov, the size of my fist," said Ina. "You're not going anywhere."

"You've got a small fist," said Alexander. "What's the big deal?"

"I'll tell you what the big deal is," she said. "You're not going anywhere, that's the big deal. Now, let me turn you so I can clean that nasty wound of yours."

Alexander turned over himself. "How nasty is it?"

"Nasty, Major. The shell ripped off a hunk of your flesh."

He smiled. "Did it rip off a *pound* of my flesh, Ina?"

"A *what*?"

"Never mind. So tell me the truth—how bad was I hurt?"

While changing his dressings, Ina said, "Bad. What, Nurse Metanova didn't tell you? She's impossible. Dr. Sayers took one look at you after they brought you in and said he didn't think you were going to make it."

That didn't surprise Alexander. He had floated so long on the periphery of consciousness. It hadn't felt much like life. Yet dying seemed inconceivable. He lay on his stomach while Ina cleaned his wound and listened to her.

"The doctor is a good man, and he wanted to save you, feeling personally responsible. But he said you had lost just too much blood."

"Oh. That's why I'm in critical care?"

"Now you are." Ina shook her head. "You weren't here to begin with." Patting his shoulder, she said, "You went right to terminal."

"Oh." His smile evaporated.

"It's that Tatiana nurse," said Ina. "She is . . . well, frankly, I think she's concentrating too much on the terminal cases. She ought to be helping the critical, but she's always in the terminal ward trying to save the hopeless."

So that's where she was. "How does she do?" muttered Alexander.

"Not too good. They're dying left and right there. But she stays with the patients until the end. I don't know what it is with her. They still die, but—"

"They die happy?"

"Not happy, just—I can't explain."

"Not *afraid*?"

"Yes!" she exclaimed, bending over and looking at Alexander. "That's it. Not afraid. I say to her, 'Tania, they're going to die anyway, leave them alone.' And not just me. Dr. Sayers keeps telling her to come and work in the

576

critical wing. But she doesn't want to hear it." Ina lowered her voice. "Not even from the *doctor!*"

That brought a smile back to Alexander's face.

"She's got some mouth on her, too. I don't know how she gets away with a tenth of the things she says to that nice man who is running ragged around this hospital. When they first brought you in, like I said, the doctor looked at you and shook his head. 'He is bled out,' he said, and he said it sadly. I could tell he was upset."

Bled out? Alexander paled.

Ina continued. " 'Forget him,' he said. 'There is nothing we can do.' " She stopped washing Alexander for a second. "And do you know what that Tatiana said to him?"

"I can't imagine," said Alexander. "What?"

Ina's voice was full of gossipy, hot frustration. "I don't know who she thinks she is. She came up really close to him, lowered her voice, looked him straight in the eye and said, 'Well, it's good thing, Doctor, that he didn't say the same thing about you when you were floating unconscious in the river! It's a good thing he didn't turn his back on you when you fell, Dr. Sayers.' " Ina laughed gleefully. "I couldn't believe her nerve. To talk that way to a *doctor*."

"What *was* she thinking?" muttered Alexander, closing his eyes and imagining his Tania.

"She was determined. It was like some kind of a personal crusade with her," Ina said. "She gave the doctor a *liter* of blood for you—"

"Where did she get it from?"

"Herself, of course." Ina smiled. "Lucky for you, Major, our Nurse Metanova is a universal donor."

Of course she is, thought Alexander, keeping his eyes tightly shut.

Ina continued. "The doctor told her she couldn't give any more, and she said a liter wasn't enough, and he said, 'Yes, but you don't have more to give,' and she said, 'I'll make more,' and he said, 'No,' and she said, 'Yes,' and in four hours, she gave him another half-liter of blood."

Alexander lay on his stomach and listened intently while Ina wrapped fresh gauze on his wound. He was barely breathing.

"The doctor told her, 'Tania, you're wasting your time. Look at his burn. It's going to get infected.' There wasn't enough penicillin to give to you, especially since your blood count was so low." Alexander heard Ina chuckle in disbelief. "So I'm making my rounds late that night, and who do I find next to your bed? Tatiana. She's sitting with a syringe in her arm, hooked up to a catheter, and I watch her, and I swear to God, you won't believe it when I tell you, Major, but I see that the catheter is attached to the entry drip in your IV." Ina's eyes bulged. "I watch her *draining* blood from the radial artery in her arm into your IV. I ran in and said, 'Are you crazy? Are you out of your mind? You're *siphoning* blood from yourself into him?' She said to me in her calm, I-won't-stand-for-any-argument voice, 'Ina, if I don't, he will die.' I yelled at her. I said, 'There are thirty soldiers in the critical wing who need sutures and bandages and their wounds cleaned. Why don't you take care of them and let God take care of the dead?' And she said, 'He's not dead. He is still alive, and while he is alive, he is mine.' Can you believe it, Major? But that's what she said. 'Oh, for God's sake,' I said to her. 'Fine, die yourself. *I* don't care.' But the next morning I went to complain to Dr. Sayers that she wasn't following procedure, told him what she had done, and he ran to yell at her." Ina lowered her voice to a sibilant, incredulous whisper. "We found her unconscious on the floor by your bed. She was in a dead faint, but you had taken a turn for the better. All your vital signs were up. And Tatiana got up from the floor, white as death itself, and said to the doctor coldly, 'Maybe *now* you can give him the penicillin he needs?' I could see the doctor was stunned. But he did. Gave you penicillin and more plasma and extra morphine. Then he operated on you, to get bits of the shell fragment out of you, and saved your kidney. And stitched you. And all that time she never left his side, or yours. He told her your bandages needed to be changed every three hours to help with drainage, to prevent infection. We had only two nurses in the terminal wing, me and her. I had to take care of *all* the other patients, while all she did was take care of you. For fifteen days and nights she unwrapped you and cleaned you and changed your dressings. Every three hours. She was a ghost by the end. But you made it. That's when we moved you to critical care. I said to her, 'Tania, this man ought to marry you for what you did for him,' and she said, 'You think so?'" Ina tutted again. Paused. "Are you all right, Major? Why are you crying?"

That afternoon, when Tatiana came to feed him, Alexander took her hand and for a long time couldn't speak.

"What's the matter, darling?" she whispered. "What hurts?"

"My heart," he answered.

She leaned from her chair to him. "Shura, honey, let me feed you. I need to feed ten other very sick people after you. One of them doesn't have a tongue. Imagine the difficulty there. I'll come back tonight if I can. Ina knows me. She thinks I've taken a shine to you." Tatiana smiled. "Why are you looking at me like that?"

Alexander still couldn't speak.

Later that night Tatiana came back. The lights were out, and everyone was asleep; she sat by Alexander's side.

"Tatia . . ."

Quietly she said, "Ina's got a big mouth. I told her not to upset my patient. I didn't want you to worry. She couldn't help herself."

"I don't deserve you," he said.

"Alexander, what do you think? You think I was going to let you die when I knew we were meant to get out of here? I couldn't get that close and then lose you."

"I don't deserve you," he repeated.

"Husband," she said, "did you forget Luga? God, did you forget Leningrad? Our Lazarevo? I haven't. My life belongs to you."

6

Alexander woke up and found Tatiana sitting in the chair. She was sleeping, leaning forward on his bed by his side, her blonde head covered with a white nurse's kerchief. It was quiet and dark in the large room, and cold. He pulled the kerchief off her and touched the wispy strands of hair falling on her eyes, touched her eyebrows, traced his fingers around her freckles, her little nose, her soft lips. She woke up. "Hmm," she said, lifting her hand to pat him. "I'd better go."

"Tania . . ." he whispered, "when am I going to be whole again?"

"Darling," she said soothingly, "you don't feel whole?" She bent over him, cradling him. "Hug me, Shura," she said. "Hug me tight." She paused, and added in a whisper, "Like I love . . ."

Alexander put his arms around her. Tatiana's arms went around his neck as she tenderly kissed his face, her hair brushing against him. "Tell me a memory," he whispered.

"Mmm, what kind of memory are you looking for?"

"You know what I'm looking for."

She continued to kiss his face lightly as her breathy voice whispered, "I remember one rainy night running home from Naira's and putting our blankets in front of the fire, and you making the most tender love to me, telling me you would stop only when I begged you to stop." Tatiana smiled, her lips on his cheek. "And did I beg you to stop?"

"No," he said huskily. "You are not for the weak, Tatiasha."

"Nor you," she whispered. "And afterward, you fell asleep right on top of me. I was awake a long time holding your sleeping body. I didn't even move you, I fell asleep, too, and in the morning you were still on top of me. Do you remember?"

"Yes," he said, closing his eyes. "I remember." *I remember everything. Every word, every breath, every smile you took, every kiss you laid upon my body, every game we played, every Bronze Horseman cabbage pie you cooked for me. I remember it all.*

"You tell *me* a memory," she whispered. "But quietly. That blind man across the ward is going to have a heart attack."

Alexander pulled the hair away from her face and smiled. "I remember Axinya standing by the door of the *banya* while we were alone and inside and so hot and soapy, and I kept saying to you, *shh.*"

"Shh," Tatiana whispered breathlessly, glancing over at the sleeping man across the ward.

Alexander felt her trying to pull herself away. "Wait," he said, holding her to him and looking around the dark ward. "I need something."

She smiled into his face. "Yes? Like what?" Alexander knew she knew the look in his eyes. "You *must* be healing, soldier."

"Faster than you can imagine."

Bringing her face flush to his, she whispered, "Oh, I can imagine."

Alexander began to unbutton the top of her nurse's uniform.

Tatiana backed away. "No, don't," she said softly.

"What do you mean, *don't*? Tatia, open your uniform. I need to touch your breasts."

"No, Shura," she said. "Someone will wake up, see us. Then we'll all get in trouble. Somebody will definitely see. Maybe as a nurse I can get away with holding your hand, but I think this would be frowned upon. I think maybe even Dr. Sayers wouldn't understand."

Not letting go of her hand, Alexander said, "I need my mouth on you. I want to feel your breasts against my face, just for a second. Come on, Tatiasha, open the top of your uniform, lean over as if you're adjusting my pillow, and let me feel your breasts on my face."

Sighing and obviously uncomfortable, she undid her uniform. Alexander wanted to feel her so much that he didn't care about propriety. Everyone is sleeping, he thought, watching her hungrily as she opened the uniform to her waist, stood very close to him, and lifted her undershirt.

Alexander gasped so loudly when he saw her breasts that she reeled back and quickly pulled her shirt down. Her breasts had grown to twice their previous size; they were swollen and milky white. "Tatiana," he groaned, and before she could back away farther, he grabbed her arm and brought her close to him.

"Shura, stop, let go," she said.

"Tatiana," Alexander repeated. "Oh, no, Tania . . ."

She wasn't fighting his hand anymore. Bending over, she kissed him. "Come on, let go," she murmured.

Alexander did not let go. "Oh my God, you're . . ."

"Yes, Alexander. I'm pregnant."

Speechlessly he stared at her shining face.

"What the hell are we going to do?" he asked finally.

"*We*," she said, kissing him, "are going to have a baby! In America. So hurry up and get well, so we can get out of here."

At a loss for better words, Alexander found a way to ask, "How long have you known?"

"Since December."

He was clammy. "You've known since before you came to the front?"

"Yes."

"You went out on the ice, knowing you were pregnant?"

"Yes."

"You gave me your blood, knowing you were pregnant?"

"Yes." She smiled. "*Yes.*"

Alexander turned his head to the isolation tent, away from the wall, from the chair she was next to, and away from her. "Why didn't you tell me?"

"Shura," she said. "*This* is why I didn't tell you. I know you—you'd be worried frantic about me, especially because you're still not well yourself. You feel like you can't protect me. But I'm fine," she said, smiling. "I'm better than fine. And it's still early. The baby is not due till August."

Alexander put his arm over his eyes. He couldn't look at her. He heard her whisper, "You want to see my breasts again?"

Shaking his head, he said, "I'll sleep now. Come and see me tomorrow." He felt her kiss his forearm. After she left, Alexander was awake until morning.

How could Tania not understand the terrors that haunted him, the fear that clutched his heart when he imagined trying to get through NKVD border troops and hostile Finland with a pregnant wife? Where was her sense, her good judgment?

What am I even thinking? This is the girl who blithely walked 150 kilometers through Manstein's Group Army Nord to bring me money so I could run and leave her. She has no sense at all.

I am *not* getting my wife and baby out of Russia on foot, Alexander said to himself. His thoughts turned to the Fifth Soviet communal apartment, to the filth, to the stench, to the air-raid sirens every morning and night, to the cold. He remembered seeing a young mother last year, sitting in the snow, frozen, holding her frozen infant on her lap, and he trembled. What was worse to him as a man, remaining in the Soviet Union or risking Tatiana's life to get her home?

A soldier, a decorated officer in the largest army in the world, Alexander felt unmanned by his impossible choices.

The next morning when Tatiana came to feed him breakfast, Alexander said quietly, "I hope you know, I hope you understand that I'm not going anywhere with you pregnant."

"What are you talking about? Of course you are."

"Forget it."

"God, Shura, that's why I didn't want to tell you. I know how you get."

"How do I get, Tatiana?" he said hotly. "Tell me, how do I get? I can't *get* out of bed. How am I supposed to get? Lying here powerless, while my wife—"

"You're not powerless!" she exclaimed. "Everything you are, you still remain, even wounded. So don't give me that. This is all temporary. *You* are permanent. So courage, soldier. Look what I found for you—eggs. I have an assurance from Dr. Sayers these are real eggs and not dehydrated. You tell *me.*"

Alexander shuddered as he thought of going from Helsinki to Stockholm in trucks on ice for 500 kilometers under German fire. He wouldn't even look at the eggs she was holding out for him.

He heard her sigh. "Why is this the nature of your beast?" she asked. "Why do you always get like this?"

"How do I get?"

"Like *this*," she said, giving him the fork for the eggs. "Eat, please—"

Alexander threw the fork on the metal tray. "Tania, have an abortion," he said adamantly. "Have Dr. Sayers take care of it. We'll have other babies. We'll have many, many babies, I promise. All we'll do is have babies, we'll be like Catholics, all right, but we can't do what we're planning with you pregnant, we just can't. *I* can't," he added. He took hold of her hand, but she yanked it away and stood up.

"Are you joking?" she said.

"Of course I'm not. Girls have them all the time." He paused. "Dasha had three." Alexander saw by Tatiana's face that she was horrified.

"With *you*?" she asked weakly.

"No, Tatia," he said tiredly, rubbing his eyes. "Not with me."

With a breath of relief but still white, Tatiana whispered, "But I thought abortion has been illegal since 1938?"

"Oh, God!" Alexander exclaimed. "Why are you so naïve?"

Her hands shook as she fought for control, and through her closed teeth she said, "That's right. Yes. Well, perhaps, I could have had three illegal abortions myself before I met you. Perhaps that would have made me more attractive and less naïve in your eyes."

Alexander's heart squeezed. "I'm sorry—I didn't mean that." He paused. She was too far away and too upset for him to take her hand. "I thought Dasha might have told you."

"No, she didn't tell me," Tatiana said in a low, agonized voice. "She never talked to me about those things. And yes, my family protected me as best they could. Still, we lived in close quarters in a communal apartment. I knew that my mother had half a dozen abortions in the mid-thirties, I knew that Nina Iglenko had eight, but that's not even what I'm talking about—"

"So? What's the problem? What are you talking about?"

"Knowing how I feel about you—do you think it's something I could ever do?"

Tightening his lips, Alexander said, "No, of course not. Why *would* you?" He raised his voice. "Why would you ever do anything that would give *me* peace of mind!"

Leaning over him, Tatiana whispered angrily, "You're right. Your peace of mind or your baby. The choice *is* tough." She threw the plate of eggs down on the metal tray and walked away without another word.

When she did not return all day, Alexander concluded that having Tatiana be angry with him was more than he could endure—for a minute, let alone

582

for the sixteen hours it took her to come back. He asked Ina and Dr. Sayers to bring her to him, but apparently she was very busy and could not come. Very late that night she finally returned, bringing with her a piece of white bread with butter. "You're upset with me," Alexander said, taking the bread out of her hands.

"Not upset," she said. "Disappointed."

"That's even worse." Alexander shook his head in resignation. "Tania, look at me." Tatiana raised her eyes to him, and there, around the edges of her ocean current irises, he saw her love for him flow out. "We will do exactly as you want," Alexander said, sighing heavily. "Like always."

Smiling, Tatiana sat on the edge of his bed and took a cigarette from her pocket. "Look what I brought you. Want a quick smoke?"

"No, Tania," said Alexander, reaching for her, bringing her to him. "I want to feel your breasts on my face." He kissed her, undoing her uniform.

"You're not going to recoil in terror, are you?"

"Just come here. Bend over me."

It was dark in the ward, and everyone else was sleeping. Tatiana pulled up her shirt. Alexander lost his breath. She bent over and pressed herself into him. Keeping his eyes open, he cupped her full warm breasts, nesting his face in between them. He inhaled deeply and kissed the white skin in front of her heart. "Oh, Tatiasha . . ."

"Yes?"

"I love you."

"I love you, too, soldier." She lightly rubbed her breasts back and forth across his mouth, his nose, his cheeks. "I'll have to shave you," she whispered. "You're very stubbly."

"And you are very soft," he muttered, his mouth closing around her enlarged nipple. Alexander could tell that Tatiana tried very hard not to moan. Once she moaned, she backed away, pulling her shirt down. "Shura, no, don't excite me. Every one of those men will wake up, I guarantee it. They can smell desire."

"So can I," Alexander said thickly.

All buttoned up and more composed, Tatiana hugged him. "Shura," she whispered, "don't you see? Our baby is a sign from God."

"It is?"

"Absolutely," she said, her face sparkling.

Suddenly Alexander understood. "That's the radiance," he exclaimed. "That's why you're like a flame walking through this hospital. It's the baby!"

"Yes," she said. "This is what is meant for us. Think about Lazarevo—how many times did we make love in those twenty-nine days?"

"I don't know." He smiled. "How many? How many zeros follow the twenty-nine?"

She laughed quietly. "Two or three. We made love to wake the dead, and yet I didn't get pregnant. You come to see me for one weekend, and here I am—how do you say, *up the stick?*"

Alexander laughed loudly. "Thank you for that. But, Tania, I want to remind you, we did make love quite a bit that weekend, too."

"Yes."

They stared at each other for a silent, unsmiling moment. Alexander knew. They had both felt too close to death that gray weekend in Leningrad. And, yet, here it was—

As if to confirm what he was thinking, Tatiana said, "This is God telling us to go. Can't you feel that, too? He is saying, this is your destiny! I will not let anything happen to Tatiana, as long as she has Alexander's baby inside her."

"Oh?" said Alexander, his hands tenderly stroking her stomach. "God is saying that, is He? Why don't you tell that to the woman in the Ladoga truck with you and Dasha, holding her dead baby all the way from the barracks across to Kobona?"

"I feel stronger now than ever," Tatiana said, hugging him. "Where is your famous faith, big man?"

"Tania, have you talked to Dr. Sayers?" Alexander was caressing her hands under his blanket, kneading her fingers, feeling her knuckles, her wrists, her palms.

"Of course. All I do is talk to him, go over all the details. We're waiting for you to walk. Everything is set. He's already filled out my new Red Cross travel documents." She purred, leaning closer to him. "That feels so nice, Shura. I'm going to fall asleep."

"Don't fall asleep. Under what name?"

"Jane Barrington."

"That's nice. Jane Barrington and Tobe Hanssen."

"Tove."

"My mother and a Finn. Some couple we make."

"Don't we?" She half-closed her eyes. "That feels very nice, Shura," she murmured. "Don't stop."

"I *won't* stop," he whispered huskily, gazing at her. *That* made her open her eyes.

A moment. They stared at each other. Remembering. Blink.

Tatiana smiled. "In America can I please carry your name?" she whispered.

"In America I will insist on it." Alexander was thoughtful.

"What's the matter?"

"We don't have passports," he said.

"So? You'll go to the U.S. consulate in Stockholm. We'll be fine."

"I know. We still have to get from Helsinki to Stockholm. We can't stay in Helsinki for a second. It's too dangerous. Crossing the Baltic Sea. It's not going to be easy."

Tatiana grinned. "What were you going to do with your limping demon? Same thing with me." She paused. "*Eugene calls to the wherryman—and he, with daring unconcern is willing, to take him for a quarter-shilling, across that formidable sea.*" Smiling happily, she said, "Your mother, you, your ten thousand dollars will get us back to your America." Both her tiny delicate hands were threaded through his.

Alexander was suffocating under the weight of his love.

"Shura," Tatiana said, her voice tremulous, "remember the day you gave me your Pushkin book? When you fed me in the Summer Garden?"

"Like it was yesterday." Alexander smiled. "It was the night *you* fell in love with *me*."

Tatiana blushed and cleared her throat. "Were you . . . if I weren't such a shy chicken . . . would you have—" She broke off, looking away momentarily.

"What? What?" He squeezed her hand. "Would I have kissed you?"

"Hmm."

"Tania, you were so terrified of me." Alexander shook his head at the memory, his body aching. "I was completely gone for you. Kissed you? I would have ravished you right on the bench by the child-eating Saturn if you had given me half a sign."

7

Alexander got stronger every day. He could get up and stand near his bed. It still hurt him to be upright, but he was off morphine completely, and now his back throbbed from morning until night, reminding him of his mortality. He was carving constantly. He had just carved a cradle out of another piece of wood. Soon, soon, he kept saying to himself. He wanted to be moved over into the convalescent ward, but Tatiana talked him out of it. She said his location and care were too good to give up his place in critical.

"Remember," Tatiana said to him one afternoon as they were both standing by his bed, his arm around her. "You have to get better so that no one thinks you're getting better. Or before you know it, they'll send you back to the front with your stupid mortar." She smiled up at him.

Alexander removed his arm. He saw Dimitri walking toward them. "Courage, Tania," he whispered.

"What?"

"Tatiana! Alexander!" Dimitri exclaimed. "No, how incredible is this? The three of us together again. If only Dasha were here."

Alexander and Tatiana said nothing. They did not look at each other.

"Tania, how are the terminal cases coming along? I just got you some more white sheets."

"Thanks, Dimitri."

"Oh, sure. Alexander, here are some cigarettes for you. Don't worry about paying me. I know you probably don't have any money on you. I can get your money and bring it to you—"

"Don't worry, Dimitri."

"It's not a problem." He stood at the foot of Alexander's bed, his eyes darting from Alexander to Tatiana. "So, Tania, what are you doing here in critical care? I thought you were in the terminal ward."

"I am. But I see my crossover patients, too. Leo in bed number thirty used to be terminal. Now he is always asking for me."

Dimitri smiled. "Tania, not just Leo. *Everybody* is asking for you." Tatiana didn't say anything. Neither did Alexander, who sat down on his bed. Dimitri continued to study them. "Listen, it was good to see you both. Alexander, I'll come by and visit you tomorrow, all right? Tania, you want to walk me out?"

"No, I have to change Alexander's dressing."

"Oh. It's just that Dr. Sayers was looking for you. 'Where is *my* Tania?' Dr. Sayers said." Dimitri smiled warmly. "Those were his exact words. You're getting to be quite friendly with him, aren't you?" He raised his eyebrows to her. "You know what they say about those Americans."

Tatiana did not nod, did not blink. She just turned to Alexander and said, "Come on, lie down." Alexander did not move.

"Tania, did you hear me?" Dimitri asked.

"I heard you!" Tatiana said, not looking at Dimitri. "If you see Dr. Sayers, you can tell him I'll be with him as soon as I can."

After Dimitri left, Alexander and Tatiana looked at each other. "What are you thinking?" he asked her.

"That I need to change your dressing and go. Lie down."

"Do you want to know what I'm thinking?"

"Absolutely not," she replied.

Lying down on his stomach, Alexander said, "Tania, where is the rucksack with my things?"

"I don't know," she said. "Why? What do you need it for?"

"It was on my back when I got hit . . ."

"It wasn't on your back when we got to you. It's probably lost, honey."

"Yes . . ." he drew out. "But usually the rear units clean up once the battle is over. Pick up things like that. Can you ask around for it?"

"Of course," she said, unwrapping his bandages. "I'll ask Colonel Stepanov." She paused, and Alexander heard her purr. "You know, Shura, the only thing I want to do when I see your back is play rail tracks, rail tracks." She kissed his bare shoulder.

"The only thing *I* want to do when I see your back," he said, closing his eyes, "is play rail tracks, rail tracks."

* * *

Later that night when she was sitting by him, Alexander said to her, "Tatiana, you have to promise me—God help me—that if something happens to me, you will still go." He held on to her when he said it.

"Don't be ridiculous. What can happen to you?" She didn't look at him when she said it.

"Are you trying to be brave?"

"Not at all," she said. "As soon as you're fit, we're leaving. Dr. Sayers is ready to go anytime. In fact, he is itching to go. He is a big grumbler. Keeps complaining about everything. Doesn't like the cold, doesn't like the help, doesn't like—" Tatiana stopped. "So what are you talking about? What can happen? I won't let you go back to the front. And I won't leave without you."

"That's what I'm talking about. Of course you will."

"Of course I *won't*."

Alexander took her hand. "Now listen to me—"

Tatiana moved to get up from him, turning her head. "I don't want to listen." He wouldn't let her hand go. "Alexander, please don't scare me," she said. "I'm trying to be so brave. Please," Tatiana said calmly, her breath shallow.

"Tania, many things can go wrong." He paused. "You know that there is always the danger I will be arrested."

She nodded. "I know. But, if you're taken by Mekhlis's henchmen, I will wait."

"Wait for *what*?" he exclaimed in frustration. Alexander had learned the hard way that the best he could hope for was that Tatiana would agree with him. If she had her own opinion, he didn't have an icy hope of talking her out of it.

His emotion must have shown on his face, because she took both his dark war-beaten hands into her flawless white ones, pressed them to her lips and said, "Wait for you." Then she tried to disentangle herself from him. He wasn't having any of it. Pulling her off the chair, he brought her to sit next to him on the bed. "Wait for me *where*?" he asked.

"In Leningrad. In my apartment. Inga and Stan have left. I have two rooms. I will wait. And when you come back, I will be there with your baby."

"The Soviet council will take the hallway and the room with the stove away."

"Then I will wait in the room that's left."

"For how long?"

She looked over at the other sleeping patients, at the darkened windows. At anything but him. The hospital room was quiet, with no sound except for his breathing, except for hers. "I will wait as long as it takes," she said.

"Oh, for God's sake! You would rather be an old maid in a cold room without plumbing than make yourself a better life?"

"Yes," she said. "There is no other life for me, so you can just forget it."

Alexander whispered, "Tania, please . . ." He couldn't continue. "And what about when Mekhlis comes for *you*? What are you going to do then?"

"I'll go where they send me. I'll go to Kolyma," she said. "I'll go to Taymir Peninsula. Eventually Communism will fall—"

"You sure about this?"

"Yes. Eventually there won't be any more people left to reconstruct. And then they'll let me out."

"Dear sweet Jesus," Alexander whispered. "It's not just you anymore. You have to think about our baby!"

"What are you even talking about? Dr. Sayers is not going to take me without you. I have no right to—no claim on—America," Tatiana said. "Alexander, I will go anywhere in the world with you. You want to go to America? I say yes. You want to go to Australia? Yes, I say. Mongolia? The Gobi Desert? Dagestan? Lake Baikal? Germany? The cold side of hell? I say, when are we leaving? Anywhere you go—I will go with *you*. But if you are staying, then I'm staying, too. I'm not leaving my baby's father in the Soviet Union."

Leaning over an overwhelmed Alexander, Tatiana pressed her breasts into his face, kissing his head. Then she sat back and kissed his shaking fingers. "What did you say to me in Leningrad? 'What kind of a life can I build,' you said, 'knowing I have left you to die—or to rot—in the Soviet Union?' I'm quoting *you* back to you. Those were *your* words." She smiled. "And on this one point I will have to agree with you." She nodded and said softly, "If I left you, no matter which road I would take, with ponderous clatter indeed, the Bronze Horseman would pursue me all through that long night into *my* own maddening dust."

Alexander said with emotion, "Tatiana—it's war. All around us is war." He couldn't look at her. "Men die in war."

A tear escaped Tatiana's eye, no matter how strong she tried to be. "Please don't die," she whispered. "I don't think I can bury you. I already buried everyone else."

"How can I die," Alexander said, his voice breaking, "when you have poured your immortal blood into me?"

And then Dimitri came one cold morning, holding Alexander's rucksack in his hands. He was limping badly on his right leg. The errand boy for the generals, the worthless lackey, constantly shuffling cigarettes and vodka and books between camps and tents in the rear, the runner who refused to bear arms, Dimitri hobbled forward, handing Alexander the rucksack. "Oh, so it *was* found," Alexander said steadily. "What happened?"

"Wouldn't you know it? Some stupidity at the embankment. Some guys . . . I don't know, they were pissed off. Look at my face."

Alexander saw the bruises.

"I was charging too much for smokes, they said. Take it, I said, take it all. They did. Beat the shit out of me anyway." Dimitri smirked. "Well, they won't be laughing for long." He came and sat in the chair under the window. "Tatiana did a marvelous job on me. Fixed me right up." Something in Dimitri's voice twisted Alexander's stomach. "She's marvelous, isn't she?"

"Yes," said Alexander. "She is a good nurse."

"Good nurse, good woman, good—" Dimitri broke off.

"That's great," said Alexander. "Thanks for my ruck."

"Oh, sure." Dimitri got up to go and then, almost as an afterthought, sat back down and said, "I wanted to make sure you had all you needed in your ruck: your books, your pen and paper. As it turned out, you didn't have any pen or paper, so it was a good thing I checked, because I put some in for you. In case you wanted to write letters." He smiled pleasantly. "I also added some cigarettes and a new lighter."

Holding his rucksack, Alexander, with darkening eyes, said, "You looked through my things?" The twisting in his stomach intensified.

"Oh, just to be helpful." Dimitri again made as if to go. "But you know . . ." He turned back. "I found something very interesting in it."

Alexander turned his face away. Tatiana's letters he had reluctantly burned. But there was one thing he could not burn. One beacon of hope for light that he continued to carry with him. "Dimitri," Alexander said, throwing the rucksack by the side of his bed and crossing his arms in silent defiance, "what do you want?"

Picking up the rucksack, Dimitri, in a friendly, polite manner, unbuttoned the flap and pulled out Tatiana's white dress with red roses.

"Look what I found at the very bottom."

Alexander said, "So?" His voice was calm.

"So? Well, you're so right. Why shouldn't you be carrying around a dress owned by your dead fiancée's sister?"

"What's the surprise to you, Dimitri? That you found the dress? Can't be *that* much of a surprise, can it?" Alexander said acidly. "You *were* going through my personal belongings looking for it."

"Well, yes and no," Dimitri said jovially. "I was a little surprised, I admit. A little taken aback."

"Taken aback? By what?"

"Well, I thought, this is so interesting. A whole dress, and there is Tatiana here at the front, working side by side with a Red Cross doctor, and there is Alexander in the same hospital. I suspected it was not a coincidence. I always thought you had feelings for each other." He glanced at Alexander. "Always, you know. From the beginning. So then I went to Colonel Stepanov, who remembered me from the old days and was very warm to me. I really like that man. I told him that I would be glad to bring you your pay so you could buy tobacco and papers and extra butter and some vodka, and he sent me to the

CO adjutant, who gave me five hundred rubles, and when I expressed surprise that all you were getting was five hundred rubles being a *major* and all, do you know what the adjutant told me?"

With a grinding of his teeth to lessen the throbbing in his temples, Alexander said slowly, "What did he tell you?"

"That you were sending the rest of your money to a Tatiana Metanova on Fifth Soviet!"

"I am, yes."

"Absolutely, why not? So I went back to Colonel Stepanov and said, 'Colonel, isn't it fantastic that our wanton Alexander has finally found himself a *nice* girl, like our Nurse Metanova,' and the colonel said he had been surprised himself that you got married in Molotov on your summer furlough and told no one."

Alexander said nothing.

"Yes!" exclaimed Dimitri in a frank and cheerful manner. "I said that *was* quite surprising because I was your best friend, and even I didn't know, and the colonel agreed that you were indeed a very secretive fellow, and I said, '*Oh, you have no idea, sir.*' "

Alexander looked away from Dimitri, sitting in the chair, and looked at the other soldiers lying on the beds. He wondered if he could get up. Could he get up? Walk around? What could he do?

Dimitri got up. "Listen, it's great! I just wanted to say congratulations. I'm going to go find Tania now and congratulate her."

Tatiana came to Alexander later that afternoon. After she fed him, she went to get a pail of warm water and some soap. "Tania, don't carry that," he said. "It's too heavy for you."

"Stop it," she said, smiling. "I'm carrying your baby. You think a *backet* is too heavy for me?"

They didn't speak much. Tatiana washed Alexander and shaved him with a razor and then dried his face. He kept his eyes closed so she wouldn't see through him. Every once in a while Alexander smelled her warm breath on him, and every once in a while her lips touched his eyebrows or his fingers. He felt her stroking his face and heard her sigh.

"Shura," she said heavily, "I saw Dimitri today."

"Yes." It was not a question.

"Yes." She paused. "He was . . . he told me you told him we got married. He said he was happy for us . . ." She sighed. "I guess it was inevitable he was going to find out sooner or later."

"Yes, Tatiana," said Alexander. "We did as well as we could hiding ourselves from Dimitri."

"Listen, I may be wrong, but he didn't seem to have as much of his usual nervous tension. As if he really didn't care about you and me anymore. What do you think?" she asked hopefully.

You think maybe this war has made him into a human being? Alexander wanted to ask her. *You think this war is a school for humanity, and Dimitri is now ready to graduate with honors?* But then Alexander opened his eyes and saw Tatiana's frightened expression. "I think you're right," he said quietly. "I don't think he cares about you and me anymore."

Tatiana cleared her throat and touched Alexander's clean-shaven face. Leaning closer to him, she whispered, "Do you suppose you can get up soon? I don't want to rush you. I saw you yesterday trying to get around. It's painful for you to stand? Your back hurts? It's healing, Shura. You're doing great. As soon as you're ready, we'll go. And we'll never have to see him again."

Alexander looked at her for interminable minutes.

Before he opened his mouth, Tatiana said, "Shura, don't worry. My eyes are open. I see Dimitri for what he is."

"Do you?"

"Yes. Because like all of us, he, too, is the sum of his parts."

"He cannot be redeemed, Tania. Not even by you."

"You don't think so?" She tried to smile.

Alexander squeezed her hand. "He is exactly what he wants to be. How can he be redeemed when he has constructed his life on what he believes is the only way to live it? Not your way, not my way, *his* way. He has built himself on lies and deceit, on manipulation and malice, on contempt for me and disrespect for you."

"I know."

"He has found himself a dark corner of the universe and wants us all there with him."

"I know."

"Be very careful with him, all right? And tell him nothing."

"All right."

"What would it take for you, Tatiana, to reject him, to turn your back on him? To say, I cannot take his hand because he does not want salvation. What?"

Her thoughts trickled out from her eyes. "Oh, he'll *want* salvation, Shura. He'll just have no hope of it."

Walking with the help of a cane, Dimitri came to see Alexander the next day. This is becoming my life, Alexander thought. There is fighting across the river, there is healing in the next room, the generals are making plans, the trains are bringing food into Leningrad, the Germans are slaughtering us from Sinyavino Heights, Dr. Sayers is getting ready to leave the Soviet Union, Tatiana sits with the terminal soldiers, growing life inside her, and I lie here in my crib and get my bedding changed and watch the world rush by me. Watch my minutes rush by me. Alexander was so fed up that he pulled back his covers and got out of bed. He stood up and began unhooking his IV bag when Ina ran up and laid him back down, muttering that he'd better never try that again. "Or I'll tell Tatiana," she whispered, leaving Alexander alone with Dimitri, who sank down in the chair.

"Alexander, I need to talk to you. Are you strong enough to listen?"

"Yes, Dimitri, I'm strong enough to listen," said Alexander, with a supreme effort turning his head in Dimitri's direction. He could not meet his eyes.

"Listen, I really am sincerely happy that you and Tania got married. I'm past bad feeling. Honestly. But, Alexander, as you know, there is one thing that's left unfinished with us."

"Yes," Alexander replied.

"Tania, she's very good, she keeps her composure well. I think I've underestimated her. She is less of a pushover than I first thought."

Dimitri had no idea.

"I know you two are planning something. I know it. I feel it in my heart. I tried to get her to talk to me. She kept saying she didn't know what I was talking about. But I know!" Dimitri sounded excited. "I know *you*, Alexander Barrington, and so I'm asking you if perhaps there is room for little old me in your plans."

"I don't know what you're talking about," said Alexander steadfastly, thinking, there was once a time I had no one else to trust but this man. I put my life in this man's hands. "Dimitri, I have no plans."

"Hmm. Yes. But you see, I understand so many things now," Dimitri said with an unctuous smile. "Tatiana is the reason you've been dragging your feet on running." He paused. "Wanted to work out a way to run with her? Or didn't want to desert and leave her behind? Either way I don't blame you." He cleared his throat. "But now I say we all must go together."

"We don't have any plans," said Alexander. "But if something changes, I will let you know."

An hour later Dimitri limped back, but this time with Tatiana. He sat her down in the chair while he hunkered down close to them on his haunches. "Tania, I need you to talk some sense into your wounded husband," Dimitri said. "Explain to him that all I want is for you two to get me out of the Soviet Union. That's all I've ever wanted. To get out of the Soviet Union. I'm getting very jittery, very nervous, you see, because I can't take the chance that you two will run off and leave me here. In the middle of war. You understand?"

Alexander and Tatiana said nothing.

Alexander looked at his blanket. Tatiana stared straight at Dimitri. And it was when he saw Tania looking unflinchingly at Dimitri that Alexander felt stronger and stared at Dimitri, too.

"Tania, I'm on your side," Dimitri said, "I don't want any harm to come either to you or to Alexander. Just the opposite." He smiled. "I wish you the best of luck. It's so hard for two people to find happiness. I know. I've tried.

That you two somehow managed—I don't know how—is a miracle. Now all I want is a chance for myself. I just want you to help me."

"Self-preservation," said Alexander, "as an inalienable right."

"What?" said Dimitri.

"Nothing," replied Alexander.

Tatiana said, "Dimitri, I really don't know what this has to do with *me*."

"Why, *everything*, dearest Tanechka, why, it's got everything in the world to do with you. Unless, of course, it's the smooth, healthy American doctor you're planning to run away with and not your injured husband. You've been making plans to go with Sayers when he returns to Helsinki, haven't you?"

No one spoke.

"I don't have time for these games," Dimitri snapped coldly, rising to his feet and leaning on his cane. "Tania, I'm talking to you. Either you take me with *you* or I'm afraid I'm going to have to keep Alexander here in the Soviet Union with *me*."

Her hand still in Alexander's, Tatiana sat stoically in her chair and then looked at Alexander and raised her shoulders to form a faint question.

Alexander squeezed her hand so hard that she emitted a tiny cry.

"There, there," exclaimed Dimitri. "That's the moment I want to see. She convinces you, miraculously seeing everything. Tatiana, how do you do that? How do you have such an uncanny ability to see everything? Your husband, who's got less of that ability, struggles against you but in the end gives in because he knows it's the only way."

Alexander and Tatiana didn't say a word. He relaxed his hold on her hand, which remained nested in his.

Dimitri folded his arms and waited. "I'm not leaving here until I hear an answer. Tania, what do you say? Alexander has been my friend for six years. I care for both of you. I don't want any trouble." Dimitri rolled his eyes. "Believe me—I *hate* trouble. All I want is to have a small portion of what you are planning for yourselves. That's not too much to ask, is it? I want a tiny piece of it. Don't you feel you'll be selfish, Tania, if you don't allow me a chance for a new life, too? Come on, now—you, who gave away your oatmeal to a starving Nina Iglenko last year, surely you aren't going to deny me so little when"—and here he looked at her and Alexander—"you have so much?"

Pain and anger tripping over each other in their race to his already embattled heart, Alexander said, "Tania, don't listen to him. Dimitri, leave her alone. This is between us. This has nothing to do with her." Dimitri was quiet. Tatiana was quiet, her fingers rubbing the inside of Alexander's palm, thoughtfully, intently, rhythmically. She opened her mouth to speak. "Don't say a *word*, Tatiana," said Alexander.

"Say the word, Tatiana," Dimitri said. "It's up to you. But please, let me hear your answer. Because I don't have much time."

Alexander watched Tatiana rise to her feet. "Dimitri," Tatiana said without blinking, "woe to him who is alone when he falls, for he has not another to pick him up."

Dimitri shrugged. "By that I take it to mean that you—" He broke off. "What? What are you saying? Is that a yes or a no?"

Her hand holding Alexander's tightly, Tatiana said, barely audible, "My husband made you a promise. And he always keeps his word."

"Yes!" Dimitri exclaimed, springing to her. Alexander watched Tatiana pull sharply away.

Tatiana spoke softly. "Every kindness is repaid by good people," she said. "Dimitri, I will tell you of our plans later. But you need to be ready at a moment's notice. Understand?"

"I'm ready this moment," Dimitri said with excitement. "And I mean that. I want to leave as soon as possible." He extended his left hand to Alexander, who turned his face away, still holding on to Tatiana. He had no intention of shaking hands with Dimitri.

It was a pale Tatiana who brought their hands together. "It's all right," she said, her voice quavering slightly. "It'll be all right."

Dimitri left.

"Shura, what could we do?" Tatiana said while feeding him. "It will have to work. It changes things a little bit. But not much. We'll figure it out."

Alexander turned his gaze to her.

She nodded. "He wants to survive more than anything else. You told me so yourself."

But what did you tell *me*, Tatiana? thought Alexander. What did you tell *me* up on the roof of St. Isaac's under the black Leningrad sky?

"We'll take him. He'll leave us alone. You'll see. Just please get better soon."

"Let's go, Tania," said Alexander. "Tell Dr. Sayers that whenever he's ready to leave, I'll make myself ready."

Tatiana left.

A day passed.

Dimitri returned.

He sat down in the chair next to Alexander, who did not look his way. He was staring into the middle distance, into the long distance, into the short distance of his brown wool blanket, trying to recall the last name of the Moscow residence hotel he had lived in with his mother and father. The hotel kept regularly changing names. It had been a source of confusion and hilarity for Alexander, who was now deliberately focusing his mind away from Tatiana and away from the person sitting in the chair not a meter away from him. Oh, no, thought Alexander, with a stab of pain.

He remembered the last name of the hotel.

It was *Kirov*.

Dimitri cleared his throat. Alexander waited.

"Alexander, can we talk? This is very important."

"It's all important," stated Alexander. "All I do is talk. What?"

"It's about Tatiana."

"What about her?" Alexander stared at his IV. How long would it take him to disconnect it? Would he bleed? He looked around the ward. It was just after lunch, and the other wounded were either sleeping or reading. The shift nurse was sitting by the door reading herself. Alexander wondered where Tatiana was. He didn't need the IV. Tatiana kept it on him to force him to remain in the critical ward, to keep his bed. No. Don't think about Tatiana. Pulling himself up, Alexander sat upright against the wall.

"Alexander, I know how you feel about her—"

"Do you?"

"Of course—"

"Somehow I doubt it. What about her?"

"She is sick."

Alexander said nothing.

"Yes. Sick. You don't know what I know. You don't see what I see. She is a ghost walking around this hospital. She is fainting constantly. The other day she lay in a faint in the snow for I don't know how long. A lieutenant had to get her up. We brought her to Dr. Sayers. She put on a brave face—"

"How do you know she was in the snow?"

"I heard the story. I hear everything. Also I see her in the terminal ward. She holds on to the wall when she walks. She told Dr. Sayers she was not getting enough food."

"And you know this how?"

"Sayers told me."

"You and Dr. Sayers are getting to be good friends, I see."

"No. I just bring him bandages, iodine, medical supplies from across the lake. He never seems to have enough. We talk for a few minutes."

"What's your point?"

"Did you know she was not feeling well?"

Alexander was thoughtfully grim. He knew why Tatiana was not getting enough food, and he knew why she was fainting. But the last thing he was going to do was trust Dimitri with anything about Tatiana. Alexander kept customarily quiet for a moment and then said, "Dimitri, do you have a *point?*"

"Yes, I have a point." Dimitri lowered his voice and pulled the chair closer to the bed. "What we're planning . . . it's dangerous. It requires physical strength, courage, fortitude."

Alexander turned his head to Dimitri. "Yes?" he said, surprised that words like "fortitude" could have come from Dimitri's mouth. "So?"

"How do you think Tatiana will manage through it all?"

"What are you talking about—"

"Alexander! Listen to me for a second. Wait, before you say more. Listen. She is weak, and we have a very hard road ahead of us. Even with Sayers's help. Do you know there are six checkpoints between here and Lisiy Nos? Six. One syllable out of her at any of them and we're all dead. Alexander . . ." Dimitri paused. "She can't come."

Keeping his voice low—it was the only way he could keep it—Alexander said, "I am not having this ludicrous conversation."

"You are not listening."

"You're right, I'm not."

"Stop being so obstinate. You know I am right—"

"I know no such thing!" Alexander exclaimed, his fists clenching. "I know that without her—" He broke off. What was he doing? Was he trying to convince Dimitri? To keep from shouting required an effort out of Alexander he just wasn't prepared to make. "I'm growing tired," he said loudly. "We'll finish this another time."

"There *is* no other time!" Dimitri hissed. "Keep your voice down. We're supposed to be going in forty-eight hours. And I'm telling you I don't want to hang because *you* can't see clear through the day."

"Crystal clear, Dimitri," snapped Alexander. "She'll be fine. And she *will* come with us."

"She collapses here after a six-hour day."

"Six-hour? Where have you been? She is here twenty-four hours a day. She doesn't sit in a truck, she doesn't sit and have cigarettes and vodka on her job. She sleeps on cardboard, and she eats what the soldiers don't finish, and she washes her face in the snow. Don't tell me about her day."

"What if there is a border incident? What if, despite all of Sayers's efforts, we're stopped, interrogated? You and I will have to use our weapons. We'll have to stand and fight."

"We'll do what we have to." Alexander glared at Dimitri's cane, at his bruised face, at his hunched body.

"Yes, but what will *she* do?"

"She'll do what she has to."

"She is going to faint! She is going to collapse in the snow, and you won't know whether to kill the border troops or help her up."

"I will do both."

"She can't run, she can't shoot, she can't fight. She'll swoon at the first sign of trouble, and believe me, there is always trouble."

"Can *you* run, Dimitri?" Alexander asked, unable to keep the hate out of his voice.

"Yes! I'm still a soldier."

"What about the doctor? He can't fight either."

"He's a man! And frankly, I'm less worried about him either way—"

"You're worried about Tatiana? That's good to hear."

"I'm worried about what she will do."

"Ah, that *is* a fine difference."

"I'm worried that you will be so busy fretting about her, you will screw up, make stupid mistakes. She will slow you down, make you think twice about taking the kind of chances we might need to take. The Lisiy Nos forest checkpoint is poorly defended, not *un*defended."

"You are right. We might have to fight for our freedom."

"So you agree?"

"No."

"Alexander, listen to me. This is our last chance. I know it. This is a perfect plan; it could work so well. But she will lead us to ruin. She is not up to it. Don't be stupid now when we are so close. This is it." Dimitri smiled. "This is what we've been waiting for! There are no more trial runs, there are no more tomorrows, no more next times. This is it."

"Yes," said Alexander. "This is it." Closing his eyes briefly, he fought an impulse to keep them closed.

"So listen to me—"

"I will not listen."

"You *will* listen!" exclaimed Dimitri. "You and I have been planning this a long time. Here is our chance! And I'm not saying leave Tania in the Soviet Union for good. Not at all. I'm saying let us, two men, do what we have to do to get out. Get out safely and, most importantly, alive! You're no good to her dead, and I'm not going to enjoy America if I'm dead myself. Alive, Alexander. Plus, to hide in the swamps—"

"We're driving to Helsinki in a truck. What swamps?"

"If we need to, I said. Three men and a frail girl, we're a crowd. We're not hiding out. We're asking to be caught. If something were to happen to Sayers, if Sayers were to get killed—"

"Why would Sayers get killed? He's a Red Cross doctor." Alexander studied Dimitri intensely.

"I don't know. But if we had to make it by ourselves across the Baltic—on ice, on foot, hiding out in convoy trucks—well, two men can do it, but three people? We will be too easily noticed. Too easily stopped. And she won't make it."

"She made it through the blockade. She made it through the Volga ice. She made it through Dasha. She will make it," said Alexander, but his heart was burning with uncertainty. The dangers Dimitri was pointing out were so close to Alexander's own anxieties for Tatiana, it was brutalizing his stomach. "All the things you say may be true," he continued with great effort, "but you're forgetting two very important things. What do you think will happen to her here once I'm reported missing?"

"To her? Nothing. Her name is still Tatiana Metanova." Dimitri nodded

597

slyly. "You have been very careful to keep your marriage hidden. That'll help you now."

"It won't help *her*." Alexander stopped.

"No one will know."

"You're wrong," said Alexander. "*I* will know." He gritted his teeth to keep the groan of pain from escaping his throat.

"Yes, but you'll be in *America*. You'll be back home."

Alexander spoke in a flat voice. "She cannot remain behind."

"She can. She'll be fine. Alexander, she's never known anything but this life—"

"Neither have you!"

Dimitri went on. "She'll continue here as if she'd never met you—"

"How?"

Dimitri laughed. "I know you think a lot of yourself, but she will get over you. Others have. I know she probably cares for you very much—but with time she'll meet someone else, and she'll be fine."

"Stop being an idiot!" Alexander said. "She'll be arrested in three days. The wife of a deserter. Three days. And you know it. Stop talking horseshit."

"No one will know who she is."

"*You* found out!"

Ignoring Alexander, Dimitri continued calmly, "Tatiana Metanova will go back to Grechesky Hospital and will go on with her life in Leningrad. And if you still want her when you're settled in America, after the war is over, you can send her a formal letter of invitation, asking her to come to Boston to visit a sick and dying distant aunt. She will come by proper methods, if she can, by train, by ship. Think of this as a temporary separation, until there is a better time for her. For all of us."

Alexander rubbed the bridge of his nose with his left hand. Somebody come and rescue me from this hell, he thought. The short hairs on his neck stood on end. He breathed more erratically. "Dimitri!" said Alexander, staring straight at him. "You have a chance, for the second time in your life, to do something decent—take it. The first time was when you helped me to see my father. What do you care if she comes with us?"

"I have to think of myself, Alexander. I cannot spend all my time thinking about protecting *your* wife."

"How much time have you spent thinking about that?" Alexander exclaimed. "You have always thought only of yourself—"

"Unlike, say, you?" Dimitri laughed.

"Unlike anyone else. Come with us. She extended her hand to you."

"To protect *you*."

"Yes. It doesn't make her hand any less extended. Take it. She will get us out. We will all be free. You will have the one thing you care about the most—your free life away from war. You do care about that the most, don't you?" Tania's St. Isaac's words swam by Alexander. *He covets from you most what you want most.* But Alexander would not be defeated. *He will never take it all from you, Alexander,* his Tatiana had said to him. *He will never have that much power.* "You will have your free life—because of her. We will not perish—because of her."

"We'll all be killed—because of her."

"I guarantee—you will not perish. Take this chance, have your life. I'm not denying you what is rightfully yours. I said I would get you out, and I will. Tania is very strong, and she will not let us down. You'll see. She will not falter; she will not fail. You have nothing to do but say yes. She and I will do the rest. You said yourself, this is our last chance. I agree. I feel that more now than ever."

"I bet you do," Dimitri said.

Trying to hide his desperate anger, Alexander said, "Let something else guide you! This war has brought you inside yourself, you have forgotten other people. Remember *her.* Once. You know that if she stays here, she will die. Save her, Dimitri." Alexander almost said, *please.*

"If she comes with us, we will all die," Dimitri said coldly. "I'm convinced of it."

Alexander turned his body forward and faced the middle distance once again. His eyes glazed over, cleared, glazed over.

Darkness engulfed him.

Dimitri spoke. "Alexander—think of it as dying at the front. If you had died out on the ice, she would have had to find a way to continue living in the Soviet Union, wouldn't she? Well, it's the same thing."

"It's all the difference in the world." Alexander looked into his stiffening hands. Because now there is light in front of her.

"It is no difference to her at all. One way or the other she is without you."

"No."

"She is a small price to pay for *America!*" Dimitri exclaimed.

Shuddering, Alexander made no reply, his heart pumping out of his chest. *The Fontanka Bridge, the granite parapets, Tatiana on her knees.*

"She will doom us all."

"Dimitri, I already said no," he said, steel in his voice.

Dimitri narrowed his eyes. "Are you deliberately not understanding me? She *can't* come."

I am just a means to an end, she had said. *I am just ammunition.*

Alexander laughed. "Finally! I was wondering how long it would take you to issue your useless threats. You say she can't come?"

"No, she can't."

"That's fine," said Alexander with a short nod. "I'm not going either. The whole thing is off. It's over. Dr. Sayers is leaving for Helsinki immediately. In three days I'm going back to the front. Tania will return to Leningrad."

Steadying his loathing stare on Dimitri, he said, "No one is going. You're dismissed, Private. Our meeting is finished."

Dimitri looked at Alexander with cold surprise. "Are you telling me you will not go without her?"

"Have you *not* been listening?"

"I see." Dimitri paused, rubbing his hands. He leaned over, propping himself on Alexander's bed as he spoke. "You underestimate me, Alexander. I can see you will not listen to reason. That's too bad. Perhaps, then, what I should do is go and talk to Tania, explain the situation to her. She is much more reasonable. Once Tania sees that her husband is in *grave* danger, why, I am certain she herself will *offer* to stay behind—" Dimitri didn't finish.

Alexander grabbed Dimitri's arm. Dimitri yelped and threw his other hand up, but it was too late, Alexander had them both.

"Understand this," said Alexander as his thumb and forefinger tightened in a twisting vise around Dimitri's wrist. "I don't give a fuck if you talk to Tania, to Stepanov, to Mekhlis, or to the whole Soviet Union. Tell them anything! I am not leaving without her. If she stays, I stay." And with a savage thrust, Alexander ruptured the ulnar bone in Dimitri's forearm. Even through the red of his fury Alexander heard the snap. It sounded like the ax crashing against the pliant pine in Lazarevo. Dimitri screamed. Alexander did not let go. "You underestimate *me*, you fucking bastard!" he said, jerking the wrist violently again and again until the broken bone tore out of Dimitri's skin.

Dimitri continued to scream. Clenching his fist, Alexander punched Dimitri in the face, and the uppercut blow would have driven the fractured nasal bone into Dimitri's frontal lobe had the impact not been weakened by an orderly who had grabbed Alexander's arm, who literally threw himself on Alexander and yelled, "Stop it! What are you doing? Let go, let go!"

Panting, Alexander shoved Dimitri away, and Dimitri slumped to the floor. "Get off me," Alexander said loudly to the stunned and grumbling orderly. As soon as the man got off him, Alexander started wiping his hands. He had yanked the IV right out of the vein, which was now dripping blood between his fingers. So it does bleed, he thought.

"What in the world happened here?" yelled the nurse, running up. "What kind of awful situation is this? The private comes for a visit, and what do you do?"

"Next time don't let him through," Alexander said, throwing off his blankets and getting out of bed.

"Get back into bed! My orders are that you don't get out of bed under any circumstances. Wait till Ina comes back. I never work the critical ward. Why does something always happen on *my* shift?"

After a commotion that lasted a good half hour, a bleeding and unconscious Dimitri was removed from the floor, and the orderly cleaned up the mess, complaining that he already had plenty to do without the wounded making more wounded out of perfectly healthy men.

"You call him perfectly healthy?" said Alexander. "Did you see his limp? Did you see his pulverized face? Ask around. This isn't the first time he's been assaulted. And I guarantee it won't be the last."

But Alexander knew: he had not merely assaulted Dimitri. Had he not been stopped, Alexander would have killed Dimitri with his bare hands.

Alexander slept, woke up, looked around the ward.

It was early evening. Ina was at her station by the door, chatting to three civilian men. Alexander stared at the civilian men. That didn't take long, he thought.

Motionless and alone, he remained with the rucksack on his lap, both of his hands inside, on the white dress with red roses. Alexander finally had the answer to his question.

He knew at what price Tatiana.

It was Colonel Stepanov who came to see him later that evening, eyes sunk deep into his ashen face. Alexander saluted his commander, who sat down heavily in the chair and said quietly, "Alexander, I almost don't know how to say this to you. I should not be here. I'm here not as your commanding officer, understand, but as someone who—"

Alexander interrupted him gently. "Sir," he said, "your very presence is a balm to my soul. More than you know. I know why you're here."

"You do?"

"Yes."

"Then it's true? General Govorov came to me tonight and said that Mekhlis"—Stepanov seemed to *spit* the word out—"approached him with a slew of information that you have previously escaped from prison as a foreign provocateur? As an *American?*" Stepanov laughed. "How can that be? I said it was ridiculous—"

Alexander said, "Sir, I have proudly served the Red Army for nearly six years."

"You have been an exemplary soldier, Major," said Stepanov. "I told them that. I told them it couldn't possibly be true. But as you know—" Stepanov broke off. "The accusation is all. You remember Meretskov? He's now commanding the Volkhov front, but nine months ago he was sitting in the NKVD cellars waiting for a wall to become available."

"I know about Meretskov. How much time do you think I have?"

Stepanov was quiet. "They will come for you in the night," he said at last. "I don't know if you're familiar with their operations—"

"Unfortunately, very familiar, sir," replied Alexander, not looking at Stepanov. "It's all about stealth and cover-up. I didn't know they had the facilities here in Morozovo."

"Primitive, but yes. They have them everywhere. You're too high up, though. They'll most likely send you across the lake to Volkhov." He spoke in a whisper.

601

Across the lake. "Thank you, sir." He managed to smile at his commanding officer. "Do you think they'll promote me to lieutenant colonel first?"

Stepanov breathed out a choking gasp. "Of all my men I had hoped the most for you, Major."

Alexander shook his head. "I had the least chance, sir. Please, do me a favor. If you yourself are questioned about me, understand"—he struggled for his words—"that despite your valor, there are some battles that are lost from the start."

"Yes, Major."

"As long as you understand that, you will not waste a second's breath defending my honor or my army record. Distance yourself and retreat, sir." Alexander let his gaze drop. "And take all your weapons with you."

Stepanov stood.

The unspoken remained between them.

Alexander couldn't think of himself, couldn't think of Stepanov. He had to ask about the unspoken. "Do you know if there was any mention of my . . ." He couldn't continue.

Stepanov understood regardless. "No," he said quietly. "But it's just a matter of time."

Thank God. So Dimitri didn't want them both. What he wanted was for them not to have each other, but he still wanted to save his own skin. *He will never take all from you, Alexander.* There was hope.

Alexander heard Stepanov say, "Can I do anything for her? Maybe arrange for a transfer back to a Leningrad hospital—or perhaps to a Molotov hospital? Away from here?"

After a spasm Alexander spoke, looking in the other direction. "Yes, sir, you actually could do something to help her . . ."

Alexander didn't have time to think, and he didn't have time to feel. He knew the time for that would swallow too soon what was left of him. But right now he had to act. As soon as Stepanov left, Alexander motioned for Ina and asked her to call Dr. Sayers.

"Major," said Ina, "I don't know if they're allowing anyone near you after this afternoon."

Alexander glanced at the plainclothed men. "It was a little accident, Ina, nothing to worry about. Do me a favor, though, don't tell Nurse Metanova, all right? You know how she gets."

"I know how she gets. You better be good from now on, or I'll tell her."

"I'll be good, Ina."

Sayers came a few minutes later, sat down cheerfully, and said, "What's going on, Major? What's this about some private's arm? What happened?"

Shrugging, Alexander said, "He lost the arm wrestle."

"I'll say he lost. What about his broken nose? Did he lose the nose wrestle, too?"

"Dr. Sayers, listen to me. Forget him for a second." Alexander summoned his remaining will to speak. What strength he once possessed had left his body and gone to a tiny girl with freckles.

"Doctor," he said quietly, "when we first spoke about—"

"Don't say it. I know."

"You asked me what you could do to help, remember? And I said to you," Alexander continued, "that you owed me nothing." He paused, collecting himself. "It turns out I was wrong. I desperately need your help."

Sayers smiled. "Major Belov, I'm already doing all I can for you. Your terminal nurse is quite a persuader."

My terminal nurse.

Shrinking into himself, Alexander said, "No, listen carefully. I want you to do just one thing for me, and only one."

"What is it? If I can do it, I will."

With a halting voice, Alexander said, "Get my wife out of the Soviet Union."

"I am, Major."

"No, Doctor. I mean *now*. Take my wife, take—" He could not get the words out. "Take Chernenko, the prick with the broken arm," he whispered, "and get them out."

"What are you talking about?"

"Doctor, we have very little time. Any minute someone is going to call you away from me, and I won't be able to finish."

"You're coming with us."

"I am not."

In agitation, Sayers exclaimed, "Major, what the hell are you talking about?" In English.

"Shh," said Alexander. "You will need to leave tomorrow at the absolute latest."

"What about you?"

"*Forget* about me," Alexander said firmly. "Dr. Sayers, Tania needs your help. She is pregnant—did you know that?"

Sayers shook his head, dumbstruck.

"Well, she is. And she's going to be very scared. She is going to need you to protect her. Please get her out of the Soviet Union. And protect her." Alexander stared away from the doctor. His eyes filled with . . . *the river Kama, with the soap on her body.* They filled with . . . *her hands going around his neck and her warm breath in his ear, whispering, potato pancakes, Shura, or eggs?*

They filled with . . . *her coming out of Grechesky Hospital in November, small, alone, wearing a big coat, her eyes at her feet; she couldn't even lift her eyes as she walked past him to her Fifth Soviet life, alone to her Fifth Soviet life.*

"Save my wife," whispered Alexander.

In an emotional voice Dr. Sayers said, "I don't understand *anything*."

Shaking his head, Alexander said, "Do you see the casually dressed men you had to walk past on your way here? Those are NKVD men. Remember I told you about the NKVD, Doctor? What happened to my mother and father, and to me?"

Sayers paled.

"The NKVD enforces the law of this great land. And they are here for me—again. Tomorrow," Alexander said, "I will be gone. Tania cannot stay here a minute after that. She is in grave danger. You must get her out."

The doctor still didn't understand. He protested, he shook his head. He became increasingly nervous. "Alexander, I will call the U.S. consulate personally. I'll call them tomorrow on your behalf."

Alexander became worried about the doctor. Could he even do what was needed? Could he keep his composure when he would need it the most? He didn't seem composed in the least. "Doctor," Alexander said, keeping his own composure, "I know you don't understand, but I don't have time to explain. Where is this U.S. consulate? In Sweden? In England? By the time you call them and they reach the U.S. State Department back home, the Mekhlis blue boys will have taken not only me but her, too. What does Tatiana have to do with *America*?"

"She is your wife."

"I have only my Russian name, the name I married her under. By the time the United States gets together with the NKVD to clear up the confusion, it'll be too late for her. *Forget me*, I said. Just take care of *her*."

"No," Sayers said. He bucked, he couldn't sit. He walked around Alexander's bed, adjusted his blankets.

"Doctor!" Alexander exclaimed. "You have no time to think this through, I know. But what do you think will happen to a Russian girl once it's discovered she is married to a man suspected of being an American and infiltrating the Red Army's high command? What use do you think the Commissariat of Internal Affairs will have for my pregnant Russian wife?"

Sayers was mute.

"I'll tell you what use—they will use her as leverage against me when they interrogate us. Tell us everything, or your wife will be 'strictly judged.' Do you know what *that* means, Doctor? It means I will be *forced* to tell them everything. I won't stand a chance. Or they will use me as leverage against her. Your husband will be safe, but only if you tell the truth. And she will. And afterward—"

Shaking his head, Sayers said, "No! We will put you in my ambulance right now and take you back to Leningrad, to Grechesky. Right now. Get up. And from there we will drive to Finland."

"Fine," said Alexander. "But those men"—he nodded in their direction—"will come with us. They will come with us every step of the way. You won't get either of us out."

Alexander could see that Dr. Sayers was grasping at what he could. Glancing toward the door, to Ina, to the shuffling, smoking men standing chatting with her, Alexander shook his head. Sayers was not getting it.

"What about him? Chernenko? I don't know him or owe him anything."

"You must take him," whispered Alexander. "After this afternoon, he finally understood. He thought I would sacrifice her to save myself because he could not imagine any other way. Now he knows the truth. He also knows I will not sacrifice her to destroy him. I will not keep her from escaping to keep *him* from escaping. And he is right. So take him. It'll help her, and I don't give a shit about anything else."

Dr. Sayers was at a loss for words.

"Doctor," said Alexander gently, "stop fighting for me. She does that. I don't want you to worry about me; my fate is sealed. But hers is wide open. Concern yourself only with her."

Rubbing his face, Dr. Sayers said, still shaking his head, "Alexander, I've seen that girl—" His voice broke. "I've seen that girl drain her lifeblood into you. I'm fighting for you because I know what it will do to her—"

"Doctor!" Alexander was nearly at the end of his tether. "You're not helping me. Don't you think I know?" He closed his eyes. *Everything she had she gave to me.*

"Major, do you think she'll even go without you?"

"Never," said Alexander.

"God! So what can I possibly do?" Sayers exclaimed.

"She must never know I've been arrested. If she finds out, she will not go. She'll stay—to find out what happened to me, to help me in some way, to see me one last time, and then it will be too late for her."

Alexander told Dr. Sayers what they had to do.

"Major, I can't do that!" Sayers exclaimed.

"Yes, you can. It's just words from you, Doctor. Words and an impassive face."

Sayers shook his head.

"Many things can go wrong. And they will," said Alexander. "It's not a perfect plan. It's not a safe plan. It's not a foolproof plan. But we have no choice. If we're to succeed at all, we must use all the weapons at our disposal." Alexander paused. "Even the ones with no ammunition."

"Major, you're out of your mind. She will never believe me," said Sayers.

Alexander grabbed the doctor's wrist. "Well, that will depend on you, Doctor! The only chance she has of living is if you get her out. If you waver, if you're unconvincing, if when faced with her grief you weaken and she sees for a split second that you are not telling her the truth, she will not go. If she thinks I'm still alive, she will *never* go, remember that, and if she doesn't go, know that she has days before they come for her." Stricken, Alexander said, "When she sees my empty bed, she will break down in front of you, her façade will crumble, and she will raise her tearful face to yours and say,

'You're lying, I know you're lying. I can *feel* he's still alive,' and that's when you will look at her and you'll want to comfort her, because you've seen her comfort so many. Her grief will be too much for you to take. She will say to you, 'Tell me the truth, and I will go with you anywhere.' You will pause just for a second, you will blink, you will purse your lips, and in that instant know, Doctor, that you are condemning her and our baby to prison or death. She is very persuasive, and she is *very* hard to say no to, and she will keep on at you until you break down. Know—that when you comfort her with the truth, you will have killed her." Alexander let go of Sayers's wrist. "Now, go. Look her in the eye and lie. *Lie with all your heart!*" His voice nearly gone, Alexander whispered, "And if you save *her*, you will help *me*."

There were tears in Sayers's eyes as he stood up. "This fucking country," he said, "is too much for me."

"Me, too," said Alexander, extending his hand. "Now, can you get her for me? I need to see her one last time. But come with her. Come with her and stand by my side. She is shy with other people around. She will have to be distant."

"Maybe alone for just a minute?"

"Doctor, remember what I told you about looking her in the eye? I can't face her alone. Maybe you can hide, but I cannot."

Alexander kept his eyes closed. In ten minutes he heard footsteps and her choral voice. "Doctor, I told you he's sleeping. What made you think he was restless?"

"Major?" Dr. Sayers called.

"Yes," said Tatiana. "Major? Can you wake up?" And Alexander felt her warm, familiar hands on his head. "He doesn't feel hot. He feels fine."

Reaching up, Alexander placed his hand on hers.

Here it is, Tatiana.

Here is my brave and indifferent face.

Alexander took a breath and opened his eyes. Tatiana was gazing down at him with a look of such unrelenting affection that he closed his eyes again and said, his lips carrying the cracked words mere centimeters from his mouth, "I'm just tired, Tatia. How are *you*? How are you feeling?"

"Open your eyes, soldier," Tatiana said fondly, caressing his face. "Are you hungry?"

"I was hungry," Alexander said. "But you fed me." His body was shaking underneath his sheet.

"Why is your IV disconnected?" she said, taking hold of his hand. "And why is your hand all black and blue, like you ripped the IV out of the vein? What have you been doing here this afternoon while I was gone?"

"I don't need the IV anymore. I'm almost all better."

She felt his head again. "He does feel a bit cold, Doctor," she said. "Maybe we can give him another blanket?"

Tatiana disappeared. Alexander opened his eyes and saw the doctor's anguished face. "Stop it," Alexander mouthed inaudibly.

Returning, she covered Alexander and studied him for a moment. "I'm fine, really," he said to her. "I have a joke for you. What do you get when you cross a white bear with a black bear?"

She replied, "Two happy bears."

They smiled at each other. Alexander did not look away.

"You'll be all right?" she asked. "I'll come back tomorrow morning to give you breakfast."

Alexander shook his head. "No, not in the morning. You'll never guess where they're taking me tomorrow morning." He grinned.

"Where?"

"Volkhov. Don't be too proud of your husband, all right, but they're finally making me lieutenant colonel." Alexander glanced at Dr. Sayers, who stood by the foot of the bed with a pasty grimace.

"They *are?*" Tatiana beamed.

"Yes. To go with my *Hero of the Soviet Union* medal for helping our doctor. What do you think of *that?*"

Grinning, Tatiana leaned into him and said happily, "I think you're going to become *really* insufferable. I'll *have* to obey your every command, won't I?"

"Tania, to get you to obey my every command, I'll have to become a general," Alexander replied.

She laughed. "When are you coming back?"

"The following morning."

"Why then? Why not tomorrow afternoon?"

"They transport across the lake only in the very early mornings," said Alexander. "It's a little safer. There is less shelling."

Sayers said in a weak voice, "Tania, we must go."

Alexander shut his eyes. He heard Tatiana say, "Dr. Sayers, can I have a moment with Major Belov?"

No! Alexander thought, opening his eyes and staring at the doctor, who said, "Tatiana, we really have to be going. I have rounds to make in three wards."

"It'll take but a second," she said. "And look, Leo in bed number thirty is gesturing for you."

The doctor left. He can't even say no to her when she is asking simple things, Alexander thought, shaking his head.

Coming close, Tatiana brought her freckled face to him. She glanced around, saw that Dr. Sayers was looking right at them, and said, "God, I won't get a chance to kiss you, will I? I can't wait until I can kiss you out in the open." Her hands patted his chest. "Soon we'll be out of the thick forest," she whispered.

"Kiss me anyway," Alexander said.

607

"Really?"

"Really."

Tatiana bent, her serene hand remaining on his chest, and her honey lips softly kissed Alexander's own lips. She pressed her cheek against his. "Shura, open your eyes."

"No."

"Open them."

Alexander opened them.

Tatiana gazed at him, her eyes shining, and then she blinked three times quick.

Straightening up, she put on her serious face and raising her hand in a salute, said, "Sleep well, Major, and I'll see you."

"I'll see you, Tania," said Alexander.

She walked to the end of his bed. No! he wanted to cry out. No, Tania, please come back. What can I leave her with, what can I say, what one word can I leave with her, *for* her? What *one word* for my wife?

"Tatiasha," Alexander called after her. God, what *was* the curator's name . . . ?

She glanced back.

"Remember Orbeli—"

"Tania!" Dr. Sayers yelled across the ward. "Please come now!"

She made a frustrated face and said quickly, "Shura, darling, I'm sorry, I have to run. Tell me when I see you next, all right?"

He nodded.

Tatiana walked away from Alexander, past the cots, touching a convalescent's leg and bringing a small smile to the man's bandaged face. She said good night to Ina and stopped for a second to adjust someone's blanket. At the door she said a few words to Dr. Sayers, laughed, and then turned to Alexander one last time, and in Tatiana's eyes he saw her love, and then she was out the door and gone.

Alexander whispered after her, "*Tatiana! Thou shall not be afraid for the terror by night . . . nor for the arrow that flieth by day . . . nor for the pestilence that walketh in darkness; nor for the destruction that wasteth at noonday. A thousand shall fall at your side and ten thousand at your right hand; but it shall not come near thee.*"

Alexander crossed himself, folded his arms, and began to wait. He thought back to his father's last words to him.

Dad, I *have* watched the things I gave my life to broken, but will I ever know if I have built them up with my worn-out tools?

Barefoot, Tania stood at attention in front of Alexander, in her yellow dress and with her golden braids peeking out from under his cap. Her face was ablaze with an exuberant smile. She saluted him.

"At ease, Tania," he said, saluting her.

"Thank you, Captain," she said, coming up and standing on tiptoe on top of his boot-clad feet. Lifting her face to him, she kissed his chin—it was as high up as she could reach without him bending his head to her. With one hand he held her to him.

She stepped a meter away and turned her back to Alexander. "All right, I'm falling. You better catch me. Ready?"

"I've been ready for five minutes. Fall already."

Her chortling squeals chimed as she fell, and Alexander caught her, kissing her from above. "All right," Tatiana said, straightening up, opening her arms, and laughing joyously. "Now your turn."

Good-bye, my moonsong and my breath, my white nights and golden days, my fresh water and my fire. Good-bye, and may you find a better life, find comfort again and your breathless smile, and when your beloved face lights up once more at the Western sunrise, be sure what I felt for you was not in vain. Good-bye, and have faith, my Tatiana.

In the Moonlight's Pallid Glamour

Late the next morning Tatiana came into the critical care ward at the field hospital, the wooden building that was once a school, and found someone else in Alexander's bed. She had expected his bed to be empty. She did not expect to see a new patient in Alexander's bed, a man with no arms or legs.

Staring at the man with incomprehension, she thought she had made a mistake. She had woken up late and rushed and then spent too many hours in the terminal ward. Seven soldiers had died that morning.

But no, it was the critical ward. Leo in bed number thirty was reading. The two beds next to Alexander had also been emptied and refilled by new patients. Nikolai Ouspensky, the lieutenant with one lung next to Alexander, was gone, and so was the corporal next to him.

Why would they have filled Alexander's bed? Tatiana went to check with Ina, who knew nothing; she wasn't even on shift duty yet. Ina told Tatiana that late last night Alexander had asked for his dress uniform, which she brought him and then left for the night. Past that she knew nothing. Ina said that maybe Alexander had been moved to the convalescent wing.

Tatiana went to check. He hadn't been.

She came back to the critical ward and looked under the bed. His rucksack was gone. Alexander's medal of valor was no longer hanging on the wooden chair that stood by the new patient, whose face was covered in gauze, oozing blood near his right ear. Absentmindedly Tatiana said that she would get a doctor to take a look at him and groggily ambled away. She was feeling as well as she could for a woman four months pregnant. Her stomach was beginning to show, she knew. It was a good thing they were leaving, because she could not imagine explaining herself to the nurses and her patients. She was on her way to the mess to eat but found a nagging tick mowing through her insides. She became afraid that Alexander had been sent back to the front, that he had gone across the lake and been made to stay. She couldn't eat a bite. She went to look for Dr. Sayers.

She couldn't find him anywhere, but when she found Ina, who was getting ready to start her shift, Ina told her that Dr. Sayers had been looking for her.

"He couldn't have been looking very hard," said Tatiana. "I've been in terminal all morning." Tatiana found Dr. Sayers in the terminal ward himself, with a patient who had lost most of his stomach. "Dr. Sayers," she whispered, "what's going on? Where is Major Belov?" She saw that the patient had mere minutes to live.

Sayers didn't look up from the man's wounds when he said, "Tatiana, I'm almost done here. Help me hold his sides together while I sew."

"What's going on, Doctor?" Tatiana repeated as she helped him.

"Let's just finish with him first, all right?"

Tatiana looked at the doctor, looked at the patient, and put her gloved and bloodied hand on the patient's forehead. For a few moments she kept her hand on him and then said, "He is dead, Doctor, you can stop suturing."

The doctor stopped suturing.

Tatiana ripped off her gloves and walked outside. The doctor followed her. It was nearly the middle of March and unremittingly windy. "Listen, Tania," Sayers said, taking hold of her hands and looking white. "I'm sorry. Something terrible has happened." His voice half broke on *happened*. The circles under his eyes were so dark, it looked as if he had been beaten. Tatiana stared at him for a moment, another moment—

She pulled her hands away. "Doctor," Tatiana said, paling and looking around for something to hold on to. "What's happened?"

"Tania, wait, don't shout—"

"I'm not shouting."

"I'm very sorry to tell you this, *very* sorry, but Alexander—" He broke off. "Early this morning, when he was taken with two other soldiers to Volkhov . . ." Sayers couldn't continue.

Tatiana listened motionlessly, her insides becoming anesthetized. She tried to say, "What?"

"Listen, they were going across the lake when enemy fire—"

"*What* enemy fire?" Tatiana whispered vehemently.

"They left to cross before the shelling started, but we're fighting a war. You hear the bombing, the German shells flying from Sinyavino? A long-range rocket hit the ice in front of the truck and exploded."

"Where is he?"

"I'm sorry. Five people in that truck . . . nobody survived."

Tatiana turned her back to the doctor and shook so violently that she thought she would split open. Without looking back, she asked, "Doctor, how do you know this?"

"I was called to the scene. We tried to save the men, the truck. But the truck was too heavy. It sank." His voice was below a whisper.

Tatiana gripped her stomach and was sick in the snow. Her pulse tearing through her body at over 200 beats a minute, she reached down, grabbed a handful of snow, and wiped her mouth. She took another handful and pressed it to her face. Her heart would not quieten. She could not stop retching. She felt the doctor's hand on her back, heard his voice dimly calling for her, "Tania, Tania."

She did not turn around. "Did you see him yourself?" she asked, panting.

"Yes. I'm sorry," he whispered. "I got his cap—"

"Was he alive when you saw him?"

"I'm sorry, Tatiana. No."

She couldn't stand any more.

"No, please," she heard Dr. Sayers's voice and felt his arms holding her up. "Please."

Straightening herself, willing herself to remain upright, Tatiana turned around and leveled her gaze at Dr. Sayers, who touched her face and said, very concerned, "You need to go and sit down immediately, you're in a state of—"

"I know what I am in," Tatiana said. "Give me his cap."

"I'm sorry. It breaks my—"

"I'll take his cap," said Tatiana, but her hand was shaking so badly that she couldn't grasp it for a moment, and when she did, it fell out of her hands and onto the snow.

She couldn't hold the death certificate either. Dr. Sayers had to hold it up for her. She saw only his name and the place of death. Lake Ladoga.

The Ladoga ice.

"Where is he?" she said faintly. "Where is he now—" She could not finish.

"Oh, Tania . . . what could we do? We . . ."

Waving him off, she doubled over. "Don't speak to me anymore. How could you not have woken me? How could you not have told me instantly?"

"Tania, look at me." She felt herself being pulled upright. Sayers had tears in his eyes. "I did look for you after I returned. But I can barely stand in front of you now when you've come for me, when I've got no choice. If I could, I would have sent you a telegram." He shivered. "Tania, let's get out of here! You and I. Let's be done with this place! I have to get out of here, I can't do it anymore. I need to be back in Helsinki. Come on, we'll get our things. I'll call Leningrad, let them know." He paused. "I have to leave tonight." He glanced at her. "*We* have to leave tonight."

Tatiana did not respond. Her mind was playing tricks on her. For some reason she couldn't get past the death certificate. It wasn't a Red Army certificate. It was a Red Cross death certificate.

"Tatiana," said Sayers, "can you hear me?"

"Yes," she said indistinctly.

"You will come with me."

"I can't think right now," she managed to utter. "I need to think for a few minutes."

"Will you . . ." Sayers let out. "Will you please come back to my office? You're not—Come, sit in my chair. You'll—"

Backing away from Sayers, Tatiana watched him with an intensity she knew was excruciating to him. She turned and walked as fast as she could to the main building. She had to find Colonel Stepanov. The colonel was busy and refused to see her at first.

She waited outside the front door until he came out.

"I'm headed for the mess tent. Walk with me?" Stepanov said to her, not catching her eye and hurrying forward.

"Sir," Tatiana said into his back, not taking a step, "what happened to your officer—" She couldn't say his name out loud.

Stepanov slowed down, stopped, and faced her. "I'm sorry about your husband," he said gently.

Tatiana didn't speak. Coming close to him, she took Colonel Stepanov's hand. "Sir, you are a good man, and you were his commanding officer." Wind was whipping her face. "Please tell me what happened to him."

"I don't know. I wasn't there."

Tatiana stood small before the uniformed colonel.

The colonel sighed. "All I know is that one of our armored trucks carrying your husband, Lieutenant Ouspensky, one corporal, and two drivers exploded this morning under what appeared to be enemy fire and eventually sank. I have no other information."

"Armored? He told me he was going to Volkhov to get promoted this morning," she said in a faint whisper.

"Nurse Metanova," said Colonel Stepanov, pausing and blinking. "The truck sank. Everything else is moot."

Tatiana never looked away from him for a moment.

Stepanov nodded. "I'm sorry. Your husband was—"

"I know what he was, sir," Tatiana broke in, holding the cap and the certificate to her chest.

With a small shiver of his voice, staring at her with hurting blue eyes, Colonel Stepanov said, "Yes. We both do."

Mutely they stood in front of each other.

"Tatiana!" said Colonel Stepanov emotionally. "Go back with Dr. Sayers. As soon as you can. It'll be easier and safer for you in Leningrad. Maybe Molotov? Go with him."

Tatiana saw him button the top of his uniform. She didn't take her eyes off him. "He brought your son back," she whispered.

Stepanov lowered his eyes. "Yes."

"But who is going to bring *him* back?"

The bitter wind whistled through her words.

How to move, how to move now, can I get on my hands and knees and crawl, no, I will walk, I will look at the ground, and I will walk away, and I won't stumble.

I will stumble.

She fell on the snow, and the colonel came over and picked her up, patting her back, and she closed her coat around her and, without looking again at Stepanov, staggered down the road to the hospital, holding on to the walls of buildings.

To hide him her whole life, to hide him every step of the way, to hide him from Dasha, from Dimitri, to hide him from death, and now to hide him even from herself. Her weakness felt insuperable.

Finding Dr. Sayers in his small office, Tatiana said, "Doctor, look at me, look me in the eye and swear to me that he is dead."

Sinking to her knees, she looked at him, her hands in a plea.

Dr. Sayers crouched down and took Tatiana's hands. "I swear," he said, "he is dead." He did not look at her.

"I can't," she said in a guttural voice. "I can't take it. I can't take the thought of him dying in that lake without me. Do you understand? I can't take it," she whispered wrenchingly. "Tell me he's been taken by the NKVD. Tell me he's been arrested and he'll be storming bridges next week, tell me he's been sent to the Ukraine, to Sinyavino, to Siberia—tell me anything. But please tell me he did not die on the ice without me. I'll bear anything but that. Tell me, and I will go with you anywhere, I promise, I will do exactly as you say, but I beg you, tell me the truth."

"I'm sorry," Dr. Sayers said, "I couldn't save him. With my whole heart I'm sorry I couldn't save him for you."

Tatiana crawled away to the wall and put her face into her hands.

"I am not going anywhere," she said. "There is no point."

"Tania," Sayers said, coming after her and putting his hand on her head, "please don't say that. Honey . . . please . . . let me save you *for him*."

"There is no point."

"No point? What about his baby?" exclaimed the doctor.

She took her hands away from her face and stared dully at Sayers. "He told you we are having a baby?"

"Yes."

"Why?"

Flustered, the doctor said, "I don't know." His hand was still on Tatiana's head. "You don't feel good. You're all cold. You're—"

She did not reply. She was convulsing.

"Are you going to be all right?"

She covered her face.

"Will you stay here? Just stay in my office and wait. Don't get up, all right. Sleep maybe?"

Tatiana made a rasping noise that sounded like an animal pressing its gaping wound into the ground, hoping to die before it bled to death.

"Your patients were asking for you," Sayers said softly. "Do you think—"

"No." Through her hands. "Please leave me. I need to be alone."

Until night fell, she sat on the floor in Dr. Sayers's office. She put her head into her knees, and sat against the wall. Until she couldn't sit up anymore, and then she lay down, curled into a ball.

Dimly she heard the doctor return. She heard his gasp and tried to get up but couldn't. Helping her up, Sayers sucked in his breath when he saw her face. "God, Tania. *Please*. I need you—"

"Doctor!" Tatiana exclaimed. "All the things you need me to be, I can't be right now. I'll be what I can. Is it time?"

"It's time, Tania. Let's go." He lowered his voice. "Look, I went to your bed and got your backpack. It's yours, right?"

"Yes," she said, taking it.

"Do you have anything else you need to bring?"

"No," Tatiana whispered. "The backpack is all I have. Is it just you and me going?"

Dr. Sayers paused before he answered her. "Chernenko came to me earlier today and asked if our plans had changed now that—"

"And you said . . ." Her weak legs weren't holding her. She sank into the chair and looked up. "I can't go with him," she said. "I just can't."

"I don't want to take him either, but what can I do? He told me, not in so many words, that without him we wouldn't be able to get you through the first checkpoint. I want to get you out, Tania. What else can I do?"

"Nothing," said Tatiana.

She helped Sayers collect his few things and carried his doctor's bag and her nurse's bag outside. The Red Cross vehicle was a big jeep without the enclosed solid steel body customary for ambulances. This one had glass covering the passenger cab but only canvas covering the back, not the safest for the wounded or medical personnel. But it had been the only truck available at the time in Helsinki, and Sayers could not wait for a proper ambulance. The square Red Cross badges were sewn into the tarpaulin.

Dimitri was waiting by the side of the truck. Tatiana did not look or acknowledge him as she opened the tarpaulin and climbed in to load the first aid kit and the box of plasma.

"Tania?" Dimitri said.

Dr. Sayers came up from behind, and said to Dimitri, "All right, let's hurry along. You get in the back. Once we leave here, you can change into the Finnish pilot's clothes. I don't know how you're going to get your arm through . . . Tania, where are those clothes?" Then to Dimitri, "Do you need morphine? How is your face doing?"

"Terrible. I can barely see. Is my arm going to get infected?"

Tatiana glanced at Dimitri from inside the truck. His right arm was in a cast and sling. His face was swollen black and blue. She wanted to ask what had happened to him, but she didn't care.

"Tania?" Dimitri called to her. "I heard about this morning. I'm sorry."

Tatiana retrieved the Finnish pilot's clothes from their hiding place and threw them on the truck floor in front of Dimitri.

"Tatiana, come," Dr. Sayers told her. "Let me help you down, we have to get going."

Taking Sayers's hand, Tatiana jumped down past Dimitri.

"Tania?" Dimitri repeated.

She lifted her eyes to him filled with such unwavering condemnation that Dimitri could not help but look away. "Just put on the clothes," Tatiana said through her teeth. "Then get down on the floor and lie very still."

"Look, I'm sorry. I know how you—"

Clenching her fists, Tatiana lunged furiously at Dimitri, and she would have punched him in his broken nose had Dr. Sayers not restrained her from behind, saying, "Tania, God. Please. No. No."

Backing away, Dimitri opened his mouth and stammered, "I said I was very s—"

"I don't want to *hear* your fucking lies!" she yelled, her arms still being held by Dr. Sayers. "I don't want you to speak to me ever again. Do you understand?"

Dimitri, mumbling nervously that he didn't understand why she should be upset with *him*, got into the back of the truck.

Dr. Sayers got behind the wheel and stared wide-eyed at Tatiana.

"Ready, Doctor. Let's go." Tatiana buttoned up her nurse's white coat with the Red Cross badge on the sleeve, and she tied her little white hat over her hair. She had all of Alexander's money, she had his Pushkin book, she had his letters and their photographs. She had his cap, and she had his ring.

They drove into the night.

Tatiana held Sayers's open map but could not have helped him get to Lisiy Nos. Through the northern Russian woods Dr. Sayers drove his small truck, as they made their way on unpaved, muddy, snowy, liquid roads. Tatiana saw nothing at all, staring out the side window into the darkness, counting inside her head, trying to keep herself upright.

Sayers kept talking to her nonstop in English. "Tania, dear, it will be all right—"

"Will it, Doctor?" she asked, also in English. "And what are we going to do with *him*?"

"Who cares? He can do what he likes once we get to Helsinki. I'm not thinking about him at all. All I'm thinking about is *you*. We will get to

Helsinki, drop off some supplies, and then you and I will take a Red Cross plane to Stockholm. Then from Stockholm we'll ride the train to Göteborg on the North Sea, and we'll take a protected vessel across the North Sea to England. Tania, can you hear me? Do you understand?"

"I can hear you," she said faintly. "I understand."

"In England I've got a couple of stops to make, but then we'll either fly to the U.S. or take one of the passenger liners from Liverpool. And once you're in New York—"

"Matthew, please," whispered Tatiana.

"I'm just trying to make you feel better, Tania. It's going to be all right."

From the back Dimitri said, "Tania, I didn't know you could speak English."

Tatiana did not reply at first. Then she picked up a metal pipe from under Dr. Sayers's feet that she knew he kept in case of trouble. Swinging her arm, she smashed the pipe hard against the metal divider separating her from Dimitri, startling Dr. Sayers nearly off the side of the road. "Dimitri," she said loudly, "you have to stay quiet and stop talking. You are a Finn. Not another Russian syllable out of you."

Dropping the pipe onto the floor, she folded her arms around her stomach.

"Tania . . ."

"Don't, Doctor."

"You haven't eaten, have you?" the doctor asked gently.

Tatiana shook her head. "I'm not thinking about food at all," she replied.

In the middle of the night they stopped by the side of the road. Dimitri had already slipped on the Finnish uniform. "It's very big," Tatiana heard him say to Dr. Sayers. "I hope I don't have to stand up in it. Anyone will see it doesn't fit me. Do you have any more morphine? I'm—"

Dr. Sayers came back a few minutes later. "If I give him any more morphine, he'll be dead. That arm is going to give him trouble."

"What happened to him?" Tatiana asked in English.

Dr. Sayers was quiet. "He was nearly killed," he said at last. "He has a very nasty open fracture." He paused. "He may lose that arm. I don't know how he is conscious, upright. I thought he'd be in a coma after yesterday, yet today he is walking." Sayers shook his head.

Tatiana didn't speak. How *could* he still be standing? she thought. How could the rest of us—strong, resolute, spirited, young—be falling on our knees, be demolished by our life, while *he* remains standing?

"Someday, Tania," Sayers said in English, "you will have to explain to me the—" He broke off, pointing to the back of the truck. "Because I swear to Christ, I don't understand at all."

"I do not think I could explain," whispered Tatiana.

On the way to Lisiy Nos they were stopped half a dozen times at checkpoints for papers. Sayers presented papers on himself and papers on his nurse, Jane Barrington. Dimitri, who was a Finn named Tove Hanssen, had no papers, just a metal dogtag with the dead man's name on it. He was a wounded pilot being taken back to Helsinki for a prisoner exchange. All six times the guards opened the tarpaulin, shined a flashlight in Dimitri's battered face, and then waved Sayers on.

"It's nice to be protected by the Red Cross flag," said Sayers.

Tatiana nodded.

The doctor pulled over by the side of the road, turning the engine off. "Are you cold?" he asked.

"I'm not cold." *Not cold enough.* "Do you want me to drive?"

"You know how to drive?"

In Luga, when she was sixteen, the summer before she met Alexander, Tatiana had befriended an army corporal stationed with the local village *Soviet.* The corporal let Tatiana and Pasha drive around in his truck for the whole summer. Pasha was annoying because he always wanted to be behind the wheel, but the corporal was kind and let her behind the wheel, too. She drove the truck well, better than Pasha, she thought, and the corporal told her she was a quick learner.

"I know how to drive."

"No, it's too dark and icy." Sayers closed his eyes for an hour.

Tatiana sat quietly, her hands in her coat. She was trying to remember the last time she and Alexander had made love. It was a Sunday in November, but *where* was it? She couldn't recall. What did they do? Where were they? Did she look up at him? Was Inga outside their door? Was it in the bath, on the couch, on the floor? She couldn't remember.

What did Alexander say to her last night? He made a joke, he kissed her, he smiled, he touched her hand, he told her he was going across to Volkhov to get promoted. Were they lying to *him?* Was he lying to *her?*

He had been trembling. She had thought he was cold. What else did he say? *I'll see you.* So casual. Not even blinking. What else? *Remember Orbeli.*

What was *that?*

Alexander often told her fascinating little tidbits he picked up in the army, names of generals, stories about Hitler, or Rommel, about England or Italy, about Stalingrad, about Richthoffen, von Paulus, El Alamein, Montgomery. It wasn't unusual that he would say a word she didn't understand. But Orbeli was a word she hadn't heard before, and yet there was Alexander—asking her to *remember* it.

Tatiana nudged Dr. Sayers awake. "Dr. Sayers, what is Orbeli?" she asked. "Who is Orbeli?"

"Don't know," Sayers replied sleepily. "Never heard of it. Why?"

She said nothing.

Sayers began driving again.

They got to the silent, sleeping border between the Soviet Union and Finland at six in the morning.

Alexander had told Tatiana it wasn't really a border, it was a line of defense, which meant there was anywhere from thirty to sixty meters between the Soviet and Finnish troops. Each side marked its territory and then sat and waited out the war.

To Tatiana the Finnish conifer and willow woods looked like the Soviet conifer and willow woods they had been driving through for the last long hours of the night. The headlights from their truck illuminated a narrow strip of unpaved road ahead. Sunrise was slow in coming toward the ides of March.

Dr. Sayers suggested that if everyone was sleeping, maybe they could just drive across and present their papers to the Finns instead of to the Soviets. Tatiana thought that was an excellent idea.

Suddenly someone yelled for them to halt. Three sleepy NKVD border troops came up to the doctor's window. Sayers showed them the papers. After thoroughly looking over the documents, the NKVD soldier said to Tatiana in accented English, "A cold wind, isn't it?"

And in clear English, she replied, "Very bitter. They say it is going to snow."

The soldier nodded, and then all three men went around to take a look at Dimitri in the back of the truck. Tatiana waited.

Silence.

The flashlight shined.

Silence.

Then, "Wait," Tatiana heard. "Let me see his face again."

The flashlight shined.

Tatiana sat immobile and listened intently.

She heard one of the soldiers laugh and say something to Dimitri in Finnish. Tatiana didn't speak Finnish, so she couldn't guarantee that it *was* Finnish, but the Soviet soldier spoke to Dimitri in a language Tatiana didn't understand, and obviously Dimitri hadn't understood either, because he did not reply.

The Soviet officer repeated his question more loudly.

Dimitri remained silent. Then he said something in what sounded to Tatiana like Finnish. After a short snickering silence from the troops, one of them said, in Russian, "Get out of the truck."

"Oh, no," whispered Dr. Sayers. "Are we caught?"

"Shh," said Tatiana.

The soldiers repeated their order to Dimitri to get out of the truck. He didn't move.

Dr. Sayers turned around and said, in Russian, "He is wounded. He can't get up."

And the Soviet officer said, "He'll get up if he wants to live. Talk to your patient in whatever language he speaks and tell him to get up."

"Doctor," whispered Tatiana, "be very careful. If he can't save himself, he will try to kill us all."

The three NKVD soldiers dragged Dimitri out of the truck and then

619

ordered Sayers and Tatiana out. The doctor came around and stood by Tatiana's side near her open door. His slender body was slightly in front of her. Tatiana, feeling herself weakening, touched Sayers's coat, hoping for some strength. She felt ready to faint. Dimitri was out in the open in plain sight a few meters away from them, dwarfed by the Finnish uniform, a uniform that would have been just right on a bigger soldier.

Laughing, their rifles trained on him, one of the NKVD troops said, in Russian, "So, hey, *Finn*, we ask you how you got your face wound, and you tell us that you are going to Helsinki. You want to explain?"

Dimitri said nothing, but stared pleadingly at Tatiana.

Dr. Sayers said, "Look, we picked him up in Leningrad, he was grievously wounded—"

Imperceptibly, Tatiana nudged Dr. Sayers. "Keep quiet," she whispered. "It's trouble."

"He may be grievously wounded," said the NKVD man, "he's just not grievously *Finnish*." The three soldiers laughed. One of the NKVD men walked up to Dimitri. "Chernenko, don't you recognize me?" he said in Russian, cracking up. "It's me, Rasskovsky." Dimitri lowered his good arm. "Keep your hand above your head!" the NKVD soldier yelled, laughing. "Keep it up." Tatiana saw they were not taking Dimitri seriously, his right arm in a sling. Where was Dimitri's weapon? she wondered. Did he have one on him?

The two other soldiers stood a short distance away from Dimitri. "You know him?" one of them asked, lowering his rifle.

"Know him?" Rasskovsky exclaimed. "Of course I know him! Chernenko, have you forgotten how much you were charging me for cigarettes? And how I had to pay because I just couldn't be without my smokes in the middle of the forest?" He laughed. "Just four weeks ago I saw you. Have you already forgotten?"

Dimitri didn't say a word.

"Did you think I wouldn't recognize you just because of the pretty color on your face?" Rasskovsky seemed to be having a very good time. "So, Chernenko, darling, can you explain what you're doing wearing a Finnish uniform and lying in the back of a Red Cross truck? The arm and the face I understand. Someone didn't like your extortionate prices?"

One of the other two soldiers said, "Rasskovsky, you don't think our runner is trying to escape, do you?" Everyone roared with laughter.

Under the glare of the lights Dimitri stared at Tatiana, who held his gaze for only an instant. Then she turned her whole body away and moved closer to Dr. Sayers, her arms tight around herself. "I'm cold," she said.

"Tatiana!" yelled Dimitri in Russian to her. "You want to tell them? Or should I?"

Rasskovsky turned to look at her, and said, "Tatiana? An American named Tatiana?" He walked over to Sayers. "What's going on, here? Why is he talking to her in Russian? Let me see her papers again."

Dr. Sayers showed Tatiana's papers. They were in order.

Looking right at Rasskovsky, Tatiana said in English, "Tatiana? What is he talking about? Listen, what do we know? He said he was Finnish. Right, Doctor?"

"Absolutely," Dr. Sayers replied, stepping forward and away from Tatiana and the truck, his friendly hand on Rasskovsky's back. "Listen, no trouble, I hope. He came to our hospital—"

At that moment Dimitri took out his sidearm and shot at Rasskovsky walking in front of Tatiana.

She wasn't sure whom Dimitri was aiming for—he was shooting with his left arm—but she wasn't about to stand there to find out. She dropped down. He could have been aiming at the NKVD man. He could have. But he missed and shot Dr. Sayers instead. Or maybe Dimitri didn't miss. Or maybe he was shooting at her—standing behind the two men—and missed. Tatiana didn't want to think about it.

Rasskovsky ran toward Dimitri, who fired again, this time hitting Rasskovsky. Dimitri wasn't quick enough to turn his fire on the other two NKVD soldiers, who, as it suspended in still life, struggled to remove their rifles from their shoulders. Finally they opened fire on Dimitri, who was thrown several meters by the force of the impact.

Suddenly there was return fire from the woods. This fire was not slow and methodical bolt-action fire—the metronome of battle: five cartridges, flip open bolt, thumb in another five, close bolt. No, this was a bursting machine-gun fire that broke apart the truck's elongated, flatton front end and the entire windshield. The two NKVD men disappeared.

The window of the cabin door above her shattered, and Tatiana felt something hard and sharp fall and lodge itself in her cheek. She tasted liquid metal, and her tongue ran over and got caught on something sharp inside her mouth. When she opened her mouth, blood dripped out. She had no time to think about it, crawling under the nose of the truck.

Tatiana saw Dimitri on the ground. Dr. Sayers was on the ground out in the open. There was an endless barrage of fire, a stifling ringing, a constant popping against the steel hood of the Red Cross truck.

Tatiana crawled out, grabbed hold of Dr. Sayers, and dragged his motionless body with her. Pulling him close and covering him with herself, she thought she saw Dimitri still moving, or was it the strobe lights of gunfire? No, it was him. He was trying to crawl to the truck. From the Soviet side a mortar shell flew into the air and burst in the woods. Fire, black smoke, screams. From *here*? From *there*? She couldn't tell. There was no here or there. There was just Dimitri making his way toward Tatiana. She saw him in the incongruous headlights, searching for her, finding her, and in the second or two when there was no noise she heard him calling for her: "Tatiana . . . Tatiana . . . please . . ." with his hand outstretched. Tatiana closed her eyes.

He will not come near me.

Tatiana heard a whistling noise, a flash, and then a charge that exploded so close that the wave pushed her head into the undercarriage of the truck, and she lost consciousness.

When she came to, Tatiana decided not to open her eyes. She couldn't hear very well, having just come out of a dead faint, but she felt warm, as if she were in the hot bathhouse in Lazarevo when she would throw hot water on the rocks and the rocks would sizzle and release steam. Dr. Sayers was still partially underneath her body. There was nowhere for her to go. Her tongue ran over the sharp object in her mouth again. She tasted metallic salt.

Sayers felt clammy. *Blood loss.* Tatiana opened her eyes, felt around on him. A small flame behind the truck illuminated the doctor's pale face. Where was he hit? With her fingers she felt around under his coat and found the bullet hole in his shoulder. She didn't find the exit hole, but she pressed her gloved hand into his arm to try to clot the wound. Then she closed her eyes again. There was a blaze behind her, but there were no more gunshots.

How long did that take? Two minutes? Three?

She felt herself starting to slip down into a black abyss. Not only could she not open her eyes, she did not want to.

How long for her life to end, to continue? How long for Dr. Sayers to sleep, how long for Dimitri to stand alone in the glare? How long for Tatiana? How much longer for her?

How long did it take for Alexander to rescue Dr. Sayers and get hit himself? Tatiana had watched it all from the Red Cross truck, positioned behind the trees on the clearing leading to the slope to the river, the slope down which Alexander ran for Anatoly Marazov.

Tatiana had watched it all.

Those two minutes of watching Alexander run for Marazov, shout at Dr. Sayers, run to Dr. Sayers, pull him out, and then drag three men to the truck had been the longest two minutes of Tatiana's life.

He had been so close to safety. She watched the shell from the German plane fall on the ice and explode. She watched Alexander fly headfirst into the armored truck. When Alexander went down, Tatiana grabbed a box full of cylindrical plasma containers and her nurse's bag, jumped down from the back of the Red Cross truck, and ran down the embankment, caught near the ice by a corporal who yanked her down and yelled, "What are you, crazy?"

"I'm a nurse," she said. "I have to help the doctor."

"Yes, you'll be a dead nurse. Stay down."

She stayed down for exactly two seconds. She saw Dr. Sayers hiding behind the armored vehicle that protected him and Alexander from direct fire. She saw him waving for help. She saw Alexander not getting up. Tatiana jumped up and ran out onto the ice before the corporal could utter a sound. She ran at first and then got scared by the crashing artillery shells and dropped onto her stomach, crawling the rest of the way. Alexander was motionless. His shredded white camouflage coat had an enlarging red stain on the right side of his back, surrounded by black ash. Tatiana crawled on her hands and knees to him and pushed the helmet away from his blood-covered head.

One look at Alexander's face told Tatiana he was about to die.

He was gray and flaxen. The ice underneath him was slippery from his blood. She was kneeling in it. Tatiana said, "Hypovolemic shock. Needs plasma." Dr. Sayers instantly agreed. While he was searching for a surgical instrument to cut open Alexander's sleeve, Tatiana took off her hat and pressed it hard into Alexander's side to slow his blood loss. Reaching down into his right boot, she pulled out his army knife and threw it to Dr. Sayers, saying, "Here, use this." She didn't think she breathed once.

Sayers cut open Alexander's coat and his uniform to expose his left forearm, found a vein, and attached a syringe, a tube, and a plasma drip to him. When he left to get the stretcher and some help, Tatiana, by this time sitting on Alexander's wound, cut open his other sleeve, got out another bottle of plasma, another syringe, another catheter, and attached it to a vein on his right forearm. She adjusted the syringe so that it dripped the fluid into Alexander's body at sixty-nine drops a minute, the maximum possible. She sat on his back pressing into him as hard as she could, her white hat and her white coat saturated in his blood, waiting for the stretcher and muttering, "Come on, soldier, come on."

By the time the doctor came back, her plasma bottle had emptied and Tatiana had attached another one. Taking off her stained coat, Tatiana laid it on the stretcher sideways, and when they lifted Alexander onto it, she wrapped her coat tightly around his wound. He was excruciatingly heavy to lift, because his clothes were wet. Dr. Sayers asked how they were going to carry him, and she replied that they were just going to pick him up on three and carry him, and he said incredulously, you are going to carry him? and she said without blinking, yes, I will carry him, NOW.

And afterward Tatiana struggled with the Soviet doctors, with the Soviet nurses, and even with Dr. Sayers, who had taken a look at Alexander's blood loss and the hole in his side and said, forget it. We can't do anything for him. Put him in the terminal ward. Give him a gram of morphine, but no more.

Tatiana hooked an IV to Alexander's vein herself and fed him morphine and fed him plasma. And when that wasn't enough, she gave Alexander her blood. And when that wasn't enough, and it looked as if nothing was going to be enough, she trickled blood from her arteries into his veins.

Drop by drop.

And as she sat by him, she whispered. All I want is for my spirit to be heard through your pain. I sit here with you, pouring my love into you, drop by drop, hoping you'll hear me, hoping you'll lift your head to me and smile again. Shura, can you hear me? Can you feel me sitting by you letting you know you're still alive? Can you feel my hand on your beating heart, my hand letting you know I believe in you, I believe in your eternal life, I believe you will live, live through this and grow wings to soar over death, and when you open your eyes again, I will be here. I will always be here, believing in you, hoping for you, loving you. I'm right here. Feel me, Alexander. Feel me and live.

He lived.

Now as Tatiana lay under the Red Cross truck in the coming of the cold March dawn, she thought, did I save him so he could die on the ice without my arms to hold him, to hold his young, beautiful, war-ravaged body, the body that loved me with all its great might? Could my Alexander have fallen alone?

She would rather have buried him as she had buried her sister than live through this. Would rather have known she had given him peace than live through another starless second of this.

Tatiana could not endure another moment of herself. Not another moment. In one more instant there was going to be nothing left of her.

Dimly she heard Dr. Sayers moan. Tatiana blinked, blinked away Alexander, opened her eyes, and turned to Sayers. "Doctor?" He was semiconscious. The forest was still. The dawn was steel blue. Tatiana disentangled herself from him and crawled out from under the truck. Rubbing her face, she saw it was covered in blood. Her fingers touched a chunk of glass stuck in her cheek. She tried to pull it out, but it hurt too much. Grabbing it by one side, Tatiana wrenched it out, screaming.

It didn't hurt enough.

She continued to scream, her eviscerated cries echoing back to her through the barren woods. Her hands gripping her legs, her stomach, her chest, Tatiana knelt in the snow and screamed as the blood dripped from her face.

She lay down on the ground and pressed her bleeding cheek into the snow. It wasn't cold enough. It couldn't numb her enough.

There was nothing sharp in her mouth anymore, but her tongue was torn and swollen. Getting up, Tatiana sat in the snow, looking around. It was eerily quiet; the bleak, bare birches contrasted somberly with the white earth. No sound anymore, not an echo, not even of her, not a gray branch out of place. Deep in the marsh, close to the Gulf of Finland.

But things were out of place. The Red Cross truck was ruined. One NKVD man in his dark blue uniform lay to the right of her. Dimitri was on the ground within a meter of the truck. His eyes were still open, and his hand remained extended to Tatiana, as if by some providential miracle he expected to be delivered from his own eternity.

Tatiana stared for a moment into Dimitri's frozen face. How Alexander would enjoy the story of Dimitri's getting recognized by the NKVD. She looked away.

Alexander had been right—this was a good spot to get through the border.

It was poorly manned and poorly defended. The NKVD troops were lightly armed; they had their rifles, and from what she could see they had one mortar, but one wasn't enough to keep them alive—the Finns had bigger shells. On the Finnish side of the border things were quiet, too. Despite the size of their shells, were they also all dead? Looking through the trees, Tatiana could see no movement. She was still on the Russian side. What to do? New NKVD reinforcements would no doubt be here soon, and she would quickly be whisked away for questioning, and then?

Tatiana felt her stomach through her coat. Her hands were freezing.

She crawled back under the Red Cross truck. "Dr. Sayers," she whispered, putting her hands on his neck. "Matthew, can you hear me?" He was not answering. He was in bad shape; his pulse was around forty, and his blood pressure felt weak through his carotid. Tatiana lay down by the doctor, and from his coat pocket she pulled out his U.S. passport and both their Red Cross travel documents. They plainly stated in English that one Matthew Sayers and one Jane Barrington were headed for Helsinki.

What should she do now? Should she go? Go *where*? And go *how*?

Climbing inside the cabin, she turned the ignition. Nothing. It was hopeless. Tatiana could see what extensive damage had been done by the gunfire to the front end. She peered through the woods across the Finnish side. Was anyone moving? No. She saw human forms on the snow and behind them a Finnish army truck, a little bigger than their Red Cross one. That wasn't the only difference between them: the Finnish truck didn't look ruined.

Tatiana hopped out and said to Dr. Sayers, "I'll be right back."

He didn't reply.

"All right, then," she said, and walked across the Soviet-Finnish border. It felt about the same, she thought, being in Finland as being in the Soviet Union. Tatiana walked carefully among the half dozen dead Finns. In the truck sat another man, dead behind the wheel, his body keeled forward. To get inside she would have to pull him out.

To get inside she *heaved* him out, and he fell with a thud onto the trampled snow. Climbing in, Tatiana tried the key, still in the ignition. The truck had stalled. She put it in neutral and tried to start it again. It was dead. She tried again. Nothing. She looked at the gauge on the gas tank. It said full. Jumping down, she went to the back of the truck and climbed under to see if the gas tank was punctured. No, it was intact. Tatiana went around the nose of the truck and opened the hood. For a minute she stared, unfocused, but then something came to her. It was a diesel engine. How would she know that?

Kirov.

The word *Kirov* sent a long shudder through her body, and she fought off the impulse to lie down in the snow again. This was a diesel engine, and she used to make diesel engines for tanks in the Kirov factory. "*I made you a whole tank today, Alexander!*" What did she remember about them?

Nothing. Between the diesel engines and the woods in Finland so much had happened that she could barely remember the number of the tram she took to get home.

One.

It was tram Number 1. They would take it part of the way home so they could walk the rest down the Obvodnoy Canal. Walk, talking about war and America, their arms bumping into one another.

Diesel engine.

She was cold. She pulled the hat down over her ears.

Cold. Diesel engines had trouble starting in the cold. She checked to see how many cylinders it had. This one had six. Six pistons, six combustion chambers. The combustion chambers were too cold; the air just couldn't get hot enough to cause the fuel to ignite. Where was that little glowworm Tatiana used to screw in on the side of the combustion chamber?

Tatiana found all six glowworms. She needed to heat them up a little so the air could get warm enough during compression. Otherwise the engine was drawing below-zero air into the cylinders and expecting it to warm up to 540°C in the one-up-one-down motion of the pistons.

Tatiana looked about her. Five dead soldiers lay in the vicinity. She stuck her hand into the small pocket of one of their rucksacks and pulled out a lighter. Alexander had always kept his lighter in the small pocket of his rucksack, too. She used to fetch it to light his cigarettes for him. Flicking the lighter on, she held the small flame to the first glow plug for a few seconds. Then to the second one. Then to the third. By the time she got through all six, the first one was as cold as before she had started. Tatiana had had quite enough. Gritting her teeth and groaning, she broke a low branch off a birch and tried to light it. The branch was too wet from the snow. It wouldn't light.

She looked around in frantic desperation. She knew exactly what she was searching for. She found it behind the truck in a small case on the body of one of the Finns. He was wearing a flamethrower. Tatiana yanked the flamethrower off the dead Finn, her jaw set and her face dark, and strapped it to her back like Alexander's rucksack. Holding the propellant hose firmly in her left hand, she pulled out the ignition plug in the tank, flicked the lighter on, and pressed it to the ignition.

Half a second passed and all was still, and then a white nitrate flame burst out of the hose, the recoil nearly knocking Tatiana backward onto the snow. Nearly. She remained standing.

She walked up to the open hood of the truck and pointed the flame over the engine for a few moments. Then a few more moments. She could have stood there for thirty seconds, she couldn't tell. Finally with her right hand she popped the ignition lever down, and the handheld fire shut off. Flinging the flamethrower off her back, Tatiana climbed into the truck, turned the key, and the engine creaked once and revved into life. She started the truck in neutral, depressed the clutch, put the transmission into first gear, and stepped on the accelerator. The truck lurched forward. She drove slowly across the defense line to pick up Dr. Sayers.

To get Sayers inside the Finnish truck required more out of her than she had.

But not much more.

After she got him in, Tatiana's eyes caught the Red Cross flag on Sayers's truck.

She found Dimitri's army knife in his boot. Walking over to the truck, Tatiana reached up and carefully cut out the Red Cross badge. How she was going to attach it to the tarpaulin on the Finnish truck, she had no idea. She heard Dr. Sayers moan in the back and then remembered the first aid kit. With mindless determination she got the kit, along with a plasma bottle. Cutting away the doctor's coat and shirt, she attached the plasma bottle to his vein, and while the plasma was draining, she looked over his inflamed wound, which was red around the entry hole and unclean. The doctor was hot and delirious. She cleaned the wound with some diluted iodine and covered it with gauze. Then with grim satisfaction she poured iodine onto her cheek and sat pressing a bandage to her face for a few minutes. It felt as if the glass were still inside her skin. She wished she had some *undiluted* iodine and wondered if the cut would need stitches. She thought it would.

Stitches.

Tatiana remembered the suture needle in the first aid kit.

Her eyes clearing, Tatiana took the suture needle and suture thread, jumped down, and, standing on tiptoe, carefully sewed the large Red Cross symbol into the brown canvas of the Finnish truck. The thin thread broke several times. It didn't matter. It just had to hold until Helsinki.

After she was done, Tatiana got behind the wheel, turned to the back, said into the small window, "Ready?" to Dr. Sayers, and then drove the truck out of the Soviet Union, leaving Dimitri dead on the ground.

Tatiana drove down the marshy wooded path, carefully and uncertainly, with both hands clutching the big wheel and her feet barely reaching the three pedals. Finding the road that stretched along the Gulf of Finland from Lisiy Nos to Vyborg was easy. There was only one road. All she had to do was head west. And west she could find by the location of the gloomy, barely interested March sun.

In Vyborg she showed her Red Cross credentials to a sentry and asked for fuel and directions to Helsinki. She thought he asked her about her face, pointing to it, but since she didn't speak Finnish, she didn't answer and drove on, this time on a wide *paved* road, stopping at eight sentry points to show her documents and the wounded doctor in the back. She drove for four hours until she reached Helsinki, Finland, in late afternoon.

The first thing she saw was the lit-up Church of St. Nicholas, up on a hill overlooking the harbor. She stopped to ask directions to *"Helsingin Yliopis-tollinen Keskussairaala,"* the Helsinki University Hospital. She knew how to *say* it in Finnish, she just couldn't understand the directions in Finnish. After she'd made five stops for directions, finally someone spoke enough English to tell her the hospital was behind the lit-up church. She could find that.

Dr. Sayers was well known and loved at the hospital where he had worked since the war of 1940. The nurses brought a stretcher for him and asked Tatiana all sorts of questions she did not understand: most of them in English, some in Finnish, none in Russian.

At the hospital she met another American Red Cross doctor, Sam Leavitt, who took one look at the gash in her face and said she needed stitches. He offered her a local anesthetic. Tatiana refused. "Suture away, Doctor," she said.

"You'll need about ten stitches," the doctor said.

"Only ten?"

He stitched her cheek as she sat mutely and motionlessly on a hospital bed. Afterward he offered her some antibiotic, some painkiller, and some food. She took the antibiotic. She did not eat the food, showing Leavitt her swollen and bloody tongue. "Tomorrow," she whispered. "Tomorrow it will be better. Tomorrow I will eat."

The nurses brought her not only a new, clean, oversize uniform that hid her stomach but also warm stockings and a flannel undershirt, and they even offered to launder her old, soiled clothes. Tatiana gave them the uniform and her woolen coat but kept her Red Cross armband.

Later Tatiana lay on the floor by Dr. Sayers's bed. The night nurse finally came in and asked her to go and sleep in another room, lifting her and leading her out. Tatiana allowed herself to be led out, but as soon as the nurse went down the hall to her station, Tatiana returned to Dr. Sayers.

In the morning he was worse and she was better. She got her old uniform back, starched and white, and managed to eat a bit of food. She remained all day with Dr. Sayers, staring out the window to the patch of the iced-over Gulf of Finland she could see past the stone buildings and the bare trees. Dr. Leavitt came in the late afternoon to check on her face and to ask her if she wanted to go and lie down. She refused. "Why are you sitting here? Why don't you go get some rest yourself?"

Turning her head to Matthew Sayers, Tatiana didn't reply, thinking, *because that's what I do—then, now. I sit by the dying.*

At night Sayers was worse still. He had a high fever of nearly 42°C, and was parched and sweaty. The antibiotics weren't helping him. Tatiana didn't understand what was happening to him. All she wanted was for him to regain consciousness. She fell asleep in the chair next to his bed, her head near him.

In the middle of the night she woke up, feeling suddenly that Dr. Sayers wasn't going to make it. His breathing—it was too familiar to her by now, the last gasping rattles of a dying man. Tatiana took his hand and held it. She placed her hand on his head, and with her broken tongue whispered to him in Russian, in English, about America and about all the things he would see when he got better. He opened his eyes and said in a weak voice that he was cold. She went and got him another blanket. He squeezed her hand. "I'm so sorry, Tania," he whispered, rapidly breathing through his mouth.

"No, *I'm* so sorry," she said inaudibly. Then louder, "Dr. Sayers," she said. "Matthew . . ." She tried to keep her voice from cracking. "I beg you—please tell me what happened to my husband. Did Dimitri betray him? Was he arrested? We're in Helsinki. We're out of the Soviet Union. I'm not going back. I want so little for myself." She bent her head into his arm. "I just want a little comfort," she whispered.

"Go to . . . America, Tania." His voice was fading. "That will be *his* comfort."

"Comfort *me* with the truth. Did you really see him in the lake?"

The doctor stared at her for a long moment with an expression that looked to Tatiana to be one of understanding and disbelief, and then he closed his eyes. Tatiana felt his hand trembling in hers, heard his breath sputtering in his chest. Soon it stopped.

Tatiana didn't let go of his hand until morning.

A nurse came in and gently led Tatiana away, and in the hall she put her arms around Tatiana and said, in English, "Honey, you can do your very best for people, and they still die. We're at war. You can't save everybody, you know."

Sam Leavitt approached her in the hall on the way to his rounds, asking her what she intended to do. Tatiana said she needed to get back to America. Leavitt stared at her and said, "*Back* to America?" Leaning toward her, he said, "Listen, I don't know where Matthew found you, your English is pretty good, but it's not *that* good. Are you *really* an American?"

Paling, Tatiana nodded.

"Where is your passport? Can't get back without a passport."

She stared at him mutely.

"Besides, it's too dangerous now. The Germans bomb the Baltic mercilessly."

"Yes."

"Ships go down all the time."

"Yes."

"Why don't you stay here till April, work until the ice melts? Your face has to heal. The stitches need to come out. And we could use another pair of hands. Stay in Helsinki."

Tatiana shook her head.

"You'll have to stay here anyway until we get you a new passport. Do you want me to take you to Senate Square later? I'll take you to the U.S. consulate. It'll take them at least a month to issue you new documents. By that time the ice will have melted. Getting to America is hard these days."

Tatiana knew that the U.S. State Department, digging around to find a Jane Barrington, would discover only that *she* was not Jane Barrington. Alexander told her they could not stay a second in Helsinki—the NKVD had a long arm. Alexander said that they had to get to Stockholm. Shaking her head, Tatiana backed away from the doctor.

She left the hospital, carrying her backpack, her nurse's bag, her *Jane Barrington* travel documents. She walked to the semicircular south harbor in Helsinki and sat on the bench, watching the vendors at Market Square pack up their carts and their tables and sweep the square clean.

Calm descended again.

The seagulls screeched overhead.

Tatiana sat on the bench and waited interminable hours until night fell, and then she got up and walked past a narrow street leading up to the gleaming Church of St. Nicholas. She barely glanced at it.

In the dark she meandered up and down the harbor until she spotted trucks with the blue-and-white Swedish flag, loading small amounts of lumber lying in piles on the ground. There was quite a bit of activity in the harbor. Tatiana could see that night was the time for the supplies to get across the Baltic. She knew that the trucks did not travel by day, when it was easy to spot them. Though the Germans generally did not bomb neutral trade vessels, sometimes they did. Sweden had finally started sending all its shipping and trucking trade with protective convoys. Alexander told her that.

Tatiana knew that the trucks were headed for Stockholm because one of the men said the word "*Stokgolm,*" which sounded like "Stockholm" in Russian.

She stood at the edge of the harbor watching the lumber being loaded onto the back of an open truck. Was she scared? No. Not anymore. She approached the truck driver, showing him her Red Cross badge, and said in English that she was a nurse trying to get to Stockholm and could he please take her across the Gulf of Bothnia with him for a hundred American dollars. He didn't understand a word of what she had said. She showed him a hundred-dollar bill and said, "*Stokgolm?*" Gladly taking the money from her hands, he let her ride with him.

He didn't speak any English or Russian, so they barely talked, which was fine with Tatiana. On the way through the white-out darkness, illuminated by the convoy's headlights and by the gleaming northern lights above her head, she remembered *that the first time she kissed Alexander when they were in the woods in Luga, she was really afraid that he was going to know immediately that she had never been kissed before, and she thought, if he asks me, I'm going to lie, because I don't want him to think less of me. She thought that for the first second or two, and then she couldn't think about anything, because his lips were so abundantly passionate for her, because in her hunger to kiss him back she had forgotten her inexperience.*

Thinking about the first time they kissed took up much of the trip. Then Tatiana slept.

She didn't know how long the journey took. The last few hours, they meandered on the ice through the small islands preceding Stockholm.

"*Tack*," she said to the driver when they stopped at the harbor. "*Tack sa mycket.*" Alexander taught her that, how to say thank you in Swedish. Tatiana walked across the ice, careful not to slip, walked up granite steps and was out on the cobbled seaside promenade. I'm in Stockholm, she thought. I'm nearly free. Slowly she meandered through the half-empty streets. It was morning—too early for the stores to be open. What day was it? She did not know. Near the industrial docks Tatiana found a small open bakery, and on its shelves there was *white bread*. She showed the woman her American money. The shop owner shook her head and said something in Swedish. "*Bank*," she said. "*Pengar, dollars.*"

Tatiana turned to go. The woman called after her, but in a strident voice, and Tatiana, afraid the woman suspected she didn't belong in Sweden, did not turn around. She was already on the street when the woman ran around to stop her, giving her a loaf of warm crusty white bread, the likes of which Tatiana had never smelled, and a paper cup of black coffee. "*Tack*," Tatiana said. "*Tack sa mycket.*"

"*Varsagod*," said the woman, shaking her head at the money Tatiana was offering her.

Tatiana sat on the bench at the docks overlooking the crescent of the Baltic Sea and the Gulf of Bothnia and ate the whole loaf of bread and had her coffee. She stared unblinkingly into the blue dawn in front of her. Somewhere east of the ice lay besieged Leningrad. And somewhere east of that was Lazarevo. And in between was the Second World War and Comrade Stalin.

After eating, she walked around the streets long enough to find an open bank, where she exchanged some of her American money. Armed with a few kronor, Tatiana bought some more white bread and then found a place that sold cheese—in fact, all different kinds of cheeses—but even better, she found a café near the harbor that served *her* breakfast, and not just oatmeal, and not just eggs, and not just bread, but *bacon*! She bought three helpings of bacon and decided that from now on that was *all* she was going to have for breakfast.

The day was still long. Tatiana didn't know where to go to sleep. Alexander told her that in Stockholm there would be hotels that would rent them a room without asking for their passports. Just like in Poland. She found that beyond belief then. But Alexander, of course, was right.

Not only did Tatiana rent a hotel room, not only did she get a key to a room that was warm, that had a bed and a view of the harbor, but it had its own bathroom and in the bathroom was the thing that Alexander had told her about, the shower thing that poured water on her from above. She must have stayed under the hot stream for an hour.

And then she slept for twenty-four.

It took Tatiana over two months to leave Stockholm.

Seventy-six days of sitting on the pier bench looking east past the gulf, past Finland, to the Soviet Union, while the seagulls cried overhead.

Seventy-six days of—

She and Alexander had planned to stay in Stockholm in the spring while waiting for his documents to come through from the U.S. State Department. They would have celebrated his twenty-fourth birthday in Stockholm on May 29.

Austere Stockholm was softened by spring. Tatiana bought yellow tulips and ate fresh fruit right from the market vendors, and she had meat—smoked hams and pork and sausages. She had ice cream. Her face healed. Her stomach grew. She thought of remaining in Stockholm, of finding a hospital to work in, of having her baby in Sweden. She liked the tulips and the hot shower.

But the seagulls wept overhead.

Tatiana never did go to Riddarholm Church, Sweden's Temple of Fame.

Finally she took a train across the country to Göteborg, where she easily slipped into one of the holds on a Swedish trade cargo vessel bound for Harwich, England, carrying paper products. As during her passage from Finland to Sweden, she and her vessel were surrounded by a heavily armed convoy. Since Norway was German-occupied, there were quite a few incidents of bombings and sinkings in the North Sea. Noncombatant Sweden wasn't having any of it, and neither was Tatiana.

All was quiet as she crossed the North Sea and docked in Harwich. To get to Liverpool, Tatiana took a train, which had the *most* comfortable seats. Out of curiosity she bought herself a first-class ticket. The pillows were white. This would have been a good train to take to Lazarevo after burying Dasha, thought Tatiana.

She spent two weeks in dank and industrial Liverpool, until she found out that a shipping company called the *White Star* sailed once a month to New York, but she needed a visa to get on board. She bought a second-class ticket and appeared on the gangplank. When a young midshipman asked for her papers, Tatiana showed him her Red Cross travel document from the Soviet Union. He said it was no good; she needed a visa. Tatiana said she didn't have one. He said she needed a passport. She said she didn't have one. He laughed and said, "Well then, dearie, you're not getting on this boat."

Tatiana said, "I do not have visa, I do not have passport, but what I *do* have is five hundred dollars I would like *you* to have if you let me pass." She coughed. She knew that five hundred dollars was a year's salary for the sailor.

The midshipman instantly took the money and led her into a small room below sea level, where Tatiana climbed onto the top bunk. Alexander told her he slept on the top bunk at the Leningrad garrison. She wasn't feeling well. She was wearing the larger of her two white uniforms, the one she had been given in Helsinki. Her original one had long stopped fitting her, and even this one did not button well around her stomach.

In Stockholm, Tatiana had found a place to wash her uniforms called the *tvatteri*, where there were things called *tvatt maskins* and *tork tumlares* that she put money into, and thirty minutes later the clothes came out clean, and thirty minutes later the clothes came out dry, and there was no standing in cold water, no washboards, no soaping. She didn't have to do anything but sit and watch the machine.

As Tatiana sat and watched the machine, she remembered *the last time she and Alexander made love. He was leaving at six in the evening, and they finished making love about five fifty-five. He had just enough time to put on his clothes, kiss her, and bolt out the door. When they made love, he had been on top of her. She watched his face the whole time, holding on to his neck and crying and pleading with him not to end, because when he ended he would have to leave. Love. How did they say it in Swedish?*

Kärlek.

Jag älskar dig, Alexander.

As the *tork tumlara* twirled her Red Cross uniform and stockings, Tatiana was so grateful that the last time she and Alexander made love, she saw his face.

The trip across to New York took ten nauseating, spluttering days. When she arrived, it was the end of June. Tatiana had turned nineteen years old on the *White Star* line in the middle of the Atlantic Ocean.

On the boat Tatiana coughed and thought about Orbeli.

"*Tatiasha—remember Orbeli—*"

Coughing up blood, Tatiana summoned her sinking strength and the foundering energy of her heart to ask herself—if Alexander knew he was going to be arrested and couldn't tell her because he knew she would never go without him, would he have gritted his teeth and set his jaw and lied?

Yes. Everything she knew about Alexander told her that would be exactly what he would do. If he knew the truth, he would give her one word.

Orbeli.

Her chest hurt so much it felt as if it were about to tear apart her breast-bone.

When the *White Star* line docked in the Port of New York, Tatiana could not get up. Not that she wouldn't. She just couldn't. Delirious after a passage of violent coughing, she felt as if something inside her were leaking out.

Soon she heard voices, and two men came into the room, both of them dressed in white.

"Oh, no, what do we have here?" said the shorter man. "Not another refugee."

"Wait, this one is wearing a Red Cross uniform," said the taller man.

"She obviously stole it somewhere. Look, it barely buttons over her stomach. It's obviously not hers. Edward, let's go. We'll report her to the INS later. We've got to empty this ship."

Tatiana moaned. The men came back. The taller man looked her over. "Chris, I think she's going to have a baby."

"What—now?"

"I think so." The doctor felt for something underneath her. "Her water may have broken."

Chris came up to Tatiana and put his hand on her head. "Feel her. She's burning up. Listen to her breathing. I don't even need a stethoscope. She's got TB. God, how many of these cases can we see? Forget it. We still have all the cabins to go through. She's our first. I guarantee she won't be the last."

Edward kept his hand on Tatiana's stomach. "She's very sick," he said. "Miss," he said, "do you speak English?"

When Tatiana didn't answer, Chris exclaimed, "You see?"

"Maybe she has papers? Miss, do you have any papers?"

When Tatiana didn't answer, Chris said, "I'm done. I'm going."

Edward said, "Chris, she's sick, and she's about to have a baby. What do you want to do, leave her?" He laughed. "What kind of a damn doctor are you?"

"A tired and underpaid one, that's what kind. PHD doesn't pay me enough to care. Where are we going to take her?"

"Let's bring her to the quarantine hospital on Ellis Island Three. There's room. She'll get better there."

"With TB?"

"It's TB, not cancer. Let's go."

"Edward, she's a refugee! Where is she from? Look at her. If she were just sick, I'd say all right, but you know she's going to have the kid on American soil, and bam! She's entitled to stay here like the rest of us. Forget it. Deliver her baby on the boat, so that she's got no claims on U.S. soil, and then put her in Ellis. As soon as she's better, she'll be deported. That's fair. All these folks think they can come into America without permission . . . well, no more. Look how many we've got. Once this damn war is over, it's going to get even worse. The entire European continent is going to want to—"

"Going to want to what, Chris *Pandolfi?*"

"Oh, easy for *you* to judge, Edward *Ludlow.*"

"I've been here since the French–Indian wars. I'm not judging."

Chris waved Edward off and left. Then, sticking his head back into the room, he said, "We'll come back for her. She's not ready to have a kid now. Look how still she is. Let's go."

Edward was about to walk away when Tatiana groaned slightly. He came back and stood by her face. "Miss?" he said. "Miss?"

Lifting her hand, Tatiana found Edward's face and placed her palm on his cheek. "Help me," she said in English. "I'm going to have a baby. Help me, please."

* * *

Edward Ludlow found a stretcher for Tatiana and fetched a reluctant and grumpy Chris Pandolfi to help him carry her down the plank and onto the ferry that took her to Ellis Island in the middle of New York Harbor. Years after the heyday of Ellis, the island's hospital had been serving as a detention center and quarantine for immigrants and refugees coming to the United States.

Tatiana's eyes were so clouded she felt half blind, but even through her haze and the ferry's unwashed windows she could see the valiant hand offering a flame up to the sunlit heaven, *lifting her lamp beside the golden door.*

Tatiana closed her eyes.

At Ellis she was carried to a small, spartan room, where Edward laid her on a bed with starched white sheets and got a nurse to undress her. After examining her, he looked at Tatiana with surprise, and said, "Your baby has crowned. Do you not feel that?"

Tatiana barely moved, barely breathed. Once the baby's head came out, she convulsed, gritting her teeth through palpitations that felt like distant pain.

Edward delivered her baby for her.

"Miss, can you hear me? Please, look. Look what you have. A beautiful boy!" The doctor smiled, bringing the baby close.

"Look. He's a big one, too—I'm surprised you could get a baby this size out of little you. Brenda, look at this. Don't you agree?" Brenda wrapped the baby in a small white blanket and laid him next to Tatiana.

"He's early," mouthed Tatiana, staring at her baby. She placed her hand on him.

"Early?" Edward laughed. "No, I'd say he was right on time. If he were any later, you'd be having him back in—where are you from?"

"The Soviet Union," Tatiana said indistinctly.

"Oh, dear. The Soviet Union. How did you *ever* get here?"

"You would not believe it if I told you," said Tatiana, lying on her side, shutting her eyes.

"Well, forget all that now," Edward said brightly. "As it is, your boy is a U.S. citizen." He sat by the chair near her bed. "That's a good thing, right? It's what you wanted?"

Tatiana suppressed a groan. "Yes," she said, pressing her swaddled son to her feverish face. "It is what I wanted." It was hurting her to breathe.

"You've got TB. It hurts right now, but you'll be all right," he said gently. "Everything you've been through, it's all behind you."

"That's what I'm afraid of," whispered Tatiana.

"No, it's good!" the doctor exclaimed. "You'll stay here at Ellis, get better—Where did you get a Red Cross uniform? Were you a nurse?"

"Yes."

"Well, that's great," he said cheerfully. "You see? You have a valuable skill.

635

You'll be able to get a job. You speak a little English, which is more than I can say for most people who come through here. It'll separate you from the chaff. Trust me." He smiled. "You're going to do very well. Now, can I get you something to eat? We have sandwiches with turkey—"

"With what?"

"Oh, I think you'll like turkey. And cheese. I'll bring it for you."

"You are a good doctor," Tatiana said. "Edward Ludlow, right?"

"Right."

"Edward—"

"It's Dr. Ludlow to you!" Brenda, the nurse, exclaimed loudly.

"Nurse! Let her call me Edward if she wants. What do you care?"

Huffing, Brenda left, and Edward took a small towel and wiped Tatiana's tears. "I know you must be sad. It *is* frightening. But I have a good feeling about you. Everything is going to be just fine." He smiled. "I promise."

Through her grieving green eyes, Tatiana looked at the doctor and said, "You Americans do like to promise."

Nodding, Edward said, "Yes, and we *always* keep our word. Now, let me get our Public Heath Department administrative nurse for you. If Vikki is a little grouchy, don't worry. She's having a bad day, but she's got a good heart. She'll bring you the birth certificate papers." Edward stared at the boy warmly. "He's a cute one. Look, he's got a full head of hair. A miracle, isn't it? Have you thought about a name for him?"

"Yes," said Tatiana, weeping into her baby's black hair. "He is going to have his father's name. Anthony Alexander Barrington."

Soldier! Let me cradle your head and caress your face, let me kiss your dear sweet lips and cry across the seas and whisper through the icy Russian grass how I feel for you . . . Luga, Ladoga, Leningrad, Lazarevo . . . Alexander, once you carried me, and now I carry you. Into my eternity, now I carry you.

Through Finland, through Sweden, to America, hand outstretched, I stand and limp forward, the galloping steed black and riderless in my wake. Your heart, your rifle, they will comfort me, they'll be my cradle and my grave.

Lazarevo drips you into my soul, dawn drop by moonlight drop from the river Kama. When you look for me, look for me there, because that's where I will be all the days of my life.

"Shura, I can't bear the thought of you dying," Tatiana said to him when they were lying on the blanket, having made love by the fire in the dewy morning. "I can't bear the thought of you not breathing in this world."

"I'm not crazy about the thought of that myself." Alexander grinned. "I'm not going to die. You said so yourself. You said I was meant for great things."

"You are meant for great things," she replied. "But you better keep yourself alive for me, soldier, because I can't continue to live without you." That's what she said, looking up into his face, her hands on his beating heart.

He bent down and kissed her freckles. "You can't continue? My cartwheeling queen of Lake Ilmen?" Smiling, he shook his head. "You will find a way to live without me. You will find a way to live for both of us," Alexander said to Tatiana as the swelling Kama River flowed from the Ural Mountains through a pine village named Lazarevo, once when they were in love, and young.